S0-CAG-458

THE SHAAR PRESS

THE JUDAICA IMPRINT
FOR THOUGHTFUL PEOPLE

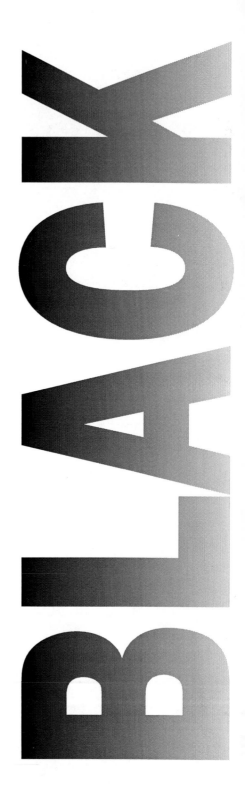

A novel by
Yair Weinstock

translated by
Miriam Zakon

A riveting novel
of suspense,
conspiracy, mystery
and revelation

A
SHAAR
PRESS
PUBLICATION

© *Copyright 1998 by* Shaar Press

First edition – First Impression / February, 1998
Second Impression / July, 2001
Third Impression / January, 2009

ALL RIGHTS RESERVED

No part of this book may be reproduced **in any form,** *photocopy, electronic media, or otherwise without* **written** *permission from the copyright holder, except by a reviewer who wishes to quote brief passages in connection with a review written for inclusion in magazines or newspapers.*

This is a work of fiction. Names, characters, places, and incidents are either the product of the author's imagination or are used fictitiously. Any resemblance to actual persons, living or dead, or locales is entirely coincidental.

THE RIGHTS OF THE COPYRIGHT HOLDER WILL BE STRICTLY ENFORCED.

Published by **SHAAR PRESS**
Distributed by MESORAH PUBLICATIONS, LTD.
4401 Second Avenue / Brooklyn, N.Y 11232 / (718) 921-9000

Distributed in Israel by SIFRIATI / A. GITLER
6 Hayarkon Street / Bnei Brak 51127

Distributed in Europe by LEHMANNS
Unit E, Viking Business Park, Rolling Mill Road / Jarrow, Tyne and Wear, NE32 3DP/ England

Distributed in Australia and New Zealand by GOLDS WORLD OF JUDAICA
3-13 William Street / Balaclava, Melbourne 3183 / Victoria Australia

Distributed in South Africa by KOLLEL BOOKSHOP
Ivy Common / 105 William Road / Norwood 2192, Johannesburg, South Africa

ISBN 10: 1-57819-196-3 / ISBN 12: 978-1-57819-196-3 Hard Cover
ISBN 10: 1-57819-197-1 / ISBN 13: 978-1-57819-197-0 Paperback

Printed in the United States of America by Noble Book Press
Custom bound by Sefercraft, Inc. / 4401 Second Avenue / Brooklyn N.Y. 11232

Dedicated, with love, to S. and T.,
sufferers of cystic fibrosis, and to their parents,
for their generosity and warmth.

S. and T., as well as hundreds of others in Israel
with cystic fibrosis, embody the verse,
"Let every soul (neshamah) praise G-d."
Our sages explain:
"For every breath (neshimah) that a man takes,
he must praise the Holy One, blessed is He."

These people feel each breath — and thank Him for it.

May G-d, in His vast mercy, give them many more
breaths, and grant them years of life.

Acknowledgments

For the idea brought to life in words, the spirit enveloped in letters, the thoughts woven together by a writing hand — for these undeserved gifts, I thank my Creator.

My warm thanks:

To my dear wife, for her encouragement and support and her wonderful suggestions;

To my brother, Rabbi Chaim Chanoch *Shlita* of Ashdod, for his diligent help and unparalleled devotion;

To my dear children, for their careful scrutiny and well-turned phrases;

To the staff of *Kol Hashavuah,* and its editor, Rabbi Asher Zuckerman, for hosting me so warmly through the year;

To Miriam Zakon, who so deftly translated this work into English;

And to the thousands of readers of this novel in its original form, who served as unequaled critics and lovingly stood by me through the year. The stream of reaction became a flood as time went by and the story, and its message, took form. I was highly encouraged by the positive words and excellent suggestions.

The Holy One, blessed is He,
found no vessel of blessing for Israel,
except that of peace.

1

A deep blackness hung over Mt. Carmel. At 1 o'clock in the morning the electric company's main generator overloaded, and all the streetlights blinked off and on and then went out. The mountain was bathed in darkness.

The white Mercedes raced down the mountain at high speed. Passing automobiles honked, while other drivers tried in vain to capture the driver's attention by blinking their headlights. The car was flying at more than 100 miles per hour. It was clear that this could end only one way: in disaster. A steady hand gripped the wheel, a strong hand that knew to the last moment when to turn the steering wheel, how to take each dangerous curve with breathtaking precision. Yet, to the drivers on his right and left, in his lane and in the oncoming one, one thing was obvious: The madman at the wheel of the Mercedes was determined to kill himself by plunging over the cliff.

Inside the Mercedes, the passengers subscribed to that theory as well.

"Manny, slow down," shouted Udi Dinar, sitting next to the driver in the front seat. "If you want to commit suicide, do it when you're by yourself!"

In the back seat sat a curly-haired young man with a sensitive, handsome face. His green eyes, normally alert and clever, stared ahead, unfocused; his head spun. He wondered if the dizziness was a result of the drinks that he and his parents had guzzled at the party. Or perhaps it was caused by the trees flashing wildly by on both sides of the dark road. They did not look at all like trees, but rather like black giants racing quickly, as if a still more fearsome giant was pursuing them.

"Beautiful, beautiful," Gili, the young man, murmured. Colored dots danced merrily before his glazed eyes. "Another giant, and another. Abba, why are the giants running so fast?"

Udi Dinar didn't turn around. "Quiet down, Gili," he said angrily. "Beautiful, he says! Manny's trying to kill us and my son is hallucinating as though he is on drugs. The wedding left me a bit woozy too, but get a hold of yourself!"

In the driver's seat, Manny was amused. "Udi, you're afraid of dying? Not me! And by the way," he continued without pausing, "what did you decide to do about the book?"

"What book?" Udi asked, puzzled.

"'What book,'" Manny repeated impatiently. "The gold-plated one, of course!"

"Manny, one last request from someone sentenced to death," interjected Udi's wife, Monica, from the rear next to Gili. "What are you talking about?"

"Oh, of course," Udi said, rubbing his forehead. "The book of *segulos*. Yes, I've decided to put it up for sale. I've spoken with Dr. Ralph Stern of Sotheby's regarding a public auction. He's appraised it at $100,000 for an opening bid. I told him I wouldn't let it go for under $650,000, and he said he'd get me someone in London who'd give me 250,000 pounds sterling for it. Think of it, Manny — 250,000 pounds!"

"Udi, you've got no sense of values if you let it go. You can't sell it! It's priceless!"

Udi sounded amused. "That's true, I don't have any values. But you know what? I need money now, a lot of money, to develop the studio in Givatayim. The book can help me, and it will really live up to its name: *The Vessel of Blessing*. Think of it," he continued with a gleeful laugh, "one quarter of a million pounds sterling! That vessel is truly blessed!"

"Where is the book?" Manny asked.

"Here," Udi pointed to the glove compartment beneath the front window.

"That's what I thought." Manny swallowed hard, and suddenly slammed down on the gas pedal. The speedometer edged towards 110 miles per hour.

"Manny," Udi's voice had the edge of hysteria, "stop! You're not a fighter pilot!"

"Oh, please, slow down," Monica added her panicky voice to her husband's. She was sitting in the back seat next to Gili, whose stoic tranquility did not calm her at all. "Manny, do you want to kill us all? I'm begging you, stop! Or at least let Gili take over!"

"G-d forbid," Udi murmured, "that's all we need, for Gili to drive. Look at his eyes; he's completely out of it."

"Gili's fine," Monica yelled, never moving her gaze from the scenery racing swiftly by. "Manny, stop it. Now!"

Stop!

Manny eased the pressure on the gas pedal. The car slowed until it came to a complete stop on the side of the road. He jumped out of the driver's seat into the fresh night air. A mischievous expression rested on his face as he walked towards the back window.

He bent one knee. "Please, Mrs. Dinar, move over to the front seat."

"What?"

"You wanted Gili to drive. By all means. He'll drive, and you'll keep an eye on him."

"Manny, get back to your seat," Udi cried out impatiently. "Stop these stupid games. Gili can't drive. He's drunk. Just slow down!"

"No!" Monica and Manny both said. "Let Gili drive!"

Monica swiftly dispatched her husband to the back and sat down in the front seat. Gili put his hands on the steering wheel and pressed down on the gas. The Mercedes lurched forward.

A few hours earlier...

The Country Galei-Gil, Kiryat Motzkin's elegant wedding hall, was jammed with people. The son of Ehud and Monica Dinar's close friends was getting married, and hundreds were invited to the lavish affair. Guests arrived bearing expensive gifts and displaying gold-rimmed invitations. The Dinars were members of a posh set, part of Israeli high society. Udi served as the dynamic chairman of the Tzalmon Film Studios, while Monica had climbed to a top position in Israel's Foreign Office.

The champagne flowed freely at the joyous celebration. The father of the groom, a noted diplomat, was surrounded by a cortege of powerful personalities from the political sphere; in the outer circle gathered the small fry, basking in the glory of their brush with greatness. Witticisms drew peals of laughter; the gaiety escalated from moment to moment.

Manny, clutching a shot glass of whiskey, approached a chuckling group. In the center of the circle stood the groom's distinguished father, standing with Manny's good friend Udi, who held a drink in one hand and a large black olive in his mouth.

"Hey, gang," Manny said, elbowing his way through, "have you heard the latest?" He told over a joke that he'd thought of just then; his talented delivery and its caustic, contemporary political message made it an instant hit. At the same moment Udi downed his drink. He began to splutter, coughing up the liquid, pointing desperately to his throat.

"Help!" Monica gave a panicky cry. "He's choking! Udi, cough it up, clear your throat!"

Udi's face turned scarlet; seconds later it was purple, then blue... The others stared in paralyzed horror, watching a man suffocate, unable to stop the tragedy.

All but Manny.

Manny sprang behind Udi, who was frantically trying to get oxygen to his gasping lungs. He encircled him with his long arms and gave a strong, sharp blow to his chest. Udi coughed, and a large olive pit came shooting out of his mouth. He took a deep, relieved breath. Saved!

"Manny did it," the guests murmured to each other as the panic faded. "He saved Udi from certain death."

Manny wasn't paying any attention to the praise. He was busy giving his friend a drink of cold water. Then he had another task: to calm down Monica and Gili.

He turned to them with a grin. "You know I don't do this for free," he quipped, as he poured them each a drink. "You'll have to pay me waiter's wages. Now calm down and drink up."

The image of Udi near demise had shaken them up. They didn't wait to be asked a second time; the liquor flowed.

❧✦☙

And now the alcohol was taking its toll. Gili's hands trembled on the steering wheel. The Mercedes swerved from right to left, wildly passing other cars. At least a dozen traffic laws were broken in as many minutes.

"Gili, be careful," Udi murmured from his seat in the back, "the police are going to stop you."

"Police? What police?" Monica said heavily. "I don't see any police!"

"Look, there's a helicopter circling us," Udi pointed towards the black sky.

"Abba, you're seeing things," Gili laughed. "There's nothing there!"

"Gili, have pity. Stop for a minute."

"Just one second, right after this curve," Gili muttered. A wave of nausea overtook him, and the Mercedes veered to the next lane.

"I shouldn't have given in to back-seat drivers," Udi said plaintively. "Go rely on a baby of 17½."

Gili was offended. "Almost 18," he said huffily.

"Excuse me, a baby of 18."

At that moment a thick red fog descended over Gili's aching head. "I can't see anything!" he called out frantically. "I can't see!"

"Gili!" Monica yelled, but she was too late. The car turned right and raced towards the shoulder of the road. Udi leaned forward and tried desperately to grab the wheel and get control of the car. He gave the wheel a mighty push in the other direction; unbelievably, impossibly, the car wouldn't respond. Remorselessly, it flew to the right, off the road.

2

The car skidded on the road's shoulder. Gili, suddenly sober, tried to hit the brakes and bring the car to a halt; instead, his foot hit the gas and the Mercedes raced down the cliff.

The powerful car tore through the steel barrier. It left the road behind and went flying into the yawning chasm below.

Two cars that had been following the Mercedes screeched to a stop. The drivers jumped out and cautiously approached the edge of the road, but in the deep blackness of the night they could not distinguish any shapes in front of them. They listened intently for cries of help, but the sole noise coming from the trees down below was that of the nocturnal birds, frightening, somehow, in the stillness of night.

"What should we do?" asked the elder of the two, a tall man whose white hair stood out starkly against the darkness. The second driver, a thin young man, bent over towards the shoulder and tentatively explored the ground with his foot. After a second he pulled back in fear. "I don't know," he said. "Just tonight, it's pitch black. I'm afraid I'll slide down. We've got to call for help."

A third car approached and slowed down near them. An energetic and resolute figure leaped out of the car. "What happened?" he asked.

"A car went over the cliff," the older man sighed.

"What are you waiting for? We've got to call for help! Every second is critical for those people down there!"

The man raced to his car and stooped inside. "Lucky stiff, he's got a cellular phone," the older man muttered, as the other emerged holding the small instrument in his hand.

They waited as the man spoke swiftly into his phone. He returned to the two men after a few minutes. "I've spoken with Magen David Adom and the police. They're on their way. Will you wait to tell what happened? Or can't you stand the sight?"

The older man glanced at his watch. "Look, there's not much for me to tell. What can I say? He was driving like a drunk, weaving from the right lane to the left and back. Suddenly he went off the road and drove straight to Heaven. It's 2 o'clock in the morning and I know this procedure — it takes hours. I've got to be at work early tomorrow morning. I'll leave you my name."

The younger man turned to the other man. "I should have been home two hours ago. My wife won't know what to think. Would you agree to wait here for the police and the ambulance?"

"Fine," the man answered, "leave me your names if they need you to testify, and you can go."

By the light of the headlights he carefully wrote out the details on a scrap of paper: names, addresses, phone numbers. Then the witnesses hurriedly prepared to leave the site of the accident.

The older man turned to the younger. "It's a miracle that this fellow turned up. I haven't the energy for this kind of thing. No one could have survived such a crash. I'll tell you the truth: I've got a weak heart and I can't bear to see them pull the bodies out of the wreckage."

"Me, too," the younger man said fervently. "I'm very sensitive; I won't sleep for months because of this."

They gave one last apologetic look at the dark abyss. Moments later the two cars left the scene.

His first feeling was pain. Terrible pain. He felt as if all his ribs were shattered. He tried to move his hands but could not: The right hand was encased in a plaster cast, the left attached to a thin tube.

"Ima, the pain, I can't stand the pain," he groaned.

"Can you open your eyes?" He heard a pleasant voice. With heroic effort Gili managed to pry his lids open. "What happened? Where am I?"

He was lying in a bed between snow-white sheets. A stranger in a white robe stood over him, speaking gently. "Good, you've opened your eyes."

"What happened to me? Where am I?"

"You're in the hospital," the man answered. "You were hurt in a car accident three days ago. I'm your doctor, Doctor Macks."

Three days!

"Are you telling me I've been unconscious for three days?" The question was on his lips, but he suddenly felt a weakness, a heaviness, coupled with a throbbing headache. His brain felt as if it were being torn into tiny pieces. The question remained unasked.

"Where am I?" he whispered again. There was no sign of the doctor. *I must have fallen asleep,* Gili thought lazily, as his eyes closed.

Two more days passed, days in which lucid moments alternated with feverish, intermittent dozing. Doctors came and went, asking him questions that seemed to have no bearing on anything. They held low-voiced consultations at his bedside. He could hear words, phrases, from outside the fog that enveloped him. "...symptoms of partial amnesia...possibility of irreversible brain damage..." He understood the terminology. "Gili was a bright boy, an excellent student..." but the terrifying words made no impression on him; it was as if they were speaking of another patient.

In the early hours of the morning Gili sat up in his bed and looked out the window. A glistening sun shone on the courtyard. A pair of white doves nestled in the branches of a nearby tree, exchanging endearments in the language of birds. They stared at him with round, innocent eyes and continued to coo with a tranquility that worked magic on him.

The thought flashed through his head like lightning in the darkness. *Abba, Ima, Manny. Where are they? What happened to them? What in the world happened to me?*

With a surge of energy he straightened up in his bed. He became tangled in the intravenous tube. Impatiently, he pushed the pole away from him. The doves in the nearby tree flew away in fright. The magic disappeared.

For a minute he sat deep in thought. Finally, he nodded his head, as one who has come to a decision. He pressed on a button near his bedside.

The duty nurse arrived immediately. "Did you call me?"

He shot a volley of questions. "I want to know where my parents are. What happened to my father and mother? Why don't I see them here?"

The nurse looked confused. If this one had amnesia, he was breaking a world record for recovery.

"Why am I here?"

Yes, it was amnesia. He didn't remember a thing...

"I'm well and healthy. Why am I here?"

The nurse stood, at a loss. "Wait a moment," she said, and she bolted to the doctors' consulting room. She returned with the head neurologist, Professor Amnon Neuberg, and Gili's own doctor, Dr. Macks.

The doctors examined him with various instruments. After giving him a tranquilizer they spoke with him to see if he remembered anything of his arrival at the hospital and why he had been admitted.

"We were traveling back from the wedding," Gili said, "from the hall...its name was Country something. Manny was driving too fast, and I took his place at the wheel. Then I became dizzy and confused."

"And then what?" The fateful question.

"Then..." Gili shook his head in a supreme effort of memory. Nothing. "I don't remember what happened to me. The car went crazy, started off the road. Abba grabbed the wheel, trying to straighten it, to get it back to the right lane. Suddenly—boom! Blows from all sides, the car is falling, disintegrating, crushed."

He murmured the last few words. His eyes grew round, his face white. The doctors looked at him in sympathy as his memory of the accident returned and the grim facts struck him brutally.

One and one make two; two parents who had been with him in the car!

"Abba! Ima!" The screams echoed through the corridors, screams heavy with fear and despair. "Are they alive?"

"Your mother is alive," Dr. Macks said.

"And Abba?" His lips quivered. He knew the answer, but had to hear it verbalized. His muscles tightened, a reflexive defense against the terrible blow about to fall.

"I'm sorry about your father. We received the final word from the Abu Kabir Forensic Institute three days ago."

What were they talking about?

"There were four of you in the car, right? The police found two moderately wounded people outside the car — you and your mother. You were saved because you were thrown from the automobile. You were lucky — you came out with nothing worse than broken bones."

"What happened to the car?"

"It was completely burned. The police investigators said they never saw a car so badly damaged."

Gili nodded. His rapid breathing broke the strained silence. The doctors waited for him to calm down somewhat, then they continued the story.

In the car they had found the remains of what had once been Gili's father, and Udi's good friend Manny, Menachem Schwartz. A few broken teeth, some bones found among the heaps of ashes and slags of molten metal were sent to the Forensic Institute, where the final dismal results came through, identifying them as belonging to Ehud Dinar and Manny Schwartz.

"We've put off the funeral until today," Dr. Macks explained, just a shade defensively, "as we thought it appropriate that his only son participate. We waited until you were fully conscious and aware."

Gili tried to erase the awareness; he longed to disappear from this place, this time. But deep inside he knew — that terrible night, and the horror of his father's funeral — he would never forget. His disabled mother, her arms in casts, supported by her sisters, murmured meaningless words under the influence of strong tranquilizers. Gili had resolutely refused offers of sedatives: He wanted to deal with the pain fully conscious.

But as he walked behind the coffin late at night, supported by his friends, surrounded by their love and affection that did nothing to mitigate the pain, he regretted his decision to spurn tranquilizers. It was too much to bear. The earth trembled beneath his feet; it was not the same world, this world without Abba.

It was almost midnight when the somber crowd trod the narrow paths of the cemetery. Gili felt trapped within a nightmare. It wasn't true: Soon he would awake from this disturbed sleep to the brightness of a wonderful new morning.

He knew that these were no more than a child's longing to escape reality. *Gili, accept the facts and learn to live with them,* he whispered to himself.

Later, in their home, under the constant supervision of a doctor, the dam of his mother's unshed tears broke, as the full dimensions of the tragedy finally set in. Gili sat, frozen. A psychologist sat beside him, encouraging him to open the barrier he'd built around his heart. Gili answered him curtly: "Are you also responsible for the death of two men, including your own father?"

The psychologist grew silent and left after a few minutes. Gili didn't regret his departure; he had no patience for the pitiful attempts to calm him. He wanted to feel the pain, to soak it all up.

The telephone rang and Gili stood to answer it. An unknown voice spoke on the other end of the line. Though Gili replied with reserve, the voice would not cease. As the seconds passed, Gili's frozen face relaxed, brightened. When we speak of the light at the end of the tunnel, we refer to moments such as these. Gili could see a light shining, there, at the end of the darkness.

3

The beam of light that brightened Gili's tunnel had a name. It was called Rabbi Yosef Friedman.

That night, when they had returned from the cemetery, Gili felt as though his world had ended.

There are traffic accidents in this world; there are orphans. His accident wasn't the first nor the last. Neither was he the only young man to lose a father. But since his youth, all who knew him recognized that the most developed aspect of Gili's personality was his conscience. He could feel his father's piercing, accusing gaze staring at him even now from above, searing his heart with a burning flame: "Gili, why?"

That question, he knew, would follow him to his very last day on earth.

His heart had crumbled beneath the pain. The psychologist sitting next to him on the white leather sofa could offer him no succor.

And then Rabbi Yosef Friedman had called.

"Call me Yoske," he'd introduced himself. The name meant nothing to Gili.

Gili's evident coolness had not deterred Rabbi Friedman. "I knew your father very well, Gili; I was his good friend. I still remember your *bris*."

Gili longed to slam down the receiver. This friend of his father's was upsetting him even more than the psychologist.

"I have a lot to say to you," Rabbi Friedman said hastily, trying to hold onto the conversation so clearly slipping from his grasp. "I'd like to speak with you. Alone."

"I don't know you," Gili answered frostily.

"You're wrong," Rabbi Friedman said tranquilly. "You know me well. Do you remember Purim in Haifa's Hadar neighborhood? You were wearing the Khomeini mask, with a turban on your head."

The memory brought a reluctant smile to Gili's frigid features. How could he forget that Purim celebration, the marvelous party that had, surprisingly enough, taken place in the house of a remarkable religious Jew whom Abba had hugged closely. Gili had been shocked to discover that Abba had a friend who looked like a real rabbi. That's right, Abba had called him Yoske. The man's face had been a revelation to Gili: It had been a cheerful face that spoke of endless tolerance. So much love radiated from that aged countenance. At the time Gili had thought how different this man was from the short-tempered people who surrounded him. The old man had the patience to play with him, a 10-year-old boy, and to speak to him as an equal. They talked for about an hour like two old friends.

The dust of eight years covered that first and only encounter. And now here he was, Rabbi Friedman, arising from the past. How sad that it was happening at such a time, in such a way.

"I was your father's close friend from the time of his youth," the relentless voice continued, "and I have a lot to tell you."

Gili's curiosity was aroused. "How did you hear what happened to Abba?"

Rabbi Friedman was silent for a moment. "Friends don't forget. Your father, may he rest in peace, wanted to renew our ties. I think the time has come."

Gili could feel the friendship in those simple words. How he wanted, needed, a good friend in the sea of misery surrounding him.

"Do you want to visit us?" he heard himself ask.

"Gladly," Rabbi Friedman said. "If I can, I'll come tomorrow evening. Ask your mother."

Gili looked over to his mother, sitting between two of her sisters, her face a frozen mask. A heavy silence lay over the room, like a threatening cloud. A few close friends from her office sat nearby, silent also, as if afraid to shatter the mourner's stillness.

"It's okay, you can come tomorrow," he said quickly.

Rabbi Friedman arrived the next day. He had hardly changed from the day of that merry Purim celebration. His face still radiated an inexplicable inner light and a gleeful vitality. All eyes in the house were drawn towards him. There seemed to be an impassable gulf between the black-clad rabbi and the young men with their long hair, earrings, and fashionable clothing.

Rabbi Friedman ran his hand over his brow. A look of astonishment appeared on his face. "Where are my horns?" he said in mock astonishment. "Have I forgotten them at home?"

His comment broke the ice. Rabbi Friedman was endowed with a wonderful sense of humor, a magical charisma and unusual ability of persuasion. But over and above that, he radiated deep integrity, without a trace of hypocrisy. He was absolutely himself, himself and no other!

The young people wouldn't leave him alone. The conversation slid into a debate on matters of religion and science. Rabbi Friedman managed to confuse them completely when he proved that they knew little of the science that their school had so diligently instructed them in, let alone Judaism, of which they knew absolutely nothing.

Gili felt uncomfortable. Though Rabbi Friedman aroused a companionable feeling within him, still, the man was strange and different. Besides, Gili's friends' obvious embarrassment was not pleasant to witness. It was Rabbi Friedman himself who helped dispel the strained atmosphere with a fascinating story that transported its listeners far away, until the entire unpleasant exchange was forgotten.

Rabbi Friedman remained there for several hours, long after the young people and other visitors had taken their leave. He spoke with Gili about a variety of topics, making certain not to enter into any additional debates with him. Several times it seemed to Gili that his visitor was hesitating, trying to decide whether or not to say something. Gili longed to encourage him: "If you've come to me, what are you afraid of? Tell me!" But he dared not speak. Rabbi Friedman peered deep into Gili's eyes, closed his own eyes, and grew silent.

Before he left he gave Gili his address and phone number, with the request that he call him whenever he wanted to. "Even at 2 in the morning," he said, with a frankness that allowed for no argument. "Except, of course, for Shabbos," he added with a smile, "when my phone is disconnected. But if you want to join me as a guest for Shabbos, I'll be happy to have you."

Gili didn't know what to think after "Reb Yoske" had departed. Later, he reviewed the conversation. Odd, Rabbi Friedman had hardly spoken about Abba. He hadn't said a thing about his relationship with him, particularly on how the two had met in their youth. This mysterious man had somehow enchanted him more than anyone he'd ever met; at the same time, he found him oddly repelling. Reb Yoske was religious, very religious. He'd opened a gate to some strange and distant place, but Gili, had no desire to visit there. Absolutely not!

But that night, seeds were sown.

Life gradually returned to normal. Gili and his mother slowly recovered from the terrible blow. Monica continued working at the Foreign Ministry; Abba's two partners ran the Tzalmon Studios. The growth surge the studio had experienced under Udi's guidance came to an end, for there were few who combined Udi Dinar's business acumen with his dynamic energy. Gili graduated high school, was drafted, and wore his khakis for three years. But Gili's particular talent came to the fore only after his army service. From the time he'd been a youngster he had felt a need to write. Now he studied journalism, and eventually he presented himself in the offices of the popular newspaper, *HaYom HaZeh*, as a prospective reporter.

"Any particular sector you'd like to cover?" asked Eric Meisels, the assistant editor, after reading several articles which Gili had written and that had previously been published.

"Whatever you need," Gili said confidently.

Eric gave him a thoughtful glance. Many enthusiastic young people, newly released from the army, visited his editorial office looking for work. The majority barely knew how to hold a pen in their hands, their writing talent was so meager. Several, however, did show evidence of journalistic talent. Some of his best reporters had started this way. This youngster with the flashing green eyes seemed to fit in the latter category. It was a judgment based more on instinct than logic, but his instincts were often correct. He decided to give him a tough assignment, and see how he would do...

"Tomorrow they're dedicating the new branch of the Klalit Health Fund in Ashkelon. The treasurer of the Histadrut will be there, along with some Knesset members and other political figures. I want you to cover the event."

Gili stared at him in shock. For a moment it seemed that he would stalk out of the room, mortally offended. Finally, he gave a slow nod of his head and asked for details of when the affair was to take place.

The next evening Gili returned with his sample article, his eyes flashing.

Pleased with yourself, youngster? Ami Kedmi, the paper's senior editor, laughed to himself, though outwardly preserving a careful decorum. "Give me the material," he said curtly. After Gili left he began to skim through the story. His sharp, experienced eye glanced over some of the phrases Gili had used.

It was enough. He called his assistant, Eric, into the room. They read the article together, open mouthed.

This novice had described a dry and boring event in scintillating style. He had taken an insipid affair and made it come alive with detail. Against all odds, he'd made it interesting.

"There's great stuff here," Ami told Eric, impressed. " I think we've caught us a live one. This kid was born with a pen in his hand; if he has to describe an old-age home he'll make it exciting!"

And so Gili began his career as a journalist. He fit in easily with the staff and wrote extensively on a large variety of subjects. He had a keen sense of what would be of interest, an unusual understanding and, above all, personal and intellectual integrity, an integrity that almost reached the point of fanaticism. He wouldn't compromise. "I shall never lie," he stated to the newspaper's editor, when Ami tried to educate him in some facts of journalistic life. "Either I describe it as it happened, without exaggeration, or I don't write. Description by special order? No such thing!"

Ami ground his teeth. If another reporter had spoken to him in this way, he would have sent him flying out of his office, and his paper — but not Gili Dinar. Despite the vexation caused by his overactive conscience, Gili advanced quickly from cub reporter to respected columnist for *HaYom HaZeh.*

4

Benny Gabison was Gili's colleague at the news desk. They were more or less the same age, and Benny had joined the staff one month after Gili. It was only natural that the two should work together in one of the small cubicles in the cavernous newsroom. Their personalities clicked almost instantly. The chemistry between the two was obvious as they both pursued the latest scoop diligently. They worked together on many issues, and their professional relationship soon blossomed into a deep friendship.

"What do you think of that twosome, Benny and Gili?" Ami asked his assistant, Eric. "A strange partnership, no?"

The assistant editor shrugged off the question. "They're good staffers who regularly bring me solid, sensational stories, and that's what matters."

"But I can't figure out how they work together!" Ami persisted. "Have you ever thought about it? They're two complete opposites. Gili is the serious type, intelligent but not brilliant. He's a deep thinker who analyzes everything that comes his way. He's sensitive and cares deeply, particularly about injustice. I've never met anyone as straight as he is."

"And Gabison?" Meisels' curiosity was roused, as he discovered a new facet to his editor's personality. The man was a budding psychologist!

Ami stubbed out his cigar butt into an overflowing ashtray and stroked his stylish cigarette lighter with clear-cut pleasure. "Benny is just the opposite. You know him: He loves the good life, enjoys his luxuries. He's clever as a fox, as sensitive as a piece of asphalt, and refuses to concentrate on anything for more than a few minutes. He jumps from topic to topic like a hyperactive grasshopper, except when he's working on a story. Then a 10-ton crane can't budge him from the computer monitor."

"And that's what's important," Eric said dryly. "For my part, let him spend his entire life at the beach. So long as he hands in his stories by deadline."

"When it comes to that, Benny and Gili are bold printing presses in human form," Ami laughed. "Every write-up a scoop!"

"Remember the gas station scandal?" Eric said, his eyes lighting up.

"And what about the exposé of the Knesset cafeteria? It was Gili who uncovered it!" Ami reminded him.

"And the stock market manipulation," Eric added.

"Not to mention the armament industry embezzlement scheme."

"And the x-ray machine leakages? Have you forgotten that one? It was Gili and Benny who exploded the story."

"In short," Ami concluded, "Gili and Benny are the star reporters on this paper."

❦❦❦

It was precisely the traits that were so different from his own that caused Gili to like Benny. Benny's gaiety and his constant smile, his refusal to take anything seriously, even the cigar that hung eternally from the side of his mouth that so repelled Gili at first, all these things endeared Benny to him.

And so when Benny's behavior began to change, Gili didn't know what to think.

"Benny, what's going on?" he asked him one day, as he was working on a story. "You're different somehow."

Benny didn't raise his head from the computer monitor glowing before him. "What do you mean?"

"It's a week already that you're so serious. It's not like you. Is something bothering you?"

Benny finally pulled his eyes off the flickering display. It was only then that Gili noticed how bloodshot his friend's eyes were. It would take a serious crisis to keep his friend up at night.

"Yeah, I'm in trouble," Benny confessed, his face reddening for an instant. "More accurately, they want to get me into trouble."

Gili cautiously approached his friend and took his hand. "Benny, how can I help? I'll do whatever you ask."

"No, it's not what you think. It's not drugs or crime," Benny gave a little laugh and grabbed his hand back. "An old friend has asked me to join him in something, and I don't know what to do."

"You're talking in riddles. To join him in what? A trip to Turkey or Thailand?"

"I've had enough of searching for my roots in Thailand and the Himalayas," Benny said solemnly. "It's actually the opposite. To take part in a seminar run by the *Arachim* organization in Teveriah."

"A seminar for *ba'alei teshuvah*?" Gili's face distorted with displeasure. "Sure, go. They'll brainwash you and you'll wind up putting on *tefillin* every Shabbat."

"What are you talking about?" Benny retorted. "Do I look like such a wimp?"

"You don't know. It's awful," Gili insisted. "I heard from friends who went. Speeches all day and night, they don't let you sleep, and when you're dead on your feet from fatigue you're ready to agree with anything they tell you. From the seminar straight to Meah Shearim."

"Exactly the opposite," Benny said heatedly. "If you're looking for intellectual challenge, your place is in the seminar. My friends who took part told me that the debate was on a very high intellectual level, much deeper than anything they heard in any philosophy class in college."

Gili stared deeply into Benny's eyes, that were as blue and deep as the sea. Two or three tiny black spots, like islands in an ocean, floated within the blue of his left eye. Normally, a mischievous spark flitted within his glowing pupils, but now the flash was gone.

"Benny, you're already taken in," Gili said, shocked. "Who's gone and brainwashed you?"

"I'm not brainwashed," Benny objected strenuously. "I told you, an old friend who went to high school with me aroused my curiosity. I'm trying to decide whether or not to register. The intellectual challenge and the intense debate intrigues me."

Gili lapsed into thought. "Be honest. Of the two of us, I'm the one who's the philosopher. Since when are you interested in theology?" He hesitated. "You know what, sign me up too," he sighed. "I want to come along and see for myself."

"Great," Benny said happily. "With you around, it won't be boring!"

"That's certain," Gili laughed roundly. "You'll see: I won't give the lecturers a moment's peace. They won't have an easy time with me."

They arrived in Teveriah during an unusually hot week. It seemed a good time to spend hours paddling in the cool, refreshing waters of the Kinneret, in the shadow of the mountains of the Golan, beneath the sparkling blue sky. To avoid embarrassing Benny's friend, though, they decided to attend the first lecture, just to try it out for a short time.

They tried it out, and they were fascinated. From the very first words they were enmeshed in some kind of magical bond. The teaching faculty opened new vistas before them, revealing worlds they didn't know existed — their own world, the world of Judaism.

Now they sat through their 10th, or perhaps 12th, lecture: They had long since stopped counting. The topic was "Evolution or Creation?" The lecturer stood before an audience of about 200, who were divided into several groups. There were those who were fascinated, whose souls had thirsted for Jewish tradition, whose eyes sparkled when they heard a Torah verse or the wisdom of *Chazal*. Others were interested only in an intellectual, academic way. A few were entirely indifferent, bored, or at least pretending to be, but these were a small minority. And, finally, the most difficult of all — the "anti's," wanting only to discredit the lecturer, to destroy him and prove his words false. These were the ones who knew everything about everything, brimming with self-confidence. They sat in their corners exchanging glances, waiting to pounce on any blunder, on any mistaken word.

Gili and Benny were part of this last group.

Gili lay in ambush, like some hungry lion seeking prey. The lecturer, Rabbi Weisgall, was an elderly man with a thick beard, whose eyes sparkled with intelligence. Those in the know said that he was himself a *ba'al teshuvah*, a top physicist, who, before making *aliyah*, had been an aide to the Chief of Staff of the French army. He spoke an imperfect Hebrew with a heavy French accent, his grammar not differentiating between male and female, past and future. Though he was not a very good speaker, the audience was attentive. "He's got something to say," was the general consensus. His premises were solid, his analysis lucid, his conclusions clear-cut and sensible.

He began with a shaky proof, the "scapegoat" of his lecture, an easy kill for his attackers. The listeners perked up: This one was going to be fun! A hail of questions and objections rained down upon him. He answered tranquilly, and readily agreed that there was some weakness in his argument. During the course of the question and answer period, he himself brought down his own initial hypothesis.

Now everyone was listening intently. This was a good speaker, one who agreed with his audience!

It soon became clear, though, that the attackers had fallen into a trap, wasting their ammunition on a decoy. Now it was time for the incisive proofs. Each new step drew closer to a specific goal; each was even more credible and unequivocal. Towards the end of the lecture the listeners reached a turning point; the astonished crowd couldn't say a word. The speaker serenely sipped a cup of tea, while for five minutes no one opened his mouth.

Rabbi Weisgall had galvanized the group with his assertion that the sciences of biochemistry, statistics, and molecular biology completely discredited the theories of Darwin.

"The argument that the first living cell was created accidentally is nonsense. The odds of creating one DNA chain accidentally is 10 to the 40,000th power, an infinite number, a statistical absurdity."

The lecturer gave a smile. "Professor Fred Hoyle, one of the world's great researchers, said that the chances of all the elements of one living cell accidentally coming together in one place are the same as a tornado hitting a junkyard and creating a Boeing 747 from the wreckage!"

A dissenting murmur filled the room. "Yes, yes, you're right," Rabbi Weisgall hastily said, "many noted scientists believe as you do. They took Hoyle to court in Alaska for libeling Charles Darwin, and he won!"

The audience quieted down. Rabbi Weisgall continued. "And even if all the parts of the first living cell somehow came together, they couldn't have survived, for they would not have had a membrane to protect them. Without this shield, contact with oxygen would have destroyed the cell. The Theory of Evolution is a fairy story," the lecturer concluded sharply. "Simply examine the cell in its complexity, this incredible factory of life. Think of the billions upon billions of cells in our bodies, and remember that for us to manufacture just one would take a plant the size of New York City. We still lack the technology to do what one single cell does! And we have billions of these cells in our bodies!"

Most of the listeners nodded their heads in fervent agreement. The speech had filled their hearts with awe. The most cynical among them was hard put to discard the speaker's firm words.

But as always, when there is no intelligent rebuttal, there comes, instead, the spiteful, teasing questions. "Why do you throw rocks on Shabbat?" "Why are there demonstrations on Bar Ilan Street?" "Why don't you serve in the army?" "Why do you wear long black coats?"

The lecturer answered well, though briefly, all questions put to him. Finally, the last questioner's turn came. "Why are you so strange?"

"Strange?" The lecturer's brow furrowed in puzzlement.

The questioner, a long-haired young man, explained. "I went to visit the Kotel. I wanted to be impressed, to feel its atmosphere. Suddenly, somebody shoved me. 'Nu, nu, move, you're blocking the Kotel.' A man with a thick beard stood there, not letting anyone get near him, as if his prayers wouldn't be answered if he couldn't see the Wall. The *chazzan* chanted the word 'Holy,' and a man wearing a Turkish turban rolled his eyes around and screamed 'holy, holy,' at the top of his lungs, while leaping up like an Olympic broad jumper. What does it all mean?"

The lecturer joined the others' laughter at the description. "The Kotel is a magnet," he said. "This magnet pulls in many people, peculiar people, some of them not even Jewish. Does that contradict all that I've said?"

Gili was the "bad boy" of the seminar. He continued to ask difficult, incisive questions, that generated debate and discussion. He seemed to represent Israel's youth, growing up in the laps of atheists, stubbornly battling belief in G-d. He made the lecturers work. By his side sat Benny Gabison, the clown of the group, his jokes relieving the frequent tension.

☙❧

"So what do you think of that twosome, Benny and Gili?"

A layer of dense smoke hovered over the staff's conference room. It was siesta time, 2 in the afternoon, but those present were completely awake.

"I'm worried about them," Rabbi Gleisel, the event's coordinator, sighed. "Gili is a confirmed atheist. I can't find a tiny crack in his wall. Benny is just a comedian who manages to ruin everything. Every time I grab everyone's attention with a minute of serious conversation he's there with his jokes and I have to start all over again."

"There's nothing to fear from atheism," Rabbi Weisgall interjected. "We've seen that the greatest *ba'alei teshuvah* began as atheists."

"I haven't forgotten that," Rabbi Gleisel exhaled a pungent wisp of smoke. "The one I think won't go anywhere is his friend, the comedian. I don't understand what he's looking for here."

☙❧

The telephone rang, as agreed, at 3 in the morning.

The man politely asked the others in the room to leave for a short time and go to the waiting room. He calmly lifted the receiver. "Any progress?"

The voice on the other end spoke quietly, almost in a whisper. "So far, nothing."

"If so, the trip was a waste of time. I'm disappointed in myself. I did not expect this," he said frostily.

"We have two more days. We'll see, maybe there'll be a change. Tomorrow there are many deep speeches on the agenda. He thinks seriously about all that he hears."

The man mused for a moment. "Tomorrow, something is going to happen," he declared. "I can see it. It fits in with what I expected. But you have to help a little. Give him a gentle nudge and he'll be off on his own."

"Good night."

"Good night. Good luck."

5

The last evening of the *Arachim* seminar includes a symposium lasting deep into the night. No one knows exactly how or why, but occasionally these change direction; the planned hours of intense debate and fatiguing discussion turn, instead, into a time of holiness and spiritual growth.

Some time in the middle of the night the lecturers relinquished the microphone to those taking part. One after the other they approached the lectern and revealed the innermost recesses of their hearts. Many of them, their voices choked with tears, announced how they had finally found that which had eluded them all their lives. The world of Judaism had been revealed to them in all its beauty, its roots and many layers. They hoped to maintain their contact with *Arachim*. Others, still more enthusiastic, declared their intention to change their lives and begin to observe the *mitzvos*. There were, of course, those not touched by all the excitement around them, remaining aloof and controlled. Two of these spoke. Rotem, an Afula businessman, said, "I heard new things, but people are too complicated to change in one minute. Maybe I'll come to another seminar, but I don't want to commit myself to anything." Eddie, an interior decorator hailing from Eilat, was even more blunt. "I'm sure everything we heard is true; I feel that both in my heart and my mind. But I'm simply not willing to give up on my enjoyment of life. Shabbat without a car is no Shabbat! I know this sounds terrible, but it's the truth. Maybe in a few years I'll become a *ba'al teshuvah* and I'll know that the foundation was laid over here!"

Many eyes turned to Gili. The tall, curly-haired journalist had garnered considerable attention over the past few days. Until yesterday he'd remained adamant and rocklike in his opposition to the lecturers. What would he say now?

"Gili, are you going to speak?" Benny asked.

"I think so," he said.

"What are you going to say?"

"You'll find out now."

He approached the lectern with long strides. Everyone waited impatiently for his words.

"We've heard Eddie," Gili began. "He described very well all that I'm feeling."

Murmurs of both disappointment and agreement sounded from all sides of the room. The lecturers glanced at each other and nodded their heads slightly. Rabbi Gleisel muttered something; it might have been the words, "I told you so."

"I, too, felt as Eddie did," Gili explained quietly. "More than that, I knew I was considered the prime heretic here, until my eyes were opened. I wasn't a heretic at all; I was an ostrich, hiding my head in the sand, cowering behind silly theories whose time had come and gone. But I understand Eddie. Even if you know that you've made a mistake, that you should change your life, who can give up on all the joys of this world? But on deeper reflection I realize that this is simple laziness!"

Every person's gaze was directed as him; the large auditorium was absolutely silent. Gili continued. "I want you all to know that I've decided to try. To investigate. I know it's not easy, that it will demand daily self-sacrifice, but, having decided without a doubt that 'Moshe is true, and his Torah is true,' I don't have a choice. You have to make sacrifices for truth. I scorn laziness," he looked at Eddie, "and plan on continuing to work with our staff of lecturers!"

A deafening roar broke out, a thunderous round of applause. Gili closed his eyes; he hadn't expected this reaction. He didn't see the mass of people surrounding him, grabbing his hand. He felt a rush of air surrounding him. Benny Gabison pushed through to his side. "Gili, wake up, you're still alive," he said with a mischievous grin.

"No," a lawyer from Tel Aviv corrected him, "he's just starting to live."

"Was I right?"

"Absolutely. The change was incredible."

"I knew it two months ago." The voice on the line was confident, satisfied, as always. "I know him from deep within. I can read his thoughts like an open book."

He wanted to tell the voice to stop exaggerating, as he would have any braggart, but not this one. He was afraid. The man on the other end of the line had power, a power you could feel emanating from him.

"In a short time there will be a drastic change," the voice continued. "First it will be step-by-step; then he'll begin to run. You'll soon see that I was right...as always. Shalom."

The line was cut; the voice hadn't bothered to wait for a reaction.

He gritted his teeth, happy that the man couldn't hear him.

Gili and Benny returned to Tel Aviv, to their work in the newsroom. Anyone who thought that Gili had spoken on a wave of emotion and would not follow up was wrong.

He turned to the addresses he'd been given at the end of the seminar, and wove a strong connection between him and the *Arachim* organization. The process began with attendance at a weekly class. Then came Shabbat spent in the home of a Torah-observant family. With small but confident steps he approached a life of Torah and *mitzvos*.

And Benny wasn't far behind.

Gili could hardly believe the change in his good friend. It seemed so strange. True, it was Benny who'd been the motivating force behind their attending the seminar. But now he simply tagged along behind Gili.

"Listen," he tugged at Benny's shirt sleeve one afternoon, "we're best friends, but it doesn't mean that you have to copy whatever I do."

Benny's eyes flashed. "I'm copying you?"

"What else? Have you gone crazy? Have you really decided to become a *ba'al teshuvah* and give up everything?"

"I'll ask you a riddle. Who said: 'You have to make sacrifices for truth'?" A mischievous smile lit up his face.

"Don't go quoting on me," Gili answered. "Seriously, have you thought about what you're doing and where it will lead? What about the restaurants, the fun, the Friday nights?"

"And what about you?" Benny retorted.

"I've made my decision," Gili answered confidently. "I'm leaving the paper."

"What?"

"You can't be in two places at once. Tel Aviv is a garbage dump. I'm going to Yerushalayim. To a yeshivah."

"Gili, no!"

"I've decided, and that's that."

Benny, shocked, took a few moments to recover. When he spoke, it was in measured, reasonable tones.

"You're making a big mistake. But you'll be back. You're a writer, it's in your blood. Now you think you'll be able to study Torah day and night. A friend of mine went to yeshivah and ran away after a week. What did he tell me? 'It's easier to chop wood from morning to night than sit and learn all day.' It's not easy, and it's not for you. You're not built for it; you were born to write. You'll be back."

The words pierced mercilessly through Gili, powerful and unyielding.

"And what about you?"

"I'm not burning my bridges," Benny said, his words chosen carefully. "I also want to learn Torah and keep the *mitzvos*, but why can't I continue working? Writing is my life. G-d gave me a talent; it's wrong to misuse it."

"You're really talking like a *ba'al teshuvah*," Gili said, amazement coloring his voice. "So you're staying with the paper?"

"I'll be here, and I'll save your place. When you want to come back, and it will be soon, let me know and I'll tell Ami to take you on again."

"You're wrong. I won't be back. I've tasted the sweetness of Gemara learning, the excitement. Your friend, the woodchopper, didn't understand a word of it. He came to the Gemara to study an ancient Aramaic text. He missed the Heavenly code hidden among its lines. I'll go to yeshivah and there I'll stay. 'Let me sit in G-d's house all my days,'" he ended emotionally.

"You're like Yosef the dreamer," Benny laughed.

"...the dreamer," Gili repeated the word as if in a trance. Suddenly he grabbed his head, as if to hold it together. There was a terrible hammering in his brain, as a sudden flash of blinding light pierced through his skull, illuminating a vast, deep cavern for a split second. The whole affair lasted just moments, but Gili swayed like a drunk and almost collapsed. Fortunately Benny noticed his face, devoid of all color, grabbed his arms and held him up.

"Gili, are you all right?" he asked anxiously.

"Fine. Completely fine," Gili reassured him, though his face was still ashen. "I guess I didn't sleep enough this week."

"Take care of yourself, Gili," Benny said affectionately. "You've got to be responsible. You're all that your mother has, after all."

"Okay, I'm going." Gili hated overt shows of emotion. He grabbed his papers hastily and threw them into his fine leather briefcase. "I've already said goodbye to Ami and Eric and everyone else."

"How did Ami take the news?" Benny asked.

"He almost fell off that oversized recliner of his. You should have seen him: His eyes almost bulged from their sockets. He turned red as an overripe tomato. I never saw him so upset. He claimed that the rabbis had practiced voodoo on me, or hypnotized me. I tried to calm him down for almost an hour, but nothing helped. He's furious with me, and won't even say goodbye."

Benny laughed at the description. At the same time he felt slightly anxious, and insisted on accompanying his friend and former colleague into the elevator. He walked Gili to the building's entrance and followed him with his eyes until he saw his car drive out of the parking lot.

Gili raced home. The awkward incident in the newsroom had upset him. Benny must have noticed that something was wrong. It had happened to him several times, but until now only when he'd been at home. With the exception of his mother, not a soul knew about these attacks. He reviewed the conversation he'd had with Benny, knowing that it was a specific word that had triggered the explosion.

Ami had been angry but his assistant, Eric, had reacted differently. He'd shaken Gili's hand warmly, wished him luck on his new path, and added, "I admire you and I envy you, Gili. I admire your inner strength that lets you take such a step. And I envy you your tranquility. From today on you're out of all the headaches. You'll be in a true paradise, a paradise of serenity. I would give millions for such peace of mind."

Gili laughed. "Peace of mind..." If only Eric knew how disturbed he was, how overwrought, he, too, would have joined in the bitter laughter.

These attacks. They had begun a year ago. At first it had been a swift, blinding flash; a month later, another had followed. Recently they had become more frequent. They were strange attacks that hit him with no warning. Suddenly his vision would dim and his head begin to swim; he felt as if lightning were hitting his brain, as if some sort of imprisoned thought was bursting out of its cell. He lost his grip on reality during the attacks.

His mother, concerned, had gone with him to consult the neurologist who'd attended him after the fatal car accident.

"There's nothing to do about it, it's one of the results of the accident," Professor Neuberg had explained. "I already told you in the hospital that, according to the police and Magen David Adom findings, you were fortunate in having been thrown from the vehicle before it caught fire. While you, Mrs. Dinar, escaped with nothing worse than broken bones, Gili landed on his head. As a result of the blow Gili experienced a mild seizure in the brain. In layman's terms, Gili had some internal bleeding, not very much, in the brain's interior. The CAT scan showed indications of the seizure on the brain's left hemisphere.

"It's possible," the doctor chose his words carefully, "that there was some brain damage, very slight, but irreversible."

What power words could wield! Take one word, "cancer," and you had sheer terror. And those three awful words, "irreversible brain damage," bringing in their wake terrifying images: wheelchairs, paralysis, unimaginable handicaps.

Monica and Gili grew pale.

"Don't panic," the doctor hastily tried to lighten the atmosphere of horror that his words had evoked. "A man's brain contains some 50 billion cells called neurons, and even a larger number of cells that connect those neurons to each other. If you think of these cells as electrical wires, imagine that 1,000 wires have been burned. Only 1,000, out of 50 billion!"

"So should we go to an electrician?" Monica was incensed and spoke sarcastically. Who was he talking about, some guinea pig in a lab? This was her Gili, her only son, her whole world, and he was dismissing him with these silly words.

"Mrs. Dinar," the doctor's face grew scarlet with anger. Luckily the residents studying under him were not present to see this. "This is a standard way of explaining a difficult concept. You don't have to take it like that; it's not fair." He began to clarify his words; though her tart rejoinder had been uncalled for, it was not a good idea to have a powerful government employee criticizing him.

Neuberg turned to Gili. "What you're going through are, in laymen's terms, called 'blackouts,' a short circuit in the brain. It's a kind of black hole in your consciousness. During the moments of this short circuit, you're disconnected from everything; it's a state of unconsciousness that lasts a split second. You'll have to learn to live with it, and you can live with it until the ripe old age of 120. No one dies from it."

So had Professor Neuberg spoken several months earlier. Though Gili bowed his head before the dictum of the learned professor, Monica refused to accept his judgment. She used her contacts to gain access to Gili's medical records from the Haifa hospital and sent them to Hadassah Hospital in Jerusalem. To her chagrin, the top neurologists there simply confirmed Neuberg's diagnosis.

But recently, Gili had begun to suspect that all the doctors were wrong. They had spoken of blackouts, short circuits, of a cutting off of his brain. Absolutely not! The opposite was true: This was not darkness, it was a blinding light. And it wasn't the random event the neurologists saw. It seemed to him that certain key words brought it on.

Today, he'd managed to pinpoint one of those words.

Dreams!

6

The automobile was enveloped in flames, illuminating the darkness of the valley with its bright glow.

He sat on the wet grass and watched the fire through a haze. He couldn't understand why he could not see clearly, why everything seemed wrapped in a fog. In the deepest recesses of his unconscious mind he knew that there was something wrong with this fire.

Gili awoke in a cold sweat, his body trembling and his heart thumping wildly. He was awake now, yet still he felt the same sense of danger he'd experienced in his dream.

"Ima," he called quietly. He felt the need for her presence as he had when he'd been a youngster. *What's happening to me? I'm as scared as a little boy,* he whispered to himself.

A deep silence prevailed in the house. Gili glanced at his watch. 2:15.

Ima's sleeping. Don't wake her, Gili. But his legs seemed to have a life of their own. They took him to her room.

Even before he'd reached the door, he could hear the muffled sobs.

"Ima," he called quietly, "do you need help?"

The sobbing stopped. There was the sound of gentle footsteps and the door was opened.

"Gili, why aren't you asleep?"

Her eyes were red. The thought suddenly struck him: *Who knows how many nights she spends crying?*

He answered with the same question. "Why aren't you sleeping?"

"Let's go to the kitchen for a cup of coffee, since we're both awake anyway," she suggested.

They sat in the breakfast nook and sipped slowly, thoughtfully, like two people searching for the right words, the difficult words, and not finding them.

Monica broke the silence. "Since Abba's gone you're my whole world, Gili. Why are you doing this to me?"

"Doing what?"

"Gili, stop playing games."

"Okay," Gili surrendered, "I believe absolutely in the correctness of the path I've chosen. I have to go and learn."

"And there's no yeshivot here in the area? You've got to leave me alone and go to Jerusalem?"

"Tel Aviv is empty."

She swiveled her chair round and round. Her coffee grew cold, untasted. "There are schools for *ba'alei teshuvah* here in Tel Aviv."

"I want to learn Torah from the source," he said resolutely. "From the great rabbis and scholars. To sit by a *shtender* and learn for six solid, uninterrupted hours without once standing up, not to hear a lecture on how nice it is to learn Torah. I want the Torah itself. Can't you understand?" He grabbed at his chair until his fingers turned white. "To learn with intensity. To understand the G-dly logic hidden in the ancient words!"

Monica looked at him for a long while, unaware of the tears in her eyes.

"You're so like your grandfather. I knew it! I knew the circle would turn back," she sighed.

"What? My grandfather? Which grandfather?" Gili was confused.

"You didn't know any of your grandparents. I'm talking about Abba's father."

"What was his name?" Suddenly his family history interested him.

"He was a good Jew. Udi loved and admired him, though he didn't accept his way. He was very religious, a great rabbi who spent his whole life learning those big texts. His name was Shmuel Dinburg, a Yerushalmi Jew. He came from an old neighborhood, Batei Ungarin I think. How your father upset him."

"You mean Abba left a religious life?" The question came out, a shout.

"Did he ever!" Monica said in a strained voice. A concealed sigh battered at the depths of her heart, until, refusing to be stifled any longer, it escaped quietly. An echo seemed to fill the walls of the house, whispering brokenly of days long forgotten, speaking of ancient struggles and fateful decisions. "How proud we were of our lifestyle. How we mocked the old ways. We hardly noticed the pain of our parents, as they broke their hearts over us."

Gili poured out her coffee, stone cold now, and brought her another steaming mug. *She's speaking about more than one child, Gili.* "Ima, you too?"

"A little."

"Meaning?"

Monica sipped slowly. "Your father did a 180-degree turn. He came from an ultra-Orthodox Yerushalmi family, he learned in yeshivah. Then he crossed all the red lines, became completely unobservant. I didn't have such a far road to travel. My parents were traditional, they admired religion. But they suffered too, when together with many of our traditions, I abandoned my given name, Rachel, and became Monica, a complete secularist."

Gili thought of what he'd just heard. Even in this melancholy situation, one could almost smile. They sit, a mother and her son, drinking strong coffee in the middle of the night when they should have been sleeping, gathering their strength for the next day. At 3 in the morning you find out that your dead father, a confirmed secular Jew, had been a yeshivah student, a Torah-observant youth. You learn that you didn't even know your mother's given name. These conversations could only take place now; in the stark light of morning, one didn't discuss these things.

"You know, Ima, I have a recurring dream. A very disturbing one."

"You dream about Abba?" A flash of life twinkled in her tired eyes.

"Not at all." The light that had appeared in her eyes dimmed. "I dreamed about Abba in the summer." The light came back, stronger now. "I miss Abba so. His smile, his laugh, his warm hug. It's like...like not having enough air to breathe." His throat tightened with unshed tears. "Sometimes I feel that I'm going mad from longing and...from regret."

Monica swallowed her own tears with difficulty. "Regret?" Her voice shook. "What's to regret? Did you do anything on purpose?"

"Because of me, Abba and Manny Schwartz turned into ashes."

Monica sighed. "Yes, Manny too."

"Who was Manny?" Gili asked. "I met him for the first time on that terrible night."

"No, you actually saw a lot of him, but you were a baby. When you were little he used to visit. He was Abba's best friend in yeshivah." Monica's voice was soft and far away. "For a few years he kept up the connection between us; then he just disappeared. Two years ago he began to visit Abba in the studio, but he didn't come here."

Gili hardly listened. His eyes were tightly shut. "If I hadn't drunk so much at the wedding, I wouldn't have lost control of the car."

"Enough. Don't live in the past. If you pick at a wound, you only invite infection."

"But you can't heal if you don't cleanse the infected area." Gili wouldn't give up.

"Gili, you can't alter the facts. Abba was killed! That's reality. Irreversible."

"Yes, I know. Irreversible damage." Gili ran his hands over his scalp, as if to try and heal the wound in his brain.

"You were telling me about a dream," Monica reminded him.

Gili hesitated. He had begun to regret his earlier talkativeness. "You won't laugh at me?"

Monica shook her head. A wrinkle composed of bitterness and hurt appeared on her forehead: She was aging rapidly.

"A strange dream, I've already had it about a hundred times. I'm lying on the wet grass, and the car is burning up. The flames are getting closer to me and I want to get up and run away, but I can't. I just lie there, helpless, until someone comes and pulls me from the flames. And all the while I'm feeling that there's something wrong with the fire."

Obviously an unconscious response to the trauma, Monica thought. "Maybe you should see a psychologist? You wouldn't speak to the psychologist who wanted to help you after the funeral. You've internalized the tragedy. It's got to come out, one way or the other."

"It could be," Gili admitted. "But that's not what I meant, why it bothers me. I see everything as strange, confused. There's a terrible sense of danger."

"Danger to whom? To you?"

"No, to Abba. I feel that Abba is in terrible peril."

"That's right. That's what really happened. He was in danger of being burned up, if the fall hadn't already killed him. But that's all in the past now, dear. Abba is not here any longer, and there's nothing we can do." Monica rose from the chair and sighed. "Wherever Abba is now, there's no danger..."

"Ima," Gili walked after her towards the door. His eyes held a pleading look. "I didn't tell you the most important part. In the dream, something isn't clear. That is..."

"Go to the bathroom, Gili. In the middle portion of the medicine cabinet, on the top shelf, you'll find a bottle of Valium." Monica spoke in a tone that brooked no argument. "Take a pill and go to bed."

☾❀☽

The line was long, as it was every night. A colorful group of people waited for their turn to enter the room. Here was a place where the early hours of morning were the most productive time.

When one of the visitors left the room, he closed the door behind him and dialed a number.

Two rings, three, five, six. Finally, someone picked up.

"Were you sleeping?" he asked coldly.

"Yes, I usually do sleep at night, if you don't mind," the answering voice muttered between yawns. "What time is it anyway? 3:30 in the morning? What do you want from me? I've got a busy day tomorrow."

"I told you once that sleeping at night is a bad habit. The night is an excellent time for thought, for study, for work. Everything is quiet and you can concentrate properly. Sleep for an hour and a half during the day: That's enough!"

"Maybe for you, but I need seven hours at night."

"You could also survive on an hour and a half. I'll teach you how another time, sleepyhead."

He's not normal, he thought to himself. *You can see that he doesn't get enough sleep.*

"So you think I'm crazy," the cold words came out of the receiver. "I work 22 hours a day; you work barely half that. So which one of us is not normal?"

A full minute passed before he recovered. *He reads minds!* "What do you want?" he asked weakly.

"Have you spoken to him recently?"

"No."

"Arrange some kind of meeting with him soon. Find out what's going on. I want to know if he's ready."

"Okay." *Just let me get some sleep.*

"Get some sleep. Good night."

A loud noise assaulted his eardrums as he stood on the threshold of the yeshivah. Hundreds of students, married and unmarried, learned aloud, most of them seated, crouched, before desks and *shtenders,* a few standing or pacing up and down the narrow aisles and between the chairs. He was astounded. *How can they concentrate with all this noise? It's louder here than in a factory!* A few curious individuals cast a momentary glance at the jeans-clad young man wearing a backpack. The young man stared back.

A man in a long black jacket seated by the eastern wall hurried towards him with long strides and greeted him with a wide smile.

"Gili Dinar?" He pumped his hand with obvious delight. "Welcome. It's good to meet you. Rabbi Schmidt. I've heard a lot about you from the *Arachim* staff."

"Good or bad?"

"A little of both." The smile never left his face. "First, you were something of a troublemaker. The teachers didn't know what to do with your questions. Are you a scientist?"

"No, just a fledgling journalist."

"You're humble, I see. So how does a journalist get such a broad knowledge of the sciences? You must be an intelligent young man. That will be a big help in your learning Gemara."

Gili stood uncomfortably. "Do you 'buy' students with flattery? It looks like you've been expecting me. Who told you about me?"

Rabbi Schmidt didn't flinch under the onslaught. "I'll tell you the truth. I saw you in Teveriah. I was up at the seminar for a short visit. And as for the 'flattery,' I disagree. You asked if I heard good or bad about you. What did you think I would tell you? It's permitted to say something nice about a person where applicable. It will make the difficult beginning a bit smoother. Afterwards, you'll have to work very hard to earn a small compliment."

That was Gili Dinar's first encounter with the yeshivah.

Ein Yisrael
5718 — 1958

The ancient motor heaved and squeaked. The aged *HaMekasher* bus exerted itself and finally reached the stop.

"Ein Yisrael," the driver announced. "The boy who got on at Beit Dagan must get off, or pay an additional 20 *agorot* to go on to Tel Aviv."

He rose clumsily, his suitcase in his hands, and got down onto the narrow sidewalk. His bones ached from having sat upon the hard wooden seat for such a long time. It had been an arduous journey, begun in Jerusalem, passing through Beit Shemesh and Ramle, and terminating at the Beit Dagan junction. He'd then boarded the bus that reached Tel Aviv via the small moshav, Ein Yisrael. Legend told of an ancient spring that had been located there. The moshav, and the yeshivah located there, were named for this *maayan*, this water source of days gone by.

He studied the small map that he had sketched on a scrap of paper torn from a notebook before he had begun his journey. Left, and then down to the dirt path. The small, unyielding suitcase seemed heavier than its actual weight. Despite his best efforts, his eyes grew moist. How he had longed for this day, how he had looked forward to it. "On Rosh Chodesh Elul I'll be learning in Ein Yisrael!" he had bragged to all his family, during summer vacation. How happily he had packed his belongings into the battered suitcase. He was grown up! A young man, 15 years old. Traveling to study in a distant yeshivah, far from his mother's apron strings, far from his strict disciplinarian father and his harsh teacher.

But now his heart was filled with longing. Even for Abba...

You haven't even reached the yeshivah and you're homesick already? he railed at himself. But the tears continued to collect in the corners of his eyes, moist and salty. He felt a lump in his throat.

If not for the people passing nearby, he would have burst into tears.

Abba, Ima, he murmured, *I miss you so. Abba, why did you make me leave home? Couldn't I have learned in a yeshivah in Yerushalayim?*

A worker in a khaki shirt and shorts approached him with swift steps. "Excuse me, do you have the time?" the young man asked.

The worker paused. "A quarter to three."

I'm late! he thought in a panic. The trip had taken much longer than he'd expected. Almost two hours on the road! Afternoon classes began at 3:15. He still had to walk from the main road to the moshav and find his place in the dormitory. *What about my roommates? Will they be friendly? Easy to get along with?*

Everything bothered him now. He longed to cross over to the other side and wait for the bus returning to Jerusalem. But what would he say to Abba? "Hi, I missed you, I ran away from the yeshivah before I even entered it..."

And it was his own fault that he was here! He had wanted to show Abba that he was independent, that he could learn without his father's constant surveillance.

It was on a summer's evening, sitting around the Shabbat table, that he'd made the solemn declaration: "I want to learn in a yeshivah away from Yerushalayim." He waited for the ceiling to fall in on him. To his utter astonishment, his parents, his father, Shmuel, and mother, Devorah, seemed delighted with the idea. "Excellent. It will be good for you. A yeshivah in a small settlement will make a man out of you. You won't be able to hide behind your mother's apron strings anymore."

With Abba, to say it was to do it: He immediately embarked on an intensive investigation of the options. There weren't all that many, sparing him a lot of trouble. A good friend recommended Ein Yisrael: "The Rosh Yeshivah is one of the great scholars of our generation; the *mashgiach* is a giant, like one of the old school, a first-class *mussar* personality."

Abba was enthusiastic, and so here he was, Abba's "Moishike," dragging his feet slowly and unwillingly on the long dirt path that led to Ein Yisrael.

It was a blistering hot day. And if. a heat wave weren't enough, an oppressive east wind howled around him, blowing brown earth from nearby fields directly at him, soiling the Shabbos suit that he'd worn in honor of his first day in the yeshivah.

I didn't need this, he thought. *Everything is against me today, even the weather.*

The dirt path came to an end. A small sign on a barbed-wire fence announced "Ein Yisrael."

A short walk and one already had a sense of the place. Young boys and older students walked feverishly between the small houses and the metal sheds. Everything was quick; a feeling of frenetic activity filled the air. He was caught up in the rush.

"Shalom. You must be the new boy from Yerushalayim."

A tall, bespectacled young man thrust out a big, sweaty hand. He was holding a long list, and he swiftly glanced at the names written in pencil on the paper. "Not him, not him," he muttered, running over the ones which had already been checked off. "Yes, here's your name. Go to the long shed on the other side, room number five. Your roommates are Yosef Friedman, Chaim Ozer Schmidt, and Menachem Schwartz."

Hard beds with metal frames, shabby straw mattresses. The window was closed to keep out the howling, sand-filled wind; inside, the atmosphere was suffocating. He put his suitcase on the mattress and rifled through his pocket for the small key.

Oh, no. It's gone.

"3:15!" He heard the shouts through the corridor. The sound of footsteps told him that the boys were rushing to the *beis midrash*. To the first class of the summer term. Only he was standing here like a fool, his suitcase before him, his new Gemara locked inside. How could he learn without it? A stifled sob rose from his throat; he grabbed a handkerchief from his pocket and wiped his face.

A strong hand landed on his shoulder.

"It's always like this on the first day. All beginnings are hard."

A smiling student stood before him, giving him a friendly once-over.

Confused, he pulled the handkerchief away. "I...I have a cold, and this wind is making my eyes tear."

"It's okay, it's okay," the smiling young man told him. Unspoken, but obvious, were his words: "I understand. You don't have to be embarrassed."

A small piece of metal appeared in his hand. "Maybe this will help?"

Impossible. His key! "Where did you find it?"

"Here, on the floor." The student pointed to the cracked flooring near the bed. The boy had sharp, deep eyes, eyes like none he'd ever seen before. "I assume this is yours."

"Right."

"Good. Now leave everything and come to the *beis midrash*. The *mashgiach* doesn't like people coming late on the first day. Oh, by the way, we haven't introduced ourselves. My name is Menachem Schwartz. I'm from Antwerp. What's your name?"

"What? You're from Belgium?" He looked at the young man in unconcealed surprise.

"Yes. What's the big deal?"

"You haven't the trace of an accent."

"That's it? Yes, I look and sound like a born and bred Israeli."

They walked quickly to the yeshivah's old building, chatting like old friends.

A hushed, holy atmosphere filled the *beis midrash*. Dozens of students were already *davening Minchah* with bent heads. The two entered quietly and were soon indistinguishable among the others.

That was Moshe Dinburg's first encounter with the yeshivah.

7

He had known it wouldn't be easy. But so hard?

Gili threw his things in his green backpack, a feeling of frustration overwhelming him as he prepared to go home. All right, he was admitting defeat. It was unpleasant, absolutely humiliating. But there was no alternative: he just couldn't stay here any longer.

Preferring not to say goodbye to anyone he stealthily tiptoed down the quiet hallway. All the others were in the *beis midrash*. No one would see him leave. Would they figure out that he'd fled? So what, let them.

"Hey, Gili, where are you going?" Rabbi Schmidt appeared and stopped him in the doorway.

"Home."

"What's the matter? A crisis?" Rabbi Schmidt didn't sound surprised.

"Benny was right," Gili answered.

He told Rabbi Schmidt about Benny Gabison and his pessimistic forecast, how he had predicted that Gili would not be able to stand it in yeshivah. He spoke of Benny's friend, who had run away from yeshivah after just a few days, who preferred chopping wood to learning Talmud.

In a low voice he remembered his initial enthusiasm, how he had so longed to see the G-dly light in the Gemara.

"And now I see nothing. In the seminar they spoke about the meaning of life, about reality and illusion. We discussed the Torah and the prophecies. They shattered my beliefs in Darwin and evolutionary theory. That's what pulled me to yeshivah. I come here and what do I find? Suddenly I'm spending hours on involved debates about lost objects that haven't even negligible value. Did you ever hear of three men who managed to lose half a penny? I'll tell you the truth, I don't understand a thing. It doesn't mean anything to me."

"So that's it? Off you go? Do you always give up so easily?"

Gili was offended. "I'm no quitter. But this is different. I'm sick of it!"

"So quickly? You've been here all of two days. Stay here for a week, do *mishmar* on Thursday night. Then we'll hear what you have to say."

"*Mishmar*? Translation, please."

"You learn all of Thursday night, right up to sunrise. We'll see you after that, after you've tasted the sweetness of a difficult *Tosafos* at three in the morning. Wait till you've toiled over the razor-edge logic of the '*Avnei Miluim*' when everything outside is dark and silent, when only the stars are twinkling in the blackness and whispering, together with you, the secrets of the universe, and you feel a spiritual happiness like nothing you've ever experienced. Let's see you do that!"

Gili wheeled around. These words intrigued him.

"But explain to me, what's the point of this exaggerated precision, of the Sages' obsessive interest in every dot and letter, on valueless objects worth less than a penny?"

Rabbi Schmidt gave the question some thought before replying. Finally, he said, "First of all, to answer your specific question, I hope you won't be offended if I tell you that it seems you didn't understand the Gemara on the topic of a coin lost by three walking together. More generally, all the world agrees that the Jews are the most ethical nation on this earth. Do you want to know why? From this meticulousness, from going down and examining every tiny detail. Only those willing to delve into the deepest layers, on a penny and half a penny, and who can then agree that the law of a penny is like the law of a hundred dollars, only such a nation can rise to the greatest heights."

"That's true," Gili said, suddenly remembering his history classes. "All the great empires of the past declined because of their moral decadence."

"And decadence begins with a penny, excuse me, half a penny," Rabbi Schmidt intoned in mock solemnity, ending with laughter.

Smiling, the two crossed the threshold into the yeshivah. Gili's backpack lay forlorn near the doorway as he began learning intently with his *chavrusa*.

Ein Yisrael
5718 — 1958

Night. The hour was late and the entire dormitory was asleep. Even the most diligent in Ein Yisrael had gone to bed. From the mists of slumber the Belgian student, Menachem Schwartz, heard a muffled cry, relegating it immediately to the world of dreams. But the cry grew louder, more urgent. Groggily, he thought of the nightly concert given by the moshav cats, usually right under his window. He turned over, anxious to go back to sleep, and suddenly realized that this was no cats' choir: Moshe Dinburg, his roommate, was sobbing beneath his blanket.

"Moishike, is that you? Calm down," he whispered. "You'll wake up Yoske and Ozer."

Moshe froze. Slowly he pulled his head out from the blanket. "Did you hear something?" he said, his confusion apparent.

"Come, let's go outside for a while," Menachem suggested gently.

They strolled between the dormitory huts. In those days of poverty and want, streetlamps were sparingly installed, with large spaces between them. The feeble light couldn't compete with the night's blackness. Countless stars gave off pale sparkles in the dark heavens above them, sending warm greetings to the pair of young men. The frosty air hinted at the fast-approaching autumn; the two figures in pajamas shivered slightly in the coolness. They walked silently near the boggy sand dunes that surrounded the yeshivah dormitories. Hardly aware of their meanderings, they reached the moshav's orchards. The night chill had coated the fruit with drops of dew, and they emitted a heavenly scent. Menachem and Moshe sat down on the hard earth, beneath one of the trees, and breathed in the sweet, fresh smell.

"So what is it? Still missing home?"

"A lot," Moshe answered honestly.

"You don't like the yeshivah?"

"I like it a lot. But family is family. I'm homesick."

"You have to get used to it. It's hard for me, too. I'm a little further from my house than you are. You'll travel to Yerushalayim sometimes; I'm here until Pesach. That's a full half-year. Tell the truth — you don't enjoy the yeshivah?"

Moshe hesitated. It was hard, fooling Menachem. "You're right, it's hard for me. I'm not used to learning for so long. Ten hours! I just can't do it."

"Who said you have to learn for 10 hours?"

"So what should I do?" Moshe asked heatedly. "Just fool around?"

"That's not what I mean," Menachem explained placidly. "Don't talk about '10 hours.' That makes it hard on you. I, for instance, learn only five minutes. How? Very simple. I tell myself, Come, let's go learn for five minutes. Anyone can learn for a few minutes, right? After five minutes, I tell it to myself again. Over and over. That's the way to solve your problem!"

"Oh, I should fool myself?" Moshe argued. "But don't I know that in the end I'll wind up learning for 10 hours?"

"No! Instead of repeating those frightening words, '10 hours,' over and over again, make it easy on yourself. Whisper the magic words 'five minutes'! It works! Your brain believes what you tell it; tell it 'only five minutes,' and you'll see how it will calm down. In a day or two there'll be a real change for the better."

"How old are you, Manny?"

"Fifteen, just like you. Why?"

"That's good adult advice. You must have heard it from the *mashgiach*."

"No, I haven't spoken more than two sentences with him," Menachem admitted. "Moshe, if you're complaining about how tough it is, what should I say? You came from a background that's similar to this one; you learned in *cheder* from morning to night. You've made the transition from a poor house to a poor yeshivah. Compared to you I come from a wealthy place, and in my school in Antwerp we never learned Gemara for more than a short period of time. I'm just as homesick as you are. Believe me, if I could I would run back to Belgium tomorrow. It's hard, but is that a reason to cry? What's with you?"

He said those last words with such emphasis that Moshe felt a pang of shame, as if the *mashgiach* had reprimanded him. "You're right," he muttered, his embarrassment showing in his voice, "I've been acting like a little boy. You won't hear me crying again."

They had passed the dormitory.

"By the way, why did you call me Moishike?" Moshe asked.

"Isn't that what they call you at home?"

"My father does, but I don't like it. Everyone else calls me Moishy."

"Okay, Moishy it is."

But the question continued to gnaw at Moshe: How had Menachem known his father's nickname for him? The name appeared only in his father's letters to him. Had Menachem read through his mail? Impossible!

In any case, in the next few weeks Moshe became Moishike to everyone in yeshivah...

That was the first of their heart-to-heart talks. Other nocturnal walks followed, as Moshe became captivated by the personal charisma of his new friend. Officially they learned together in the morning; in reality, they were inseparable all the time.

The *mashgiach*, Rabbi Shmuel Bergman, wasn't terribly pleased with the friendship, despite the help that Menachem gave to Moshe in those first difficult days. His finely honed pedagogical instincts defined the differences between the two. Moshe was a sensitive soul with a compliant character; Menachem, with his tough, steely disposition, immediately dominated the relationship. Rabbi Bergman's heart told him that nothing good would come of this friendship, and he did all he could to separate the two. He looked for another friend for Moshe Dinburg, choosing the reticent Yoske Friedman to fill this role.

In truth, Moshe himself felt drawn to Friedman, whose personality so matched his own. But a silly quarrel that sprang up between Dinburg and Friedman put an end to the budding friendship. The *mashgiach* investigated the cause of the problem, and discovered...Manny!

In the war between the elderly, experienced *mashgiach* and the young Belgian student, Menachem Schwartz, sly and unyielding, surprisingly emerged victorious. In all his years Rabbi Shmuel could not remember meeting such a sophisticated young man. Manny Schwartz won the hearts of almost all of the students in the yeshivah; but for the most part he preferred to spend his time with the youngster in the Yerushalmi garb.

Rabbi Schmidt was right. And wrong.

After the initial difficulties, Gili made a breakthrough. He began to taste the sweetness of the Gemara learning. His intellectual enjoyment when he mastered a difficult point of logic was unprecedented; he'd never enjoyed such an adventure. He knew that he was touching absolute truth, and he felt as if he'd climbed the world's highest peak. His own personal Everest seemed to grow taller with each passing day, and the spiritual joy that the Gemara gave him increased enormously with time. He spent days and nights deep in his learning, revealing intellectual capabilities that enabled him to unravel difficult *sugyos*. Though many clamored to learn with him, Gili insisted on learning only with Rabbi Schmidt, with whom he forged an intense bond.

Three wonderful weeks passed in this manner. Then, unsolicited and unwanted, came the crisis.

Gili, the on-the-spot reporter, suddenly found himself sitting in front of an open Gemara, daydreaming about his former profession. He felt drawn to the drama and excitement, the secrets and the searches. He felt a deep desire to once again experience the adventure.

"Gili, are you with me?" Rabbi Schmidt asked him from behind his *shtender.* "It seems that you're engrossed in some sweet dream, or maybe in some terrible nightmare."

"That's right," Gili confessed quietly. "I miss the paper."

"You've tasted the sweetness of Torah, entered a paradise on earth, and now you want to run away?"

"I want to learn, but the writing is drawing me like a magnet."

"It's a shame, Gili. You've got to bear down and persevere. These are just fantasies. Did you know that the imagination is the kiss of the *yetzer hara*? Be strong, give yourself a chance. You can't do it all in one day; there are many for whom the process of return is a long and arduous one, with one step forward and two back."

But in the following days the situation only became more acute. In the place of the first rapture came despair and frustration. Rabbi Schmidt explained that these were merely challenges and would disappear; Gili himself couldn't understand the conflicting emotions that beset him.

Two months of this seesaw existence passed. For every hour of satisfaction and growth came two days of increasing discomfort.

On that afternoon Gili entered his room and found a guest sitting on his bed, reciting *Tehillim*. "Benny," he shouted happily, "Hi! What are you doing here?"

Benny shut the *Tehillim* and moved his sunglasses onto his thick hair. He jumped off the bed and gave Gili a warm, heartfelt hug.

"Our Gili! I hear you've become a real scholar!"

"Stop it," Gili laughed. "I'm trying to learn a little."

"'Let me dwell in the house of the L-rd all my days'? But do you get any time off for good behavior?"

"It's tough," Gili said, suddenly gloomy. "I'm like a person dying of thirst in the desert who finally reaches an oasis and discovers a sweet water well. He begins to drink a bit, and suddenly finds himself missing the burning sands!"

Benny was silent. Inside, Gili thanked him for not bursting out into a chorus of "I told you so." He sat down next to his old friend and offered him something to eat.

It wasn't long before he'd figured out what had brought Benny to him.

"Benny, are you serious?"

"Gili, I told you then, I'm keeping your seat warm."

Gili wanted to jump with joy, but he kept his cool. He was torn between the desire to learn and the equal desire to write. "I want to return to the paper, but I've just begun to discover the hidden glory of the Torah."

"Gili, you've got to come back. It's essential. Listen and you'll understand why."

Benny spoke of the grim reality that the religious community faced every day: the distorted picture of them presented by the secular media. Most newspapers had a reporter specializing in religious affairs; without exception these were confirmed secularists, lacking even a minimal understanding of religion, now assigned to report on the activities of the religious community. They presented their public with a twisted, inaccurate view of a primitive, barbaric group whose underpinnings were lies and perversions.

And now, Benny said, there was an opportunity to improve the situation somewhat. Ami Kedmi and Eric Meisels, the editor and his assistant, who hadn't despaired of Gili, were offering him a position on the paper as specialist in the affairs of the religious community. A reporter of the stature of Gili Dinar, a man well known in Israeli society, writing sympathetically of the religious lifestyle, and with first-hand knowledge of his subject, in the widely distributed newspaper *HaYom HaZeh*: Those words would carry weight.

"Gili, do you get it? It would be a position of great power, a reporter who is a *ba'al teshuvah*, someone who's run the entire route. It'll be a dream!"

"It's stupid. I'm not looking for positions of power."

"Okay, and what about the *kiddush Hashem* that you can make? And the *chillul Hashem* that takes place every day, as journalists distort our image among the public. Is that also stupid?"

Gili stood up and motioned to Benny to join him at the window. They saw an ancient Yerushalayim alleyway before them. It was twilight and men were rushing to *daven Minchah* before sunset.

"Look, Benny. I've discovered a new world here. These people couldn't care less what the outside world thinks of them. They live for truth and are prepared to die for it. No radio, no television, no newspapers. Completely cut off from all written and electronic media."

Benny wouldn't give up. "Let's go talk to Rabbi Schmidt."

Gili leaped up in shock. "Benny, don't tell me you've talked with Rabbi Schmidt about this!"

"As a matter of fact, I did," Benny laughed. "He's waiting for you in his office."

"I've thought about you a lot, Gili. In all honesty, with your hand on your heart, do you want to learn or do you want to write?" Rabbi Schmidt's words were sharp; they pierced through him until he could feel the pain.

"That's not fair," Gili protested. "I've tried and I've tried. Learning is a taste of paradise."

"Yet despite that you've not succeeded in your learning." Rabbi Schmidt was pained. "Generally, I wouldn't let someone with your talents leave. I would give you a year's trial, certain that at the end of the year you would be one of the best in yeshivah. But you are not the ordinary *ba'al teshuvah*. In your case it is possible that I should permit a temporary departure from yeshivah, though not from Torah."

Gili's eyes roamed through the small office, over the pictures of the rabbis adorning the walls, the desk overloaded with papers, the shelves sagging beneath their load of *sefarim*. This was his first visit to this room; if it was any indication of the yeshivah's financial situation, it would seem it was in no great shape. Aside from some outdated office equipment and many *sefarim*, there was nothing there.

"If it is your desire to leave for a while, then you may leave."

They say that the eyes are the windows to the soul; Gili was certain that Rabbi Schmidt's were windows to heaven. There are people whose eyes are empty. Rabbi Schmidt's were full, expressing so much. Gili stared into the clear blue eyes, trying to delve deep into the man's soul. What did he really think?

"Gili, you're considered one of the country's top journalists. We're surrounded by a sea of hostility. Please make sure we are treated fairly in the press. Go in peace and come in peace. I'm certain you'll return here, and then it will be for good." Rabbi Schmidt stood up and held Gili's hand for a long moment. True friendship seemed to flow from the soft hand to the steely one. Gili had searched for Rabbi Schmidt's soul within his eyes; here, now, in this sensitive hand he could find it. This hand spoke in a language of its own, whispering of love for others, of deep emotions that words could not articulate.

When the mouth cannot speak, the heart opens!

8

The lights in the head office of the General Security Service were on at one in the morning, though on the outside, one could see nothing through the sealed windows. The conference room was still quiet, but all felt that the storm was about to break. Around the large oval table sat six out of 15 branch heads. This was no secret meeting; officially, it was not taking place at all.

None of those attending were surprised at the absence of the regular inhabitants of "the cube," the secretaries, typists, and security guards who were normally quartered in the far left-hand corner, in a cube-shaped area cordoned off by paneling. The topic was too sensitive, too secret to be shared.

The head of the GSS, known only as "S," fixed questioning eyes upon the six who'd been taken into confidence. *Good men, all of them, men who can be relied on. And "K"? Does he also have the necessary criteria? He's been vetted, his recommendations are superb. And yet, I'm not certain. Will his religious past make problems?*

He slowly examined each face: "G," his deputy, a quick-thinking, bright man full of creative ideas; "M," head of the Department of Psychological Warfare: "S" had spoken with him already. The man was brilliant; too brilliant, perhaps. "B," head of the Jewish Affairs department, a strong, brave man who wouldn't be afraid to make tough choices. But he was overeager; he needed a firm hand to rein him in. "T," head of the Manpower Division; "K," head of the Arab sector; "H," head of the Anti-Terror Unit. The seventh man sitting with them, the only one whose name was permitted to be mentioned, was Mutty, liaison officer.

Good men, all of them, men who can be relied on.

With a slow gesture he pulled out his tobacco pouch and filled his pipe with fine Empora leaves. He flicked open a lighter and inhaled the scent with pleasure.

What does he want? What's happened? Seven men, one shared thought.

Good, let them get a little nervous, he laughed inwardly. *It won't hurt them.*

He blew a smoke ring upward and began to speak in a quiet tone. "Okay, let's begin. As you see, no one besides us is here in the room. This is an ultrasensitive topic, classified. Even in our own service, which is always discreet, there are different levels of confidentiality. This is top secret! This stuff is explosive; it can lead to absolute chaos. Remember, one word and everything is lost."

Quit the introduction and get to the point. Again, a thought common to all seven.

"I will ask 'B,' head of Jewish Affairs, to open the meeting."

B. began. "We're facing an acute problem. We tend to overlook it, but it's growing day by day." His tone was solemn.

"What are you talking about?" K. breathed the words. Perhaps his instincts were telling him something.

"You'll hear. I'm not keeping secrets here. We're talking about a minority in the country, a minority that is growing all the time. And I'm not talking about the Arab sector. The establishment tends to treat it with contempt, because of its size. We feel that though it's a small minority, we're the only ones who realize that it is growing at an incredible rate. We haven't any reliable sources of information within it. We've tried to place agents within, as is our usual policy, but because it is such a homogeneous group, they've immediately been spotted. They were kicked out within days! The group has finely honed instincts; they are highly intelligent, very suspicious, and immediately catch on to any duplicity.

"Until now," B. continued, "no agency has succeeded in estimating its size. Not only do we lack formal figures, but the Central Bureau of Statistics and other research agencies haven't managed to do so. But with the help of top statisticians in the field we've managed to put together a confidential assessment, and the results have caused a ringing of the alarm bells.

"According to our evaluation, which may not be accurate and if anything is underestimating the numbers, today, in the year 1988, this minority comprises 11 percent of the State. So, you ask, what's the problem? That's just about one tenth of the population! But an expert who will join us in a few minutes will explain how this minority, within less than two decades, shall actually form a majority within Israel."

"Maybe you can tell us exactly whom you're talking about. It's not Arabs, okay. Is it Druze? Christians?" H.'s voice, like his face, was somber.

B. was silent for a long minute. He placed the fingertips of his hands together, forming a human tent. The tension in the room grew with every passing second. All the participants stared at him, mesmerized, while he continued to play with his fingers, as if trying to put off the moment. Finally, he took a deep breath and spoke quickly.

"I'm talking about the *chareidim*, the ultra-Orthodox," he said.

Ein Yisrael 5723 — 1963

Life in Yeshivas Ein Yisrael was shrouded in seriousness and sanctity. The Rosh Yeshivah, Rabbi Aharon Rapaport, and the *mashgiach*, Rabbi Shmuel Bergman, were outstanding personalities in the Jewish world. The Rosh Yeshivah was unique in his genius, reflected in the lessons he gave; the *mashgiach* was renowned for extraordinary piety, and for his lectures in ethics, that harked back to the style of the Lithuanian yeshivos of Mir and Kelm. The students learned with extraordinary diligence. Many of them were above average in talents and understanding, with some excelling in their analytical skills. A small number of youngsters stood perpetually in the warm glow of their *mashgiach's* presence. These were students destined to take their places as the next generation's *roshei yeshivah* and *maggidei shiur*.

The *beis midrash* was no more than a rectangular wooden hut, long and narrow, with thin walls that allowed in winter's cold and summer's blazing heat. One lone ceiling fan tried valiantly to keep 100 suffering boys cool. But neither soaring temperatures nor plunging thermometers decreased the diligence. Some of the boys felt it was not enough; these became members of the "Sixty Club." Their goal: to study even during their leisure hours between classes, and to ultimately learn 60 hours each week.

Occasionally the yeshivah boys themselves gave *shiurim*, young men hardly older than their students. Astonishingly, they were able to command the respect of their students, though less than two years separated them.

But with all the privation, there was plenty of youthful exuberance. And one of the reasons for the joyous atmosphere was the dining room where the boys ate their daily and Shabbos meals.

Yeshivas Ein Yisrael suffered from abject poverty. The meals served were skimpy. On Friday nights, at the end of dinner, the still-hungry students were given plates laden with chickpeas, as a means of augmenting an otherwise unsatisfying meal. The famished boys filled themselves up on the peppery treat until they felt ready to burst. When no one wanted to even see a single round chickpea, Moshe Shipper of Jerusalem would get up and collect all the leftovers. Amazingly enough, he managed to eat every last one of them without ever getting a stomach ache. The boys used to claim that he could even eat nails, since his intestines were obviously made of forged steel. It was certainly a fact that no one ever matched his record of eating 60 sabra fruits at one time, which he had done on a wager with a friend, but that's another story...

But the impoverished meal couldn't daunt the young men, who would sit and sing Shabbos songs for hours. They sang slow, emotion-filled songs that contributed much to the special atmosphere of the yeshivah.

But all this was considered trivial: what was important was the learning. Ein Yisrael was at its best; it prospered and flowered.

Manny Schwartz and Moshe Dinburg grew up; they were already 19-year-old young men sporting mustaches and fuzzy beards on their chins.

Four years had passed since Moshe had entered yeshivah. He'd long since forgotten the crisis of his first days there; with Manny's help, he'd inured himself to yeshivah life. The two had become best friends, with Manny often visiting Moshe's home in the Jerusalem neighborhood of Batei Ungarin. Many times the *mashgiach* wondered if he hadn't been mistaken in his conviction that their remarkable rapport boded nothing good.

One year later came the great change, one that left its indelible mark on many lives for years to come. It was a bright, sunny morning when the two left the yeshivah grounds; a few hours later they entered the giant army camp in Tzrifin. Three years later, their army service ended, the two had no vestige of religious observance left. Moshe Dinburg, bareheaded, had become Udi Dinar. Rabbi Shmuel Bergman could have patted himself on the back — his fears had not been misplaced — but his anguish at the fate of his two students was so sharp that he felt no sense of satisfaction in being proved right.

No one knew precisely what had come over the two prize students of the yeshivah and caused them to stray so far from its path. The riddle remained unsolved, a black mark on the proud escutcheon of Ein Yisrael.

Tel Aviv 5758 — 1988

"Nonsense," K. objected. "The *chareidim,* ultra-Orthodox, posing a danger to the state? Fantasy!"

"You know, when we called you here we took your background into account. Despite it, you were invited to join us." B. carefully prepared his pipe, held the lighter to the tobacco, and inhaled deeply. "Tell me if we made a mistake."

K. sat in offended silence for a few seconds. He would not give in. "Anyone familiar with the *chareidim* know that the majority of them are quiet, highly intelligent people. Why create an imaginary enemy? Let's concentrate on the Arab states, our true foes. Have you solved the problem of Iraq and Iran? The *chareidim* simply pose no threat to our lives here in Israel."

S. took the floor. "We've heard your opinion. We respect it, and disagree with it 100 percent. We are convinced that the enlightened secular majority will be frightened enough to leave the country. By the way, this business of 'highly intelligent people' doesn't bolster your argument, if you think about it. Gentlemen, when you leave here and go home, think about what you've heard at this meeting. Next time we get together I want a detailed simulation of what may happen in this country when this minority succeeds, because of its growth and political strength, in capturing control of the government."

"May we know how many years you're talking about?" This was G., the brilliant assistant to the department chief, speaking with scarcely concealed mockery. "With all due respect to our theorists, it seems to me these fears are exaggerated. They've lost all sense of proportion. Danger from *chareidim?* I have a few *chareidi* neighbors; they are as quiet as sheep."

"In another 10 years, when you're standing with your bags packed in Ben Gurion Airport, fleeing to Los Angeles before the religious flood, you'll hang your head and ask who was wrong!" S. unleashed his legendary temper, as he always did when faced with even a hint of opposition. "I also have met many pleasant *chareidim.* I'm speaking of a group, not of individuals. Are you familiar with the demographic picture of these people? They are expanding exponentially, a child a year! A religious family has eight to ten children, sometimes more! I know, there's nothing to do to stop it. Israel isn't China; we can't pass a 'one child per family' law here. We're even helping them in a roundabout way, with all the benefits that obviously we will continue to offer; they are getting stronger and stronger.

"We have several plans for keeping them in the minority. For example, the government is considering bringing tens of thousands of *olim* from various countries to counterbalance the growth of the religious. I'm hoping to hear other practical plans from all of you.

"You'll now hear the report of Professor Theo Mitchell, a worldrenowned demographic expert from Harvard University, and visiting lecturer on the Tel Aviv University faculty. Professor Mitchell, please."

A side door opened and a man in his 50s entered the room. He was graying, and his tailoring was impeccable. His fashionable glasses and high-domed forehead added to his academic demeanor; the title professor seemed tailor-made for him. He gave a slight bow before the participants and after a few pleasant introductory words turned to a screen on the wall.

For the next half-hour the men heard a fascinating and convincing slide presentation. Mitchell showed the demographic patterns, natural increase, and the incredible growth of the *chareidi* public over the past 40 years.

"From 1980 on, a new factor came into the picture, one that would change the entire scene, and give the *chareidi* sector a huge boost. That is what is known as the *teshuvah* movement. It is difficult to measure with normal statistical tools, but its strength is easily perceived, and lately its momentum is almost unparalleled. What the laws of demographics didn't quite do for the *chareidim*, the *teshuvah* movement did."

Mitchell spoke in elegant English, but the participants understood every word. At the end of his speech they remained immobile in their chairs. Their guest had aroused terrifying thoughts within them. He'd used sophisticated phrasing and deliberate ambiguities; he'd avoided spelling out a clear position, bringing examples from countries all over the earth. In a frosty and confident tone he'd described how minorities that had grown rapidly had taken over the governments of many countries. Iran and Algeria were two examples. "Empirical evidence backs up my theoretical assertions. There's no reason why the same thing that happened in many countries should not happen here in the Middle East. There is the distinct possibility that you will wake up one day and find that the nation you've built out of your blood and sweat no longer belongs to you. You'll have become a secular minority persecuted by the government theocracy."

S. stared at his underlings. *Good, Mitchell has laid the groundwork. Now it's time to strike, while the iron is hot.* "We've heard the learned opinions of Professor Theo Mitchell. Thank you so much," His slight nod indicated to the professor that his time was up. Mitchell quietly left the room. Two security guards met him and escorted him out of the GSS headquarters.

K. lifted a finger. "Discussion?"

"No discussion." S. was firm on the point. "I want detailed ideas from each of you on how to deal with the problem. We need ideas: how to minimize the influence of this group, that's growing without stop. I expect you to do sound fieldwork and return here with your 'homework.' We'll meet two weeks from today, at this same time."

K. drove home recklessly, almost causing an accident when his Opel swerved into the oncoming lane at high speed. A few cars shrieked to a stop at the very last second. K. escaped back to his lane just seconds before the onslaught of the furious drivers. They were justified, he decided, in their anger; still, he couldn't control his driving. His thoughts were drawn relentlessly back to the meeting.

No wonder it wasn't official. K. excelled in practical solutions, but now he felt cut off from reality. *If I hadn't heard it myself, I would never have believed it. To sit and plot against a good and loyal community, that never did and never could do anything harmful; to decide people's futures as if they were no more than dolls, statistics to play with...*

K. himself came from a *chareidi* family. His parents, brothers and sisters were *chareidim.* Only K., influenced by neighborhood friends, had taken on the secular life. He'd made his way in the outside world, and eventually found himself in the General Security Service.

And where were you until now? he laughed bitterly at himself. *Don't we always think of people that way, as if they were mere objects? Now you've decided to wake up?*

K. knew his friends intimately. Men changed when they were in power. With a wave of the hand they decided the destiny of thousands. It did something to you: In your head, men, groups, entire communities became raw materials to work with.

And when this power was secret, it grew even greater. You were protected by the curtain of confidentiality, and in the name of the security of the state you could do almost anything.

Yes, you had a superior who was responsible for you and kept his eye on your actions, but there was a lot of leeway...

K. was skeptical about the possibility of the government's involvement in S.'s schemes. He thought briefly of trying to go public, but quickly reconsidered such a dangerous idea. If this was all coming from "above," who knew what kind of trouble he could land in?

As he parked his car in his private space, among the villas of Herzliya, he knew what he had to do.

Go to his brother-in-law!

M., head of the Department of Psychological Warfare, also knew what he had to do. He had been the first to hear of S.'s concerns, and within days he'd come up with a splendid plan of action. S. had been astounded when he'd briefed him yesterday. "Ingenious!" he'd said. "But it seems just too crazy, too grandiose. Who could possible carry it out?'

M. told him.

S. hesitated. "Think about it again. It's too difficult, too elaborate, too complex. There must be simpler ways."

That was yesterday. M. knew his confederates well, and was certain that two weeks from now, after he'd gotten all the routine memos from the others, S. would agree that his plan was the only one that would work, and he'd give him the green light.

He would do it all!

9

The massive office building owned by *HaYom HaZeh* hummed with life, a hive of activity filled with reporters, inputters, proofreaders, photographers, and editors. Cellular phones rang. Optical scanners read dozens of color photographs and placed them in the memory banks, a few more bytes of data in the gigabyte memory of the latest in high-tech computers. These photos were then prepared for color separations and final printing in the giant rotary presses. Laser and ink-jet printers discharged rough drafts and polished final copy into the impatient hands of waiting journalists. In fact, it was business as usual during these hours before the paper was "put to bed" and sent to the printer.

This was the newsroom on Monday at 7 p.m. And suddenly everything grew silent, a momentary lull born of surprise, followed by a roar that shook the building:

"Gili!"

Within seconds the tall, lean young man with the green eyes and firm chin, a large black yarmulka perched on his curly locks, was surrounded by a group of enthusiastic staffers. "Gili, you've come back!" "Gili, you left with a small *kippah*, what's this watermelon on your head?" "Are you masquerading?" "Don't hit us with your *tzitzit*!"

Eric Meisels gave him a warm hug. "Gili, it's good to see you back. I'm glad you haven't become a fanatic. I was afraid you were going to excommunicate us."

Ami Kedmi, the paper's editor, came out of his office and, after shaking hands with the returning hero, put an end to the festivities with a loud shout: "Enough. Quiet down! Gili's back and he's welcome. Now everyone back to work, and that includes you, Gili!" The journalists and workers scurried back to their cubicles.

HaYom HaZeh was produced in a vast room divided by glass partitions into small offices. Every two reporters shared a space of about six square feet, enclosed by thick blue-tinted glass. In this way the journalists could keep contact with each other while enjoying a measure of privacy.

Gili returned to the familiar office, which had not changed in his absence, along with his friend Benny.

"Too bad *I* didn't leave for two months," Benny lamented. "What a welcome, what a display! Everyone loves you."

"I'm really touched," Gili said indifferently. "But if I look at them the wrong way their love will turn into hatred. Everyone's just looking out for himself."

"What kind of talk is that?" Benny said, shocked. "You've become bitter in yeshivah."

"Just the opposite. In yeshivah we were full of joy, real joy. There I learned to tell the difference between selfish love and love that's true."

"You're impossible today," Benny complained. "I can't talk to you as I used to. As soon as I can, I'm going to introduce you to my rabbi. He's more religious than you are, and not half as serious."

"Benny, you're seeing a rabbi?" Gili chortled.

"What's so funny?" Benny said, offended. "I'm even related to him."

"A relative?" Gili's laughter redoubled. He saw before him the image of Benny, the incorrigible clown, obediently bending a knee before an ancient and venerable, white-bearded rabbi.

"Maybe let me know what's so funny," Benny grumbled. "You're dying of laughter and I'm not even allowed to know why?"

"Nothing," Gili answered, taking hold of himself. "I'm just wondering who your rabbi is, that's all."

"You should meet him," Benny said enthusiastically. "He's terrific. I'll take you to him as soon as I can."

"Does he have a long white beard?"

"No, actually he's relatively young. A brilliant man, full of the joy of life. Rav Avram Rosenthal. Haven't you heard of him? Half the country knows who he is. He moved here from America some years ago."

Ami Kedmi stuck his head in. "Gili, you've got an assignment. Tomorrow you go to Jerusalem to cover the Judaica fair there."

Gili was disappointed. "Judaica? That's a dead field. Find me something more interesting."

"You'll be surprised to learn that Judaica is still alive and well," Ami replied. "There's drama there, and intrigues, and even violence. You'll find something hot there, I'm sure. Four o'clock tomorrow, at the Holiday Inn. Don't be late."

⊙⋟⋞⊙

A large cloth banner waved in the strong wind: Welcome to the International Judaica Fair, Jerusalem, sponsored by Sotheby's and the Israel Antiquities Commission.

Gili hesitantly entered the hotel. This was his first assignment since he'd become observant, and he didn't much like it. Was Judaica, then, a religious issue? Benny had told him that Ami was anticipating reports on the mosaic of *chareidi* life, with all its factions and trends. Instead, they were sending him to cover a Judaica fair, one great, big bore. At least there was going to be an auction: That would inject a touch of drama into an otherwise dull happening.

The hotel wore an air of palpable heaviness. A blast of frigid, air-conditioned air hit him as he entered the immaculate lobby. Well-dressed visitors stood around the display tables, examining the articles with interest: ancient books carefully preserved in display cases, under heavy glass, holy articles encased in silver that had not lost their glitter despite the passing of years. There were treasures of handwritten documents and letters of historical interest, amulets, prayer books, illuminated *Haggadahs*. Everything gave off an air of antiquity. Suddenly Gili found himself fascinated by the display.

"Are you a collector?" A well-groomed muscular young man sporting an elegant bow tie and dress suit suddenly appeared at his side, holding a large leather bag in his hand. "Welcome. I'm a guide to the exhibit."

Gili politely explained his function there, hoping his escort would go elsewhere. Instead the young man grew even more insistent. "A journalist? I've got some interesting material for you."

The tour guide led Gili through the display cases. Gili heard all about filigree and incunabula, books produced during the first years of printing, between the years 1440 and 1500, and the huge price that such books fetched today. Gili rolled his eyes when he found out that a rare incunabulum could go for up to several hundreds of thousands of dollars.

"The first printing of *Rashi's* commentary on the *Chumash*," his escort explained, "as far as we know, no longer exists. If you'd find it in your house, you'd have won the lottery: Its value would exceed half a million dollars."

"I don't believe it. *Rashi's* commentary isn't rare: It's found in every *Chumash*."

"But the incunabulum is particularly rare; there isn't even one full edition in the entire world. Experts in the field claim that the text differs somewhat from today's editions."

After a time they grew tired and flopped down happily in the exhibit's comfortable chairs.

"Tell me more," Gili asked from deep in the recliner. "I'm a complete ignoramus when it comes to this field."

The man spoke at length of the market for antiquities, astonishing Gili when he told him the prices of the rarest items.

"You're telling me that sane men are prepared to pay millions for some ragged sheets of paper?"

"You got it." The guide drummed his fingers. "You're lucky a sensitive collector didn't overhear you, or he would really have told you off."

Gili leaned back with a smile. The guide continued to speak. "Many people have a deep reverence for antiquities, which hold fragments of our glorious past. Even thieves know the value of these collections: That's why we have such heavy security here. We keep a close watch. There are gangs of criminals who wander through the aisles; we've got to be careful.

Suddenly something is missing and we haven't a clue where it's gone. And that's not all: The worst danger comes from the 'title-page bandits.'"

"Title-page bandits?"

"You heard me. They are bona fide visitors who show interest in a specific book. No one is watching and suddenly the title page of some ancient book is smuggled out. Sometimes the title page is worth more than the contents of the book itself, particularly if it includes an autograph or seal of a well-known personality who owned the book. For example, the *Tur Choshen Mishpat* that was printed in Berlin in the year 5543 (1783) isn't particularly rare and is worth only about $200, but if the title page includes the signature of the Gaon of Vilna? Oh, boy! That changes the entire picture; the book's value goes up by about 10 or 20 times!"

"Those thieves sure know what they're doing," Gili laughed.

"And how! They inflict tremendous damage. Many books lose their value without a title page. That's why we've placed all of the really valuable books under lock and key. But what happens when a potential customer comes and wants to touch the book with his own hand? Can we say no? That's how some of the most valuable title pages are stolen. There are also forgers, and shady dealers who sell their material, and all sorts of charlatans and fakes." The man sounded very professional in his assessment.

"You know, we haven't even introduced ourselves properly." Gili held out a hand. "Gili Dinar. I'm with *HaYom HaZeh*."

"You're the famous Gili Dinar?" The guide's mouth hung open. "Why didn't you say so immediately? It's good to meet you. I'm Bumi Porat."

"Nice meeting you, Bumi." Gili gave a slight nod. He was about to put another question to him, when a commotion at the hotel entrance caught their attention. Bumi jumped up excitedly. "That's the 'King of the Antiquities,' Big Yaakovi, coming. I must be there to greet him."

Gili chased after Bumi.

An entire entourage entered the lobby. At its center stood a tall man, of imposing dimensions. There was a small knitted *kippah* on his head, which concealed only a minute part of his bald pate. His scarlet cheeks resembled two apples.

The lobby suddenly bustled with activity; everyone surrounded the group, with a few lucky ones succeeding in making their way to the man and pumping his hand.

"It's Big Yaakovi," the whisper could be heard throughout the room, "the greatest of the collectors. Now things are going to get interesting."

Gili couldn't understand the excitement generated by the appearance of this giant, this "Big Yaakovi." He grabbed Bumi Porat and demanded an answer: What was going on? Wasn't the public auction not scheduled for another two days?

"Kid," Bumi gave him a belittling look, "the public auction is a joke. The drama is going on right now!"

After a few minutes Gili understood where Big Yaakovi's power lay.

A visitor to the exhibit examined each display in two or three minutes; a slower guest needed five or six. Those in a hurry took about one minute. Big Yaakovi gave each display no more than 10 seconds. He raced between the cases, gave the items a hurried perusal, made a swift, professional assessment, all the while scribbling in a small pad. He gave the impression of a lightning-fast, sharp brain; it seemed he knew the entire Judaica market by heart.

An entourage of five or six followed him from place to place. Gili joined the caravan, right behind Yaakovi. The collector stopped first near a square glass case, firmly fixed a small pair of glasses on the bridge of his nose, and read the explanatory label: "*Siddur*, Roman custom, Soncino edition, 5246, starting price $40,000."

He wrote a few words in the pad and murmured something unintelligible. Gili, standing behind him, strained his eyes and saw the scribbles: "Consult with A.R. tonight."

At the next display, Yaakovi once again read the description: "*Passover Haggadah*, Venice, 5263." Gili again stared at the trader making marks in his pad. This time, though, Yaakovi noticed the journalist; he gave Gili a penetrating look and asked, "And who are you, sir?"

"He's okay," Bumi said quickly. "That's Gili Dinar, the journalist."

The trader gave him a painful slap on the shoulder. "Why didn't you say so? I thought it was one of those idiotic ushers. Gili, do me a favor, give me a good write-up."

At the next stall the exhibitor removed a *sefer segulos* printed in the 16th century from the locked case and gave it to Yaakovi for his perusal. He leafed through it, held one of the pages to the light. Without hesitating he scribbled, "Forgery? Check with A.R. this evening."

They approached the exhibition of ancient Jewish ritual objects. Yaakovi scrutinized a silver snuffbox. The case was faintly inscribed with the words, "A gift sent to our Rabbi, the G-dly kabbalist Rabbi Yosef Yuzfa Halpern, may he live, from the youngest of his students, Avraham Abba ben Chava of Dermashtadt."

Yaakovi froze; he examined the case again, and stared at the marked price: $2,000.

"How'd it get here?" he whispered to himself. "And the price? Good. I'll buy it again."

This time he wrote nothing in the pad.

The group had reached the last of the exhibit. Yaakovi sank into the nearest recliner; Gili sat down opposite him.

"What do you say, my young friend?" Yaakovi put his brawny forearm on Gili's shoulder. "Fascinating, no? I live, breathe, and eat Judaica, 24 hours a day. You take a group of ancient writings, 500 years old. Let's say it's a *sefer segulos*. Let's call it *The Vessel of Blessing*. You buy it for $20,000 from its owner, a senile old man who has no idea of its value. After two years you sell it for half a million, and you're rich! Hey, what's wrong?"

This time the attack was a prolonged one. Gili lay in a heap on the carpet. In the large room confusion reigned. A young man holding an attache case raced over from the other side of the hall. "Don't touch him," he warned, as he ran over. "I'm a doctor."

It was 60 seconds before the attack passed. Gili stirred, stood up, shook himself. He dusted off his jacket, hardly noticing that he stood in the middle of an interested circle of onlookers.

He looked around. The noisy hall grew silent. Everyone stared at him in anxious curiosity.

"There's nothing to worry about," Gili turned to the crowd. "I just lost my balance for a minute. It could happen to anyone."

"Are you all right?" The doctor asked him. "It seemed to me that you'd lost consciousness."

"Don't exaggerate. Medical science doesn't call a minute's dizziness a loss of consciousness."

"Just let me examine you," the doctor insisted. The two went to a side room, where the doctor checked Gili from head to toe.

"Very strange," he exclaimed, as he hit Gili's knee with a small steel hammer. "Your reflexes are fine. But your pupils are enlarged and you're blinking too much, an indication of possible irregularities in the brain."

Gili's heart skipped a beat. "How do you know that?"

"I'm a neurologist! I recommend an immediate EEG."

He had to get away from this man, quickly. "Listen, Doctor," Gili was already tying his laces and straightening his tie. "I feel fine now. Give me your phone number; if I don't feel well I'll give you a call."

He dashed out of the room and raced to the lobby. Yaakovi had disappeared, along with his retinue.

"I knew it," he muttered.

He examined the booths he'd looked at with Yaakovi. The Roman *Siddur* was fine; the *sefer segulos* also seemed unchanged. He stood next to the snuffbox and stared.

The case had been stolen! Another had been substituted in its place!

Few would have noticed the minute difference. The original case said 'Halpern'; here, the forger had written "Halperin." Otherwise, the forgery was perfect.

At the lobby's entrance Gili bumped into Bumi Porat. "I have something interesting to show you," Gili said, pulling him earnestly towards the exhibit. "Your 'Big Yaakovi' is nothing more than a first-class forger! Come and see how he took advantage of the confusion in the hall to replace the snuffbox with a top-notch forgery."

"Impossible," Bumi objected. "Let go of my arm, please. You can say what you want of Yaakovi, that he drives a hard bargain and takes advantage of his workers, that he pays late and..."

They had reached the stall. "Here," Gili called out triumphantly. "Take a look at the catalog, at the picture of the case. See how "Halpern" is spelled in the catalog, and how it's spelled here. What do you say now?"

Bumi stared intently at the photo and then at the item itself. He gave Gili a strange look.

"What do I say? I say that you're seeing things!"

"Seeing things?"

"Absolutely. Look at what's inscribed on the case."

Gili bent down and stared. Then he straightened, as if struck by lightning. Bumi was right: The name "Halpern" was clearly inscribed!

Someone was making a fool of him.

But how?

Bumi disappeared, returning a moment later with the young doctor in tow. "I asked you before if you were okay," the doctor grumbled. "Come along, we're going to the hospital. Now."

Gili didn't argue. As he sat in the doctor's speeding car, he thought of the term he'd heard years ago in the hospital: irreversible brain damage.

Perhaps the doctor and Bumi were correct, and he was experiencing another attack. What had the neurologists said? The brain is a gigantic communications center that ceaselessly takes in and processes data via relays in the brain. If there is a cutoff between parts of the brain, we misperceive data. Was that what was happening to him? Were the events that had just passed nothing more than a dream, a fantasy, or was there another explanation?

He was lost in thought as he tried to catalog the day's events in chronological order. First, there had been the encounter with Bumi Porat. Then Big Yaakovi had come on the scene, and the mysterious "A.R." whom Yaakovi wished to consult so urgently. Then Yaakovi had said the words that had caused Gili's blackout. Finally, there was the exchanged snuffbox case, or was there?

Someone was orchestrating these events, with split-second timing. Someone was pulling at his strings; he was dancing to someone else's tune. But whose?

With the screeching of its horn the car approached Hadassah Ein Kerem Medical Center. The doctor stole a glance at Gili, making certain his patient hadn't lost consciousness again.

Gili wanted to jump out and shout, I never felt better in my life. The car sped to the Emergency Room. Now Gili felt completely calm. He'd made up his mind: He would play the game, until he'd unearthed the identity of the mystery man and understood his obscure motives.

A group of doctors and nurses surrounded his bed in the E.R. They poked and prodded, inserting needles and tubes. He heard the words: infusion, liquids, plasma, EEG, oxygen. Twenty milligrams; no, double that to 40.

Words, words surrounded him, so many words, but Gili concentrated only on himself. He again reviewed the situation but his initial optimism had dissipated. His heart sank. It was hard to do battle with an unseen enemy. And how much harder the game was when you didn't know any of the rules!

10

G ili was admitted to the hospital, where he underwent a battery of tests. He hadn't had a stroke, that much was clear: All the results were normal. However, due to his past medical history he remained hospitalized. For three days he lay in the Intensive Care Unit, electrodes attached to his head registering every tiny vibration.

At his discharge his doctor, Professor Martin Prince, an expert neurologist, spoke to him. "All the tests were normal; you're completely healthy. Nothing abnormal happened to either your brain or your body. But there was one interesting finding in all this."

"Which is..."

The doctor pulled a long roll of paper out of Gili's medical file and unfolded it onto his desk. "These are your EEG results. Look at the wave pattern: Everything is quiet and normal. And suddenly, a storm: mountains and valleys, massive changes, lines going up and lines going down. This indicates very deep thinking. Immediately afterwards, a straight line, continuing for two to three seconds. That's your famous 'blackout': a brief loss of consciousness. We scrutinized it closely, but were unable to figure out why it happens. But it seems that very intense brain activity is the catalyst that sets it off. I would have liked to know what you were thinking about then, what caused the short circuit."

"I would also love to know," Gili answered wryly.

Dr. Prince sighed. "Excellent. We're both on the same wavelength." He walked towards the window and peered out at the woods of the Judean Hills. Then he turned towards Gili. "We dream of the day we'll be able to photograph thoughts electronically. You'll think, and we'll watch a movie... Ah, it's the fantasy of every neurologist and brain researcher. But it's still in the realm of science fiction. We can't observe your thoughts on our monitors. So if you can possibly remember what thoughts were in your mind that may have triggered the blackout, you'll be making our lives and yours easier."

"I told you, I would love to. I'm trying to pick up the thread, but the minute the picture seems a little more distinct, it disappears."

Dr. Prince didn't understand. "You are a man of higher than normal intelligence. Can't you explain yourself more clearly?"

Gili wasn't happy at the prospect of sharing his deepest feelings with this doctor. Would he suspect him of insanity? The young man's eyes, darting to and fro, revealed his turmoil.

"I don't want to pressure you," the doctor apologized. "If it's too hard for you, you don't have to. I'm trying to help you, not make things more difficult."

"No, no, I'll tell you. It's all connected with the car accident that I was in five years ago, when I was about 18 years old..."

Intrigued by the story, Dr. Prince let his telephone ring unanswered and ignored the incessant buzzing of his intercom. Finally his secretary knocked hesitantly and entered, to tell the doctor that 10 people were waiting for him in the anteroom.

"Let them wait," Prince answered shortly.

The room was bathed in clear light, as the sun's rays highlighted the philodendron blooming on the windowsill. Gili kept his eyes focused on the sunshine peeking in from between the green leaves.

Prince listened intently, filling his open notebook with Latin words and complicated medical terms. He tried fruitlessly to catch Gili's eye, hoping to glean from his gaze just what words set off his loss of consciousness.

But the neurologist had to content himself with merely listening. A specialist such as he could learn a lot from someone's words, just by the nuances evident in the speaker's tone, rhythm and emphasis. "Halting intonations," he wrote.

Gili finished. Prince stared at the list he'd compiled. "Very interesting. It's a complex story, with several factors influencing your reactions. I'll study it in the next several days; you will be hearing from me. In any case, you can call me any time; I will make myself available for you."

Gili was satisfied. In the doctor's office he had acted disappointed as he asked Dr. Prince if he had drawn any conclusions from the story. The professor was cautious, simply reiterating that he would study the material rather than issuing a hasty opinion. Gili predicted what he would recommend: Go to a psychologist; the patient is riddled with feelings of guilt.

As he sat in his car, speeding towards Tel Aviv, Gili couldn't help but smile. He had carefully considered his words to the neurologist, deleting pertinent details. Several times he had halted, trying to remember what it was he should not say; Prince had built an entire theory on these "halting intonations"...

Yes. Gili had seen the words the doctor had scribbled in his notebook, in one surreptitious glance. Gili was an expert in reading things upside down, in speed-reading, and he possessed a photographic memory; whatever he saw was etched in his mind.

It was only that terrible night that eluded him. Parts of it seemed to dance before him, teasing, eternally slipping out of his grasp. No blackout, this; rather, a giant mental block perched squarely in his brain, ensuring that the hazy pictures never sprang to vibrant life.

His Mitsubishi slipped into Tel Aviv. Finally, the building came into view. The huge red letters gleamed against the white facade: *HaYom HaZeh*. Beneath them, smaller orange neon lights blared their additional message: The Newspaper of Tomorrow.

Gili felt deeply content. He had woven his plan carefully, and in a few moments would begin to put it into action. Piece by piece.

Tel Aviv 5748 — 1988

After two weeks the branch heads met once again. This meeting, like the last, was completely classified, not appearing even in the protocols and minutes of the GSS. Again, the meeting took place after midnight.

Everyone had brought carefully delineated ideas and suggestions and various scenarios as to what would happen in the event of *chareidi* domination of the country.

Swelling with self-importance, the branch heads sat in their upholstered seats around the oval table. Even K. had brought a document with him, which, shorn of its jargon and verbosity, gave the noncommittal recommendation that the *chareidi* community be closely scrutinized during the next few years. He knew that no one would take his suggestion seriously, because of his past as part of the *chareidi* community. Yet he knew he had to stay in the picture at all costs.

S., head of the GSS, asked the branch heads to summarize their findings in a few brief sentences.

G., his deputy, opened the floor with a sophisticated idea. "The government of Israel, be it of the left or the right, should take advantage of the housing shortage among the *chareidim* and disperse them throughout the country. Let them sell the *chareidim* apartments in small cities at discount prices. That way, the *chareidim* will not get an absolute majority in any of the large or midsize cities. Eventually the Knesset will change from a population-based membership to one based on regions, in which each area chooses its own representation."

B., head of the Jewish Affairs Division, reacted negatively. "You'll get the opposite results of what you planned! The *chareidi* public is increasing exponentially, with its high birth rate. Place them into all the cities and you're simply giving them the chance to outnumber us everywhere!"

"And what do you suggest?" S. asked.

"Persecute them!"

"What?"

B. took a deep breath. "I've thought about this deeply. We have no chance against them. Time and demographics, plus the *teshuvah* movement, are all working in their favor. If we don't do something drastic to convince them to leave they will take over the land. Take Jerusalem as a model. In a few more years Jerusalem will be theirs, with a *chareidi* mayor at its head. We have no choice: We have to make their lives so tough that huge numbers of them will run to Brooklyn."

"What do you suggest?" G. asked sharply. "That we shoot at them? Starve them in labor camps? Attack them with bulldogs and Rottweilers?"

The others grinned. The frigid atmosphere melted somewhat. His colleagues' smiles pierced the arrogant mask that normally dominated B.'s haughty features. Through clenched teeth, he hissed, "I will not dignify my colleague's comments with an answer. I recommend taking steps that will inflict mortal wounds on the *chareidi* pocketbook and turn their economic life into a nightmare. Set the tax people on them, the income tax auditors. Have squads investigate every *chareidi* business and close any that are operating illegally. Start with the flourishing black market in clothing that is sold in practically every apartment; end with the vendors of religious articles. Disturb the *kollelim* and yeshivot with twice-weekly inspections by the Ministry of Defense and the Ministry of Religion. We can send them the..."

S. waved away the eager suggestions. B. stopped in mid-sentence. "All of this will simply boomerang. Experience has shown that such foolishness simply strengthens their community resolve. I had expected better of you, not this small-time Nazi wickedness. The Middle Ages and the Inquisition are over. Okay, continue. What about you, K.?"

"The *chareidi* community is as disciplined and obedient as G. claimed at our previous meeting," K. replied. "But the future danger will only come about if it is united. In my opinion, the quarrels and splits among them are so great that the threat of *chareidi* hegemony is simply not relevant at this point. I recommend keeping close surveillance on them in the coming years to see how things develop."

After a moment S. continued. "And what does T., the head of the Manpower Division, recommend?"

"Let's infiltrate the *chareidi* youth. Develop meetings between young people from secular and religious backgrounds. Entice their youngsters into secular activities. We've seen in the past that the majority of religious

Jews who have abandoned their Torah lifestyle did so after peeking out of their ghetto into the larger world and seeing what they were missing. All the many pleasures that a secular lifestyle can offer will beckon to them. Even the religious want to have fun."

M., head of the Psychological Warfare unit, snorted. "Dreams! Except for a few dozen marginal young people, no *chareidi* youth worth anything will buy it. *Chareidi* education is effective and of the highest quality. A yeshivah student who finds his satisfaction in prayer and enjoys the intellectual stimulation of Talmud learning won't be tempted to go out 'onto the street' or dance in a discotheque. They're not brainless idiots, longing to break out of the ghetto walls. There are individuals, yes, who want to leave the community, but they are the exceptions."

"And what do you have to suggest?" T. exclaimed huffily.

"A lot."

"So let's hear it," S. said mildly.

"Gladly." M. spoke at length, in great detail, for nearly an hour. By the end of his lecture the others were frozen in their places. After they'd recovered their composure, the room hummed with a babel of voices. Some reacted with fervent enthusiasm, terming their colleague a genius; others called him a prophetic madman. On one point, though, there was common agreement: M., in his masterful and creative vision, had gone farther than any of them. His plan was riveting and completely unexpected, and if successfully implemented had an excellent chance of destroying the *chareidi* world from within.

"Hey, Gili, what have you been up to?" Benny gleefully welcomed his friend as he entered their cubicle. "I wanted to visit you in the hospital, but the doctors watched over you like a treasure. No visitors, friends are not welcome."

Gili dropped down into his seat. Benny offered him a can of cold soda, which Gili received with thanks. "They didn't want me to think too much. The doctors wanted to figure out what was happening in my brain."

"But they didn't succeed," Benny laughed. "What did I hear on the news this week? In Hadassah, researchers have uncovered a man without a brain..."

Gili threw the can at him, and missed. The soda leaked out, landing in a brown and sodden pool on the floor.

"Hey, don't get mad, you'll destroy my computer," Benny complained. "And speaking of computers, what about the report on Judaica? Are you going to write it up?"

"And why not? I'm as healthy as an ox."

"Nu, so get on with it. Back to work."

Gili heaved himself over to the computer. "Before I start, I've got to get a few details cleared up. Get me Bumi Porat or Big Yaakovi."

"Who are they?"

Gili clapped a hand to his forehead. How could he have forgotten? Benny hadn't been with him at the Judaica fair. He brought Benny up-to-date on some of the details. Benny set out on a telephone chase, until he'd caught up with Bumi. "Big Yaakovi" was a name without a number; no one could figure out where he'd come from or to where he'd disappeared.

Gili set up a meeting with Bumi Porat. The young man didn't live far from his own home, in the Ramat Aviv Gimmel neighborhood of Tel Aviv. Two hours later the two young men met in a dairy restaurant near Diezengoff Square.

The restaurant bustled with activity. Bumi crammed pancake after whipped-cream-and maple-syrup-drenched pancake into his mouth, washed the whole thing down with cream-topped coffee, and lauded his host's taste. "I never thought a kosher restaurant could serve such delicious food." Gili himself barely touched the hot, tempting crepe set before him: He had work to do.

He interrogated Bumi for two solid hours. Bumi was generous with details, giving a colorful description of the public auction, providing specifics of what items had been sold there.

Gili wanted to know who'd purchased the snuffbox.

"Of course, Big Yaakovi. He bought it for $2,500."

"And where did he go? Where does he live?"

Bumi took a sip of water and drummed his fork on his plate. Gili took the hint.

"Waiter, bring my friend a cup of cappucino with cream, and four cheese and raisin blintzes."

Bumi laughed quietly, a sound that raised Gili's blood pressure. Impossible: This kid knew something, and he wouldn't talk. How could he pull the information from him?

The waiter brought the tray, staggering under the load. Bumi's eyes lit up as he prepared to enjoy this encore performance. Gili clenched his teeth.

"You know that I have finished my story."

"That's interesting. Send me a copy," Bumi said indifferently.

"Why not? I think the write-up should interest you. Do you understand? It will include stories about Bumi Porat, on 'Big Yaakovi,' on the snuffbox and, particularly, on Yaakovi's little pad."

For the first time that evening Bumi began to sweat. "What are you talking about?"

"On that small, pretty little pad, and on the mysterious Mr. A.R. whom Yaakovi planned to consult."

Bull's-eye. Bumi's plate lay before him, forgotten and unattended. He stared at Gili, his eyes veiled. "You wouldn't do that, would you? "

"Why not?" Gili said, with affected innocence. "The public has the right to know."

"Listen, let's make a deal. You don't write about A.R., and I'll give you Big Yaakovi's address." Bumi was nervous; his eyes moved tensely from side to side.

"I'm not agreeing to anything. Give me Big Yaakovi's address and then we'll see."

"I've got a friendly suggestion for you. If you write about A.R., have your will written up first."

"That's the way it is?"

"Absolutely."

"Okay, you've got a deal."

The next day, Gili paid a visit to the residence of Big Yaakovi.

11

I t was twilight on a hot summer's day when Gili stood before the locked gates of Yaakovi's house, in the northern Tel Aviv neighborhood of Ramat Aviv Gimmel. Gili felt foolish: Here he was, some two short blocks away from Bumi Porat's house, and what a job it had been to squeeze the address out of him!

The huge villa stood out among its smaller neighbors like a hen amidst her chicks; it was the only one that boasted a tall gate and was surrounded by barbed wire. A small sign told those who still were not persuaded to keep away that this home was protected by the Maoz Security Company.

Rosy-tinted rays of sun did a melancholy dance over the trees surrounding the villa. Evening shadows descended upon the neighborhood, as it began to darken. Gili buzzed the intercom bell again and again, until he was finally answered. "Gili Dinar? Who's that?" The metallic crackle emerging from the intercom didn't sound at all like the deep voice of Big Yaakovi.

"The journalist from the Judaica fair."

"Who?"

"The reporter who fainted in the Holiday Inn last week," Gili shouted into the intercom.

There was a short silence followed by a buzz. The metal door responded to Gili's impatient shove and opened wide.

A swarthy young man came running up. "I'm Yaakovi's assistant; come with me." Obeying some obscure instinct, Gili imprinted a picture of the courtyard on his memory. A stone path meandered through a rose garden. On the left was a gigantic kennel; two huge wolfhounds restrained by metal chains prowled aimlessly behind its gate, waiting for night, when they would be let loose to guard against thieves. Though they strode swiftly, Gili managed to see three garages, a late-model Cadillac parked in one of them. The man was wealthy, that was clear.

They entered a large anteroom, near a stairway that led to the second floor. Gili felt as if he were in a museum. Big Yaakovi had exquisite and lavish taste, which ran to the antique: Gili had never before seen a house furnished almost entirely in the 17th-century decor.

His eye skimmed the wonders of the civilized world, cunningly hidden among the heavy furnishings in a masterful feat of architectural design. Modern halogen lights gave off their electric glow from amidst antique candle-lit chandeliers. Cool air blew from vents concealed by dark wood paneling. Gili was certain that within the old-fashioned telephones lay state-of-the-art equipment.

Impressionist paintings by some of its greatest masters hung upon the walls. Each was worth well into the hundreds of thousands of dollars; the artwork alone justified the alarm beams concealed within recesses built into the furnishings.

Big Yaakovi awaited him in his study, at the end of a long hallway. It took Gili a few seconds to recognize him. The low chair in which he was ensconced obscured his height. He was dressed in a blue sports suit which contrasted sharply with the professionally tailored suit he had worn at the fair. Inspecting the writing table before him, Gili was tempted to ask if it was here that Ferdinand, King of Spain, had signed the warrant of expulsion against the Jews. But the closed-circuit monitor that maintained a vigilant eye on the street in front of the villa surely had not stood on Ferdinand's desk.

"So what do you think of my house? Never seen anything like it, hey?" Yaakovi was delighted with Gili's obvious wonder.

"To be perfectly honest, no, I haven't," Gili said openly. "You breathe history here."

"Just wait," Yaakovi crowed. "You haven't seen anything yet. Let's see what you'll say when you've seen my collections, on the third floor."

"With your permission, I'd like to get down to business immediately."

"What's the hurry? You young people today have no patience. First of all, we haven't introduced ourselves properly. I'm Pinny Yaakovi, the greatest of collectors in the Middle East." Modesty and humility weren't the man's strong points, that was clear.

"Pleased to meet you." Gili extended a confident hand. "Gili Dinar, religious affairs journalist for *HaYom HaZeh,* and former investigative reporter."

"The newspapers have written a lot about me." Yaakovi leafed through a black notebook. "Hmmm, here's one: 'Yaakovi is the biggest of them all.' Interesting, it was actually in *HaYom HeZeh* five years ago."

Gili politely read the first lines of the story: "Pinny Yaakovi is one of the most colorful men I've ever met in my career. He is a man of boundless energy and lightning-quick thought..."

The notebook was suddenly torn out of his hands. "Let's get down to the essentials," Yaakovi said. "You're obviously interested in Judaica, not in me. What do you want to know?"

He was impulsive too; Gili would have to be careful.

"I'm particularly interested in rare manuscripts," Gili answered.

"Aha! You've gotten right to the heart of it!" Yaakovi said enthusiastically. "First of all, you'll find money, a lot of money! The price of an antique manuscript escalates to a million dollars, depending on its rarity, quality, and authenticity, that is, how certain we are that it's not a forgery. But aside from the finances of it, the acquisition of rare manuscripts is an exciting and fascinating area, absolutely incomparable. It's the love of my life; my whole world."

"Mr. Yaakovi, my readers will undoubtedly ask: It's a lot of money, but exciting? What can be so exciting about a sheaf of old papers? Contemporary people live for today, not in the past."

Yaakovi held his head in two balled fists and fixed crafty eyes upon him. "Do you want to know the truth, or a string of cliches for a foolish public?"

"Foolish? No such thing! Today's readers are mature and intelligent; you can't fool them. A reporter who doesn't bring in the goods, with stimulating and interesting stories, will soon find himself unemployed."

"Intelligent? Mature?" Yaakovi chuckled. "Okay, that's not what we're discussing. Manuscripts? Have you ever heard of classified documents whose statute of limitations runs out and are published after a certain number of years?"

"Of course. After about 50 years have elapsed."

"That's right. The ban on publication eases up with time. An old secret is no longer a secret, right? But here, in my room," Yaakovi gestured theatrically at the bookshelves sagging under the weight of books reaching up to the ceiling, "here are secrets 500, 800 years old that are as important today as they were then. Publicizing them, even today, could cause the earth to tremble. It would bring on diplomatic crises. I could destroy many well-known personalities, in Israel and throughout the world, with revelations of some of their family history and secrets."

This was getting interesting. "I assume you're not exaggerating. An 800-year-old secret can cause an earthquake?"

"Absolutely!" Yaakovi answered hotly. "Only a boor like you, the product of the national ignorance and stupidity of the Israeli educational system, wouldn't understand this. Do you know what could happen within the Christian world if I would publicize some of the manuscripts of the Vatican? I could create a major schism between England and France if I would release just two letters written by Admiral Horatio Nelson to the media."

"So you do not limit yourself to the world of Judaica?"

"Mister, to be known as 'the greatest collector in the Middle East,' and perhaps in all of Asia, doesn't earn the title with one measly collection! I own the most comprehensive and rare stamp collection in the world, with items that cannot be found anywhere else on the globe. A series of Australian stamps on the Bible was taken out of circulation by the Sydney government at the request of the Chief Rabbinate, because G-d's name appeared on them. They were all recalled — but I've got two of them. I have a rare collection of antique timepieces, ancient coins, paper currency, one-of-a-kind religious objects. I have a suitcase full of silver ingots stamped with the signet ring of the members of the British royal family throughout the generations. I even own a collection of walking sticks."

The collector turned his attention towards a corner of the room, in the direction of a stand filled with old canes.

"That's also a collection?" Gili chuckled.

"You don't think so?" Yaakovi wasn't offended. "Bring me the stand, but carefully."

Gili stumbled beneath the weight of the walking sticks. "Heavy?" Yaakovi grinned. "Soon you'll understand why." He pressed on the silver head of one old-fashioned walking stick. There was the faint click of a spring being freed. The silver head opened and a thin, sharp metal prong flew out.

"An incomparable weapon," Yaakovi murmured. His hand pointed towards several innocent-looking canes. "These are rifles." He gently pulled the end of a green stick, then touched the handle. Gili could clearly see the safety catch of the gun. "Now it's loaded," the collector pointed it towards the face of the astonished journalist. "Have you ever wondered why so many heads of state carry walking sticks or umbrellas? There are laws against carrying rifles, you know, but when arms are forbidden, even walking sticks can shoot! Ha, ha!" The collector clearly enjoyed his little witticism.

Gili feverishly took notes, trying to keep up with his host's dizzying pace. Yaakovi placed reading glasses on the bridge of his nose and skimmed through a leather-bound book that lay atop a pile on his desk. Gili could see the Arabic script. "This is a very ancient manuscript, the notes of the doctor Ibn Saud. The things written here are as timely as something written today. He writes, for example, that if a person has a 'mukah,' known in today's parlance as a boil, he should put a mixture of tomatoes and spiders' webs on it and he will be healed. Sounds incredibly primitive, no? Professor Caspi, one of Tel Aviv's top doctors, told me that there are antibiotics currently available which are composed of a modern combination of — tomatoes and spiders' webs!

"Surely an intellectual such as yourself knows this," Yaakov added mockingly. "You feed your readers their weekly portion of culture, don't you? The intelligentsia? Pseudointellectuals, with an overwhelming dearth of wisdom! In Israel today we have the culture of a flock of sheep.

One animal leads and the others follow. Everyone reads the same paper and talks about it over the weekend. If the investigative reporter wakes up feeling aggressive that morning, and he looks around for prey, tomorrow the entire nation will be shocked to find that their bread contains ingredients that cause liver failure! The next day a journalist from a rival paper wakes up, jealously sharpens his pencil, and so we find out that our apricots are sprayed with material that causes leukemia. The heads of the Broadcasting Authority, green with envy, tell the nation of Israel that night that a top officer in the Navy took bribes to give someone a government contract."

Gili couldn't get a word in edgewise. Yaakovi continued spouting information: "And that's the intelligentsia? The empty pursuit of scoops? In my eyes a wise man is one who knows wisdom; anyone who doesn't understand what is hidden in the past doesn't understand what's happening in the present!"

Yaakovi lifted himself from the chair and ponderously stood up. Now his considerable height was apparent. With unexpectedly swift steps he approached one of the shelves and pulled out a brown leather-bound book. "*Sefer Avnei Shoham* is a kabbalistic manuscript, practical kabbalah from the 16th century. If you could understand it, you could perform miracles.

"You must realize," Yaakovi said in a husky whisper, "in my room there is no distinction between past, present, and future. The flow of time has no meaning here, everything is one. Ancient books are ticking time bombs: one false move and 'boom!' you've destroyed a world." He pivoted around from the bookshelf to his upholstered chair and fell leadenly into its depths.

Now he was calm; his guard was down. *A good time to strike.* "And what about books of *segulos*?"

"*Segulos*? I have dozens of such books. What exactly are you interested in?"

Careful, Gili; it's a minefield out there.

"You spoke about a *sefer segulos* at the fair. It was just when I fainted." *Wrong. It was what caused my longest blackout ever.* "I remember the name. It was something like 'Holds Blessing,' I believe."

"The full title is *The Vessel of Blessing*," Yaakovi's lips twisted in displeasure. "I just mentioned it casually."

Gili resolved to outmaneuver the slippery collector. This one wouldn't slip through the net. "That book interests me."

"Why?"

"My late father had a book with a similar title. I'd forgotten all about it; you reminded me at the fair. *And that was what brought on my attack and unconsciousness; but you won't hear that from me.* The book is no longer in my possession and I'm interested in it."

Yaakovi clucked in commiseration. "Your father didn't leave the book to you? What a shame."

Gili took a deep breath. His heart beat like a drum; with great effort he controlled his trembling. If this collector saw that he was moved, he might lose points in this strange duel.

"I was an only child. I don't have the book because it was destroyed in a fire."

Yaakovi's massive fist reached out to an antique globe and twirled it around. "The book was burned up? Terrible. You lost a lot of money."

If this was a performance, Yaakovi was a first-rate actor. The man's sorrow was absolutely authentic. *But I'm not dropping my suspicions of you, not for one minute, despite your little show.* "I know. My father planned to sell it to Sotheby's. They'd promised him hundreds of thousands of dollars."

"And what happened then?"

"There was a car accident. It was my fault. The car turned and went over a cliff on the Carmel. The car burned up, together with the book."

"If you're concerned about the world of antiques, I can comfort you. There are two more copies of the book *The Vessel of Blessing,* and both are here in my house."

Gili spoke with lowered eyes. Every word was a knife thrust in his flesh. "There were only two copies. Abba had one. Abba went up in flames to heaven, together with the book."

Yaakovi paled and leaned weakly on the arms of his chair. After a moment's tense silence he pressed a hidden button. His diligent assistant appeared almost immediately from the dimness of a hallway. "Bring us something to drink. I'm thirsty."

That "something to drink" was not long in coming. The quick-witted assistant gave his instructions a broad interpretation, and returned within minutes with a tray laden with carafes of coffee and hot cocoa, bottles of bubbling soft drinks, and three plates groaning under their load of fragrant freshly baked cookies, pastries filled with vanilla cream, rum balls and sesame sticks, and a bowl brimming with fruits of the season. He set out the refreshments upon fragile china crockery, quickly and efficiently as was his wont, and disappeared quietly from the room.

Pinny Yaakovi hadn't attained his girth by fasting on Mondays and Thursdays. Before his guest had completed the blessing on a cup of coffee, the host had bolted down half the cookies; his hand hovered over the remaining ones. "Eat," he said through a full mouth, pointing to a plate of honey cookies. "My wife is the queen of the kitchen. She could have made a fortune through her gastronomical talents. But she saves them just for me. And with good reason: Why work when her husband can make a million in a day?"

"Every day?"

"What do you think? There are 'dead months,' but suddenly everything wakes up. Not long ago I sold a manuscript, one of a kind in the entire world, of an ancient commentary on *Maseches Berachos*. Oxford University paid me $700,000 for it."

Gili didn't know what he believed and what he didn't. It seemed that the man was an unrepentant blowhard with delusions of grandeur. Yaakovi continued his narrative, punctuated by the sound of gulping food. "It was a manuscript that I'd bought in Nablus 20 years ago, for $5,000. The Arab seller was convinced I was an idiot, prepared to pay good money for some worthless papers. But I have a sixth sense; I felt that this was an ancient, original manuscript. I looked through it for only two minutes, and kept a poker face. You can't show enthusiasm or the seller's meter starts ticking too fast: One second's interest can cost you $1,000! I bought it there and then, checked it carefully at home, and found a treasure! It was the last, lost section of an original manuscript written by one of the first giants of the Talmud, a section whose existence was known, but one which had never been seen. I negotiated with both the British Museum and Oxford University and finally sold it to the University, which offered a better price. Not before I had it photocopied, of course. The copy will be donated free to a Jerusalem institute specializing in the deciphering and collecting of ancient commentaries. That's my modest contribution to the world of Torah and yeshivot."

"How generous," Gili said, half-teasingly, quickly adding something to allay his host's suspicions. "How did you know it wasn't forged, there in Nablus?"

"As a matter of fact, I didn't. I was risking $5,000." Yaakovi stared at the few remaining rum balls, lying orphaned and alone on the plate, minding his manners and waiting for the first opportunity.

"There's just as much luck as knowledge involved here. Even the greatest experts sometimes mess up. But if you're familiar with the field you know that every book has identifying 'fingerprints.' Watermarks, for example. All incunabula or ancient manuscripts have watermarks on their pages."

"Watermarks? Like those on currency?"

"Exactly. Bring me that book, please." Yaakovi sent Gili towards a shelf on the room's far wall. With the journalist's back to him, he gave a mighty lunge for the rum balls, finishing them off before Gili had returned.

Yaakovi wiped his hands with a napkin, then held the book under the desk lamp, staring at the pages beneath its strong white light. "Look here and tell me what you see." Gili approached and squinted. "It looks like menorahs."

"Very good," the collector praised him. "That's a watermark in the form of a multibranched menorah, engraved into the paper by the manufacturer. It tells us that the book before us is from the years 1640 to 1740.

"Every era has its own identifying marks. If they offer me a manuscript written on rag paper and I see lines throughout the page, I know that this is truly a book from the 14th or 15th century.

"Not long ago," Yaakovi continued, swept away by his own eloquence, "a friend brought me an incunabulum, a *machzor* for the holidays in excellent shape that had been printed in the 14th century in Wadi Al-Charar. I checked the book: The paper was authentic 14th century, the letters those of Al-Charar. I handled the *machzor* and told him, 'This is a forgery; it was printed now.'

" 'You're right,' my friend shouted in wonder. 'That's what Professor Keidar of the Hebrew University told me, after examining it for two weeks!"

" 'And I knew it immediately,' I told him, 'just by touching it. Every page of an incunabulum has minuscule bulges. How did they print in those days? They made a plate of either bronze, wood, or stone, and arranged the letters within it. They smeared it with ink and 'ironed' the page with a mechanical blow. The letters bulged out of the reverse side of the page, and the paper felt rough to the touch. But this book was printed on a modern press, and the paper felt smooth.'"

Yaakovi was now completely mellowed; it was time to strike.

"If you're such an expert, why do you have to consult with someone?"

"Me, consult?" The collector's vanity was touched.

"At the fair, you wrote in your pad to discuss something with A.R. Who is this person who is a greater expert than you are?"

The dig struck home. Yaakovi erupted from his seat like a missile shot from its launcher. His cheeks were scarlet with anger. "Don't stick your nose into something that doesn't concern you, you arrogant fool!"

"Why are you so upset?" Gili asked tranquilly. "Have a bit of snuff; it'll calm you down."

"Snuff?" Yaakovi tried to get hold of himself. "What are you talking about?"

"I'm talking about the snuffbox given as a gift to the kabbalist Rabbi Halpern."

The swollen veins in Yaakovi's neck returned to normal; he calmed down. "Are you referring to the snuffbox that I bought at the public auction? Say so, then. Why are you going around in circles? Do you want to see it? Wait a minute."

A small locked vault stood at his left. He opened it hurriedly using a secret code that Gili couldn't decipher. For a minute he rummaged through it; soon, a silver box gleamed in the white light.

"Here is the pretty little box that cost me $2,500. I saw it in New York two years ago, and I had my eye on it then. At the time one of my friends bought it for $1,000; he grew tired of it and put it up for sale again. This time its value on the antique market went up."

Fairy tales, thought Gili. "May I see it?" he asked pleasantly.

"Certainly."

Gili held the box and turned it from side to side. The name Halperin was written out fully... Something smelled bad here: In the catalog, it had been written Halpern.

"Thanks for your cooperation." He stood up politely to take his leave. "You'll find the write-up in the weekend edition, including a mention of the mysterious A.R."

Yaakovi was afraid, that much was certain. His red face turned white all at once. "Listen, you won't mess me up, after all the information I've given you absolutely free?"

"Why not?" Gili confronted him. "I'm not afraid of this A.R."

"You don't understand," Yaakovi growled. "I'm not afraid of him either. But he's too respected a man to involve in this."

"Respected?"

"Yes." The secret was squeezed out of him. "He's like a chassidic rebbe, one of the most important men in Israel. Thousands wait for an audience with him."

"Give me one guess," Gili said dryly. "He's called Rav Avram Roosenthal, and half the country knows him."

"That's right," Yaakovi said in wonder. "How did you know?"

Gili was already in the hallway, being escorted by the ubiquitous assistant. "Professional secret. I'll find my own way to him," he called gaily. "I'll be seeing you again. I haven't heard everything I want from you."

12

G ili found himself stuck in the midst of a huge traffic jam on his way back from Big Yaakovi's house. As always, he used the time to formulate his plans. He had written entire stories in half-hours spent stuck in his car.

A significant question remained: If this Rav Avram Roosenthal was as great a rabbi as Benny Gabison and Pinny Yaakovi had made out, why were they afraid of him? A second question: What was the secret of this man, who managed to inspire such awe in a millionaire businessman of Yaakovi's caliber?

The questions wouldn't be answered by themselves: Gili would have to investigate, diving into unknown waters.

The traffic finally started moving; Gili eased his car towards the newsroom. Once inside he found Benny banging on a keyboard, his eyes glued to a grayish paper as he copied the contents of the document directly onto the computer. "Hi, Gili, what'd you catch today?"

"You," Gili answered, hanging up his jacket.

"Sardine fishing is prohibited," Benny chuckled. "You know, I'm a protected species: danger of extinction. You should go for the whales."

"I caught one of those too."

"Who?"

"Rav Avram Roosenthal."

Benny slowly pulled his eyes away from the monitor. "Gili, I thought we were joking."

"I'm very serious." Gili sat down backwards in his chair, his arms embracing the backrest, his hands clenched together tightly. "Benny, you said you would take me to your rabbi. I want to do it today!"

"Have you got a problem?" A mischievous flicker lit up Benny's eyes. "Rav Roosenthal specializes in problem-solving, all kinds. But there's a long line: If you want to make an appointment for Chanukah, try calling on Purim."

"What's this foolishness? Didn't you say you were close to him? Get me in now!"

Benny stared at him intently. "You're crazy, Gili. To get into Rav Avram on the same day you ask to come? The Prime Minister couldn't do it on such short notice! The best I can do for you is get you an appointment for next week."

Gili jumped up angrily. "Thanks loads. I'm very grateful."

Benny moved uneasily in his own seat. "Gili," he said in his most endearing voice, "what's the rush? You want me to give it a try? Okay, I'll try."

He looked into a small address book and dialed a number. "This is the home of Rav Avram Roosenthal," a tinny voice announced. "Please leave your name and number."

"Zabik, it's me, Benny Gabison, from the paper," he cried. There was a click as the receiver was picked up.

After a short argument Benny turned, with a glowing face, to Gili. "You're in luck. I pressured Zabik, the rabbi's *gabbai,* and he's arranged an interview for you tomorrow night."

"Night? What time?"

"I forgot to mention that the rabbi is a night bird. Two-thirty in the morning. I'll come with you."

The streets were quiet at 2 o'clock in the morning. Occasionally, the headlights of a lone vehicle pierced the fog. "Everyone's asleep, and I've got to wander around with you," Benny whined.

"Keep complaining," Gili said, his hands on the wheel. "It's important. Your griping is keeping me awake."

"You won't have a chance to nap; we're almost there," Benny said with a yawn. "Another 10 minutes."

The car entered a quiet neighborhood at the outskirts of Petach Tikvah. Benny guided Gili towards a large apartment building. The parking lot was full and Gili circled several times until he found a place.

"A parking problem here? At the end of the world?" Gili asked, astonished."Who comes here in the middle of the night?"

"You do," Benny answered laconically.

Suddenly their musings were interrupted by a shout. "You're going to Roosenthal? Stay away! He's a dangerous impostor!"

They turned in the direction of the voice and saw a middle-aged *chareidi* man. Again he shouted, "All the *gedolim* are opposed to him. Don't go!"

Benny was furious. He lunged at the man, but Gili held him back. "Let's go in, Benny. We came to see the rabbi, not get aggravated by cranks."

Two minutes later Gili saw a strange phenomenon: The night had disappeared! Inside, the building resembled Tel Aviv's Carmel Market at noon. A jammed elevator took them up to the seventh floor; they found themselves in a hallway that had the smell and sound of a busy public place. A broad spectrum of people, of all ages and ethnic backgrounds, occupied all the chairs in front of the rabbi's door, leaving none empty. Here and there arguments erupted over possession of a place, a seat, a number: The line stretched endlessly.

"I don't believe it," Gili rolled his eyes and stared at his watch. "It's two-thirty in the morning and it looks like noon. Where are the neighbors? Doesn't anybody complain about the terrible noise?"

"The neighbors are *tzaddikim*," an elderly Yemenite woman explained.

"'Good for a *tzaddik*; good for his neighbors.' They've been influenced by the rebbe," a young black-suited man swathed in bandages added, as he leaned on a set of crutches.

The door was opened for a split second. A freckle-faced young man stuck a thin neck out of a dim hallway. "Number 95," he called, in a voice that hinted of the transition from youth to manhood. A young man in chassidic garb stood up and walked quickly towards the door, as if frightened that someone would take his turn. He vanished into the darkness.

"Lucky man," an envious voice whispered, "he's only been waiting two hours."

The crowd grumbled impatiently, complaining about the long line and the lateness of the hour. Some had been here before and they soothed the others. "It's worth the wait; Rabbi Roosenthal solves all problems," they explained.

Every few minutes the elevator disgorged another load: young people in jeans and tricot shirts beside yeshivah boys with suits and ties; singles looking for a match and couples on the verge of divorce. A collection of troubled faces came together in this lobby at 3:15 a.m.

Gili was perplexed by the phenomenon. He nudged Benny in the ribs. "Why don't we hear about this? How is it that it hasn't gotten publicity in the papers?"

"Rav Avram loathes publicity," Benny explained. "When he heard I was a journalist he warned me not to write a word about him."

"Do we have a chance of getting in?" Gili felt a stab of excitement. "There are at least 100 people before us."

"It'll be okay," Benny said complacently. "Come with me."

They descended a floor. Benny knocked on an unmarked brown door three times, waited a moment and then gave two more quick raps. After another second's wait, he gave four more slow bangs.

There was the metallic sound of a chain being disengaged. The door opened a crack, and a suspicious eye peered out at them, flashing hostility towards Gili. The eye roamed farther and landed on Benny lurking in the background.

"Benny, is that you? You frightened me." There was a relieved sigh as the door swung open, revealing a swarthy, robust young man. "Hi. You must be Gili; pleased to meet you. I'm Muli, assistant to the head *gabbai*, Zabik. Pardon the suspicious welcome, but we can't cope anymore. There are so many pests trying to get into the Rav, all I need is for someone to find out they can enter through here."

The rabbi's residence was apparently spread over more than one apartment in the building. Perhaps he had no neighbors at all to protest the noise volume?

They climbed a set of steps to the rabbi's home. Benny spoke first, his eyes alight with pride. "You should know that the rabbi is the wisest man I've ever met; his wisdom is almost unnatural. Providence chose him as a messenger to earth, to help all the unfortunates here."

The three were now standing before a door. Gili stood absolutely still, his penetrating gaze observing his friend. "Welcome back from Teheran; you really are brainwashed," he said.

"You don't like my new style?" Benny laughed.

"You've really turned into a fundamentalist."

The smile never left Benny's pink lips. "When you see Rav Avram, you will also speak like this. You'll be ready to follow him through fire and water."

Gili spoke slowly, patiently. "It won't happen to me. No spiritual leader will cause me to lose my own identity."

Benny kept laughing, the perverse laughter of one who knows that victory is assured. "You asked me to get you an emergency appointment? Five minutes and you're in. Good luck."

☙❧

Gili stood in the darkened corridor and waited impatiently for the previous visitor to leave. His alert glance surveyed his surroundings carefully. He was impressed by the simplicity of the apartment but wouldn't jump to conclusions.

The door opened and a young man walked out, his face a stunned mask. He almost bumped right into Gili.

The rabbi's *gabbai*, Zabik, appeared, an appointment calendar in his hand. "Mr. Gili Dinar is invited to enter," he called in a courteous and official voice.

"That's me," Gili answered gently.

"Please," the *gabbai* extended a hand towards the door, "enter."

Every man has certain images etched upon his memory forever. Men with a propensity towards nature's lavish displays keep upon their hearts the incredible sight of Niagara Falls, the unforgettable vision of hundreds of meters of crystal waters leaping and dancing over the mighty rocks down to the chasm below, or the sight of a multicolored rainbow stretching over the horizon, joining heaven and earth. A person who has stood breathless before the snowy Alps, their peaks perforating the skies, will not forget them in a hurry. Many nature lovers have awoken with the dawn to watch the sunrise from the top of Masada, while the world's expert photographers have tried to capture sunset upon the waters in their attempts to immortalize the scarlet ball falling into an azure sea, imprinting it upon celluloid for eternity.

But there are others not astonished by nature's inanimate wonders and the grandeurs of its scenery. Unusual human drama, images that others almost ignore, fill them with astonishment. Gili, with his boundless curiosity and eagerness to learn about others, entered the dusky room and stared in intense concentration at the bent man sitting in the simple office chair, feeling as though he were standing before one of nature's wonders.

There was a slight, almost imperceptible fragrance in the air, a sweet smell Gili could not identify. A tiny table lamp illuminated the small desk but left most of the room in darkness. Rabbi Roosenthal's face, too, remained in shadow. Gili, sitting, saw from within the dimness the man's ordinary western dress. Here were no turbans, no robes in the style of the miracle worker. A frozen, Sphinx-like countenance stared at him from behind half-closed eyelids.

With his sharp senses Gili immediately felt the man's intense power, a power that filled the room and radiated outside of it. Irrationally, Gili felt that this was a dynamo capable of powering an entire factory, simply with the strength of this concentrated intellect. He knew instinctively that he had never encountered such a force before. In the past, his feelings had proved to be accurate: He never erred.

"Sit," Rabbi Roosenthal said in a quiet tone.

Gili sank into a comfortable leather chair. For an instant he wondered at a host who showed his guests more consideration than he had for himself.

"You're Gili Dinar, the journalist?"

"That's right."

"What brings you to me? You're a successful reporter who has everything he desires. Usually people with problems are the ones who come here."

He spoke in fluent Hebrew, with only the trace of an accent revealing his American origins.

"And who doesn't have problems?" Gili said. "But I haven't come because of them. I've come to see how you operate."

Gili awaited the protest at his blunt and disrespectful tone, the surprise at his arrogant request. But he was wrong. Rabbi Roosenthal met the challenge.

"Okay," Rabbi Roosenthal said, "I'm prepared to let you do so. But there's a problem. The people who come here do so with the confidence that their personal lives will be revealed only to me. Would you invade their privacy?"

"I didn't mean to sit here while you met with people. I wanted to hear your policies, how you influence others."

"And this was so important that you had to come here at 3 o'clock in the morning?"

Rabbi Roosenthal stood up. Unconscious of it, he walked into the circle of light, his penetrating glance falling on Gili's face. His eyes burned with a cold, hypnotic light. He approached Gili, speaking in a serene voice. His fingers gently touched Gili's outstretched palm.

"You're battling with yourself. You've come to me for help. Don't be embarrassed to admit it. Bigger and better men than you have come to me."

Gili felt the energy radiating from Rav Avram's fingers. Everything went blurry. "Rabbi, you're wrong. I honestly want to learn about you."

"I've never been wrong," the warm fingers pulled away. "Heaven has blessed me with an understanding as unerring as an x-ray. Do you want to know why you've come to me? I'll tell you! You're lost in a maze of troubles, pursued by deep feelings of guilt. A sharp pain stabs through you and you want to ease the burden of suffering and hurt, to take a break from the perpetual agony. Benny Gabison has told me a little about you.

You're wondering if you haven't made a mistake, leaving behind your happy secular lifestyle and entrapping yourself in the inflexible life of a Torah observer. In the deepest recesses of your heart, you haven't yet convinced yourself wholly of the truth of Torah. My friend, you need help, but your vanity doesn't allow you to seek that help, as if you were just one of the masses, so you hide behind your facade as an investigative journalist."

The burning eyes didn't relent for a minute. Two warring powers fought within Gili: One longed to flee from this perceptive, plain-spoken man before him; the other was drawn to him.

Suddenly he remembered his father's words to him, spoken when Gili was just a youth: All men are equal; don't humble yourself before anyone.

The thought injected him with renewed energy. He withdrew a little from Rav Avram, taking up his usual challenging stance. A wild thought blazed through his head: *Who's the one who is hiding something here, you or I? Why the dim light, why not use a normal bulb?*

"Excellent," Rav Avram said delightedly, "I love your kind of man, whose face conceals nothing!"

Gili broke out in a sweat. *I didn't say a word to him...*

"Yes, yes," the rabbi grinned broadly, "what are you worried about? You're an open book to me. I know you better than you know yourself. You've come to me to help strengthen yourself; why are you so ashamed?"

Gili felt a sudden weakness. This rabbi was powerful: He must have learned some form of mental telepathy in the Far East. Gili had once read in a science journal of a monastery in Tibet which passed on to its members the secret of total concentration, training them to become mediums with the gift of clairvoyance. Was that Avram Roosenthal's secret? Or was he working with the powers of darkness?

Gili gathered his last remaining strength. "I'm not amazed by your conjectures. Any average kabbalist or 'miracle worker' can do what you've done, hitting a bull's-eye by knowing what goes on in most people's lives. You could have figured out all that you've told me, relying only on the information given to you by your lackey, Benny Gabison."

"I'm not a miracle worker, I'm a simple man trying to help people. I don't have lackeys, and your judgment of Benny is unfair," Rav Avram said in quiet, measured tones. "You have no idea how dedicated Benny is to your welfare; he truly loves you. Do you know when he first told me about you? A week ago, when you were hospitalized with a possible stroke. He came to me, totally distraught, and wept like a baby. I'd never seen him cry before. He told me that he had a close friend, a journalist who'd lost his father in a car accident, who now found himself in mortal danger. He is as concerned for you as your mother is, though you're her only son."

The man's loving tones tugged at his heart. Gili, almost swept away, remembered the practical words he'd once heard from Rav Schmidt: Respect him and suspect him.

"So Benny told you I'm an only child."

"Benny told me three things about you. One, you were in a car accident. Two, it was feared you'd had a stroke. Three, you are an only child. All the rest, I just knew."

Gili quickly surveyed the dimly lit room. On the wall behind the rabbi hung a large number of *"kemeyot"* written on both metal disks and parchment. Kabbalistic signs pictured the ten *sefirot,* large numbers of interlocking circles, and many worlds interwoven one inside the other. All reflected the Torah's hidden wisdom.

"Is that the secret of your power?" Gili asked, pointing towards the wall. "Or just part of the scenery, the props you use to maximize the effect on a credulous, foolish public?"

Rav Avram grinned once again. "May your lips be blessed! Your words are a pleasure to hear. I hadn't expected a young Israeli of the 90s to speak so. I like you, young man. I appreciate bravery and honesty. They enable me to harness heavenly energies."

"Tell your stories to someone else," Gili said, standing up. "It's not long ago that I crossed the borders and became observant. But even in that short time I learned to sense who was a true rav. Rabbi Schmidt, Rabbi Weisgall and Rabbi Lieberman of 'Arachim': They don't need these magical posters of yours."

"They were your teachers?"

A brief nod.

Rabbi Roosenthal said, "If you stay with me, I will teach you the difference between the power of the sages of revealed Torah, and that of the hidden Torah. It's a fascinating topic that can't be explained quickly. But to give just a short summary: The rabbis whom you've mentioned are like small-time shopkeepers doing a meager business. My dear fellow, a true kabbalist who understands just what kabbalah is and how to work with it is a Rothschild, a Reichman, a Safra. Not in money, of course, but in eternal treasures, in boundless spiritual possessions."

"That's what you say," Gili whispered doubtfully, as the image of Rabbi Schmidt poring over his Gemara flashed suddenly before his eyes: the furrowed brow, sleep-deprived, weary eyes lit up with internal satisfaction and sheer serenity. Gili thought of the spiritual treasures of his friends in the yeshivah for *ba'alei teshuvah* whom he'd left behind in Jerusalem's Beis Yisrael neighborhood. He felt a strong longing for them. Were any of them in the *beis midrash* now, at four in the morning? Yes, Tully Amit was probably sitting and humming contentedly as he concentrated on the *Sefer Kuzari* or one of the books of the Maharal of Prague. Two benches away would be Rafi Marciano, the *masmid*, engrossed in some difficult Talmudic concept. Did these not possess spiritual treasures?

"And I tell you that you still don't understand the difference. Of course the Talmud contains vast spiritual wealth, but the kabbalah is the internal dimension that contains the external as well." Once again, Gili was shocked. *He's playing telepathic ping-pong with me. I think to myself and he answers me aloud. What is the source of his power?*

"It's late, and difficult for the people outside." Rabbi Roosenthal ended the interview, escorting Gili to the door. Before parting he added that the topics they had discussed necessitated much exhaustive study before they would be clarified. Gili could return at any time: The door was open to him. Could he come during the morning hours, Gili asked. The rabbi assured him that he could come whenever he pleased, just by calling first for an appointment.

When he descended to the lower floor he heard the people gathered there pouring out their wrath on the hapless head of Zabik the *gabbai*. The rabbi's assistant declared that there had been a special emergency. Gili's father had told him, as a child, that he was special; somehow, Zabik had reached the same conclusion.

Benny had waited for him downstairs, cat-napping on a folding cot. Gili drove him home, Benny asking from between half-closed eyelids how it had gone; by the time Gili had framed a reply the eyes were totally shut, and Gili found himself talking to someone fast asleep. Gili drove mechanically, like a robot. The darkness of night was slowly giving way to dawn and it was easier to drive than before, despite the thoughts chasing through his brain as he reviewed the events of the past hour.

Before the meeting he had armed himself with a heaping dose of *chutzpah*, and during the encounter itself he had fearlessly attacked Rav Avram, but the wise rabbi had not taken up the gauntlet. Conversely, Rav Avram had appeared as one of the rare breeds, wise and powerful, charismatic and exciting. Gili saw in him incomparable powers of domination. Rav Avram recognized each individual's weak points and used them, achieving mastery over others through their own vulnerability. Gili feared their next meeting: The rabbi would overcome all of his defenses, he suspected, and ensnare him with his charisma, as he had all the others.

When he let Benny, still yawning, out of the car, he played with a heretical thought, wondering if he should simply not return for another meeting with the rabbi. While he parked the car by the yellow beam of the streetlights, he found himself torn by two opposing forces. As he fell into bed for the few hours of sleep that remained to him, his decision was made.

Gili had to learn more about this Rav Avram: Who he was, what motivated him, why he only worked at night. And, most important of all, what his expertise was in the arcane world of Judaica and antiquities!

There was no question about it: They would meet again.

13

few hours later, in the newsroom of *HaYom HaZeh*, Benny apologized for his previous indifference. "I was collapsing from fatigue. If I don't get a good night's sleep, I'm not even human."

"You're barely human even after you've slept," Gili teased. "Tell me, how do you manage with a rabbi who only works at night?"

"Don't ask. It's a complete disaster," Benny lamented. "Rabbi Avram is always down on me. He calls me 'sleepyhead' because I require seven hours of shut-eye a night. He's got his own special philosophy. It's called: Sleep No More."

Gili didn't understand. "Sleep is a basic necessity of every normal man. Who can survive without sleep?"

"Rav Avram Roosenthal," Benny said confidently. He told Gili of his rabbi's unique creed. Sleep, Rav Avram believed, was a mental, rather than a physical, need. The body can make do with an hour's rest; it's the brain that needs all that sleep.

Gili made a dismissive gesture. "What's the difference? The fact is that most people sleep six or seven hours a night, with a few exceptions who are satisfied with four or five."

"And that's where we get to the rabbi's innovation," Benny explained excitedly. "Rav Avram clarified the matter with researchers in a sleep laboratory in Virginia. They told him that sleep during the day is of higher quality, more concentrated, and better for the brain than sleep at night. Rav Avram tried it out on himself and proved that one and a half hours of sleep during the day is just as good as seven hours at night."

"Maybe for him. Not for me," Gili dismissed the strange theory.

"You took the words out of my mouth. I told him precisely the same thing. Do you know what he told me? That I'm lazy, and that 30 of his followers are already doing what he does, working all night and making do on one and a half to two hours of sleep in the afternoon."

Gili thought of the bustling, energetic atmosphere in the waiting room during the late hours of the night. Of the *gabbaim*, utterly and astonishingly awake. Of the freckle-faced young man.

"Who was that boy, the one who announced the visitors?" Gili asked.

"If I don't finish this write-up, and Eric yells at me, I'm going to blame you," Benny warned. "I haven't even written two sentences today."

"Who was the freckle-faced kid?" Gili repeated.

"You're a pain," Benny grumbled. "He's Choni, the rabbi's son."

"Oh, my first discovery. By the way, doesn't the rabbi's wife resent the evening marketplace in her house? Or is she also a member of the league against sleep?"

"Sherlock Holmes, you can't stop asking questions. Rav Avram has no wife. He's single."

"You just told me he has a son."

"An adopted son," Benny took a sip from the can of soda that rested perpetually on his desk and spoke in a quiet, sad tone. "Two adopted sons, to be exact. Though Rav Avram never married, he's not alone, and not only because of the crowds who come to visit him. He adopted two unfortunates. Choni has had a tragic life, an orphan whose parents are alive. In his short life he's attempted suicide and was thrown out of four yeshivot. His father doesn't want to have anything to do with him. Rav Avram is raising him in his home. Paysi came from an institution. He's a deaf-mute from a broken home."

Gili opened his mouth to speak several times, but didn't manage to utter even a syllable. He saw Rabbi Roosenthal in another light, the light of charity and kindness. *And I was so rude to him,* his heart thudded. Rabbi Roosenthal truly aided unfortunates, just as Benny had said the night before.

"You know, Choni made a good impression on me. Could you arrange a meeting with him?"

"Maybe you can leave me in peace," Benny grumbled, his attention reverting to the blinking monitor before him. "My story today came out completely messed up because of you."

"Benny, I want to meet Choni."

"Okay, on your next visit. But you'll go alone; I want to get a good night's sleep."

"Certainly, Sleepyhead."

Eric suddenly entered their cubicle. "Gili," he yelled, "your computer isn't even turned on! You haven't written a thing yet! What about that writeup on Kiryat Sefer? If it's not on my desk in two hours, you're fired!"

He exited with the slam of a door. Benny and Gili exchanged grins. Eric never fulfilled any of his dire threats. Gili continued smiling for the next half-hour, while he sat writing up his story. He had found an excellent excuse for still another visit to that charming, yet infuriating, rabbi.

From his earliest youth, Gili had always searched for the human dimension in every event. Choni was that human factor. Gili just had to meet him.

❧❦❧

Monica lay on her bed. A severe case of the flu had kept her homebound the entire week. She was speaking with a close friend in the office, catching up on all the latest happenings at work. Her friend, glad to take time from her schedule to entertain a sick colleague, had happily gossiped with Monica, relieving her boredom somewhat.

The roar of an approaching motorcycle didn't manage to wrest her attention away from the call. It was only when the cyclist rang her bell that she hurriedly said goodbye and went to the door.

A postal service worker held a heavy helmet in one hand; in the other, he waved an envelope and large pad. "Registered mail, please sign."

After she'd signed and the postman had left with a roar, she looked curiously at the envelope. It was addressed to Gili; the name of the sender wasn't evident.

She suddenly felt herself shivering. *These are not flu symptoms,* she thought. *I'm afraid!*

There was no rational reason for her sudden terror. Gili had often received such unmarked envelopes in the past. But since the tragedy, Monica had become very high strung. Groundless fears were now part of her life.

Gili didn't like her to open his mail. He was very sensitive about his privacy. On the other hand, perhaps this was something that should be hidden from him? The envelope was feather light, as if it were empty.

Something that should be hidden from him? What kind of nonsense is this?

But I'm afraid...

He'll never know...

Monica placed the envelope over a boiling tea kettle. The steam moistened the gum on the envelope, which opened easily. She removed a small piece of paper. The text was short, printed from a computer: "My dear Gili, This is an appeal from a friend. You're wandering around in perilous places. Break off contact immediately; your life is in danger!"

The paper slid through trembling fingers. Monica's lips and mouth went dry. Who was threatening Gili, and why? She had but one child, and he was in danger!

When Monica had chosen to live as a secular Jew she had cut herself off from her roots. But suddenly she felt an irresistible urge to pray. "Please, my G-d, watch over my only son. He's my only comfort, now that Udi is gone. If something happens to him, take us both together then..."

Like a sleepwalker she staggered towards the bookshelf. There she found an old *Tanach* that had belonged to Udi. She hadn't read the Bible since her elementary school days. She skimmed through the pages, searching fruitlessly for *Sefer Tehillim*. Where was it hidden? Despite her panic she seemed to recall that *Tehillim* was placed somewhere between the prophet Yechezkel and the sufferings of Iyov. Why couldn't she find it? Was it because tears were blurring her vision?

She continued to skim through the book.

A small paper flew out from among the pages, landing on the carpet. This was a day for scraps of paper. She bent down and picked it up.

Udi's handwriting, so painfully familiar, stood before her. They were small, carefully crafted letters, written in a beautiful calligraphic hand. "The book of *segulos*, *The Vessel of Blessing*, written by the *chacham* Rabbi Ezra Albertzloni. Salonika, 5234 (1474), with three parts. The first part, the wisdom of the soul. The second part, the wisdom of the countenance. The third part, the wisdom of the deeds."

Beneath these words was a blank line, followed by more of Udi's writing: "Remember! This is the title page of the book of *segulos*. This valuable book was inherited by my father from his father, Rabbi Moshe Dinburg of Shidlitz, for whom I was named. He inherited it from his father, and on and on, until my great-great-grandfather, Rabbi Tzvi, 'the *sofer* of Salonika,' a disciple of the author who received it from him as a gift. My father, may he live, told me that the book is unique. It is very rare and is worth a fortune. It is written in the author's handwriting, on parchment made from the hide of a deer. There is no copy like it in the entire world! Father has told me secretly that one day I shall inherit it, if I succeed in my studies. This book has been in our family for 500 years and shall continue to be passed on, generation to generation. I've written this as a keepsake, today, Sunday, 5 Shevat, 5721, at one in the morning, in my room in the dormitory, Yeshivas Ein Yisrael, while my roommates, Manny Schwartz, Chaim Ozer Schmidt, and Yoske Friedman are sleeping soundly. Signed, Moshe Dinburg."

Monica broke down in wild sobbing. She had never seen her Udi from this perspective, a young, eager yeshivah student, full of joy and the naivete of youth. When she had met him, some years after this had been written, he was already using the name Udi Dinar. He was cynical and cold and there was no sign left of this endearing innocence. Only one thing remained of the old life: the book.

Monica remembered the book well, the first time she saw it in Udi's hands, two weeks after their marriage...

"What's that junk you're carrying?" Monica asked, staring at the package wrapped in tattered cloth. Udi held the bundle tightly, as a mother holds her infant. Since their wedding, two weeks earlier, they hadn't managed to unpack all their gifts and their belongings. Now they were busily setting things out on shelves and in closets. The work was endless, especially because Udi and Monica told each other the background of each and every item they unpacked. They stood and laughed, content and happy, with the wonder that only a newly married couple can feel.

"You're insulting me," Udi said with a smile. "Don't call our good-luck charm junk."

"Good-luck charm? Since when do you believe in those?" the young wife asked, astonished.

"This is the most expensive item we have in this house. Do you have any idea how much it's worth?"

"You're driving me crazy! What's inside?"

Udi unrolled the yellowed linen cover and revealed the contents of the bundle: an ancient book, bound in brown leather.

"You're making such a big deal about an old book? I was sure the package was full of diamonds!" Monica was disappointed.

"That's right. This book is a real diamond!" Udi said solemnly. He told Monica of the great value of the book that he'd inherited from his father, Rabbi Shmuel Dinburg, who had died suddenly of a stroke two months after his "Moishike" had joined the army and flung the *kippah* from his head.

Udi leafed through the parchment pages, showing her words written in large vowelized letters. "These are the names of angels," he told her. "My father told me that someone who is versed in practical kabbalah can make the angels swear by their own names, and they will then come to serve him and change the laws of nature for him."

Monica shook her head in disbelief, dissatisfied that her modern husband should display evidence of such a superstitious streak. Udi didn't answer. Deep in his heart he knew she was right. He hadn't bothered putting on *tefillin* in years and hadn't felt a pang of conscience, and yet he treated this book with awe and reverence.

But Abba had spoken with such confidence, and had told him of the miracles his own grandfather had performed with the power of the charms and kabbalistic secrets hidden in the book. Abba was a strict disciplinarian, but he was not a liar, of that Udi was certain. Abba was the very symbol of integrity, his heart and his lips were as one. Occasionally he would tell his family tales of the holy book; each time he would remember still another miracle his grandfather had wrought with its aid.

"Have you ever heard a father lie to his son?" Udi asked. "I don't believe Abba made up the stories."

"If those stories are true, you should learn from them and change your life," Monica retorted. "You're living a contradiction. If there really are angels who can be called upon, then the entire Torah is true. If part is true, then all is true."

"You know what?" Udi said despondently, "That's just the way it began for Manny and me. It was actually because of this book that we started to have doubts and, finally, lose our belief. We tried secretly to make use of the powers within it a few times, and nothing happened. Those were the first cracks in the wall of our faith, for both of us."

Monica could hardly believe what she'd just heard. "Are you serious?" she stammered. "You and Manny Schwartz, two bored schoolboys, stood in a dark room and whispered 'abracadabra' and, when no hocus-pocus appeared, you threw away your *kippot* and enlisted in the army!"

"No," Udi said angrily, "it wasn't like that at all. One day maybe I'll tell you every detail of the events that sent us out of the yeshivah, as if we were carried on a tidal wave. But that was the beginning."

"And your father, what of him? You said your father would never lie to his children."

"That's true," he admitted quietly. He could hear the voice of his *mashgiach*, the saintly Rabbi Shmuel Bergman, speaking: "Remember, students, a father doesn't lie to his children. You won't find a person who asks his children to believe something that he himself does not. If a Jew told his son he stood at Mt. Sinai when God gave the Torah to him and his nation, it is a sign that these things really did happen. Six hundred thousand fathers were there and saw this. They told this to their sons. And thus are these truths handed down from generation to generation."

"If my father, Rabbi Shmuel Dinburg, a man whose very essence was honesty, a modest scholar and one who feared God, if he lied to me, the world would come to an end!

"But if he did not lie, I'm in a bind, because it is all true. The entire Torah!"

Udi put a quick end to the theological discussion. "The book is a treasure. Any way you look at it, it's worth a fortune."

He wrapped the book back into its cover with the same love he had shown before. That week he bought a steel-lined safe and locked the book within it. The contradiction didn't disturb him too much. The book was holy and valuable and placed in a heavy metal box for safekeeping. And life was secular, and everything was wonderful...

❧❧

The door opened. Gili saw his mother standing near the bookshelf, two scraps of paper in her hand, her eyes moist.

Gili ran over to her. "Ima, has something happened?" He gently stroked her hand.

Monica shook her head. Thank G-d, nothing had happened to her Gili. Here he was, healthy, whole.

"Gili, they didn't come after you? Lock the door. I'm afraid."

Gili shrugged his shoulders and quickly shut the door. "Ima, I asked you, what's happened?"

"I'm embarrassed to tell you, Gili, but today I opened your mail. An anonymous letter came for you and I'm so afraid."

Gili read the brief note. His brain hummed like a beehive. "Who is this friend that doesn't like my visit to Rav Avram Roosenthal? Who is threatening me?"

Monica carefully examined the postmark. "It was mailed from Haifa. Does that tell you anything?"

"Nothing," Gili replied, massaging his temples wearily. "Absolutely nothing."

Monica looked deeply into Gili's eyes. "Tell me the truth. I won't be angry with you. You know I'm liberal, open minded, even with regard to religion. I don't mind that you've become observant. Now tell me, where do you spend your time?"

Gili told her of his nocturnal visit to the rabbi.

"Very strange," Monica said.

"What's strange?"

"The whole thing. The times he sees people. If he wants to help them, why force them to come at such hours? What's wrong with daytime? I have a lot of questions about the whole concept of kabbalists. Which of them are charlatans, and which of them are real? But what really upsets me is who would threaten your life after one visit to a rabbi's house?"

Gili noticed the second piece of paper. He read it eagerly. Monica watched his eyes fly over the lines, seeing him grow pale as he took in the contents.

"Gili, what's the matter?" Monica asked, frightened.

Gili gave her a hollow look. He felt that his brain would burst with the flood of hazy memories, as they writhed within him, looking for a way into his consciousness.

"It's nothing, Ima," he whispered weakly. His body went limp. He grabbed at the embroidered tablecloth. A blue vase full of flowers crashed down to the floor. Monica dashed forward and grabbed his arms, trying to break his fall. With a great effort she managed to get him to the sofa. "Gili, what is it?" she asked in concern. "Another blackout?"

Gili shook his head in assent.

"What's going to be?" Monica wrung her hands in despair. "The attacks don't stop. We can't go on like this! We've got to travel abroad. We'll find the world's top neurologist!"

Gili shook his head. "No, Ima, I'm curious about these attacks; I want them to continue."

Monica ran to the kitchen and returned, a cold drink in her hand. "Drink, Gili. You're frightening me with these crazy ideas."

Gili waved the scrap of paper. "Something I read now awoke something dormant in my brain. I feel that some day everything will burst forth, all the memories."

"Gili, what are you talking about?"

"I'm talking about this!" Gili again read the words his father had written as a youngster, long before his only son had come into this world. "The book that Abba had is the key to the whole mystery. One day I'll have a gigantic blackout, one that will explode throughout my brain, and then the whole picture will become clear."

Monica was very disturbed. "I think you should see a good doctor right away. You're being unreasonable. Who knows if something new hasn't happened to you?"

Her voice choking, she burst into tears, collapsing weakly into a chair and coughing uncontrollably. Gili, too, lay drained on the couch, frustrated and angry with himself. On the wall facing him he could see one of the marvelous pictures taken by his father, a professional photographer. It was a picture of a tiny baby pigeon, its downy feathers tangled, trying fruitlessly to leave its nest, giving a noiseless cry towards its white-winged mother hovering helplessly over it, unable to reach her young. It was a picture that tugged at the heartstrings of all who viewed it in the Dinar home. The pigeon's poignant despair was moving, though no one could articulate exactly why. Gili was the only one who knew Udi's professional secret, just how he'd created the picture that had won a prestigious award. He'd covered the nest with glass...

"You understand, Gilichik, sweetie," Udi had smiled, the small wrinkles near his eyes crinkling up in glee, "no one can see the transparent glass. I shot the pigeon and the nest at such an angle that the rays of light passed through it. What people see is a mother pigeon and her chick, helpless, grabbing for each other and clucking in despair."

Gili was only 6 years old, but was already full of curiosity and questions.

"Abba," he asked, his wide eyes full of wonder, "is that allowed?"

"Why not, cutie?"

Gili spoke slowly. "Abba, imagine someone putting me on a train that's going to go down a cliff, and he'd see you running after me on the platform, screaming Gili, Gili, and then he would say that he did it only to take a picture of how the two of us are so miserable. Would you agree to it?"

Udi understood. He was stunned by his son's logic, childish and incisive at the same time, and by the mature conscience and well-developed vocabulary of the 6-year-old. His first reaction was to give him a strong hug and raise him high into the air. Afterwards, he explained to his sweet little boy that the analogy wasn't quite right because it just took a second or two and then he removed the glass covering and rewarded the pigeon with a rich lode of birdseed. The main thing was that the photo had garnered an important award in Paris and was now registered, under his name, in the international photo agency, Photo Image Bank.

But on that day they each lost their fascination with the famed photo. Gili never made peace with the injustice done to the feathered creatures captured by the camera's lens; Udi always remembered his son's sensitive conscience, which lashed at him from the eyes of a bereaved mother bird.

Oh, what are you, you photograph? Just a silent, dead picture, colored paper, or reality, frozen in time eternally?

Gili felt like the chick, caught in a transparent trap. The solution was so close, and occasionally he almost reached it. But he stuck his hand out to touch it and it was gone, leaving him alone and bereaved. Just a few damaged brain cells, that was all, the transparent partition standing between him and the solution. If only he could create them anew. But everyone knew that a dead brain cell could never come back to life. Irreversible...

14

ili lay on the couch half an hour, recovering. Then he took a deep breath, did some exercise, and drank a glass of cold water. He glanced at himself in the mirror and, seeing that he'd returned to normal, turned to say goodbye to his mother.

"Maybe you want to stay home today?" she pleaded with him. "You just had a blackout."

"I feel great, Ima. Can't you see?"

She gazed at his face. The color had returned to his cheeks. "But someone is threatening you."

"Oh, come on, Ima."

Monica stared after him as he left the house, his step jaunty and confident. She was flooded by a wave of maternal love and anxiety, and fought the temptation to run after him and bring him back.

Stop it, Monica. He's not a little boy anymore; you can't embarrass him publicly. She sighed and remained at the window, her eyes following the car as it roared down the street.

Gili parked the car not far from Rav Avram's house and considered his next move. He was planning to surprise the rabbi with an unexpected visit.

They had agreed that Gili would first make an appointment. The rabbi would most certainly not appreciate his sudden appearance at 4 o'clock in the afternoon. Gili considered five different excuses.

As he prepared to leave the car, Gili put on a pair of sunglasses and a cap with a large visor. He hoped to conceal himself among the others. If he were recognized before the right time, the element of surprise would be lost. The situation could change in just one minute.

The large building looked different in the light of day. There wasn't a trace of the bustle of the night before. The stairwell was empty and the elevator sat quietly, as if waiting just for him.

He examined the mailboxes. The name Roosenthal appeared on only one of them. Two boxes were unmarked; presumably they, too, belonged to Rav Avram. Clearly, though, the building did have other tenants, quiet neighbors or apathetic ones, who didn't care that their building turned into an open marketplace every night. Or perhaps they'd all become devotees of the rabbi's policy against nocturnal sleeping? A sudden mischievous image rose in his mind, of the rabbi leading his neighbors in a "no-more-sleeping" workshop: "Goldstein, you slept four hours yesterday? To the punishment cell! Green, you haven't slept three nights. Excellent. You've earned the 'Good Neighbor Award.'"

You're dreaming, Gili. You've got a lot of work to do, and you're standing here, dreaming.

The numbers flashed in the elevator's indicator: 4, 5, 6. Gili exited and took a long hard look at the hallway. Nothing strange here. Two doors bearing people's names, one door unmarked. He put his palm over the peephole and knocked. Three regular knocks, two quick ones, and four slow bangs.

There was the sound of footsteps on the other side. Someone approached the door and tried to see who was outside. Gili smiled victoriously: Except for a black circle, he would see nothing...

The chain was pulled, the lock turned twice, and the door was opened.

Gili found himself standing before a tall, impressive-looking boy of about 14 who, despite the large hearing aids that protruded from his ears like antennae, was extraordinarily handsome. *He must be Paysi,* Gili thought, the institutionalized deaf-mute from the broken home, abandoned by his family and adopted by the rabbi. He was one of the unfortunates who seemed to inherit all the troubles in the world.

But that was Gili's assessment of him. The lad's face didn't show a trace of misfortune. His eyes darted curiously back and forth as he scanned Gili's face with a searching look. He made a sign with two of his fingers, opened his hand and waved it in the air in a series of quick curves and lines.

As Gili had never learned sign language, he could not interpret the silent gestures. He came as close to the boy as he could, and asked loudly, "Are you Paysi, the rabbi's son?"

The youngster nodded his head energetically and clapped his hands with joy. He opened his mouth and moved his lips several times. Gili read the message: "Come with me."

"Should I go with you?"

Another energetic nod. Paysi whipped a small notepad out of his pocket and scribbled something quickly. This was his most effective means of communication, Gili noticed, the way he could be best understood.

He put the message into Gili's hands, who shuddered slightly at the strange handwriting. With difficulty, Gili managed to make out a few words: "Are you the reporter?"

Gili nodded. "How do you know?" he asked loudly.

Paysi wrote once again, letter after letter, sweating with the effort. The result: "Abba told me you would be coming this afternoon, and he drew a picture of you."

Paysi pulled a folded sheet of paper out of his back pocket. With a few bold lines, someone had made a detailed sketch of Gili's features.

"Your father drew this?" Gili marveled. Rav Avram could have built a career as a top caricaturist. He certainly possessed a wide variety of talents.

Paysi wrote once again. Gili swiftly read the words: "Wait until Abba calls you on the intercom."

Are we dealing with a prophet? How did Rav Avram know that I was on my way here? I didn't tell a soul! Gili suddenly felt like a wild animal caught in a trap.

Paysi didn't waste a minute. While Gili was still lost in thought, he flew lightly through the large apartment preparing refreshments on a wooden table. The neck of a bottle of expensive brandy stuck out from amidst cubes of ice in a sparkling aluminum bucket. Paysi poured Gili a small cup without waiting for him to ask.

Gili downed the brandy with pleasure. Rav Avram undoubtedly had good taste. The brandy had a fruity texture that, when chilled, slid smoothly down the throat.

Paysi watched his every move, his alert eyes following him without embarrassment. Gili felt uncomfortable under the scrutiny and made a great play of turning towards the window.

The intercom buzzed into life. "Gili Dinar may come up," Rav Avram's melodious voice came through. "I'm waiting for him."

⚬❧❧⚬

In the light of day Rav Avram looked very different. The darkness had concealed him; now, one could see a soft, benevolent face, a man dressed in a light robe giving off a pleasant, peaceful feeling. He was walking down the long hallway near his study; it seemed that he was waiting for something. When he saw Gili and Paysi his face cleared.

"Here's our investigative reporter," he said jovially. "Welcome."

Gili scanned the rabbi's face. He had a high, domed forehead and a turned-up nose. A pair of light eyebrows lent him a tranquil look, but his deep eyes gave off a gaze as sharp and sagacious as a surgeon's knife. Gili began to understand the secret of the man's force. If the Creator equips you with a pair of eyes such as these, you can easily understand a man's soul. He was a handsome, impressive person, with a light-blond beard and thin frame that radiated health and strength. Rabbi Roosenthal looked younger than his years; Gili estimated his age at no more than 45. The fact that he wasn't married seemed like something out of a Greek tragedy: A man who helped and advised the entire world was left, himself, without a family, with only two unfortunate children whom no one else wanted to raise as his own.

"Paysi," the rabbi clapped his hands, "you can go and rest now."

The lad looked at him longingly but went down the stairs without protest. The rabbi turned to Gili. "Come into the room, we've got something to talk about."

Even his room looked less mysterious and threatening in the glow of the hot sun's rays. A spartan, simple bed stood on one side; the blankets looked untouched and Gili felt a sudden urge to find out if the rabbi had had his daily ration of sleep. Two of the walls were covered with shelves filled with the Talmud, Midrash, Chassidic tomes and, particularly, books of kabbalah. There was a huge collection of all sorts of kabbalistic works, their bindings worn, clearly by frequent use.

The wall behind Rav Avram's back was decorated with kabbalistic symbols, talismans, and illustrations of the *sefirot*. Only small areas of the wall were uncovered, peeking out from behind the furniture, revealing aging wallpaper that featured charming blue flowers. Several framed pictures of renowned *rabbanim* were on the desk. There were dozens of scraps of paper in every conceivable spot; even an ignoramus could figure out that these were requests customarily given to kabbalists bearing the name of some sick person or someone looking for the right match.

"Gili Dinar has come to find out why I only work at night," the rabbi said with a broad smile. "I've met a lot of curious people in my time, but none quite as impudent as you are."

Gili laughed. He felt too mellow in this comfortable recliner. His host's amused tone left no doubt: The rabbi didn't care to do battle with him.

"The first question that needs clarification: Are you a prophet? How did you know I was coming?"

Rav Avram allowed himself a half-smile. "It was to be expected. You told me you planned on coming back after our discussion last night. You work on the paper in the mornings. What else could I think?"

"And what about your receiving people at night? People come here because they're in trouble and need help. Why do you make it harder for them by forcing them to come here at so late an hour?"

The rabbi's face grew serious. He thought for a moment and stared at Gili with his piercing gaze. "I think I can trust you and reveal the true reason. Know, then, that the wisdom of kabbalah says that during the first hours after midnight and up until dawn the atmosphere is pure and holy, free from pollution and sin. During those hours it is easier for me, and for all true *rabbanim*, to rehabilitate a man's soul and direct him on the proper path."

Gili hastily rose up and approached Rav Avram at the window.

"How is it that I hadn't heard about you until just a short while ago? And what, what is your great power?"

Rav Avram rested his arm on Gili's shoulder. "Relax. Take a deep breath. It's not healthy for you to get excited; you've had enough blackouts. High blood pressure is a mortal danger for you. You may not grow too angry or emotional, you must be tranquil, without heart-stopping terrors or mad adventures."

Gili found himself under the rabbi's hypnotic spell: He was already breathing deeply and his heartbeat returned to normal. His violent emotions dissipated, leaving him mellow and serene.

He spoke with absolute honesty. "Thank you for your wise medical advice. But with all that, I'd like an answer to my question."

"Okay, I accept the challenge," said the rabbi, much taken by Gili's youthful exuberance. "Come, look down at the street below, study it, and tell me what you see."

Gili lowered his glance towards the yard and quiet noonday street. He saw automobiles languidly traveling through the narrow road, pedestrians scurrying on their way, cats lolling carelessly in the sun. Elegant lavender orchids bloomed in the well-kept garden.

"I meant for you to look at people, not cats and flowers," the rabbi explained. "What do you see?"

"Nothing special. Just ordinary people, like everybody else."

"That's your first mistake: There is no such thing as an ordinary person. Every person is unique unto himself, an individual."

"You're giving me a philosophy lesson? I learned philosophy in high school."

"You learned nothing in high school. You only received a diploma. If you had to take a test today, you wouldn't get a passing grade. But that's not what we're talking about. You hear the word 'person' and immediately talk about philosophy."

Rav Avram paused for a moment. The two sat near the desk, and he continued.

"You asked what power I have. My power comes from the word human. I am a specialist in humanity. I asked you what you saw in the street.

The answer is: people who think they are people, but they are wrong. They are just a caricature of the marvelous creature the Creator made, the creature called 'man.' The people you saw on the street live in a crooked, distorted world; life passes by them but not within them. They don't know how to live and thus find themselves awash in misery. I set them straight, as the Creator meant for them to be, and thus all their problems disappear."

The shoemaker goes barefoot, Gili thought mockingly, *you can straighten everyone else out, but not yourself.*

"To my great sorrow, I suffer from an ailment whose cure is not contingent upon me or my good will, and therefore I have not built a family, if you wanted to ask," the rabbi said, his eyes veiled. This time he managed to shock Gili into near-panic. He felt himself laid bare, transparent, before the eyes of this brilliant rabbi. Rav Avram could read his mind!

"I don't read minds," the rabbi said quietly, almost to himself. "I hear thoughts. Every thought is a world in itself, a complete creation. I hear how it is woven and created, how it manifests itself within your head. I hear your thoughts, as if you'd said them aloud!"

"Enough!" Gili shouted, scarlet faced. He felt as if he were suffocating; with trembling fingers he pulled at his necktie.

In a split second Rav Avram had loosened the knot and was pouring cool water down Gili's burning throat. He waited silently for a few minutes, while his guest regained his strength.

Gili tried desperately to muster the last remaining vestiges of rebellion. "Enough! I don't want to hear more! You know me through and through, you know all my weaknesses and psychoanalytical shortcomings, Dr. Sigmund Freud!"

"You too could read thoughts, if you wanted. I wasn't born with this ability." The rabbi spoke soothingly. "I've invested many years of thought and meditation into it, and I learned kabbalah. Have you ever heard of the saying of *Chazal*: 'The thought of sin is worse than sin'? When I was a yeshivah student of your age, I didn't understand why. We accept that action comes as a result of thought; we know that action is more serious than thought; so why should the thought of a sin be worse than the sin itself?"

The rabbi approached the bookshelf. His hand slid over the spines of dozens of books of kabbalah. Gili's gaze followed him, entranced.

"The question bothered me until I learned kabbalah, in these books, and I discovered the power of one lone thought. A man sins? It is one sin. But if he thinks of sin? Woe to him, for each tiny thought creates a new reality, another sin. Hundreds of sins in a few moments of thought! More, when a person sins with his body, in reality the sin is not complete; there is always something missing in the action. But the imagined sin, that in the mind? It is complete, for the imagination can fill in all the details, in full color."

"That's true!" Gili jumped to his feet. "Rabbi Schmidt told me a similar idea. A cream cake is nothing more than a combination of flour and margarine, sweetened. But in the imagination of a youngster fasting for the first time on Yom Kippur, when his stomach is empty and grumbling, that awful margarine turns into an earthly delight, a bursting, sweet torte dripping with chocolate."

"Absolutely. The cake is just a parable," Rav Avram agreed. "You're a diligent pupil. If you want to I can teach you how to grab life and play it with the proper notes. You'll have a seminar with me on a subject unknown to the world: absolute pain control!

"But be patient. You don't learn how to create a man in one day. I assure you, when you leave me, you'll be an absolutely new person. I'll build you from scratch, from top to bottom. You'll have control over yourself, as a pilot has control over his ultramodern jet. You'll never be depressed or angry; nothing will disturb you. Have you heard of the Chazon Ish? He was the most tranquil person in the world; not even the philosopher Diogenes could compare with him. You can live in serenity, just as the Chazon Ish did: Enjoy every moment of life, be in eternal paradise!"

Gili's defeat hurt. He felt the pain of the rabbi's total victory: Yet, it was a pain infinitely sweet. He was conscious of his complete rout. He'd come to win and was leaving, won over. He had been vanquished by the strong hands of the rabbi and, most shocking of all, he loved it!

Am I a masochist? he asked himself. *No, I don't enjoy being bested. But today I have discovered absolute truth.* This was a thrilling adventure, the likes of which he'd never encountered in his life.

When Gili left the rabbi's house at dusk he understood that his friend Benny, too, had undergone a spiritual metamorphosis similar to this. He knew that Benny had been right: He, Gili, would also go through fire and water for Rav Avram!

15

"**M**r. Journalist! Mr. Journalist!"

The Mitsubishi's motor was already running, and it was about to pull out of the parking lot, when Gili heard the shout over the noise of the engine.

Choni, the rabbi's adopted son, raced towards him with Olympic swiftness and approached the half-opened window.

"Are you leaving?" he asked eagerly.

"Yes. Why?"

"You were just with the rabbi, right?"

This one's just as curious as Paysi, Gili thought. "What's it your business?" he said harshly.

The young man was taken aback. "Just asking. I saw you leave the rabbi's room. You know? He doesn't speak so long with anybody. I'm Choni, the rabbi's son. Can I join you?"

Gili blinked and suddenly Choni was in the car, settling comfortably down in the front seat next to the driver.

"You can drive. I won't bother you."

Gili shut the motor and gave Choni a frigid look. "What's this all about?"

"Why are you so upset? I have to be in Tel Aviv. Don't you take hitch-hikers?"

Gili longed to ask this uninvited guest why he wasn't in yeshivah now, but then he remembered what Benny Gabison had told him. If the kid had been kicked out of four yeshivos, undoubtedly he wasn't enrolled in a fifth one.

He started the engine again. "I only take well-behaved hitchhikers."

He turned his head to make certain he didn't bump any of the other cars in the lot. It was then that, in the day's waning light, he noticed Paysi standing near the building, amidst the blooming orchids, giving them a look laden with sorrow. Gili ignored him; Paysi soon vanished.

"Where did you want to go with me?" Gili asked Choni.

The youngster rifled through his pocket and pulled out a packet of cigarettes. He offered one to Gili.

"No, thanks." Gili declined the offer. "Your father, the rabbi, lets you smoke?"

"He's not my father, and he can't tell me what to do," Choni snarled. His words were poisonous with anger and bitterness.

Choni lit his cigarette with trembling fingers. He inhaled deeply and tried unsuccessfully to blow out a smoke ring. "Look," Choni added, obviously frightened by his own words, "it's true he's adopted me, but he can't tell me what I can do and what I can't."

"How did you meet him?" Gili again tried to get hold of the conversation.

"It's a long and boring story. I'm sure you don't want to hear it. Why should you be interested in an animal like me?"

The car moved forward. At one of the intersections they got caught in a massive traffic jam: A truck full of chickens had dropped its squawking load onto the highway. Hundreds of them clucked on the road, as furious drivers tried to gather them into their crates.

The sun had already set. By the light of the waning day they were two shadowy figures within the automobile.

"You know something? Animals interest me," Gili said offhandedly.

"Monsters too?"

"Monsters are my specialty."

Choni scrutinized his face. Gili's expression was carefully innocent.

Choni began to speak.

Gili soon realized that Choni needed just one thing: attention. And Gili was willing to give him what he needed, in large quantities.

Gili didn't rush to the newsroom even when the traffic jam finally cleared up. He parked the car on the corner of a quiet street. Choni continued to speak.

❦

When Yochanan was born, his parents, Shaul and Penina Vardi, felt the stirrings of true joy in their luxurious, attractive home in a central Jerusalem neighborhood. A boy, after five girls! Drunk with happiness, the parents were certain they would do anything for their son. For a time Penina Vardi neglected her job as the manager of an exclusive wig salon to take care of her Choni. She left the wig business in the hands of her skilled employees, keeping an eye from a distance with the help of her telephone. Even her husband, Shaul Vardi, a well-known businessman in the *chareidi* world who frequently complained, "I have no time to breathe," and whose constant byword was, "I need 30 hours in the day," abandoned his business dealings almost entirely, curtailed his trips abroad, and spent that first year in the house with his sweet little son.

The baby's sisters were incredibly jealous of the child, each showing her resentment in a different manner. It began with little Dini, 3 years old, who physically lashed out at the infant with every opportunity, and ended with the eldest, Daniella, who turned silent and introverted.

It wasn't the toys, beautiful clothing and other goodies heaped upon the baby which roused the envy of his sisters. They were jealous of what lay behind the endless gifts: their parents' obvious preference for him. Their parents had been business people first and foremost; the children grew up as best they could, given into the hands of top-quality babysitters and nannies. They were flowers nurtured with only droplets of parental love. They couldn't bear to see the endless attention heaped upon little Choni.

But their jealousy did not last long.

After they'd drunk deeply of their cup of delight in their new son, the pair returned to business. Shaul busily jumped from this important meeting to that urgent conference. Penina returned to her exclusive salon, leaving the house at ten in the morning and returning home late at night.

One-year-old Choni suddenly tasted the bitterness of being bereft of a parents' love. The most dedicated babysitter couldn't give him the authentic feelings to which he had grown accustomed. Suddenly he didn't see his father except for some stolen minutes here and there. His mother tried to fill the gap, but when she heard the impatient honking of the waiting cabbie she was off, leaving him desolate.

"Iba, Iba," the desperate child cried as he stood by the door after Penina had left the house.

"Say 'Ima,'" his sister Dini corrected him.

"Iba, Iba," Choni continued. No error, this, but an example of a child's instinct: In one fell swoop he had lost both Abba and Ima!

Shaul would return home for short intervals, but even then he would always be on the phone. The house boasted three telephone lines, all of them constantly busy: The hard-working man of business could speak to three people at once. At the same time no one could match Penina's golden hands, and all of the women clamored for her personal expertise. The money rolled in but the parent's emotional ties stretched thinner and thinner. The girls were well trained, and learned to bask in the rare word of affection or a random gesture of fondness gleaned from their busy parents. But Choni was too young. The spoiled one, the favorite, now battled for every crumb of attention.

The youngsters in kindergarten drew a small house, flowers, a large, laughing sun glowing down on it. Little Choni drew a home bathed in the darkness of night, with flowers drooping in the blackness. "I have no sun," he explained seriously to the worried teacher. This was more than just a warning sign: This was a full-fledged red alert, a scream reaching the heavens. But the ones who should have awakened did not awaken; the fragile flower continued to yearn for a little water, a few rays of sunshine to brighten its world. He waited and waited for love, for attention, that was not there to be had.

Choni remained faithful to his mother, waiting for her every day near the doorway. Perhaps today she would surprise him and come to eat lunch with him. But Penina returned home late at night, when Choni was already asleep. She snatched a kiss for her little angel and collapsed, exhausted, on her bed.

And Choni continued to draw withered flowers even as he, too, withered. But only his melancholy eyes revealed what his mouth could not express.

When the first signs of violence were spotted, a child psychologist warned Penina, "A babysitter is not a mother. You must spend more time with him."

Penina sighed and took a week off from work. She kept Choni home from kindergarten and stayed with him from morning until night, walking through parks and joining him on the play equipment to the sound of his laughter. Choni was the happiest child in the universe.

It lasted exactly a week.

When Penina returned to her work after the short vacation she vowed to do it again from time to time. But that was the same week she received the surprising invitation from a top wig manufacturer in New York to come, all expenses paid, to their offices and learn new design techniques, in preparation for her appointment as their head distributor and manager of their company's Israeli branch. That very week, she boarded the plane for New York.

Choni took it hard. Little by little he turned into an incredibly demanding, self-centered child. Eventually, his rage erupted. His environment took its revenge, pushing him farther and farther away; the lad found himself on an endless cycle of animosity and rejection. The more his friends rebuffed him, the more of an egoist he became, and the greater his penchant for resentment and bitterness. In elementary school the situation was just barely endurable, and as an adolescent the bitterness finally ripened into a full-blown disease. Choni was angry at the whole world without knowing the reason why, and no one could tolerate him.

In his first yeshivah he so embittered everyone's lives that the other students finally issued an ultimatum to the principal: "It's either him or us."

When he was expelled, Choni returned home with his head bowed. He lay on his bed, covered his head with a pillow, and wept and wept, until he fainted. He felt destroyed by the humiliation; his anger and resentment thudded within him until his heart felt it would burst. Dini found him on the bed, unconscious, almost suffocated beneath his pillow, his breathing weak and labored. Somehow she managed to get her panic under control and call an ambulance.

Thus Shaul and Penina Vardi, together in Los Angeles, found out that their son had been expelled from school and had attempted suicide. Shaul satisfied himself with a call to his brother, Rabbi Yaakov Vardi, *rosh yeshivah* of "Kavod HaTorah." Rabbi Yaakov capitulated to the pressure exerted over the international cables from Los Angeles, making the worst mistake of his life when he agreed to mix family bonds with his personal business. He expressed his willingness to accept Choni into his yeshivah. The boy, overcome with emotion, was released from the hospital and, white faced, made a solemn vow to his uncle: "From today and onwards I'm going to change. I learned my lesson; I'll take hold of myself," he said with absolute sincerity.

Choni tried, but the deprivations of his youth were too much for him. His violent outbursts overcame him before he could even think about them. Rabbi Yaakov was forced to dismiss his nephew before he destroyed the delicate social balance of the yeshivah that had been built up with such great effort. Too late the devoted uncle realized that his good nature had destroyed his relationship with his family. His brother Shaul never forgave him the slight; this anger remained even after the father himself had cast away his son.

"I was expelled again. I thought I'd get used to it," Choni said dryly. "But I was wrong. It hurt even more the second time."

The stigma of violence clung to Choni like some foul disease. But his uncle, Rabbi Yaakov, beset by feelings of guilt, didn't abandon him. Using all of his connections he managed to get the youth accepted into a more appropriate school, a Jerusalem yeshivah for "special" cases, where the boys learned for half a day and expended their considerable energies doing manual labor in the afternoons. But the brawls did not stop, not even there.

"Today I realize that I was just an obnoxious person, looking for excuses to fight. If I was not worthy of my parents' love, I would make myself hated by all the other students. That *rosh yeshivah* brought Rabbi Avram into the picture and he tried to rehabilitate me by putting me into a high school, hoping that a change of scenery would prove settling to me."

In his new school Choni's situation deteriorated even more; he would spend the day wandering between the dining room and the dormitory, burning with a boundless hatred. He hated them all, whatever their head-covering, be it a black yarmulka or knitted *kippah*. And, like a boomerang, the hatred returned to him, until finally the other students forced the administration to expel him.

"And that's it," Choni ended his melancholy story in simple language. "Today, I'm Zabik the *gabbai's* assistant."

Gili had drawn his own conclusions. It was clear that Choni's emotional outlook was completely distorted. He hated heaven and earth and directed all his feelings of love inward, towards himself. Gili also understood why the boy was so egocentric: From the age of 1 he had grown up without parental love, and one who does not receive, cannot know how to give!

"You work with Zabik all night?"

"Yes. I bring him the lists of the visitors, sometimes take care of registration, when Zabik isn't there, and buy him the cassettes."

"Music cassettes?"

"Music? You're making me laugh. No, blank cassettes. Not recorded tapes. What did you ask? Music? Yes, yes, we love music, that is, chassidic music, Werdyger, Fried. They're great, right? I was at an Avrohom Fried concert not long ago. Listen, he's great."

The young man was completely tangled up in his own words. He began to stutter and then blushed. Gili took pity on him, and threw him a life preserver. "Where are you heading?"

"Wherever you're going. I'd like to see the inside of a newsroom. Would they let me in?"

If you've got nothing to do, don't do it with me. With difficulty, Gili swallowed his words.

Benny and Gili took him through the large building. Choni was fascinated by everything he saw. The staffers explained the different equipment to him.

"This is an optical scanner. You see, I put the picture on the glass surface and close the cover on it. Now watch the computer screen. See how nicely the computer rebuilds the picture..."

"And this state-of-the-art machine scans pictures for our color magazine. The pictures are processed in PhotoShop, a computer program that develops photos."

"This is the computer room. Their fax-modems are all in use now. Watch the numbers on the screen: They indicate how many files have been read by the modem. The reporter can sit in his house, or even in the desert or jungle, and send his copy over a telephone line, using his laptop computer. All he needs is a modem and a telephone line, even a cellular phone will do. Miraculous, no?"

"These are the fastest laser printers available. In another minute they'll print out the write-ups we've received on the modem."

"I'm Gideon, the rewrite man. There are many reporters whose writing skills are deficient. They write horribly, to be more accurate. I rewrite their stories, put in a little 'spice,' so that even the author doesn't recognize it when it's published!"

"This is the darkroom. Here they photograph the pages that are ready for film, and prepare them to be made into plates."

And on and on...

They reached one of the most interesting areas of the building, the office of Eric Meisels, assistant editor. They found him writing hastily in a notebook. "Hello, young man. Hello, everybody. Gili, I have a new project for you. Starting next week I want you to visit all the chassidic courts and the various yeshivot in Israel. Every week you'll write an article synopsizing one court and one yeshivah. You'll start this week with Jerusalem, with the Kiltzer *chassidim* and Yeshivah Torah Lishmah."

"It's about time," Gili said, his face beaming. "I've been waiting for this for three months."

"Good. You'll begin the series next week. Now excuse me, I'm busy."

He continued his feverish scribbling, paying no attention to his visitors. The three took the hint and quickly left the room.

After a three-our tour Benny and Gili were completely wiped out, though Choni seemed prepared to go on forever. His face fell when Benny reminded him that Rav Avram's "office hours" were about to begin, and that Choni was needed at Zabik's side.

Gili was still curious about these two boys that Rav Avram had adopted. What was the reason for that melancholy look that Paysi had worn when Gili had driven off with Choni? Why had Choni begun to stutter after he'd let something slip? What was so important about buying blank tapes?

He would learn sign language, and get Paysi to tell him.

Gili sat in front of his computer, gazing unseeingly at the screen. He'd been given a tough assignment and he wasn't certain just how to approach it. He'd learned a little about the world of yeshivos as a result of his stint in a *baal teshuvah* yeshivah, but the world of chassidic courts was a complete mystery. Gili decided to view it as a new, exciting challenge. After a few fruitless minutes spent staring at the blank screen, he turned off the computer and set to work organizing his thoughts on pen and paper — the tools that had never let him down. He sat, doodling, still trying to muster his thoughts. Suddenly it became clear to him: He was a complete ignoramus when it came to the world of *chassidus*! Yes, he knew that there were rebbes, and he knew that the rebbes had *chassidim*, but that was the total extent of his knowledge! He knew nothing!

"I've got to find an expert in *chassidus*," he whispered to himself. Perhaps Benny knew someone, but he wasn't in the office. An hour had passed since Gili had brought Choni back to Rav Avram's house, an hour of useless daydreaming. He suddenly felt a deep despair. He began to wonder at the wisdom of transferring from an investigative journalist, a position at which he excelled, to a reporter on religious affairs. Did the fact that he, himself, had become religious justify the decision?

The telephone rang.

In other days, Gili and Benny had constantly argued over who would answer the phone. Both were busy and each pushed the responsibility on the other. Even the simple buzzing of the intercom could set off a major battle between the two reporters, who resented every interruption. All who phoned them, without exception, complained that no one answered the phone until it had rung at least 10 times.

Gili grinned. This incredible boredom was doing something to him; he picked up the phone on the second ring.

"This is Zabik, Rav Avram's *gabbai*. Please wait a minute, the rabbi wants to speak with you."

Gili waited impatiently. The music on the line suddenly stopped; the rabbi's voice came on.

"Hello, Gili. A few minutes ago I started to think about you. It was sudden, and for no apparent reason. That's astonishing, because normally I control my thoughts, and they do not control me. I decided that if that happened, you must need my help."

"Need help? Me?" Gili laughed. "Nothing's happened to me."

"You're keeping something from me. I'll call you in about 10 minutes. In the meantime, try to jog your memory."

He hung up the phone.

It was barely six hours since Gili had left the rabbi's house; six brief but adventure-filled hours. He had unearthed some corners of the *HaYom HaZeh* building that he had never known existed. But what had profoundly moved him was his conversation with Choni, that wounded soul who was suffering so much. If he didn't get help, Choni might try his nonsense again, perhaps for the last time.

But the top story of the day, of many days, was reserved for Rav Avram Roosenthal. Gili tingled with pleasure as he recalled the powerful conversation he'd had with the rabbi, the strange things he'd heard from him. Gili felt a deep admiration for him, the kind that, no doubt, a devoted *chassid* felt for his rebbe.

One minute. One minute. Rebbe...*chassidim*...

Fool! Idiot! Rav Avram had felt from afar how you've spent the past hour biting your nails in desperation because you didn't know what to write. And who could help you better than Rav Avram himself, whose speciality was being a "rebbe" to his "chassidim"!

He looked at his watch. Five minutes had passed. Another five, and the rabbi would call again. He sat impatiently by the telephone, awaiting its ring as he would the messiah.

His fax machine rang and spit out a single page that contained a few words. He went to see what it was.

"Gili. This is your second notice, in case you haven't understood the first. Your life is in danger. Stop contact with the negative elements you've connected with lately. Danger!"

16

There was no signature or identifying mark. On top of the page, though, was the phone number of the fax machine from which it had been sent. It began with the area code 04, the code for Haifa and its environs.

The earlier note had also been sent from Haifa. Was it the same person?

"So what's the explanation?" Rabbi Schmidt used to ask in yeshivah. How Gili longed to return to his beloved *shtender,* to the warm, embracing arms of the Gemara. He felt pressure being put on him from several different sources. Someone wanted something here; there must be a logical explanation for what was happening.

A quarter of an hour had already passed. Rav Avram hadn't phoned him. Gili had never imagined that he would sit in nail-biting tension waiting for the ringing of the telephone, that much-detested instrument.

Twenty minutes, 25, half an hour. What had happened?

After 45 minutes had passed, he prepared to leave his office. If Rav Avram was testing his nerves, he would show him.

The phone rang. Zabik spoke. "Gili, the rabbi wants to speak with you."

After a few seconds Rav Avram came on the line. "Gili, are you angry with me?"

His voice softened Gili's anger. "Uhh...." He was at a loss.

"Of course you're angry. I said 10 minutes and they turned into 50. There was an urgent case here. You shouldn't know of such troubles: A 28-year-old man was about to get engaged when suddenly, at the last minute, the girl's family changed their minds and broke it off. The cakes were already on the table. You can understand my sorrow; such suffering here. But let's get back to business. Have you thought about what we spoke of before?"

Gili was, first and foremost, an incurable busybody. "Would you allow me to ask how the man was when he left you?"

"Feeling better."

"How do you do it? When someone comes to you, completely broken, what do you say to such a person, how do you change him?"

"I've told you, if you want to learn, I'm prepared to teach you. I'm actually looking for a student such as you."

"Before that, there's something else that's disturbing me. I've received two threats to my life."

"Threats?" Gili could hear the rabbi treading lightly here. "Who is threatening you?"

Gili told him of the letter and the fax. Rav Avram didn't seem to take it too seriously. "It's probably some harmless fool. I can guess who it is."

"Who?"

"One of our neighbors who hates us because of the noise we make at night. He follows our visitors and the minute he finds one who is known, a celebrity like you for example, he threatens him."

Another secret revealed: The problem of neighbors hadn't been solved. The neighbors were angry; some, very angry indeed. One of them was even willing to threaten other's lives. "What have you done to him?"

"My assistant, Zabik, was a bit hasty, and without my knowledge sent all the complaining neighbors a little gift in my name. Since then they've kept quiet."

"What did he send?"

Rav Avram almost choked on his laughter. "The book *The End of Life,* with commentaries and annotations. The most unpleasant neighbor also received an extra present: two personally inscribed *yahrzeit* candles. I found out afterwards, and everything I've done to calm him down hasn't worked. He's furious!"

There was a silence on the line. Gili didn't react. After a few moments, he said, "I don't think it's one of the neighbors. The letter and fax came from Haifa."

"So that's a problem? I've got a brother in Haifa. Is it hard to arrange for him to send a letter or fax for me? There's nothing to worry about. And now back to reality: How can I help you?"

Gili told him of his new assignment and of the difficulties that he was suddenly facing, as he began to write his masterpiece on the *chassidus* of Kiltz and realized that he was treading on uncharted ground.

"Nu, that's why I called you. I felt that you were in trouble. Your topic is a fascinating one. In the next few minutes I'll give you a framework that you can use for all the chassidic courts in Israel. Take a pen and paper and write."

Gili pressed the speakerphone. Rav Avram dictated, and Gili wrote it all down.

"Title: Chassidic dynasty. Subtitle: the rebbe and his assistants. Chapter heading: A. The court's structure. B. Political strength. C. Family members. D. Possible heirs. E. Alliances and enmities in the court. F. Intriguing stories. G. Behind the scenes. H. Who makes the rules in the court. I. Exact number of *chassidim*. J. Interrelationship between *chassidim* and the rebbe. K. Weak links. L. The ideology and spiritual principles of the court.

"You're beginning next week with a fairly small group, Kiltz. I know them intimately. I'm interested in how you'll do the write-up. Go to them, write what you want, and come to me before you bring the material to Eric Meisels."

"Excellent." Gili was pleased; Rav Avram had eased his path.

"Before we finish up, one more point. When you're here, I'll give you an outline for writing up the world of the yeshivos. I have first-hand knowledge of most yeshivos."

"Even better." Gili was floating in the clouds. What great fortune he'd had, meeting up with Rav Avram, the man who would open all doors before him. The outline was complete, and Gili was on his way!

The following day, before noon, Gili prepared to leave the newsroom on his way to Jerusalem to begin gathering facts for his first story in the series, with the chassidic court of Kiltz and the Lithuanian yeshivah Torah Lishmah as his initial subjects.

His beeper gave a shrill call. "The rabbi asks that you call him. Urgent."

"The rabbi." Was there another besides Rav Avram?

He immediately dialed Zabik's phone number, and was surprised to hear Rav Avram's pleasant tones on the line. "Gili, you're on your way to Jerusalem? Pass my way, please. Choni wants to go with you. He's dying of boredom. Do me a favor."

Gili had always loathed tag-alongs. The thought of Choni chattering beside him made his temper rise. "Forgive me, Rabbi, but I like peace and quiet. It's hard for me to concentrate when someone is with me."

"Choni won't bother you. I guarantee it. This is your chance to combine kindness with work. Think about it from the Jewish perspective."

This was the time for Gili to gently tell the nuisance to find himself another sacrifice. But Rav Avram was not a nuisance — he was a man of great power who'd opened his eyes a little, and who in the future would reveal many secrets to him.

"But what will Choni do with me? He'll be completely bored."

"Just the opposite. He loves this kind of thing. Gili, you should know that Choni has a good head and a youthful perspective on matters. He can help you."

Gili reached Rav Avram's house half an hour later. In the dingy stairwell he passed an elderly man holding several heavy baskets. The man gave Gili a dark and knowing glance. Gili longed to ask him, "What did I ever do to you?" but then remembered what the rabbi had said about his angry neighbor. *Look into his eyes, Gili; he may be the man who sent you those threats.*

The house was empty of visitors. All of the rabbi's *gabbaim* were there: Zabik, Muli, and two other young men whom Gili hadn't met before. In answer to his question Zabik explained that Rav Avram was reeling under the heavy burden and simply couldn't meet everyone who wished to speak to him; thus, from time to time he broadened his circle of helpers.

"Burden?" Gili raised an eyebrow.

"No, not a burden, a flood," Zabik corrected himself proudly. "In the past weeks the number of visitors has grown from night to night. The Rabbi has already extended his visiting hours, from ten at night to five in the morning, and even those aren't enough. We're falling apart."

"Why don't you make one of the rooms into a reception area?" Gili asked. "Why does everyone have to sit outside near the stairs?"

Zabik sent him an angry look and hissed something from behind clenched teeth. To Gili it sounded as if he'd said, "Let them pay!"

The question of money had finally reared its head. Gili looked around at the rabbi's residence. He was forced to admit that it was humble, at best; miserably poor, at worst. The cracked and peeling paint lent a cheerless air. The kitchen was in the style of the late 1970s; the color scheme was a dull, depressing maroon. The beds used by his cadre of assistants were old and simple, with shabby mattresses that sagged down to the floor.

In sharp contrast to those miracle workers who amassed treasures from the naivete of others, Rabbi Roosenthal didn't take a penny, Benny and Choni had told him. He devoted himself to the Jewish people solely for the sake of Heaven. How, then, did he manage; who paid the four assistants; where did he get the money to support his two adopted sons, Gili wondered. He would have to clarify the situation soon. Perhaps Rabbi Avram needed financial assistance and was ashamed to ask for it?

Gili looked for Choni, but the young man was not to be found in any of the rooms. Had the rabbi brought him here for nothing? Perhaps Choni was resting. He opened one of the bedroom doors in search of Choni, and then heard voices coming from the next room:

"Rav Avraham, I can't take any more. The burden on my shoulders is enormous.

"It's my son. He is a manic-depressive. Few people know about it, since we were living in Europe at the time. My son is already older, he's

27, and his condition is stable. He learns in a well-known Bnei Brak yeshivah, and not a soul there knows of his past. Now an excellent girl has been suggested for him. Can I allow him to marry without worrying about the possibility of another eruption of the symptoms? Or is this a terrible injustice to do to the girl?" The man's voice broke.

"If your son comes to me, I'll have an answer for you," Rav Avram declared. "I can detect whether there are indications of recurring manic-depressive episodes. If the boy is, indeed, liable to episodes, one may not do such a thing to the girl. On the other hand, I can cure him. There's something to talk about: Send him to me."

Gili tiptoed out of the room. The next room over was not the rabbi's study. What was going on here? He stealthily walked towards the room where the conference was going on. The door was shut. He put his ear to it.

"I thank you so much, Rav Roosenthal."

"Call me Avram. I'm a simple man."

"You're a great *tzaddik*."

"Goodbye and all the best."

There was the sound of heavy footsteps in the room. In a panic, Gili raced backwards but, to his astonishment, the door didn't open. Gili approached once again. He could hear a strange sound, like that of someone watching a video in fast-forward. Then another conversation began:

"What, exactly, are you afraid of?" It was Rav Avram's voice.

"The dark. Death. Since I was at the cemetery for my grandfather's funeral," a young boy answered.

"When was that?"

"A year ago. The funeral took place at two in the morning. From then on, every night, whenever I get into bed, the nightmares begin."

"Can you tell me exactly what happens?"

"It's hard. I'm afraid enough as it is."

"You mustn't push away the fear. When you hide fear in your heart, even the smallest fear, it becomes a gigantic demon that can eat you up. Take the fear out." There was a long silence, and he began again. "Is it hard for you? I understand. Do you want me to tell you what happens to you? Okay. You get into bed and go under the blanket. You immediately remember that your grandfather lay in the same way. The sheet that covered him didn't conceal the lines of his body; since then, you've been terrified. You saw that and you panicked, your beloved grandfather suddenly turned into a body, silent and strange. You wanted to be strong and you peeked in when they prepared the body, right?"

"That's...that's right," the boy stuttered.

"And then you went to the cemetery. Who asked you to, were you one of the gravediggers? There you felt death approaching you, for you, too, would one day die. One feels death close by in cemeteries, particularly in the darkness. And since then you're afraid of death, you think often of that black day when you, too, will lay, silent and cold as your grandfather, and the angels of death will begin to lash at you. You see the dead in your dreams: skeletons, skulls, black souls pursuing you..."

A thin shriek came from the room, followed by the sound of weeping. No, not weeping: it was laughter.

Gili opened the door with one swift movement.

Choni was lying on the bed, laughing. He was listening to a recorded conversation issuing from a sophisticated stereo system. On the bed by his side dozens of tapes lay scattered. When he saw Gili his eyes almost popped out of their sockets. His face contorted in an expression that was composed half of frozen, mocking laughter and half of sheer panic.

"What's going on?" the two of them said at the same time. But Choni's voice faded first, as the panic overwhelmed him.

"I asked you first," Gili thundered. "But you don't have to tell me. I understand it all. You had a slip of the tongue yesterday, didn't you. You buy empty cassettes, don't you? Why? I'll tell you why. So that you can tape the rabbi's confidential conversations and listen to them! You should be ashamed of yourself! How dare you invade people's privacy like this!"

Choni curled into a ball on the bed. He put his arms around his head, as if to ward off oncoming blows. He gave a loud wail and then settled down into dejected weeping.

The door opened. Framed within the doorway stood Rav Avram and his two assistants, Zabik and Muli. He motioned to the two of them and they immediately left.

Rav Avram and Gili remained, staring at each other. A thick, almost palpable feeling of oppression hung in the atmosphere; the tension was almost too great to be borne.

Rav Avram regarded Gili with a penetrating glance, looking him over slowly, as if he were seeing him for the first time. Gili felt that glance squeezing the life out of him: It was as if his soul were being pulled apart for inspection. His knees buckled; he almost fell.

"What have you done, Gili? Do you know what you've done?" The rabbi slammed one fist into the other. His voice was deep with sorrow. "You've destroyed the work of half a year in one reckless moment."

Choni jumped off the bed and raced out of the room, whimpering like a baby and wiping his nose on his sleeve.

"Do you know what's happened here?" Rav Avram demanded, when they were alone in the room.

Gili didn't manage to answer. He felt overwhelmed with guilt. Rav Avram looked at him pityingly, then took his trembling hand and led him to the bed. He remained standing.

"Never approach a boy like that with a frontal attack. You think I didn't know what the poor fool was doing? Who knows how many times he secretly taped my conversations, absolutely intimate discussions, family secrets, illness both physical and mental, other tragedies? I understood it all, just as you did, the moment I entered the room, but I didn't discuss it directly. The first rule in treatment: Take detours."

Gili still hadn't found the right words. No matter: Rav Avram didn't wait for him to speak. He continued. "Today it's the fashion to pave by-pass roads, highways that go in circles. For Choni I've paved the 'intelligence-bypass road.' I have to detour around his poor, crooked mentality to reach his soul. I've worked with him for half a year, with excellent results, until you came and destroyed it all in an instant."

Blushing with shame Gili tried to stammer some words of apology. Rav Avram had returned to his stoic calm. His eyes were frigid. "There's no reason to apologize. It's always possible to straighten that which has been twisted. I don't accept the concept of 'irreversible.' One can always turn the cycle and correct everything. Oh, the tapes will be destroyed today. Now take Choni and drive with him quickly to Jerusalem. I don't want to see him until the weekend."

The fallout from the dismal confrontation stayed with them until Gili had passed Sha'ar HaGai on the Jerusalem-Tel Aviv Highway. All of Gili's attempts to lift the heavy cloud were fruitless. Choni turned inward like a clam going into its shell, and managed to change Gili from accuser to accused. Wasn't it he who had eavesdropped behind the doorway, who had invaded Choni's privacy with a heavy hand, who had sinned again and again and again?

"Oh, keep quiet. Please. Let's hear some nice music," muttered Choni. Gili, sighing deeply, turned on his compact disc player. From the four speakers came the beautiful tones of a well-known boy's choir singing *Lev tahor bara li Elokim* in harmony, in a slow, moving tune.

They slowly nodded in time to the music, whispering the poignant words of the song: "Do not forsake me; do not take Your holy spirit from me." A salty tear fell from Gili's eyes. His father, Udi, had loved this melody and often hummed it, much to Gili's amazement.

Choni, too, was taken by the notes of the song. He suddenly opened his mouth, after about three minutes of silence.

"My uncle was here on that terrible day."

"What are you talking about?"

The car was passing by the *chareidi* community of Telz-Stone. Choni pointed wordlessly towards the ravine on the right side of the highway. "Don't you remember what happened here?"

Gili's face darkened. Two different memories flashed in his mind, side by side. "You mean bus number 405?"

"That's right. My uncle, Rabbi Yaakov Vardi, was driving behind the bus. He once told me what he saw. I have a good memory; I can tell you the story word for word. 'At the time I didn't know that a terrorist was on the bus. I couldn't understand what had happened to the driver, why the big, sturdy bus was turning towards the right, towards the ravine. I thought I was dreaming. It was impossible that a sane driver would drive down the cliff, together with all his passengers.' "

Gili blinked nervously. His hands trembled on the steering wheel; he felt himself losing control of himself. Choni continued to imitate his uncle, a self-satisfied smile on his face. "'And then, to my horror, I saw the bus jump to the right, burst over the guard rail and fall down the cliff into the trees, as if a gigantic hidden hand had pushed it with a huge fist and sent it flying."'

With a screech of his brakes Gili managed to pull over to the side of the highway. Dizziness overcame him and sparks flashed before his eyes. His head lolled weakly upon his arm, still clinging to the wheel. Another blackout, another in the endless series. And now he knew exactly what had brought it on. He saw another car speeding swiftly down the Carmel on a particularly dark night, its young driver in a drunken stupor not managing to control it as it was pulled to the left, towards the dark chasm beneath.

But why was it that whenever he remembered the accident something exploded in his mind? Colored lights danced before him, as if trying to illuminate the deep, endless darkness.

Choni awoke from his trance and looked at him in obvious astonishment. "Why did you stop? Boy, you're white as a sheet."

"It's okay," Gili managed to whisper weakly. "Just give me a minute or two and I'll continue."

"Can you drive?" Choni asked anxiously. "People who look the way you do are usually taken to hospital morgues."

"Do I look so terrible?" Gili made the effort of a smile.

"A corpse looks more lively." Choni, too, gave a grin.

"Thanks for the encouragement." Gili gave Choni a slap on the back. "Could a corpse do that to you?"

Choni began to laugh. "You're just showing off. And I thought we would both be finished here on the road."

They heard the sound of honking horns. A few cars had stopped, their concerned drivers sticking their heads out of the window. "Do you need help?"

"Thanks, we're managing," Choni answered.

A Safari van stopped near them. "You don't look too great," the driver yelled.

Gili stuck his head out. "Thanks everyone, but the show is over." He sent the car surging forward, leaving the others behind, until he reached Jerusalem's usual traffic jam near the Sakharov Gardens interchange.

Compared to the difficult scene at Rav Avram's house, the encounter with the *chassidus* of Kiltz, and the rebbe who stood at its helm, was a breeze.

The modest dwelling of the chassidic court of Kiltz stood in the Nachalat Bayit neighborhood of Israel's capital city. It was an unfinished building, whose greyish concrete walls still awaited their facade of Jerusalem stone. The building including a medium-sized *beis midrash*, a yeshivah high school, a guesthouse, and a *mikveh* in the basement.

Rabbi Yehoshua Schneidman, the group's diligent and active administrator, received them enthusiastically in his office. He was a decisive person in his 50s, whose eyes radiated vitality and life. His round eyeglasses gave him an academic look, and his long silver-streaked beard lent him an air of dignity.

Gili voiced a desire to meet with the rebbe himself, Rabbi Mendel Shiffman.

"The rebbe can't receive you now," his administrator explained. "He's preparing for prayers."

"What prayers?" Gili asked, surprised. After all, it was two in the afternoon.

"*Shacharis,* of course."

Now it was the reporter's turn to meet up with the chassidic world, with its own unique perspective. Rabbi Shiffman was one of those who *davened* late because he spent hours in preparation, immersing himself in the *mikveh,* learning Torah, and preparing himself for an audience with his Maker. Rabbi Schneidman explained that the rebbe toiled mightily to prepare and purify his body and soul together in preparation for his eternal encounter with his Creator.

"I'd like to see him pray," Gili said fervently. The prayers of one after such preparations surely differed from those of ordinary people.

Choni walked around impatiently, his hands jammed into his pockets. "Enough. What's there to see, anyway? I'm interested in the building. May I look around?"

"Certainly," the administrator said graciously. "Would you like a guided tour?"

Choni sulkily refused the offer. "I'll be okay on my own," he said. Gili sighed.

"Your brother?" the administrator asked sympathetically.

"No. You needn't worry. He's a good boy, but the stars seem to have been against him from the moment he was born. Ill fortune seems to dog him at every step, and he can't seem to succeed anywhere. My rebbe, Rav Avram Roosenthal, sent him with me, hoping I'd help ease his boredom, but it seems that he's not happy. Excuse me a moment."

He raced out of the office. In the next few minutes he searched through all three floors of the building. No sign of Choni.

Gili returned to the office breathing heavily, apologizing for the interview that had ended before it had even begun.

"It's all right," Rabbi Schneidman smiled pleasantly. "I'm always busy, so the time wasn't wasted. So now, how can I help you?"

Gili eyed the outline Rav Avram had given him. Reflecting, he pulled his eyes away from the page. With what question should he begin?

As he sat, his eyes fell on the window behind Rabbi Schneidman's back. Through it, he could see the street in front of the building. On the sidewalk across stood a public telephone. A young man in a blue short-sleeved shirt was speaking into the phone, his lips almost touching the receiver, as if he were afraid that his words might fly away into the air, into the ears of those who should not overhear them.

The boy was Choni...

17

ili turned away from the window and began a lively discussion with Rabbi Schneidman. The chassidic court of Kiltz consisted of only 300 families, he learned, but the rebbe's admirers numbered many times that amount; the rebbe's personality and piety drew throngs to him. Despite devoting most of the hours of the day to intense Torah study, lengthy prayers, and countless immersions in the *mikveh,* the rebbe was completely aware of the day-to-day happenings about him: The world outside was as familiar to him as the streets of his own Nachalat Bayit neighborhood.

The door opened with a bang. "Good news: I'm back," Choni announced, wiping the sweat off his brow. "Do you have any cold drinks here? You can die from the heat."

"We've been waiting for you," Gili said. The thread of irony in his voice was too subtle for the boy to catch and he continued to speak. "Go on, I'm not here. Ignore me."

"I don't understand," Rabbi Schneidman said, surprised. "If you've been through the building, how did you manage to miss the soda machine on the second floor?"

Choni rushed outside before the two could see his burning cheeks.

After a few minutes he returned, three cold cans in his hands. "Drink, my brothers, drink and enjoy." When he had quenched his thirst he collapsed into a chair next to Gili; during the rest of the interview he didn't utter another word.

Gili would have been thrilled if everyone he interviewed would cooperate with as much enthusiasm and sympathy as Rabbi Schneidman. After an hour the journalist had most of the story planned. He had all the statistics he had asked for; Rabbi Schneidman hadn't concealed anything from him. It was only when he touched upon the sensitive question of the rebbe's health that Rabbi Schneidman moved uneasily in his chair.

"The rebbe is no longer young. He's 83 years old. But with care and Heaven's help, he will live until 120. We believe with perfect faith that we will be able to receive Mashiach with the rebbe at our head."

Gili breathed an "amen" to the fervent declaration, but somewhat to the chagrin of Rabbi Schneidman, he wouldn't drop the subject. "What do you mean, 'with care'? Who takes 'care' of the rebbe?"

Rabbi Schneidman grew evasive. Suddenly there were urgent matters that needed to be dealt with. He offered Gili a cup of marvelous Colombian coffee. Gili refused. He'd had ample experience with such diversionary tactics; he pressed on, not yielding an inch.

Rabbi Schneidman caved in quickly. All was not perfect in the court of Kiltz, and the root of the problem was the rebbe himself.

"Do you know what it's like to be the rebbe? To hear, day after day, hour after hour, the woes and troubles of the people whom you love? To hear that this one is dying of a terrible disease, that one will never bear children, a third cannot afford even one chicken for his seven hungry children for Shabbos? Can you imagine the terrible burden, as you take on each and everyone's sorrow as if it were your own?

"Our rebbe would spend hours crying after he'd said goodbye and given the last visitor a blessing. And finally, he could take it no longer."

"And..." Gili prompted. He noticed the beads of sweat forming on Rabbi Schneidman's brow. The room's temperature was comfortable; clearly, telling this tale was no easy task for the man.

"He made a bargain with his Creator."

The image rose, unbidden, in Gili's mind of stories of individuals who had sold their souls to the devil in exchange for their hearts' desire. Despite himself, he laughed. "A bargain with G-d?"

Rabbi Schneidman gave him a stern look. "You're a bright young man; bright enough to know how little you know of such things. Our rebbe, like his ancestor Rabbi Levi Yitzchak of Berditchev, enjoys a relationship with the One On High that is not like yours or mine. He couldn't bear to see such suffering and be unable to help, he told his Creator. Let Hashem give him the power to heal, the power to soothe, by granting his blessings special merit. And in return..."

"In return?"

"The rebbe vowed never to say no to a supplicant. No matter when someone would come to him, no matter how many would beseech him, he would not sleep until he had spoken to all, had blessed all."

"That's a fascinating story," Gili said, honestly impressed. "And the rebbe has, since then —"

"The rebbe will not leave his study until everyone awaiting him has had an audience. No matter how long it takes."

"And the bargain?"

"The rebbe kept his side; the Creator, too, has adhered to His."

"Meaning?"

Rabbi Schneidman paused, choosing his words carefully. "No one can have complete power over this imperfect world. There is death, there is inescapable sorrow. But the blessing of the rebbe has an effectiveness far above what one can expect in our mortal lives."

Gili's eyebrows rose in wonder. Now here was a story! A rebbe whose blessings worked every time, guaranteed.

"No wonder so many come to him," he murmured.

Rabbi Schneidman's brow furrowed in anxiety. "That's our problem exactly. Though we have not publicized our rebbe's special power, in our small world his gift is known. Many come to him and though his heart is great spiritually, it is also weakened physically. The strain is incalculable, and yet he will not refuse an audience. Despite his protests that there was no need, we had a top cardiologist examine him. He told us that the rebbe, with proper care, could live for many more productive years. But he needs rest: a two-hour nap every day, and eight hours of sleep at night."

"And did the rebbe follow the doctor's orders?"

Rabbi Schneidman gave a snort, a sound built half of scorn and half of frustration. "Listen? If we're lucky, if everything is quiet, the rebbe retires at midnight, having seen people for seven to eight hours. He's up at five, beginning his day. A nap! On Shabbos, after the *cholent*, a 15-minute doze! And when we beg him to slow down he smiles at us and tells us that he's just fulfilling his part of the bargain!"

"And the people keep coming."

"They do, indeed. Many have realized that his blessings are powerful. Some say he has *ruach hakodesh*."

"What?" The concept was new to Gili.

"He can perform miracles. He knows of things that he hasn't seen, he feels things happening in other places; he can read minds."

Now this was familiar language. "My rabbi, Rav Avram, too, can read my mind as if it were an open book."

Rabbi Schneidman wasn't impressed with the marvelous news. "Yes, so I've heard," he said with a rather sour face, his fingers drumming lightly on a shiny fish-shaped metal ashtray. "Reading other's minds in and of itself is no great feat. It is a man's *yiras shamayim*, his fear of G-d, that determines his greatness."

With a smile of thanks, Gili stood up to leave. Choni had disappeared a few minutes before Gili ended the interview. Gili found him in the *beis midrash*, his hair still wet from immersion in the *mikveh*.

"I've spoken to the rebbe," Choni whispered. "He shook my hand and blessed me." The youth pointed towards the eastern wall. A frail, bent figure wrapped in a *tallis* stood immobile near the tall *amud*.

"While the rebbe finishes his prayers, it's worthwhile to look around at our *beis midrash*," Rabbi Schneidman whispered, his pride apparent. "Notice the ornamental windows. That is an ancient Jerusalem manner of building, though this building is relatively new. The chandelier with the golden arms is a genuine antique and has been in use for at least 400 years. The rebbe inherited it from his grandfather, Rabbi Kalman Shiffman of Kiltz. It is said that it hung in the Great Synagogue of

Amsterdam, brought there by the Jews of Spain fleeing the Inquisition. Because of its symbolic significance it is insured for a vast sum."

They examined the antique chandelier, and looked with interest at the dark-red velvet *paroches*, drawn across the wooden doors of the ark, that was embroidered in gold with the names of the donor and his parents. They scrutinized the screen that enclosed the women's gallery and the two candles lit in silver candlesticks in a metal box that hung over the cantor's *amud*. But most often their gaze returned to the rebbe, still standing bent in prayer. "He's not short, but when he stands before G-d he tries to dwarf himself, to pull himself in as much as he can." Rabbi Schneidman volunteered the explanation.

Half an hour later the rebbe left the *beis midrash*. He walked towards his modest study, Rabbi Schneidman escorting him on one side, Gili on the other. At the door he motioned to them to enter.

The rebbe extended his hand. Gili's rough palm quivered helplessly within the rebbe's delicate, silk-soft grasp. The rebbe spoke a respectable Hebrew with a heavy European, Ashkenazic accent. He asked Gili his name.

"Dinar?" His face grew serious. "The prophet Daniel saw the heavenly River Dinar in his prophecy. Di Nar. In Aramaic it is two words, 'of fire.' A holy name you possess! The Midrash states that the River Dinar is created from the perspiration of fiery angels who serve before G-d's Holy Throne, and that the souls of the wicked burn within it."

Gili's cheeks blazed fiery scarlet. *If Abba would have known, he wouldn't have changed his name from Dinburg.*

The rebbe once again pressed his hand. "And what is the source of the Dinar family? Was that your grandfather's name as well?"

"No, my grandfather was Rabbi Shmuel Dinburg. My father changed his name to Dinar, and also switched from Moshe to Udi." Gili couldn't understand the sudden urge he had to reveal all to this aged rebbe.

"Ahhh, your grandfather was Reb Shmiel Dinburg?" The rebbe's face glowed. "I learned with your grandfather in the Chayei Olam *cheder*. We were in the same class. He was a special boy. *A kleine velt*, it's a small world. Your father was his only son, Moshe Dinburg. I was his *sandek* and said the blessings at his *bris*." The rebbe gently drummed on his cheek. "How your grandfather loved him. 'Moishike,' he called him. How much anguish he felt, when his only son turned from the proper path. His heart couldn't take the suffering and simply gave out. Just two days before his stroke he was with me. He wept bitterly. 'I have nothing left in this world. My Moishike, my only son, the joy of my life, has thrown his *kippah* off his head, and has become completely defiant.' I spoke to him, assured him that his son would repent one day and bring him *nachas*, true joy. But alas, my words fell on deaf ears; he would not be comforted. Now I see that I was right: Your father has repented. Look, here is his son, wearing a large *kippah*."

Gili was engulfed in turmoil, a maelstrom of emotion that exploded within his soul, searching desperately for an outlet. He cleared his throat and tried to speak, but nothing came out but bitter tears.

"I'm sorry," he finally said, hiccuping like a child, "I'm sorry to disappoint the rebbe, but my father is no longer alive. The gates of repentance are closed to him forever and who knows what judgment he was given above? I just hope that his terrible death was his atonement."

The rebbe's eyes dimmed and burning tears dropped onto his cheeks. "What? What a tragedy! I can't believe what I'm hearing. When did it happen?"

"It's already five years." Gili's shoulders heaved in a choked sob. "Five full years for me to feel incredible waves of longing, night and day. Dear Rebbe, my world was destroyed when I was 18 years old. I became an orphan, and I can't bear the pain. My heart goes out to my father. I loved him so, and I still love him. I see his smiling face before me as if he were still alive. You're the first to hear a word about this. I'm living in a cruel world, a hard world that has no place for emotions. Someone who cries is considered a weakling but you, Rebbe, you are such a good person, and I'm not embarrassed."

Rabbi Schneidman quietly left the room; Gili silently thanked him for his consideration. It seemed as if the emotional encounter had drained the venerable rebbe. With great effort he arose on swollen feet and turned towards the doorway, leaning on a silver-headed walking stick, talking quietly to himself all the while, obviously moved. "But I was his *sandek*. How could he have died unrepentant? Didn't I bless him? Didn't I say, 'Living G-d, our Portion and our Rock, may You issue the command to rescue the beloved soul within our flesh from destruction, for the sake of His covenant that He has placed in our flesh...' How did Moishike Dinburg fall into the depths of the River Dinar? And I was his *sandek*..."

Gili was left alone in the room. The rebbe's murmurings as he spoke to himself, his pained wonder, cut into Gili's flesh like white-hot knives. He checked his small tape recorder. It was working! The conversation had been taped. This was certainly a conversation that deserved to be recorded. Let Choni hear this, not the intimate secrets that he'd taped without ever asking permission!

After a few seconds he walked towards the sink in a corner of the room and rinsed his face. He hadn't cried like this since the accident; this had been a passionate weeping, an explosion of stormy emotion. Even during those terrible days after the accident he hadn't shed a tear and now he'd cried like a child. But how wonderful it had been. All the suffering and agony, the burden of his ravenous longings, all had been washed away, leaving him pure as a newborn.

18

"You've got to understand the background of the yeshivah world in order to understand its marvelous revival today. You won't be able to do justice to the write-up on our yeshivah without such background," the *rosh yeshivah* of Yeshivas Torah Lishmah, Rabbi Shemaryahu Mirinski, known to all as "Rav Shmerl," said earnestly.

"In that case I'm afraid we won't finish until tomorrow," Gili said wearily. "Don't worry, I did my homework before I left Tel Aviv."

The meeting had come about as a result of considerable persuasion by Rabbi Zimel Mirinski, the *rosh yeshivah's* brother and the principal of the yeshivah, in order to ensure that Rav Shmerl meet with the journalist. "What do I need it for?" the *rosh yeshivah* had complained. "The vast majority of journalists work in the sewers; they're a bunch of blood-sucking leeches. I don't understand the benefits of an interview. Exposure in a secular newspaper, I'm afraid, will lead to nothing but trouble."

"You're absolutely right," Zimel said, calming him. "But you should know that if we slam the door in the journalist's face, he'll slander the yeshivah. If we cooperate, there's a chance that we'll get a favorable write-up. And maybe a few philanthropists will be persuaded to think positively about us when they read it, and a bureaucrat or two will give the new building a stamp of approval."

"Nu, nu," Shmerl grumbled, loosening his tie. To give a class for an hour and a half, to decipher an incredibly difficult contradiction in *Rambam* on a hot summer's day in front of 50 young students, was no easy task. The sweat streamed down his face. "Contributions resulting from a story in a secular paper? *Ich gloib nisht*, I don't believe it. Look, I understand your point of view. The financial burden that you are bearing weighs me down too, and no one wants a new building more than I do. But remember this: Nothing good can come out of something evil. If you ask me why I'll agree to be interviewed by this garbageman, I'll tell you, only because I'm afraid of *chilul Hashem*! That is the sole reason I'm willing to meet with the reporter, so that he won't dump a libelous mountain of lies upon us. The reporter will probably be some gentile dressed like a German skinhead, with two rings in his nose and three in his ear, a gentile who doesn't know a thing about Judaism and who won't understand one word of our conversation. And there's one condition: I must see the report before it's published. Without that, there will be no interview and no story!"

That argument had taken place yesterday, before Choni and Gili had even left to Jerusalem. Now Choni and Gili were standing in Rav Shmerl's office. The window looked down upon a small plot of earth strewn with empty soda cans, deflated soccer balls, and a hardy weed or two. Nearby, a fence-rimmed building site caught the last pink rays of sunset. A sign proclaimed it to be the future home of Yeshivas Torah Lishmah. And a much-needed home it was, Gili thought, taking in the poorly lit hallways and the tiny closet that served as the *rosh yeshivah's* office in the old, creaking building.

"I know the details about the 'mother of yeshivos,' the well-known Volozhin Yeshivah, and the general history of the yeshivah world. Our readers don't want history, they want news. We delve into current events; we don't research through dusty encyclopedias. Rav Shmerl, I want to know how the yeshivah works today, in a modern world, on the brink of the 21st century," Gili explained. "As you can see, I, too, have sat upon the yeshivah benches, and I hope to soon return there. I'm not a complete ignoramus. If background is critical, give me the background of your yeshivah."

During the next few minutes Gili and Choni heard a sincere outpouring by Rav Shmerl on the personalities who had founded the yeshivah: his father, Rabbi Simcha Mirinski, and his father's friend, Rabbi Yosef Dov Warshaver. "Imagine," Rav Shmerl said emotionally, "how the two *roshei yeshivah* wore themselves out seeking donations. One summer's day they walked, in their heavy, hot shoes, one painful step, another painful step, on the city's broiling pavement. This was before they'd paved the streets of Bnei Brak. They searched for the home of a certain donor who lived in the strange, unknown neighborhood of Givatayim; it took them an hour each way, and they never did meet him! I asked my father why he didn't take a taxi. 'Impossible,' he said. 'This money belongs to the yeshivah.'

"These were the role models that we grew up with. They were extremely poor, toiling only in Torah, modest, never asking anything for themselves. They feared G-d and carefully dotted every 'i' and crossed every 't' when it came to *halachah*. They sacrificed themselves for Torah. These were the heads of yeshivos in the previous generation, those who laid the foundation for Torah in Israel in its first years. From their sacrifice emerged the incredible flourishing of Torah institutions two generations after the Holocaust. Today, we see a momentum in the world of yeshivos; with Heaven's mercy we see them thriving in an unparalleled way. Every year hundreds of new students join and more and more yeshivos are opened, for young people, for adults, even for special children. We've never known such a phenomenon."

"And what's the reason for it?" Gili asked.

Rav Shmerl laughed and pointed towards the sky, colored at that hour with wave upon wave of pastel color, delicate hues that no human hand could have painted. In a corner towards the west hung a tiny orb, radiant in powerful shades of red and orange; further, luminous clouds of deep purple drifted lazily. The center of the sky was dominated by pink; eastward, it was as if a dividing line had been sketched in between the pink and the deep blue of the darkening east.

"Crazy," Choni whispered. "Really wild."

"Don't talk like that," Gili scolded him. "Choose from these words: a beautiful sunset, lovely, stunning, thrilling. Do you see what a rich language we have, how many strong words and phrases I've just handed you? Why do you young people choose to speak so inadequately: wild, crazy, nuts. What's 'crazy?' Who will go mad from such a sunset? What's so wild about it?"

The Mirinski brothers laughed inwardly, in complete agreement with Gili. This young sympathetic reporter had surprised them from the moment he had entered, his head not shaved and sporting no earrings. He had captured their hearts immediately.

Rav Shmerl once again pointed towards the sky. "On the verse, 'Who is a rock (*tzur*) like our G-d,' the Gemara says, 'Who is an artist (*tzayar*) like our G-d.' You've seen this incredible sunset," he turned towards Choni with a smile. "Could a man of flesh and blood have painted something like it?"

Choni shook his head in a negative gesture.

"This is your answer. There, in the heavens, G-d commanded the blessing. Only He does it all. His Heavenly wisdom 50 o years ago brought upon us a Holocaust, for our sins, destroying a third of the Jewish people. That same Elevated wisdom has now decreed a wave of blessing; it has brought a flood of students to the gates of the yeshivah.

"Two generations ago, the experts were predicting the inevitable demise of Torah Jewry as the Holocaust and assimilation jointly took their terrible toll. Today, we do not face the problem of too few students; we are blessed with the challenge of too many."

"Too many?"

"Twenty years ago, this old building was just about suited to our needs. We now have students crammed into every nook and cranny, and still we must refuse many who clamor to learn here. In the winter we learn wearing our coats, with only the words of Torah to warm us; in the summer we stifle."

"And the new building?" Gili cocked his head towards the building site, now barely visible in the growing darkness.

"Ah, the new building. My brother, Reb Zimel, has put his heart and soul into the project. Fund-raising, that eternal bane of *roshei yeshivah* — he's assumed the entire burden, allowing me to stay here and teach. With G-d's help, we're waiting for final government approval on our building plans, and we'll be ready to begin construction."

As Reb Zimel took Gili around the yeshivah, he saw only too well the reason for the *rosh yeshivah's* grievances. Yet, despite the unattractive, overcrowded surroundings, the yeshivah was a dynamic, throbbing, living place.

As he watched the scores of students arguing over their *shtenders* in the *beis midrash,* his gaze fell upon a dreamy-eyed young man peering intently into a *Chumash.* Something about those clear blue eyes were familiar; he'd seen that face before. Not in a yeshivah — in a completely different setting.

It was only as he passed the Geha Junction, near Bnei Brak, that Gili remembered just who that young man was.

19

Rav Avram glanced swiftly through the prepared stories. "Top-notch work. You're a very talented journalist. Would you give me five minutes to read it carefully?"

"What a question!" Gili, flattered, would have gladly kissed the rabbi's hand. He certainly could give him five minutes of his time.

Rav Avram sat in his darkened room. Outside, a heat wave raged; inside, the shutters remained closed and the air conditioners worked diligently to keep the temperature down. Gili marveled that the ascetic rabbi would invest in a device as hedonistic as an air conditioner; heat and cold didn't seem to be elements that could disturb such a steel-tempered personality.

Paysi entered the room. When he saw Gili he made a face and rolled his eyes. Gili suspected that the boy was trying to tell him something. He handed him a piece of paper and motioned for Paysi to write.

The boy gently removed Gili's hand and pointed to the next room.

"What is it?" Gili asked.

Paysi tried hard. Trembling with the effort, he stared with beseeching eyes at Gili, as if to say, "Why don't you understand me?"

Rav Avram lifted his eyes from the sheaf of papers. "Gili, don't you understand? Paysi wants you to go to his room with him."

Gili left with the deaf boy. They reached the end of the hallway, three doors down from the rabbi's consulting room. Gili had already counted six rooms in the large apartment, and he assumed that there were still more. Had Rav Avram combined two apartments, or was this just one large one, he wondered.

Paysi's room gave the impression of being occupied by one who was determined not to waste an inch of space. Pictures and posters of *gedolim* covered the walls. On the closet and in every corner were stickers reminding him not to lose his faith, to know that there is no despair in the world, and to be aware that being constantly happy is a great mitzvah.

But the poster that most touched Gili was the one which asked three piercing questions:

Have you acted honestly in business?

Have you set aside times for Torah learning?

Have you awaited salvation?

These were the questions, Gili had heard, that a man was asked when he was taken to judgment following his demise. The simple reminder chilled him. How was it that this Paysi, this unfortunate wretchedly sick boy, could feel so close to Heaven?

He put his mouth close to Paysi's ear and said loudly, "Did you want to show me your stickers?"

Paysi shook his head in denial. Gili decided to clarify a point that had been bothering him since he'd met the boy. "How much can you hear?"

Paysi grabbed a notebook that had been flung on his bed. He skimmed through it, looking for an empty page, and scribbled, "Almost nothing. I read lips."

Gili remembered the first time that the boy had opened the door after he'd given that special knock. How had the lad heard the sound? He wrote his question down on the paper. Paysi wrote down his reply: "The blinking red light."

"What light?"

"They've made me a device that blinks when someone knocks." The line had cost him a great deal of effort. The handwriting grew less legible with every letter, and ultimately resembled the scribblings of a chicken.

Gili decided to put an end to this exhausting, strange dialogue. "Why have you called me here?"

Paysi tried to answer with motions of his fingers and hands, with shrugs of his shoulder and nods of his head, but Gili didn't understand a thing. The boy grabbed the notebook in despair and wrote crookedly, "Learn sign language, so that I can speak with you, tell you things."

Paysi favored him with his melancholy glance and pointed to the line he'd written.

Anger, despair and pity combined within Gili into a physical pain. He felt intuitively that Paysi could help him more if only he wanted to. The boy knew something. Gili stared deeply into Paysi's eyes and suddenly turned away and left the room, leaving Paysi alone, depressed and sorrowful.

When Gili had left Paysi grabbed the paper, tore it into tiny pieces, and threw it in the wastebasket.

Rav Avram had finished reading the stories. He had particularly enjoyed the report on the *chassidim* of Kiltz.

He had only two suggestions. The first was for Gili to focus more on the relations between the rebbe and his *chassidim*. "That's a vitally important detail," he explained. "I don't mean the superficial relations, such as Chatzkel the *chassid* goes to the rebbe's *simchahs*, and the rebbe goes to the wedding of Chatzkel's son, I'm talking about something much deeper."

The second suggestion fell on Gili's head like a bomb.

"Skip the story about the rebbe's 'bargain' with G-d. Don't mention a word about it."

"But why in the world should I delete it?" Gili asked, astounded. "It's got drama, poignancy, a touch of the mystical — all the elements of a hot story."

Rav Avram fingered his blond beard and sighed. "Look beyond the 'hot story,' Gili. Suppose you — like all humanity — have a problem. Suppose you read in a prestigious newspaper that a man exists who will solve that problem. What will you do?"

Gili grinned. "I'm no fool. I'd go to him."

Rav Avram did not answer his smile. "Fool or not, you would go to him. Now multiply that by a thousand — thousands of people clamoring to see the rebbe of Kiltz; desperate people grasping at their last hope. And the rebbe agreeing to see them all because of the vow taken years ago. You'll kill him, Gili — you will kill him!"

I wouldn't have dreamed of such a thing, Gili thought in wonder. But despite Rav Avram's unyielding, fine-honed logic, he was still torn between loyalty to his newspaper and to his rabbi. All his journalistic instincts were aroused. *Gili, you're a reporter first and foremost. You've got a scoop: Don't let it go.*

"My responsibility is to write the truth. Am I responsible for the consequences?"

Rav Avram picked up his head from the papers. "My friend, I have news for you. You certainly are responsible. You are going to be the very first, the herald of a change in journalism. Your words will only bring good to this world. Even more: No more *lashon hara.* Your stories will be the finest, grade A pure. You'll no doubt find shortcomings in the *chareidi* world. But you won't print them."

"My public will abandon me immediately," Gili protested. "A newspaper isn't a book of ethics."

"Slander is prohibited even in a newspaper; I've never heard of any halachic permission to libel someone in print. Gili, don't worry, your stories, your untainted stories, your responsible stories, will be the best in the newspaper *HaYom HaZeh.* Everyone will ask, 'Who is Gili Dinar, who writes so interestingly?' "

As Gili prepared to leave, he fired a parting shot, much like the last attack of a sullen little boy who knows his father is right. "I have a journalistic conscience too. I found out another little secret during my interview, one that I decided on my own was too 'hot' for print."

Rav Avram raised an bemused eyebrow. "Do you want to tell me what it is, or do you want me to guess?"

Goaded into speech, Gili burst out, "Do you know who is learning in Torah Lishmah? Ron Limor is one of their many students."

The Limor Affair, as journalists had taken to calling it, had burst on the scene two years earlier, with the breakup of the marriage of Dan and Yael Limor. Divorce was nothing new in Israeli society, but when the ex-husband was Dan Limor, one of Israel's preeminent industrialists, and the ex-wife Yael Limor, founder and leader of the country's largest left-wing political party, the marriage's end was duly noted in the newspapers.

The story moved from society columns to front-page headlines when the custody battle began. Both parents wanted 16-year-old Ron, the brilliant only child of the stormy marriage. A phalanx of Israel's top lawyers appeared for each side. Yael, always on the road on her party's behalf, was not a fit mother for an adolescent, Dan declared; a boy's place was with his mother, and not with a father who took his first-class seat on an airplane as casually as most people boarded an Egged bus, insisted Yael.

And then Ron vanished. And the furor really began.

The police were called in, and because of Limor's political connection, the General Security Service. Two days after the boy's disappearance, after tens of thousands of shekels had been expended in fruitless searches, Limor received a call on her unlisted number. It was Ron, contrite at the trouble he'd caused. He had had enough of being pulled in two different directions. He was going to make it on his own, with the 350 fifty shekels he had saved over the years. He loved his parents but could not live with them, either of them. And a judge was not going to decide his destiny.

Though the widespread searches were called off, Yael and Dan didn't give up on finding their wayward son. But despite vast sums of money expended on private detectives, and though the police had kept the file open, with the exception of monthly phone calls — too brief to be traced — assuring them of his well-being, Ron Limor had decided his own custody case.

"And I saw Ron Limor learning in a corner of the *beis midrash*. He had a scraggly little beard, but I recognized him. After all," Gili concluded dryly, "his face was plastered over every newspaper in the country for two solid weeks, until some other sensational story pushed it off the front pages."

Rav Avram's eyes glistened. "Ron Limor, a *baal teshuvah*. Not surprising, really: his parents, though misguided, are dedicated idealists. The boy's *neshamah* must have been searching for Torah."

Gili couldn't help but be proud of his discovery. "I realized right away that I couldn't print his whereabouts. The boy must be 18 by now and he has every right to live on his own, in his own way. And if his parents should find out where he was, who knows what pressures they might bring to bear on him?"

Rav Avram bestowed a wide smile on Gili. "You're a rarity, Gili: a journalist with a conscience."

The two articles appeared in the weekend edition of *HaYom HaZeh*'s magazine, and did actually garner substantial praise. For the first time a secular newspaper had captured the positive aspects of *chareidi* society.

Rabbi Zimel Mirinski was the first to call. "Congratulations! An incredible story. My brother was apprehensive, and wanted to check out the story before publication, but you were wonderful."

Rabbi Schneidman called a few minutes later. He, too, thanked Gili. "By the way, I notice that you didn't write about the antique chandelier in the *beis midrash*. You left out a nice journalistic tidbit. Why?"

"Are you looking for thieves?" Gili answered.

Rabbi Schneidman swallowed his exclamation of shock. "You're even more ethical than I had thought. Good for you!"

Gili blushed: That last omission, too, had been Rav Avram's idea.

His friends also came to pat Gili on the back. "Good work," they encouraged him. But Gili couldn't help but feel a little bitter, thinking of all he hadn't written. And according to Rav Avram, these were only the first of many scoops that would never see the light of day.

And all for the sake of peace!

In the following weeks Gili Dinar was one of the busiest reporters on *HaYom HaZeh*. A new series seemed to take over the newspaper, a series with a logo of its own: "The Jewish Viewpoint: Rebbes, dynasties, and yeshivos in modern Israel."

Every Friday the color magazine of *HaYom HaZeh* included two stories in its center fold, one on the chassidic world, one on the world of the yeshivah. The chassidic article gave a full-color look at one of the many sects in Israel, from the largest to the smallest. The yeshivah report took a weekly peek at one of Israel's many institutions. The two stories combined into an engrossing narrative that sent the newspaper's sales figures flying off the charts. Secular Israelis who had absolutely nothing to do with religion, and certainly not with *chassidus* or the self-contained world of the yeshivah, waited impatiently for Friday's magazine, for Gili Dinar's articles. Gili opened a fascinating window into the world of the *chareidim* for the secular reader. Rav Avram had been correct: The reports were finely sifted, free of any hint of slander, and yet enjoyed sustained success, perhaps because of the lack of smut: even the secular reader had grown tired of such underhanded tactics. Gili didn't lay sentimental drivel before them. He didn't resort to saccarine-sweet, old-fashioned literary tricks, and despite his loyalty to his fellow *kippot*-wearers, he didn't merely pat them on the back, in "with us everything is perfect" style.

He had a unique approach, his own personal style, that gave his stories their special flavor, and endeared him to his public. He brought the reader, even the most ignorant one, deep into the issues. A felafel vendor in Jerusalem could feel at home in the study hall whose image had been tarnished by the secular press until now. The simple housewife in Afula and the successful Tel Aviv stockbroker suddenly felt a deep connection with the "*tish*," a chassidic rebbe's table. Somehow the image of those "black" yeshivah students seemed less daunting than they had in the past.

With the help of heaven, Gili had become an artist. Not an artist utilizing oils on canvas; he used the most modern of tools, a computer, a monitor, a printer. But the high-tech equipment didn't stop him from breathing his own soul into his essays. He sketched each chassidic court in its many variations. His writing was powerful, razor-sharp, enhanced with fine human emotions. He wrote of the *chassidim* of Gur as one who had been a Gerrer *chassid* from birth, described the courts of Viznitz and Belz with all their nuances just as a dedicated Viznitzer or Belzer *chassid* would have done. His writing had atmosphere and life, color, sounds and images. Readers lifted their eyebrows and asked themselves how a man, secular from birth, could describe in such rich detail worlds that had been so foreign to him until a short time before. Gili took the courts of the *chassidim* and the study halls of the yeshivos and poured them into the pages of his newspaper, between the words and the letters on the newsprint. The stories included many photographs, but they were almost unnecessary. The picture that was drawn in the mind of the reader was vivid and colorful, the images three-dimensional, so real you could almost reach out and touch them. The report seemed to have taken on a life of its own in the dead pages of the newspaper.

The next series brought extraordinary stories about the *teshuvah* movement. Gili visited several such yeshivos, and with his own background as a student in one of them it was no wonder that his reports reached new heights. Gili brought out the human dimension of the *teshuvah* movement, finding a new angle that none had seen before. He shared with his readers the soul-searching of recent *baalei teshuvah*, brought them to the peaks of spiritual heights in the wake of the first vast discoveries of the light of Judaism, descended with them to the depths of the soul during the difficult passages as one made a 180-degree turn in one's life. The public adjusted its reading glasses and declared in astonishment, "Is that how it looks? I didn't know..."

There was something else readers didn't know: For the first time in the history of Israeli journalism a "spiritual committee" was deleting sentences and even entire paragraphs from an enlightened and unaffiliated secular newspaper.

Gili's fax machine toiled long and hard during that time. He faxed every story to Rabbi Avram Roosenthal even before he'd handed it in to Ami Kedmi, the editor-in-chief, or to his assistant, Eric Meisels. Rav Avram advised Gili as to what was permissible to publicize, what should be deleted, and what must be censored!

Within four months Gili had examined the vast majority of chassidic courts in Israel. The larger yeshivos, too, were treated to publicity from a world they'd never dreamed of.

Gili would never forget one special day. His telephone buzzed. Ami Kedmi, the editor himself, was on the line. "Gili, come here now."

Gili shuddered slightly. The man's tone sounded threatening. But what could have happened, particularly after a series that had garnered such praise?

Ami and Eric were waiting for him. Ami, impatient as usual, was holding a fax that he'd just pulled from the machine.

"Read it," he commanded, thrusting the paper into Gili's hands.

Gili was confused. "What's happened?"

"Stop asking questions! Read it!"

Gili nervously began to scan the paper. After a few seconds his eyes lit up and a huge grin split his face.

TO: Mr. Ami Kedmi

Editor-in-Chief, *HaYom HaZeh*

Dear Mr. Kedmi:

The presidium of the Journalists' Council have proposed granting their 1995 "Golden Pen Award" to reporter Gili Dinar, for his successful series, "The Jewish Viewpoint: Rebbes, dynasties, and yeshivos in modern Israel." This monumental series, "The Jewish Viewpoint," is a masterpiece of the journalist's craft and has made a significant contribution towards the unification of a divided nation. Therefore the presidium have unanimously recommended Gili Dinar as the nominee most deserving of the "Golden Pen Award," as the top journalist of the year 1995.

Sincerely,

Chaim Tzadok

President, Journalists' Council

"So what do you have to say?" exulted Ami.

Gili cleared his throat. "I don't know what to say. I'm flabbergasted."

"Do you know what this means?" Ami shouted. " 'The Golden Pen!'

That's Israel's top prize! My lad, you did it! You took first place!"

Eric Meisels was euphoric. "Imagine yourself, in *The New York Times* or the *Washington Post*, investigating chassidic dynasties all over America and garnering the Pulitzer Prize. Do you understand? The top journalist's prize in the world! You can do it!"

"Eric, don't get carried away," Ami warned him.

"No, really," Eric said excitedly. "Why shouldn't Gili go to America and bring us honor there?"

"Eric, that's not to be discussed. We need Gili here."

A heavy silence descended. Gili felt the tension between the two. For some time a covert struggle had been going on between Ami, the editor, who lacked writing talent but was the trusted representative of the wealthy shareholders and owners of the paper, and Eric Meisels, assistant editor, a journalist in every bone of his body who felt a strong bond with all other reporters.

Gili preferred to be out of the office during these difficult moments. He longed to tiptoe out of there, but Eric cut him off. "Come on, Gili, let's show the fax around and have everybody celebrate."

"You're such an innocent," Ami said in mocking tones. "They'll celebrate? Here, in the city of Sodom? What you mean to say is: They'll burst from jealousy!"

"There are good people in Sodom too," Eric said firmly. "Come with me and I'll show you how the gang is happy for him."

Ami didn't bother with a reply. He sat heavily down in his executive armchair, picked up the receiver and began to dial.

As they walked down the long corridor Gili asked,"Do you really want me to go to America? Or were you only trying to provoke Ami?"

"What do you think I am? Gili, don't be so suspicious. I think if you were working for *The New York Times* you'd get the Pulitzer, no doubt about it."

"Are you trying to kick me up, or out?"

"Neither. I'm just trying to teach you something, but you don't want to hear," Eric sighed, all trace of his former exultation gone.

"Tell me again. Clearly."

Eric glanced over his shoulder, then turned around to make certain that no one was listening to their conversation. He hesitated for a moment. Finally, he said, "I can't speak; they'll kill me."

"Eric, are you trying to give me a nervous breakdown?"

Another sigh. Instead of entering the newsroom, fax in hand, the two paced up and down the corridor. After a prolonged inner struggle, Eric said a short sentence. "Gili, open your eyes. You've become a pawn in a chess game."

Gili worked through the facts hastily. Eric was trying to tell him something. But what in Heaven's name could it be?

"Whose side am I on? The white, or the black?" he whispered.

Eric once again looked right and left. "In this game the black is dressed as white, the white is dressed as black. But I think they're all gray."

20

In his fascination, Gili hadn't realized that he was squeezing Eric's arm in a powerful grip. Eric gave a yell, or as much of a yell as he could while still whispering. "Let go, please."

The clenched fist loosened, but Gili remained all wound up. "Eric, I need an explanation. What are you trying to tell me?"

"I'm not sure. What I've hinted to you until now is enough." Eric gave Gili's leg a gentle slap, turned around, and began to walk towards his office.

Benny stuck his head into the corridor. "Gili, phone!" he shouted.

Gili hurried back to his shared quarters. The receiver was resting on the desk, waiting for him. He grabbed it roughly and put it next to his ear. "Yes?"

The voice was muffled, as if the speaker was trying to disguise his voice. "Gili Dinar?"

"Yes? Who's this?" His voice shook slightly.

"That doesn't matter. Tell me, are you stupid? Don't you understand what you've been told? I've sent you a letter, I've sent you a fax. Your life is in danger!"

"What kind of danger?"

"Stay away from certain people whom you've recently gotten close to. Don't you understand?"

"What will happen to me?" Gili asked, clenching his teeth.

"What happens to anyone who sticks his nose in places where it does-n't belong."

"Who are you?" Gili shouted.

The line was cut on the other end. Gili could hear the shrill sound of a dial tone; it sounded like an air-raid siren in his ears.

He breathed heavily, raced to the cooler and downed three cups of water, one after the other.

"Gili, what's up?" Benny looked worried. "What did they say to you?"

"Move, Benny. Move!" Gili yelled furiously.

Benny was shocked. Gili — sensitive, calm Gili — speaking so harshly? Gili raced to the door, turned, and gave a weak smile. "Sorry about that. I'm in a rush."

With loud, heavy steps Gili walked to the elevators. He stopped, looked around him. No, no one was following, not even Benny. The elevator arrived with a genial ring. It was empty. Gili sent it back down to the lobby from where it had come; he himself retraced his steps, sped towards Eric's office, and put his ear to the smoked-glass door. He didn't hear a sound.

Slowly, slowly he opened the door. The room was empty. Strange, Eric had just returned to his office a few minutes before. Where had he disappeared to?

And what had he meant? "A pawn in a chess game ... black dressed as white..."

In his agitation he placed his hand into his pants pocket. Suddenly he felt a paper rustle between his fingers. In his overwrought state the meaningless noise sounded like an artillery shell going off. He pulled out the paper. Had he forgotten to throw away a shopping list?

The letters were printed, impossible to identify. They swam before his eyes; he could hardly put them together into words, sentences. His eyes widened.

"Gili, destroy this paper immediately after you've read it. I can't go into detail, because then I'll be in the same boat as you, and we'll drown together. Your fabulous series on the chassidic courts and yeshivos... Doesn't it strike you as odd that a secular newspaper is interested and sympathetic to the *chareidi* public? Why?

"You've fallen into the mire, into the hands of dangerous scoundrels. This business smells from top to bottom. You're asleep, you're blind. Wake up! You were once clever. Ask the right questions, use your gray cells..."

His sight was hazy as he ripped the note into small pieces and lit a match to burn them. *Eric Meisels, you sly fox, you slapped me on the leg and placed the note into my pocket. You've run home because you're afraid to speak; you've left me here, utterly confused.*

That afternoon Gili drove to Rabbi Avram Roosenthal's home. Dozens of questions raced through his mind. Today he would clear everything up, every last detail. The letter from the president of the Journalist's Council was stowed in his attache case: He wondered how Rav Avram would react to the glad tidings.

For the first time since he had begun to frequent Rav Avram's residence, Gili noticed something out of the ordinary. But it wasn't the trees, beginning to drop their yellowed leaves in this autumn season, that caught his attention. Rather, he saw a large truck standing before the building. The words "Express Movers" were proudly displayed in gigantic letters on the truck's green canvas cover. Movers bent their backs beneath heavy loads as they carted out an apartment's contents. The building's elevator seemed in constant use. Supervising the staff was Michoel Wolfin, a resident of the sixth floor, an immigrant from Russia known by the strange name of "Sha-sha" because of his penchant for yelling "Shhh..." every night to the people assembled on the seventh floor. "Shhh...shhh...quiet!" was his nightly battle cry.

Fury clouded Michoel's vision as he saw Gili. He left the workers and stood before him. "Thank G-d I'm through with this," he thundered. "After years of suffering, my troubles are over. I'm running away. I've already told your rabbi that I'll never forgive him for the theft of sleep. He'll pay for his abuse of the people who live in this building night after night."

Should he try and calm Michoel down? But the man didn't want to hear; he wanted to be heard. There was nothing for Gili to do but leave as quickly as he could. The elevator was still in use. Gili snuck away towards the stairwell and raced up the seven flights. The angry resident ran after him, his shouts echoing throughout the building. "Your rabbi is like a *parah adumah*, a red heifer, do you hear? He makes the impure pure, and makes the pure impure! That's your rebbe. He helps the unfortunate, the deaf-mutes, the big *tzaddik*... But he's made all of us deaf. Tell your rabbi, the thief, that the price of apartments in this building has gone down by $20,000 because of him!"

Sha-sha stuck with him up to the seventh floor. His breath came heavily and quickly but his shouts didn't abate. When Gili saw Zabik waiting in front of the rabbi's door he gave a sigh of relief. The two entered and slammed the door, mere inches in front of Sha-sha. "You'll see!" Michoel roared, his face scarlet, to the closed door. "It will come to court yet! Scandal!"

Choni stood behind the door, amused at the sight. The shouts echoed through the building for some time still, until the man grew tired and returned once more down the steps. Choni turned and looked at Zabik. The two burst into noisy laughter. "Scandal, courts. Sha-sha, shhhh!" Choni imitated his neighbor, his shoulders heaving like a boat on a stormy sea, in a wave of hysterical laughter.

Gili stared at them in disbelief. His frozen features couldn't conceal the fury that overtook him. Zabik patted his shoulder. "Gili, why so serious? Why don't you laugh, man?"

"You can ask? A man's blood is roused, and with good reason, and he's yelling. What's so funny about that?"

"I'll laugh twice as much at Sha-sha's shenanigans," Zabik announced, though his face grew more serious. "If you had any idea how much we've suffered from that man you wouldn't defend him so strongly. Who do you think bought his apartment from him if not Rav Avram, at full market price, without a discount of one cent? From today on Sha-sha's apartment has become the Rabbi's waiting room. No more stairways! Aren't you glad to hear it?"

This was not the time to get involved in petty arguments, Gili decided.

"Can I go into the rav?"

"No. He's asleep."

"What?" Gili said, shocked.

"What do you mean, 'what'? The rav is also human."

"Yes, but..." What of the rabbi's strongly held theory that one needed no more than one and a half hours of sleep a day?

"You can come in, Gili." The rabbi's drowsy tones were heard from his room.

"I don't want to disturb," Gili apologized from behind the door.

"You're not disturbing. Come in."

Gili respectfully entered the room. The shutters were closed and a small night light gave off a yellow beam near the bed. Rav Avram was lying down beneath a light blanket that showed off every line of his emaciated body. The rabbi's face looked weary; his eyes were bloodshot and Gili saw, for the first time, dark circles underneath them.

"I'm going through a difficult time," the rabbi said reluctantly, as if confessing. "I'm tired. Very tired."

"Are there a lot of people expected?"

"That, and more."

"More?"

"Many more people are coming, there's more work to do. Gili, the problems are very grave. There are a lot of unfortunates in the world. It's terrible."

An atmosphere of intimacy and closeness hung in the room. Gili sensed the rabbi's affection in a way he never had felt before. This was the kind of moment that never came again. He decided to grab the opportunity: It was time to take all the rabbits out of the hat.

"Why are you standing?" the rabbi broke into his thoughts. "Take a chair and sit by me. We've got a lot to talk about."

"Yes, I have so many questions, I don't know where to begin." Gili pulled over a chair and dropped down into it. He felt comfortable, free.

"Let me help you organize your thoughts," Rav Avram smiled. "First question: What's my system? How do I deal with people?"

"That's right," Gili nodded. That was the first question that he'd prepared; he'd asked it before. But now there was still another, more critical, question: Who are you — Rav Avram Roosenthal? But that would wait for another opportunity.

"This doesn't get written down," Rav Avram warned him. "Not on paper, not in your computer. These things get inscribed into your heart."

"I'm all ears."

"Good. You've asked me how I operate. You've heard, no doubt, of homeopathy, of self-healing — who hasn't? My system can be described in two words: spiritual homeopathy. What homeopathic doctors do for the body, I do for the soul."

"You're speaking a foreign language," Gili, who always preferred straight talk, complained.

"Patience, my boy," Rav Avram waved a finger at him. "Soon you'll understand everything, and you'll be astonished when you see how simple it is. It's just a matter of practice."

Rav Avram sat up in bed, and leaned comfortably on two large pillows. He gave Gili a burning glance and asked, "Tell me, are you normal?"

Gili burst out laughing at the absurdity of the question.

"Don't laugh, I'm very serious. Give me a simple answer. Do you consider yourself a normal man?"

"Very."

"That is to say, you consider yourself eminently sane?"

"Absolutely."

"Is that so? And what would you say if I were to make you mentally ill within a short span of time? I could do it," Rav Avram declared. "Not only you, but anyone."

"Just like that?"

"Absolutely just like that! Every person has his Achilles heel, a weak point in his mental structure. I'm an expert in finding out where that weak point is; I can open it wider and wider, until the most normal, balanced person will be screaming and acting like a lunatic."

"Everyone?"

"No exceptions."

"Nonsense!"

Rav Avram grew silent and closed his eyes in concentration. Gili quickly regretted his impetuous outburst. *You are certainly lacking in manners, Gili. You can tell you didn't learn "fear of your rabbi as fear of Heaven" when you were a youngster. That's how you speak to a great rabbi?*

Rav Avram laughed silently, a laugh brimming with enjoyment and serenity. His wise eyes saw Gili's confusion and he laughed more, his body heaving. "You know, Gili, there are some things about you that I really like, but most of all I love your *chutzpah*. You're impudent, but you're honest."

Quiet descended upon the room for some minutes.

"Gili, do you want to earn a million dollars? I'll give you a million dollars if you can find me one person on this entire globe who doesn't suffer from one of these symptoms: sensitivity; nerves; fears; worries; melancholy; feelings of inferiority."

"You've just lost a million dollars," Gili cried out, a mischievous light sparkling in his eyes. "Here I am!"

Rav Avram smiled. "Very funny. Listen, Gili, there's no such person! Our modern era has changed mankind into a mass of nerves and fears, popping pills in order to sleep. Bring me whomever you like; in a few minutes I'll pinpoint his weak spot. Give me some time to broaden the breach. It doesn't matter who — man, woman, Chinese or Swede or Ethiopian, professor or shepherd. There's no one, no matter how sane, who can't be turned mad."

The young journalist wasn't made of soft, pliant clay: Gili was a matchless opponent. "These symptoms that you've described, who doesn't have them? I myself am sold on sleeping pills. But from there to madness?"

"What's going to be? You don't understand the first thing of what I've told you," Rav Avram said in despair. "How do you want to be my student? This, then, is my credo: Every person has a perforation in his soul. That's the way G-d created us, perhaps so that we not become overly proud, that we know how little we really are. If you know how to widen the hole and make it larger, you can manipulate any person's mental balance, no matter who he is! But I use this knowledge to heal men, not to make them sicker."

Rav Avram sank deep into thought. He sat up in his bed and hung his head between his knees. For a brief moment Gili seemed to see an image of a Biblical prophet in some artist's masterpiece. The rabbi's magnetism was working again: Gili began to think that there might be something to his theories. But still there was a trace of doubt in Gili's next words.

"Okay, I accept your premise as true for unstable personalities, but you say you could turn a healthy, intelligent man insane too?"

"Easily. Even the most normal of men has some small percentage of lunacy within him, but he suppresses it. Here you are, for example, living in constant fear of a dread disease entitled 'second-rate journalist.' Isn't that true, Gili? The fear that someone may say you're not a top-notch-reporter can drive you mad, under the right circumstances. I know the secret of those circumstances."

Wordlessly Gili rummaged through his attache case and pulled out the letter from Chaim Tzadok, president of the Journalists' Council. Rav Avram read through it with increasing enjoyment; he then pumped Gili's hand happily. "Congratulations, Gili. You see? Without even an iota of libel you've managed to grab first prize!"

"And a second-rate journalist at that," Gili said dryly.

"Gili Dinar is the best! And do you know why? Because his fear of being second-rate is pushing him ahead! Your brain has been sending you subconscious commands from the age of 7, from the day you saw the hope in the eyes of your mother and father, how much they wanted you to bring home an honor certificate. If you thought you'd fail, you wouldn't want to live!"

Gili hardly noticed that he had risen from the chair, round eyed. "How do you know that?" he asked in a choked voice. "It was exactly like that. My nightmares always revolve around my career as a journalist. Day and night I think about how not to mess up, how to uncover the next successful story."

"You don't have to tell me, I read it in your eyes. That's you. You have some other fears as well," the rabbi's eyes grew sly, "but now is not the time to discuss them.

"It's not only you. Everyone is touched by something. We all live on the edge, on the thin line between madness and sanity. What G-d does is bring forgetfulness to people so that they don't think too much about their troubles. But if I were to tread on their toes I could free them from their sanity in no time!

"I know, soon you'll find me some spiritual Samson, a person completely healthy in his outlook. Don't you worry, even the mightiest harbor some dark secret: Knock on it and the demons come racing out. The best of men have dark secrets!"

"And then what? What do you do with them?" Gili asked eagerly. *You're getting closer to understanding human behavior, Gili.*

"That's where the homeopathy comes in, the self-healing. I isolate the weak spot and magnify it. For example, is so-and-so, the lawyer, a nervous type? I tell him of an incomparably nerve-wracking situation."

Rav Avram laughed. "You know, I'm an expert in describing things so that they seem almost real. I speak and he sees it before him. I'll draw him the courtroom, the accused whom he's defending successfully, the weakness of the case against his client in the face of this defense. And then suddenly everything turns around; the accused says something wrong and incriminates himself absolutely. The prosecution makes hash of the false defense, the judge becomes hostile, the accused is found guilty. The whisper goes around among the lawyers: You lost your case. You're losing your touch. The phone stops ringing, there are no new appointments, you sit in your beautifully decorated office and wonder how you can sell it. You're worth nothing! Within five minutes everything's turned upside down, the starched, tailored lawyer is sweating, angry and nervous. Here, in my office, he begins to scream like a madman."

"This really happened in the past?" Gili was white.

"Hundreds of times. Hundreds of people have screamed here. You could have seen respected men here in positions that would have led you to bring them right to an asylum," Rav Avram said tranquilly. "But that's just the beginning, the bitter pill of the medicine. Now the soul begins to build up immunities. I travel with the patient through the straits of his consciousness and show him, in the second and third stages, that there is no place for worry. I close the wounds; the patient feels like one newly born. His soul is now 100 percent healthier, with only 5-percent instability."

"You do this in one visit?" Gili asked in disbelief.

"What do you think? The average patient comes 20 times. Until he's found a balance in his psyche."

"And money?"

"I work for nothing," Rav Avram's face glowed. "I don't even take a nominal fee."

Gili tapped his fingers on his knees. "But why? You could be rich, even if all you took was $50 a visit. That's not much."

Rav Avram suddenly stood up from his bed, walked to the window and opened the shutters. The darkened room was bathed in sunlight. Gili rubbed his eyes; Rav Avram didn't even blink. His self-control was certainly inhuman. "You see this room. It is obvious to me that it's lacking in luxuries. I've got different priorities. I don't need money."

"But who pays for this house? Where do you find the money to support four helpers, Choni, Paysi?"

"I have an inheritance," Rav Avram said; Gili wasn't certain if he was serious or not. The rabbi returned to bed and sat down. His hands were clasped behind his back and he leaned on the wall.

"Did you want anything else?" he asked wearily, his eyes half-closed.

Gili hesitated. It seemed as if the rabbi was failing. Perhaps he would wait for another time. "I wanted to ask," he heard himself say, "who you really are, Rav Avram Roosenthal. Where did you come from? What are your values? I've learned about a mitzvah that comes from a sin; how is it possible that you try to help people at the same time you make your neighbors miserable? And why are people afraid of you? A millionaire dealer in antiquities known as Big Yaakovi was afraid to give me your name. His liaison, Bumi Porat, told me that I should dig my own grave before I meet you. Benny Gabison is absolutely frightened of you. He's a journalist, yet he hasn't written a word about you. Why?"

Rav Avram spoke with his eyes closed shut. "I've got a very good filter against publicity. In fact, I'm hermetically sealed."

After a short moment Gili continued his list of unanswered questions. "Eric Meisels has warned me that I've fallen in with scoundrels, and others threaten my life over the phone. What's going on here?"

Rav Avram's head lolled. He seemed to have fallen into a light doze. Gili longed to get up and leave the room. Today he had had surely broken every rule of good behavior. Rav Avram suddenly awoke and said, in a sleepy tone, "What did you ask? Why are they afraid of me? Good question. That's a topic for a discussion, a discussion, a discussion, a complete..."

His head again dropped for a few seconds. Then his entire body grew limp on the bed, and he fell into a deep sleep.

Gili looked worshipfully at Rav Avram's shining face. A strange feeling overcame him suddenly, as if he'd seen this face somewhere before. Then the thought struck him: Only a newborn could fall asleep so suddenly in front of another person, without any adult embarrassment or self-consciousness.

A newborn or a person completely drained.

Reflectively he stood staring at the sleeping rabbi for some minutes. Then he tiptoed out and quietly closed the door behind him.

The apartment was empty. Zabik, Muli, Choni and the others had vanished. But when he passed Paysi's room he heard a strange noise. He opened the door a crack and peered inside.

Paysi was lying on the bed, his eyes tightly shut. His face, usually so handsome, was distorted. His runny nose was bright red; his mouth opened and closed without emitting a sound. Gili couldn't understand what he was seeing. For a few seconds he stared at the contorted face, until it suddenly dawned on him.

Paysi was crying. Soundlessly.

The cry of a mute.

Gili waited several seconds longer. He felt his heart breaking in sorrow; his eyes grew moist without his even realizing it. How he wanted to go to Paysi and embrace him, comfort him. But no: Paysi was a shy, sensitive youngster who wouldn't forgive himself if he knew that Gili had seen him in his weak moment.

He stood near the apartment's door, ready to leave, but felt a sudden urgent desire to see Rav Avram one more time. He had looked so gentle in his sleep...

Quietly, quietly he pushed the knob of the bedroom door.

Rav Avram was in a deep slumber. Gili approached and scrutinized him once again. He saw the rabbi's head begin to nod to and fro, as if he were going through some fierce inner struggle. Suddenly his eyes flew open. He saw Gili and sat up in bed. Gili was shocked by his mentor's awesome self-control. If he had been in a deep sleep, a tractor couldn't have awakened him.

"What did you ask? About Big Yaakovi? Listen, you've overstepped the boundaries. You're impossibly insolent! I should have thrown you out of here."

Now here was a rebuke, a positive rebuke. Gili was wounded. This was the first time since he'd met the kabbalist that Rav Avram had spoken so.

"Don't be insulted," the rabbi calmed him. "I said I should throw you out. There are many things a person *should* do. Come with me into the kitchen. We'll drink a cup of strong Turkish coffee and bring up old memories."

In the next hour Gili learned the dreadful story of the merchant of antiquities, Big Yaakovi.

21

Pinny Yaakovi climbed to his position as Israel's largest dealer in antiquities from the slums where he was born. His father, Meshulam Yaakobovitz, was a great Torah scholar, but for his daily bread he worked as a teacher of young children in Talmud Torah Meah Shearim in Jerusalem. During family celebrations Meshulam was the one always asked to speak. Listeners would soak up his lucid words and honey-sweet reflections. Impossible to imagine a *nitzadah,* the *sheva berachos* held on *motzaei Shabbos* — a Jerusalem custom that fell into disuse in the 1940s — without him. Participants would sit around tables laden with slices of leftover challah intermingled with cigarette butts. Blending with the sound of thunderous singing would be the words, growing louder and louder, *"Nu, Meshulam, zug shoin eppis,* Come on, Meshulam, say something already." Meshulam would shrug his shoulders in a gesture of refusal; again came the cry: "Nu, nu, Meshulam." After repeated pleas, who could say no?

Meshulam would stand and speak. He would tell a parable, describe an event. He compared life to a 10-stringed harp. After each of life's epochs a string snaps, until it is the turn of the very last string... When his tear-filled voice would intone the words, *"s'geit platzin der letste strone,* the last string is about to break," listeners would join him in weeping.

Meshulam possessed, too, many joyous speeches, rich in humor, that brought his listeners to uncontrollable laughter. There was his popular story of the City Council of "Committee City," that would meet time after time on the burning issue of the day: In light of a water shortage, should the water in the *mikveh* be changed once in two months or once in three? For seven days and seven nights the Council met, arguing over what to do. At the end of their deliberations they came up with a firm resolution: to meet again to discuss the matter. The refrain — "to meet again to discuss the matter"— sounded wonderful in Yiddish and brought waves of hysterical laughter in its wake.

The men of Jerusalem loved to listen to him. Of the 10 measures of criticism that descended upon the world, nine are granted to Jerusalem — and yet they listened to his speeches eagerly. With eyes half-shut and faces glowing with contentment, with the fragrant smell of tobacco wafting through the air and cups of sweetened water in profusion, they announced in evident satisfaction, "*Ah mechayah*! He's giving us diamonds!"

Meshulam possessed a vast store of spiritual wealth and cultural treasures, but Jerusalem wits used to say that if he would write a *sefer* it would be titled, "The Poor Man's Wisdom."

The Yaakobovitz family lived in a one-room apartment in Meah Shearim, adjacent to its open-air market. Ten people lived in the large, stuffy room with the arched walls: Meshulam, his wife, Rivka, and their eight children. Dusty webs hung from the ceiling, with both spiders and their prey suspended limply in their gluey threads. Vast numbers of flies and mosquitoes buzzed near the dead insects. Rivka Yaakobovitz was a sickly woman who spent most of her day in bed, sighing deeply. At the age of 40 she was admitted to the Rosenblatt Hospital for the mentally ill in the Jerusalem neighborhood of Givat Shaul; she never returned home. The unfortunate family tried to hide the fact, but in Jerusalem of old there were no secrets. The youngsters grew up in terrible neglect: Deficiency and desertion, deprivation and dirt worked hand in hand in the miserable Yaakobovitz household.

Pinchas Yaakobovitz was Rivka and Meshulam's eldest child. He was a sensitive boy, delicate and scrupulously clean. For him life in his parents' musty home was one long nightmare. From the age of 7 Pinny dreamed of being rich, of living in a wonderful palace surrounded by an army of servants. There was no chance of his dream ever coming true, Pinny knew; he would be a beggar just as his father, Meshulam, was.

At the age of 7 Pinny had no idea that he had inherited his father's rare bibliographic talents. But when he was 14 he went rummaging through the bags of *genizah* in the Yeshuas Yaakov synagogue, better known as "the *shtieblach*" of Meah Shearim. He found, among the heaps of ripped *siddurim* and *Chumashim*, a sheaf of writings that looked different from the rest, and decided to take it for himself.

That day, when Meshulam returned from his work in the Talmud Torah, Pinny showed him his find. "Abba, what's this?"

Meshulam skimmed hastily through the ancient writings. Suddenly he gave a shout. "It's the *sefer Noam Elimelech* of the *tzaddik* Rav Elimelech of Lizensk, a first edition! This is worth a lot of money! Where did you find it?"

Pinny told his father, and from that day forward continued to burrow through the sacks of *genizah* of "the *shtieblach*," as well as other collections throughout Jerusalem. Occasionally he would find valuable manuscripts. With the sale of these antiquities to merchants and collectors the family's economic situation slowly began to improve. But Pinny wasn't content: He wished to keep all his treasures for himself. He understood, though, that economic necessity forced him to set aside the passion for collecting that was beginning to grip his very soul, at least for the time being.

Pinny developed a unique sense for unearthing antique manuscripts, books, and letters. He created a sweeping network among Israel's dealers and knew just how to bargain and obtain the highest price. Slowly he created a substantial collection of rare and precious items. Along the way, he drifted from the way of life that he had learned from his father, though he never shed his *kippah*. "I'm a religious man," he would openly declare.

Pinny was a dedicated collector. If he heard that an old man living in Petach Tikvah owned a bundle of letters written by the rebbe of Gur, the *Chiddushei HaRim*, for example, he would travel there that same day and begin bargaining with the oldster. With a sour face he would pay the old man half the asking price; a year later, he would sell it to a wealthy Gerrer *chassid* from America for four times the amount. Sometimes things moved even faster. One day he heard that a woman from Australia who was visiting in Kfar Saba had the manuscript of *Paamonim*, an ancient philosophical work whose value was beyond measure. Despite his immense girth, Pinny raced to Ben Yehudah Street and hailed a taxi to Kfar Saba. He paid his driver 60 lirot, a huge sum that was about one third of the average worker's monthly wage at the time, to drive to Kfar Saba, wait for him, and drive him back — a concept unheard of in those impoverished days. After two hours of hard bargaining he had snared the prize: *Paamonim* changed hands for the princely sum of $2000. As he left the tourist's home he met a competitor who had taken public transportation, and who was left helplessly gritting his teeth at his opponent's victory. Four years later Pinny sold *Paamonim* to a fledgling Brazilian dealer for $50,000.

Pinny kept about 70 percent of his acquisitions for himself, amassing a sizable horde of antiques and valuables. An expert assessor from Sotheby's estimated his collection of manuscripts at about $20 million. And that did not include the many other collections in Yaakovi's home!

And then things became complicated. Yaakovi had reached the summit of success: From there, he had no place to go but down. Troubles come in threes, the folk saying goes; Yaakovi could confirm that. Within a short time the blows rained down from all sides. The first misfortune: Yaakovi lost several hundred thousand dollars on unsuccessful deals. Second, he experienced a serious setback as thousands of immigrants from the former Soviet Union came to Israel, bringing with them considerable numbers of previously unknown manuscripts that cut deeply into his share of an already tight market. Finally, the third problem: Several members of the Israeli mafia, angry because he had sold them items that turned out to be forgeries, threatened his life if he didn't return their money to them. In trying to get out of the muck he only fell in further. Of course, he could have sold some of his rare manuscripts in exchange for ready cash, but within the obese body of "Big Yaakovi" lived the soul of an undersized squirrel. To sell his manuscripts? Impossible! Yaakovi stepped confidently upon the path to destruction: He borrowed a million dollars on the black market and found himself facing the sharp teeth of the Israeli mafia...

Rav Avram stared at Gili over the empty cup. He took a deep breath and continued the story.

"And then he came to me, beaten, his soul destroyed. He was threatened by the mafia, trembling for his life. I asked him how he had managed to get involved with the Israeli mafia, and he told me a terrifying story of a flourishing industry of forgeries. That's how I found out that Yaakovi would sell undetectable copies of original manuscripts that were part of his voluminous collection. He sold to several dealers, the top echelon of the underworld, forged incunabula, for hundreds of thousands of dollars, thinking that the fraud would never be discovered. But it was discovered fast enough. He received a threatening letter: 'You can drive in an armored Cadillac and wear eight revolvers, but if you don't return the money we'll bury you alive in cement in a new housing project. No one will ever find your body!'

"Yaakovi was deathly afraid. In his despair he searched for any way out. A friend of his told him about me and he decided that I, as an American rabbi who was very different from others, and who lived in the secular world as well as the spiritual one, could help him. I had a graphologist study the handwriting in the threatening letter and I then told Yaakovi that if he valued his life he should return the money, no matter what, because the one who'd penned the letter was a criminal with murderous intent. Yaakovi listened to me, sold several of his manuscripts, and repaid the debt."

"Yaakovi sold manuscripts?" Gili whistled incredulously. He remembered with a grin the fat collector. Yaakovi thought that Gili hadn't noticed how his host had grabbed all the cookies on the plate the minute Gili's back was turned... But with all his weaknesses, Yaakovi was one tough man.

"Yes. Did you forget that he was working with me? I have a certain influence on people," Rav Avram said dryly. "First I rescued him from the claws of the mafia. Later, I decided it was time to put an end to Yaakovi's activities. He'd cheated dozens of honest men out of tremendous sums of money. Even if they weren't threatening his life, did they deserve to sustain such losses?"

"What did you do?" Gili asked tensely.

"G-d has granted me a precious gift, the talent of autosuggestion. Do you know what that is?"

"Of course I do!" Gili jumped up, like the prize pupil in a classroom. "Autosuggestion is a form of hypnotism, the deepest form of persuasion. Rav Avram, are you trying to hint to me that you have parapsychological powers, like Uri Geller, who can bend a fork without touching it or stop a watch with a look of his eyes?"

"Perhaps. I've never tried my powers on solid objects. The clock and the fork do quite well without me." Clearly, the rabbi was a little insulted by the comparison. *Parapsychology? Me? You don't understand very much, do you, Gili Dinar? My power comes from another wellspring entirely, one you'll never be able to tap.* "I work with people, in order to help them. That's my specialty. I don't even have to look into your eyes in order to control your thoughts and cause you to think as I wish you to think. I can control you by telephone; a dial tone is enough to create a radical change within you. At first I tried to bring Yaakovi back through pleasant means: I explained to him the severity of the prohibition against theft. But when I saw that I was wasting my eloquence on him, I used the power of suggestion. I brought 'Big Yaakovi' to the edge of insanity and linked together, without his being aware of it, a lack of integrity with melancholia and thoughts of suicide. Whenever 'Big Yaakovi' wants to cheat someone he suddenly gets depressed, he loses his desire to live, without understanding why..."

"That's unethical!" Gili yelled, his face scarlet. "You could have forced him to suicide!"

"If I had the slightest fear that I would accidentally cause someone to harm himself, I would have closed up my clinic long ago," Rav Avram said serenely. "My power is to bring a person to the edge, without letting him ever cross over. A foot before the red line, a moment before the point of no return, I pull him back. How? I control his soul from afar, as if through remote control. Slowly Yaakovi realized that I wanted only his good. I created a fixation on sanity within 'Big Yaakovi'. He changed his ways, but he's still terrified of me; he fears me as he fears the angel of death. He consults with me on all his business deals, in order to prove to me how fair and honest he's become: he won't budge an inch without me."

"And that's the reason for his notes at the fair, to consult with A.R., to discuss it with A.R." Gili finally understood the antique merchant's inexplicable behavior. But the deeper he delved into the thoughts of this rabbi, the more questions he had, the more riddles remained unanswered...

"And Bumi Porat. Why did he tell me to prepare a will if I consulted you?"

"Bumi, too, is afraid of me. He was involved in a sordid business deal, and as Yaakovi's assistant he followed in his boss' footsteps. I saw within him signs of, let us call it crookedness, so I placed a great fear of me within him."

"But why did they warn me? What have I done wrong?"

Rav Avram rose from his seat. "Have you noticed? The coffee grounds have all dried out. Look how long we've been talking. Soon people will begin to come, and Zabik and Muli haven't returned yet."

Gili caught the rabbi's robe. "Just two more questions. The rav knows that I'm with him completely, but what should I do? I'm fanatically straight. If something doesn't seem right to my conscience I can't bear it."

"Your conscience is selective, just as you are. It's asleep and awake at the right times." Rav Avram sighed; his words pierced Gili like the stab of a knife. "Put the kettle on the fire and we'll drink another cup of Turkish coffee, and you can get the answer to the question you put to me in my room: 'Who are you, Avram Roosenthal; what are your values? How do you help one person while making others miserable, your neighbors for example?' "

❧❦

Gili filled the kettle from the tap; as he did so, he decided to buy the rabbi an electric kettle and a water filter as a gift. The house was certainly suffering from considerable neglect. As if to confirm his thoughts, a large fly buzzed in at that moment through the open kitchen window and landed on the garbage pail. A moment later it flew off again and landed squarely on a plate of cookies sitting on the table. Rav Avram didn't take his eyes off it. Gili's face wore an expression of disgust as he waved his hands over the plate, but the fly stuck firmly to the sugar crumbs on top of the cinnamon cookies and avoided Gili's motioning arms.

"No, don't do that," Rav Avram protested. "I'm enjoying him. Everyone is a messenger: This green fly has been sent from heaven to help clarify my next words. Don't be insulted, Gili; answer me honestly, with your hand on your heart: Are you any better than that green fly?"

"I feel, once again, that I don't understand a thing." Gili wiped the sweat off his brow. Suddenly, it had become very hot...

"I don't mean you personally," Rav Avram explained. "But in my opinion journalists are flies. They make a living from humanity's garbage; they settle on its open wounds. Like the fly, they search out filth and, just like the fly, the higher the pile of dirt, the happier they are!

"My distaste for journalists is well known. How did Eric Meisels put it? You've fallen into a gang of scoundrels... Pinny Yaakovi and Bumi Porat both know my feelings for journalism. They understood that you planned on interviewing me and examining me to my core. Because I handled them with an iron hand, they suspected that you, too, would get similar treatment."

"And why have I gotten better treatment?" Gili was baffled: From the moment he'd met him, the rabbi had shown him favor. "Actually, I have an even tougher question: If journalists are flies, why were you so pleased when I was assigned to examine the yeshivos and chassidic courts?"

The rabbi smiled patiently: It seemed that the world's entire store of patience was at his command. "I have never hated another person. If I'm disgusted by the smell of the man who cleans the sewers, it doesn't mean I hate him. What does the Gemara say? *The world cannot be without perfumers; the world cannot be without tanners. Lucky is he whose profession is in perfumes; unfortunate the man who is a tanner.* Journalism in and of itself is a marvelous instrument; without journalism there would be corruption everywhere, graft would be rampant in government. The task of journalists is to be society's guard dog. There's nothing wrong with the reporter's job, but sometimes the journalist loses his balance and instead of ferreting out corruption he looks for cheap sensations and, in the worst case, squeezes money and favors by threats of revealing secrets of someone's past. That's what I call a fly, living off garbage!

"When you first came to me I immediately sensed, through my inner radar, that you are a good man, not at all corrupt. That's why I brought you closer to me. Benny Gabison, too, I've brought into my circle despite his being a journalist. Benny is afraid of me, that's true. He is a positive person without any reason to suspect me of anything; his fears are childish: He is certain that I can read his thoughts. You know, the only truly private place you have is your mind. You are the master there. If you think that last island of privacy is being invaded you feel threatened. You needn't be afraid of me. The Chazon Ish writes in his letters that fear and love cannot live together; one does not love whom one fears. Only the fear of G-d's greatness does not conflict with love of Him; that is something completely different."

Rav Avram gazed at the fly, contentedly sipping up the grains of sugar, and again stopped Gili's hand. "Does the rule forbidding harming living things include flies? What do you say, Gili?

"And so, when they offered you the position of reporter for religious affairs, I was pleased. I knew I would be able to do the unbelievable: create a spiritual presence within a secular newspaper. What I did with *HaYom HaZeh*, at least in your stories, was what they do with the *chareidi* dailies. Funny, no? Through you, the secular world learned the beauty of a Torah life. Your series did more than earn a prestigious journalism award: It has made an immeasurable difference in many people's lives, both in this world and the next!"

Sometimes a person weeps from sheer joy. Gili felt his throat tighten. Not long ago, he had lived in spiritual darkness; now he was bringing others back to a religious existence. Gili turned to the kitchen window, his eyes misty with unshed tears as he stared out at the darkness. Evening already? He stared at his watch: His conversation with the rabbi had lasted four hours!

Rav Avram smiled and said, "Okay, what's left? Yes, your last question."

"You asked who I am. My full name is Avraham Yitzchak Roosenthal. I was born in Flatbush, a neighborhood in Brooklyn, and I learned in one of the most prominent yeshivos in the States. I was born with a silver spoon in my mouth. G-d granted me good fortune: From my earliest youth, everything I touched flourished. That's the reason I have so many enemies. I admit my detractors, like my admirers, are many in number!"

"Who could hate you?" Gili protested. "You've helped thousands of people."

Rav Avram sighed. "Who hates me? Perhaps Eric Meisels, your assistant editor. Various rabbis: Unfortunately, my ways are not always understood by the more conventional. Some of the neighbors whose sleep I've disturbed; these Israelis are absolutely wild about sleep. The average Israeli loves to sleep, while I make do with one and a half to two hours a day. Yes, I know it's forbidden to disturb neighbors at night. But my priorities are different: While this is not a halachic decision, in my opinion, it's preferable to help many, even if a few individuals suffer a little from it.

"When I came to Israel with a small inheritance from my grandfather in my pocket, I could have bought two apartments in this building. This area was considered the slum area of Petach Tikvah and the apartments weren't expensive. In the meantime some things have changed. I invested a little of the money in the stock market during the good years, and I doubled my capital. Today, I buy every apartment in the building that is put on the market, so as not to disturb the neighbors."

Gili was silent.

"Do you have any other questions?" Rav Avram asked.

"None." *Something about Eric Meisels isn't quite right, but I'm not sure what.*

"Good."

The door opened noisily. Zabik, Muli and Choni entered, breathing heavily. Choni approached the rabbi. "Shalom, Abba. Don't ask! Sha-sha messed up the elevator before he left; we had to walk up the seven flights."

Gili was enraged to hear about Sha-sha's vandalism, but the rabbi spoke serenely. "Really? We should call the repairman immediately, and have the elevator fixed tonight. We can't have hundreds of people climbing 112 steps."

Rav Avram stopped before the window that overlooked the parking lot, casting a reflective glance outside. He squinted, straining his eyes, and a look of shock passed over his features for a swift moment. But when he turned to Gili the serenity had returned to his countenance.

"Gili, don't wait here. Go home immediately."

It was a command that was to be obeyed without hesitation. Gili flew down the stairs, wondering why the rabbi had sent him home so urgently.

Maybe he wanted to let me be alone with my thoughts. If I wasn't embarrassed, I would stand in the middle of the street with a sign: Rav Avram Roosenthal is the gadol hador.

That's it: Eric Meisels is jealous! He's jealous, and perhaps he hates him too. Meisels and his revolting hints: a gang of scoundrels... Who knows? Maybe he's behind the threats, the phone calls, letters, faxes. He should be ashamed of him-

self! Well, every tzaddik has his opponents. The main thing is: I know the truth. And I'm lucky.

Gili was the happiest of men as he left the building. All of his difficult questions had been answered, fully and in detail. Rav Avram's methods had been laid clearly out before him. An incredible therapist had led him into his own Holy of Holies and revealed all his secrets. Slowly Gili, too, would learn how to use them and help unfortunates.

In one tiny corner of his brain, a warning bell tolled ominously. He saw a man stretched out beneath his Mitsubishi as if searching for something. When the man heard Gili's footsteps he straightened out and ran away. In the dim light of the parking lot Gili couldn't make out his features. The warning bell grew louder.

Gili bent down and examined the chassis of the car. There was nothing suspicious there, and yet the figure that had lain beneath it had aroused nebulous suspicions within him.

What do they want from me?

22

youth sat on a bench in the Charles Clore Park near the Tel Aviv beach. The other benches were empty in the cold weather; the park was deserted.

He stared at the blinking lights of two boats floating in the distance, tiny pinpoints reflecting back from the darkness of the water. A frigid wind blew, bringing the foaming surf towards the shore. The waves broke upon the rocks, spraying the air with millions of droplets of sparkling water. The breeze wafted the salt smell to his nose, and he yearned for summer's days, when he could cavort among the waves.

A Suzuki motorcycle approached with a thunderous roar and stopped nearby. A tall man in a winter jacket descended and sat down, as if by coincidence, on the bench near the man. They sat silently and stared at the stormy sea. "A cold night, no?" the cyclist said. "Have you brought the goods?"

"The goods" were wrapped in an attractive package within a black leather case. Nonchalantly, the man exchanged that briefcase for another, identical one, that he'd brought with him. "You have 50 blank tapes. We'll meet in two weeks."

"Dunno." The youth sounded hesitant.

"Why not?" The man was curt.

"It's getting harder every day. It's not like before, when he agreed. Now he's fighting. Every day I have to find a new way."

The man opened a briefcase and pulled out a crisp 200-shekel bill. "Take something on account. The rest will come next time."

The youth angrily threw the bill onto the grass. "That's all?"

The man bent down and retrieved the money, not at all offended. He pulled out another bill and handed them both to the youth.

"That's better," he muttered, as if unimpressed. Funny, he would have been perfectly satisfied with 200, and had merely flung the bill down for the sake of a little drama and a little business. He crumpled the reddish bills, stared at them to make certain they weren't counterfeit.

The cyclist left first. The youth sat for 10 minutes, gazing at the dark water. Then he rose and left, his fingers playing with the bills in his pocket.

Since he had identified Ron Limor as a student in Yeshivas Torah Lishmah, Gili had felt a powerful urge to return to the yeshivah and find out more about their famous pupil, and how he had come to study there.

Gili, he told himself proudly, *you've done well. You gave up a sensational scoop to save someone. You have to meet him, see who he actually is.*

On Thursday afternoon, the *HaYom HaZeh* newsroom was almost deserted. The weekly magazine was already being distributed in stores, to be sold the next day with the Friday paper. Benny Gabison leaned back in his chair, his arms hugging the nape of his neck, his face wearing its usual bland mask of indifference. His bored gaze took in Gili, busy putting a bag containing two croissants into his briefcase.

"Where to?"

"Jerusalem. Yeshivas Torah Lishmah."

"I thought you'd finished with that foolishness."

"You're right, I have. And that 'foolishness' ended with the Golden Pen Award. But I have this urge to see the place again."

"Listen to a friend's advice." Benny straightened in his chair; his fingers rested on the desk in front of him. "Stay away from places you've written about, as you would from fire."

"Why?"

"If you wrote negative things about them, they'll be angry. If you wrote good things about them, they'll feel they owe you something, and are sure you've come to collect on the debt. Gili, the world is an ungrateful place."

Gili's brown eyes widened. Benny's entire body exuded an air of discontent. What was bothering him?

"You know what, why don't you come with me? If they want to hit me, you can protect me."

"Leave me alone." Benny had leaned back again, his hands once more hugging his neck tightly. "I'll see you when you get back." He patted his stomach. "I've got a feeling here in my gut that you're heading into a minefield."

Gili smiled."Have a good day."

"Have a good minefield."

What did you need this for? Gili thought, when two hours had passed. *Benny was right; you've walked right into a minefield!*

It was evening when he had reached Yeshivas Torah Lishmah. The building looked much as he remembered it — dingy, worn, its peeling paint and cracked windows stuffed with cardboard all proclaiming the yeshivah's dire need for a new building. Only one thing seemed to have changed: the crowded, dynamic and vibrant feeling that had filled the crumbling walls on his last visit seemed to have disappeared. A few young men stood on the steps smoking; others chatted in desultory and aimless fashion in the hallways. Gili, looking into the *beis midrash*, was shocked to find it almost deserted.

As he walked, puzzled and increasingly uneasy, towards the yeshivah office, a door flew open and Rav Zimel stepped out. When he saw Gili his Adam's apple worked up and down in his throat and his eyes narrowed.

Gili felt his heart lurch within him. Ignoring the vague fears that were slowly taking form, he gave Rabbi Zimel a small, unconvincing smile.

Without waiting for an invitation he headed into the office, followed by the obviously furious principal.

Rabbi Zimel pulled a wallet out of his jacket pocket. "How much do I owe you?"

"For what?"

"Funeral expenses. After all, you dug our graves for us."

Gili stared. His mouth grew dry; a cold sweat broke out on his forehead. "What are you talking about?"

"I'm talking, Mr. Award-Winning Journalist, about the end of our yeshivah, the end of our dreams. I'm talking about the person who revealed the whereabouts of Ron Limor!"

The story tumbled out in half-sentences, unfinished phrases. Obviously, Rabbi Zimel had been holding his wrath inside; now, like a flood of dark angry water, it crashed through the walls of the dam, engulfing everything in its way.

In a fog, Gili heard the tale. How Ron Limor, in despair, had run away from his unhappy home and lived on the streets for several weeks, falling prey to the horrors of homelessness in an uncaring city, sleeping in abandoned buildings, surviving by stealing chocolate bars from blind kiosk owners and begging half-shekels from commuters. How a *kiruv* worker from Bnei Brak had found the youngster, sick and despairing, vomiting in a corner of Tel Aviv's sparkling new Central Bus Station. How he'd seen, not a dirty panhandler, but a young Jew in distress, and brought him to his home, his doctor, and his *beis knesses*. How the boy had prayed, murmuring unfamiliar words with the fervor that brought him to the attention of the *shul's* rav.

"He started by going to *shiurim* with *baalei teshuvah*. But he's bright, very bright, and soon he was ready for a mainstream yeshivah. No one would touch him — no one dared. If his parents would find out that a yeshivah had been hiding their son... destruction! No one dared, but Rav Shmerl. He *farhered* the boy. Amazing! In a few months, he knew more than most of our students had learned in years. An *ilui*, that's what Rav Shmerl called him..."

For about a year Ron Limor had learned, living among the other students. Only a few — his *rosh yeshivah*, Rav Zimel, the benefactor who had originally found him — knew his identity. To the others he was Ronny Lichtenstein, an unusual boy who spoke much in learning, and little about anything else, particularly his past. At the behest of the *rosh yeshivah*, Ron called his parents occasionally to assure them of his well-being, but even now, at the age of 18, he was not ready to confront them or the lifestyle that he had rejected.

And now the tale turned ugly. "It wasn't three days after your visit that the police came into our building. No warrant, no explanation, no apology. They grabbed Ron and hustled him out into a car. He called us a few hours later, broken. His parents had been behind the 'abduction.' He was in their home now, facing their recriminations and fury. Finally, the two had something to bring them together.

"He's 18 and they couldn't keep him against his will. He moved in with his grandmother, his father's mother, who remembers her own parent's traditional life and who has agreed that he can stay with her as a *shomer Torah u'mitzvos*. He's in trouble with the army; without a deferment, he's officially AWOL and may face charges. He doesn't dare step into any yeshivah, not wanting to arouse his powerful parents' animosity against any institution.

"And our yeshivah? His father, the industrialist, managed to get our mortgage commitments canceled. And why not? He plays tennis with the bank's CEO every Shabbos. His mother has put them all on our tracks: Income Tax, the army, the zoning authorities. You know in this country how the bureaucracy can have you at their mercy. A new building? Sorry, we lost the files, you'll have to submit the plans again, only the approval committee won't be meeting for another eight months. The *rosh yeshivah* is broken, broken. He's gone to America to try and raise funds to keep us going, to replace the government monies that have somehow failed to materialize. The *kollel* missed last month's paychecks; most of the young men, desperate, are looking for new places.

"No one knew of Ron Limor's presence here. No one knew — until you came. To dig our graves."

Gili found one small comfort, as he staggered outside, pale and trembling, to his Mitsubishi. He rejoiced from the bottom of his heart that he hadn't seen the Rosh Yeshivah, Rabbi Shmerl Mirinski. To stand before the gaze of the Rosh Yeshivah? He couldn't have borne it.

"Masochist!"

"No, I just want to see what's happening at Kiltz."

"You're looking for trouble."

The dialogue was being held between Gili and the reflection that looked back at him from the mirror in his Radisson Moriah Plaza hotel room in Jerusalem. When he left Yeshivas Torah Lishmah he had decided to spend the night in the city, to say Friday's sunrise prayers at the Kotel, and then to go to the Nachalat Bayit neighborhood and spend Shabbos with the Kiltz *chassidim*. What could be simpler?

"You're killing yourself," his exhausted reflection told him from the mist-covered mirror. *"What will you do if you find out that in Kiltz, too, they want to eat you alive?"*

"I don't care," Gili told the figure coming out of the mist. *"I must know what's there."*

He was certain he had fallen asleep the moment his head hit the pillow, but when he closed his eyes he immediately saw before him the image of Rabbi Zimel Mirinski screaming at him. The destruction of Yeshivas Torah Lishmah lay on his conscience like a heavy stone. What had he done? Though he wouldn't publicize Limor's presence in the yeshivah, he had let fall some broad hints in the newsroom that he had suppressed a sensational story. No doubt one of the reporters, hungry for a scoop, had put two and two together and had scampered off to Yeshivas Torah Lishmah to find out just what Gili Dinar had been hiding.

At least whoever it was didn't get his byline on the story, he thought bitterly. There hadn't been a word in the papers: Obviously, the parents' reach extended to the country's printing presses.

After two hours of fretful tossing and turning he turned on the light and stared at his watch. Three in the morning. What luck that he had brought his Valium along. He would take a pill and sleep until dawn.

As he rummaged through his travel bag the phone rang, a loud and raucous sound. He would have to speak with the switchboard; to wake up to that at three in the morning...

"Gili Dinar?" The voice was deep and hoarse. Gili's mouth went dry and his heart began to thump wildly.

"Yes. Who are you?"

"It doesn't matter." The anonymous voice sounded terrifying. "You're a fine person. You write stories and destroy people and institutions. You've made an enormous contribution to the destruction of the *chareidim* in this country. Soon you'll visit Kiltz and find that you've destroyed it, too, just as you did Yeshivas Torah Lishmah."

"Who are you? What do you want?" Gili shouted, trembling.

"You'll have an interesting Shabbos in Kiltz. *Shabbat shalom* to you, Gili Dinar, a *shabbat shalom* in hell. Ha, ha, ha..." The hollow laugh echoed in his ears.

He jumped up from bed. *It was just a nightmare! I was asleep until now, I dreamed that I couldn't sleep... But the phone did ring. How could it be?*

He paced the floor for hours, trying to understand what was happening.

The phone rang once again, obstinately and remorselessly. "Mr. Dinar?" It was the switchboard operator. "You ordered a wake-up call at first light. Good morning, and have a nice day."

◌⤜⤛◌

Gili longed to *daven* next to the huge stones until his soul was cleansed and purified. They say that prayers said at this place are immediately received; how he wanted to pour out his heart, verbalize all that was disturbing him, and have his *tefillos* accepted on the spot.

With fervor, with feeling, he would cleanse his soul between the cracks of this wall, leaning upon these stones, which possessed a soul of their own. You spoke to the stone and felt it had an ear to hear, a heart to understand.

This wall has ears...

His left hand leaned upon the wall, his face was buried within it. A single tear dropped down, flew through the air for an instant like a sparkling diamond, and moistened the page of his *siddur. Master of the Universe, set me upon the right path; show me the truth.*

A magical atmosphere covers the Kotel plaza in the hour before dawn. One who has never been there for sunrise prayers cannot understand. The air is clear, pure; a delicate bluish hue floats above while a refreshing, gentle breeze strokes your face and harmonizes with the chirping of the white pigeons flying above in bewitching circles. The pigeons soar upward and descend to the plaza to peck at the bread crumbs some merciful soul has left for them. Gili's wounded spirit, too, flew up and down, just as they did.

Gili arrived at the gray concrete building of Kiltz on Friday afternoon. He didn't tell anyone that he was coming, and went directly to the *beis midrash*. The windows were small and the area was almost in complete darkness.

His eyes turned towards the antique chandelier that hung in the middle of the sanctuary. Where was its beautiful light?

The chandelier was gone!

A coil of electric wires attached to the ceiling marked the place where the missing chandelier had hung. A large hole, black as night, marred the domed ceiling. These were the sole desolate signs that the historic chandelier had ever hung there.

A few young people were sitting and learning the weekly *parashah*. They sang each verse twice, in a pleasant sing-song, repeating it a third time with the Aramaic translation of *Onkelos*.

Gili joined them, and after a few minutes he sensed eyes piercing his back. He wheeled around. Yes, as he had thought, Rabbi Yehoshua Schneidman was standing there, staring at him with a serious face. His grim countenance changed almost instantly into a broad smile as Gili turned towards him.

He approached quickly, his hand outstretched in welcome. "Gili, *shalom aleichem* and welcome."

"How's everything?" Gili asked, bracing himself for the worst.

"Thank G-d." The answer was spiritless, melancholy.

"What happened to the chandelier?"

Rabbi Schneidman gave a deep sigh. "It was stolen."

"How?"

"Even the police don't know. One morning, about two weeks ago, we entered the *beis midrash* and everything became black before our eyes, quite literally."

"That's why I didn't want to write about it, not to attract too much attention." Gili tried to comfort himself, but the knot in his stomach grew bigger and bigger. It was a nightmare, like the one he'd had in the hotel; soon he would wake up and find that reality was much more pleasant.

"I've come here for Shabbos. Is that okay?"

"What a question. You'll be my guest for Shabbos. You'll sleep and eat in my house."

"I'd like to speak with the rebbe if I can."

Again that sigh. "Haven't you heard? The rebbe sees no one."

Shabbat Shalom in hell. "What's happened?"

"We had always feared this. The rebbe's load has been increasing even as he grows weaker. But he wouldn't slow down. Finally, last week, he had a mild heart attack."

"What do the doctors say?" Gili asked, shocked and concerned.

"He'll be fine — if he can be persuaded to decrease the stress and strain in his life. That's about as simple as asking the sun to move from north to south."

23

The bereft court of Kiltz had one source of merriment left.

In the middle of the silent portion of *Shacharis*, when the large *beis midrash* was quiet and each of the congregants was concentrating deeply on his prayers, a fearful cry suddenly broke the stillness: *"Zy shtil, tziganer, ferd-goniff!* Quiet, gypsy, horse thief!"

Gili shuddered. A glance at those around him hinted that the shouts were not to be taken seriously.

And then came a threat, in a softer and calmer tone: *"Ich vill dir patchen,* I'm going to slap you." A yell followed, again splitting the air of the *beis midrash.* *"Zy shtil,* Be quiet!" Finally, the threat again: *Ich vill dir patchen.*

Gili rapidly finished his prayers, turned around and looked around him. His keen eye soon uncovered the source of the disturbance. An elderly congregant wrapped in a *tallis* stood on the western side of the *beis midrash,* beneath an illuminated memorial plaque, leaning on a metal walker. His entire body trembled. He surreptitiously glanced from behind his thick glasses, as if to gauge what impact his shouts had on the others.

A young man wearing a black *kappatah* and sash whispered to Gili, "That's Fishele Mamaliga."

"Fishele what?"

"Mamaliga. He's nicknamed for a Rumanian food, mamaliga, made of cornmeal. You know, these nicknames just take on a life of their own. He's an old man suffering from schizophrenic paranoia. The poor man was imprisoned in Siberia for some years and became mentally ill. He thinks the KGB is after him. According to him they've set a spy onto him, a KGB agent who follows him day and night. One minute the old man is surrounded by Jewish horse traders; the next, he's Fishele Mamaliga, furious at the spy and threatening to hit him."

"Why do you allow him to *daven* here, you should forgive my asking. He's disturbing all the prayers! The place for such a person is an asylum!"

"We thought so too," the young man admitted. "But the rebbe, *shlita*, won't let. The unfortunate Fishele has gone through enough in his life, the rebbe explained, and if he would be committed to an asylum he would die immediately. So Kiltz has turned into his own hostel, and we have a free show every Shabbos."

"You can't calm him down?"

"Just try it," the boy laughed. "When you tell him he's disturbing the prayers, he doesn't understand what you want from him. 'I'm shouting?' he asks in wonder. 'It's not me, it's him, the spy! Hit him, kill him, the scoundrel doesn't give me a moment's rest.' Wait a minute. If you're lucky, you'll hear even more interesting things."

Gili was captivated by the intriguing drama. When the Ark was opened Fishele heaved over on his walker and warned his adversary, loudly, not to interrupt the Torah reading. "I'll show you, cruel spy, you won't come here. Soon I'll bless the congregation; I'll bless them quietly, so quietly that you won't know where I am."

Immediately after his solemn declaration Fishele rolled towards the *Sefer Torah* and kissed it warmly. All eyes followed him as he returned to his place. He stopped, breathed deeply, stared at the congregation from behind his thick glasses, and said in a roar: "Blessed are you, precious Jews, let G-d fulfill your desires for the good, and only happiness and wealth be your lot for all of your days." Suddenly, in a drastic turnabout, he screamed wildly, "You're all accursed gypsies, horse thieves!" He then muttered quietly, "You're so smart, you KGB agent, where were you a minute ago, when I blessed them? Ah, you didn't know where I was! I've won!"

Even the walls seemed to humor Fishele. Only one serious old man walked over to Fishele and rebuked him. "Don't give us your honey, nor your sting: Don't bless us and don't curse us."

"Me, curse?" Fishele Mamaliga was insulted. "It was the KGB agent, may his name be blotted out. Choke him, let him stop hounding me!"

When they went to the Schneidmans' house after prayers Gili expressed his astonishment at the patience that an entire congregation had shown to Fishele's raucous outbursts.

"It's what I told you," Rabbi Schneidman confided. "Kiltz has one common denominator left: Fishele Mamaliga. We love him, even though he's mentally ill. He's a good man, and just, and besides that, he brings a little color into our lives. Aside from him, there is nothing lighthearted to lighten our day, now that our rebbe is ill."

Once again your words have been borne out, Rav Avram. The world is truly full of misfortune. Who revealed the secret of that ancient chandelier, an inheritance from the days of the Marranos? The Inquisition itself did not destroy it, the thieves of Amsterdam let it alone, not until you, Gili, with your two left hands, touched it, and suddenly... Here was a chandelier and now, nothing. It seems to me that Choni eyed that chandelier when we were here. But Choni could not arrange such a theft, not by himself. To rip out a heavy chandelier and smuggle it out, in a building full of people? Only an experienced gang of expert thieves could have pulled off such a stunning coup. Maybe Choni was just the courier. He was speaking to someone on the phone when I was in Rabbi Schneidman's office, and he thought I didn't see him. But that was before we had ever seen the chandelier... What happened first? I'm completely confused.

And how have we gotten to a point where a paranoid schizophrenic is considered the most joyous thing in Kiltz?

What's gone wrong?

☙❦❧

Though his host could not have been more gracious, Gili sensed throughout Shabbos that Rav Schneidman was withholding something. Finally, with Shabbos's end, Gili taxed him with it.

"And you... are you angry with me? Do you feel I'm to blame for what's happening here?"

"I blame you? Heaven forbid. But from the time you visited us, a holocaust has come upon us. We had managed to shield our rebbe until you came.

"But I didn't write about the rebbe's gift in my story!" Gili protested earnestly.

"The story? That's true. But what else besides the story?"

"What are you hinting at?"

His host crumbled a piece of the cake his wife had set before him, until it was almost as fine as flour. How much energy, how much fury, would it take for him to crush it into molecules, into atoms, Gili wondered. Rabbi Schneidman lifted his eyes. "When you were here last you talked about your rebbe. You said he could read minds. Who is your rebbe?"

Now it was Gili's turn to be enraged. "I ask that you keep my rebbe out of the picture. He's a holy man, a *tzaddik,* a pillar of goodness in our generation."

"When did you learn to speak in hollow cliches?" Rabbi Schneidman taunted him. "I put together reports in that kind of language all the time for the *chareidi* press releases. I knew the style — empty words, meaningless descriptions — before you were even born. The question is why, immediately after you visited us, an invisible hand stirred our tranquil pot. We've investigated and discovered that your rebbe, Rav Avram Roosenthal, was the one who disseminated news of the rebbe's powerful blessings, news that would cause a heart attack as surely as high blood pressure would in another man."

Gili burned with anger. The unfairness of it all — it had been Rav Avram who had pointed out the ramifications of printing the story! And now he was being blamed for it!

"I'll clarify the matter," Gili promised. "I'll speak with Rav Avram. I'm not convinced that it was he."

"It was, and it's a waste of time talking about it," Rabbi Schneidman declared decisively. "Your rebbe clapped his contriving hands, and caused us terrible damage, irreversible damage."

He looked at his watch. Could Gili Dinar pick up the phone? Yes, Shabbos had been over for some time. A shame that he had waited until now, but it wasn't too late; much could still be salvaged.

His tongue moistened lips dry with tension. He punched in the number of the Radisson Moriah Plaza in Jerusalem and asked for Gili Dinar's room. The phone rang several times, unanswered. The hotel's answering machine went into operation with a recorded message.

After the "beep" of the machine he spoke quickly. He managed to compress the fateful message into 30 seconds, then put down the receiver with a sigh of relief. Tomorrow they would meet in the Shmarkaf Cafe, and the heavy stone that lay on his heart would roll off.

As he hung up, there was another slight click, as if somewhere else someone had put down a receiver. In his haste he didn't notice it. He hurried to the Toyota parked in the lot and started the engine. His wife, Dafna, had the flu and hadn't wanted to join him for a visit to their daughter in Yokneam.

Sometimes the flu can save someone's life...

He was troubled. The scheme of destruction had begun to let blood much more quickly than he had imagined, and now he regretted his co-operation. No matter: He would reveal all, and save whatever could be saved.

A smile of anticipatory pleasure played over his lips as he thought of his 3-year-old granddaughters. Those adorable twins were impatiently awaiting his arrival in Yokneam. He glanced at the back seat, at the huge teddy bears in their cute wrapping paper. He imagined his granddaughters' squeals of delight at the sight of the woolly bears.

He had reached the portion of road between the Arab village of Fureidis and the settlement of Bat-Shlomo.

The giant truck was traveling without lights. It jumped out at him from the darkness like a black demon, leaped out of its lane and landed with all the force of a tractor-trailer.

In the space of a moment the Toyota had become a bloody piece of broken metal.

The well-oiled machine glided smoothly on its accustomed course: Once every two to three weeks the recorded tapes were replaced with blank ones, on the bench in the Charles Clore Park, during the darkness of deep night. The blank tapes were taken by the young man in order to be recorded; the full ones were brought by the older courier to a large, capable staff well versed in many languages, who had learned to identify every mumbled word. These staffers transcribed the tapes. Most conversations were in Hebrew, but hours were also spent on translation from English, French, Yiddish and German, and even the Swiss-German dialect spoken in parts of Switzerland. Every spoken word was transcribed. The staffers were a fount of information: They could compare the items discussed on tape number 376 with something similar discussed on anonymous tape number 759. Their work was painstaking: thorough, clandestine, and penetrating.

The information was then transferred to a staff of 10 keyboard operators who manned the computer terminals. The data was prepared for use in four databases: on diskettes; in the central computer's hard disk; in the "unabridged book," a secret file that included all the information, without analysis or editing; and in the "abridged" version, another classified file that comprised only the relevant information, edited and arranged by individual subjects.

All four databases were under the jurisdiction of S., the head of the G.S.S. The "abridged version" was in the hands of M., head of its Psychological Warfare Division.

Gili felt the full force of the shock after Shabbos. Late that night, after the discussion he had had with Rabbi Schneidman, he returned to his room in the Radisson Moriah Plaza.

At one in the morning he realized that he would not be able to sleep without taking a pill. A long night lay ahead of him. He hadn't slept much at his host's home; the anguish of learning of the rebbe's illness and the theft of the chandelier had weighed down his soul on Friday night. *I'm getting addicted to Valium,* he thought anxiously, as he downed the two pills with one gulp.

A deep sleep, heavy as lead, descended upon him as soon as his head hit the overstuffed pillow.

After about an hour the phone rang several times, then a few seconds later it rang again. Every few seconds the caller tried, getting the hotel's answering machine after several rings. Then he would hang up and call yet again. Gili couldn't tell if he was coming down from heaven or up from a deep chasm. His awakening was tortured, difficult as rising from the grave. He just couldn't get up.

The telephone wouldn't stop. It rang yet again.

With tightly shut eyes he groped towards a switch, and turned the light on in the expensive Tiffany-style lamp at his bedside. He picked up the receiver.

"Gili, you've finally woken up." It was Benny Gabison, his voice near hysteria.

"What's happened?" Gili asked heavily. A tornado raged within his brain; dozens of tiny hammers pounded in his temples.

"Are you sitting down, Gili? Hold on to your chair or bed, I have something horrible to tell you."

"I'm lying down. What's happened?" A hacksaw had joined the tiny hammers.

"*Baruch dayan ha'emes.* Eric's been killed."

Gili gave a loud cry. "What? Eric Meisels? When, where, how did it happen?"

"A few hours ago. *Motzaei Shabbos.* He was traveling to visit his daughter in Yokneam. A tractor-trailer swerved from its lane and smashed his Toyota. He was killed instantly. What a tragedy."

"Who was with him?"

"Luckily, he was driving by himself."

Gili asked about the funeral arrangements, and Benny explained that it was still too early to speak of it. The policemen hadn't completed their investigation of the accident, and the family was just being notified.

"How do you know about it?"

"Ami Kedmi told me five minutes ago. The police called him after they found Eric's press card in his pocket. They asked him to go with them to inform the family. What a tragedy! Gili, what's going to be?" Benny sobbed weakly. Gili couldn't even manage one word of comfort. Finally, he hung up, heavy hearted, with mutual wishes for better news.

He put out the light and folded his hands beneath his head, gazing vacantly at the dark ceiling above him, thinking of the accident.

But the ceiling wasn't dark, after all. A small red dot danced across it. *Wonderful, now you're hallucinating.* No, this was no hallucination; it was real. Something was winking from below, and was reflecting on the ceiling. He pushed himself up on his elbows and stared at the telephone.

A round red light blinked from the ivory instrument. A quick glance at the hotel's instruction booklet taught him to press one of the buttons and hear a recorded message.

"Hello, Gili." It was Eric Meisels' voice coming over the phone, a voice that sounded very upset, almost frenzied. "I need you urgently. It's eight-thirty in the evening, and you must have made *havdalah.* Why aren't you in your room? I can't talk to you in the newsroom, they're watching me there. We'll meet tomorrow night at nine at the Shmarkaf Cafe. I've decided to teach you how to play chess, on the white side... I have a lot to tell you. I'm going to open your eyes. We'll talk!"

How was it that he hadn't noticed the blinking light before he had gone to bed? He must have been too tired. Only now did the dimensions of the tragedy begin to sink in. He felt an enormous surge of regret pass through him. *Eric was going to open my eyes and tell me something. He spoke about a chess game. And I didn't want to talk to him since his strange note to me. I thought that he was motivated by personal interests. But maybe he was right. Here, he wanted to reveal a secret, and now he's dead. Was I blind? What have I missed?*

Or perhaps his death wasn't accidental after all? Maybe this innocent accident wasn't all that innocent. Who could have wanted to kill such a good man?

Now you're calling him a good man. Two days ago you accused him of base motives.

What had Eric proposed to reveal? What a terrible missed opportunity! Instead of pressuring Eric to tell all he had known on that day, Gili had allowed him to slip away and afterwards, in anger, had stayed away from him.

It was comfortable in the elegant, air-conditioned room but Gili suddenly felt himself trembling. *Eric was put out of the way because of what he was going to tell me, and the murderer knows exactly what my next step will be. He heard the conversation. He has an advantage over me: I heard the message at three in the morning, while my anonymous foe heard it at eight-thirty, and went to work immediately. He has another advantage, too. He knows who I am. And I don't know who he is...*

Gili, you're next in line.

I need someone to guide me out of this maze.

Tomorrow morning I'm going to Rabbi Schmidt.

24

"We proved from this that the words of the *Rosh* don't contradict the logic of *Tosafos*, although it seems to from its language. The opposite: His words complete theirs."

Five-thirty in the morning. Ten married young men sat in a circle around Rabbi Schmidt in the yeshivah, men striving to understand a Gemara before leaving for a day's work.

Gili stood next to the doorway and listened. His heart yearned to join them, to sit peacefully and delve into the Gemara while his mind was clear and alert after a night's sleep. With no fear of threats on his life, without wrenching memories of his good friend, dead in a car accident — accident? — his shattered body being brought to burial, perhaps today.

Just like Abba...

Rabbi Schmidt stood behind a large *shtender*. For a moment he raised his head from the Gemara, and their eyes met. His face lit up momentarily with an inner glow. He smiled and gestured to Gili as if to say: Wait a bit.

At six exactly the *shiur* came to an end and the listeners dispersed. Rabbi Schmidt rushed towards Gili. "You've come back to us?"

"Soon," Gili said, his face revealing nothing. *If I can stay alive.*

"Gili, something is bothering you."

"That's right. That's why I'm here."

Rabbi Schmidt locked the door. They were alone, seated next to each other.

"I don't drink before *davening,* but if you want a cup of coffee I'll make you one in the kitchen." Rabbi Schmidt was all hospitality and goodwill. Gili refused. His mouth felt dry, but to bother Rabbi Schmidt was unthinkable.

"Okay, what's new?"

Gili told him everything, from the beginning of his relationship with Rav Avram until Eric's accident, and the recorded message that he had listened to only after his friend's death.

Rabbi Schmidt did not take his eyes off his student as he spoke. When Gili had finished the rabbi closed his eyes and thought with intense concentration. A lazy winter sun rose slowly; golden rays made their way through the yeshivah's eastern window, creating a bronze frame around their silhouettes on the opposite wall.

Rabbi Schmidt agonized over what to say, how to say it. The picture that had been painted before him seemed dark with trouble, but who knew better than he, as one who brought others back to observance, how sensitive and crucial was the question of *emunas chachamim,* belief in our leaders.

A *baal teshuvah,* on the beginning of his road back, is like a newborn. He does not yet know what is permitted and what is forbidden, what is urgent and what should be delayed, what is vital and what is less important. In his lack of confidence he grabs hold of rabbis as a spiritual anchor in a sea of doubts. His rebbe, he is certain, is the Moshe Rabbeinu of his generation. If one undermines his vision of his rebbe, his entire spiritual world can collapse like a house of cards. Demolish the image of the rav and you've destroyed his world!

After a few difficult moments of soul-searching, Rabbi Schmidt began to speak, carefully weighing each word. "I have a disagreement with Rabbi Roosenthal. I believe in our circles many feel his *derech* is unusual, to say the least. According to what you've told me, we seem to have a different set of priorities. I believe the end never justifies the means." He smiled behind his beard. "Stealing the sleep of an entire building for years? Judaism doesn't allow such a thing, even if you want to help many others. To bring a man to the edge of madness in order to cure him? A wise man once said, 'The road to *gehinnom* is paved with good intentions.'"

Chaos. The earth has split; the sky has fallen in, Gili. Rabbi Schmidt hasn't attacked Rav Avram, and yet you are drowning. Look how simply he's spoken, his words so clear. Strong as rocks. Rav Avram's way is so much more clever, so much more intelligent...

But where does it lead?

"Let me suggest something to you," Gili said, his voice trembling. Outside there was a great bustle: The yeshivah was preparing for *Shacharis*. Gili knew how careful Rabbi Schmidt was with his time. He made use of every minute, all 60 seconds of it. Gili was aware of how much effort Rabbi Schmidt was putting in to listen patiently and pleasantly to him, to give him the impression that he, Rabbi Schmidt, had all the time in the world.

"I'm open to all suggestions," Rabbi Schmidt said affably.

"I'm certain that Rabbi Avram Roosenthal is a great man, but perhaps he is making a mistake. He's a great man, but perhaps he needs someone outside, someone who can open his eyes and set him on the right way. Someone to explain to him what you've just told me now."

"What are you trying to say?"

"I'm asking, pleading," (*amazing how much the voice can tremble; I've turned into a quivering old man...*) "that Rabbi Schmidt come to meet Rabbi Roosenthal."

"What? What do I have to do there? My way is not his."

"I'm begging you, Rabbi Schmidt." Gili touched Rav Schmidt's fingers. His green eyes gazed beseechingly at the wise eyes, eyes touched with goodness, that stared back at him.

It worked. Rabbi Schmidt's heart melted. "When do you want to go to him?"

"Whenever the Rav can."

Rabbi Schmidt skimmed through his crowded appointment calendar. "I have a *shiur* in yeshivah this morning, a lecture this afternoon. We'll see what happens tomorrow."

"There's no need," Gili interrupted. "Rabbi Roosenthal only sees people late at night. I can arrange an appointment for us at two this morning."

Rabbi Schmidt was shocked. For the first time, he understood what Gili had been talking about. "When does he see people, this Rav Avram?"

"Up until five in the morning."

"He's been destroying the residents' nights, night after night!" His palms lightly slapped his cheeks, ran through his graying beard. "I'm sorry, I don't have many hours to sleep. If I give up my small ration, how will I give a *shiur* at five tomorrow morning?"

Gili would not relent. He grabbed the rabbi's hand. "Just this once, for my sake. Can't you do it?"

"Okay, tonight. What time?"

"Midnight."

⟩⟩⟩⟨⟨⟨

It was a difficult and dreary Sunday in the *HaYom HaZeh* newsroom. The dreadful news of Eric Meisels' tragic death cast a pall over the stunned staff members, the journalists, photographers, printers, and Eric's other friends. The driver of the truck, according to police, was a drunken minor; this was not his first conviction.

Just another auto accident?

Late that evening, after the melancholy funeral, Gili drove to Jerusalem to pick up Rabbi Schmidt and bring him to Rav Avram's "clinic." Rabbi Schmidt tried fruitlessly to nap on the way. Finally he gave up and told Gili that as long as he was traveling to Petach Tikvah, he had decided to consult Rav Avram over a complex family matter. "After all," he gave an embarrassed chuckle, "since you say he is such a wise man, maybe he can help me."

Gili would never forget that night. Never.

When they arrived Rabbi Schmidt was astonished at the bustle going on in the building at one-thirty in the morning. "I've never seen such a thing," he said. "Perhaps I was mistaken in my harsh judgment. Throngs of people, from all backgrounds, make such an effort to be here at an inconvenient time. It seems we're not talking about just another 'miracle-worker.' They say that people have an instinct; if hordes come here, there is something to be found."

They sat on a wooden bench among the crowd. Gili went to try and use his influence: Let Rabbi Schmidt see how powerful he was here. He went down to the sixth floor and gave the pre-arranged knock on the door. Muli opened it, and Gili whispered to him, "Tell Zabik I've brought an atom bomb with me tonight — one of the greatest of Jerusalem's *roshei yeshivah*. A respected, well-known man wants to come to Rav Avram for advice. Try to see to it that he doesn't have to wait."

"I'm not impressed by *roshei yeshivah*," Muli said nonchalantly. "They can wait with everybody else."

Anger surged through him. "Call Zabik immediately," he barked wrathfully. Muli insulting Rabbi Schmidt!

Muli got nervous. "Wait a minute," he said, and he left for the seventh floor. Zabik, the head *gabbai*, quickly materialized before him. "I hear you're angry," he said.

"Yes, I am. I brought a most respected visitor, a Torah great, a famous *rosh yeshivah* from Jerusalem who wants to consult with Rav Avram. At five in the morning he's giving a *shiur*. Can you make sure he doesn't have to wait more than 10 minutes?"

Zabik was the embodiment of goodwill. "Why are you upset? You've brought a guest; he'll get all the respect due him. I just brought a couple on the verge of divorce into the rabbi. It's a tough case — both spouses had been married and divorced previously, and now they're looking to 'return to their roots' and divorce each other! When they come out, in a short while, happy and content, your rabbi can go in. By the way, I'm a bit surprised: I thought Rav Avram was enough for you; I didn't realize that you also shared him with Rabbi... what is his name?"

"Rabbi Schmidt," Gili turned scarlet. "I knew him before I met Rav Avram."

"Oh, I'm just joking." Zabik smacked a bony, powerful hand on Gili's shoulder. The tense journalist almost snapped in two. "Everything will be fine. Mr. and Mrs. Break-Up will leave and Rabbi... what was his name?"

"Rabbi Schmidt."

"That's right, Rabbi...Schmidt will go in. The two of you wait for me on the seventh floor. When Mr. and Mrs. Divorce leave our rabbi, Rabbi Schmidt will go in."

Zabik's tone was less than respectful, and his sudden attack of forgetfulness when it came to Rabbi Schmidt's name seemed to have been done consciously.

As Gili walked up to the seventh floor he was flooded with mixed emotions. He was angry and upset with a boorish *gabbai* who thought he ruled the world; he hoped desperately that when his two teachers met they would find common ground and all their differences would be ironed out quickly.

Rabbi Schmidt sat hunched over a small Gemara. He struck an alien note in this jumble of humanity swarming all around him, a tiny dot of spirituality. Just on this night, when Gili hoped to flaunt before his first teacher the elite men and women who came to stand before Rav Avram, the crowd seemed much more of a rabble than ever before. *Rabbi Schmidt seems like a rose among thorns,* Gili thought, his mind going to the verse in *Shir HaShirim.* If he could, he would have bypassed this demonstrative crowd altogether and brought Rabbi Schmidt into Rav Avram's room this very minute. No matter: In just a few minutes it would happen, and with official sanction.

After half an hour doubts began to steal into his heart. A robust young man left the apartment quickly, passing the elevator and walking towards the steps. A few steps behind him came a young woman, her eyes reddened. Zabik walked out, an appointment calendar in his hand. His eyes scanned over the anxiously awaiting crowd. He waved a finger at a balding, chubby man whose gray coat hung negligently over his shoulders. "Mr. Mikuver, please."

Gili shuddered as if he had been whipped. He wanted to get up and scream, "I'm next. You promised!" but the presence of Rabbi Schmidt restrained him. How he wished he could take Rav Avram's place as a mind reader, and know exactly what Rabbi Schmidt was thinking. *Is that all you can do? Where is your much-vaunted influence, your wonderful close relationship to the kabbalist, the great psychologist...*

What a humiliation. For the first time he understood the cliche "between a rock and a hard place." Powerful emotions pulled him between two men whom he loved and respected. Each of the two personalities had influenced his way of life in differing ways. When you're torn between your rabbi, who refuses to meet your other rabbi, you get a taste of death's bitterness. If only he could have dug himself a hole and hidden there until the horror had passed. What an embarrassment.

The quiet drama that went on in that room that night did not end with the exit of Mr. Mikuver. Then came the turn of a respected matron. The hostility of her unblinking face quickly put an end to any thought of attempting to take her turn in line. After half an hour two well-dressed yeshivah students entered.

Zabik motioned to Gili to join him near the elevator. "Listen," he said in a low voice, his face looking somewhat embarrassed, "While that wonderful couple, Mr. Problem and his wife, Mrs. Worries, were inside, I told Rav Avram that you had come with Rabbi Schmidt from Jerusalem. He seemed surprised and asked me twice what our respected guest's name was and why he'd come. 'He'll come in right away,' he told me solemnly. 'Right now I'm working on a matter of life and death. After this couple they can come in immediately.' But after the Quarrelsomes left it was poor Mr. Mikuver's turn. Don't be jealous of him; he's got more troubles than you have hairs on your head. And after that came that elderly woman. What was with her? Oh, that's right, she claimed she has a serious problem. And when she left I reminded him that Rabbi Schmidt was waiting. 'Yes, I know,' he answered, 'but two students who are left without a yeshivah for the winter term can't wait any longer.' If you want to stay, I'll keep reminding him every 15 minutes."

"Thank you very much," Gili answered frostily, "you're a real comedian, aren't you? Do you know anything except stupid jokes about divorcing couples?"

Zabik looked offended. "You haven't a shred of humor! I told you, I'm doing my best. You want some friendly advice, free? Take your rabbi and go right back to Jerusalem."

Gili was taken aback. "Why?"

"I have a feeling that Rav Avram isn't interested in seeing him," Zabik answered, abruptly turning away.

Not interested in seeing him. Nonsense, he doesn't even know Rabbi Schmidt...

The hour hand on the small clock in the room remorselessly approached the number 4. Gili lost the last vestige of patience. "I'll be right back," he whispered to Rabbi Schmidt. He went down to the sixth floor and again knocked in the secret code.

Muli, surprised, could not stop the furious journalist as he strode into the house. "What are you doing?" he protested weakly, but Gili did not give him a backward glance. He jumped over a banister and took the steps three at a time.

When he got to the upper level he looked around him. Choni was sitting and reading by a dim orange light in the anteroom near the Rabbi's office. "Choni, where's Zabik?" he demanded.

Choni did not lift his eyes from the book. "I'm on duty now. Zabik's taking a short nap."

Excellent. Zabik could not stop him. He listened intently to what was going on behind the closed door. One of the students was speaking quietly.

He knocked on the door and, without waiting for a reply, opened it and walked in.

The room was in semidarkness, as usual. The fluorescent lamp gave off a tiny circle of white light onto the table. But six startled eyes could see Gili, even in the dimness.

There was a short, shocked pause. Rav Avram swiftly got control of his emotions. "Gili, did you get permission to enter?" he asked, his voice restrained.

Gili chose not to answer directly. He walked over to Rav Avram and whispered harshly into his ear, "Tell them to leave."

Rav Avram acquiesced before Gili's overwhelming fury. "Would you mind waiting outside for a few minutes?"

The students stood up, their reluctance obvious, and left. When the door closed Gili collapsed on the chair and burst out crying. "Why are you doing this to me?"

"What are you talking about?" Rav Avram seemed honestly perplexed.

"I brought one of the great rabbis here, an outstanding genius, the head of a respected yeshivah. I was promised we wouldn't have to wait more than 10 minutes. His Torah has been humiliated now for three hours, as we waited together with all the porters and watermelon salesmen. I don't know where to hide, I'm so embarrassed."

Rav Avram plucked a hair from his thinning beard. "You're oversensitive. What's the rush? There were urgent cases here that couldn't be put off."

"And how do you know that Rabbi Schmidt's affair could be put off?" Gili retorted. "Have you spoken to him already?"

Rav Avram grew angry. "Gili, enough! I like your honest and direct approach, but I won't tolerate interference in my concerns!"

Gili softened and retreated. "I'm begging you. Rabbi Schmidt has to return to yeshivah. In another hour he has to give a daily Gemara *shiur.*"

Rav Avram wouldn't make a promise. "These boys are waiting for me since last week. The minute I finish with them I'll receive Rabbi Schmidt. Now please leave and wait in the lobby."

He walked Gili to the door and again called in the students. Gili leaned against a small sink near the bathroom and breathed deeply. Zabik was right: Rav Avram was not interested in meeting with Rabbi Schmidt. He could see clearly how Rav Avram had looked for an excuse which he found in the form of two boring students.

Zabik surprised him from behind. His hard hands violently grabbed Gili's shoulders. "How dare you enter without my permission?" he panted in fury, pulling at him wildly.

Gili reacted as he had been taught in his antiterrorist training: His foot kicked backwards, landing in Zabik's stomach. Without hesitation he pivoted around and landed a strong right to his foe's chin. Zabik, shocked, flew backwards. Gili, freed from his viselike grip, grabbed Zabik's hands with all his might and slammed them together. "If you dare attack me again, this will be your last day in this house," he hissed between clenched teeth.

Zabik landed on the floor, breathing heavily. "You're a wild man! Rav Avram won't tolerate this."

"Look who's talking," Choni emerged from the shadows and approached the two opponents. "One word to Rav Avram, and I'll tell him the truth," he threatened the *gabbai.*

The boy approached Gili and looked at him admiringly. "Teach me that. A backwards kick, a turn, a fist right in the face. Beautiful and clean."

Gili put an affectionate hand on the shoulder of his new fan. "Choni, I learned those moves in the army, before I became religious. And I can tell you, as one who has experience, that there's nothing to look for on that side. It's a pity, every day that you're not in yeshivah. Better to learn how to 'take on' a tough Gemara and 'conquer' a confusing *Tosafos*."

The boy's eyes grew round. "You mean to tell me that street life isn't a lot more fun?"

"No! With a capital 'N'! I've had everything you dream about: night-clubs, discos, sports, entertainment. Listen to me, the spiritual pleasure of understanding a difficult concept in Gemara is a million times greater."

"That's interesting," Choni said. "Good night. That is, it's already good morning. See you, Gili."

From the floor Zabik's blazing eyes followed the two parting at the door.

It was Rabbi Schmidt who didn't stop comforting Gili all the way to Jerusalem. Gili, broken and depressed, could find nothing to placate his tormented soul. The double humiliation was not to be borne: the humiliation to Rabbi Schmidt's Torah learning, and his own personal shame. They had whipped him, they had cast him adrift: They had promised Rabbi Schmidt would enter immediately, and ultimately kept him outside.

Gili had wanted to leave the waiting area as soon as he had returned there, but Rabbi Schmidt wanted to test the promise of this "wonder worker." The two students in search of a yeshivah left after about 20 minutes. Zabik then crept in slowly, averted his eyes from Gili and Rabbi Schmidt, and announced to the nearly 50 people still waiting, "The rabbi doesn't feel well; he can't see anyone else tonight." Words of disappointment and protest followed his figure as it vanished inside.

"I've heard of such things happening," Rabbi Schmidt murmured, his eyes half-shut and his body swaying to the rhythm of the speeding car. He had not slept a moment this night, and would be late for his early morning class. "If he says he doesn't feel well, he must have become too tired to see anyone else."

"Why did he do this to me?" Gili whispered in a broken voice. He was finding it hard keeping the steering wheel straight between his trembling hands.

"Who?"

"Rav Avram."

"Ah, Rav Avram." Rabbi Schmidt's face fell upon his chest, as he drowsed lightly.

Gili felt that he had lost points in front of Rabbi Schmidt. He had certainly lost them to Zabik the *gabbai*. And something told him that Rav Avram had lost a few points of his own.

25

It seemed that Rav Avram was right: A man *could* live without sleep.

Gili arrived in the newsroom on Monday morning on the verge of collapse. He tallied up the sleep of the past few nights. Thursday night, in the hotel: two hours. Friday night in Kiltz: three and a half. *Motzaei Shabbos*, at the hotel once again: before and after the tragic news of Eric Meisels, another two hours. Sunday night: the frustrating visit to Rav Avram's with Rabbi Schmidt. Sleeping time: zero.

It's a wonder that I'm not seeing spots before my eyes!

The *HaYom HaZeh* building was in a ferment. Everyone was talking about the late Eric Meisels and his newly appointed replacement, Tzvika Bloom. Ami had chosen Tzvika, the paper's veteran reporter of national affairs, as his assistant, relying on his tenure and extensive experience.

Gili hadn't dreamed for a moment that he was in line for the job; the sensitive and complex position of editor was not in the realm of a young journalist, no matter how talented. With all that, he felt a slight pang of jealousy. No other reporter on *HaYom HaZeh* had ever won the Golden Pen. Despite that, he had not even been considered for the post.

"Gili, you look out of it," Benny declared when he walked into their shared office. "Your eyes are all black and swollen."

"I'm putting our rabbi and teacher's philosophy into practice," Gili answered bitterly. "According to Rav Avram, this is how a person is supposed to look."

"I hadn't heard that he recommended getting punched in the eye," Benny said.

Gili was annoyed. "What punches? Can't you see that I'm dying of fatigue?"

"So go to sleep," Benny suggested. "No one will notice. Everyone's talking about Eric Meisels and his 'heir,' Tzvika Bloom. I'll do your write-up for tomorrow's paper. What was your assignment?"

A board with his work schedule hung on the wall. Eric had posted the latest assignment two days before his death. Benny skimmed the paper. "You were supposed to cover the problem of foreign workers in Bnei Brak tomorrow. I'll focus on describing the hardship endured by the residents of the neighborhood, and the negative consequences of the proximity of the workers to the children. Another few days and there will no longer be such stories: Unlike his predecessor, our new assistant editor, Tzvika, is antireligious."

Gili nodded wearily in assent. "Got you. Thanks, Benny. I'm going home."

His eyelids drifted downwards. On the unsteady legs of a drunk he made his way down the hallway. From the office of Tzvika Bloom came the sound of celebration, as the paper's journalists came together noisily. Eric Meisels' office was silent and deserted, with the door open just a crack.

Sleep? He could catch up on sleep later. Cold sober now, his fatigue-induced stupor completely gone, Gili felt compelled almost against his will to rummage through Eric's office. Perhaps he would find something among the drawers, some key to the mystery. What had Eric wanted to reveal to him? What terrible secret had he paid for with his life?

Gili tiptoed in. The desk drawers were locked but the key was in its usual place in the ashtray. That was one little secret he had known for a long time. With trembling fingers he burrowed into the top drawer, where the important documents were kept. He kept an ear cocked towards Tzvika's office. If the noise there would die down, he would leave immediately.

He recognized the well-known logo of the mammoth American newspaper, *The New York Times*, printed on an envelope that bore American stamps and a United States postmark. The envelope had been opened; with his heart thumping he pulled out the sheet of paper inside.

Gili had mastered both English and French, thanks to his father, who had urged him to study the two languages in school until he was fluent. From among the closely printed letters two words stood out: Gili Dinar.

Gili swiftly read through the letter.

The editor-in-chief of *The New York Times* had turned to Eric Meisels with the request that Gili Dinar be transferred to his paper. He wanted Dinar, who had written a colorful, exuberant, and poignant account of the various Orthodox groups in Israel. "Our newspaper is developing a series of reports on Orthodox factions in America, and we would like to take on Gili Dinar, winner of the Golden Pen, as a *Times* staffer."

The letter was dated about the time that he had completed the series for *HaYom HaZeh.*

Gili suspected that his invitation to join the prestigious American paper was backed by one of the newspaper's owners, the millionaire Josh Hamilton, a well-known tycoon who was associated with the Republican party, which desperately needed the Jewish vote in order to win the presidency. What could be simpler than to appoint a religious Jew to the staff?

Eric had known what he was talking about when he suggested that Gili travel to America and try for the Pulitzer.

Gili put the letter back from where he had taken it. Ami Kedmi certainly knew about it; there was no reason to hide it from him. He locked the desk and slipped out of the room.

Benny Gabison surprised him in the hallway. "Still here? I thought you'd gone already."

Gili hesitated. He didn't want to arouse his friend's suspicions. "I'm on my way to bed," he said honestly.

Benny followed him until his Mitsubishi had disappeared from view.

While he was driving home he tried to organize his thoughts. *Who are you, Gili Dinar?* he asked himself. *An ethical person, fanatically straight, and*

yet, at the same time, burning with ambition, desiring with all your might to reach the pinnacle of success. They appointed me as reporter for religious affairs. I did a top-notch series that aroused jealousy. I touched the chassidim of Kiltz? They've been destroyed. I rubbed shoulders with Yeshivas Torah Lishmah? Everything there is ruined.

And that's only one example. Those were my masterpieces, the first in the series. Afterwards I wrote about most of the chassidic courts in Israel, examined many of the large yeshivos.

If Kiltz and Torah Lishmah are any indication, I'll soon be getting some very unsympathetic calls from every religious group. Who knows what destruction I've sown? The stones are going to fall on me from every direction! An unknown person has threatened my life two, three times; Eric Meisels was left in pieces on the Haifa-Yokneam road a day before he was to open his mouth to tell me something. The administrators of the religious institutions all want my head. What do I have left here in Israel?

And so it was decided: *I'm running away to America. I'll become the religious affairs journalist for The New York Times. They'll appreciate me there. I'm a shoo-in for the Pulitzer.*

But he needed Torah, he needed a *chavrusa,* an outstanding American scholar who could learn with him three, four hours every day.

Rav Avram had told him he had learned in the States. Good; surely he would not refuse to give Gili a recommendation to his former *rosh yeshivah* there, asking to admit him as a part-time student and to arrange a top study partner for him.

⊙⋛⋚⊙

Monica was at work when Gili returned home. It was eleven in the morning. Would Rav Avram speak to him now? It was possible.

He punched the numbers on the phone lightly. His heart pounded. What would he say if Zabik answered the phone? How many hours had elapsed since their scuffle?

"Hello?" It was Choni's voice. Gili was relieved. "Choni, please call Rav Avram to the phone."

The rabbi came on immediately. "Good morning, Gili. Are you angry with me?" His voice sounded a little nervous.

"The truth is, you humiliated me last night in front of Rabbi Schmidt." (*And I know why you refused to see him. You were afraid that he would rebuke you for your unconventional ways and zigzag methods. You can criticize the entire world, but if you think someone will have something negative to say to you, you'll find a thousand and one reasons not to meet with him.*

"You feel sorry for Rabbi Schmidt, but not for me?" Rav Avram complained. "I explained to you how things had gotten confused last night. Bring him tonight and we'll receive him with great honor."

"No, thanks. Rabbi Schmidt isn't a ping-pong ball."

"As you wish." Was that a sigh of relief that Gili heard, or was it just his imagination?

"I didn't call about that. I have a question."

Rav Avram sounded interested. "Go ahead."

Gili told him everything: about Kiltz, and Torah Lishmah, the wall of fury that was blocking his every step. He told him of the threats, the fears, *The New York Times*, the Pulitzer, attending yeshivah in America.

Rav Avram listened to the lengthy monologue without interjecting a single comment of his own. He stayed silent for five long minutes, even after Gili had finished and awaited his farewell blessing. The passport was in order in his drawer. A visa for the U.S., an airline ticket, a farewell to Ima and on to New York...

Rav Avram broke the silence, pouring cold water on Gili's feverish dreams.

Gili was shocked to hear Rav Avram's fiery objections to his American scheme. America was wonderful, *The New York Times* was Mount Olympus, the Pulitzer was prestigious and shiny, but everything paled in comparison with Gili's mission to Israeli journalism!

"Do you understand, Gili?" Rav Avram declared fervently. "Gili Dinar is a symbol! You've become the ethical guidepost for Israeli journalism. You're showing it a new way: pristine journalism, without slander or bloodsucking. This is worth everything else, and certainly balances out this childish pursuit of prizes and honor."

"And the anger, the threats coming in from all sides?"

Rav Avram spoke bluntly. "You're a coward, running away from battle. It's tough for you here, so you flee to the United States. It won't all be roses at *The New York Times,* I can promise you that. The journalistic jungle of America is many times more brutal than that of Israel. Where are you going to run to then? And this yeshivah is not geared for *baalei teshuvah.* You won't find your place there. And how will you leave your widowed mother by herself?"

Gili objected strenuously. "There's no place left for me here. I'm threatened from all sides. Zimel Mirinski and Yehoshua Schneidman are furious with me, and they're probably not the only ones. I haven't yet heard what they're saying about me in Gur and Viznitz, in Mir and Ponovezh. Who knows what trouble I've left behind?"

"Stop feeling so sorry for yourself," Rav Avram shouted. "Are you a baby? Some anonymous coward is sending you faxes and you run for shelter. Go out and fight! Next time you get a threatening fax, find out from where it was sent. You can check with the phone company for the information. Instead of cowering and apologizing tell this Kimel and Schneidmaster that they're ungrateful. You wrote a glowing report on them and they attack you. You destroyed Kiltz and Torah Lishmah? They were destroyed without you. These events were decreed in Heaven, measure for measure. What holiness is there in an entire congregation that stands and laughs at some unfortunate, what did you say his name was?"

"Fishele Mamaliga," Gili repeated the strange nickname.

"That's right, the unfortunate Fishele. If you bring him here to me, I'll try to cure him. But to stand and be amused, to laugh at mental illness? Cruelty! And though the staff at Torah Lishmah meant well, was it right to let a young boy sever every tie to his family, no matter how difficult his home situation? Why didn't they try to bring *shalom bayis* to the Limor family? And why do they blame you, who was so careful not to print a hint of their little secret?"

There was something in that! He felt the blood begin pulsing anew in his veins. Rav Avram, it seemed, was right: What did Zimel and Schneidman have against him? What had he done to them, after all?

"I'll think about it," Gili promised, ending the conversation. Rav Avram's words had persuaded him.

But not entirely.

What had happened to the chandelier in Kiltz? A routine burglary? Just as Eric's death was a routine accident? And what of the theft of the neighbors' sleep? *And, above all, why should he care if I go to the United States for a few years, returning laden with honors? From there my road would be clear to open my own, independent newspaper, and to take all the papers of Israel by storm!*

Understanding dawned suddenly. *Rav Avram thinks I've got the brains of a sparrow, if he thinks I bought his explanation. No, there are too many holes in the story. Only his objection about Ima, about Monica — Rachel — was strong and valid.*

I know a man, a man possessing a logical mind and unclouded vision, a man without any vested interests. That man is Rabbi Schmidt — and I am returning to him. This time everything will be clear.

Crystal clear.

He could sleep later, Gili assured himself, as he passed by the Castel Ridge, his eyes occasionally shutting. The sun's rays blinded him painfully, but at the same time they helped him concentrate on his driving. He knew he should not be driving in this state; if he fell asleep at the wheel it would be the end.

With a supreme effort he reached Jerusalem. Luckily, he got caught in a tremendous traffic jam at the entrance to the city, near the Sakharov Gardens' exit, a jam that allowed him to catch a refreshing 15-minute nap.

The shrill sound of impatient honking blasted him into wakefulness. The traffic jam had eased and drivers behind him could not understand what was holding up the white Mitsubishi, until they noticed Gili's head drooping towards the steering wheel. They saw it, and they honked.

He reached the yeshivah at lunchtime. Rabbi Schmidt was eating alone at his desk. "I'm a bit tired," he apologized, with a faint smile.

"Too bad you weren't stuck in the traffic jam with me," Gili laughed. "Strange how refreshed you can feel after a few minutes of sleep. Rav Avram is right, at least in that: You don't need to sleep a lot..."

An interested smile split Rabbi Schmidt's face. "I see he's really grabbed hold of you, this rabbi of yours. Only I had no luck with him. Now tell me a bit more."

Gili told him everything, from his first introduction after Benny Gabison's words to the last conversation, two hours earlier, the one that had spurred him on to making a thorough examination of the entire topic.

Rabbi Schmidt's clear blue eyes gazed fixedly upon him throughout. Occasionally they would fog up, as if sleep were overtaking them. At the end of the story Rabbi Schmidt gave an enormous yawn covered by his hand. "I have something to tell you, but first — a little sleep."

They went to nap in one of the lecturer's offices. Despite his fatigue, Rabbi Schmidt found it hard to doze off. Memories of times past flew through his head, keeping him wide awake: anecdotes, a story here, an incident there. Slowly the memories made their way up from the abyss of forgetfulness, flowing through his mind, first in a thin stream, then in a mighty, unstoppable river.

"Gili, are you asleep?" he whispered.

"No. I'm thinking."

"That's exactly what I'm doing," Rabbi Schmidt chuckled. "Sleep is one of the things that can only come about subconsciously. The more you want to sleep, the more it eludes you. In the meantime, I've been remembering my days as a youngster in yeshivah."

It was noontime, but the skies were dark. A wintry wind pushed dark, rain-soaked clouds through the sky. A long streak of lightning illuminated the room for a second with a huge explosion of white light. It was followed by a powerful roll of thunder. Drops of heavy rain danced gracefully along the window, washing away the summer's dust.

The two jumped up and recited the proper blessings.

"We can always sleep later," Gili comforted Rabbi Schmidt with a smile. Steaming cups of tea emitted transparent clouds of vapor. Rabbi Schmidt gazed vacantly at the dissipating mist.

"What yeshivah did you learn in?" Gili broke his reverie.

"Yeshivas Ein Yisrael."

Gili stared at him. "What, you learned in Ein Yisrael?"

"That's right," Rabbi Schmidt murmured. Gili seemed excited about something; what was so interesting about this?

"What years?"

Rabbi Schmidt tapped his forehead. "Give me a minute to remember. That's right, I entered Ein Yisrael in Elul 5718 and learned there for seven years, until I married."

Gili decided to conceal his involvement. "Why are you thinking about your youth?"

Rabbi Schmidt grinned again. "My *baalei teshuvah* brought with them a slang expression that contains a good deal of truth. 'Suckers never die; they just get replaced.' And I say: 'Charlatans never die; they just get replaced.' "

Gili gazed at him through narrowed eyes. "Meaning?"

Rabbi Schmidt gave a confused laugh. "Don't be insulted by the comparison, but our history is full of such swindlers. The same beliefs, identical actions. Rav Avram Roosenthal is, in my mind, the reincarnation of dozens of such 'rabbis' in the past. Your story, for example, reminded me of an old friend, one of the students at Ein Yisrael, a schemer from Belgium by the name of Menachem Schwartz. We called him Manny. Oh boy, there was never anyone as sly. He had a powerful personality, and managed to dominate people. He had sharp psychological instincts and a unique talent to identify a person's weaknesses, and he used his rare powers to dominate others. I was his *chavrusa* for two years. He didn't manage to exercise his power over me, but he made a test case of Moishike Dinburg, who was sensitive and softhearted, and he controlled him like an expert jockey does his horse."

Rabbi Schmidt, lost in his memories, didn't notice Gili's face, empty of all expression, grow pale. His eyes seemed lacerated with bitter suffering. "Manny Schwartz came to us from Antwerp. I'll never forget him. He was a true manipulator, involved in everything, his hand everywhere, pulling strings, but with incredible astuteness he managed to stay hidden behind the curtain. The *mashgiach*, Rabbi Bergman, *shlita*, used to call him the *koch lefel*, the one who stirred the pot. I thought about Manny because of what you told me happened in Kiltz and Torah Lishmah. Manny did the same thing, on a small scale, in Ein Yisrael: He would use his talents to make trouble between friends, not out of nastiness but so that each of the quarreling schoolmates would prefer him, Manny, over the other. Manny also liked to do favors to one person by putting down another. He had a perverse set of priorities. He never asked another for advice, though one of the great men of the generation was sitting on a bench 10 feet from him, the pious *mashgiach*, student of Rabbi Yerucham Levovitz of Mir, my rav and teacher, Rabbi Shmuel Bergman, *shlita*, who is considered one of the last great men of the *mussar* movement."

Rabbi Schmidt downed the now-cold tea in two gulps, and said *borei nefashos*. He was on another, distant planet, far away from Gili, who stared at him open mouthed, his face bathed in cold sweat. Despite the frigid air, his shirt was drenched with perspiration. "Manny was always right, and loved to prove it in a thousand ways. Woe to him who criticized Manny. I remember how he 'took care' of getting a *chavrusa* for Moshe Shiffer. He destroyed an existing partnership, pulling Yaakov Tzovri from Yoske Friedman with some clever tactic, thus leaving Yoske without a *chavrusa* for an entire term! But the main thing — Moshe Shiffer got his *chavrusa*. His goal justified all the means, thought it left a trail of corpses behind him."

"And Moishike Dinburg?" Gili asked weakly, his voice sounding like the croaking of a frog. An old, hoarse frog. Thousands of tiny explosions were taking place within his brain, preparing for the great blast, the next blackout.

"Moishike was pathetic, a boy with a weak personality, spoiled and sensitive. He came to us from the Batei Ungarin neighborhood in Jerusalem and couldn't find his place in the strict Lithuanian yeshivah. Manny dominated him completely; Moishike felt blessed in his friendship, though at first he was uncomfortable with his domineering personality and tried to tear himself away from beneath his sway. Even the *mashgiach*, that most expert of pedagogues, couldn't manage to break the bond between them. To the outsider it seemed that there was no greater friendship than that of Manny Schwartz and Moishike Dinburg. Only an eagle eye could see that Moishike was completely defeated. Later, the two joined the army and left their religious observance behind. From then on I've never heard of either of them, neither Manny nor Moishike. I would love to meet them."

Gili began to slide down in his chair. On the brink of unconsciousness he thought, I'll say nothing, for now. Rabbi Schmidt doesn't have a clue that I am the son of Moishike Dinburg, and he hasn't the faintest idea of the bitter fate of Abba and Manny Schwartz, dead in an accident — because of me.

Rabbi Schmidt's expression was dreamlike; he concentrated on his own inner vision, and saw nothing of what was going on around him.

Gili was already on the floor, a foot away from him, and he continued to speak. "I see many points of comparison between Manny Schwartz's tactics, and the actions of the 'baba' Saadiah Bozgolo, whom hundreds of men and women wait to see, here in the Beit Yisrael neighborhood. In my opinion Bozgolo is a con artist. To my great sorrow — I know this will hurt you, but it is my opinion — your Rav Avram Roosenthal, too, seems to me to share the same characteristic. Manny Schwartz, the 'baba Bozgolo,' and Rav Avram Roosenthal are three branches nurtured from the same rotten root. That's what I said to you, the charlatans are just replaced. If you look through Jewish history, you'll find hundreds of personalities like these in every generation... Hey, what's happened?"

Gili lay on the linoleum, unconscious. Rabbi Schmidt had not witnessed the phenomenon of these "blackouts," and he quickly called for help. One of the students, a former army paramedic, put Gili's head back and lifted his legs up, to help the blood flow to his brain. A second student bathed his temples with cold water.

Slowly Gili swam back to consciousness, his eyes blinking and his entire body trembling. He strongly objected to sending for a doctor, and recovered with the help of four cups of mineral water.

"Are you all right?" Rabbi Schmidt asked worriedly before he left. "Maybe we should take you to the emergency room?"

Gili refused. "There's no need. Unfortunately, I'm used to these incidents."

Rabbi Schmidt was perplexed. "You have epilepsy?"

"No, This is a 'blackout,' a kind of hole, a short circuit in the brain. Not actual unconsciousness, but a lightning swift loss of consciousness, lasting just a few seconds. I've suffered from these blackouts since I was in a car accident and sustained a head wound." He wouldn't reveal his secret, the reason for this particular blackout. But he was convinced: The puzzle pieces were falling into place. The picture was growing clearer.

Rabbi Schmidt nodded in comprehension. "I'm sorry to hear about it. May it be His will that you are cured soon."

"Amen," Gili answered fervently.

As he returned to Tel Aviv, Gili plotted his next step. During the *shivah* for his father he'd rummaged through the room used for storage, and had found closely written diaries penned by his father in the past. The hurt of the loss was so fresh then that merely looking at his father's handwriting was enough to provoke unbearable feelings of guilt within him. Two years before he had chanced upon them once again, but they had seemed to be nothing more than old diaries, irrelevant and uninteresting.

Now his curiosity was aroused. Perhaps he could find, among these traces of the past, a document or fact that would shed light on the blackness and help him formulate his future plans.

Rabbi Schmidt had, unknowingly, opened a door open before him. Up until this day he knew only of a triangle: Moshe Dinburg, Manny Schwartz, Yoske Friedman.

Now the triangle had become a square. The fourth corner was Chaim Ozer Schmidt. He, too, had been in that class in Ein Yisrael, though he had no knowledge of the fate that had befallen Manny Schwartz and Moishike Dinburg.

Gili would wipe the dust off those old diaries. Interesting to see if Abba would mention Rabbi Schmidt. And, particularly, what he would have to say about Manny Schwartz.

26

afael and Shulamit Brent were the parents of three lovely daughters. Rafael longed for a son. Oh, how he wanted a son! He prayed constantly for one, prayers said with a fervent, burning longing.

Years later, Rafael was to hear a talk by a well-known lecturer, who declared that a person should not make specific demands of Heaven, for how could he tell if his request would be for his own good? Better for a person to simply pray that G-d do what is right in His eyes, and allow the Creator to work things out from His infinite perspective.

Hundreds of men sat in the large auditorium listening to the speech, among them one whose eyes blazed with a strange light. Rafael Brent sobbed unashamedly, weeping aloud, drawing the gaze of the others upon him. "Woe is me," he cried, "if I would have known, I wouldn't have prayed for a son."

But he didn't know it at the time, not when, after his three daughters, he merited a special gift: twin girls.

He felt himself ill used, and began praying for a son three times a day.

The tragedy came suddenly. Shulamit, the wife of his youth, awoke that morning ashen faced, asking for a cup of water. When Rafael returned with the drink, Shulamit was lying inert on the floor. A fully equipped ambulance arrived almost immediately, but there was nothing for the doctor to do but sign the death certificate.

For two years Rafael struggled to raise his five daughters by himself. But he knew that he couldn't go on like this. He needed someone who could help carry his heavy burden.

When he married Dina, a young widow, Rafael felt as though a heavy stone had fallen from his heart. After a little more than a year, on the night of the *seder* in 5739 (1979), an infant with a wrinkled face and red cheeks made his appearance, coming into the world not with a cry, but with a cough. There was no one happier than his father, Rafael. The newborn was given the name Pesach, in honor of the holiday, but his sisters quickly changed it to Paysi.

And the troubles began...

The new mother, who had never had children of her own before, would feel a salty tang when she would kiss her little Paysi. She assumed it was a baby's normal smell. The infant continued to exude a salty perspiration, to eat a lot but not gain weight, but no one could explain the phenomenon. When he was one month old they realized that the child was wheezing desperately. They rushed him to the emergency room, where they told the attending physician that the child was always hungry and gave off a salty perspiration.

The doctor froze. "Nurse," he interrupted the mother, "take a sweat sample, urgent, for testing."

The perspiration showed high levels of sodium. A further examination found high levels of chlorine, which is considered an accurate marker for the genetic disease that the doctor had suspected, and feared: cystic fibrosis.

Rafael and Dina underwent genetic testing which determined that each carried the defective gene and that any future children had a one out of four chance of carrying the disease.

The sky had fallen down upon them. They had never heard of this hereditary illness; even the name was difficult for them to pronounce. In the clinic for CF in Beilinson Hospital they received their first informational literature: "Cystic fibrosis is the most common genetic disease in the western world among Caucasians. One out of every 20 people carries the gene."

They read about the nature of the disease: Unlike a healthy person whose drainage system works properly, and whose mucus is flushed out by the blood and lymph systems, CF sufferers have mucus whose texture is too thick to flow properly, and so their glands become blocked.

Rafael Brent wanted to understand more. So what if the saliva did not drain properly? He began to rummage through medical libraries, looking for data on the disease. He searched through the hospital library and found a thin, scientific pamphlet, "Research on Cystic Fibrosis." He photocopied it and sent it out to be translated into Hebrew. When he read the cold, dry lines, his eyes grew dim: "At first, and most importantly, the disease harms the lungs. CF is characterized by chronic lung disease and a blockage of breathing passages by viscous phlegm that creates a fertile ground for the growth of germs. As a result of the phlegm's viscosity, victims suffer from repeated infection in the air passages that can cause irreversible damage, destroying lungs and creating breathing insufficiency. That is the terminal phase of CF patients."

That was that. Not saliva; not mucus. A fatal disease! *Rafael, stop reading. The more you know, the more it will hurt.*

He couldn't stop. "CF is a pan-systemic disease that can damage the liver, the pancreas, and even the heart (particularly in times of increased perspiration, such as summer), and cause diabetes. CF victims suffer from damage to the pancreas's secretion of enzymes. Their body cells need double the amount of energy of a healthy person, and without a high-calorie diet they can also suffer from severe weight loss..."

The translated pages fell from between paralyzed fingers and landed on the ground. Rafael couldn't even bend down to pick them up. For years he'd prayed for a son... *I begged, I wanted, I cried, I broke through Heaven's gates. The prayers were answered. All the prayers. But there are prayers that one shouldn't say. There are requests that one shouldn't make!*

My Paysi, my sweet, beautiful baby, has so little time to live. The tears ran down his cheeks. Other tears, tears of blood, flowed, not from his eyes, but from the deep pit of his heart. *Paysi, my poor little boy.* All of his short life would be fettered by medicines, medical treatments, limitations. Massive physiotherapy, two or three times a day, an hour at a time, in order to drain the thick phlegm from clogged lungs. Every few months the unfortunate boy would have to go to the hospital to receive high-dose intravenous antibiotic treatment. He would have to take 40 to 50 pills daily to make up for the enzyme loss and improve his digestion.

Just in order to breathe, my sweet little Paysi will need the amount of calories that a full-grown adult takes in for all his needs for two days... In order to grow and develop, Paysi would need two or three times the amount of calories of a healthy person. But the illness harms the intestines! How could he digest all that high-calorie nutrition?

And all the treatments, what would they accomplish? Paysi would, perhaps, live to see his 25th or 30th birthday. And then?

Rafael was an introverted, reserved man, deep and reflective. He thought and thought, made the reckonings, until despair had worked itself deep into his marrow.

He grew profoundly depressed. He managed to come out of it for a short time with the help of his *rosh yeshivah*, a man with whom he had shared a strong bond for many years. "G-d gives life; thank Him for it every day, for every minute of life. Who are you to complain about Him?"

"But it's my son," Rafael sobbed bitterly.

"He's my son, too," the *rosh yeshivah* joined him in his tears. "But G-d's thoughts are deep, very deep, impenetrable." He spoke in the singsong of the Days of Awe, in a thin voice, as he affectionately stroked the trembling hand of his suffering student. "He judges alone, who can dispute Him? As He wishes, so He does.'"

Rafael wept.

Dina buried her head in the sand; an ostrich, what she did not know would not hurt her. But Rafael, clever Rafael, continued to gather information, and his new knowledge horrified him.

Paysi, the baby himself, knew nothing. He continued to develop, unaware of what awaited him in the future, and showered his contagious smiles on all those around him.

When Paysi was three months old, the second blow struck.

At this age, the majority of babies take their first steps in communicating. Paysi, though, remained indifferent, not reacting to the words of his mother and sisters. He was quiet for most of the day, except, of course, when he coughed to clear his lungs. He would answer Dina's smiles with his own toothless one, but as soon as she turned her face away from him, and he was dependent on his hearing, he stopped responding.

Dina, hysterical, turned to the CF clinic. "Is there a connection between the disease and hearing loss?" she asked worriedly. "We've never heard of it, but come immediately," they answered.

Paysi was examined. It turned out that a rare complication of the disease had interfered with his hearing, as the drainage in his ears became blocked. As a result he suffered from chronic infections and fluid in the inner ear. More medication was added to the already huge dosage that Paysi ingested. He drained bottles of antibiotics every day in order to avoid lung infections, but they were of no use in protecting his ears and hearing. Doctors put tubes in his ears to help drain the fluids, but his hearing continued to deteriorate. The Brent home had been full of talk of physiotherapy, antibiotics, enriched nutrition, inhalators, and blocked lungs; now, discussion turned to audiometers and audiograms.

Paysi underwent surgery on his ears when he was 2 years old, and the doctors succeeded in salvaging 10 percent of his hearing. Left almost deaf, unable to hear ordinary conversation, his speaking ability never developed. Thus the youngster was given still another title: deaf-mute.

Rafael was sunk in a deep depression. With all the joy of life gone, the lightning of his eyes turned ominously into a dangerous spark — a spark that doctors in certain kinds of hospitals would have recognized. Perhaps if he had received immediate treatment they could have saved his sanity, but the entire household revolved around Paysi and his illness.

They were lying there, just as he had left them — three notebooks bound in cardboard. The first notebook: "Moshe Dinburg, Yeshivas Ein Yisrael, Elul 5718 - Nisan 5722. Diaries and notes."

The second notebook: "Iyar 5722 — Tishrei 5724."

The third: "Cheshvan 5724 — April 1968."

The change from the Jewish to the secular date in the last notebook expressed the dramatic change in lifestyle by the diaries' author. Gili didn't have to delve deeply in that last notebook to find the description of the abandonment of yeshivah and the first notes from the training camp in the Negev.

He brought the diaries to his room, locked them in a drawer, and waited for the optimal time.

The hour was late, and Monica was ensconced in the deep leather sofa in the guest room, reading a thick book by the soft light of a lamp. Gili knew that if he didn't get her to go to sleep she was perfectly capable of staying up until three in the morning and then coming in to check on him. And that, he was determined to avoid.

"Ima," he said gently, "you should go to sleep."

"What are you plotting, my scheming journalist?" Monica smiled wearily. "I know I should be suspicious when you send me off to bed."

He wanted to tell her how right she was, but he remained silent. Instead, he went into his room and lay down on his bed, fully dressed beneath his blanket.

About 15 minutes later Monica entered the room, glanced swiftly at her only son, and then left. Two minutes later her shutter was closed and the light extinguished.

He waited, unmoving, for 15 minutes, then walked over to his mother's room and listened to her even breathing. She was a light sleeper, Gili knew, and any small noise might wake her. Returning to his own room he lit a small bedside lamp and lay down comfortably, his temple leaning on his fist, and again gazed at the even, beautiful handwriting. In the yellow light, the small calligraphic letters, undoubtedly written with a Rolex fountain pen, looked like little glittering diamonds.

Gili entered the time machine that swept him back 37 years, to Yeshivas Ein Yisrael.

Wednesday, 18 Elul 5718 (September 3, 1958)

Today I know it: My place is here in yeshivah.

Up until yesterday I thought about running back home, to Jerusalem. I knew that Abba would beat me with a stick or strap, but I was so homesick I was prepared to accept the blows and go home.

But Manny Schwartz didn't stop encouraging me, with both pleasant and sometimes stern language. I really admire his strength of conviction. He's come from Antwerp, in Belgium, and hasn't once complained that it's hard for him. If there's anyone I owe my toughening up to, it's Manny. Because of him I don't give in to my homesickness — not like spoiled Tommy Deshevski, who came here from Detroit, all aflame with the ideal, "exile yourself to a place of Torah," and, in two days, evolved into a big cry-baby, turning his sheets into wet rags with all his tears at night.

Friday, 27 Elul 5718 (September 12, 1958)

The tension before the Day of Judgment has reached its climax. The mashgiach is turning us inside out, demanding that we seek out G-d in our prayers on Rosh Hashanah. How did he put it yesterday during his shmuess? "Hashem's spirit approaches every man's heart, just to the degree that the person is ready to accept it!"

Manny Schwartz asked my forgiveness for a trick that he played on me on my first day here. When I was looking for the key to my suitcase, I found that I had lost it. How I had cried; I was so homesick, and I was terrified that I'd be late for class. Then Manny turned up, my key in hand, and asked if it was mine. He told me he found it on the floor.

Today Manny confessed that he'd picked my pocket the moment that he'd seen me. "I saw immediately that you were a naive Yerushalmi, and I wanted to shake you up a little." He's got incredibly fast hands — he told me — and if he wanted to be a magician, he could make a good living.

I think he may have rummaged through my suitcase on other occasions too. How did he know my nickname, Moishike, that is only written by Abba in his letters to me?

I'm afraid of Menachem Schwartz!

Gili skipped over half of the notebook, and jumped to the middle of the year 5719.

Motzaei Shabbos, Tu B'Shvat 5719 (January 24, 1959)

I really love yeshivah life. If I would have given in to my own self-pity and run away, I would have been a complete fool. Tommy Deshevski, home-sick, ran back to Daddy and Mommy in Detroit before Rosh Hashanah and hasn't returned. The mashgiach told us that in twenty years Tommy will again make his sheets wet with tears, crying over why he didn't overcome his homesickness and stay in yeshivah, never becoming a real Torah scholar.

There's nothing like yeshivah life. Learning with a chavrusa, the sweet melody of the Gemara, the even sweeter understanding of Rashba and Rambam. The discourses of the mashgiach, the tzaddik. The friendships, the singing in the dining room on Friday nights. How beautiful to hear Itzik Chalamish and Eli Kagan singing the heartrending melodies of the Modzitzer chassidim deep into the night. We follow the ruling of the Chazon Ish and don't use electricity on Shabbos, and the dim light of the kerosene lamps just adds to the magical atmosphere.

From the yeshivah comes the scent of heaven. From the outside it looks impoverished and unfortunate, with its tin huts. We sleep on mattresses whose straw is sticking out and the mosquitoes are our honored guests, yet inside us it is all light.

Last week we had a fight, my chavrusa, Chaim Ozer Schmidt, and I. With hindsight I see that I've lost a good friend, a refined boy with an aristocratic nature. When we were succeeding in our studies and our shouts made the entire yeshivah tremble, Manny would smile and call us, "the head opposite the brain." When I asked where he found the phrase he smiled, opened the siddur to the hineni muchan that we say before putting on tefillin, and showed me the sentence: "the head opposite the brain, so that the soul that is in my brain..."

The cause for the quarrel was tiny. Ozer was looking in my notebook, the one that I use for writing notes on Rav Daniel Shlenkeh's lessons. In the margin were some sentences that talked about Ozer Schmidt in less than flattering terms: "a bore, dolt, dreaming fool."

Schmidt brought the notebook to me, his face as red as fire. "That's what you think of me?" I looked and grew pale: The handwriting was just like mine!

Interestingly, someone had told me about half an hour earlier that Ozer had called me, in the dining room, a weak personality. I told Schmidt that I could swear I hadn't written the words, but because he'd talked against me in the dining room there was no way that we could resolve our difference. He denied that he'd said a word against me, and added, "The best defense is a strong offense: You're trying to fool me. Look, it's your handwriting!"

When I examined the writing I saw that someone had very successfully forged mine.

Who could it be? I searched my memory. I remember in a conversation once in the dining room, when Schmidt wasn't there, someone — I can't remember who — had called him a bore. Even if I had thought so — and I don't — would I have been crazy enough to write it in my notebook, black on white, in a notebook that half the yeshivah looks through regularly, first among them my own chavrusa, Chaim Ozer Schmidt!

In the meantime, there's a deep hatred between us...

That's what Rabbi Schmidt had been referring to: the classic work of Manny Schwartz, the one who caused others to quarrel. Poor Abba hadn't remembered who had said those words against Schmidt, but Gili had no doubt who had said what, and who had done the forgery, copying the handwriting of Moshe Dinburg and spreading the rumor that Chaim Ozer Schmidt had spoken against him.

When a person is living close to an event, the small details obscure the big picture. From the distance of 37 years Gili could see what Abba could not. If only he could have gone into the notebook, traveled backwards in time, reached Yeshivas Ein Yisrael, and whispered in the ears of a sensitive and innocent boy from Jerusalem to stay away from Manny Schwartz as from fire...

Onwards, to the first summer in yeshivah:

Motzaei Shabbos, Behar-Bechukosai, 22 Iyar 5719 (May 30, 1959)

Summer descended on us suddenly. The yeshivah is as hot as an oven, but students in the know tell us that when these heat waves pass over, the rest of the summer isn't as bad.

Last week the mashgiach was as boiling as the sun. Manny staged a performance for him that we'll never forget.

One of the residents of Ein Yisrael (the yeshivah is located within Moshav Ein Yisrael; that's where it got its name), whose name was Tzion Batat, was a porter, until he lost his job because of a slipped disk in his back. Batat became very poor, because he didn't know any other trade.

Manny decided that the yeshivah should take care of him. With the declaration, "You shall build a world of lovingkindness," he stirred up all the yeshivah, using his cronies, while he himself stayed in the background.

In the middle of the first seder, when the mashgiach had gone, as usual, to his house nearby for half an hour, the entire yeshivah emptied out. The boys made a long convoy towards the home of Tzion Batat, the unemployed porter, and brought him gifts. One brought him a cup of milk, another half a loaf of bread, a third a piece of cheese wrapped in paper. Manny's friends had taken these things from their portions at breakfast. One of the boys had even lined a wooden orange crate with straw and brought 20 eggs to the porter. Five broke along the way... Among the rest, were the following products: fruits, olives, herring, a pair of white girl's socks (!), two packages of Escot cigarettes (maybe he smokes), three packages of dried beef tongue under top-notch kashrus supervision (a gift from our American friends), and three cans: black shoe polish; anchovy paste; and sweetened condensed milk.

When the mashgiach returned from his house to the beis midrash, he saw, to his astonishment, that "ein Yisrael" — there was no Yisrael — in Ein Yisrael! Growing more and more nervous he went out to look for his little lost flock, wandering back and forth and not finding a soul! He had almost collapsed from worry when the celebrations came to an end (with most of the foodstuffs eaten in the wild party that took place at the unfortunate man's house!) and we returned, tired but satisfied, to the yeshivah.

Reb Shmuel almost fainted when we proudly told him of what we'd done. Like all good students of Kelm he had forced himself to master his emotions, but now we could barely recognize him. His face grew red as a beet. "Lies, lies!" he shouted, his hands waving back and forth. "This is a mitzvah that comes from an aveirah. If you were honest in your motives, an entire yeshivah wouldn't have come to this waste of Torah study, not to mention the gluttony ... that alone is a sign that you only intended mischief!"

He conducted a thorough investigation that put him on Manny's trail. Manny denied doing wrong, and pointed an accusing finger at the ones who had made such fiery speeches in the dining room on the subject of loving others.

Three of the boys were suspended from the yeshivah for a week: Yoske Friedman, Manny Schwartz, and me, Moshe Dinburg Yoske went to Haifa, Manny was sent to his uncle's house in Pardes Chana, and I traveled home. Naturally, "boring" Chaim Ozer Schmidt was smarter than all of us. He hadn't followed Manny's lead and had kept a low profile during our "chesed" project.

On the way home to Jerusalem, at Ramle's Central Bus Station, a boy came onto the bus. His deep, clever eyes danced. "Manny!" I cried happily. We fell on top of each other, and burst out laughing.

Manny spent the week with us in Batei Ungarin. Abba was very angry at us: "If the mashgiach threw you out of yeshivah, this house is not a sanctuary. Get out to the beis midrash, " — and he waved his finger threateningly — "if you don't learn the same amount you would in yeshivah, you don't get any food here!"

After two days in which we diligently learned in the neighborhood's largest shul, Abba forgave us and sat us down late at night for a heart-to-heart talk.

I could spend a lot of time describing the scene in the Batei Ungarin neighborhood: the special types that live there, the early rising of Yudel Cohen the "Vekker," who wakes everyone up for davening, the smell of the cooking fish issuing from every kitchen on Friday morning. But more than anything, I love to sit on the porch at night, listening to the neighborhood's nocturnal noises.

The three of us sat beneath the domed sky on the long communal porch shared by the second floor of the "driter tzeil," the third line of houses in the neighborhood. The place was bathed in silence, except for the sound of Torah learning coming from a nearby beis midrash, the sweet melody of the Gemara.

Abba and Manny found common ground. Manny told him about the person who had had the most influence on him in his life, the rebbe Reb Itzikel, head of a chassidic court known as Pshevorsk in Antwerp, that city of diamonds. Abba was very impressed by Manny's stories of the great tzaddik and wonder-worker who had served as Manny's role model since childhood. "If there is a corner of Torah and chesed in Antwerp, it is the home of the rebbe," Manny said with chassidic fervor, his clever eyes burning. That's how he captured Abba: He's always had a soft spot for eyes that shine with intelligence. "Wait a minute," Abba said, dashing into the house in his brown slippers. I understood what he had gone to bring, and I was right: After a minute, Abba came out with a package wrapped in white linen. "This is our family talisman," he said with a radiant smile. "The ancient, valuable book, The Vessel of Blessing."

There was a strange fire in Manny's eyes as he saw the sefer. I don't want to call it greed, but he just seemed to go crazy. He reverently skimmed through the book; when he saw the name of the author he jumped up as if bitten by a scorpion. "I recognize this sefer!" he cried excitedly. "I recognize it! My father told me about it!"

"How do you know of it?" Abba asked, surprised. "This is the only copy in existence. It wasn't printed, it was written on deer hide. Have you ever heard of incunabula? It was printing in its infancy. They are among the most valuable books in the world. Well, this book is worth more than an incunabulum."

"The author was my grandfather," Manny answered composedly.

"The golem of Prague was your grandfather," Abba laughed. "The author was a Sephardi, Rabbi Ezra Albertzloni, one of the great scholars of Salonika, in Greece. And you're an Ashkenazi for generations."

Manny sat silent, upset. If his head had been transparent, I'm sure we would have seen the wheels turning around in his brain. After a few seconds of thought, he said, "The author's son traveled to Poland, where he married a native and assimilated among the Ashkenazim."

"That's the best you can come up with?" Abba teased him, but his eyes were thoughtful. His head nodded back and forth, as if trying to dislodge old memories that had almost been forgotten. Suddenly, he spoke. "Maybe you're right; there's a kernel of truth there. I remember that my father, may his memory be blessed, told me when I was a child that the book was not handed down to the author's son, because he had turned to evil ways. The author left it to his student, Rabbi Tzvi HaSofer of Salonika, and we are his descendants. He, too, was a Sephardi, though we, his children, are complete Ashkenazim."

"My father told me," Manny began hesitantly. It sounded as if he was contradicting Abba, but his face was serious. "...he told me that our grandfather, the author, wrote a will bequeathing the book to his son, unless his son turned wicked, because it was a very holy work. His son didn't really turn to evil, but he didn't exactly follow his father's ways. That gave his father's student the chance to claim that the son didn't deserve the book, and that it should go to him. That's what I heard."

A cool Jerusalem wind stroked our faces. It seemed that Abba hadn't heard Manny's last words. It was 1 o'clock in the morning when he revealed to us the true nature of the rare book, "one of the most precious books in the world," he emphasized.

"The sefer The Vessel of Blessing that I am holding in my hand is essentially a book of segulos, charms, but its great worth lies in the three gates.'"

"Three gates?" I asked.

"There are three parts, called gates: the wisdom of the soul, wisdom of the countenance, and wisdom of the deeds. The wisdom of the soul and the countenance are interconnected: Together, they teach how to recognize the nature and traits of man. You can know him better than he can know himself, for good and for bad. The wisdom of the deeds is practical kabbalah — and that's where the danger lies."

"Danger?" Manny asked.

Abba lowered his voice, as if he were ready to reveal some top-secret information. "Do you know what kabbalah is?"

"A little," I replied humbly.

"Good. You've heard of kabbalah from 'on high,' superficially, and you've probably only heard of theoretical kabbalah. Not practical kabbalah."

"And what is practical kabbalah?" Manny asked eagerly.

"Slow down," Abba patted his shoulder and gave him a smile through his thick beard. "Let's go in order, from easy to hard. Theoretical kabbalah includes the study of the secrets of the world, the structure of the upper world, the seven levels of heaven, the creation of the world, and the various powers that rule within by the ten 'sefirot' that bring the G-dly light to the physical world. This kabbalah speaks of the sparks of holiness and those of impurity that are spread throughout the world, and the means of correcting those that need such 'tikkun.'"

"Not interested," Manny tapped his fingers impatiently on the metal railing of the narrow porch. "What's practical kabbalah?"

Abba hesitated before speaking. "Practical kabbalah is the knowledge of how to use the names of the angels — pure and impure — in order to do something that is impossible by the laws of nature. But be careful, young men — it's playing with fire! There used to be certain chosen individuals who could use G-d's Name to call upon the angels to fulfill all their desires.

But someone who is unworthy, who uses powers that are forbidden to him, is putting himself into danger. They say that even great men who concerned themselves with practical kabbalah — their children went astray. The author of this book can confirm that."

Manny sat, reflecting. Finally he said a few words that terrified Abba.

"If I had that book I could be like Rabbi Itzikel, I could lead thousands of chassidim, rule them."

"What are you saying?" Abba said heatedly. "Theoretical kabbalists have excommunicated more than one person who indulged in practical kabbalah, because they used heavenly powers in a way that is forbidden. Aside from that, even if you wanted to, you couldn't understand a word of the book."

"I could," Manny insisted stubbornly.

"You're dreaming," Abba closed the subject. But before I went to sleep I noticed that he had hidden the book in a new place, deep behind his ancient Vilna Shas.

He was afraid of Manny Schwartz!

27

The hours passed; Gili read and read some more. An entire world unfolded before him from the pages of the diary. Five years after his death, his father had opened a wonderful window before him, a window on his rich, beautiful inner life. The real portrait of Udi Dinar — Moshe Dinburg, in Moishike's first incarnation — was revealed before him, in living color. Abba was a bashful, sensitive yeshivah student, diligent in his studies, stable in his world view. How had he been sucked into a whirlpool that had relentlessly pulled him from behind the walls of the yeshivah, outside the Jewish observance in which he had so passionately believed?

And what had moved him to write such a detailed diary? Had he felt so alone, he who had such a close friend in Manny Schwartz?

Friend? Foolishness — Manny Schwartz was a dictator, a schemer who dominated Moshe Dinburg with an absolute mastery. Moshe-Udi had felt that this marvelous friendship was nothing more than a hidden expression of Manny's need to rule. The diary was his last refuge, the only private corner allowed him. Even wily Manny, possessor of a thousand eyes, didn't know of its existence. Many times Moshe-Udi wrote the entries in the middle of the night, when his roommates, Manny Schwartz and Yoske Friedman, were already fast asleep.

It was four in the morning. Gili's brain was leaden; his joints ached from fatigue. If he had a rooster, it would have been crowing before the dawning day. But the diary was engrossing, fascinating: Perhaps he would find within it other hints to his actual, present-day situation?

Sunday, 6 Tammuz 5719 (July 12, 1959)

It's hot. Very hot.

In the yeshivah they've hung one lone wall fan, and suddenly everyone wants to sit in the center of the beis midrash, beneath the fan.

They put in the fan after what happened to Moshe Shiffer. The oppressive heat led some of the students to do something crazy. A betting craze broke out in yeshivah. Last Sunday Yoel Minkus bet Moshe Shiffer ten lirot that he couldn't eat 100 sabra fruits. The background of the bet: Moshe Shiffer's declaration that he had a cast-iron stomach and could eat rocks if he wanted.

On Monday morning Yoel went to one of the moshavnik's homes and bought an entire case of thorny, green sabras. The entire yeshivah (!) gathered between Shacharis and breakfast to help peel the prickly fruit and see how Moshe Shiffer did with 100 sabras on an empty stomach.

"They're not ripe." Moshe wrinkled his nose at the sight of the greenish fruit.

"Coward," Yoel Minkus teased him, "looking for a way out of the bet."

Moshe Shiffer picked up some sabras that looked just like green eggs. "And if I perish, I perish," he quoted, clamping his eyes shut. He made the blessing and threw five sabras into his mouth in one shot.

Ten, 20, 30, 38... 45... The sabras were actually as hard as rocks, and not at all tasty. Moshe writhed, clenched his teeth, and reached 50.

"I can't do more," he confessed, beaten. "I'll give up the money. The sabras are completely unripe."

Yoel held a 10-lira note in his hand. "Eat 10 more and I'll give you the whole thing," he offered.

"Eat!" half the yeshivah advised him. "10 lirot!"

"Don't eat," the other half said. "The sabras aren't ripe."

Moshe ate another 10. His face was contorted with nausea, but he ate — and almost choked.

Yoel handed him the bill. "My word is my word," he declared ceremoniously.

The students went off to breakfast.

After two days Moshe was doubled over in pain. The green sabras had turned into stone in his intestines! Sixty stones on an empty stomach...

He was raced to Assaf HaRofeh Hospital. The doctors took an x-ray and diagnosed a severe intestinal blockage. They began to prepare him for surgery.

Moshe turned pale. "Abdominal surgery is done under general anesthesia?" he checked with a nurse.

"Certainly."

"That's all that I need," Moshe was filled with fear. "People who get anesthesia sometimes go to sleep forever."

When he was handed the white hospital gown and sent to undress, he jumped out the window and hitchhiked back to the yeshivah.

The worried mashgiach heard his story with a horrified expression. "What have you done?" he shouted. "You've put your life in danger!"

"I don't want to die," Moshe wailed.

Fortunately, Rabbi Bergman is a bit of an expert in medicine. Two older students took on the nursing job. They closeted themselves with the pain-wracked boy and dosed him five times with a mixture of castor oil and warm water.

Rabbi Bergman swung like a pendulum between the beis midrash and the room where the sick boy was being treated. He listened at the door to hear if there were any results, nodded his head and returned to the beis midrash. One hundred and fifty pairs of frightened eyes followed him each time he came and went. "Not yet," the whisper spread like fire in a field of thorns. "Not yet."

After the fifth try the mashgiach overheard a consultation.

"It's not working. What can we try next?" one of the boys said.

"Boiling water. That would do it," the other said.

"No!" the mashgiach screamed in horror from the other side of the door. "Do you want to kill him? Try once more with warm water and olive oil."

Someone quickly brought a bottle of olive oil from the kitchen. The mashgiach led the entire yeshivah in Tehillim. After about half an hour one of the "nurses" came and yelled excitedly, "Mazel tov! It's working!"

Moshe Shiffer was miraculously saved, but the administration had learned its lesson. The brutal heat did something to the boys.

A fan! We called it the Minkus Ventilator...

The lion's share of praise went not to the two "nurses" but to Manny Schwartz. It was suddenly revealed to all of us that Manny was involved behind the scenes and it was he who suggested the treatment that helped Moshe. Rabbi Bergman praised the wisdom and medical knowledge of the young Belgian. "One mitzvah brings another," he said in his measured, tranquil tones, his arm around Manny's shoulders in a warm hug. "After you saved a person, who is considered an entire world, continue to do well in your studies."

Manny modestly bent his head.

Dawn broke. The last stars winked out, one after the other, disappearing into the lightening sky. Gili shut the diary and hid the notebooks deep within a drawer. Paradoxically, the more tired he felt, the further sleep felt from his burning eyes.

He had never seen his father with such a clear perception. It was like viewing him through crystal-clear glass. Here he was, Gili Dinar, graduate of top schools, progressive institutions, with educational enrichment and the latest in technology. On the other side, Moshe Dinburg, a Yerushalmi lad, graduate of the old-fashioned Talmud Torah Meah Shearim. And when it came to the pen, who could choose between them? True, the style occasionally reflects a young man's immaturity, but with all that it is brimming with a richness of language, clarity of perception, and a level of writing that is many times higher than yours, you spoiled, intelligent young man.

Your writing talent is an inheritance from your father, Gili Dinar. Your father, Udi Dinar's, obsessive interest in his chosen profession, photography, becomes *more and more a riddle. Why hadn't he developed his writing talent, his obvious creativity?*

Gili jumped out of bed. "I can sleep later," he whispered the mantra of the past few days. In another year or two he would get some rest and calm down.

Just the thought of what he was planning filled him with fear. His emotions were running through his veins, unchecked. *Calm down,* he whispered to himself. *Be logical and balanced.*

But there was no control. He tiptoed out of the house. The Mitsubishi raced in the dawning light of day towards the old Yarkon Cemetery. Gili recalled another journey, a journey that ended in an abyss and a fire that took his father away from him.

When Monica had awakened after the accident, her first question was, "What happened to Gili and Udi?"

The doctors had kept her under sedation with anesthetics and painkillers and for three days Monica had hovered on the brink of consciousness. It was necessary: Otherwise, she would have suffered the torments of hell. Her head had been badly hit and both her arms were broken. Another benefit: This gave them a bit of breathing space until the situation was clarified. The Abu Kabir Forensic Institute had not yet made final identification of the bodies, a young man lay unconscious, and Monica herself was still undergoing tests to verify if there was further injury. By the afternoon of the third day, though, progress had been made. The bodies had been positively identified, Gili had awakened, and the results of the tests had proven that except for her broken arms and some local damage to her head there were no further injuries.

And when the narcotics had worn off, she had asked her question. "Where are Udi and Gili?" Slowly, ever so slowly, the doctors had told her...

Her broken cries echoed through the entire wing. She screamed like a wounded beast. Udi, her husband, dead. Burned alive, together with his old friend, Manny Schwartz. Gili, her only child, his brain damaged. "Internal bleeding in the brain," the doctor explained.

Why was she still alive?

She wept for two solid hours. She would have cried for longer, much longer, but life is cruel and must go on. A young doctor had approached her and gently asked if she had given any thought to a final resting place.

"No. I want to see my son, but I don't have the strength to tell him," she answered weakly.

"He already knows," the doctor assured her.

The young man escorted her to the neurological ward. When she saw Gili lying in bed, weak and bandaged, all the pain returned. She sighed bitterly, came close to Gili and burst into tears. She almost choked as she tried, to no avail, to gain control of herself.

The doctor was sensitive, but his voice was laced with firmness. "Mrs. Dinar, calm down. This isn't healthy for either of you."

"I know." The tears rolled down her cheeks. "The two of us are healthy, so healthy. What a shame to spoil such pictures of health."

The doctor slipped out of the room.

With a great effort of will, she managed to control her emotions. "Gili, do you know what happened?"

His lips were purple and swollen. "I heard. Abba is dead," he whispered. "And Manny. I did it."

"You're not guilty. Efraim, the driver, is. Why didn't he want to come with us to the wedding?" she said bitterly. "If he had come, everything would have been different. Gili, where shall we bury Abba?"

"Should I know? Where everyone goes, in Holon."

"No. I want the Yarkon Cemetery. I want him to stay close to home." She spoke from amidst a raging flood of emotion, almost in a singsong.

"The Holon cemetery is just as close," Gili murmured.

"No, it's too big. Udi will be lost there."

Gili was too confused, too full of pain, to deal with her strange logic.

Though Monica had little liking for Manny, her husband's childhood friend, in view of the circumstances there could be little doubt: Manny would be buried next to Udi. "Beloved and pleasant in their lives, and in their deaths they were not parted," she said, with just a trace of mockery.

The memory of that day lay like a stone in Gili's heart, as he sped down the Bavli neighborhood and onto the Northern Ayalon highway. When his parents married, the Bavli neighborhood had been considered a luxury area; even after most of the nouveau riche had deserted to Ramat Aviv Gimmel, Udi had not wanted to leave his beautiful apartment, and so they had stayed on.

At this early hour the road was completely empty, and Gili stepped on the accelerator. A frigid wintry wind howled in through the open car window and rushed through his hair. He held onto his coat lapel, trying to protect himself, but did not close the windows. To his left the scenery raced by, too familiar to grab his attention. Shikun Lamed; Ramat Aviv Gimmel; the giant Pi-Glilot gas refineries. When he turned right onto Highway 5, towards Raanana and Ariel, he thought of his father's intriguing diaries. First-class reading material. Why had they been hidden away?

The Mitsubishi continued its swift pace, passing Kfar HaYarok on the right and Ramat HaSharon on the left. After the Morashah Junction he approached the cemetery.

The name "Yarkon" was confusing, as there were two cemeteries with the same name, one near the other. But other than the shared title, they had little in common. The old Yarkon was small and well tended, with the graves hidden between rows of cypress and China trees that gave off abundant shade. The "new" Yarkon was almost barren. Makeshift metal huts served visitors and held the *chevra kadisha's* equipment. The cemetery was growing rapidly, the second largest cemetery in the entire Greater Tel Aviv area.

At a quarter to six in the morning, not exactly a routine time for a visit, Gili stood pensively next to the graves of Udi Dinar and Manny Schwartz. His eyes glanced at the shining marble stone: "Here lies a good man, Udi (Moshe) Dinar, z'l, son of Rabbi Shmuel Dinburg. Taken from us at the age of 47. 29 Cheshvan 5750 — November 27, 1989."

Words that said nothing, that could not describe a person. Nothing more than an identity card of the dead. A few details to let one know who was buried there. *If only you knew, my dear father, how much you are in my mind... Recently, I've been visiting your inner world through your private diaries. I will read them all, from the first word to the last.*

Almost unwillingly he read the second stone. "Here lies our beloved R' Menachem (Manny) Schwartz, z'l. Born in Antwerp. He loved to help everyone. Died in a traffic accident on Monday, 29 Cheshvan 5750, November 27,1989, when he was only 47 years old."

His monument had been chosen by Manny's family in Antwerp. Monica had tried to word her husband's stone differently, but even a blind man could see the similarities. The graves, one next to the other, bore the same date of death, the same age. It gave even the casual visitor something to think about.

Gili, too, was lost in thought. Udi and Manny. What a contrast. *Forgive me, deceased Manny Schwartz, but in the last few days your persona has been revealed to me. And it's not very pleasant.*

But he was dead...

So, only the righteous died?

Gili was certain that anyone who saw him now would swiftly send him to an asylum. Here he was, a young man standing in a cemetery before sunrise laughing wildly. But the joke that Abba had told him was so apt, so full of true Jewish humor: "There was once a man who took his young son for a trip to the cemetery. When they left, the youngster turned to his father. 'Daddy, I want to be a thief.' The father, shocked, asked him why and the young boy answered innocently, 'Every gravestone has such nice things written on it — an upright, honest man; the best of men; a *tzaddik;* a good man. I didn't see any that had words such as "Here lies Yaakov Cohen, the well-known thief," or "Shimon Levi, head of Israel's crooks." It seems that thieves don't die. They live forever — so I want to be a thief.'"

Gili, enough! an inner voice chided him. *Manny was a schemer, but the analogy isn't quite right...*

The phrase "Thieves don't die" sounded familiar. Hadn't Rabbi Schmidt said something similar when he'd spoken of Manny's intrigues, of the kabbalist Bozgolo of Beit Yisrael, and of Rav Avram Roosenthal? He'd put them together into one big package.

The kabbalist Bozgolo, Gili decided, bore looking into.

The Beit Yisrael neighborhood of Jerusalem. An ancient, one-story stone house. A large courtyard covered with weeds. A group of chickens cackling and contentedly pecking at the floor. Gili picked his way carefully on the path paved with pieces of broken cement and entered.

Even as he entered the waiting room, Gili could feel the antagonism to Rabbi Schmidt's comparison growing within him. Religious people came to see Rav Avram. True, there were many plain folk among them, of all types: Ashkenazim and Sephardim, *chassid*im and Lithuanians, young and old. But there were learned people as well.

In the long line that waited to see the kabbalist Bozgolo he couldn't find even one *chareidi* face. The atmosphere resembled Tel Aviv's Carmel market at noon. The vast majority were nonreligious, simple men and women, some wearing *kippot* to show their respect.

The line moved with excruciating slowness. A sign on the kabbalist's door proclaimed, "Five minutes with the rav. Many are waiting!" Gili appreciated the thought, comparing it to the circus that went on in Rav Avram's stairwell. But the reality was quite different: The visitors ignored the sign and stayed significantly longer than the five minutes allotted them.

After an hour and a half of sitting on a hard wooden bench, Gili approached the *gabbai,* a young Yemenite man with curly *payot* and a perpetual smile.

"Hey, son," he said, "how much time do I have to wait?"

The young man looked at him with clever eyes. "How much?" he answered the question with another.

Gili understood. A small bribe might speed things up. He loathed the idea — but he had his own special brand of bribe. "I'm a journalist," he whispered.

Ten minutes later Gili entered the "baba's" room.

His enmity escalated from moment to moment. Gili was furious with Rabbi Schmidt. He was highly insulted by the comparison he had made. There was just one similarity between Rav Avram and Baba Bozgolo: The two met people in a half-lit room. And with that any resemblance ended.

Baba Bozgolo looked like a graduate of a school for "babas." He was clothed entirely in white, a snowy-white cloak reaching down to his ankles, a white turban on his head. He wore white cloth shoes and sat in a large reclining chair. He was a fat, beefy man, a little clumsy, and his sly eyes gave off sparks as he examined his visitor. Still, Gili decided to withhold judgment. He sat silent for some time.

"What does his honor want?" Bozgolo asked.

Gili framed a possible answer from among several possibilities. "I need help," he finally said.

"You have children?"

"No wife."

"So say so. When was his honor born? The secular date, please."

"March 22, 1973."

Bozgolo jotted down the numbers on a large sheet that was prepared on his desk.

"Your name and your father's name," the kabbalist tapped his finger on the desk.

"Gili ben Udi."

The kabbalist wrote the names down, calculating their numerical value, and began to make crosses between them and Gili's birthdate. He wrote again and again, whispering something in Arabic. Finally, he declared, "I think you've made a mistake in the name. The reckoning doesn't come out right."

He knows something, at least, Gili thought, impressed. He had purposely not given his full name. "The rav is right," he said, pulling out his identity card. "My full name is Gil Shmuel ben Moshe." Yes, his father had named him for his grandfather, Shmuel Dinburg.

"Didn't you say Udi?" the kabbalist asked.

"His real name was Moshe. Udi was the name he adopted when he went to the army."

"I understand," the baba murmured, writing the name down once again. His eyes immediately lit up. "Now everything works out," he said in satisfaction. He added some other jottings and asked to see Gili's palms. His eyes carefully read the lines of both hands. He leaned back in his chair and gave off an audible breath. "Good; now everything is clear."

"So?" Gili said, amused.

The kabbalist gave him a strange look. "They want to kill you."

Gili paled. The words fell like bombs on his head. The baba suddenly wore the aspect of one who saw far beyond normal mortals. "Who?"

The kabbalist gave him a severe glance. "Who? A good question. You're not a criminal, are you? You look like a fine young man."

Gili nodded. "Watch yourself," the baba warned him. "Your life is in danger!"

The threat was not new. Five months had passed since the first warning. But this sounded more concrete, more real. "When will they kill me?"

"Soon."

"What can I do?" Gili asked, caught in the belief that the baba knew what lay before him.

"What shall a man do to be saved from the pangs of the Mashiach?" the baba hummed serenely. "Say much *Tehillim*. But there is one more thing. A great evil eye hovers above you. You have had much success, you are talented and your best friends are eating you alive with their envious looks. If you remove the eye, the killer will leave you."

"How do we remove the evil eye?"

"That's my job," the kabbalist murmured. "Give charity. It is said that charity saves from death."

"How much?" Not the first time the question had been asked in this house.

The kabbalist thought for a moment. "I must guard over you. You must give charity for your 248 organs and 365 sinews. We will protect your entire body from harm. That comes out to $613, plus another $72 for the holy 72 that is good for protection, plus $26 for the holy Name, that surrounds you on all sides, plus $18 for the word 'chai.' And another $21 for the word ach' from the phrase '*ach tov l'Yisrael,*' only good for Israel. That comes out to $750."

Gili pulled out his checkbook. "Why not 750 shekels? I get paid in shekels, not dollars!" he complained.

The kabbalist grimaced. "The shekel is *sheker,* false! The shekel is not valuable currency. Try buying something in Japan for shekels... The dollar is accepted throughout the world. If you prefer, you can pay in pounds sterling or German deutsche marks."

Gili wrote a check for 2500 shekalim. "Make it out to Yeshivat Mechalkel Chaim," the baba instructed him.

"I rounded it off upwards. That won't disturb the reckoning?" Gili asked wryly.

"No, more doesn't hurt," the baba explained serenely. Suddenly, his face hardened into sternness. "I hope that his honor gives the money with a full heart. Because if it is given under duress, we can't help him at all."

"That's okay," Gili blushed scarlet. "I make a good living and I can afford it."

The baba leaned over, opened a drawer and pulled a round gold-colored pendant hanging on a thin gold chain. "Inside is a holy amulet. Put it around your neck and the holy names will guard you."

Hesitantly Gili pulled the chain over his head and hung it on his neck. The baba followed his actions closely. "Excellent," he clapped his hands in satisfaction. "You have now been saved from certain death. Come back to us in another month. If you come to me a few times, we'll solve all your problems."

Gili left the room awash in fury and confusion. Rabbi Schmidt had insulted Rav Avram for no reason, as far as he was concerned. Bozgolo wasn't a complete fool, he clearly knew something of the mystic world — he had hit a bull's-eye on the threat to Gili's life. But he was certainly a greedy kabbalist! How could Rabbi Schmidt compare him to Rav Avram?

Gili was very angry. His feet took him directly from Baba Bozgolo's home to the yeshivah, located in the same neighborhood. He was already forming the first sentences of his speech to Rabbi Schmidt. He would be polite, but would demand an apology.

To insult Rav Avram?

28

All the professional sentences, the polished words, flew out of his head the instant that he climbed the yeshivah's steps. Gili was frustrated and embittered, confused and nervous. Most of all, he was afraid. For several weeks he had been behaving like a hunted rabbit. In his car he would continually glance backwards to see if any other automobile was trying to overtake him; when he walked he constantly glanced from side to side. He had analyzed the situation several times since he had found himself caught in the labyrinth, but still he found that everything was hopeless. And Rabbi Schmidt's words, his comparison of Rav Avram to Baba Bozgolo, had infuriated him.

Rabbi Schmidt was coming down the stairs, and they met in the middle. Immediately after asking his rabbi how he was, Gili burst out, the hurt in his voice apparent, asking how his rav could so insult a precious person and describe him as a rogue and charlatan, when he was clearly the opposite.

Rabbi Schmidt went down with him to the yeshivah's courtyard. They grabbed two light garden chairs and sat down to talk. Gili, in a rage, hardly noticed as he pulled out a flower that had pushed its way from between the cracks of the cement blocks of the courtyard floor.

Rabbi Schmidt's eyes followed him. Too late, he tried to stop the destruction. "Why did you do that?" he asked.

Gili's fingers pulled the light purple petals apart. When he was a child his father had told him that during the siege of 1948 the women of Jerusalem had used this flower, known as a *chubezah*, to prepare a kind of mock gefilte fish. "What did I do?"

Rabbi Schmidt pointed to the flower. "Why did you uproot it?"

Gili's angry face cleared somewhat; a thin smile appeared. "That's an unusual combination: the head of a yeshivah who is also a member of the Society for the Protection of Nature."

Patiently, Rabbi Schmidt explained, "Our world is made up of four types of creations: the inanimate, the plants, the beasts, and the 'speakers.' Each one serves its Creator from its own unique position. You have just changed this from a plant to an inanimate object."

"Something to think about," Gili said admiringly. The Gemara says that each and every blade of grass has an angel appointed over it, which hits it over the head and commands it to grow. Could Rabbi Schmidt, then, see those angels? He carefully placed the green stem on the ground, as if mourning its young life, cut off before its time.

"I understand that you paid a visit to Baba Bozgolo, down the next street. What did you see there?"

Gili gave a vivid description of the baba. Rabbi Schmidt laughed aloud several times during the narrative. But Gili, single-mindedly, persisted in his question. "How could you compare the two?"

Rabbi Schmidt suddenly jumped out of the chair. "Gili, I have a feeling that we'll still talk about Rabbi Roosenthal, and about many things. I'm rushing to deliver a speech to a group of doctors who are *baalei teshuvah*. I'll tell you in short: I am firm in my belief that there is no serious difference between the two; the variations are merely technical ones. Baba Bozgolo works with the simple people and Rabbi Roosenthal with the more intelligent, and so he is much more sophisticated. I think Rav Avram has some secret source of power. His mastery over others certainly should be examined."

Gili bit his lip. Rabbi Schmidt had something personal against Rav Avram; nothing was as simple as he had thought. Perhaps he had been insulted that night that Rav Avram had refused to see him, and had harbored a grudge ever since. He would not let go. "Rav Avram doesn't take a cent from the people who come to him; my very first visit to Baba Bozgolo cost me 2500 shekels."

Rabbi Schmidt stood at the yard's entrance. Before leaving, he turned around and said, "That doesn't make him a bigger *tzaddik*. He has other motivations. Perhaps it's a passion for domination that drives him. Go see for yourself!"

⚘

The car slid towards the exit from Jerusalem. At the last minute Gili turned left towards Sderot Weizman. He crossed Rechov Herzl, passed through the Beit HaKerem neighborhood, turned right onto Rechov Yefe Nof. From there, he made his way down Rechov Pirchei Chen into the heart of the Jerusalem forest.

He wanted to think, to think deeply. The forest was the ideal spot.

He parked his car and began to descend into the loneliness of the pine trees. There was a feeling of moisture in the air left over from the previous day's rainfall; the atmosphere was delightfully cold. There is nothing like clear, frigid air for deep meditation.

His energetic steps sank into small puddles of mud. He ignored the dirt sticking to the soles of his shoes and pulled out a notebook. Perhaps getting things into writing might help, when his brain alone had failed.

1. **Buy a cellular phone.**

Gili had a deep and abiding resistance to the purchase of a cell phone, despite heavy pressure by his fellows in the newsroom. His deceased editor, Eric Meisels, had very much wanted him to get one. "You're cut off, the last of the Mohicans, the only journalist in the world without a cell phone," he had shouted at him more than once. But Gili was adamant. "I like to think," he told Eric. "If I had a cellular phone I'd be talking on it all day and I wouldn't have any time left for thought."

"Cellular?" Rav Avram had laughed, when his opinion was sought. "Once upon a time when someone talked to himself in the street, everyone knew he was insane. Today he's got a 'pelephone.' Not long ago I saw someone walking around with two cellular phones, one on, one off. He was phoning himself, enjoying hearing the words, 'This subscriber is not available at this time.' Then he switched to the other phone..."

Rav Avram suggested that schizophrenics invest in cell phones, and that the children of Alzheimer's patients and other sufferers from senility equip their ailing parent with the miracle instrument to avoid unpleasant encounters in the bus or street.

But now Gili had a change of heart. If he had had a cellular phone on that *Motzaei Shabbos* he would have been reached at the critical moment — and Eric would still be alive.

2. The book, The Vessel of Blessing. Thorough clarification.

There was more than one question mark surrounding this particular work. It was possible that within its pages lay the key to the entire mystery. In his diary his father had declared that the book was the only copy extant in the world, written by a scribe on the hide of a deer. He had noted the same thing on the note that had fallen from his *Tanach*. But "Big Yaakovi" had specifically said that he owned two copies of *The Vessel of Blessing*. Which of the two was authentic? Was it possible that someone had copied the book at some later date and printed it, thus allowing two copies to fall into the hands of the great collector?

Impossible. Before the accident Abba had said that the director of Sotheby's had told him of a collector in London who would pay a quarter of a million pounds sterling. A book that had several copies extant in the market could never command such a price.

Rav Avram Roosenthal had told him that "Big Yaakovi" was a master forger of ancient works. Perhaps he had forged the book? But there can be no forgery without an original. Gili could see no point of contact between his father and "Big Yaakovi."

Interesting how everyone had their eye on the book. Manny Schwartz had longed for it even as a young yeshivah student, 36 years earlier. And that very same book had been the topic of his last conversation before he was incinerated, along with the *sefer*!

Everything was wreathed in mystery. Rabbi Schmidt had hinted that Rav Avram Roosenthal had his power from some outside source, not from within. Had a copy of the book fallen into his hands, perhaps with the help of "Big Yaakovi," with whom he had such a close bond?

Sparkling drops of water danced between the pine needles. Gili, lost deep in thought, stared at them through unfocused eyes, seeing them as one gigantic drop that had captured the sun's rays within it. Could it be that Rav Avram had wanted to possess the book, get it from "Big Yaakovi" in order to learn its secrets — the secret of domination? Could his power come from the book?

Bad idea! First, the man had shown his mastery almost from birth. Second, the affiliation between "Big Yaakovi" and Rav Avram had begun after the rabbi had already exhibited his spiritual dimension. Third, the chances of "Big Yaakovi" having forged a book that he had never seen were almost nil. Fourth, even if Rabbi Schmidt was correct, Rav Avram could not have gotten hold of the book, which had burned up in the con-flagration after the accident. Period.

And yet Yaakovi had spoken with assurance about the two copies in his library. In the Holiday Inn, when they first met at the Sotheby's ex-hibit, he had mentioned the book, and not by chance.

I've got to infiltrate Yaakovi's library and check the two copies — if they re-ally exist.

Impossible. Gili clearly remembered the collector's fortified treasure house in Tel Aviv's Ramat Aviv Gimmel. His sixth sense had instructed him to memorize the house's layout, with its electrified fence, closed-circuit monitor, attack dogs, security men, digital safes. If he were a stuntman in an action film he would somehow manage to scale the high walls of the gi-gantic villa in some audacious, unrealistic exploit. But he was not an actor.

The wind whistled through the trees. When he had left Tel Aviv that morning he'd been wearing only a thin shirt; now the Jerusalem chill made its way through his bones. He longed for a hot drink to soothe his throat and warm him up, chase away the unrelenting cold, but he would-n't let up, and instead searched deep within himself, remorselessly seeking answers.

Absolute zero. Yaakovi's home was one of the best guarded in Israel. There was no way to break into it.

With languid steps he retraced the path to the parking lot, stuck the keys into the car door with a gesture of despair. Suddenly a blinding light illuminated his weary brain. A plan, brilliant in its simplicity, had sud-denly popped into his brain — in the blink of an eye.

G-d's salvation comes — in the blink of an eye.

"Living with cystic fibrosis is like living with a time bomb, one that may go off at any moment. It is a daily battle with the genetic disease, one of the worst to strike Caucasians, an illness which attacks the lung function and the digestive system. It takes a tremendous physical and psychological toll of both the sufferers and their families. That's why we've invited you here."

Thirty couples sat in the large lecture hall, all of them parents of children suffering from CF. Dr. Daniel Kreiff, a pulmonary specialist, explained to them how to deal with a CF patient, and how to ensure that their own daily lives not be destroyed by the child's special needs.

In the middle of the speech a power line short-circuited and the lights dimmed. Most people would not remember an unimportant incident such as that for long. But Dina Brent would remember it for years: Dr. Kreiff's thin lips, which looked like a gash upon his face, a gash that opened and closed; the one bulb that stayed extinguished even when the light had come on once more. She sat, wounded, bitter, not hearing even one sentence. Under extraordinary circumstances, her reactions were extraordinary.

From the time they'd discovered Paysi's illness the house had shuddered beneath the onslaught. The boy needed constant medical intervention. He had physiotherapy three times daily. Every month he underwent routine tests, blood tests, lung function tests. Summertime became a nightmare: The boy perspired, lost salt. He had to drink endlessly, and he rebelled. They wanted to send a social worker, but Dina refused: Let them not see her husband Rafael in his humiliation.

The others in the lecture hall had arrived as couples, dealing with their terrible burden together. Only Dina did not come with her husband, bringing, in his stead, Chedvi, her eldest stepdaughter, who had turned 12 only the week before. They had celebrated her *bat mitzvah* at a friend's house. Rafael Brent had been discharged from the hospital after a nervous breakdown. He stayed in the house, a brooding, melancholy presence, spending most of his time in bed staring vacantly before him. Occasionally he would don slippers and drag himself into the kitchen, rummage in the refrigerator and shelves looking for chocolate and cookies, as he burst into loud shouts. The windows of the Brent home were shut even in summer; Dina hoped the neighbors didn't hear the strange noises that Rafael would make. Her wounds bled endlessly: When he would make his occasional visits outside, the neighborhood children would surround him. His medication and uncontrollable gorging had swollen his body. His breath came heavily and with great difficulty. "The train's coming," the children would laugh behind his back.

Now she looked at the 29 other couples who filled the large lecture hall and she felt her throat tighten. The men's eyes sparkled with determination, with the resolve to deal with the challenge that the terrible illness had set before them, to lend a hand to the suffering mother and patient alike. She prepared herself for the difficult question: "Where is your husband?"

Dr. Kreiff continued speaking after the electrician had seen to the lighting problem. "In order for you to help your sick child, you must feel what he is feeling."

"How can we do that?" some of the parents asked.

"I'd tell you to use your imagination, but that's not enough. Here is the answer," Dr. Kreiff announced dramatically.

A fully uniformed nurse entered the hall with a package of drinking straws in her hand. She handed each participant a thin straw.

"When do we get to drink?" someone shouted, to the laughter of the others.

Dr. Kreiff didn't smile. "Let each of you take your straw, put it in your mouth, put your lips around it, and hold your nose with your fingers."

Everyone obeyed. There were no more confused giggles or comments. Dr. Kreiff's seriousness had sobered all of them.

"Now," Dr. Kreiff instructed them, "all of you breathe only through the straw. Five minutes. But without fooling — not through the nose, and without opening your lips."

Everyone inhaled. The hall was suddenly filled with the sounds of labored breathing. Dr. Kreiff watched them with interest. The sounds grew shriller and more filled with effort with each passing second. After a minute several of the mothers flung away the straws. "Terrible," one groaned. "I'm suffocating," another exhaled.

Others tried their best to complete the five-minute requirement. Their faces grew scarlet with supreme effort. They fought for every breath. But no one managed to last the full quota.

Dr. Kreiff's smiled. "Who wants to try again, this time through the nose?"

Only one parent volunteered. He placed the straw in his nostril and breathed heavily through it. After one minute he writhed like one suffocating, opened his mouth wide and took a deep breath. The exhibition was complete.

Dr. Kreiff struck while the others were recovering. "That's it," he said quietly. "A normal person hardly notices his breathing. He inhales and exhales 24 hours a day, breathes an average of 15 times a minute, 900 times an hour, 21,600 times a day. And he hardly notices a single breath.

"Your children, compared to this, feel every single breath. Why? Because they fight for it, fight their constant suffocation.

"You found it hard to breathe, but you could have begun to breathe normally whenever you wanted. Your children cannot! This is their life — a battle for every breath. There are children who breathe like that father who almost suffocated in one minute. Others don't have to try as hard — they breathe as you did when the straw was in your mouths. They breathe that way all day long! That simple action called breathing becomes a terrible problem when you're speaking of CF. Every breath entails work. They grow fatigued easily, their pulse races even when they are sitting down or lying in their beds. They are running all the time."

The hall was filled with the hum of emotion. "My little one breathes like that often," one mother sobbed. "I never understood until now." She took the straw and once again tried the experiment.

One of the parents asked permission to speak. "Thank you. No description could have compared to this hands-on demonstration."

Dr. Kreiff acknowledged the thanks with a nod. "One more important thought. You have to be aware of your son or daughter's every complaint. Pay close attention to every simple complaint and, in particular, talk to them a lot. Preventive treatment is most important, before the illness grows worse. The more you speak with your children, hear how they are feeling, the better you can avoid irreversible damage."

A flood of questions erupted. The parents could identify with his simple language. They had heard all the horrifying statistics until now; the time for bitter crying was behind them. Now they wanted to talk about the small problems of day-to-day life.

Dina Brent could feel the pain in her heart, a pain almost physical. Dr. Kreiff had stressed the importance of communication; all the parents had spoken of it. She longed to stand up and ask one simple question. "Doctor, what do I do when my son can't tell me he's suffocating, because he is mute? How can I speak with my little Paysi, ask him what hurts him and when, if he can hear almost nothing?"

That's why she'd brought Chedvi. The girl was old enough to learn something about the sickness. She would help ease Dina's burden, help her with Paysi's inhalation when he needed it, occasionally take him to the physiotherapy clinic. Take part in the difficult task of giving medicines to a 3-year-old. Paysi loathed the medications and fought mightily against them. They had given her a special spoon with a hollow handle, to ensure that every precious drop of medication would be swallowed. She would lay the restless boy on the bed. "Paysi, just one more spoon," she begged him, bent over near his hearing aid.

Paysi would jump out of bed and give a silent laugh, his eyes twinkling in enjoyment. Dina had to race after him through the house, finally getting him back to bed. He would twist his mouth as the hot liquid slid down his throat, trying to spit it out, while Dina firmly held his lips shut.

And that was only one medication, one of the 10 he received. Multiply that by five times daily! He needed several types of antibiotics to inhibit the growth of nests of bacteria, others to thin his mucus. Medication to replace the missing enzymes in his pancreas, medication to help break down the fats that he'd eaten, medication that provided chlorine vital for his lungs, vitamins to strengthen his skinny body...

The deaf child enjoyed the tumult of being chased and laid down on the bed; it was only because of it that he finally agreed to do the favor of bolting down the nauseating stuff. Dina rejoiced when the medication was taken, but she would be exhausted, falling on her bed totally fatigued.

Ventilating him was another ceremony, one even more daunting. When he was just 8 months old, Paysi was already frightened of the nebulizer's thrumming vibrations, and he would vanish at the sight of the mask. But when he would feel himself suffocating, he knew with the sharp instinct of infancy that the equipment helped him, and he would fall onto his bed with a weak whimper and bring his face close to his mother, waiting for her to put the lifesaving mask on his mouth and nose.

It was a heartrending image to see the 1-year-old desperately searching for the oxygen mask, but at least it kept Dina from still another battle. The nebulizer saved the youngster from suffocation more than once; on his worst days, little Paysi used it 10 times daily.

Dina, on the verge of collapse, needed help. She hoped that Chedvi would agree to assist her, if she heard a speech on the matter. But Dr. Kreiff's words terrified the young girl, and seeing 30 couples barely breathing through their straws horrified her.

"Ima," she said, pulling at Dina's sleeve — she had called her Ima from the day she'd met her, with absolute unself-consciousness — "is Paysi going to die?" Her eyes were round with fear.

She'd forgotten that the lecture hall was completely quiet. Her words exploded like a thunderstorm. Dina felt the grim looks all around her. "Chedvi, if we know how to take care of him, he will live."

"But the doctor called it a time bomb," Chedvi sobbed.

Dina felt new strength within her. She lovingly patted Chedvi. "Life is a gift from Heaven. Paysi will live for as long as the Creator decrees. Not one day less!"

Twenty-nine couples fervently clapped their hands. The thin crack in Dr. Kreiff's face widened, and finally began to resemble a mouth. And when the audience had quieted down, the doctor stood before them and applauded.

❧❦

The door bore a simple wooden sign: Vayden Family. Here lived one of Israel's most prestigious antique dealers, a 40-year-old Jerusalemite who knew the entire market by heart, particularly that of ancient manuscripts. For more than 20 years he'd made his living through these rare books and letters. A good living: Moshe Vayden could have lived in a luxury villa, but he had chosen the simplicity of this Jerusalem neighborhood.

Gili had heard Moshe Vayden's name during the course of his reports on Israel's *chassidic* and yeshivah worlds. Vayden was a central figure in the *chassidic* court of Brigal, and his name had come up in the article on that sect.

The door opened and Gili found himself standing before a sweet-faced youngster with curly *payos.*

"Do you want Abba?" the lad asked endearingly. "Come in, he'll be right with you."

Gili waited for the head of the household in a room laden with books. From the next room came the chant of Gemara learning. Moshe Vayden was studying *Maseches Nedarim* with his *chavrusa,* and the two were arguing fervently. Gili listened with interest: He was familiar with the *sugya* from the short time he had learned with Rabbi Schmidt. When he could, he would startle Vayden and his *chavrusa* with Rabbi Schmidt's position.

A half-hour later, when he was done learning, Moshe Vayden, walked into the room wearing a thin silk robe. He was a dark-skinned man with a noble brow. His face was wreathed in smiles and exuded good cheer. He glowed with pleasure when Gili repeated his words in Gemara. "You look pretty young to me. When did you manage to learn so much?"

"When I learned with Rabbi Schmidt," Gili explained.

"And what brings you here?" Vayden asked. "You haven't come to study *Nedarim* with me."

Gili looked at him watchfully. Moshe Vayden radiated honesty and integrity. One could tell him what was happening.

After a half hour, when the entire episode of *The Vessel of Blessing* had been set forth, Vayden said anxiously, "It's not a simple story. I know Yaakovi, and he knows me."

"From where?" Gili said, surprised.

Vayden explained. "The market for antiquities is quite limited. Everyone knows everyone else. You can only survive if you have sharp instincts. Yaakovi has the caution of a tigress, the ears of a cat, and the sense of smell of a good hunting dog. You can't fool him."

"There's no way to get the book away from him?" Gili's arms fell to his sides in despair.

Vayden thought for a moment. "Look, the market for antiquities is hermetically sealed. Not even a piece of paper gets lost, not to mention a book of such rarity."

Vayden proceeded to illustrate his point. "Two years ago, a young man came to me, very distraught. His son was seriously ill. That week he'd found out that I was a collector of antiquities and that I possessed an original letter from the holy Admor of Strizhov, who lived 150 years ago. This young man said he was a member of that *chassidic* dynasty, and he begged me to lend him the rare letter for a few days. 'If we put the holy letter beneath the pillow of my sick son, he will get better quickly.' Nu, could a person say no? The letter was given, with ceremonial promises that it would be returned swiftly. After a week the boy's father came to me, completely hysterical. The *segulah* worked, the boy had recovered. But the boy's older sister, who didn't know of it, had washed the sheets without checking them, and the letter had been destroyed in the washing machine.

"I assured the young man that I wasn't angry," Vayden continued. "I was naive and believed him. But what happened? After about a year the 'laundered' letter turned up in the market. The young man had sold it for several thousands of dollars. A friend, another trader, offered to sell it to me. There, go and laugh...

"And that's just a small piece of paper," Vayden concluded. "You're talking about a book worth hundreds of thousands of dollars. It is impossible to get it away from him, and if I show any sudden interest his suspicions will be aroused — why am I suddenly asking about a book that's not on the market?"

"So there's nothing to be done?" Gili asked hopelessly.

"Who said so?" A spark gleamed impishly in Vayden's eyes. "In two months Sotheby's is having a public auction in Tel Aviv. Their catalog is being finalized right now. I'll fill the world market with rumors of heightening interest in the book *The Vessel of Blessing*, and create a demand for it. One of two things is possible: Either Yaakovi lied about his two copies, and the book actually is no longer in existence, as you believe. If so, he will undoubtedly keep quiet. But if the book does exist, even a forgery, Yaakovi will not be able to withstand the temptation of putting it up for sale. Half a million, three quarters of a million dollars is a pretty nice sum by all reckonings. He may fall in the trap — even the most careful of cats sometimes do."

29

"Five factors create demand and fix the price of antiquities in general, and ancient writings in particular. 1) The importance of the author and his personality. The more important the writer, the more expensive his manuscript. There's no comparison between a letter written by the Baal Shem Tov and that written by a chassidic leader who lived 50 years ago. 2) Rarity. The price of an item goes up in direct proportion to the number available. For a trader, the fewer copies, the better. 3) Age. The older an item, the more it's worth. 4) Authenticity. The ability to prove that the item isn't forged. 5) And most important of all — the contents."

Moshe Vayden was giving Gili a crash course in the antiquities market, as they spoke over country-style bread and a plate of warm casserole. Gili's mouth stopped crunching the brown bread for a moment. "And what do you mean by the word 'contents'?"

Vayden forked a steaming piece of potato from his bowl and put it in his mouth. Unlike Gili, he continued to eat as he spoke. "You don't understand it?" he said, surprised. "Let's speak of a hypothetical situation. Let's say we find a note from the Gaon of Vilna. It's a shopping list for his son, listing the groceries he's to buy. That's important and valuable, but it can't be compared with, say, a kabbalistic manuscript of his."

Gili took a spoonful of saffron-colored soup. "Okay, I get it. And what's the price of a book such as *The Vessel of Blessing*, for example?"

"You've gotten to the heart of the matter," Vayden pushed away his now-empty plate and carefully wiped his mouth with a napkin. "That book is a problematic one. Its true value is enormous, because of its incredible contents. On the other hand, it has no real value today, because no one can understand it."

"So who would want to buy something that has no value at all, for all practical purposes?"

"Let me finish," Vayden said. He turned towards the children's room. "Shmelki, please bring me *mayim acharonim*." He returned to Gili. "I was about to say that if the book were for sale, it's possible that it would have great demand, because it meets the first four criteria, and also because it's regarded as a good-luck charm. How did your grandfather put it? 'The talisman of our family.'"

Little Shmelki brought a cup and small plate and the two recited *Birchas HaMazon.* "It was wonderful meeting you," Gili thanked his host with a smile at the end of the meal. "The soup was just what I needed."

"Tell that to my rebbetzin," Vayden laughed impatiently. "She's in charge of the gastronomy department. We'll meet in another two weeks. I have a feeling that since the company's founding in 1744 Sotheby's sales charts haven't taken off the way they will now. It's going to get interesting around here."

🙢✸🙠

The Israeli branch of Sotheby's is located in a small building in Tel Aviv, at Rechov Gordon 38. The office's fax machine chimed and spat out a piece of paper. "Rina, I'll give you ten-to-one that this is also about that book, *The Vessel of Blessing,*" the secretary said to a colleague as she stooped over the in-basket. "Look, 20 faxes, all on the same book."

"Where are they coming from?" Rina asked from her inner office, surrounded by dozens of valuable paintings on wire hangers.

"From where aren't they coming? From branches all over the world, particularly America —New York, Philadelphia, San Francisco. I understand demand for it from London, Paris, Toronto, Sao Paulo and Johannesburg. There are large concentrations of Jews in those places. But why should *The Vessel of Blessing* interest our branches in Milan, Venezuela, Sydney, and even Hong Kong and Singapore! I don't get it. How can there suddenly be such a great demand for a book I never heard of before yesterday?"

"Ask Rivka if she has an explanation for the phenomenon," Rina said, as she continued cataloging the pictures in a huge notebook.

But Rivka Sachar, manager of Sotheby's Tel Aviv branch, couldn't explain the mountain of faxes. Even her superior, David Breuer-Weill of the London branch, who was visiting Israel at the time and was consulted, had no idea. How could they know that Moshe Vayden had enlisted his many contacts all over the world and initiated in ways only he could know a wave of rumors on the impending sale of one of the three existing manuscripts of *The Vessel of Blessing?*

The antiquities market is alert and frenetic. Wherever Jewish merchants lived the word got out: A rare and valuable book, which until now was the exclusive property only of the Dinburg/Dinar family and the collector Yaakovi, was soon to be put on the block by Sotheby's Israeli division. The rumors grew: The Dinburg/Dinar copy had been destroyed in a terrible fire that consumed both the book and its owner. Only two copies remained, those belonging to Yaakovi — only two copies in the entire world! And now one of these was up for sale. The market grew nervous, collectors and traders were frantic. They called and faxed Sotheby's offices throughout the world, asking for confirmation of the rumors — and the Tel Aviv fax machine droned on and on.

When Rivka Sachar phoned Pinny Yaakovi, she felt the eyes of the worldwide network of Sotheby's upon her. The world of antiquities was in an uproar, and she would be the first to know the answer.

Pinny Yaakovi was taken completely by surprise. Until Rivka Sachar's call he hadn't heard a thing. No one had approached him. His sharp trader's instincts, though, were faster than a Pentium computer chip. "I've considered selling the book, but the price is astronomical," he said warily.

"That is —"

"A minimum of $700,000," he said, sounding unconcerned.

Mrs. Sachar swallowed a shout. "That must be a very rare book," she said admiringly. She felt giddy, almost drunk: The commission her office would receive would be almost 10 times as much as the highest they had ever gotten for a single item. The valuable oil painting of the Austrian Jewish artist Isidore Kaufman, "Portrait of a Rabbi," had been sold for $70,000, and that was considered top dollar in the Israeli market.

"Rare isn't the correct word," Yaakovi interjected. "There are only two copies left in the world, and both are in my hands!"

"You know that we're putting together a new catalog for our January sale. Would you like to insert *The Vessel of Blessing* into it?"

"Certainly."

"Our photographer will call you within the hour to make an appointment to photograph the book."

Yaakovi was adamant. "I want a policeman too. And I want this absolutely clear: The book will not leave my house until its sale."

"You don't want it displayed at the pre-sale exhibit?" Sachar's disappointment was obvious.

"No! I don't trust your safes. There are too many eyes on *The Vessel of Blessing.*"

After he had hung up, Yaakovi looked gratefully towards the decorated ceiling. Three quarters of a million dollars were raining down upon him, without the least bit of effort on his part. Someone up there was taking good care of him.

挀❧

After two weeks Moshe Vayden decided to act. Gili called Yaakovi's home. "Here is speaking Francois Germaine of Paris. I visit as a tourist to Israel," he said, with a heavy French accent. "Can you be telling me of the book *Weasel of Blessing*?"

"That's *Vessel*," Yaakovi corrected him. "Who sent you to me?" he asked suspiciously.

Gili was ready for the question. "In Paris all say, Big Kobi has the most valuable book in the world," he whistled in amazement. "They say, half a million dollar."

"Eight hundred thousand," Yaakovi countered.

"Ooh, la, la!" Gili again showed his amazement. "That is much money. I have much money, money like water. But I can pay only 600,000."

"We'll see," Yaakovi answered. He was still suspicious. "Why are you so interested in the book?"

"I want to buy *zee* book," he said, as Vayden almost fell off the couch laughing at his accent. "Your father comes from Greece."

"What are you talking about? My father is a Jerusalemite," Yaakovi said fiercely.

"I am confusing in Hebrew. Not your father, my father, comes from Greece, Salonika. So do I search for the writings of Rav Albertzloni."

"Come to the public auction at the Holiday Inn in Tel Aviv in another month and a half and you can buying the book," Yaakovi imitated Francois's French accent.

"You not understanding? I wanting to see the book in your house, if it is beautiful to me I will give you the check immediately. We have no need of Sotheby's. If you do not so desire, then *pardon* and shalom."

Yaakovi hesitated. A foolish French millionaire was begging him and he was putting him off? "One minute," he said urgently, before the receiver was hung up. "You want to come to my home? Please do! Whenever you wish it."

Gili took a deep breath. "I to come tomorrow afternoon, with my friend, Morris. He is understanding Judaica and antiquities."

For my part you can bring the Messiah. The main thing is that you bring a big check, Yaakovi thought happily.

It was "pipe night." Four of the division heads were heavy pipe smokers, not to mention S., head of the GSS, who was their model. S. was a regular frequenter of fine tobacco shops, and it was from him that they'd learned how to fill, draw and puff on a pipe, and what brand of tobacco was best. Following in his footsteps, they'd bought Captain Black tobacco, with a cherry flavor, and, when the trend changed, switched to Empora, with its red label, filling the hallways of the GSS with the aroma of fine apples. The minute he would decide to switch to Bourkenrif, or choose a whiskey-flavored tobacco, or mint, or sherry with a touch of vanilla, the others would follow. *I do something, and everyone stands at attention*, he laughed to himself.

The conference room was filled with a white haze. The vents just couldn't cope with the clouds of smoke being puffed into the air minute by minute.

"I think it's time to activate 'Operation Puppeteer Rabbi,'" S., head of the GSS, announced.

"You're moving too fast," M., head of the Psychological Warfare Division, argued. "Have you ever had a piece of meat that was served too raw? Let my plan mature a little longer, and then you can pull them out of the pot one by one, soft as macaroni."

The debate grew intense. Some of the division heads sided with M., but when it came time for a decision they all showed their unswerving obedience to the dictates of the GSS head.

Despite everything, the meeting ended without a final determination. But S. had already decided to activate part of the plan.

He would increase the dosage of "Operation Puppeteer Rabbi," he thought, with just a touch of satisfaction.

⏎⊰✦⊱⏎

Moshe Vayden and Gili took a taxi to Ramat Aviv Gimmel the next day at noon, reaching the locked gate of the Yaakovi home. Vayden had been careful to travel in his traditional Yerushalmi garb: a long *chalat* with a wide sash and a low, wide-brimmed felt hat. The strong wind threatened to blow the black hat away, and he held onto its brim to keep it steady.

Gili was dressed in the garb of a French tourist. He could speak a fluent French, like one who only a few hours earlier had boarded an Air France jet in Paris's Orly Airport. He wore a light cream-colored suit by Yves St. Laurent, set off with a bow tie, and he was surrounded by the delicate scent of fine aftershave. As an additional protection he was wearing gold-rimmed Cartier glasses.

Vayden was satisfied. "Maybe your mother would recognize you behind all these '*shmattes*,' but since you've only visited Yaakovi once, let's hope he won't remember you."

"We also met at the Judaica fair," Gili reminded him nervously.

"Nonsense. The odds of him identifying you are minuscule," Vayden waved away his trepidation with a wave of his hands. "Come and prove your ability as an actor."

Gili laughed inwardly. Vayden didn't dream how close he had come to the truth. In his drama club in school, Gili had been considered first rate; his friends had always assumed that Israel's top theatrical company would be glad to have him join the troupe.

Next to the well-remembered intercom Gili saw something new, a red light bulb. So Yaakovi had added an electric eye to his security. Vayden looked at a shiny metal circle on the other side of the gate in astonishment. "What's that?"

"He's got everything," Gili explained. "Including an infrared sensor. It looks like Yaakovi lives in mortal fear of burglars."

The sensor appeared to be working; even before they'd hit the intercom button the red bulb flashed to life.

"Who are you?" a voice croaked.

He should fix the intercom, Gili thought to himself. *His voice sounds awful. Just like last visit.*

"Moshe Vayden and a friend," the trader identified himself. *"Bonjour,"* Gili added.

"Moshe Vayden?" the croak asked in surprise. "Ah, he calls you Morris. Okay, come on in."

When they heard the buzz they pushed open the gate. They crossed a garden in full bloom and walked up the steps to the second floor.

◌⃰✺◌

The house was as beautiful as before. A fireplace gave off a pleasant warmth. Gili's sharp eye noticed a few changes: two new oil paintings, another stand near the desk that housed an impressive array of antique pipes. Pinny Yaakovi himself had lost a little weight since Gili had met him last; he looked pale and distressed. Gili wondered how many threats he'd garnered since then from the mafia heads.

Despite his appearance, Yaakovi was full of affected smiles and good cheer. He gave several forced laughs at Vayden's witticisms. "So let's get down to business," he finally said. "I love a good Yerushalmi joke, the humor of Meah Shearim where I was born. But Mr. Germaine hasn't come to Israel to hear jokes, he came for this."

He pointed to a corner of the desk, to a square object bulging out from under a thick, bordeau-colored leather covering. He picked up the leather-bound package.

Gili breathed deeply in excitement. He recognized well that ancient binding.

"This is the book *The Vessel of Blessing*," Yaakovi declared ceremoniously. "One of the two copies extant. The second is guarded in a safe in the basement."

Gili's heart beat wildly and his breath came quicker. *This cannot be Abba's book, that was burned up; if so, my grandfather, R' Shmuel Dinburg, was wrong. There were three copies, not one as he claimed.*

"Oh, that is the book? *Tres joli, monsieur.* May one see it?" It was hard to speak: His dry tongue almost stuck to his palate.

Yaakovi carefully lifted the book and handed it to Gili. "Look at it as much as you like. Soon it will be yours, and then you can learn it by heart," he said happily.

"*Tres bien,*" Gili said. As he opened to the fateful title page he looked for his father's name — and didn't find it. Vayden read the words together with him: "The book of charms, *The Vessel of Blessing,* by the *chacham* Rabbi Ezra Albertzloni. Salonika 5234 (1474), with three gates. The first gate is the Gate of Wisdom of the Soul. The second gate is the Gate of Wisdom of the Countenance. The third gate is the Gate of Wisdom of Deeds."

"That's the book, there's no doubt about it," Vayden said, deeply impressed. "I've heard so much about it and never seen it. Even when I began as a trader, I remember hearing about *The Vessel of Blessing*. It was said that whoever could understand it and follow its instructions could control anyone he wanted."

Yaakovi was enjoying himself. "It's a unique work. No one can understand a word of it, but that's not our problem. If someone were to make a serious study of it, he could turn over the world with it."

Gili skimmed through its pages, looking at the kabbalistic sketches with an uncontrollable emotion. Yaakovi whispered to Vayden in Yiddish, "He's very serious. Why did he bring you?"

Vayden whispered back. "For my skill. He doesn't trust himself. He knows you can sell him 'a cat in a sack.'"

Yaakovi smiled and looked with pleasure at Gili, engrossed completely in the book. "So let's get down to business," he said impatiently. "How much time does he need to look through it?"

"Just another minute or two. Now I want to check it also."

Yaakovi was insulted. "You don't trust me? Sotheby's does. Look what they've written in their catalog."

He pulled out a color brochure that had been printed for a previous sale and pointed to a page headed "Terms of Sale." "Here, read it," he said triumphantly.

Vayden read the tiny print of the first paragraph: "The authenticity of possession of the item as outlined in the catalog is insured as detailed in the provisions of warranty, unless otherwise stated."

"That's not enough for you?" Yaakovi crowed. "The great Sotheby's believes me and you don't? I guarantee that this is an original, with no suspicion of forgery!"

"One minute," Vayden stopped him. "See what else it says: 'Each piece is being sold as is, and neither we nor the seller are warranting the truth of statements made in the catalog or any description of the items' condition.'"

"Enough of this foolishness!" Yaakovi shouted angrily. "I assure you, on the word of honor of Yaakovi, and no one has ever known me to break my word, that the book is the original, not a copy or a forgery."

Gili awoke and put down the book. "*D'accord*, I making a deal," he said to Yaakovi. "If you agreeing to leave Sotheby's, I to pay you *tout de suite* with a check, half-million dollar."

Yaakovi grew furious; this Frenchman was no fool. Angrily, the trader grabbed hold of one of the walking sticks that were displayed nearby. Gili blinked nervously. He well remembered the secret Yaakovi had revealed on his previous visit: The innocent-looking cane hid a murderous gun. His nervous twitch had not gone unnoticed by the collector. "We were speaking about $800,000" he barked.

"*Mon ami*," Gili stuttered, "if Morris telling me it is worth it, I will be giving more."

Moshe Vayden didn't understand what was going on. He stood calmly looking at the book, and put one of the pages to the light. "What are you doing, checking the watermark? You don't believe me?" Yaakovi demanded angrily.

Vayden ignored his protests and put down the book. "Mr. Yaakovi, you must forgive Monsieur Germaine. But $800,000 isn't chicken feed." He eagerly grabbed at Gili's left sleeve. "But it's worth it. Beyond a doubt, the book is authentic."

Beyond a doubt, the book was a forgery. They had prearranged the signal: If the book was authentic, Vayden was to pull at Gili's right sleeve.

"*D'accord*, excellent. Good. I thinking about this a few days and returning here to give money and take the book."

He straightened his suit and stood up. "*Merci, merci*, thank you, Monsieur Kobi, it was very nice. I will be seeing you."

"What? You're leaving?" Yaakovi shouted. "You're not buying the book?"

"I buying the book, in a few days," Gili explained. "*C'est la vie*, I must think well on this."

Yaakovi jumped up from his upholstered chair, his face purple with rage. "You've been putting me on!" he screamed at Vayden in a thunderous voice. "It's a conspiracy; you've signaled him somehow."

Vayden looked at him, offended. "Conspiracy? You're suspicious of us for nothing! Francois, why don't you want the book? It is authentic, without a doubt."

Gili looked at him in astonishment. "I not wanting? I wanting to think a little. Why is he making the roar of the lion? *Pardon*, I am buying the book in a few days," he explained to Yaakovi.

The collector looked at him unbelievingly. "You're coming back here?"

"Like clockwork," Gili answered confidently.

Yaakovi's voice held a warning tone. "Vayden, for your own good I hope that you're telling the truth. If I find out that you've been playing games, or that you suspect me of forgery..." He stopped and left his words hanging in midair.

They called a cab and left the house. The electric eye gazed unblinkingly at them until they'd disappeared from sight. Afterwards, Yaakovi picked up the phone. "Give me M.," he said nervously. He waited a moment and began to speak again. "Meshulam, you were right. Gili is on to it. He's very suspicious. He masqueraded as that young man, Francois Germaine of Paris, speaking a very convincing French. But your father is no fool: I played along, pretending I hadn't identified him, but I recognized him right away. Just to make sure, I threatened him with one of the canes. You should have seen how pale he got. Why should Germaine of Paris get nervous because of a simple walking stick..."

The voice on the other end asked something. "I'm not a neurologist; don't speak to me in doctor's terms," Yaakovi replied. "Brain episode, blackouts... foolishness. His mind is alert, and how. He's a great danger!"

The line went dead. Meshulam thought for a moment; his expression became dreamy. Meshulam was known among his friends as "Babyface." Even at the age of 40 he still had the countenance of a child and an innocent look that often deceived his victims. But that innocence had vanished now; his eyes were loaded with a dangerous light as he turned on his computer diary and searched for the file known as "Gili." When the file appeared on the tiny digital screen he pressed "enter" and then typed in one word: Liquidate.

∽❧∼

They entered the cab and made themselves comfortable in the back seat. "Where to?" the driver asked.

"The Central Bus Station," Gili replied.

"No," Vayden interrupted. "Take us to 38 Gordon Street."

Luckily, the driver was a relaxed sort of fellow, unlike most of his colleagues. "Okay, Gordon it is. But next time, why don't the two of you decide before you come in, you and your Frenchie friend."

"Why Gordon?" Gili whispered.

"You'll see," Vayden answered.

Gili was still completely hypnotized by the book. "How did you spot the forgery?" he asked.

Vayden rubbed his hands in pleasure. "You would never have caught it. But for me it was really quite simple — and that's why he was afraid of me. The book could have been an original, or a copy printed almost at the same time. There are no later copies, that I know. Now I knew it wasn't the original, because it was printed on paper rather than deer hide. But it couldn't have been a copy from that era. The paper of the 14th and 15th centuries is linen, with identifying marks throughout. There were no such marks here. That was new paper, that went through a process to make it seem aged with the aid of certain acids."

Gili didn't get it. "Yaakovi is no fool. How could he imagine that his forgery wouldn't be spotted? In his interview with me, he himself told me the signs of a forgery. Didn't he realize that someone would uncover the fraud?"

The cab rode through the Tel Aviv streets. A heavy rain poured down outside, and windshield wipers worked continuously to keep the front window clean. They approached the city center.

Vayden explained. "Yaakovi is a swindler, but sometimes he makes unprofessional mistakes. How many times did he get involved with the mafia, each time miraculously escaping their clutches? I wouldn't be surprised to hear that they'd found his dead body in some seedy hotel. Woe to those who start up with people like that."

The taxi reached the address. They rang Sotheby's bell. After they had been scrutinized through a peephole, they heard a buzz from the intercom.

"Shalom," said Vayden, "I've come to buy your new catalog."

The secretary didn't conceal her astonishment. "It just came back from the printer an hour ago. How in the world did you know?"

Vayden smiled modestly. "Instinct."

The catalog was placed before them on a desk, still exuding faint traces of the printing press. Vayden skimmed through it hastily. "Here it is, *The Vessel of Blessing*. Now you have your answer: This is why I came here. I wanted to know if Yaakovi had cheated us," he whispered. He showed Gili a photograph of the leather-bound book. The relevant details of the book, written in English, were printed beneath the picture. The cost of the book at public auction was set at $600,000 - $800,000.

"That's our most expensive item," the secretary said proudly. "Are you interested?"

Gili skimmed through the glossy pages of the catalog. Suddenly, his blood seemed to freeze with him.

In the section on ritual objects, among the antique and ultramodern silver menorahs, was a full-page color picture. And from that picture, caught in the white light of the flash, sparkled the 20 stems of the chandelier that had been stolen from the *beis midrash* of the *chassidim* of Kiltz.

30

Moshe Vayden saw Gili's body stiffen and his hands tremble. "Has something happened?"

Wordlessly, Gili pointed to the color photo. Vayden looked at the picture and murmured quietly, "The best of Judaica. That is a very ancient and very valuable chandelier."

"Not Judaica. Loot," Gili hissed. "This pretty little object was stolen from the *beis midrash* of the *chassidim* of Kiltz."

The secretary interrupted the conversation, her fury obvious. "Excuse me, young man, but read what it says on the facing page before you slander Sotheby's. I could take you to court."

And indeed the write-up stated, in English, that the chandelier that was up for sale was one of two identical pieces that had been brought from Spain by Marranos as they fled the Inquisition. The item's cost was put at between $300,000 and $400,000.

"Who's put it up for sale?" Gili asked, his voice tinged with doubt.

The secretary hesitated. "That information is confidential."

Gili pulled out his journalist's identification card. The threat was sufficient: The secretary leafed through a thick notebook and said, "Mr.

Manfred Strum, an American Jew of Dutch extraction, has offered it for sale. It was his personal possession for many years."

"Naturally," Gili agreed, the sarcasm in his voice almost undetectable. "Undoubtedly his grandfather was the one who made it."

On their way to Jerusalem Gili told Vayden all about the *chassidim* of Kiltz and the theft of the chandelier just a short time ago. "Isn't this a question just begging to be answered?" he ended.

"Okay, let's say this 'Mr. Strum' is a front for the thieves. There's a way to find out if this was the stolen chandelier. You can have it professionally checked, to see if it matches with the little that was left of it in Kiltz."

"To do so means involving the police, and that's not so simple," Gili protested. He preferred working by himself, and wouldn't reveal all of his thoughts even to the honest Jerusalemite.

The bus on which they were traveling passed Ben Gurion Airport. Gili stared at the planes parked on the runways, an old habit of his since he'd been a youngster fascinated by the huge metal birds. "You know," he said, turning to Vayden, "since we left Yaakovi's house, a few things have been bothering me."

Vayden leaned back in his seat. "Let's hear."

"Okay," Gili nodded, his eyes taking in the passing scenery. "First, why did Yaakovi forge the book, if there was no demand for it all this time? And how did he manage to get a copy?"

Gili's eyes roamed over the sodden fields on either side of the road. He continued. "So the question is, how did Yaakovi manage to forge the book and make two copies, without ever having seen the original? The book was never placed on the market, and then it was burned up!"

Vayden flung out his hands restlessly. He also felt lost in the fog — just like Gili.

❧❀❧

When Gili left the Central Bus Station, he noticed a man also walking towards bustling Rechov Yaffo.

"You're not dreaming, Gili, it's really me," Rabbi Schmidt laughed. "What are you doing here?"

"I just returned from Tel Aviv. And you?"

"I wanted to travel with a student of mine who is on his way abroad. Because of my busy schedule, I couldn't go with him to the airport so I came here instead. But you didn't understand my question: You've got your Mitsubishi. Why would a car owner be using buses?"

"Just slumming," Gili laughed. At that moment, a thought flashed through his mind. *This isn't a coincidence. Providence has sent Rabbi Schmidt to me.*

He escorted his rabbi back to the yeshivah and then sat closeted with him in his office for a long while. He began with a history of the book *The Vessel of Blessing*. Rabbi Schmidt, lacking the background of the story, was at a loss.

Gili had tried to put off this hour. An introvert, he loathed personal confessions. But there was no choice.

Rabbi Schmidt heard his story in astonishment. "I would never have believed it," he repeated again and again. "It's amazing how you managed to hide from me the fact that you are the son of my good friend Moshe Dinburg. I never put Dinar and Dinburg together. Your father only changed a few letters of his real name."

And his identity...

Rabbi Schmidt's wonder turned to horror when he learned of the terrible fate of his two childhood friends. He jumped up and sat down several times, cries of pain and sorrow issuing forth. "Oh no! Six years and I never had an inkling."

His anguish was honest, his pain sharp and piercing. He called out their names — Moishe Dinburg and Manny Schwartz — dozens of times. When he added the words "may their memories be blessed," hot tears poured from his eyes. "The *mashgiach*, Rabbi Shmuel Bergman, *shlita*, undoubtedly didn't hear of his students' bitter end, dead without the chance of *teshuvah*. I would have heard from him if he had; he's very close to me."

Gili could almost feel his heart shrivel up within him; a lump grew in his throat. "You know," he said, his wound apparent, "actually, it was Manny, who seems from your stories like a schemer and manipulator, who at least merited death as a believing Jew. After he left the army he returned to a life of Torah and *mitzvos*. My mother has told me that he wore a black *kippah* and a *tallit katan*, and returned to observance. Only Abba, the sensitive one, the one with the sweet personality, stubbornly clung to his secular lifestyle, up until his last day on earth."

He burst out crying. The image of the rebbe of Kiltz wailing at his father's death sprang before his eyes, the rebbe walking with such effort on swollen feet as he cried, "But I was his *sandek*, how could he have died without repentance? How had Moishike Dinburg fallen into the destruction of the River Dinar?"

All Gili's hurt came to the fore: the agony of being orphaned that gnawed at his soul constantly, the longing for his father that pierced his flesh day and night. The report on Kiltz that had turned into a debacle and had had such terrible consequences. The rebbe of Kiltz, ailing and bedridden. The persecution of Yeshivas Torah Lishmah, the justifiable anger of the brothers, Shmerl and Zimel Mirinski, the threats on his own life, the sudden frostiness in his relationship with Rav Avram.

Everything exploded at once. His hidden wounds tore apart with a terrible, awesome power. He was overcome by weeping. He cried in a welter of confused emotion, wept for everything at once. Later, his pain became more structured: He thought of the loss of his father, and a wave of tears came. He remembered the troubles he'd engendered: more tears. Each wound brought with it more sobbing, more pain.

He sat thus for an hour, his head in his hands, his shoulders trembling with a weeping that had no beginning and no end.

Rabbi Schmidt sat and stared at Gili, his heart weeping with his student. Occasionally he would pat his shoulder encouragingly. Realizing that the pain had not yet eased, he opened a *Tehillim* and began to pray for Gili, that he should succeed in the future, that the hands of evil ones be kept away from him.

Finally, after an hour, Gili lifted his head. His eyes were rimmed with red, but the frightened, tortured look within them was gone, replaced by a wonderful tranquillity. Hope and faith looked out of those green eyes. He scorned danger and stood straight and strong against all the challenges that faced him.

"You're a new person," Rabbi Schmidt said thankfully. "Now you can tell me all about the book."

Gili cast away all doubt and presented a clear picture. Rabbi Schmidt listened intently for half an hour, making a supreme effort at understanding, but not managing to pierce the mystery.

Finally, he said, "Gili, believe me, if you could see my brain, you'd see it's squeezed dry as a lemon. But I can only find one thread."

"And that is?" Gili said impatiently.

"Go and learn sign language."

"What?"

Rabbi Schmidt's eyes grinned at him. "You've told me about Paysi, the deaf boy who lives with Rav Avram. Maybe he knows something. You know, no one is cautious around him.

"You've got a good head? You know English and French? So you'll know sign language too. Go and learn Paysi's language."

The Brent household revolved around Paysi 24 hours each day. There were another seven people in the home — his parents and five sisters — and his father was in desperate need of emotional support himself, but Paysi stood firmly in the center from morning to night.

His daily schedule was exhausting. When he awoke he had his daily regimen of antibiotics, cortisone, medications, chlorine substitutes, and capsules to break down the fats in his diet, a function that his damaged pancreas could no longer process. All this was in addition to a large variety of vitamins and medicines to build up his strength.

Paysi's sisters couldn't neglect their schoolwork, so only Dina was left in the house. (His father, Rafael, was also there, but he couldn't deal with anything.) After giving him his medicines, Dina began to feed him.

Even as an infant, the doctors had emphasized to Dina the need to fatten him up. "Your son will be terrifyingly thin," Dr. Kreiff and his staff had warned her. "There are several reasons for this. Every breath is an effort and takes great energy. His cellular needs are three times as high as normal. The breakdown of fats in the pancreas is flawed. His intestines are damaged and he suffers from chronic infections. All of these cause the calories to be burned up; his energy comes from a broken, clogged tap. He will constantly lose fat, yet he is the one who needs great reserves, in order to stave off infection.

"The normal intake of a CF patient looks like the dream of an insatiable glutton." Dr. Kreiff gave his flinty smile. "At the time when most of the modern world is changing its diet to low fat, high-fiber foods, CF sufferers do the opposite. They must eat a lot, foods high in carbohydrates, sugars, proteins and fats. Whatever has been forbidden to dieters is a must for CF victims."

Paysi had to eat well and eat a lot, but his appetite was small. Dina knew that his very life depended on the amount of food that she could get into his emaciated body. It took nerves of steel and a will of iron in order to put a spoon into the child's mouth, another spoon, another spoon, without giving up, knowing that after an hour of such feeding Paysi was apt to open his mouth and vomit everything out, occasionally including the medications as well.

At the age of 30, Dina was a broken woman; her heart's despair extinguished the sparks of life within her. Her nightmare was of a deadly microbe that tended to grow in the lungs of CF sufferers and could cause irreversible damage. Paysi, weakened because of the viscous mucus that wouldn't drain, was a prime candidate for such an attack.

Because of this threat, he received physiotherapy. Twice a day he went to a professional, who would bang on his back and put him in different positions. The banging and the vibrations moved the mucus through the breathing passages, helping him to cough it out. But the physiotherapist had to be careful that Paysi not cough too strongly, or he could contract emphysema or begin to bleed internally.

Fortunately, Paysi was a happy, carefree little boy, one who loved life despite its burdens and the high costs of each and every breath he took. He would lie on the couch and ask the physiotherapist in sign language, "When will you stop hitting me?"

"When you'll get better," the physiotherapist would reply, in the little sign language he'd learned in order to communicate with his deaf patient.

"And will I get better?" Paysi would immediately ask.

A tear would ooze from Dina's eye.

The professional physiotherapy treatments were very expensive, costing approximately 1500 shekels a month. The family reeled beneath the economic burdens. Paysi began getting his treatments at home — and the standard matched the training.

When he grew older Paysi began other physical activities. Swimming and exercise are an integral part of the CF sufferer's daily treatment. He learned to swim at 7, and would get to a pool twice a week. Happily, the boy took to the water like a fish.

Not every day followed the exact same schedule. Dina simply couldn't do it: She was tottering beneath the heavy load. Paysi's half sisters did what they could to help their mother, but Dina could only rely on the capable Chedvi for help. Chedvi, the eldest, was a good-hearted girl and she became Dina's right hand.

At the age of 18 Chedvi married. After she left the house, Dina felt as if she were treading water, trying desperately not to drown. Just at that time Paysi grew ill and twice needed hospitalization. When he was released his appetite disappeared completely, his weight went down drastically. After two months Paysi weighed only 40 pounds. "Anorexia," announced the doctors, hospitalizing him still a third time for force-feeding. Fats and liquid vitamins were injected directly into his stomach, as if he were a goose to be stuffed. But due to the doctor's persistence, Paysi survived.

The next attack began in the morning. Paysi awoke with the sun's first rays, thought the words *"Modeh Ani."* His eyes glanced at the bowl prepared since last night for *netilas yadayim.* But when he reached for the cup, he felt a sudden pain in his chest. Paysi was used to aches and to having difficulty breathing, but this was different: The pain cut through his lungs like a sharpened knife. He carefully breathed in, slowly, slowly, and exhaled. And the knife grew ever sharper. He felt as if his lungs were exploding, as if the air within them was whistling out into his stomach. It was a horrible feeling.

He tried to scream for his mother, but none of the exercises he'd learned at his school for the deaf were of any help now. He gave off a tiny squeak that didn't reach the door of his bedroom. The pain grew worse, the air filled his body. Panic overcame him. In despair, he began to push a chair back and forth over the floor.

"Who's making so much noise so early in the morning?" demanded Penini, the older of the twins, as she hid her head beneath her pillow.

"Paysi thinks he's allowed to do everything," Shiri, her twin sister, complained, turning over to her other side and pulling her blanket over her bright-red hair.

The scratching sounds didn't stop, and finally reached the ears of Dina, through the thick fog of sleep. She jumped anxiously out of bed. "Something's happened to Paysi," she screamed, racing barefoot to his room.

She found him on the brink of unconsciousness. His face was blue and his eyes were bulging from their sockets. When he saw her, a spark of life twinkled in his frightened eyes. "Call an ambulance," Dina shouted, rousing the entire household. "Penini, Shiri, I don't understand you. You're in the room next to him; didn't you hear anything?"

She was furious, but there was no time for anger: She had only begun his treatment when the ambulance arrived.

Dina held Paysi's hand during the ride to the hospital. He was unconscious, despite the large quantities of oxygen flowing into him from the mask they had placed over his mouth and nose. She whispered words of *Tehillim*, praying desperately that her only son not slip away from her. "Paysi, I'm watching you, don't leave me," she whispered in a trembling voice. Even the case-hardened medics averted their eyes from the heart-wrenching scene.

In the emergency room the doctors managed to stabilize his condition. He was transferred to the pulmonary intensive care unit. The CT showed a phenomenon known as 'pneumothorax.' After three terrifying hours the doctor on duty came out to explain what had occurred.

He could have simply told her that this was a lung problem typical of cystic fibrosis sufferers, and that in a few days there would be a marked improvement in his condition. But it was her ill fortune that this was Dr. Shafrir, an exacting doctor who enjoyed speaking to patients and their families in unintelligible medical jargon. He came out into the hall, and Dina rushed towards him. Had the doctor been as well versed in understanding people's faces as he was in diagnosis, he would have seen her silent cry for help, the arteries swollen with fear, the lips pulled back in terror, the entire face resembling a rubber band stretched to the breaking point. But he thought only of how he could show his vast medical knowledge.

"Mrs. Brent, your son has pneumothorax."

Her heart leaped in fright. "Pnorex? What did you say?"

The doctor pulled himself up in self-importance. "Pneumothorax. Air in his chest. That is, he has a tear in his lung, and as a result air is going into his thorax, the lung is swelling up like a balloon and then deflating, like a balloon that has a hole in it. The phenomenon is connected, it seems, from the chronic problem of air in the lungs, which destroys the surrounding tubes as a result."

All Dina could understand was his example of the burst balloon. It was a horrifying image.

"Does that mean his lungs are deflating and getting smaller from minute to minute?" A deep despair punctuated her every word.

"Mrs. Brent, don't put words in my mouth," the young man, who'd just completed his six years in medical school, reprimanded her. "I told you your son has pneumothorax. If it were something minor we would have given him pulmonary treatment, including oxygen and bed rest, and the air would slowly have returned to the lung, without any other intervention.

"But the x-ray and CT have shown that your son has lost 25 percent of his lungs. Therefore we've placed a tube in the thorax through which the air can flow, until the lung regains its full capacity. Afterwards, through that same tube, we will inject materials that will cause a chemical reaction in the membrane of the lung wall. This reaction will cause the membrane to adhere and the holes to fill. We'll be using Tabrine Hydro-chloride, which is the accepted treatment for difficult patients such as your son."

"Stop confusing me with Latin. Speak in the language of a human being," Dina burst out. "Will Paysi live?"

The learned doctor's inflated ego was actually fragile as an eggshell. His wounded dignity begged for vengeance against one who dared pierce through it. This small woman had screamed at him right there in the hallway, in front of many others!

"My dear woman, I suggest that you pray," Dr. Shafrir said frostily, as he disappeared from sight.

Dina spent the entire day at Paysi's bedside. He had returned to consciousness but slept the whole time, under the influence of painkillers. A ventilator pumped filtered air into his lungs, while the tubes placed within his chest drained the air bubbles out. Towards evening she left the room and met her five stepchildren, their faces frightened and pale. "Ima," the twins, Penini and Shiri, hugged her tight, bursting into tears, "we're sorry we didn't run to him this morning. What's happened to Paysi? The doctors told us that he's very sick."

Chedvi stood up from the bench, a *Tehillim* in her hand and her eyes moist with tears. She tried to say something to Dina, but she was too choked up to speak. "Ima," Chedvi finally whispered, her hand gently patting Dina's, "Ima." She couldn't add another word. Their eyes met, eyes that spoke in a language that has no words, in a language that needs no words. Each felt the other's heart in a way she had never done before. Chedvi was ready to give her life for this strong woman, who had bestowed upon her the love of a true mother, who had never allowed the barrier of "stepmother" to grow between them.

And now these eyes held a horrifying pain. Chedvi, looking into their depths, was frightened by what she saw. She could see the despair, terrible in its totality. Dina, Chedvi knew, had heard the wings of the angel of death fluttering in that hospital room.

Dina gave each a warm kiss. They were all wonderful, and had come to help her. One asked to stay for the night with Paysi, a second volunteered to be with him the entire day tomorrow. Dina felt a wonderful feeling of warmth in her heart.

Sisters in sorrow...

"Tonight I'm staying with him," she said determinedly. "Tomorrow, one of you can take over for me."

After they had gone, she once again sat near Paysi's bed, murmuring words of *Tehillim*. Occasionally she sent a worried glance at his ashen face. No, the doctor had not said those words — I suggest that you pray — for no reason; Paysi's condition was serious. It was a fact: even the other doctors had told the twins so!

Had she only known that it was Dr. Shafrir himself who had said those frightening words...

Dina was convinced that Paysi was fighting for his young life. Late that night a veteran nurse came on duty, and exempted her from the nightlong vigil. "I'll go into his room every 10 minutes," she told her, her voice tinged with pity. "Go to sleep, *mamaleh*. Get your strength for tomorrow."

Dina was exhausted to her very marrow; she had no energy left to protest. She pulled her aching legs towards the elevator and pressed the button. After a five-minute wait a passing nurse told her that both elevators were undergoing repairs in the basement.

She walked to the empty stairwell. After what she had undergone that day, an eight-story descent seemed like no big feat, but after only a few steps she began to feel dizzy. She carefully edged towards the steel railing and held it tightly. As her glance slid downward, she began to sway back and forth. The railing, spiraling down eight stories, seemed to reach down to infinity, as if reflected in endless mirrors, one next to the other. Her weakness and dizziness had her completely in thrall.

With white fingers she gripped the railing and breathed deeply. Dull sounds echoed from outside, exploding into horrifying noise here in the deepness of the stairwell. "He has a cut in his lungs...deflating like a balloon with a hole...difficult cases such as those of your son...my dear woman, pray...

"Pray....pray...pray." The words echoed endlessly.

The echoes grew louder, louder, turned into deafening shouts. "No, no!" she begged, covering her ears with her hands. But the cruel sounds only got worse. Thousands of ravens flew past her, shrieking. "Paysi is very sick...very sick...the doctors told us...told us...very sick...sick...sick..."

She grabbed the railing again, as if trying to avert the inescapable calamity. But the ravens' dreadful cawing grew louder, and again she covered her ears. Her head bobbed from side to side, her body shook like one drunk. She stumbled past the railing. Her legs buckled as they fell off the stairs...

And then Dina was flying through infinite space, between brightly lit clouds, and she mocked them, for she was lighter than they. She was as light as a feather dancing in space; all the worries and pains and fears and despair, the ocean of tears, the endless bitterness — all that she left far behind her.

31

"**B**y all indications, it was vertigo," the police investigator explained to Chedvi. "That's a dizziness caused from a fear of heights." He stopped for a moment, narrowed his eyes, and asked in a hard voice, "Had your mother ever shown suicidal tendencies? Had she ever spoken about wanting to kill herself?"

"Heaven forbid," Chedvi shuddered. "Ima was full of the desire to live, despite all of her troubles."

The officer jotted down her words in his small notebook. "We have outside evidence that Mrs. Brent did not commit suicide. A few moments before the incident she was seen standing near the elevators, and the nurses told her that they were under repair. This indicates that she hadn't planned on going down the stairs. Our investigation has also found that no one else was there: She wasn't pushed. So what is left? Vertigo!

"Your mother got close to the rail, looked down and grew dizzy. A person can become spellbound, lose his judgment, and do exactly the opposite of what he should do. Have you ever seen a snake hypnotize a dove? The unfortunate bird is capable of flying away, and instead it approaches its waiting captor. Your mother did the same. Instead of moving away from the railing she bent towards it. That's the only way we can explain how she fell down."

The hospital's administrator listened to the police officer's words with a serious face. He turned to Chedvi. "The administration will compensate your family for the tragedy, and we will raise the railing at least half a meter."

"Money won't bring our mother back," Chedvi muttered, her face white as the bandages the hospital used. "And a higher railing won't save her."

She stood surrounded by her four sisters in the lobby of the hospital, near the morgue. After the representatives of the law and the hospital had left them, the five sisters began to wail. Suddenly they realized just how much their stepmother had meant to them. Chedvi was married, with a home of her own, expecting her first child. But now they were all orphans, with a father who needed constant help after his own nervous breakdown, with a brother who needed 24-hour care for his terrible illness.

They were lost. With her death, the warmth that had sheltered them was gone.

After the funeral Chedvi went to the hospital. She was surprised, as she entered the intensive care unit, to see that color had returned to Paysi's face. "Where is Ima?" he gestured to her.

Chedvi licked her dry lips. She had prepared for this moment and yet suddenly felt her knees go weak, a weakness that sent her reeling. She grabbed at the bedstead.

What should she say?

She hesitated for a moment and decided to spare him the truth until he had recovered and could handle it. "Ima caught a cold. She's in bed at home," she signed to him.

Paysi was still confused from all the strong medication they had doled out to him. He believed her.

Astonishingly, Paysi made a quick recovery. The pneumothorax, as the doctors termed the tear in his lungs, turned out to be a reversible illness. The monster was not as frightening after all.

Chedvi cried day and night. "If only Ima would have known how quickly he'd get better. If only she had known... If only the elevators hadn't been under repair just that night... If only..."

There was one more "if only" that Chedvi couldn't know: if only Dina had not spoken to Dr. Shafrir.

The young doctor had been shocked to learn the identity of the woman who had fallen to her death. When he replayed the conversation he had had with her that day, he felt a sharp stab of conscience. He dedicated himself completely to Paysi's health, and the results of his efforts could soon be clearly seen.

Go and tell a mound of earth that Paysi was getting better...

After a week Paysi returned home. He ran from room to room looking for Dina. "Ima," his lips moved in longing. "Where is Ima?"

For two days they kept it from him. Ima went away, Ima is here, Ima is there. After two days they called Chedvi. The five sisters sat around him. They all had learned sign language, but only Chedvi was capable of telling him the bitter news.

Paysi looked at them without comprehension. Why were they all here around him? Why were they all so sad?

Chedvi's palm pointed upward, her index finger linked to it on the side of the thumb, first on one side of the jaw, then on the other. That was the word "Ima" in sign language. Afterwards she used her hands to show wings flying.

"Ima is a butterfly?" Paysi signed.

Chedvi did not smile. She could have broken the news quickly, by signing the motion of someone lying down on the floor. She could have, but she did not want to. How would Paysi take it?

Penini whispered, "Why not just write it down and be done with it?"

Chedvi shuddered. To see those words in print — Ima is dead — would have a fatal effect on a little boy. *G-d of the universe, show me what to say — that is, what to sign, because I cannot speak.*

Her eyes were turned to heaven, and all the other eyes in the room were turned to her, but no inspiration came. She felt the terrible pressure increasing. *What's happening to me? Why can't I find the words, the signs?*

Maybe a miracle will happen, and Abba will get back to normal. Why don't we have a father like other people, a father that can take on these hard challenges, a father that we can lean on on such a terrible day?

"One minute," she told her sisters, "I'm going for Abba."

She tiptoed into the bedroom.

Rafael Brent was lying in his bed. The windows were closed and the smell of perspiration lay heavy in the room. Gold- and silver-foil candy wrappers lay in heaps on the floor. He was just in the process of taking a large piece of chocolate out from its crackling wrapper. He threw it into his mouth with a quick gesture and swallowed it with pleasure, making loud sucking noises.

"Abba," Chedvi said gently.

He snorted in anger. She was interrupting his unalloyed enjoyment of the chocolate! "What do you want?"

"Abba, look, Paysi is back from the hospital. We're out of ideas: Maybe you can tell him what happened to Ima?"

He looked past her as if she did not exist.

She begged. "Abba, can't you wake up? Have pity on yourself. You were such a happy person, so successful and talented. Wake up, Abba, wake up. Be what you used to be. Abba, why won't you answer me?"

Again he gazed at her vacantly, as he lazily threw another chocolate in his mouth. Suddenly the awful realization dawned upon her: She had not had a father for a long, long time. Her real father had died long ago, leaving only a heavy body that lacked any life or movement, an empty shell of a man that they called Rafael Brent. She had had a mother who had been both father and mother to them. Now she had lost both of them.

Chedvi's shoulders sagged as she returned to the room. Drori, Simi, Penini and Shiri looked at her hopefully, but from her drooping face and trembling lips they understood the answer.

She sat once again across from Paysi, searching for the right movement, but a large lump grew in her throat. Her face grew contorted and the tears began to fall. A terrible weeping burst out of her. The others followed, Drori and Simi, Penini and Shiri. They sat and almost choked on their tears.

And then Paysi understood. His one source of support in a dark world, his beloved mother, was gone.

And as Paysi wept his silent cries, making no sound, his face wet and his entire body trembling, the girls' hearts tore open. They fell upon each other, their screams reaching the street beyond. Neighbors opened their windows and heads popped out; youngsters stared at the Brent home. Everyone understood; everyone wept.

The entire neighborhood mourned. They mourned Dina, taken in her prime in a terrible accident after a life of pain and sorrow. They mourned for Rafael, her unfortunate husband, left alone, clearly destined for a psychiatric hospital now that his wife was gone. They mourned for the five orphaned girls, who had twice lost their mother.

And they mourned for Paysi.

Dina had sheltered Paysi with all her strength. She kept the news of his cystic fibrosis a deep secret, as classified as Israel's nuclear capabilities. But like that classified information, it was a secret shared by all. Everyone in the neighborhood knew that Paysi was not only deaf, but that he was suffering from something much worse.

The Brent home was shattered. The neighborhood mourned for a home destroyed, a home whose light had suddenly been extinguished.

Neighborhood residents organized to help the stricken family. They started a fund in their name, opened a bank account for them. Hearts were opened wide, and large sums came in within a few days. But they could not solve the biggest problem: What to do with Paysi? Who would take care of him?

The neighborhood rav organized a confidential meeting. As a result, community leaders found a religious family that had a child with cystic fibrosis. Paysi was sent to them as a foster child. The happy boy turned melancholy. His carefree, optimistic nature changed to one of sadness. He was very close with his sisters and did not want to be among strangers. He wanted to stay with his sisters but they did not know how to take care of him. Drori got engaged and Chedvi had given birth to her first child and was busy as only a new mother can be.

Slowly he developed a tenuous connection in that home with Yisraelik, the CF sufferer. But something had broken within him.

When Paysi turned 13 his foster father came to Rav Avram Roosenthal and poured his heart out. The boy was refusing his treatments, his health was failing. His foster father could no longer take on the responsibility.

"Bring him to me," Rav Avram said. "I want to meet him."

The chemistry between the rabbi with the riveting eyes and the young deaf boy was felt instantaneously. Rav Avram held a board with the letters of the alphabet on it in order to communicate, but there was no need.

And so Paysi went to live in the house of Rav Avram Roosenthal. To protect Paysi's privacy, Rav Avram and his assistants decided to change his identity somewhat, and thus Benny told Gili about the deaf boy who had come from a broken family and was taken from an institution. The description was more or less accurate, except for the "institution."

❧❧

"When G-d closes a door, He opens a window. When the mouth can't speak, the hands do," Dr. Motty Kanarik, well-known administrator of the school for the deaf, "A Voice in the Silence," said. "You can express yourself as well with your hands as with your tongue. Deaf people communicate among themselves, and with the outside world, just as quickly and just as well as you do. But what's the problem? You have to learn their language! Just as you would learn French!"

He handed Gili a book on sign language and said, with a smile, "If that's not enough for you, take this." He offered him another thick notebook.

Late that night, after a hard day in the newsroom, Gili perused the books. The notebook was the older of the two and consisted primarily of pictures of people expressing themselves with their hands, their faces; actually, their entire bodies. The notebook began with a "table of hand forms."

The palms of the hands — Gili learned — can be formed into 10 basic forms, and from this one can make thousands of gestures and expressions. He skimmed through the newer book, built around sketches of various expressions. It contained hundreds of pictures of people signing something with their hands. And there was a "table of hand movements," horizontal movements, diagonal movements, elliptical movements, circular movements...

Resolutely Gili began to memorize some of the basic vocabulary.

Morning — hands going down and up in a rainbow movement, palms closed. Noon — the right hand moving the length of the mouth in a double horizontal movement, in the "closed fingers" form. Night...

He did not check how one signed "night," feeling that in another minute he himself would be surrounded by night, by an abyss of darkness. He felt giddy. He had never known that sign language was so rich; it left him wordless and astonished.

Why should I work so hard, the thought came to rescue him. *I'll learn the sign language alphabet and speak with Paysi by spelling out words.*

He opened the alphabet chart of the Society for the Deaf in Israel.

Despair overcame him. The chart included 33 letters — the 22 letters of the Hebrew alphabet, and eleven vowelized or final letters. There were another nine vowels, totaling 42 signs.

I won't give up, Gili decided. In order to speak with Paysi he need only learn the basics. The rest he could fill in with the help of notes and an alphabet chart.

Until dawn he memorized about 200 basic words in sign language. It was hard, it was exhausting, but his phenomenal talents once again came to the fore. He retained it all.

❧✦❧

"Your moment of truth is arriving. If you don't abandon this business — you will die."

Gili and Benny examined the fax that awaited them in the office. The anonymous menace hadn't bothered to disguise himself; he had written the words in his own handwriting, not using a computer or even printing them.

They looked at each other. To whom was this addressed, to Gili or to Benny?

"Has your life ever been threatened?" Gili asked.

"Threatened? Sure, every day crazy drivers would threaten me. But since I sold my old jalopy of a Daihatsu and began taking cabs I haven't gotten any complaints. Certainly nothing by fax," Benny answered.

"This is either the third or fourth one that I've received. I wonder if it also came from Haifa." Gili checked the sender's number. "Absolutely;

it's area code 04. I wonder who it is. Some eccentric sits in Haifa and sends me threats, and I should be scared?"

You're an ostrich. Baba Bozgolo also warned you that they were planning to kill you.

"You can check with the phone company to see who sent it to you."

"Leave it alone," Gili shrugged. "It doesn't bother me. No one dies from a fax."

He did not tell Benny the real reason for delaying. Gili was beset by a deep terror. His death was just a matter of time; he was living on borrowed hours. Up until now he had been certain that these faxes were part of a carefully laid plan. But now he was taking an entirely different tack.

He took the fax with him. Dr. Shoshani, one of the country's best-known graphologists, lived not far from Gili's house. Gili had an idea of who the anonymous sender was. Now he wanted to confirm it with a handwriting analysis.

"Blessed is He Who brings the dead back to life," Rav Avram chortled. "Gili, where have you disappeared to? We haven't seen you for thousands of years."

Black rings beneath them emphasized Rav Avram's deep eyes. His cheeks were sunken and his skin almost transparent; tiny veins protruded from his temple. He was very tense, his fingers opening and closing constantly. This was new to Gili: There was no trace left of the serenity that had characterized Rav Avram.

"A thousand years, like a day," Gili paraphrased the well-known verse of *Tehillim*. "And how is the rav?"

"It's hard," the rabbi answered casually.

"Hard work? Many people?"

"Hard decisions," he said, in a brief moment of candor.

"What?"

"Nothing. They're waiting for me in the room." Rav Avram retreated hastily.

Gili stood behind the closed door. He did not have to eavesdrop to hear a stormy debate going on between a man and a woman, with Rav Avram trying to insert a sentence now and then.

It was noontime when Gili had reached Rav Avram's home for a visit. After the rabbi had locked himself in his room Gili wandered through the apartment. No one was there but Paysi, who lay on his bed reading.

"Do you want to go for a walk?" Gili signed to him.

A huge grin split the pale face. "You've learned my language?" his fingers asked.

"A little."

"I'm happy, so happy," Paysi signed. "Yes, I want to go with you."

A burst of energy suddenly enveloped the emaciated figure. He leaped off the bed, put on a blue woolen sweater, pulled on his shoes and stood by Gili's side. "Where to?"

"Patience." This time Gili did not need special signs: he used the universal gesture, and Paysi understood.

As the Mitsubishi drove away from the parking lot, Rav Avram stood at the window and stared at the white car so rapidly disappearing from view. His eyes gleamed with a sudden moisture.

☙❧

They reached Ganei Yehoshua, a large park near the Tel Aviv area, and wandered through its large grassy lawns. It was a fairly warm winter's day and hundreds of youngsters had responded to the sunshine's invitation and played happily and noisily on the varied equipment scattered around.

They sat on a bench staring at the children cavorting in the distance. Paysi had a hard time taking his eyes off them. A sudden coughing spasm overtook him. Gili tensed up: He had never heard such a wracking cough before.

"Are you cold? Maybe you shouldn't be sitting outside?" Laboriously he put the sentence together, using dozens of signs.

Paysi gave him a gloomy look. "It doesn't make any difference."

"Why not?"

Another coughing fit. He tried unsuccessfully to bring up the sputum. Gili was scared. "Are you okay?"

Finally, Paysi managed to swallow. A red warning light lit up in Gili's head. This coughing reminded him of tuberculosis.

"Do you have a contagious illness?"

Paysi shook his head in a negative gesture.

What was happening here? Gili was upset. Suddenly the boy seemed very pale.

"What's the matter with you? You're not all right."

Paysi nodded his agreement this time. He gestured to Gili to give him a pen and paper. Gili looked at his thin fingers as Paysi wrote two words:

Save me.

❦

After two hours his head was filled almost to the bursting point. What he had learned this day from Paysi, during two hours of signing, writing, and pointing at an alphabet chart, was beyond anything he could have imagined.

"I am very ill," Paysi told him, in his unique manner of communication. "I have a bad case of cystic fibrosis. My lungs have been destroyed by chronic infections. I can hardly breathe. I urgently need a heart and lung transplant."

"Heart and lung transplant?" Gili repeated in shock. "When?"

"Yesterday, two days ago. With every day that goes by my chances of survival go down. Some of my friends have already undergone such a transplant by the famous surgeon, Dr. Magdi Yakub of London. Only I am stuck, and it's because of Rav Avram."

"What?"

The boy's innocent eyes carried a terrible burden of anger and bitterness. "The rabbi's house is the last place I should be, from a medical standpoint. Because of him I missed a summer trip to Davos, in Switzerland, to a camp for sufferers from CF. Because of him I don't receive appropriate treatment. And especially, because of him I missed my chance to have the transplant in England. Rav Avram doesn't understand a thing about cystic fibrosis; he's always busy with other things.

"I spend entire days in the house. I don't learn, don't do necessary physical exercise, don't swim. I should be swimming every day, it clears my lungs. Rav Avram promised my foster father everything but instead of giving me money for the pool he sends me twice a week to some stupid reflexologist in Ramat HaSharon. I have to eat full meals, foods high in calories, carbohydrates, fats and protein. They used to bring me food from restaurants; now, in Rav Avram's house, I get crackers and salty cheese. My life is hanging by a thread. If I don't get a transplant soon, I'll die. Save me!"

Gili scrutinized the youngster. Only now did he notice how thin the boy had become. He looked terribly run down. His emaciated body couldn't weigh more than 100 pounds.

"And there's something else. The doctors say that my liver has also been partially effected." Paysi's eyes spoke of deep sadness. "I'm afraid I'll need a liver transplant too."

That was the last straw. This boy was ill, critically ill, and no one was doing a thing.

"So why does he keep you, for G-d's sake?" Gili screamed into Paysi's ears.

The boy's blue eyes looked fearfully at him. "Do you promise not to tell?"

"Of course. I'm your friend."

"Then I have a story for you."

32

C honi Vardi and Paysi Brent were Rav Avram Roosenthal's adopted sons. Unfortunates both, each with his own miserable destiny. Both 15 years old. It would seem that the two should be good friends, brothers in pain.

Actually, two people could not be more unlike.

Paysi was the incarnation of purity and integrity. Innocence shone from his fine eyes. Choni, on the other hand, was a neurotic, confused personality, finding his satisfaction in strange practices.

"Choni has tapes of all of Rav Avram's conversations with his patients," Paysi told Gili. "He thinks I don't know about them. He's hidden them in a closet in his room: about a thousand audio tapes. Every two weeks or so he gets a load of blank ones and returns them full. His drop-off point is at Charles Clore Park, near the Tel Aviv beach. I followed him there."

"Does Rav Avram know of it?" Gili asked. He remembered Choni's sadistic laughter as he listened to a young man confess his deep fear of death to Rav Avram. Rav Avram had promised that the tapes would be destroyed that very day... One thousand tapes!

Paysi again grew terrified. He looked around him like a scared rabbit. Gili stroked his hand warmly. "I'm with you," he signed.

Paysi asked for the alphabet chart and quickly pointed at the letters. Gili combined letter with letter, word with word. "Rav Avram seems to object to it, but Choni forces him. A man used to come to the house regularly, a tall, muscular man on a Suzuki motorcycle, and Rav Avram himself would give him the tapes. Then they had a fight; the man came and screamed at him, and Rav Avram screamed back. From that time on Choni is in charge of the tapes. Rav Avram tried to stop him, and Choni threatened him. I don't know with what. Rav Avram is very afraid of him. He gives him 500 shekels every month to keep him quiet. That's why there's no money for me."

"But who needs the tapes? Who's interested in them?"

Paysi stroked his bottom lip in a gesture that said it clearly: "I don't know."

"Really?"

"Really, I don't."

"But you haven't yet told me why he keeps you."

Paysi again pointed to the chart. He built a sentence that roused dismal thoughts in Gili's head: "I'm part of the scenery."

Rav Avram had painted himself as a man of extraordinary kindness, a man willing to give of himself boundlessly for the sake of others. He had never married so that the burden of a family would not keep him from helping unfortunates — this according to Paysi — 24 hours a day.

The home of Rav Avram was the embodiment of goodness and love, kindness and charity. Such a home needed four or five ill-fated wretches to wander about. Zabik, a convicted felon who had turned *baal teshuvah*. Muli, a recovering alcoholic. Choni, a living orphan, a boy thrown out of his father's house.

And Paysi, the deaf-mute, the boy from "the institution." Actually, a cystic fibrosis sufferer.

Rav Avram had surrounded himself with the luckless, the ill fated, the miserable.

"He brought me to him to help me, but he sees me as an abandoned puppy who needs a bone thrown to him once in a while." Hot tears flowed down his cheeks. "Did he ever try to speak with me? Did he try to learn even two or three signs, as you did? Did he once try to understand what is going on in my heart? He helps everyone else, but ignores those close to him!"

Gili rubbed his brow. What did this remind him of? Oh, yes, Choni had told him the same story. His father, Shaul Vardi, running from morning to night to help others, traveling to distant countries... and throwing his only son out of his home!

The path was strewn with leaves that had fallen from the park's trees. The withering foliage glowed in the golden sunlight and drifted slowly in the gentle breeze. Another terrible coughing spasm shook Paysi's thin body. How could he ask Paysi to uncover the identity of Choni's anonymous employers, Gili worried, if the boy needed a heart-lung transplant, not today, but yesterday!

Someone wearing a brown woolen sweater knit with a pattern of white diamonds suddenly pushed between the two, placing a friendly arm around Gili's shoulder. Gili, lost in thought, looked up, startled.

He saw Choni's smooth face looking at him, a green and black baseball cap perched backwards on his head. His face showed open curiosity.

"Choni, what are you doing here?"

"Exactly what you are. I came to take a walk in Ganei Yehoshua," Choni answered innocently. "It's good to breathe a little, no?"

"That's right," Gili agreed. Paysi's face had paled. He, like Gili, had realized that Choni's presence here was no coincidence. The boy had followed them.

For the first time since he'd met Paysi, Gili was grateful for the boy's handicap. Even if Choni had been standing right behind them the entire time, he wouldn't have understood a word. Paysi's spoken vocabulary was quite limited, and of sign language Choni knew nothing.

"I'll take Paysi home. Want to come along?" Gili offered.

Choni pushed together dozens of withered leaves with his foot, kicking them into a large pile and then viciously scattering them back onto the path. The yellowed foliage flew in the breeze, just barely touching the grass.

"No, thanks. I'm waiting for a friend," he said, jogging away from them.

"The writer is a relaxed person, thoughtful and diligent. He has tremendous discipline and self-control of the highest order. He has strong desires and passions and yet lives a most inhibited life. He has very high standards, extraordinary sensitivity, takes things to heart and yet at the same time puts in great efforts at restraining himself. The form of the writing and its flow attest to superior intelligence: the Writer is a wise man. On a scale of one to ten in ethics, I would give him a ten."

The graphologist Meir Shoshani was a tall man, whose graying hair framed still youthful features. He gave Gili a scrutinizing look as he handed him a 10-page report analyzing the handwriting of the anonymous sender of the fax. Gili quickly scanned the first few lines. Shoshani charged a tidy sum for his professional work; Gili knew that he was paying more than 70% over the usual market price. But it was well worth it. The north Tel Aviv graphologist was much in demand, and he had managed to paint an exact portrait of the writer. Only a photograph was missing.

Shoshani accepted the 1000-shekel check with a frosty face. "There's something strange about this," he told Gili almost nonchalantly.

"And that is —"

"The writer is under constant emotional strain. He is afraid of something external. And yet paradoxically he is a very relaxed person. I have worked with all segments of the population, and have only found this paradox among the religious. The professional literature of graphology has no term for this. It took me years to figure out that this was the fear of a greater power. The religious call it 'the fear of Heaven.'"

Gili understood what Shoshani was hinting at.

"And that's very strange. Excuse my asking, but why should a religious, G-d-fearing man fax such terrible threats? 'If you don't leave this business alone — you will die.'" He stared again at the piece of crumpled paper. "But that's your business, whether or not you want to involve the police."

Gili thanked Shoshani and returned home. He had already figured out who had written the fax, but had looked for some way of confirming his suspicions. Now Shoshani had done just that. He called Bezek's directory assistance and received a number in Haifa's Neve Shaanan neighborhood.

This afternoon he'd work in the newsroom. And tonight, he would travel to the port city.

Gili returned to the newsroom, but his mind was elsewhere. He parked the Mitsubishi in its usual spot, on a small side street nearby, seven stories beneath his office window. As he parked he bumped lightly into a Buick parked in front of him.

The driver of the Buick was sitting inside, a newspaper unfolded on his steering wheel. He jumped out of the car, furious. "Look what you did!" he cried angrily.

The Buick was not even scratched. Gili calmed down the ill-tempered driver, apologized, and left. The Buick's driver once again sat down and scanned the newspaper, waiting until Gili was no longer in sight. Then he walked towards the Mitsubishi.

Gili couldn't concentrate at all. For a half-hour he sat dreamily next to a pile of papers. Benny Gabison spoke to him, but he didn't answer.

"What did you say?" he said, abruptly waking from his reverie.

"Good; you're awake. I asked you what was happening in Rav Avram's house."

"Everything as usual. But Rav Avram looked exhausted. Something is really bothering him."

"That's what he looked like to you?" There was a strange undertone in Benny's voice.

"That's right."

"What's bothering him?"

"Am I a psychologist? Ask him?"

Benny didn't ignore Gili's outburst. "Seems to me that you're the one that's bothered. You're nervous, dreamy, and haven't done a thing for the past half-hour."

"That's right, boss."

"I want to know what's bothering you."

"Would you leave me alone!" Gili answered angrily. "Let me dream in peace."

But Benny was worried. Gili's dreams, he knew, were often the precursors of his blackouts. "Gili, look in the mirror. You're white as a sheet. Maybe you should get to a doctor, now."

Gili closed his eyes. Benny was right: A terrible pain suddenly skewered the left side of his head. He rummaged around for his medication but found none; even the Tylenol had disappeared. The headache grew worse from moment to moment.

He stood up. "I'm going to the pharmacy."

Benny jumped up. "No!" he yelled. "Don't get up from your chair. Sit quietly. What did you want to buy?"

"Tylenol, Optalgin. Something."

"Give me your keys. I'll get it for you."

A white fog had begun to descend upon his brain. He felt too weak to stand up. "Benny, thanks. I really couldn't drive now."

"Save the thanks for your *shadchan* on your wedding day." Benny grabbed his key ring. "Anyway, I miss driving. It's been two weeks since I sold my old Daihatsu. And I won't get the new Applause until..."

"Come back quickly," Gili interrupted him. "I think I may faint."

Benny quickly poured him two cups of Coke. "Drink up and hang on. I'll be back in a minute."

He sped into the hallway and raced to the elevator. He had no intention of buying Tylenol for anyone: He was running to get the car to the building's entrance, hoping to force Gili to go to Ichilov Hospital's emergency room.

When the elevator reached the lobby he shot out like a rocket, in his frenzy dashing into a young journalist not quick enough to get out of his way. "One side!" he called belatedly to the young man doubled over on the floor. Breathing heavily he reached the side street, opened the door, and sat down in the driver's seat.

The green Buick pulled swiftly away from the other side of the street, the driver giving nervous glances out of his side mirror. That wasn't Gili Dinar! He had memorized the description he'd been given: Gili Dinar, 24 years old, curly brown hair, green eyes, no glasses, straight nose, thin, muscular body, tall. He had deliberately provoked the argument with him in order to confirm his identity.

The young man flying into the car like a tornado was dark, wore glasses, had a flattened nose and a chubby body. But it was too late. The Buick sped away as if pursued by demons.

Benny closed the car door, turned the key, and heard the engine hum into life.

It was the last sound he ever heard.

Gili drank the Coke thirstily. Since the accident, the stress of heavy concentration had often made him ill. And from the moment he had left the office of Meir Shoshani he had constantly been thinking of what to do and how to do it.

He wondered how much time it would take Benny to get to the pharmacy. Benny would surely take a short spin around town before he returned. After all, it had been two weeks since he had been behind a wheel...

A huge explosion shook the exterior of the *HaYom HaZeh* building. The windows shattered, the shards falling into the room, their tinkle the bearer of bad tidings.

Frightened cries came from the long hallways. "There's been an attack!" "Something's exploded!" "It must be a bus!" "Those cursed terrorists again!"

With a great effort of strength Gili shook off the fog. He pulled himself towards the window and looked with blurry eyes out at the street.

Nothing had happened on the main street. Traffic was flowing as usual. But on the side street, seven floors down, just beneath his office window, a reddish streak of flame engulfed what had once been an automobile.

Gili had to look twice at the horrifying sight in order to confirm that it was his Mitsubishi that was going up in flames, and that his good friend Benny Gabison had paid for his friendship with his life.

"Good for you, Gili Dinar. Good for you. What a shame you're a journalist. You could have been a great detective. How did you find me?"

Rabbi Yoske Friedman met him at the door and whispered the words right into his ear. He had changed from the time that he had paid a visit to Gili after Udi Dinar's death, six years earlier. His beard had grown longer and whiter and small wrinkles now surrounded his eyes. But the eyes themselves still twinkled with the same spiritual brightness that Gili remembered.

"How'd you get onto me?" Rabbi Yoske smiled. "Tell me quietly."

"I used my head. Haifa, threats that aren't fulfilled, a person not trying too hard to hide, faxes, avoiding telephone use. But it was the last fax that gave you away completely. You wrote it in your normal handwriting. The graphologist told me we were talking about a religious, G-d-fearing person. Nu, who else but Rabbi Yoske Friedman? You gave me quite a scare, until I figured out it was you. You wanted me here. Well, here I am." There was something theatrical about all this whispering. They behaved like two actors trying to tell a secret while the audience listened.

Rabbi Friedman smiled modestly. "I don't quite agree with the graphologist on the subject of my fearing G-d. Would that my soul were in as good a condition as my body... But you were right that I was afraid of speaking on the phone. I don't know if anyone listens to my lectures, but to my phone calls I know they're listening."

He wrote something quickly on a paper and handed it to Gili. "Begin speaking normally. I suspect that my house is bugged."

Gili stood, his face a mask. So here in Haifa, too, he had not found a lifeline. Rabbi Yoske was pursued, just as he. But who was pulling all the strings?

Yesterday's tragedy still struck deep within him. The terrible flood of emotion didn't leave him for a minute. Everyone was talking about it. "Top journalist assassinated in booby-trapped car!" the headlines screamed that morning. But it seemed that Rabbi Friedman had heard nothing.

Gili chatted for a few minutes of this and that, and then scribbled on the paper, "Why did you frighten me with those threats?"

Rabbi Friedman's habitual smile vanished. He rose from his chair and stood next to an old buffet. A simple menorah, some old candlesticks, a silver goblet and an esrog box glinted in a mirror.

"How is your mother?" he asked out loud. He then sat down again and wrote, "Gili, I told you I was here for you 24 hours a day. Why didn't you come to me?"

From here on the conversation took two tracks: out loud and in writing.

"Ima is fine." (For what?)

"Give her my warmest regards." (You were taking your first steps in the Jewish world. Why didn't you come to consult with me, before you fell into the hands of scoundrels?)

"And what is the Rav doing?" (Did you and Rabbi Chaim Ozer Schmidt learn together in yeshivah?)

"I'm teaching in a yeshivah." (Of course, your father and me, and Schmidt, and Manny Schwartz. We were a foursome. And there were others: Moshe Shiffer, Yoel Minkus, Yaakov Gluft, Eli Leiker from America. Those were the days...)

"What yeshivah is that?" (Who is the scoundrel?)

"Matnos Kehunah." (Don't you understand by yourself?)

"And how many students does the Rav have?" (Is it Rav Avram?)

"Thirty." (I'm not certain, but he is certainly different from any other rabbi.)"I love teaching." Rabbi Yoske's eyes gave off a quiet fire. He continued to write.

(He's a lone wolf. He never served other rabbis and *gedolei Torah* and his way is not conventional. He has exceptional beliefs, not accepted by the consensus of *rabbanim*.)

"And I love to learn Torah. But I don't have the time." (I'm not afraid to ignore a consensus.)

"No time is no excuse." Rabbi Friedman grabbed Gili by the shoulders. (Listen to a friend's advice: Sever your connection with Rav Avram. Do it slowly.)

"You're right. I'll look for a *chavrusa*." (I did that already. But why the threats?)

"Good luck." (You poor kid, did you think I was threatening you?) Rabbi Yoske's tense body relaxed somewhat. (I just wanted you to know that they were after you. They used you, they are still using you, without knowing it you're like a puppet in the hands of men without conscience.

I think that Rav Avram is cooperating with them, voluntarily or by force, in a huge scheme that the GSS has woven against the *chareidi* sector of Israel. They want to destroy the *chareidi* community from within. They needed someone to find out the community's secrets. They will sow conflict and controversy, pit one man against his brother. It will seem natural, as it were, but the GSS is pulling the strings.)

He wrote with increasing speed. (From the moment you began snooping around, a certain person was appointed to lead you off the track. And he has many helpers... I knew it would be like that and that's why I told you even at the beginning of the process that they wanted to kill you. I'm not certain you weren't followed here.)

"Tomorrow I'm going back to my studies." (That's true. Yesterday they tried to kill me.)

"What will you learn?" (How?)

"*Maseches Nedarim.*" (My friend was killed in my place.)

"`That's good. *Maseches Nedarim* helps stretch the brain." (What!)

Gili had had enough of the double dialogue. Quietly he wrote of the horrible murder of Benny Gabison, who had died in the flames in Gili's car. Rabbi Yoske didn't manage to swallow a cry of shock, disguising it as a sudden cough.

"It's stuffy in here. Let's go get some air on the porch," he said, giving a slight wink. Gili nodded in comprehension.

On the porch they could speak without worrying about hidden microphones.

33

They stood on the porch gazing at one of Israel's most spectacular night views: the port of Haifa with its refineries floating upon a sea of lights, dancing in the dark waters.

"I'm sick of trembling like a frightened rabbit and writing notes," Rav Yoske leaned upon the railing. "Here I can be sure there are no eavesdroppers."

"Why should the GSS listen in on a lecturer in a yeshivah? What's so interesting about your household conversations?"

Rav Yoske gently avoided the question. "Gili, the incident that I have been faxing you about almost took place yesterday. They almost murdered you."

"I know. They meant to kill me, but Heaven protected me, and I don't know in what merit. The assistant editor of my paper, Eric Meisels, was also assassinated, an hour after he told me on the phone that he had something to reveal to me. A few days earlier he had told me that I was just a pawn in a chess game — and that I was on the black side. What did he mean?"

In a sudden wave of weakness, Rav Yoske sat down heavily on an old lounge chair. He sighed and murmured something unintelligible.

"What did you say?"

"Nothing. At this point, the less you know, the better."

Gili wanted to leave. Rabbi Friedman invited him to stay for dinner, but Gili refused. Since yesterday he had lost all appetite for food and was living on water alone. The blackout that had threatened to overcome him, and that had so frightened Benny Gabison, had, paradoxically, lifted because of the trauma of his friend's murder. The emotions had overcome the body!

Gili wondered what that blackout would have revealed. It would have been another in a long chain of such blackouts, episodes that blasted the barrier that had been built up in his brain, a barrier that hid one fateful memory. The memory that was trying, without success, to leap out at him. It was a memory, he was convinced, that would get to the heart of this maddening mystery.

Rabbi Friedman stopped Gili before he could leave. He rubbed his temples in deep thought. "A little bird told me that Rav Avram Roosenthal gets his powers from an ancient book of kabbalah."

Gili returned Rav Friedman's steely gaze with his own. He measured his words as a miser measures his gold coins. "You're referring to *The Vessel of Blessing*."

Rav Yoske jumped up in panic. His head hit his neighbor's porch overhead. "So you know?"

"Didn't you say I was a detective?" Gili smiled.

His host disappeared for a moment, returning with a laden tea tray. Reluctantly Gili poured himself a steaming cup from a pink ceramic pot decorated with tiny blue flowers.

"It's from Shanghai," Rav Yoske explained with a smile. "I have a friend, an importer, who sometimes brings me 'bargains' from the Far East."

Gili spoke slowly, his eyes riveted in wonder to a miniature drawing of a red-tiled country home next to a golden wheat field. "From my father, may he rest in peace, I inherited an aesthetic sense, an appreciation for beautiful objects." He shook his head. "But I'm just dreaming. Rav Yoske, if you want cooperation, you have to reveal your sources. How do you know that Rabbi Avram depends on an ancient book?"

Rav Yoske pushed a plate of lemon-flavored wafers towards him. "Have something to eat," he urged him warmly.

Gili unenthusiastically nibbled at a wafer. "You didn't answer me. And I've got another question too: Does Rabbi Avram have that book in his possession now?"

Rav Yoske was firm in his refusal. "For reasons I can't divulge, I prefer not to reveal everything at this time. But my source is inside information — and that alone is a lot to tell you. At the right time and place, and I suspect that will be soon, you'll be the first to know who it is, and not to satisfy your curiosity but because we'll have to consult together for a way to foil the GSS plans before they bring ruin down onto the *chareidi* population in Israel."

"Okay, without revealing your sources. But what am I supposed to do now? One man against an unstoppable apparatus. Should I wear a bulletproof vest? Maybe they'll shoot me on the way home."

"They won't shoot you. The GSS lost points in their murder of your friend. Whoever gave the order to blow up your car will take a time-out for some renewed thinking. Take my advice, get yourself a friend from among Rabbi Avram's household."

"Who? Zabik the *gabbai* who loathes me since I punched him out? Or Choni, the little spy?"

"Neither. There's a boy there, sweet and sympathetic. In my opinion he can do a lot for you, if you only know how to speak with him."

"Paysi."

The rabbi sighed. "That's right. Paysi is a true unfortunate, deaf, mute, a sufferer from cystic fibrosis. I believe he has a very elevated soul. He is an intelligent lad who suffers deeply from his enforced loneliness. If you save him from destruction, you'll have done a very important act of kindness. I believe he knows something about Rabbi Avram, perhaps about his kabbalistic book. Rabbi Avram doesn't suspect him at all."

Gili returned to Tel Aviv heartened by Rabbi Friedman's words. He spent his time on the bus in deep thought about the rabbi and his hidden sources of information.

"My source is inside information," Rav Yoske had said.

Who?

Benny Gabison's funeral took place at the "new" Yarkon cemetery the next morning. It was decidedly out of the ordinary, of definite interest to those who were familiar with the heads of the GSS. Gili walked slowly down the asphalt pathway behind the coffin, together with Izzy Lapidot, *HaYom HaZeh*'s military affairs reporter. Izzy's blinking eyelids were working overtime today. "I can't believe what I'm seeing, whom I'm seeing," he whispered, shocked, to Gili.

Gili leaned towards him. "Who?"

"Something smells rotten here," Izzy hissed into Gili's ears. "Benny Gabison must have been an agent or something. I've identified at least two members of the GSS here. And there's a third one. I don't understand why they're openly revealing themselves so carelessly."

Gili had long since stopped being surprised. "Whom have you identified?"

"Quiet," Izzy suddenly whispered. "They're looking at us. Walk away from me slowly, be natural, as if nothing had happened."

Gili followed the instructions. With small steps and bent head he followed the mourners to the grave.

When the *chazzan*'s voice began the "*Kel malei rachamim*" prayer, a sound rippled through the assemblage. "He's coming! The rebbe is coming!"

"Who's coming?" Ami Kedmi, editor of *HaYom HaZeh*, asked a young man standing on the side of the path.

"Our rebbe," the young man swelled with pride, smoothing his tousled hair as if to mark the occasion.

"Our rebbe, Rav Avram," another added in a pronounced Moroccan-French accent.

Rabbi Avram Roosenthal stepped out of a luxury car that belonged to one of his wealthy supporters. Dozens of his ardent *chassidim* waited impatiently for him. The mass of people approached the grave, pushing aside all that stood in its way.

With closed eyes and clenched arms Rabbi Avram stood, surrounded by his admirers, listening patiently to the throaty flourishes of the cantor.

Standing alongside the freshly dug grave Rabbi Avram eulogized "sweet Benny," in a voice quiet and controlled. But when he spoke of "the hands of evildoers who had cut off his life," his voice broke. "Our Benny, all your life you were happy and made others happy. You went to Heaven in a storm, and your innocent blood shall bubble and froth like that of the priest Zecharyah, until the one who has spilled it is called to judgment."

From a distance Gili could see several men eyeing each other. He was not able to identify any of them. After two minutes the men left the cemetery.

❧❀❧

Izzy tried to mask his initial strong reactions. "So we saw them, the 'great men,'" he said mockingly. "Who doesn't know them? B, head of Jewish Affairs; H, head of the Anti-Terror Unit; and M, head of Psychological Warfare."

"If all you know is their initials, who do you think you are, anyway?" a young reporter teased.

Izzy willingly met the open provocation. "That's no secret," he sneered. "Boaz Shamir, head of the Jewish Section. Hadar Paz, Anti-Terror. And Meshulam Yaakovi, head of Psychological Warfare."

Gili grabbed frantically onto a nearby headstone. Was the name Yaakovi a mere coincidence? Moshe Vayden had told him about Rabbi Meshulam Yaakobovitz, "Big Yaakovi's" father. So Pinny Yaakovi had named his son Meshulam, for his father.

In the undeclared war they had waged in Yaakovi's house, when Gili had gone with Moshe Vayden, he had assumed that he had been the victor, successfully fooling the gullible antiques dealer. But it was Yaakovi's game, one-zero. Francois Germaine... Gili blushed at the thought of what a fool he'd made of himself in front of Yaakovi. And immediately afterwards had come the murder attempt. No wonder: If the son was one of the heads of the GSS, undoubtedly the father, too, was in the picture.

He left the cemetery and stood at the side of the road, lost in thought. What was Rabbi Avram's part in all of this?

"Gili!" the familiar voice of Rabbi Avram himself called to him from within the luxury car. "Where are you headed?"

"To work."

"Get in."

Rabbi Avram was sitting in the latest model Grand Prix. He waved Gili in. A well-dressed young man sat behind the wheel. "Who is our guest?" he asked Rabbi Avram, with a pronounced American accent.

Rabbi Avram smiled. "Gili, please meet Jimmy Schwartzman of the U.S., a good friend of ours. He's an industrialist who supports us occasionally. Eh, Jimmy?" He gave the driver's back a loving pat.

"I'm here to collect unemployment insurance," Jimmy answered.

Rabbi Avram laughed heartily. "Jimmy, this is Gili Dinar, one of Israel's top journalists. He was a good friend of Benny Gabison. Let's take him to his newsroom."

"Benny was killed in my car," Gili said to the driver in perfect, unaccented English. "He was killed accidentally; they really wanted my blood." He gave Rabbi Avram and the driver each a piercing glance, waiting for their reactions.

"This is so stupid," Jimmy fumed, stuck in the traffic leaving the cemetery. He hadn't heard Gili's words, or he didn't want Gili to know he'd heard. "Why does someone who wants to get out of the cemetery have to drive three miles in one direction, turn into the opposite lane, and go back another three miles, until he's reached the cemetery gates? Why doesn't this place have a normal exit road?"

Rabbi Avram ignored Jimmy's complaint and turned to Gili. "Do you have any idea of who would want to kill you?"

"Your neighbor," Gili pushed the thorn in deep. "Your angry neighbor, Michael Wolfin, 'Sha-sha,' as Choni and Zabik call him. When I asked you who was sending me the threatening faxes, you said it was your neighbor."

Rabbi Avram didn't reply. A silence descended upon the car, a heavy, brooding quiet. Gili pressed together his fingertips nervously. *I was too hard on him,* he thought. *I'd better do something.*

He threw a question into the silence. "The GSS leaders know that any novice military affairs reporter knows who they are. How did they dare come to the funeral so openly?"

Rabbi Avram pointed towards the left. At that moment they were again passing the cemetery, after their six-mile detour, on the way to Tel Aviv. "Not long ago, when the entire country was in turmoil after the murder of Prime Minister Yitzchak Rabin, there were many conspiracy theories flying about. People accused — and some still do — the GSS of involvement in the assassination. What did your friend Benny Gabison report about that?"

Gili could remember it clearly. "Benny was a big security man. He defended them strongly and came out violently against the conspiracy theories. Everyone remembers his two stories on the GSS, articles so flattering they sounded like advertisements."

"And that's the answer," Rabbi Avram said. "Benny came to consult me before writing those stories. He didn't hide from me the fact that he'd been a GSS agent in the past. He wanted to know if there was some kind of ethical problem with his writing the story. I told him not to worry: We need a strong GSS, and such rumors weaken its deterrent capability. The heads of the GSS came today to tell him, 'Thank you.'"

"They told him 'thank you' two days ago, in my Mitsubishi," Gili muttered. "Why did they reveal themselves?"

Rabbi Avram again pointed at the cemetery rapidly disappearing in the distance. " I think that the GSS wanted to announce that it is not hiding. Maybe it's a hint to the Gabison family: 'We didn't kill him. Don't worry: we'll take care of it.' Before his parents start asking for an investigative committee to find out how their beloved son was killed. Before they start making noises."

"Who's that madman on the road?" Jimmy complained, pointing to a black Chevrolet that was speeding behind them. "I wouldn't let that drunk behind a wheel!"

The "drunk" in the Chevrolet approached the Grand Prix, put on a burst of speed, and suddenly bumped right into them. "He's really crazy!" Jimmy yelled, opening his window. "Wild man, drunk!" he screamed at the driver. They tried to see who was in the driver's seat, but the Chevrolet had tinted windows.

The black automobile approached them from the left lane and began to push the Grand Prix towards the shoulder of the road. "He's trying to turn us over!" Gili shouted in fear.

Rabbi Avram's pale face looked at him from the rear-view mirror. His forehead was wet with sweat; his lips were whispering quietly. He looked terrified.

The Chevrolet moved back and then again approached, bumping them like an angry beast. "Mamma, help, they're going to kill us," Rabbi Avram shouted in Yiddish.

Gili didn't lose his cool. He grabbed his cellular phone and dialed the police. "Help! We're in a green Grand Prix on Road #5 towards Tel Aviv, near Kefar HaYarok. A black Chevrolet is driving next to us, trying to run us off the road and turn us over. Help us!"

The policeman sounded interested; something exciting was finally happening on the road. "Stay in the Grand Prix. We'll be there soon."

The Chevrolet hit them twice more, hard bumps that turned their stomachs. It was only thanks to Jimmy's steady hand on the wheel that they managed to stay upright.

The attacking Chevrolet passed them and then reversed, backing straight for their front windshield.

"Careful!" Gili screamed. "Get down!"

The car swayed like a boat on a stormy sea, but miraculously only the front headlights were shattered. The Chevrolet leaped ahead and disappeared.

Jimmy Schwartzman pressed furiously on the gas pedal. Like a demon he pursued the Chevrolet, but was stopped by a red light at the next intersection. The Chevrolet didn't bother halting... and disappeared from sight.

Two patrol cars approached, their sirens wailing. The policemen took their testimony and quickly broadcast warnings on their two-way radios. Roadblocks were set up all along the nearby roads. Gili didn't have the shadow of a doubt of what would happen and, as he expected, the Chevrolet had vanished without a trace.

Someone wanted to tell him: You're still the target.

But they knew that Rabbi Avram was in the car with me, Gili thought. *They could have killed him along with me! It looks like Rabbi Avram and I are in the same boat after all...*

A hazy picture suddenly jumped into his mind. As he concentrated upon it, he remembered every detail, as if it were happening now. It was that same evening that the elevator had broken down in Rabbi Avram's house.

Rabbi Avram is looking out the window at the parking lot. And then he sends him racing out of the house. "Gili, don't stay here, go home immediately." Gili wants to stay, to help with the elevator, and Rabbi Avram actually pushes him out the door. And in the darkened lot he finds a man bending beneath his car.

Yes. Rabbi Avram is on my side. How is it that I didn't see it before? He saved me from death that night. They wanted to boobytrap my car even then.

And maybe now they were trying to kill Rabbi Avram?

His head was spinning with these new thoughts. Rabbi Avram had revealed himself today in his weakness, his fears. The know-all psychologist had screamed "Mamma" in Yiddish like a frightened child. (*Why not English? Wasn't it true that under terrible strain a person reverted to his mother tongue?*) His steel-plated armor had developed a few chinks.

On second thought, Gili decided, it was rather endearing. Every person had the right to some weakness. Even the legendary Rabbi Avram!

After two barren hours, with nothing written and a mind dry as a desert, Gili fled his office. The room, empty of Benny's joyous and lively spirit, seemed like a grave to him and threw him into a bleak depression. He hailed a taxi and made his way to Rabbi Avram's, glancing constantly into the rear-view mirror to see if anyone was following him.

Zabik met him at the door, clearly angry. "Why have you come? Rabbi Avram doesn't feel well. Don't go in to him."

"I know. We shared the same adventure," Gili replied, walking straight into the rav's room, ignoring the *gabbai's* obvious fury.

He expected to see someone slightly nervous. But Rabbi Avram had gone way past that. His cheeks were sunken and pale with panic. He was lying down in his bed, his eyes darting back and forth. "Gili, what's happened? Why have you come back?" he croaked in terror.

Gili took a deep breath. "I've come to take Paysi for a bit of air. Is that okay?"

"Okay? What kind of question is that? I should have done it myself! But there's no time. What will you do with him? After all, he can't hear or speak."

"We'll take books with us," Gili answered lightly. "*Liar,*" his conscience whispered to him.

"Very good," the rav said. "It's a great kindness on your part. Do you know sign language?" he asked suddenly, giving Gili a sharp look.

"Just a few signs." Gili's heart skipped a beat. Choni had clearly reported on their encounter in Ganei Yehoshua.

Rabbi Avram thought for a moment. Then he said quietly, "Take him. He has no one in his world. He's an invalid and mildly retarded and doesn't take in what's going on around him. Take care of him, keep him out of the wind, and make sure he takes his peninsula."

"Peninsula?"

"Don't you understand? His pills. He has to take about 20 peninsula capsules. Why are you looking at me like that?" Suddenly he realized his error and laughed. "Excuse me, did I say peninsula? I meant penicillin. I'm so tired, I'm getting my words mixed up. Yes, Paysi has to take many different medications, many vitamins. Penicillin. He's very sensitive to cold."

And that was Rabbi Avram's minimalist version of cystic fibrosis: He's sensitive to cold.

Gili considered whether or not to reveal to Rabbi Avram that he knew the secret of the cystic fibrosis. No, he mustn't show that he had so much information; Rabbi Avram might realize that Gili and Paysi were communicating clearly.

"Take care of Paysi and of yourself," Rabbi Avram said in sudden fright. *The accident today did something to him. He's turning into a Yiddishe mamma.*

This time they went to Givat HaShelosha, a heated pool not far from Rosh Ha'ayin. Paysi was thrilled to the core: He frolicked like a little boy, had a contest with Gili over who could do more laps. But after only five laps he grew tired and left the water, sitting weakly on a chair, his eyes following Gili's energetic swimming.

Two minutes later Gili left the pool. He wrapped the boy's emaciated body in a towel and sat down next to him.

"Tired? Want to go home?" he asked solicitously. A wave of tenderness radiated from his heart towards the youngster trembling with cold.

Paysi pulled his hands out of the towel. Gili put the alphabet chart next to him. "I want a lung transplant. There's a doctor in London, an

Egyptian, Dr. Magdi Yakub. He's a world-famous surgeon in heart-lung transplants. He transplanted lungs in my friends."

"Paysi, whatever you want. But tell me, can you shadow Rabbi Avram?"

The fingers raced over the chart. "Easily."

"See if he uses a book called *The Vessel of Blessing*."

The fingers slowed down, hesitated. "In his own room it's a little bit hard. He has a metal safe beneath his desk and he locks everything there, a digital safe with two rows of numbers. Each row has six digits. Twelve digits all together! He uses it often when he sees people; sometimes he sends people out in the middle of a consultation, and then he opens the safe. Then he calls them in again. Sometimes he locks himself in between visits."

"Can you shadow him, and write down the numbers?"

"I'll try. I'll have to have a chance."

"You'll have a chance soon." Gili's fertile brain had already come up with a wonderful plan to force Rabbi Avram out of his office during his consulting hours.

"I'm glad to see two such good friends."

Muli, Zabik's second-in-command, rose out of the warm water, his athletic body dripping, and shiny puddles sloshing around his feet. He stood next to their chairs, his eyes curiously looking at the two towel-clad young men. And, particularly, at the alphabet chart.

34

Gili and Fishele Mamaliga left Jerusalem at midnight. Gili's rented Honda Civic raced over the empty roads, and they reached Rabbi Avram's residence in 40 minutes.

Gili had thought that the crowd would be small, but he was wrong: More than 100 people waited impatiently to enter the rav's small room, each man with his problems, his troubles, his entanglements.

Attention turned to the elderly Fishele from the moment he walked in, with his brownish-reddish cap dotted with white sweat stains and his bent body wrapped in a dark woolen coat. His wispy gray beard framed a tormented face. Two black points of light surrounded by rings of white and red peered out from behind thick black glasses. These were the eyes of a wise man, yet madness blazed within them as well. Fishele pranced into the room and sat down heavily on a chair that a well-mannered young man offered him.

Rabbi Avram's waiting room had finally been moved from the stairwell to a quieter spot, the apartment of Michael Wolfin, "Sha-sha." With his departure, "Sha-sha" had bequeathed a modicum of quiet to the building.

Zabik had made other changes as well. A bell would ring with each new appointment, and he had installed the type of number system that was prevalent in medical clinics. There were separate waiting rooms for men and women, hot and cold water, and a small kitchen from where a tantalizing aroma drifted.

"Have you been in our new kitchen?" Choni asked with a grin. "Come on in." Gili followed him in, his nostrils quivering slightly as he gently sniffed. Impossible! There, bubbling merrily on a gas range, were huge pots filled with *cholent*, a mass of brown beans, potatoes, and giant rolls of *kishke*.

"What's this?" he asked, shocked.

"A gift from the rav's friend, Jimmy Schwartzman of America," Choni answered, filling a plate with the pungent mixture. "Jimmy said: 'We can't have people sitting here all night without feeding them something.' So now they've got *cholent*, and fish, and *malawach*, and black coffee. Everything under the top *kashrus* supervision. Eat, Gili, and give some to your guest."

Gili shrugged and went back to the waiting room. He took a number for Fishele, number 108. When he asked where they were up to, he was told that number 33 was about to enter.

"We'll be here until morning," he said impatiently to Fishele. "Stay here a minute. I'll get you in."

He descended to the sixth floor and entered Rabbi Avram's apartment in his own preferred fashion. Muli answered the pre-arranged knock. At Gili's request, Muli didn't lock the door. "I'll be in and out all night," he explained. After a moment he opened the door to Rabbi Avram's room, paying no heed at all to Zabik's dark looks.

"Rebbe, I've brought him."

Rabbi Avram blinked and stopped in the middle of a heated discussion between a worried father and his daughter, a pale girl of 16. "Whom did you bring?"

"Fishele Mamaliga."

"Who?"

"Don't you remember? Fishele Mamaliga, the schizophrenic from Kiltz, the one who's got a spy after him. By the way, Fishele told me that the spy's name is Yona. Maybe that will help you with his treatment."

"What do you want from me?" Rabbi Avram blinked in confusion.

"You promised that you would treat him. When you were criticizing the *chassidim* of Kiltz you told me that you could cure him of his mental illness. So I brought him to you tonight."

"Wonderful," Rabbi Avram complained. "We spoke about him two months ago and suddenly you remembered to bring him."

"I'll be in with him right after these people," Gili declared. "Rabbi Avram, your greatest admirer is entitled to a little favoritism once in a while, no?"

Without waiting for the rav's answer he walked out towards the waiting room. By the shouts and screams that he could hear as he approached, he knew that Fishele had started his theatricals.

The old man stood on a chair, speaking in a loud roar to 10 giggling high school students who were enjoying the show. "Good evening, everyone. I am Fishele Mamaliga. Yona the spy is after me."

"What a lovely name, Mamaliga," a young man said, delighted, as he rubbed his bristly chin.

"Mamaliga is just a nickname," Fishele explained solemnly from the heights of his chair. "My real name is Fliedermaus. Yona is a KGB agent. He's told me that a group of his friends, former KGB spies, are plotting to steal nuclear missiles from America and blow up all of Israel."

"We're all going to die?" the high school students said in chorus.

Fishele grew enthusiastic. "Of course not! Tomorrow I'm going to Tel Aviv, to the American ambassador, and I'll reveal the plans. Don't worry."

"No problem, we're saved!" the boys crowed. They were growing rowdy now; the elderly schizophrenic was adding a little spice to the evening. A boy who seemed to be the leader of the group pulled off his Walkman headphones from his head and yelled, "Hey, gang, here he is: the savior of mankind!"

The group shouted and laughed. Two youngsters in tricot shirts grabbed Fishele's arms, pulled him down from the chair, and began to dance wildly with him. Many of the others waiting joined the fun and accompanied the dancers with exuberant singing. A pony-tailed man with one earring joined the circle, holding a compact disc player in his hand. He turned the volume up, and stereo sound filled the entire building.

"Quiet!" came shouts from the stairway. "You're going too far!"

Furious neighbors banged on the door. One particularly angry resident, wearing blue pajamas, was the first to fly into the apartment. He was followed by a mass of enraged people, who began tussling with the young men. "Enough, let us sleep!"

More and more neighbors appeared, screaming and cursing. Five years of anger and bitterness erupted suddenly, like a raging river overflowing its banks. There was complete chaos in the building.

And suddenly, as if someone had pulled a plug, the incredible noise just stopped. Complete silence reigned. Rabbi Avram Roosenthal, hearing the unprecedented clamor, had hastily finished his interview with the man and his daughter, and sent them home. He ran downstairs with his light robe flapping, his eyes flashing lightning. Zabik, Muli, and Choni followed him like three dark shadows.

༺❧⦿❧༻

Paysi hastily jumped out of bed. For two hours he had lain there pretending to sleep, waiting impatiently for this moment. Gili had instructed him yesterday. "When you hear something going on and feel the floor shaking you'll know that Rabbi Avram has run downstairs, and then go into his room."

"Who says he'll run down?" Paysi asked, and Gili had answered, "He'll go and all his assistants will go with him, or my name isn't Gili!"

And Gili was right. Through his hearing aids Paysi could even make out the distant sound of singing. The building was in an uproar — and suddenly the apartment was empty!

He raced to the darkened consulting room, whose door had been left open wide. No one saw him as he climbed with catlike stealth and swiftness up the bookcase. The top shelf was completely empty. He pulled himself onto the shelf as Gili had instructed him and crouched into it, his heart beating like a drum from the tension and excitement.

Paysi had told Gili of the empty shelf on their way back from the pool. Gili had scrutinized the boy's emaciated frame and had asked if he could squeeze his way onto it for a short time. "Sure," Paysi answered happily. And then Gili had laid his plans.

Paysi had made his own arrangements as well. From his vantage point he could see the rows of digits on the safe. His small binoculars gave him a clear view of each number. But the crouching boy remained hidden. One would only see him if he decided to turn on a light.

Paysi prayed that no one would suddenly decide to turn on that light.

"What's going on here?" Rabbi Avram asked quietly.

No one dared answer. Here and there men in pajamas sidled away towards the exit.

"I asked what's going on." Rabbi Avram slashed the group of high school youths with two flaming eyes. "Why have you come here? To go wild?"

A young man in torn jeans found his courage. "We want to become *baalei teshuvah.*"

"You want to know what's going on? I'll tell you!" Fishele Mamaliga emerged from the group. He scrutinized Rabbi Avram's furious face and murmured to himself, "I don't believe it. It's Yona!" He looked again with his deep eyes and muttered, "Yes! Yona the spy, without a doubt!"

And before anyone could stop him, Fishele's fists were churning mercilessly into Rabbi Avram, beating him to the ground with the strength of madness. "It's you, Yona the spy, the traitor. All these years you've been running after me and cursing all the Jews. You should be ashamed of yourself, trying to steal America's missiles and destroy us!"

Rabbi Avram lay on the cool tiles of the floor. The old man continued flailing at him, bending over the paralyzed rav and hitting him with all his strength. "I'll teach you. You'll go back to Russia, to Siberia!"

Zabik and Muli stood like statues, hardly believing the absurd, unbelievable scene taking place before them. Gili, though, kept his presence of mind, coolly pulling Fishele from behind and rescuing Rabbi Avram from the merciless fists of the furious old man. Finally, Zabik and Muli escorted the rav, white and shaken, to his room.

A yeshivah student poured Fishele a cup of cold water. "Calm down, Grandpa," he said gently to him. "Drink and calm down."

Fishele took a sip and burst out in hearty laughter. "Did you see how I laced into him, the spy, Yona?"

"What have you done?" Gili asked furiously. "You've insulted an important rabbi!"

"What rabbi?" Fishele spat in contempt. "A spy!"

For the next half-hour Gili tried to calm Fishele down and explain his terrible error to him. All the while he felt his cheeks burning, as dozens of men identified him and asked what a top journalist was doing with an aggressive psychotic. Finally, Gili grabbed Fishele's arm. "Come with me, you're coming now to apologize to Rabbi Avram. You've hurt him badly."

The door to the apartment on the sixth floor was still open. They walked up the interior staircase to Rabbi Avram's room on the seventh floor.

Zabik heard the heavy footsteps and ran outside to see the intruder. "Gili!" he yelled furiously, "you're impossible! How dare you bring him here after what he did to the rav!"

Gili calmly helped the old man up the steps. Zabik stood at the top, ready to block them with his own body. But Gili spoke tranquilly. "Zabik, Fishele made a mistake. It was an accident. He wants to apologize."

"It was a terrible mistake," Fishele wailed weakly. "I mixed up Rabbi Avram Roosenthal and Yona the spy. I have to say I'm sorry."

The angry *gabbai* did not know what to say. Taking advantage of his perplexity, they slipped inside.

The apartment was quiet and dark. A round fluorescent light gave off a dim light in the long hallway.

Zabik followed them, muttering suspiciously. "Wait here, there are two inside. When they leave, go in to apologize. If I were the rav I would never forgive you."

"And that's why he's a rav and you're the assistant to the assistant," Fishele answered with a loud, provocative laugh.

After 15 minutes the door opened. Two elderly men walked out into the hallway. "Are you finished?" Gili asked.

The older of the two looked at him suspiciously. Was he trying to push ahead? "No," he said firmly. "The rav asked us to wait outside for five minutes. We'll be going back in soon."

The two whispered eagerly to each other. "You can come in now." Rabbi Avram's voice could be heard from within the room.

After 10 minutes the two left, satisfied and joyous. Rabbi Avram walked them out, speaking in conciliatory tones. When he saw Fishele sitting waiting for him, his face grew grim and angry. "Gili," he yelled. "This is too much! How dare you bring that madman here?"

"I came to ask forgiveness," Fishele whined. "It was a mistake."

Rabbi Avram rubbed his aching stomach. "Certainly," he said mockingly. "You almost destroyed my liver by mistake."

Fishele began to cry bitterly. "But I didn't mean you. Really."

"So who?" Rabbi Avram said, coming closer to the old man.

"I meant the evil Yona," Fishele answered. With a great effort he pulled himself out of the chair and jumped towards Rabbi Avram. "Do you understand, Rabbi? Yona the spy, who came with me from Russia."

"Nu?" Rabbi Avram prompted him impatiently.

"What, nu? He's entered your body! Why don't you throw him out? Spy, get out of there!"

And his fists once again hit the rav's thin body as he hurled horrifying blows at him. "Throw him out of yourself, of me, of all of us. All of Israel shall suffer from him!" The hands of the old man were now around the rav's throat; Rabbi Avram gasped for breath, his mouth open and tongue lolling.

Once again confusion and panic reigned, as everyone's attention was riveted to the drama. No one noticed Paysi tiptoeing out of Rabbi Avram's room. Zabik and Muli were red faced in their wrath. This time they went immediately to rescue their rabbi, pushing Fishele towards the door. "Gili, we won't forget this," Muli warned him. "Have you lost your mind? No man ever lifted a finger to the rav, and now this happens — twice!"

"Who would have thought that the crazy old man would behave like this?" Gili shot back, upset and furious. "Rabbi Avram asked me to bring him here for treatment."

He turned his anger on Fishele. "Idiot, what have you done? We came so that Rabbi Avram could cure you, take out this dybbuk of Yona the spy. And now you've spoiled everything!"

He left the house with Fishele in tow. His shouts echoed through the hallways. "Where did you learn to behave like that to rabbis and great men? You haven't any manners at all!"

The elevator swallowed his voice as they swiftly descended. Zabik and Muli watched as they left the building, with Gili berating the old man until they were in the car.

The automobile turned onto the next street. A great wave of laughter overpowered Gili; the Honda swayed like a drunk. He pulled over and shared his mirth with Fishele, laughing until the two were doubled over, their stomachs aching.

"How was I?" asked Fishele, thrilled with himself.

"You really overdid it!" Gili answered, the tears still running down his cheeks. "I thought you'd make a little scene, but to hit Rabbi Avram like that — twice!"

"I only hit him once," Fishele protested seriously. "The second time, it was Yona the spy that hit him."

Another wave of hysteria overcame Gili. The vision of Rabbi Avram, shocked and unbelieving beneath the old man's fists, put him into such a gale of hysteria that it was several minutes until he could continue driving.

But deep in his heart he worried just a little about Rabbi Avram's reaction, and the wrath of the rabbi's assistants. When he had talked with Fishele of a "small, pleasant scandal," he had never dreamed that he was letting a genie out of a bottle. He had thought Fishele would be satisfied with his solo performance in front of the boys of the Malik school in Tel Aviv — brought there for a fee of 20 shekels each — and it had never occurred to him that Fishele would take their "little scandal" quite so far. Still, the main thing was that their diversionary tactic had succeeded beyond their wildest dreams. Rabbi Avram had been pulled out of his room twice in one night.

And Gili knew that the rav had opened his safe on that very night.

The letter reached Gili's house two days later. Paysi had worked diligently to make the short letter legible.

"Dear Gili. You're a genius. Rabbi Avram didn't know a thing because of the confusion. I saw everything when he asked the men to leave in the middle of their conversation and opened the safe. The combination is: first row 3,2,0,4,2,8; second row 7,3,2,5,4,7. Yours, with love, Paysi. P.S. Gili, I'm very depressed and don't feel well. Have you spoken with Dr. Magdi Yakub?"

Gili had mixed emotions as he read the letter. His plan had succeeded; this was a good start — but Paysi was very, very ill!

He decided to put the ball in Rabbi Yoske Friedman's court. He undoubtedly knew of a philanthropist who would have Paysi flown immediately to London.

Now he had to wait until Rabbi Avram was out of the house. And then the road was clear and smooth before him.

* * *

The opportunity came that week. Pinny Yaakovi's youngest daughter, Tammy, was marrying Yaakov Prezance, son of the Belgian millionaire Milton Prezance, in an incredibly elegant wedding in the glittering Recital Ballroom in Ramat Gan, a suburb of Tel Aviv. Rabbi Avram had been asked to officiate. Before sundown he left with his entourage — Zabik, Muli, Choni. After all, who wanted to miss a millionaire's wedding?

Only one person stayed behind in the house that evening.

Paysi.

"Someone has to keep an eye on the house. Who wants to stay?" Rabbi Avram had asked.

Everyone pointed at Paysi. He was not feeling well anyway; how could he possibly enjoy the wedding?

Paysi accepted the task calmly, without any signs of protest or sadness. The others knew that Paysi had long since learned to mask his feelings.

Half an hour after the others had left, Paysi opened his door to a guest. Though time was short, Gili stopped for a moment to peer at the boy's gaunt face. What he saw worried him. "I've spoken with an important rabbi. He'll see to it that you'll be flown to London in the next few days. It's being taken care of."

Light returned to the melancholy eyes. "I feel very sick," Paysi signed to him. "Muli took me to a big doctor in Beilinson Hospital today. He told Muli that I'm weakening, and that they've got to take care of me."

"Muli told you that?"

"No. I read the doctor's lips."

Gili gave Paysi a warm hug. "Paysi, with G-d's help you'll have a full recovery."

Paysi walked him to the rabbi's room. He was coughing without a stop and breathing with difficulty. Gili decided to fax Rabbi Yoske once again. Paysi was flickering out like a candle in the wind!

Rabbi Avram's door was locked, but Paysi knew where a spare key had been secreted.

And now they were in the rabbi's holy of holies.

35

They stared at the safe. "It's big," Gili whispered appreciatively. Rabbi Avram had bought a safe with unusual dimensions, built wide and deep and very low. It was hidden beneath his desk, safe from the eyes of his many visitors. His dim lighting took on a grim aspect: Perhaps he sat in the darkness because he had something to hide.

Gili had memorized the combination by transforming the numbers into letters and making a mnemonic.

The room was dark and the digital numbers glowed mysteriously. Gili had worn thin rubber gloves as a protection against any who might look for fingerprints. Miraculously, his fingers didn't tremble as he pressed on the numbers.

He coded in all the digits — and nothing happened. Gili waited tranquilly; he knew that many computerized safes had some kind of delayed-action mechanism. After 60 seconds the door slid smoothly and noiselessly on its well-oiled hinges.

The safe was illuminated inside by a dim bluish light. Gili whistled in wonder when he saw its inner dimensions. It was much larger than it seemed from outside. It was scrupulously organized and contained a large amount of varied objects.

Paysi nudged him with warm fingers and gestured, "What is it?"

The safe contained three shelves. On the top shelf lay a few large notebooks. Gili opened a purple-orange one. He immediately recognized the draft of the stories he'd written that he had sent to Rabbi Avram for checking. Several paragraphs that had been omitted in the final versions were outlined in yellow highlighter. These were paragraphs deleted from the final, printed version, following the instructions of Rabbi Avram, who had termed them *lashon hara* or warned that they could have negative consequences. There were scores of intimate details that were best left unpublicized, details whose publication could ignite the fires of controversy. The hidden secrets of many different groups, that had been scrupulously censored from his beautifully written stories, had been carefully guarded in this archive of Rabbi Avram.

Why had the rabbi saved them? How had he used the censored paragraphs? Why had he kept them? So that after his death he could show them to the Heavenly Tribunal as proof of his good deeds?

The second shelf contained hundreds of audio tapes, each carefully numbered. Gili thrust his hand towards the back, as if to measure its depth. To his great surprise the shelf moved forward on hinges. There, in the back of the safe, he saw an ultramodern tape recorder. Wires leading out of the safe through tiny holes were attached to three microphones concealed in the desk, beneath the formica top.

They bent down and inspected the desk from underneath. "You see," Gili signed to Paysi in the dim light, "this room is a recording studio! All the conversations that Rabbi Avram has had with his followers have been taped!"

Gili returned to the safe, his senses dulled. At that moment he wanted only to die. The destruction of an idol is truly a traumatic thing. This must be how Terach had felt after his little boy Avram had destroyed his statues.

Gili thought that nothing else could touch him, but when he bent down to the third shelf, the bottom one, he stopped, breathless.

There on the shelf lay, in all its beauty, a thick, leather-bound book, golden tassels hanging from each of its four sides.

He didn't have to open the book to know what it was.

The Vessel of Blessing.

Gili's hands trembled as he pulled out the book. This work that he held in his gloved hands was much more beautiful, more impressive by far than the forgery he'd seen in Yaakovi's house. The book gave off the scent of antiquity, though it was extraordinarily well preserved.

He opened the book at random and skimmed a page. Without a doubt this was the real thing, written on pliable animal hide, slightly rough on one side, smooth as marble on the other. It glowed bluish in the dim light of the safe. Gili couldn't wait another instant: He quietly pulled the shutter up a crack.

Now he could see the binding in its natural color, something between brown and black. It was very old and yet shone in the light as if it were new. With respect bordering on awe he opened the tome. The words were covered with tiny, beautifully formed calligraphic letters. Gili was not particularly well versed in the scribal arts, his connection with *sofrim* being limited to the day he'd bought his *tefillin*. But despite his ignorance he was convinced that this book had been written by an expert scribe.

He brought the book closer to the window. The black letters shone, reflecting the light like glimmering pearls.

"Like new," he signed to Paysi. Again he touched the strong hide and examined it minutely. The parchment was yellowing and thin; deer hide, without a doubt.

Paysi watched in wonder as Gili leafed through the book. They saw mystical pictures flash before them, holy names, circles, diagonal lines, angels' names...

The book was divided into three parts. He could have named them by heart, even half asleep: The first gate is wisdom of the soul, the second gate is wisdom of the countenance, the third gate is wisdom of the deed.

He tried to understand random sentences from the beginning of the book but gave it up immediately: These kabbalistic concepts were too deep for his understanding. *Why does he hide such an incomprehensible book?* Gili thought. *What are its great secrets?* And then his gaze fell upon the second part, "Wisdom of the Countenance." He read a little, astonished. The style was antiquated, but it was sharp and clear. Here were detailed instructions on how to identify a person based on his facial features.

Forehead, nose, nostrils, mouth, eyes, right eye, left eye. Deep eyes or protuberant ones, eyebrows, upper lip, chin, right cheek, left cheek, ears, temple, neck, hair, beard...

Gili decided to put the information to a practical test. He built a profile of Paysi based on *The Vessel of Blessing*. In the short time that he'd known the boy, he had already learned much about his character.

The book was 100 percent on the mark! *Good-hearted, long-suffering, physically poor but possessed of a rich soul, honest, a man of integrity who can keep a secret, one who does not speak ill, one who doesn't speak much at all...*

It was a specific, detailed analysis. Now Gili understood why Rav Avram had allowed him to come close to Paysi. Rav Avram knew perfectly well that the widely held view of Paysi as a semiretarded invalid was wrong, but he was depending on his muteness and, even more, on Paysi's characteristic of keeping secrets.

But he hadn't taken into account the terrible anger of the sick boy over the neglect of his cystic fibrosis.

The third part, "The Wisdom of Deeds," included thousands of practical suggestions for all kinds of life's troubles — family, education, business, matchmaking, fears, illness of the body and, particularly, mental illness.

It was from here that Rav Avram reaped his vast wisdom; within the pages of this book he found an answer to each person's problems. That was why he would sometimes ask his visitors to step out in the middle of treatment: He couldn't always remember the text by heart.

For a full hour Paysi and Gili looked through the book, forgetting that Rav Avram was due back from the wedding at any time.

A 10-piece band with the newest in audio equipment and two famous singers entertained the crowd in the Recital Ballroom. The visitors were surrounded by polished mirrors that flattered them from all sides; crystal chandeliers spilling over their light and sparkling glass walls lent an air of opulence that was indeed impressive. Cameras in every corner constantly gave off their own lightning flashes.

The rich, varied menu was in itself a celebration and was fitting for a wedding celebrated at a millionaire's standard. It began with thin slices of veal in a pepper sauce and *pâté de foie gras,* accompanied by a dry chateau wine, vintage 1956, and individual melon baskets filled with a sweet-and-sour fruit cream. Jacketed waiters laden with heavy trays made their way between the tables and ambushed those who had not yet eaten something from the mountains of delicacies.

The highlight of the evening was the personal gift to each of the participants: a vintage bottle of burgundy. The bottle itself was made of pure silver engraved with the monogram of the bride and groom. A few of the relatives and close friends were called into a side room and surprised with a small, beautifully bound leather book with its title, *A Time for Everything,* engraved in gold. When they opened the book they found, inside, a luxury gold Chevalier watch.

"Miserly Pinny has decided to spend his last cent tonight! The watch alone costs a small fortune!" the guests whispered, their eyes gleaming with the brightness of the gold.

Rav Avram sat at the dais, dozens of his admirers standing behind him ready to snap up his every word. The groom, Yaakov Prezance, a graduate of a *hesder* yeshivah, cut the huge *challah* and gave generous slices to everyone at the table. Rav Avram seemed to have no appetite; he didn't even taste a crumb of the fragrant *challah.* A waiter approached. "Please, Rabbi, what would you like? Stuffed capon, filet steak, or duck roasted in our special sauce?"

Rav Avram graciously declined the tempting plates on the tray. He whispered something to the bride's father, Pinny Yaakovi, shook his hand and left the hall. A long trail of admirers followed him towards the exit. The hall grew silent for a moment, then the band burst out in song.

When the last of Rav Avram's admirers had left, a young man approached Pinny and asked him something.

Pinny looked at his assistant, Bumi Porat, said a few words and nodded his head in a negative gesture. The young man disappeared, his face evidencing dismay and shock.

"Paysi, we've got to get out of here. Rav Avram can come back any minute." Paysi nodded his head. Gili stood next to the safe, ready to replace the book, when he suddenly remembered: He hadn't looked at the title page, the most important page of all!

He opened the book again and looked for it. There was no title page!

"How could it be?" he whispered. A book with no title page? He remembered Bumi Porat's words in the lobby of the Holiday Inn in Jerusalem that first time he'd met "Big Yaakovi." From that first encounter, everything had grown so complicated. It was then that Bumi had told him of the "title page thieves," who wandered through the exhibits and stealthily made off with those precious pages, selling them for astonishing prices. Had the title page of *The Vessel of Blessing* fallen into those greedy hands?

Gently he felt the edge of the missing page. He could see that it had been carefully cut out by a sharp instrument so close to the binding that one could hardly see it had been removed. But his fingertips could feel the slight cut on the parchment. Such perfect work could not have been done by even the most expert of thieves under the pressure of time, when every second could bring exposure. No, this was done almost scientifically, a cut done for a specific purpose, one so pressing that it justified the destruction of such an ancient, valuable tome. Perhaps the title page would bear witness to a terrible miscarriage of justice?

Gili locked the safe with the secret combination, removed any signs of his presence and quickly left the room. Paysi buried himself in his bed, covered his face with his oxygen mask, and took deep breaths of Ventolin. This was no show: Thick mucus had almost suffocated him after an hour in the dusty room.

The Honda Civic roared out of the parking lot 10 seconds before Rav Avram's car entered.

Rav Avram gave the disappearing car a glance fraught with meaning.

"I can't go on this way. My head is about to explode!"

Gili paced the length of the room, back and forth, back and forth. He began at the closet at one end and made his way to the bookshelf at the other. His computer monitor danced with light but Gili ignored it. He was talking, as if to himself, letting his mother, sitting on a recliner near the window, share his thoughts though he knew she could not understand them.

"This puzzle has been driving me mad for the past six months. I'm a pawn in someone else's chess game. I'm a puppet on a string. Someone is standing behind the curtain moving around the bunch of rags whose name is Gili wherever he wants."

"Wonderful, wonderful!" Monica said dryly, clapping her hands. "Can I ask for some background?"

Gili walked even more quickly. It seemed to him that he was closer than ever to the riddle's answer. He was missing just one spark that would set the wick aflame. "Ima, do you honestly want to hear? Here goes: 1. Why is the title page missing? 2. How did Rav Avram Roosenthal get the book? 3. Why has he hidden it in his safe? 4. Who is standing behind — "

"Enough! Enough, Gili!" Monica interrupted the flow of words. "I don't want to hear anything. I'm afraid. Every time you delve too deeply you get a blackout. I'm begging you, Gili. The world is moving ahead. You can't ruin your life trying to find a book that's been burned. Abba is dead — don't die on me, too. Find yourself someone, rebuild your life. You're a grown man; it's time you built your own house. I so badly want sweet little children to fill up this big home. Since Udi's death our house has been cold and empty, like a huge refrigerator in a miser's home."

Her voice broke. Gili closed his mouth in humiliation. His first thought was to ask her if his own presence in the house meant nothing. *But,* he asked himself, *when was the last time you were in the house without barriers, without secrets, without impatiently telling Ima, "I have no time now, I have to finish this story!"?*

This chase, this chase after the book and the one who was hidden behind it, would drive him insane. He knew he was at the verge of finding the solution, and yet still sensed that one imperative piece of the puzzle was missing.

He put on a light woolen overcoat and walked into the evening's darkness. "Ima, I'm going out to get some air."

"Take care of yourself, Gili," Monica called out worried. "Don't look for trouble."

He walked through the streets. The security measures he had taken had become habit by now. As he left the house he looked all around him. Before he entered the car he bent down and looked beneath the chassis. As he drove he checked his mirrors constantly to see if anyone following him. He was certain that at some point a car would turn up behind him. "They" undoubtedly knew that he was nearing a solution. They weren't fools.

There were still many questions. He analyzed them one by one.

The fact that Rav Avram had *The Vessel of Blessing* in his possession meant nothing. Perhaps Gili's grandfather, Rav Shmuel Dinburg, had erred when he said there was only one copy in existence. Perhaps its author, Rav Ezra Albertzloni himself, had written more than one. Hadn't authors in those times worked to write more than one copy of their work — *Rashi*, the *Baalei Tosafos*, *Rambam*, *Rashba*...? The list was long. Who was to say that *The Vessel of Blessing* was different?

But why was the title page gone? Was it to conceal certain lines? Gili had found a copy of the text not long ago in his father's diary, those warm words written by Rav Shmuel Dinburg to his son:

> *"This holy book is for you, my dear son Moshe, to mark your growth in Torah and fear of G-d. May it be His will that this book accompany you throughout your life, as it did me and my father, generation through generation for five hundred years, until my forefather, the tzaddik Rav Tzvi Sofer of Salonika, beloved student of the author, the tzaddik and kabbalist Rav Ezra Albertzloni, who gave him the book as a gift. May their merit guard us. Your father, the humble Shmuel Dinburg."*

But Abba's copy of the book had been destroyed together with him, in the blazing automobile!

He hardly noticed that he had driven onto the highway. He passed the Kfar Shemaryahu intersection and continued on towards Haifa. *Do I know where I'm going?* he asked himself. *I'll let the Master of the Universe guide me.*

He drove into the night, not knowing where his car would lead him. He let his hands guide the steering wheel, hoping that things would work out by themselves. The cool breeze energized him; despite the lateness of the hour, his brain felt as clear as fine wine.

The lights on the road showed a gas station nearby. He checked the gauge: almost empty.

The Honda slowed onto the round island on the highway and came to a stop in front of the pump.

"Yes, sir?" The gas attendant seemed familiar; his pleasant face awoke something in the back of Gili's brain. A cigarette butt hung from the attendant's lips. "Have you heard the news? Gasoline prices are going up tonight at midnight. How much do you want?"

Gili checked his wallet. "Fill it up," he said. At the same moment, he grabbed his head between his hands. *I've been here before. The same question, the same voice — the same man. He had that pleasant face, that cigarette butt in his mouth.*

And suddenly Gili knew the answer — and the cerebral celebrations began. Colored fireworks exploded in his brain without warning, illuminating the darkness of that night. In a millisecond the black picture had grown light and he could see those forgotten minutes, even as unconsciousness covered all.

The attendant topped off the tank and approached the driver for payment. His eyes widened in astonishment.

Gili was lying unconscious in his seat.

36

Rav Yoske Friedman returned from yeshivah at 8 p.m. tired and drained. The daily yeshivah routine was exhausting if one took it seriously.

Rav Yoske took everything seriously. His lectures in the yeshivah in Haifa were masterpieces, each carefully thought out and crafted. Selected young men from the elite of the yeshivah world followed him enthusiastically in order to learn his "ten questions and one answer" method of learning. He made a deep analysis of each concept, giving sharply honed proof that each *sugya* was a united whole, if only one could penetrate its core.

Force of habit sent him to his fax machine. A few notices awaited him, but only one seemed to shriek its cry for help: "Paysi's health is deteriorating rapidly. Urgent that he receive heart-lung transplant. Gili."

Rav Yoske had never met Paysi, but he had heard of him from Gili. He also had heard of the well-known activist Rav Zishe Tzimer, who worked with extraordinary success on bringing sick people from Israel to hospitals abroad for transplants.

Now Rav Yoske faced a difficult challenge. Zishe was an activist who worked 18-hour days. Getting through to his multiline phone was one of the most difficult and frustrating experiences a person could undergo.

Nevertheless, he would have to call him.

It took an hour to finally get through to the office. "Good evening," the secretary said. "How can I help you?"

"I need Rav Zishe Tzimer urgently. It's an emergency!"

The secretary was not impressed. "Stay on the line. Rav Zishe will be on within the hour."

She was about to transfer the call. Rav Yoske, with all the impatience of a man about to be trapped with piped-in music for a solid hour, shouted, "One minute! Help!"

The secretary's finger remained dangling. "Did you want to say something?" she asked politely.

"Yes." He breathed deeply; at least he was still speaking to a human voice and not some digitised musician. "Tell him we're talking about an urgent transplant, a boy with a severe case of cystic fibrosis."

It worked! "Why didn't you say so before?" she asked. "Rav Zishe will speak with you within five minutes."

The five minutes stretched to fifteen. After three classical songs had come and gone he heard Rav Zishe's pleasant voice. "Yes?"

Rav Yoske provided all the details that he knew. When he finally hung up the phone he felt a stone lift from his heart. Everyone knew that though Zishe Tzimer took care of the entire gamut of human illness, his particular strengths were in three fields: malignancies, heart trouble, and transplants. And transplants were his specialty.

Rav Yoske could be calm now: Rav Zishe's well-oiled *chesed* machine had begun its work. He could imagine the ambulance pulling into Ben Gurion Airport within the next few hours. Inside would be the doctors and nurses who would accompany Paysi, the most modern medical equipment, all the necessary paperwork — passport, tickets, medical records, x-rays and CT scan — everything. Two days from now Paysi would be breathing normally, a newly transplanted heart and lung in his body.

Rav Yoske was certain: No one could stop Zishe Tzimer!

The gas attendant poured a strong stream of water on Gili's face. Gili moved his head and rolled his eyes. He stared around him without comprehension.

"Good morning," the attendant said. "You awake yet?"

"What happened to me?" Gili asked, rubbing his temples.

"That's what I'm asking," the attendant laughed. "I filled your gas tank and when I got back to you you were fast asleep!"

Gili suddenly understood. The words "filled your gas tank" had brought on the blackout.

"I guess I was just overtired," he told the worker as he took his change.

"Take some free advice. Drive right to an emergency room," the attendant murmured, his cigarette butt dancing between his lips.

Gili raced out of the gas station. Now he knew exactly where he wanted to go. He would reconstruct that night, the night of the wedding and the accident, from the starting point.

The Honda sped down the highway towards Haifa. Here it all began...

☾☽

Udi, Monica, and Gili were traveling to a friend's wedding in the Country Galei-Gil hall in Kiryat Motzkin. Efraim, Udi's faithful driver, had begged off with a headache; Gili was taking his place. After they'd passed the Kfar Shemaryahu junction they stopped for gas. The attendant came over and told them, "Gas prices are going up tonight. Fill it up?"

"To the top," Gili answered. Udi had looked angrily at the attendant. "Young man, do you want to blow up this station? A cigarette, here? Right next to the gas pumps?"

The attendant pulled the unlit butt from between his lips. "Never make an accusation until you've checked your facts," he said serenely. "It's not lit. It just helps calm my nerves."

Udi apologized. "I'm so sorry."

"No big deal," the pleasant-faced attendant shrugged.

From there they had gone on to the wedding. When they reached Haifa Gili, in a sudden burst of economy, stopped at a gas station and again filled up, topping it off, "before the prices go up," he explained. When he parked the Mercedes in the lot the gauge clearly showed that it was full.

When they left the wedding hours later they were exhausted and confused after Udi's close call with choking. It was Manny Schwartz, of course, his friend, who had saved his life.

Despite his confusion, Gili noticed that the gas tank was almost empty. "They drained the gas out of the car! Thieves are also worried about the rising prices," Gili had said sluggishly. But his words hardly registered: Everyone was in a daze.

Now, driving to the Carmel once again, he remembered his recurring dream. He was lying on a bed of wildflowers watching the blazing car go up in flames like a bonfire on Lag B'Omer. All through the dream he felt that something was wrong with the fire.

Something was wrong. Very wrong. If there was no gas in the tank when they left Kiryat Motzkin, how had the car been incinerated in a raging inferno of smoke and flame?

Had the fire come later? Had someone doused the wreck in gasoline and lit a match?

Gili could remember where the car had crashed. It was on one of the roads leading down the Carmel. Their presence there, too, was a result of their daze: Manny should really have taken the short route through Haifa, but he had gotten lost and somehow wound up on the mountain. When he had reached the summit he had begun to speed like a madman. Monica had begged him to stop, and then Gili took the wheel. Two minutes later the Mercedes had plunged into the ravine below.

It was a little after midnight when he saw the lights of the Carmel in the distance. On the night of the accident there had been a short circuit in the mountain's main generator, and all the street lights had been extinguished. Now they gave off a sparkling blue shine.

He remembered exactly where the Mercedes had skidded off the shoulder and flown into the ravine. After his release from the hospital he had come here a few times in the company of a police officer in order to reconstruct the accident. He had agreed very reluctantly, and was too frightened to gaze down into the ravine below. The trauma was still too fresh and aching. Afterwards, when he had recovered somewhat, he had traveled there many times. He would come, meditate, think of his father's death. But he never went down the wadi; even in the light of day he was terrified to climb down. Now, after midnight, in the darkness, he was prepared to do so!

He stopped at the spot. The place had not changed very much; essentially it looked exactly the same.

Gili parked the Honda on the road's shoulder, as far as he could from the streetlights. He left the car and gazed fearfully into the inky depths below. He could feel his heart thudding wildly. He took a deep breath and climbed over the metal railing.

With hesitant, careful steps he began to climb down. At first the descent was gradual, but after a few yards it became steeper and steeper. Lights of passing cars above him rent the darkness, but the hazy yellow lights were rare: Few cars passed here at this time of the night. Gili hoped that no driver would stop to investigate the deserted car parked on the side of the road. He was filled with terror and tension; the sound of each engine broke his concentration. And he needed every bit of concentration he could muster.

After he had descended about six yards he pulled a flashlight out of his coat pocket.

He was surrounded by thorns and low trees, themselves as black as the night. To his left he saw a large mound of sand.

A cold sweat broke out on his brow and his body began to tremble uncontrollably. He approached the mound and shuddered, as if he had stepped on a corpse.

He forced himself to calm down, breathed deeply and stared around him. The ground was soft here, full of pebbles and grasses, a lot of grasses. If the Mercedes had fallen here on the sand it would have received a soft, cushioned blow, and all its passengers would have survived the crash.

His flashlight lit up the slope. Fifteen yards below him he saw a black circle of earth. Holding the flashlight between his teeth he crawled down, hanging on to every thorn bush and boulder, his body trembling. Occasionally pebbles dislodged by his legs would roll explosively down beneath him. When he reached the circle he could see the broken stump of an olive tree. The trunk was very wide and stood sturdily amidst the dirt and pebbles, a huge boulder of a tree that could certainly have stopped the Mercedes' crashing fall. And that's what the official report said had happened.

"It was a miracle that the car crashed into the trunk," the police had told them after the accident. Black scars on the face of the trunk had lent credibility to their theory.

Gili stared above him at the mountain. It was about 10 yards from the road to the tree. If the heavy Mercedes had fallen down into the tree the car would have been split in two; surely, no one could have come out alive from such a crash. *Where have my brains been?* he asked himself. *How did I buy such a stupid story?*

So everything was one big lie. Even the fire, it seemed, had been staged. Why? To burn people who had died in a car accident? What cannibal had incinerated the corpses?

A few yards further down, the descent ended in a valley of thick pine trees and natural forests. The car certainly could not have reached down there, not unless it had been flung there like the scapegoat hurled down to *azazel*.

Gili sat himself down on the tree stump and counted out the possibilities on his fingers. 1. The soft mound. They did land there, according to the police report. 2. The tree trunk. They could not have crashed into it; otherwise, all of them would have been crushed. 3. Further down, into the woods — even clear that they could not have survived such an accident.

So where had the car landed that night? Where had it stopped? And when had it burned up?

And if the car had, indeed, crashed into the tree, how was it that Monica and Gili had been thrown onto the cushion of grass and wildflowers? They were sitting in the front, were strapped into seat belts, and yet the two passengers in the back, Manny and Udi, had been trapped in the burning car. The odds of the seat-belted driver dying in an accident such as this were much greater than those of the back-seat passengers — and yet here the opposite had happened.

Suddenly, without any introductory blackout, Gili knew. He could remember exactly what had happened after the accident. The suppressed memories that had tried so hard to push through the veil of his memory suddenly burst forth, after six years, and stood before him, clear and bright.

⊙❧☙⊙

He was sitting on the cushioned floor, a good distance from the Mercedes. The car was not on fire! His hand felt the piercing of a thorn; his legs seemed paralyzed. He tried to move but his body would not respond. *It seems that I've died;* the thought flashed through his head. *Silly, the dead don't see what's happening around them.* And Gili could see shadowy figures surrounding the car. Someone had pulled Monica out and left her not far from him. When the figures came closer to him he closed his eyes and pretended to be unconscious. Now he knew that this had saved him from death, although he had not understood a thing then. He had been completely dazed, uncaring, disconnected from what was going on around him. He saw his mother lying on the ground next to him unconscious and felt nothing, neither sorrow nor pity. A blessed tranquility had fallen upon him, a strange tranquility, like the feeling one got after an anesthetic; like morphine...

Suddenly he understood. They had been drugged! All of them, drugged. That was why Manny had lost his way, why Udi had heard a helicopter above them. That was the reason he, Gili, had felt so dazed and lost control of the car.

Someone had wanted to kill them. Why? Who were those shadowy figures around the car? He had not made out any faces; everything was dark. The figures did not utter a word, they had worked in total silence.

He had fallen into a dazed sleep and only awoke from the heat of the blazing automobile. Unconsciously, he had known all along that something was wrong with the fire.

⊙❧☙⊙

Gili rose from the tree trunk. This night had solved part of the mystery. The fire that had burned the car up had been started after the accident. The automobile had undoubtedly landed on the soft mound, six yards beneath the highway.

The police had lied. There had been a cover-up; false facts had been placed in the file. A ruined tree stump had been placed there after the fact;

signs of charring had been made in the wood. It had been singed in some laboratory somewhere, to help lend authenticity to the story.

Who could be behind it? Someone with friends in very high places, someone who could do what he wanted with police investigations.

Just like the Chevrolet that had tried to overturn Rav Avram's Grand Prix. The police had been given a detailed description of the car, had put up roadblocks and closed highways. For nothing. They had found nothing, because the file had been closed even before it had been opened. That's what happens when an invisible hand stirs a pot, a hand with authority even higher than that of the police.

The GSS, for example.

Gili carefully climbed up the mountain, hanging on to every branch and outcropping. Beads of sweat gathered on his forehead and washed over his face. He was breathing heavily when he once again reached the soft mound of earth. He began to dig through it in a frenzy. Clods of dirt and flowers flew through the air. He hoped he wouldn't wake some sleeping snake or quick-tempered scorpion.

When he had dug about two feet he stopped and gazed at the dirt in the light of the flashlight. There were no snakes or scorpions, thank Heaven, but unidentifiable crawling creatures raced around from all sides. He bent down and filled his fist with dirt, and then sniffed it as a bloodhound might. The dirt had the smell of — dirt. No fire. Nothing.

"Hey, down there, what are you doing there?"

Gili paled and almost fell. A young man in a light shirt was standing on the edge of the road. "Identify yourself or I'm getting the police!" he shouted.

The paralyzing fear disappeared. The threat of the police was part of the lexicon of plain, private citizens, not of GSS professionals. "Don't be afraid," he yelled back, "I'm not Hamas or the Islamic Jihad. My name is Gili Dinar."

He climbed to the highway. At the last minute his feet wobbled and he almost rolled back down into the wadi. The light-shirted man extended a hand and helped him up.

"You scared me," the young man complained.

"Look who's talking," Gili dusted off the dirt from his clothing. "I nearly had a heart attack."

The young man apologized. "I was passing by and I saw a Honda too close to the edge, as if it were going to fall. Like that night, six years ago. Suddenly all my memories were aroused. I stopped to look, and I heard noise from down below..."

Gili froze. "Did I hear you right? Were you here six years ago?"

"Absolutely." The man was happy to share his story. "I remember it like yesterday, how the Mercedes went off the road and rolled down below. Oh, it was terrible."

Gili approached him, his eyes narrowed. "You were there that night?" he muttered.

"Why do you want to know?"

"Because I was in the Mercedes!"

The man looked at him in fright, as if he had seen a corpse rising from its grave. "You were in that accident?"

"Yes."

"And you weren't killed?"

"I was hurt, but my father and his friend were burned up."

The man was a few years older than Gili. "I work the night shift at the Dan Panorama Hotel, on the top of the mountain; I come home every night around this time. Since that night I have nightmares. Sometimes I see myself falling into the wadi."

"What happened that night?" Gili had to know.

"We were driving behind a Mercedes, me and another car, being driven by an older man. We saw the white Mercedes zigzag on the road, veer left, drive right over the barrier and disappear into the dark. The two of us stopped immediately and tried to figure out what we could do. It was pitch black and we could hardly see anything. For a minute it seemed to me that I had seen wheels turning around a few yards beneath me, but I wasn't certain. Suddenly an Opel pulled up. Its driver was very efficient, and he took care of everything. He wrote down our names, told us he'd call the police and Magen David Adom, and all but chased us away from there. You know what? At the time I was happy, because I'm not one of your hero types, but the next day it seemed a bit strange to me."

Gili waved his hand impatiently. "What did the man look like? Tall, fat, with a knitted *kippah* on a bald head?"

"No, not at all. He was middle aged. I only saw him for two minutes; how much can I remember? But he certainly wasn't fat or bald."

"And the fire?"

"What fire? There was no fire!" The man pulled away from Gili's grip.

"Are you sure?" Gili's throat had tightened.

"Nothing is sure," he said. "When I was here there was no fire. But the next day the newspapers said that a car had fallen into the ravine and had been burned, with two of its passengers trapped within. I called the police and asked if that had been the accident that I'd witnessed, because as far as I knew there'd been no fire. They explained that the gas tank had exploded later."

Gili was shocked. To be so stupid? "Think about it," he said frostily. "The emergency services came immediately, right? And they stood by with folded hands and let two people burn to death without lifting a finger? Didn't you understand that the man who sent you away didn't want to call help? He only wanted to set the car on fire once you'd gone!"

The young man was astonished. "I never thought of that!"

Gili again grabbed his hand. "You saw a first-degree murder committed here. Two innocent men were killed. Why didn't you stay? Why didn't you say anything?"

The young man made a face and pulled his hand away. "I don't owe you anything. In the army they taught us not to make a fuss if we wanted to get home in one piece."

Gili thought of the mess he had become tangled up with since he had pushed himself in where he was not meant to be. "You're right," he said. "But now I need your testimony. Would you mind giving me your identification?"

The young man did not protest. Gili wrote down his name, address and phone number in his personal memo pad. The man's name was Effie Green, a resident of Herzl Street in Haifa.

Before dawn Gili had arrived home and flung himself, fully dressed, onto his bed, weak and drained. When he made a reckoning of his position he felt even worse. His chances of success were close to zero; no, they were absolute zero. This was a war of a single man against a huge organization. "They" knew who he was, but he didn't know who they were (almost). The GSS had been writing the script and they had predicted most of his moves before he had even made them. He had to get a few steps ahead of them, find a place they had never dreamed of.

Gili needed the best advice available. He knew only one man who could give him the spiritual perspective and outlook he needed. Not to mention a blessing.

The sick, old rebbe of Kiltz.

But the rebbe wasn't seeing anyone, and his administrator, Rabbi Schneidman, blamed the rebbe's illness on Gili himself!

But Gili had one thing up his sleeve. Something he knew Rabbi Schneidman could not resist.

Zishe Tzimer was surrounded by the jangling of phones. He had called Paysi's doctors in Beilinson Hospital and clarified the seriousness of his illness. He shuddered at the simplicity of the prognosis: The boy's lungs were collapsing and he was nearing the end.

Paysi's one hope for life was a lung transplant.

Zishe immediately phoned Harfield Hospital in western London and asked to speak to the renowned surgeon, Dr. Magdi Yakub, who had specialized in heart-lung transplants for CF sufferers for the past decade. The doctor got on the line and heard an update on Paysi's condition. He gave a slow whistle.

"Rabbi Tzimer, Rabbi Tzimer," his voice sounded exultant, "you've fallen on me from heaven. They brought a young man here this afternoon. He'd been in an accident and was clinically dead. His blood type is rare, O-negative. Two hours ago my secretary started looking for potential transplant recipients. There's a long list; twenty sick children in Europe and America are waiting. Some of them are the right size for the organs, but only your Israeli boy has the needed blood type."

One circle closed. Now Rabbi Zishe worked without losing a moment. "Go to the house of the Interior Ministry director," he yelled to his assistant, Mendel Levi. "Get her out of her home. I need a passport in two hours."

Zishe got his staff working at a dizzying pace. He was racing a merciless clock; for Paysi, the sand in the hourglass was running out.

After two feverish hours Paysi's long-dreamed-of trip had become reality. His passport and ticket were ready, his medical records had made the trip from the hospital to the offices of Rav Zishe's "Refuah Sheleimah" organization, and Beilinson Hospital had volunteered a doctor and nurse to accompany him. Only a fully equipped ambulance remained to be sent to Rav Avram's house to collect the sick boy.

At two in the morning Rav Zishe allowed himself the luxury of stretching in his chair and smiling in satisfaction. British Airways flight 660 to London would take off tomorrow morning at 6:15 from Ben Gurion Airport. According to the plans worked out with Rav Avram, the "Refuah Sheleimah" ambulance would pick up Paysi at 5:30 a.m. Rav Zishe sipped tea that had grown cold and prepared to leave the office within the next half-hour. Unless something else came up...

Sitting next to him was Pinny Klein, a new helper. This was Pinny's first encounter with an actual CF patient. After a moment's hesitation he asked, "Rav Zishe, I don't understand. What's the point of a transplant if CF is a genetic disease and the boy will get sick again?"

"And more years of life as a present, is that nothing to you?" Rav Zishe asked the rhetorical question. "Our experience has showed us that such transplants grant several more years with a much higher quality of life than before."

"And why a heart too? The heart isn't damaged, after all."

The telephone rang. Zishe held it in his hand, and continued speaking to Pinny. "It's hard to believe, but the reason is a technical one. The heart and the lungs are linked in many ways — the blood cells, the nervous system, and more. From the surgical point of view it's just better to transplant the two together." He turned his attention to the phone. "Yes, the ambulance for the CF patient. You're the new driver. I understand. What's the change? Oh, 15 minutes earlier. At 5:15. I'm not too happy about it; it's not good for the youngster to spend too much time in the airplane. But if you have no choice, that's a different story. Shalom."

He spoke to Pinny again. "A new driver. He's moving it up by 15 minutes."

Zishe Tzimer had never been involved with the GSS.

37

Rabbi Yehoshua Schneidman leaned back in his swivel chair, his arms linked around his neck. His apathetic gaze fell on the pile of papers covering his desk. He found it difficult to concentrate on anything these days, now that his rebbe was in seclusion, his health foundering.

The telephone rang. Rabbi Schneidman heard Gili's voice on the line. "I've really got nothing to say to you," he said coldly. "You and your 'rabbi' have done enough damage here."

Gili gasped. He hadn't expected such a frontal attack. "Do you want to hear some good news?"

"Good news? With our rebbe ill there is no good news." With that, Rabbi Schneidman slammed down the phone. Luckily, the receiver didn't break apart.

Gili gathered up the last shreds of his pride, gritted his teeth and went up to Jerusalem to meet Rabbi Schneidman face to face. The administrator was the only conduit to the elderly rebbe of Kiltz; Gili just had to find a way to get through to him.

And he knew a way.

When he entered the office Rabbi Schneidman gave him the look of a furious tiger. He jumped to his feet. Gili calmly sat himself down in a chair facing his desk, pulled off his woolen checked scarf and put it on the side. "A hot cup of tea, if you don't mind. It's cold out there."

Rabbi Schneidman exuded all the warmth of an industrial-size freezer. "No one can match you for *chutzpah*, Gili," he said.

Gili put the full-color, lavishly designed Sotheby's catalog on the desk and opened it to a marked page. The photograph of the chandelier stood before the administrator's widening eyes.

Schneidman got up heavily. "What's that?" he asked, pointing at the brilliant photo.

Now it was Gili's turn to be frigid. "What do you think it is?"

The administrator grabbed the catalog. "It's our chandelier!" he shouted happily. "Whose catalog is this? Does it belong to the police?"

Gili told him all about Sotheby's and Manfred Strum.

"I won't take this!" Rabbi Schneidman repeated again and again. "An identical chandelier? Nonsense! I'm going to get the police involved in this today."

Gili's analysis had been correct: In his excitement Schneidman forgot all his anger. By the time he was ready to leave, Gili had been able to make his audacious request.

Rav Avram finished seeing his visitors at 4:30 in the morning and he began to prepare Paysi for his flight. He didn't know, or didn't want to know, who was behind the hurried travel arrangements, and he listened with a stony face to Choni's excited voice. "I want to go with the ambulance to the airport, okay, Abba? You don't care, right?"

Rav Avram glared at Choni. Relations between the two were strained; Choni was going to go with Paysi to Ben Gurion, even if "Abba" were to hang a huge sign with burning letters forbidding it.

Paysi waited in his room, two suitcases at the foot of his bed, his head bent over an open *Tehillim* as he soundlessly mouthed the words. When he saw a pair of shiny black shoes approaching, he looked up. Rav Avram stood before him.

For once Rav Avram was at a loss for words. As he searched for the right thing to say his hands rifled through his jacket pocket. He pulled out a check and wrote on the back, "Good luck, Paysi. I always loved you. Come back home healthy and whole." He shook Paysi's hand; the boy felt a piece of paper crackle in his palm. When Rav Avram had left the room Paysi found a check for $7000, a contribution towards the expenses of the costly operation.

The ambulance arrived at 5:10 a.m. It pulled into the quiet parking lot and backed up almost to the lobby itself. Choni placed Paysi's possessions inside. A paramedic with the Magen David Adom symbol on his shirt rushed out of the ambulance. The driver approached Paysi from the other side with open arms. The boy looked at him suspiciously, as if afraid that he would crush him between his powerful biceps, this thickset man whose eyes were almost hidden by layers of fat. He lifted Paysi with surprising gentleness onto the gurney. The paramedic helped him get Paysi inside. A young woman in a nurse's uniform placed an oxygen mask over his face.

Rav Avram blinked. "This is the Magen David Adom of Petach Tikvah ambulance?" he asked the driver.

"Certainly, Rabbi," the driver answered as he got into his seat. "Now if you'll please move, we'll be off."

Rav Avram persisted. "They told me they'd be sending an ambulance from 'Refuah Sheleimah.'"

The driver shrugged. "What's the matter, Rabbi? You know we work with 'Refuah Sheleimah' all the time. Zishe Tzimer and I are buddies."

The explanation satisfied Rav Avram. "Send Rav Zishe my fondest thanks. I'm astonished by his dedication."

"Yeah, it's amazing," the driver answered. "Nu, let's go already. Move to the side; you're blocking my way."

The ambulance went on its way, gaining speed, its siren silent. When it passed a sharp curve it pulled up next to a parked Chevrolet and stopped. The back door flew open.

Meshulam Yaakovi and his personal assistant jumped out of the car and climbed into the ambulance. "Excellent." Meshulam examined Paysi's surprised face with an expression of satisfaction. "You did good work," he said to Choni.

The driver started the engine and sped towards the GSS garage in Tel Aviv. Meshulam's assistant, impatient, yelled into Paysi's hearing aid, "Tell us the truth, what have you told Gili?"

Paysi looked at him with terrified eyes. "Who are you?" his lips mouthed the words, though no sound emerged.

Choni turned to Meshulam. "He's a mute."

"I know!" Meshulam answered angrily. "This mute managed to tell Gili an awful lot. Six years we're working on the perfect plan and this idiot will destroy it in one minute? I want to know how far he's gone!"

Choni spoke to Paysi, carefully pronouncing every word so that Paysi could read his lips. "Paysi, cooperate, like I do, if you want a new set of lungs. Tell the GSS men exactly what you've told Gili."

Paysi turned gray with fear. Instead of flying to London for his critical operation, had he been kidnapped by the GSS?

Meshulam took hold of himself. Psychological Warfare was his department; he excelled at it. He drew a deep breath; the scarlet hues of fury disappeared from his face. Now he looked more human. "Let me speak to him," he rebuked his assistant. "Force won't work; we have to do this nicely." He spoke to Paysi very slowly. "We want to help you. Dr. Yakub is a friend of mine. One word from me and the operation will be a success, and Paysi will be healthy. Do you understand? Paysi — healthy! Don't you want that?"

Paysi nodded his head emphatically. His eyes filled with tears.

A window of opportunity had been opened; the mute boy was softening! Yaakovi felt a surge of conceit: the power of psychology!

The ambulance raced on towards Tel Aviv. The streets were still half-dark, and many street lights blinked yellow. "Operations cost a lot of money," Yaakovi radiated generosity. "I can give you money. A lot of money."

He counted out 10 $100 bills before Paysi's eyes and handed them to him. His voice was smooth as silk. "And now let's hear your solo. What did you tell Gili? What does he know about the 'Puppeteer Rabbi'? About Goldman and Kiryat Bialik? What about Mickey Gadish?"

Paysi looked at him, beseeching. "Take me to Lod," he mouthed.

"Of course, my friend, you'll go to Lod," Yaakovi whispered. "Just nod your head, yes or no. Does Gili know something about Goldman? Kiryat Bialik? Mickey Gadish?"

Paysi's eyes rolled in their sockets; he began to cough, a long and harsh attack. Small droplets of blood dripped from his mouth onto the plastic oxygen mask. He rubbed his aching ribs, almost suffocating. The doctor and nurse sitting by his side pushed away Yaakovi; the nurse touched a button marked "oxygen."

"More oxygen, Nurse," the doctor ordered. He held a needle upside down between his fingers and gave it a push; tiny drops of liquid flew up into the ambulance. In a flash he inserted the needle into Paysi's emaciated arm and infused the transparent medication directly into a vein.

"When the cortisone has opened his lungs, we've got to take him to the airport," the doctor said, his face frozen. "The boy is on the verge of death; you don't need this shame on the good name of the GSS. Think of the headlines: Israel's security establishment battles a boy dying of cystic fibrosis... Let him go."

Yaakovi trembled with rage. "It's a show," he hissed through clenched teeth. "I know these games. I won't let a plan of six years come to nothing because of him. We've got the *chareidim* by the throat; I'm ready to rip them to pieces." His voice grew shrill with hatred; his eyes protruded. "All of the terrible controversies that they've had in the past will seem like child's play compared with what's going to happen soon, when our bombs explode. They'll kill each other in the street; blood will flow... Blood! They'll be pulling out daggers on Meah Shearim and Chazon Ish. Chassidic courts, *roshei yeshivah*, even families will be torn apart by hatred and fear. Our plan is detailed and ready to be put into action."

Choni looked at him, entranced, his eyes adoring.

"And now here comes Mr. Cystic Fibrosis, a deaf-mute who knows how to communicate perfectly. He's smarter than all of them." Yaakovi put his balled fist next to Paysi's rigid face. "Just nod your head. Did you tell him or not?"

The doctor pulled off his white jacket. "I will not have anything to do with such a crime." He approached the back door and put his hand on the handle.

"Madman!" Yaakovi roared. "Do you want to kill yourself?"

He walked towards the front of the ambulance. "Proceed to the airport," he shouted. "I've had enough of this."

The driver made a swift U-turn and gunned the engine, racing towards the airport.

Paysi motioned with a weak finger towards Yaakovi. His chest heaved; his face was white with agony.

"Did you call me?" Yaakovi asked.

Paysi nodded his head in assent.

"You've come to your senses?" Meshulam's face lit up. "Finally, you've gotten smart. Let's hear what you want to tell me."

He bent towards Paysi's lips to hear his mute whisperings. Paysi put his outstretched hand into Yaakovi's beefy palm.

Yaakovi opened his hand. His face reddened in humiliation.

He was holding 10 $100 bills.

⚜

"The Sotheby's sale will take place in another month. If we threaten the company with police action, they'll have to relinquish the chandelier," Gili explained to the rebbe of Kiltz. The rebbe, though clearly weakened, seemed as alert as ever. Gili felt a massive sense of relief: The rebbe would recover. And he, Gili, was allowed to see him, even now, when he would meet with almost no one!

"Can we prove that the chandelier was stolen?" Rabbi Schneidman, sitting next to the rebbe's bedside, asked.

Gili sat quietly for a moment, looking with new eyes at the venerable rebbe. A white yarmulka perched on thinning hair, a noble, unfurrowed brow, two thin *payos* and a patriarchal beard of silver framing a waxen visage stretched as tightly as parchment. And the eyes! A pair of youthful eyes looked out from over sunken cheeks, eyes that told of goodness and wisdom. A large oil painting hung near the rebbe's bed, a portrait. The comparison was inescapable: The rebbe, Rav Mendel Shiffman, looked very much like his father, Rav Zalman Shiffman, previous rebbe of Kiltz.

Gili's gaze continued to roam around the room. How simple, how bare and impoverished. Some old furniture, a round desk, formerly bright-colored shades that had darkened with age: Here was a heart-warming simplicity that told its own tale.

"It can be done," he said to Rabbi Schneidman. "There are many ways to reveal the truth. I can think of three."

"What are they?" Rabbi Schneidman asked. "Remember, only a tiny bronze rectangle the size of a matchbox was left in the ceiling."

"The rectangle was cut from the base of the chandelier, and that's what counts," Gili declared. "First, it's possible that the identification department of the police can compare the top of the chandelier in Sotheby's with the piece of bronze that we have, by checking the marks of where it was cut off. That's not much of a chance, though, since the thieves most likely filed down the incriminating marks. The second chance is for us to check it ourselves at the pre-sale exhibit with a powerful microscope but, again, the thieves may well have destroyed the evidence."

"So what are you suggesting?" Rabbi Schneidman burst out. "Why have you disturbed the rebbe?"

The rebbe raised his bowed head and stared at Rabbi Schneidman. "Let him speak." The movement of his pale lips reminded Gili of the enchanting wings of the doves that flew by the Kotel. "He knows what he's talking about," the rebbe concluded.

Gili blushed. "I'm a journalist. I have connections in many different places. I can take the small metal rectangle remaining on the *beis midrash* ceiling to the nuclear reactor in Nachal Sorek. I'd have to have a similar piece pilfered from the chandelier at Sotheby's. The two pieces would then be exposed to gamma rays."

"Which are—" Rabbi Schneidman interrupted impatiently.

Gili explained patiently. "It's nuclear detection. They bombard the piece with neutrons."

"Slowly and clearly," Rabbi Schneidman begged. "Our chandelier is to have an atomic explosion?"

"Would the rebbe like to hear about nuclear detection?" Gili asked gently.

The rebbe smiled at Gili, the first smile he'd seen that day. "It interests me."

Gili felt sweat break out on his brow. Until now he hadn't been sure how the rebbe was going to react, but it seemed he had a very important listener. He made his explanation brief, so as not to tire the rebbe needlessly.

"When a material is bombarded with neutrons — those are a kind of atomic particle — the material collects the neutrons and becomes radioactive. Most materials give off gamma rays when they become radioactive. The nuclear reactor is a source of neutrons. We put the remaining piece of the stolen chandelier into the reactor — we don't need the whole thing, a piece the size of a sunflower seed will do — and we put inside a similar piece from the Sotheby's chandelier, and we pull them both out the minute they become radioactive. From there they would be taken to an instrument that analyzes their gamma rays and measures the energy they are giving off. These rays grow weaker in a gradual process. Every atomic substance loses its energy in a unique pattern."

Rabbi Schneidman nodded his head energetically. His face showed great concentration, but his eyes were blank. He was silent. The rebbe turned to Gili. "If each substance has a differing pattern of loss, and the piece that you examine was indeed stolen from us, I would imagine that the two pieces would show identical patterns of radiation loss?"

Gili stared, breathlessly. This elderly rebbe could have been a professor of chemistry or nuclear physics. How quickly he'd understood, even at his advanced age, these new facts.

"Exactly!" he cried out excitedly. "They examine each of the bombarded pieces and measure the gamma rays they give off after one minute, five minutes, ten, thirty, two hours. And then again after 24 hours. If the numbers they get from the two pieces are different then the secretary at Sotheby's was correct, and the chandelier is the property of Manfred Strum of America. But if the numbers are identical that chandelier will hang once again from the ceiling: This means of identification is accepted by any court."

"Now I understand!" Rabbi Schneidman enthused. "So let's go, what are we waiting for?"

Gili stared intently at the rebbe; he framed the question in his heart. The rebbe understood the undeclared request and he turned pleasantly to Rabbi Schneidman. "Perhaps you'll let me have a few moments with Gili privately?"

"Of course. But the rebbe will not overtax himself, I hope," he murmured, casting a warning glance at the young reporter.

Gili bent towards the rebbe. His voice was sharp. "The man who stole the chandelier is not only a thief; he's a murderer!"

"Meaning?"

Gili gave the rebbe a quick summary of the events that had taken place, up to his strange nocturnal encounter on the Carmel.

"So what do you say now?" the rebbe asked, at the end of his account.

"This is my scenario: "Big Yaakovi" wanted to get *The Vessel of Blessing* for free, instead of paying the $650,000 minimum. That was the price my father was asking for the book. So he drugged us at the wedding, emptied the gas tank to strand us on the highway, and sent accomplices to steal the book. The car's falling into the wadi messed his plans up a little, but he immediately set the car on fire. Abba and Manny Schwartz saw him — he murdered them and burned them up — and the book, *The Vessel of Blessing*, was stolen and given to his esteemed rebbe, Rav Avram Roosenthal, who needed inspiration.

"Maybe you should search for the book?" the rebbe suggested. "Every book has a title page. If you find it, you can see who it belongs to."

"Rebbe, you're a prophet!" Gili almost shouted. He continued to speak quickly, almost swallowing his words in his haste. "I found the *sefer,* and the title page has been cut out with a sharp knife. I assume so that Rav Avram wouldn't ask any questions. I keep asking myself the same thing: How can I prove that "Big Yaakovi" murdered my father?"

He didn't reveal still another question that was troubling him: If Yaakovi had indeed stolen the book, why had he repeatedly called Gili's attention to its existence, beginning with their first meeting in the lobby of the Holiday Inn in Jerusalem, and on through their interview in his home? Yaakovi was many things, but he was not a fool.

The rebbe leaned his forehead on his hand and dropped his gaze, lost in thought. Gili could hear the sound of ringing phones in the background, the clatter of silverware and cups being washed. Rabbi Schneidman knocked hesitantly on the door and peeked in.

"You've come just in time," the rebbe greeted him cordially. "Remind me: Doesn't our Kopel Baum work for the Tel Aviv *chevra kadisha*?"

Rabbi Schneidman rubbed his beard thoughtfully. His eyes lit up with curiosity, but respect for the rebbe kept him from questioning. "Kopel Baum is the administrator of the *chevra kadisha.*"

The rebbe rubbed his hands with satisfaction. "If your father is buried in the Tel Aviv area, his file is no doubt in the *chevra kadisha* offices there. Kopel Baum is a *chassid* of Kiltz. Show him your journalist's ID card, and if he knows I sent you, he'll find the files of your father and Manny Schwartz. And if there's anything suspicious there at all — call me right away."

38

Z ishe Tzimer stayed in his office that night until 3:30. The usual routine: This night, too, several urgent life-or-death cases had arisen for him to work on. He was on the way home at 3:45; by 4 o'clock in the morning he was asleep.

It was 5:40 when his cellular phone, whose number was a jealously guarded secret known only to a few, rang. Half asleep, he put it to his ear, his head still propped on a pillow. His closed eyes flew open in shock. "The boy is missing?" His quiet voice became a shout. "Impossible! What? Another ambulance came 20 minutes early..." The entire spectrum of emotions passed over his features: The tranquility of sleep transformed into shock, wonder, panic, fear.

Tzimer's greatest strength was his unyielding practicality. He did not waste time with reproaches. He instructed the ambulance driver to go to the airport. Then he contacted the police department with the strange story, demanding a traffic helicopter to search for the renegade ambulance. This was the first time he had ever been involved in such an affair, but even with no prior experience his cool logic stood him in good stead.

The police chopper had taken to the air a few minutes earlier when it spotted the two ambulances approaching Ben Gurion from two different directions. The ambulance bearing Paysi came from the east, from the Kefar Truman road, after a series of diversionary twists and turns. All its passengers other than Paysi and the nurse had departed on one of the turns near the new community of Shoham; a GMC Safari picked them up and vanished. From the Petach Tikvah road came the Refuah Sheleimah ambulance with its full complement of medical staffers — except for Paysi.

Near the Border Police checkpoint, at the airport entrance, the two vehicles halted. The driver of the empty ambulance stuck his head out of the window and yelled to his colleague, "The boy is here. Come and transfer him."

The second driver left the ambulance and went to the open window. "Come with me to the police," he yelled, enraged. "You've kidnapped a sick child."

The first driver blew a bubble of bright pink from a wad of gum stuffed in his mouth, watched it pop, and said indifferently, "What are you screaming about? I don't understand what happened here either. First they tell me to take the boy to Tel HaShomer Hospital, then a police helicopter radioes me to take him to the airport and give him to you guys. Nu, take the boy. The flight is about to take off; stop wasting time."

"What's your name?" the other asked.

"Armand Lismee, Petach Tikvah Magen David Adom."

The angry driver continued to grumble but conceded the point. Time was indeed short. Paysi was transferred, semiconscious, to the organization's vehicle. Five minutes before takeoff, British Airways staffers brought the patient and his medical escorts onto the plane.

Zishe Tzimer registered an official complaint with the Petach Tikvah police. The subsequent investigation disclosed that no employee by the name of Armand Lismee had ever worked for Magen David Adom.

If all chevra kadisha workers looked like Kopel Baum, there would be a long line of people knocking on the door for burial, thought Gili as he looked at the office's manager. *"It's fun to die with Kopel,"* would be the slogan of the advertising campaign.

Kopel Baum possessed two uncommon features: his beard and his smile. His beard was a patriarchal one, snowy white and gracefully flowing. The warm smile never left his endearing face. Add a pair of gold-rimmed glasses framing twinkling eyes, put a high forehead and large black yarmulke on top, mix it all with a generous helping of sympathy and human warmth and Kopel Baum was standing before you.

Even before Gili had opened his mouth a hot cup of coffee was on the desk before him. "It's a cold day," the manager said, urging him to drink.

Gili showed his journalist's identification card.

"I thought it was you," Kopel said quietly. "I've heard everything, up to the last detail." He put his fingers on his lips and whispered, "Don't say another word: The walls have ears."

With a light step Kopel Baum went to the next room, and returned staggering under the weight of a heavy cardboard box. "Nowadays, in the computer age?" Gili couldn't help the outburst. "Who in the world uses paper nowadays?"

"Everything is computerized here too," Kopel said, pointing to two computers in a corner of the room. "But I'm a little too old for Internet. My 7-year-old grandson uses a Pentium computer, and destroys spaceships regularly on his multimedia games. The young generation was born digital. He speaks Word, thinks Einstein, draws Macintosh, looks through Windows and breaks the C if the drive gets him angry." He rummaged through the files. "I was looking for it yesterday. It's supposed to be in series 11/89, but the file is missing!"

"We've got to call the rebbe," Gili said. "He told me to let him know if anything was wrong."

"Relax," Kopel grumbled. "What's your hurry? We only hurried once in our history — when we left Egypt — and even then it was because they were throwing us out."

He rifled through the papers, humming merry march tunes the entire time, until Gili was ready to scream. After an hour he pulled out a dusty notebook and placed it into Gili's hand. The two walked out onto the porch, enclosed by a lovely cherry-wood pergola.

Just like Rav Yoske Friedman, the thought flashed through Gili's head. *The GSS has turned us into a bunch of scenery lovers.*

"Do you see?" Kopel had stopped humming, just at the high point of the march. "This is your father's file. Everything fits: Udi Dinar (name at birth: Moshe Dinburg), died November 27, 1989. Cause of death: burned in a Mercedes automobile that went off the road on the Carmel. Signing on the death certificate: Dr. Yitzchak Oren, Carmel Hospital, Haifa. And here's the authorization from the Abu Kabir Forensic Institute: "Based on the bones, teeth, and body parts brought to us, we find they belong to Mr. Udi Dinar (Moshe Dinburg), a 47-year-old Jewish male born in Israel, an officer in the Artillery Corps, army ID #6774529; identification number 20942237. Sincerely, Dr. Yaakov Tur-Malka (Koenigsberg).""

Kopel gave a silent whistle. "Why would Yaakov Tur-Malka have signed?"

"What's wrong with Tur-Malka?"

"He's one of Abu Kabir's junior staffers. Usually someone else signs these documents."

Gili looked at the papers. The last one specified Udi Dinar's final resting place: (Old) Yarkon Cemetery, Block 5, Section 4, Row 16. The last grave near the road.

"And aside from Tur-Malka everything is okay?"

"Nothing is okay," Kopel answered. "The file should have been in series 11/89. Why was it found in series 5/84, in a section dated five and a half years earlier? That arouses my suspicion."

"I'm certain that's not the only time things have been misfiled," Gili said dryly.

"No," Kopel agreed heatedly. "It happened once before — when some underworld figure was assassinated." He stared at the death certificate again. "Dr. Yitzchak Oren signed this. I'd like to clarify something with him, but I can't."

"Why, because he's been 'bought'?"

"No, because he died a year ago."

"One minute." Gili suddenly remembered something. "And where's the file of Manny Schwartz, my father's friend who died with him?"

Kopel sighed heavily. "It disappeared, together with your father's file. Don't make me search for another hour."

"You know what? Right now let's forget Manny Schwartz. I'm interested in my father. So what should we do now? Go to the rebbe?"

Kopel looked at him with his sparkling eyes. "What should we do? The rebbe told me what we should do."

He whispered something into Gili's ear.

At the Harfield Transplant Center in London the pre-op preparations were almost done. Paysi lay on the operating table, his eyes shut. He'd been anesthetized some minutes earlier.

A few years earlier, a heart-lung transplant had been considered hopeless. The famous surgeon Professor Magdi Yakub was one of the men who had changed the face of medicine. He believed in a new method and contributed his own incredible talents to the research, and more than 100 CF sufferers who had reached the terminal stages had now been saved by the organs transplanted by Dr. Yakub. In the past, patients had waited for two years in London until they'd gotten the transplant; today, the process had been shortened considerably.

Ten hours after he'd reached the hospital, Paysi was wheeled into the operating room. The battery of pre-operative tests that usually took weeks had been accelerated for him. There was no choice; the donor in Brohampton, a few miles from the hospital, was failing rapidly.

In the operating theater in Brohampton, Dr. Yakub waited for word from Harfield that Paysi was ready for surgery.

Two parallel cuts were made in the chest. The upper spotlight directed five yellow-white beams on Paysi's emaciated body. The surgeon in Harfield straightened the band on his forehead that held a small, powerful light, and adjusted his telescopic lenses. He wielded his scalpel dexterously. A special white-hot needle followed the scalpel's path, sealing the cut and preventing blood loss. A small rumbling electrical drill exposed the chest cavity. The staff stared at the small pear-shaped object beating tranquilly, expanding and contracting in a single movement. The heart looked healthy.

The lungs were another story entirely: two spongy sacs whose surrounding membrane had completely lost its original pinkish-gray color, and were a sickly shade of greenish yellow. "Prepare the machine," the surgeon announced.

On the left of the operating table a nurse turned on the heart-lung machine, the instrument that would take over the functions of Paysi's organs for a short time. The surgeon cut the right artery leading into the lung, pulled the organ out of the chest cavity, and showed it to the medical staffers. "A critical case of terminal gangrene, with advanced perforations of the wall," he explained in a calm voice from beneath his surgical mask, sounding like one discussing the weather. "We've waited for the last minute; the lobes are almost completely disintegrated. Another week and the boy would have been dead."

Dr. Dan Paldot, an Israeli doctor interning under Dr. Yakub, separated the healthy heart from the sickly lungs. The heart was placed in cold storage.

When such transplants had begun, the lungs of the CF victims had routinely been sent to labs for research. But when medical advances made such research unnecessary, the hospitals began to throw them out. Paysi's lungs, however, were carefully placed in a metal container, between chips of dry ice, at the special request of Zishe Tzimer. Later, these lungs would be shipped to Israel for burial, in accord with the dictates of *halachah.*

Dr. Yakub received the call in the operating room in Brohampton just minutes after he had prepared the now-deceased donor. Immediately after the news came, Yakub began to remove the donor's organs. The heart and lungs were placed in a portable refrigerator about the size of a knapsack and rushed to a waiting helicopter. Ten minutes later Dr. Yakub and the refrigerator had arrived in Harfield, just as the staff there had completed Paysi's preparations. Dr. Yakub quickly donned his surgical garb, washed his hands and pulled on his sterile gloves. Carefully he approached the operating table. Now his work was really beginning.

The transplant began at three in the morning, and ended successfully several hours later. The heart and the lungs had begun to function. Paysi, attached to a respirator, was transferred to the Intensive Care Unit. Two people awaited him there. His oldest sister, Chedvi Pick, had arrived at Harfield during the course of the operation. For a full hour she had had nothing to do but pray from the depths of her heart for Heaven's mercy.

She was rather startled at the hospital's policy. If they felt it necessary for Paysi to have a 24-hour male nurse at his bedside, why had they chosen this man, whose face was harsher than any she had ever seen in her life?

On Moshe Dinburg — Udi Dinar's — wedding day, the groom had gone to the grave of his father, Rav Shmuel Dinburg, in Jerusalem's Har HaMenuchos cemetery.

He felt very strange. His mother, Devorah Dinburg, had told him that it was customary to invite deceased parents to one's *chupah*.

At first he'd refused. "But I don't bel—"

Devorah cut him off. "You do believe. My Moshe was and remains a believing Jew. Your horrible friend, Manny Schwartz, has brainwashed you and transformed you to Udi Dinar. I will never forgive him for leading you from the right path. Now go and ask your father to come from Heaven."

And he had gone.

He fasted, davened *Minchah* of Yom Kippur with *Vidui*, though no one was watching. And in the heat of the day he had gone with his mother to Har HaMenuchos, stood on the grave of his father, and cried in a way that he never had before.

"My dear father," he sobbed, his hot tears moistening the cold marble slab, "forgive me, I know that I shortened your life. Forgive me, I don't deserve to be dirt under your feet, but forgive me and come tonight to my wedding. Abba, bless me."

Gili had learned about this visit from his father's diary. He remembered the poignant story as he traveled with Kopel Baum to the Old Yarkon Cemetery.

Just as Udi had begged forgiveness from his father, Gili had endlessly apologized to his dead father. But Gili was speaking of something totally different. "Forgive me, Abba, for opening your grave, but the action is justified."

The rebbe of Kiltz had given them permission to exhume the body, after confidential consultation with one of the great *poskim* of the generation. The question to be answered was not merely whether or not Udi had been murdered, and how his murderer could be brought to justice. The more important question was one of life and death: Who was next in line?

Kopel had come equipped with the latest in excavation machinery. He, too, was pale and anxious. It was one thing to place a body wrapped in white shrouds into its grave; taking the dead out of the earth six years after burial, at two in the morning, in the blackness of night, was quite another.

The cemetery was deserted and completely silent. "The silence of the grave," Gili said.

"Ssssh, don't talk. Listen!" Kopel hissed.

Gili paled. "What do you hear?"

"Your hair growing," Kopel laughed. "No, Gili, don't be angry with me for the black humor. You must understand: I and all my friends in the *chevra kadisha* also were once afraid of the dead and of death, just as you are. But over the years you build up defenses. Macabre humor, for example."

They had located the gravesite. Their skin prickled as they began to dig.

After two hours they had burrowed deep beneath the earth. "That's it, we've reached it," Kopel said. "Hold the lantern, I'll crawl right into the grave."

"Maybe I should?" Gili said, and immediately regretted his words.

Kopel smiled apologetically and didn't say a word. His gold-rimmed glasses glinted in the yellow lantern light. He bent down and crawled into the grave. Gili tried to target the light into the round hole. The noises that he heard from beneath were the most horrifying of his entire life. Even so, he found the courage to occasionally whisper, "Kopel, are you all right?"

"Don't worry," came the whisper back out of the grave. "A little more and this nightmare will be behind us."

Gili could feel his hair turning white; a man would not wish such a gruesome adventure on his worst enemy. After 20 minutes that lasted an eternity Kopel climbed out of the grave. "If only I could get out like this after I'm dead," he joked. In his hands he held a closed black bag.

"What did you find?" Gili asked impatiently.

Kopel pointed to the sealed bag. "I found a good portion of a skeleton. It seems that your father was neither shot nor burned, but let's take it slow. Tomorrow I'll take the bones to the private lab of a criminal investigator in Tel Aviv. The Abu Kabir people are the most professional, but I don't trust them anymore: The documents in your father's case were certainly forged."

Kopel placed the bag into a small wooden box, his lips whispering a prayer asking for forgiveness. They filled the hole and carefully concealed all signs of digging. When they left the place one couldn't see that the grave had been opened, its contents removed.

❦

Gili stayed out of work for two days, pleading a flu. He was tense and nervous and jumped every time the phone rang. With her own extraordinary motherly instinct, Monica pretended not to notice.

Three days later Kopel finally called, using a public phone as they had planned. "Gili, I'm taking a cab to your house right now. The results are staggering."

"So tell me!" Gili shouted.

"It's not for the phone." Kopel slammed down the receiver.

Ten tense minutes later Kopel arrived, breathless, his habitual smile gone. He sat in the living room and poured himself a shot of Chivas Regal, dashed it down in one gulp, and threw his bombshell into the air: "Gili, I'm sorry to tell you this, but those are not your father's bones."

The room was silent. A thousand thoughts exploded in Gili's head all at once; he could not verbalize even one of them. With a supreme effort of will he managed to blurt out a few sentences: "If it's not my father, who is it? Manny Schwartz? Maybe they mixed them up. They were burned up together."

Kopel poured a second cup, looked worriedly at Gili's ashen face, and urged him to take a stiff drink. He pulled a large sheet of paper out of a leather case. "Just read this. We'll talk later."

Gili coughed and put down the empty cup. He could hardly hold the paper: His hands shook like an old man's. Kopel set it down on the table and Gili read it eagerly.

> "Shulman and Kuzmah, Criminal Investigations.
>
> RE: Examination of a man's skeleton
>
> We hereby declare that on the 10th day of January 1996, the head of the Tel Aviv chevra kadisha, Mr. Kopel Baum, brought to us human bones for testing.

The results of laboratory testing: No bullet holes were found, and no signs of scorching or soot. There was no evidence of beating.

After a comparison of the dental records of Udi Dinar with those of the skeleton we received, we can say with full certainty that the bones do not belong to Udi Dinar."

"So whose are they?" Gili lifted his despairing glance from the report.

"Keep reading," Kopel commanded. "Don't waste time with talk."

Gili returned to the paper.

"In the course of our investigations we determined that the skeleton belonged to someone much older than 47 years. In addition, the rate of the bones' decay, the fact that the teeth had never had any dental work performed whatsoever, and a serial number inscribed on one of the bones aroused our suspicion that the bones and skull dated from ancient times. We sent a small shard of bone to a lab in Tel Aviv University for carbon-dating. They have determined that the skeleton is approximately 1900 years old.

"In light of these findings we sent the bones to the Antiquities Authority, which identified them after comparing the serial number on the bone to their records, as bones that had been a portion of a skeleton that was in their possession, which had been stolen six years ago from their storehouse. Its original source was an archaeological dig that took place thirty years earlier, in burial caves dating back from the time of the Second Temple, located in Beit Shearim in the lower Galilee. The Antiquities Authority is holding the bones in its possession until the conclusion of the investigation.

Sincerely, Aryeh Kuzmah."

Gili couldn't say a word for almost half an hour. Kopel poured cup after cup for the two of them. Finally, Gili recovered. "I've got to see the rebbe of Kiltz. Urgently."

"I've already spoken with him," Kopel gave him an understanding smile. "He said two things."

"Which are?"

"First, if the Antiquities Authority will not return these twice-stolen bones, we'll start ringing bells and make such a scandal that the entire world will talk of it. What audacity! These may be the bones of one of the sages of the Mishnah or Gemara, from the days of Rabban Shimon ben Gamliel and his disciple, Rabbi Chanina bar Chama.

"Second, the rebbe feels you must fly to London. Immediately."

This took Gili by surprise. "London? Oh, to visit Paysi. I get it. I told the rebbe about Paysi and his transplant. But why is it so important?"

"The rebbe is certain that the boy has information that you need to have."

39

That morning would remain imprinted in Chedvi's memory for a long, long time.

"Mrs. Pick?" Zishe Tzimer had spoken to her on the phone. "I want to tell you that your younger brother Paysi flew to London an hour ago for a transplant."

Chedvi, shocked, remained silent. Paysi's serious condition had disturbed her terribly. She had turned to their Health Fund and had become ensnared in their endless, hated bureaucracy. "Three months, minimum," they had told her. She could not even have imagined this lightning-swift, one-day operation which began in Zishe Tzimer's *beis midrash.* Zishe had waved his magic wand on Chedvi, too, and 10 hours later she was boarding a plane.

When she reached bustling Heathrow Airport, confused and intimidated, she heard her name being announced on a public address system. "Mrs. Pick, Mrs. Pick of Israel," the smooth voice of the young clerk echoed throughout the terminal, "please come to the El Al counter; someone is waiting for you there."

Dazed, she walked over to the counter. A well-dressed, pleasant-faced old woman met her. "Are you Chedvi Pick?" she asked in Yiddish laced with a strong English accent, warmly shaking her hand. "I'm Rebbetzin Birnbaum. Zishe Tzimer has already spoken with me. You can stay with me in Golders Green for as long as you need."

But Chedvi actually stayed in the wonderful rebbetzin's home just to sleep. Every night the rebbetzin would pick her up in her car from the hospital and bring her home. From morning until evening's darkness had long settled on the city, Chedvi was glued to Paysi's room.

The first time she tried to enter the Intensive Care Unit a brutish, relentless guard barred her way. After she had implored and beseeched, endlessly and fruitlessly, she remembered that Zishe Tzimer had given her his confidential cell phone number and invited her to use it if she faced any difficulties. She made use of the opportunity, and Zishe, after a hurried call to Dr. Yakub, procured a special entry pass for her. This was her second encounter with the man's meteoric speed.

Paysi battled for his life. For three days after the operation his body tried to reject the foreign organs. He was given megadoses of Cyclosporen and Azatiophren, antirejection drugs necessary to keep him from joining the long list of patients who had died after transplants. He had still another problem: The Cyclosporen was a fatty substance which Paysi could not digest, and so he had to receive a large dose of enzymes that replicated those of the pancreas, in order for him to withstand the medication.

Paysi's bed was surrounded by more instruments than almost any other in the hospital. One could almost watch the miracles of technology grab hold of Paysi's soul and maintain it in his ailing body. Monitors reported in multicolored lines on his pulse, breathing, blood pressure, blood oxygen level. For the first three days he was unable to breathe on his own, and a respirator performed that task for him. His life hung on a thread, and there were moments when it seemed that the tortured body was going to give up in defeat. But it did not. Paysi possessed an iron will to live and battled with all his strength, even in moments of semiconsciousness. Top doctors gathered around him and worked ceaselessly on him. On the fourth day there was a change for the better; Paysi was slowly weaned from the respirator and began to breathe on his own.

Chedvi sat in the small anteroom near the room in the Intensive Care Unit where Paysi lay. She was permitted to enter his room only in the sterilized green garments of the operating room: soft cloth slippers, closed jacket, haircovering, a large mask over her mouth. Everything was disposable and was thrown into the garbage immediately after use.

With her heart pounding she listened to the beeping of the intimidating instruments. Every warning alarm left her breathless and panicky; she was drowning in a sea of fears and doubts. But she never regretted her presence in the hospital. When Zishe had asked her if she wanted to go she had not hesitated for a minute, leaving her husband and son at home in order to be at her only brother's bedside during these critical hours.

Chedvi had little faith in high-tech medical instruments. She had heard enough stories of how highly vaunted medical technology would malfunction, its boast of breakthroughs turning into whispers of failure. She believed, with a deep faith, that Paysi would live only if he received permission from Above. She rejoiced in the opportunity to stay at his bedside, to pray with all her soul as she bore witness to his grave condition. She repeated the entire *Sefer Tehillim* time and again, stopping occasionally when her jaw began to ache and sneaking into the room to see if there were any favorable signs. During those first few days she felt a deep depression. She found a quiet corner and sat in solitude, praying with a broken heart for her little brother: "*Ribono shel Olam,* You've tested the Brent family with seven ordeals. You took our mother, Shulamit, from us, and we accepted Your decree. You took our father's sanity and we made our peace with that. You took our stepmother, Dina, who was like our very own mother; we accepted that with bowed heads. Paysi had two trials, deafness and muteness, and yet he doesn't bear one iota of bitterness. You tested him again by afflicting him with a terrible genetic disease. The boy grew great, even with his illness! You sent Paysi out from his home; he made peace with that. Father in Heaven, don't give us an eighth trial. Enough, we haven't any strength left! Our grandfather, Avraham, underwent 10 tests for us. Enough, enough, please!"

She put her entire soul into those last words. When she had completed her prayer she felt a deep sense of tranquility, as if she knew that it had been accepted. She wiped her face with a handkerchief and sat, drained. And then her glance fell upon the male nurse.

A poker-faced man sat constantly in the room. Every six hours the shift would change, but always there would be a poker face; the nurses looked like clones. *Where do they find men with such faces?* Chedvi wondered, suspicious. They made her terribly uncomfortable. A few times she would ask the male nurse on duty, in passable English, if every surgical patient in the hospital had round-the-clock private nursing care, and what, exactly, was his function.

"And what are you doing here?" the nurse asked her, turning to enter the room to check a monitor.

"I'm his sister!" she said, her head bent.

"Relatives are allowed to visit only once a day. If you don't want to go back to the official rules, don't bother me." The threat was not subtle; she stopped asking questions.

The behavior of these male nurses was strange. They did not seem to know how to handle a sick person, they would stand impatiently near the monitor and when one of the intravenous lines would sound, indicating that the bottle of medication needed changing, they would call one of the regular nursing staff.

What in Heaven's name are they doing here? Chedvi asked herself for perhaps the 100th time. Her discomfort turned into sharp suspicions; she eyed them in open dislike.

❦

Gili decided to go underground. The game was up, the rules were gone: Someone was getting very, very serious. He could feel a vise tightening around his neck.

He took the first step: He left the country with a passport which bore the name Yehoshua Zucker. Moshe Vayden had procured it for him. "The GSS is on to me. I've got to get a new identity and leave the area," he had explained to the well-connected antiquities dealer. "I'll go to London for a day or two, and I'll keep this new identity even when I get back. I'm living on borrowed time; the sand in the hourglass is almost gone. Another day, two days —"

"They wouldn't dare harm you in the airport," Vayden said.

"You don't know them," Gili gave a forced laugh. "And if the GSS knows I've left the country, they'll go after Paysi. They'll kill him within five minutes. They won't have to work too hard, either: just turn off the oxygen for one minute."

Moshe Vayden did not like what he was hearing. "You're exaggerating."

"Oh yes?" Gili looked at him out of the corners of his eyes and told him of the strange abduction of Paysi on his way to the airport. Vayden remained unconvinced. "And maybe there really was a misunderstanding there? People tend to exaggerate the power of the GSS. You've made them into demons, monsters."

"That's right," Gili agreed. "Benny Gabison thought just as you did."

Vayden grew silent. And Gili Dinar became Yehoshua Zucker.

⚜️

"Were you ever in London?" Vayden asked Gili, on their way to the airport.

"No." Gili yawned; everything had happened so fast, he had had no time to catch up on lost sleep.

"It's a gigantic and fascinating city," Vayden said. "More than 10 million people live in its 800 square miles. It's got enough attractions to keep a tourist busy for a year: Buckingham Palace and the Changing of the Guard; the Parliament; Hyde Park; the Thames River; Big Ben; Greenwich Park in southeast London; Marks and Spencer —"

"I'm not going for fun," Gili interrupted.

"Okay. The main thing is, when you get off the plane, keep looking to the right."

"Huh? What are you talking about?"

Vayden explained patiently. "The British drive on the left side of the road. Here in Israel, we automatically look to the left when we get off the sidewalk. But in England you've got to look right; otherwise, there's a good chance you'll wind up under a car's wheels."

"Why?"

Vayden laughed. "Are you tired or has your brain rusted? When a car drives on the left side of the road, from which side does it approach the pedestrian crossing the street? Left or right?"

"Right."

"Very good," Vayden grinned. "And so don't forget, in London you look to the right, even though here in Israel you're known as a good left-winger."

Gili was tempted to punch Vayden in the arm, but to the antiquities dealer's good fortune, a large truck tried to pass them, and Gili needed both hands on the steering wheel.

🕸✥🕸

Unlike Israel, bathed in its bright winter sunshine, London was buried in clouds and fog. The plane floated towards the city through millions of grayish droplets and disgorged Gili, still sleepy, into the raucous corridors of Heathrow, one of the world's largest and busiest airports.

An official of Her Majesty's Interior Ministry checked Gili's passport. "How long have you come for?"

"A day or two."

"And how many days will you be staying?"

"I've already told you," Gili answered patiently. "A day or two."

"Do you have means to live here?" the clerk continued his litany of questions.

Gili's patience ebbed. With a sharp gesture he pulled his black wallet from his pocket and showed the apathetic bureaucrat his money, more than 2000 pounds sterling. The clerk nodded and stamped the passport.

Gili hesitated, trying to choose between a cab and London's famed Underground. Exigencies of time urged the former; he was soon sitting in a black cab watching the scenery race by. The store windows of Marks and Spencer and of Harrod's displaying mannequins dressed in winter coats reminded him of how cold he was; when he had left Israel, he was wearing nothing more than a summer jacket.

"You're Jewish?" the driver asked.

"Yes."

"I saw right away. You know, in England there are the English, the Irish, the Scottish, the Welsh, but only the Jews call themselves British." He burst out laughing. "But I'm Hispanic, myself," he said with satisfaction.

Gili continued to silently watch the passing scenery. The red, double-decker buses looked at first glance like elephants stampeding through the jungle of London traffic; on second look, though, they became trained elephants stepping carefully and lightly. The gray, sooty houses of London gave off an air of quiet stability. He suddenly felt that everything would work out right. In this optimistic spirit he finally reached Harfield Hospital, in the Hexbridge neighborhood of Middlesex, in western London. Only then did he realize that his cheerful Hispanic driver had taken him needlessly through the center of the city.

When he entered the hospital he had no idea where to go. He approached the Information Desk and inquired about an Israeli boy who had undergone a transplant.

The stony-faced young man unbent immediately. He was patient and polite. *Like all the English,* Gili thought.

"The Israeli boy?" the young man smiled. "His condition has improved. He's on the fifth floor, left wing, Respiratory Intensive Care, Room 506. Are you a relative?"

"A friend."

The young man shook his head. "You haven't got a hope of getting in."

"I need special permission?"

"That's the start."

"What else?"

The clerk did not answer.

Gili pulled out a 50-pound note from his wallet and crumpled them between his fingers.

The clerk's eyes brightened. Gili came a little closer, and the young man bent forward, his fingers balled up into fists. Gili leaned over; the money fell onto the counter.

The information clerk looked around him. None of his colleagues were paying attention to the crisp bill that was falling into his fingers and disappearing.

He melted completely and signaled to Gili to approach. The clerk hastily wrote on a paper and handed the memo to Gili.

Gili read the lines. Though he knew what was coming, he felt his heart thudding. "He's got 24-hour security. My friends tell me it's Israel's General Security Service."

Paysi was being guarded like the Kohinoor diamond. The GSS had put its people full time around the CF sufferer who had just had a transplant.

The hospital clerk still felt beholden to his benefactor, and he scribbled still another note. "The boy's sister is also with him."

A light in the black tunnel. "Thanks," Gili said, disappearing. He went up to the fifth floor and stood before the locked doors. A small sign told him that visiting hours were from 11:30 to 1:00 p.m.

That meant the door would be opened to visitors in another 20 minutes. He walked over to the public phone in the large hallway and called the hospital switchboard. "Hello, this is Harfield Hospital," a polite recorded voice announced. "Please hold and your call will be answered as soon as possible, Thank you."

After five minutes, an operator came on and transferred him to the unit. "Yes?" a nurse asked.

"I'm from Israel. Can you call the sister of Paysi Brent of Israel, Room 506?"

What luck that most of the world still takes international calls seriously... Chedvi was at the phone in two minutes. "Who's this?" she asked, obviously hoping it was her husband.

"A friend of Paysi," Gili said in a hushed voice. "Is someone listening to you?"

Chedvi's suspicions were immediately aroused. Her welcoming tone grew frosty. "Who's this, Choni?"

"No, it's me, Gili Dinar."

"Oh." The warmth returned to her voice. "Zishe Tzimer told me about you. You saved Paysi's life."

She's clever, Gili thought admiringly, *she's careful not to say my name.* He gave her a brief summary of what was happening. "You know that those creeps they've put near Paysi are GSS agents. They're here for one purpose only: to keep me from meeting Paysi. No doubt you can find a picture of me in their wallets."

"What do you want?" she asked.

"I've got to see Paysi for two minutes."

"I understand," Chedvi answered. "I've got an idea."

"Which is—"

"Paysi is getting strong doses of antirejection drugs and they affect his entire immune system. He's in a sterile room and people can only go into him in fully sterilized clothing. No one could identify you behind the mask."

Gili thought for a moment. Then he told her what to do.

Five minutes later the unit was opened to visitors. Gili joined a large group and hid among them. He slowly snuck towards Paysi's anteroom. The male "nurse" on duty dozed lightly there. Chedvi quickly picked up a bundle of sterile clothing wrapped in brown paper, put it near the door, and stealthily walked away. Gili grabbed the package and went into the bathroom.

He walked out completely covered; only his eyes could be seen from above the face mask. He walked into the anteroom.

"Who are you?" the young man woke up and jumped out of his chair.

Gili gave him a frigid glance. His voice was angry. "Sir, we have received dozens of complaints about you. You and your friends are disturbing the medical staff. Another word and you're all out of here! There is a limit, sir!"

The "nurse" flinched; only the top medical staff could speak with such antipathy and bluntness.

Gili entered Paysi's room without further protest.

He stared at the instruments with a confident gaze. The pulse-oxymeter showed satisfactory levels of oxygen in the blood. The new heart was pumping nicely, the heartbeat was regular. The intravenous was dripping at 25 drops per minute. He approached the bed and looked at Paysi's face. The boy's eyes were closed; he looked as though he were sleeping.

But the "nurse's" eyes were open wide. He followed Gili's every move from behind a glass window. Gili could feel his gaze piercing his back. Time was of the essence. He fiddled with several of the knobs, pulled out a thin needle from the patient's personal medicine cabinet in the room, and filled it with a drop of insulin. He had no idea what he was going to do next.

Paysi gave a quiet groan. His eyes remained shut.

Gili pulled the blanket off Paysi's arm and touched the bandage holding the intravenous tube in place. Paysi's eyes flew open.

"Paysi, it's me, Gili," he told him in sign language, hoping that the observant eyes watching him from the anteroom would not notice.

Paysi's eyes widened; a weak smile brightened his sunken face. The mask covered almost the entire face, but those green eyes were Gili's, without a doubt.

"Gili, it's you! I don't believe it. You've come to me from Israel?" His lips moved soundlessly.

He looked so small next to the daunting instruments surrounding him; Gili felt his throat tighten. Suddenly he was part of a life-and-death drama. He could hear the labored, spasmodic breathing, almost see the pain. Paysi's life hung on a gossamer thread. *Ribono shel Olam, make a miracle, let this young tzaddik live,* he prayed to himself.

Paysi motioned to him to approach; his eyes, too, were filled with tears. His thin hand grasped Gili's, like a child afraid to lose his mother. "You know, it says in *Tehillim,* every *neshamah,* soul, should praise G-d. With every *neshimah,* every breath, we must praise the Creator. No one understands this like a person with cystic fibrosis. I feel, with each breath, how *Hakadosh Baruch Hu* is giving me breath, blowing up my lungs one more time, giving me new life, and I thank Him, thank my Creator. And thank you, Gili: I know that if I stay alive, it's because of you."

Gili sobbed soundlessly. He felt like a dwarf next to a giant; he melted before Paysi's greatness of spirit. Paysi's body was weak but not his spirit: It was a great spirit that dwelled in this tortured form.

Paysi's lips moved once again. "Is there someone watching?"

"Yes."

Paysi nodded. "I had hoped he'd gone. No time to waste. Goldman."

"What?"

Paysi repeated, again and again. "Goldman. Goldman. Goldman. Go to Goldman."

The "nurse" outside suddenly approached the window. Gili busied himself with the intravenous tubes. Had Paysi received his insulin shot, or not? If he had gotten his daily dose, another infusion could be fatal.

Gili quickly thought for a moment, then efficiently began the "push" of insulin. The male nurse saw the doctor adding medication to the intravenous tube, as so many others had done. What he did not see was the liquid pouring harmlessly out of the needle, onto the exterior of the tube.

Gili signed quickly, "I don't understand a thing."

"Look in Kiryat Bialik. Goldman."

Gili placed the empty insulin bottle into the trash can. The "nurse" was already in the room. "Is the intravenous okay?" he asked suspiciously.

"Stupid!" Gili shouted. "Of course it's okay! Now stop disturbing the medical staff here. I'm already planning to put in a complaint — and my colleague, Dr. Yakub, won't like it one bit!"

He hurried out of the room and went straight to the nurses' station. "I'm the new doctor, McGregor," he mumbled to the nurse as she spoke on the phone. "I have to sign here." With confident hands he picked up a file that had been left on the counter. He scribbled something in Mr. Barney Lancersham's file, put it down on the counter, and walked away.

It was enough. The suspicious "nurse" was certain that this unknown, top doctor was going to cause him problems. He quickly walked back to the anteroom.

Gili stood up and calmly walked out of the unit, trying not to be conspicuous. The nurse at the station finished her call and opened the file. "The patient's condition is unchanged. 12:20 p.m. Dr. ——." She screwed her eyes up, trying to make out the signature, but it was unreadable. Strange, because Dr. William Cahan had checked the patient just a few minutes earlier.

She yawned. Either the patient's family had called in a private specialist, or another difficult doctor had joined the team.

He peeled the stifling surgical garb off in the bathroom, went down the elevator, and quickly left the impressive building of Harfield Hospital for the brisk London air. Chedvi surprised him as he walked out. She had waited for him around the corner, and breathed a sigh of relief when she saw him. "How did you manage with our lovely nurse?"

"That's one stupid spy," Gili answered hurriedly. "I outsmarted him, no problem."

White fog came out of their mouths in the frigid air, cloaking their words as they stood on the frozen street corner. Chedvi looked thoughtful. Finally, she said, "Paysi whispered something to me many times yesterday. Goldman."

Gili stood, rigid. "Paysi said that?"

"About 30 times."

"Just 'Goldman'?" Gili felt disappointed and a bit foolish: *All my efforts were a waste; I could have simply asked Chedvi.*

"No. He also said something very strange. 'The Rabbi Puppet.' No, it was 'The Puppeteer Rabbi.' Then he said, 'Tell Gili Dinar, Mickey Gadish.'"

"Mickey Gadish? The name means nothing to me."

"Nor to me." Chedvi gave a confused laugh. "But that's what Paysi said."

"Thanks for all your help," Gili told her politely. But Chedvi wouldn't let him go before she gave him a package of cookies and fruit that she had gotten from Rebbetzin Birnbaum.

"Bless you, Gili Dinar," she said emotionally. "I don't know you, but you're not like the others at Rabbi Avram's house. Paysi told me that you're a good man."

"Tell Paysi I never know what to do about compliments, and guard him well," Gili blurted out, as he fled. He hailed a passing cab and took it to the airport.

Chedvi went up to the fifth floor, her head full of matchmaker's thoughts. Gili Dinar was a nice boy, a very nice boy. Maybe Simi, her youngest sister...

She returned to the room. The "nurse" there was nervous; his apprehension was apparent. He and his colleagues had been chosen for one purpose only: to prevent Paysi from meeting with Gili Dinar. A bad taste in his mouth told him that Gili had managed to trick them. He could not prove it, but his sour stomach hinted at complete failure.

"Why did you leave the room when the doctor was here?" he demanded of Chedvi in a stern voice.

The blood left her face and her lips quivered. "Who says I have to be here every second?"

I was right, the man thought in vengeful satisfaction. *Her confusion is very suspicious.*

He paced up and down several times and then left the unit. He raced to the porch and pulled out his cellular phone.

The "nurse" pressed the buttons. He would contact his replacement, report to him on the failure of the mission, and send him running to Heathrow to head Gili off before he could get away.

Before the last digit his finger wavered. He turned off the phone and placed it in his jacket pocket.

One mistake was enough. If Gili had managed to get into the hospital wearing one disguise, he would leave Heathrow in another. Why announce his failure? If he did not say a word, no one would ever know.

40

As the plane made its way over the Mediterranean, Gili thought of the marvelous Dr. Yakub, and of the extra years Paysi would live due to his efforts.

He recalled an interview with a world-class Israeli transplant surgeon. The man had been remarkably modest, minimizing his own contributions to his patients' recovery. "No, I don't feel like a creator. I feel like the messenger of a Creator," he had astonished the readers with his personal confession. In the course of the interview he had remarked that transplanting organs was, in his opinion, a way of paying an outstanding debt. The nonreligious doctor had developed an unusual theory: "It could be that the donor and the recipient were reincarnations from previous lives," he had said. "In that life, perhaps one was a murderer and one his victim, killed through a knife in the heart or the liver. Now the murderer returns his victim's life through giving one of his own organs. A strangler gives up his lungs, one who hurt someone in the eye donates a cornea, and so on. There are no coincidences in this world: everything is guided by a wonderful Divine reckoning!"

And what's my reckoning? Gili thought, his head leaning on the small pillow, as he gazed tiredly at the scenery below him. The plane was coming down, crossing the seashore. Miniature streetlights cast their illumination on tiny highways far below. Tel Aviv grew larger with every second; the Dan region was a thick network of multicolored lights. *I went to London and brought back exactly six words: Goldman, Mickey Gadish, The Puppeteer Rabbi.* Completely inexplicable.

No! Actually, there were eight words he had brought home. *Kiryat Bialik.*

Gili had been busy since the start of this affair with unraveling secret codes. He knew that now, too, only the help of Heaven would help him decode this new mystery: The Puppeteer Rabbi, Goldman, Kiryat Bialik, Mickey Gadish.

⟨♥⟩

He landed at 1 a.m., hailed a cab and drove home. He hadn't left his Honda Civic in the airport; Moshe Vayden had driven it to the Dinars' garage, to confuse the enemy. Half an hour after his arrival he was home. Monica was fast asleep. He tiptoed into his room, opened a drawer, and pulled out his father's diary. He had a new, incredible train of thought, and here he searched for evidence of it.

Heaven's help came faster than he expected. He held his breath as he read a description of an episode that had taken place in Yeshivas Ein Yisrael in Shevat 5723.

"Unbelievable," he murmured, thunderstruck.

What had the surgeon said? There are no coincidences in the world! How had he missed such a clear sign? Providence had led that person to make the same mistake twice — at least — only so that Gili could find the truth today.

A light went on in his head. He laughed and cried all at once as suddenly he understood the entire chain of events, from the very beginning. Everything was clear, clear and simple. The Puppeteer Rabbi; the code was broken.

Gili went into the kitchen, warmed a cup of milk for himself in the microwave and gulped it down. He rummaged through a drawer, looking for the tape recording of his first meeting with the rebbe of Kiltz, when Gili had burst into tears. He found the relevant passage, and placed the tape, together with a small tape recorder, into his briefcase. Then he silently left the house.

He drove to Kiryat Bialik, searching for Goldman, eager to speak with Mickey Gadish.

The founding fathers of Kiryat Bialik apparently were nature lovers, with a particular fondness for trees and flowers. There was no other explanation for the street names that Gili passed at three in the morning, as he drove his Honda Civic through the deserted town. Rechov Cypress; Sycamore; Almond; Date; Oak; Cedar; Pine; Fig; Palm; Narcissus; Lily; Laurel; Rose...

The Honda drove slowly, its lights extinguished, between darkened streets. It crossed boulevards and lurched from streets to cul-de-sacs. Gili stared at the street signs until his eyes ached. They were history buffs, too: Rechov Menashe, Reuven, Binyamin, Rachel, Tribes of Israel Street... Only Rechov Goldman didn't exist; nor any other link to the name.

When the names began to repeat themselves, he realized he was traveling in circles. *Enough,* thought Gili in despair, shutting off the motor. *This is the beginning of the end. Like a plane: When you start spinning, you're about to crash.*

He had searched for an unusual building, a public facility, but had not seen a trace of the specific destination he had sought. Something was very wrong with his calculations.

On the edge of admitting defeat he once again started the engine. *One last search before I give up,* he told himself, setting off once again. He crossed Tribes of Israel and pulled into Chestnut.

The Honda stopped.

The building didn't look like an institution, certainly not like a psychiatric hospital. But the screams coming from within were sharp and clear in the night's quiet.

It was a standard apartment building of three stories. Its windows, for the most part, were dark. A large rose garden surrounded it. Over the doorway hung a small, illuminated sign: "The Sol Goldman Psychiatric Center."

The door was locked, of course. He looked at the bell and intercom, hesitated, then knocked lightly.

Once, twice, three times. There was no sound. Gili decided to leave. *I'll sleep in the Honda.*

Suddenly slippers shuffled near the door. The light was turned on in the lobby; someone peered at him through a peephole. Gili smiled and gave a cheery wave.

The key turned twice in the lock; the door opened. Rav Yoske Friedman came out, his eyes heavy with sleep, his hair tousled and beard unkempt. "Gili, what's happened?" he whispered in surprise. "What brings you here at 4 o'clock in the morning?"

"I need your help," Gili answered. He, too, whispered. "A personal computer and printer, and a place to sleep."

"Gladly. I just bought an excellent laser printer," Rav Yoske said. "But don't keep me in suspense. What have you discovered?"

In the lobby Gili told him of London and Paysi, of the strange error he had found in his father's diary, of his new idea and his discovery of the Goldman Psychiatric Center. "I've got to be institutionalized there and study it from the inside."

Rav Yoske rolled bloodshot eyes. "Come inside and get some sleep. We'll talk about it in the morning."

༺❧❦༻

After *Shacharis* and a quick breakfast of cold cereal, Gili sat and typed with astonishing speed. He was pouring out a veritable flood of information; his flashing fingers could barely keep up with the mighty stream of data coming out of his brain. When the input was completed he printed out five copies and placed them in five separate envelopes. With the name Yehoshua Zucker as the sender, he mailed them out to five different addresses: to his mother, Monica, directly to her office in the Foreign Ministry; to the rebbe of Kiltz; to Ami Kedmi, editor of *HaYom HaZeh*; to Moshe Vayden, antiquities dealer; and to Effie Green of Haifa.

Rav Yoske returned home from the yeshivah at noon. "The matter is settled," he said with satisfaction. "Since the story with Paysi I've had Zishe Tzimer's personal cell phone number. I spoke to him from a public phone. He'll take care of all the documentation. The district psychiatrist for Tel Aviv, Professor Stockman, will give you the referral for hospitalization, under the name Yehoshua Zucker."

Two guests arrived at 3 p.m. Rabbi Schmidt came in from Jerusalem, stopping in Bnei Brak to pick up Pinny Klein, Zishe Tzimer's personal aide, who carried the necessary papers. Rabbi Schmidt and Rav Yoske shook hands warmly; Gili remembered that the two had shared the benches at Ein Yisrael so many years before.

Rav Yoske's water bill reached dizzying heights that day. They spoke only in the kitchen, with the water pouring from the faucets in the background. Rav Yoske had, in past weeks, uncovered two hidden listening devices in his apartment, one in the bedroom, one in his guest room. He had not touched them, but his suspicions had proved well founded. Now he was careful with every word he uttered. Even with the faucets in both sinks going full blast, they spoke with lowered voices.

"You understand, Gili," Rav Yoske explained, "that Pinny has come to bring you to Goldman. I and Rav Schmidt are as known as you are; we're all marked men."

☙❧

They got into the taxi at 4 p.m. Gili was covered with a layer of makeup and looked completely unbalanced. He hoped that he would find what he was searching for before his makeup wore off.

Even without Tzimer's documents, he looked abnormal. He was squinting terribly, he was wearing a bright green baseball cap on his hair, now dyed dark black, a khaki shirt and stained pants. His shoelaces in his high-top brown sneakers were untied.

The cab let Pinny and Gili out a block away from Goldman. Gili was trembling with fear. He knew how he would get into the hospital, but had no idea how he would get out of there.

"Relax. Calm down," Pinny Klein whispered encouragingly. They sat down on a wooden bench beneath a tree. Gili pulled a small leaf down and crumbled it with his fingers. "You're nervous?" Klein asked, trying with difficulty to hide his own anxiety.

"No, I'm okay," Gili said, "but I'm trembling; my knees keep knocking together."

Pinny was actually pleased to hear it. "Good," he whispered in satisfaction. "If it wasn't so, I'd be more worried. A mentally ill person does tremble. A little saliva coming out of your mouth wouldn't hurt either."

They approached the building's gate. Klein rang the bell.

"Who is it?" a voice on the intercom asked.

"I've brought a patient," the aide replied.

"Do you have an appointment?"

Thank goodness Rav Yoske had thought of everything; Tzimer had taken care of the details. "Yes," Klein said confidently.

A small hum announced the electric circuit being completed; the gate opened. They entered a tree-filled yard, crossed a small gray path and waited.

41

A white-clad nurse looked at them apathetically. She leaned against a counter topped with formica in a soothing shade of blue, her chin in her hand. A sign on the counter indicated that this was the emergency area.

Holding Gili's hand with a firm grip, Klein led him to a bench, next to a grinning youth. Gili tried to overcome his disgust: The boy's breath smelled foul, as if he had fasted for days.

"Do you see it too?" the boy asked Gili.

"See what?"

"The picture of tomorrow," the young man answered, his eyes dreamy. He stood up from the bench and walked through the hallway, his arms spread like the wings of an eagle. "I can photograph possibilities. I can see particles."

"Charlie, go back to your room," the nurse shouted. In an undertone she explained to Klein, "The boy was a genius, a physicist and philosopher both. Look what happened to him." Then she pointed to Gili. "He's here to be admitted? Wait for the head doctor, Dr. Seiden." She pressed a button on her phone.

Dr. Seiden came down from his second-floor office. He was a man of average height with a granite face, who exuded an air of strength and inflexibility. He stared long and hard at Gili. "You brought him," he said, a question that was also a statement. Pinny nodded.

Dr. Seiden was blessed with quick understanding. "What's his problem, army trauma?"

"Exactly." Klein spoke quietly. "To be more specific, lack of army. His father is my good friend. The boy is destroying the entire family. He wasn't drafted; you'll soon understand why. His ego was terribly wounded. From that time on he thinks he's a soldier in the Givati unit. He shouts battle cries and orders all day long, and it's torturing his parents."

Dr. Seiden pulled a pair of reading glasses from his jacket pocket and put them on. He carefully read the recommendations of the head psychiatrist of the Tel Aviv district, Professor Stockman. "Yehoshua Zucker, psychotic, 25 years old, single. Clinical diagnosis: manic-depression. Treatment: lithium (shots and pills) to balance the minerals in the body; small doses of Elavil. Prozac for episodes of fright and extended depression. Cogentin shots to avoid side effects of convulsions and spasms."

He returned the papers to Klein. "It's a mild case; his place isn't here. I'm surprised at Professor Stockman. Doesn't he know that Goldman only takes those who pose a danger to society?"

Klein didn't panic. "Read the last page."

Dr. Seiden pushed up the gold-rimmed glasses that had slid to the edge of his nose and skimmed through the papers. He lifted his eyes and stared at Gili from above the lenses. "I understand that he had a particularly difficult attack recently?"

"Exactly," Pinny said enthusiastically. "When he's very depressed, Shuki Zucker grows violent and dangerous."

"Yes, sir!" Gili said aloud. He saluted and stood at attention.

Dr. Seiden clapped him on the shoulders. "He doesn't look particularly violent to me," he said doubtfully.

Klein spoke in a melancholy voice. "That's what the neighbor thought, poor old Davy Cohen, may he rest in peace."

Dr. Seiden's rocklike face softened somewhat. "When did it happen?"

"A few weeks ago." Klein had done his homework, and quickly told the story as Rav Yoske had instructed him. "Shuki was calmly cleaning his 'rifle,' an old metal pipe. Davy Cohen, his neighbor, really liked Shuki. He asked him what he was doing.

"'I'm cleaning my rifle,' Shuki answered.

"Davy Cohen forgot that Shuki was mentally ill. 'Rifle? I don't see any rifle.'

"Shuki was instantly furious. 'Not a rifle?' He was horribly insulted. 'It can fire and kill like all of them.'

"He began to run amuck, went crazy, and that's how poor Davy was sacrificed to his madness. It was terrible." He pulled a printed sheet out of his pocket. "Here are the details of the incident, and the telephone number of an eyewitness. If you need additional information you can ask him." Rav Yoske had briefed Mendy Sofer, a no-nonsense student at *Matnas Yehudah*, in the unlikely event that Dr. Seiden wanted to discuss the matter further.

"Well," said Dr. Seiden, "if that's the case, he should be in the security ward, in a strait jacket."

Klein paled. If Gili were put into a closed ward, all their efforts would be for nothing.

"Listen, it's not so simple. We've got to speak confidentially." He gave the doctor's shoulders a friendly pat, but his voice was tense. "Let's go to your office for a minute."

"Of course," said Dr. Seiden.

They walked up to the second floor and entered the director's large office. Two patients were inside, busily polishing a bronze model of an F-16 fighter plane. "My patients made this," Dr. Seiden said proudly. "Look how nicely they've decorated the office."

The room was impressive. Sculptures, drawings and large embroidered pictures were generously displayed throughout. Klein had to admit, there were benefits to being the administrator of a psychiatric hospital: an army at your beck and call, waiting to clean and decorate your office, and thank you for the privilege.

"Regarding Shuki Zucker: Look, it's true that he's a bit dangerous, like everyone here, but on the other hand that was his only violent episode. If you put him in a strait jacket you'll destroy him completely. His parents are in despair. Do you understand?" As he spoke he carefully counted out $1500 bills.

Rav Yoske had thought of everything.

The envelope containing the money landed on the desk. Dr. Seiden opened a drawer and swiftly threw it inside.

"Now I understand," Dr. Seiden announced, skimming through Shuki's papers. "Shuki Zucker will get a bed in Room 12, third floor. That's for the institution's simplest cases. Nonviolent."

Klein thanked him fervently and walked towards the door. Dr. Seiden's thoughtful gaze followed Zishe Tzimer's assistant as he left the room with decided steps and descended again to the nurse downstairs to tend to the bureaucratic end.

When the lengthy procedure had been finished the nurse turned on her microphone. Her voice echoed throughout the building on the public address system. "I need a nurse to escort a new patient to his room."

Pinny walked over to Gili and pumped his hand. "Feel good, Shuki, and hang on. Do you forgive me? You know I only want what's best for you." His voice shook, as if he were about to burst out in tears.

"Yes, sir." Gili saluted. Klein slowly backed away towards the door, looking occasionally at Gili, his face a mask of self-recrimination.

Four male nurses wearing white jackets quickly arrived. They were quiet, but their expressions, like their stance, were the sort that persuaded people to submit without a battle. The impressive escort surrounded Gili on all sides. He ascended two stories in an elevator and was brought to Ward 3. There he went through the admissions procedure, which included checking his height, weight, and blood pressure.

"You have any thoughts?" the admitting nurse asked.

"Thoughts?" Gili didn't understand.

"Thoughts of suicide," the nurse explained. "Do you ever think about suicide?"

"Why?"

"Because if you do, it's a good idea to come to us first. It would be a shame for you to hurt yourself, and then we'll have to put you into a locked ward."

A stone rolled off his heart. *So I'm in an open ward.* He took a deep breath. "I'll let you know if there are any serious thoughts of it," he promised her.

He was given a pair of blue pajamas but was allowed to keep his own clothing in a small dresser in his room. Thus he still had the makeup, the miniature tape recorder, and, most important, his cellular phone. That had an important role to play in his future plans.

Gili lay down on a foul-smelling mattress near the door. He looked uncomfortably around the dreary room. His roommates were all lying down. In a bed to the right of the window an older man who appeared neglected was hitting his head. His yellowing teeth opened in a broad grin. "So, you've also fallen in here?"

"That's right," Gili answered, mimicking the man's slow, melodic voice.

"I'm schizophrenic," the man startled him with his directness. "And what are you?"

"Manic-depressive," Gili confessed.

"They call me Jumbo. And what's your name?" a patient in a bed to the left asked. He was a youngish man, with wristwatches covering his entire forearm.

"I'm Shuki."

"Shuki, I've got a riddle for you. Is a cucumber longer or greener?"

What have I gotten myself into? Gili wondered. "Why?" he asked aloud.

"'Cause if you don't know the answer you're not in my room. We've only got intelligent people here."

Gili almost burst out laughing. *I've got myself some roommate,* he thought, stifling a smile. *I've found myself a wonderful place.*

The man wouldn't let up. "Answer already!"

Gili thought for a moment. "I could tell you that there's no difference, that just as a cucumber is long so it is green. But that's not the answer you wanted to hear, right?"

"Right. So what is it?" Excited, the young man drew closer.

"It's more green. Because it's only as long as its length, but it's green all around."

"Bull's-eye!" the young man shouted. "Good for you. You've been accepted into Jumbo's room. Now listen," he continued eagerly, "how many men in the street know the answer? That's it: We're the normal ones, and the ones outside are completely mad."

"That's right," Gili returned, "Elizabeth, the Queen of England, said something like that. 'It's true that you're the sane ones,' she said during a visit to an asylum, 'but we are the majority.'"

"I don't get it," Jumbo grumbled. He sat silent, and the conversation ended in an atmosphere of hostility.

About half an hour later Gili understood why his roommate had been nicknamed Jumbo. His many watches had been set with incredible accuracy. At precisely 7:47 their alarms all went off at once. "Jumbo!" the young man shouted. "Time for takeoff."

In the next half-hour Gili was treated to all the announcements and conversation of the cabin crew of a Boeing 747 jumbo jet: altitude, expected time of arrival, a demonstration on seat-belt use, a detailed listing of Europe's beautiful scenery that was passing beneath them...

"What a shame, what a shame," the older man clicked his tongue, as he rubbed his forehead rapidly. "He was a steward on an El Al jumbo jet, and suddenly he went crazy, and now I have to hear this twice a day. I have no energy for him. By the way, I didn't introduce myself," the man apologized. "They call me Bagel. Do you know why?"

"No, I don't," Gili confessed.

"Soon I'm going to the nurse for two sleeping pills. After that, I sleep like a sesame bagel. Do you know what that means? Jumbo only has digital watches, but I have one with a clock face. When it makes an entire circle of 12 hours, that's a bagel. But I sleep for 13 hours, from 8 at night to 9 in the morning, so that I don't have to hear Jumbo's ceremony in the morning. So that's a 'sesame bagel.'"

The head nurse in the Goldman Psychiatric Center, Bella Bar-Dror, received a visit that night from an unusual guest. "To what do I owe the honor of having a noted rabbi come visit me at home?" she asked Rabbi Yoske Friedman.

Rav Yoske calmly sat down in her foyer and counted out $2000 before her greedy eyes. A careful examination that he had conducted in the afternoon had revealed that the staff of Goldman was solidly corrupt, from top to bottom. Dr. Seiden and the chief nurse, Bella Bar-Dror, were at the forefront. A patient whose family could not find some ready cash with which to grease the staffers' palms would remain there, neglected and all but forgotten.

"You want special privileges for the patient?" Bella asked with a smile of comprehension. "A good room, clean mattress, new sheets, better food?"

"No." Rav Yoske handed her a detailed list. "I want you to follow these instructions." He left the paper on a table and stood up to leave. "When everything is done, you'll receive another $4000," he promised.

Bella glanced swiftly at the page. "What? Impossible! My entire key ring?"

"It will be worth your while," Rav Yoske promised her.

"Very well," Bella agreed ceremoniously, dollar signs dancing in her eyes.

The note had instructed her to begin that night, but Bella was bone tired, after a double shift of 24 solid hours. She went into bed, "just for two hours," she told herself. When she woke up in a panic, it was 7 o'clock the next morning.

Gili planned the next step. It was 8 p.m. An hour earlier he had eaten dinner, together with the other inmates. He hoped to begin his night's wanderings at midnight. At 10 a.m. Nurse Bella was to hand him the key ring, a sketch of the building, some important information, and the uniform of a male nurse.

The patients in the room were in a deep sleep. Gili sat biting his nails anxiously. A few patients chatted among themselves in the hallway. Gili was surprised: They were talking politics, discussing the news, the security situation, and other topics that he would never have believed possible. Only occasionally were there shouts or exchanges of the sort that reminded him that this was an asylum for the mentally ill. At eleven-thirty the nurse shouted at them and sent them back to their rooms.

When the place had grown absolutely silent Gili went under his blanket and, trembling, telephoned Rav Yoske. They had arranged a code between them.

"Ima didn't come," Gili said.

Shocked, Rav Yoske was silent for a moment. Two thousand dollars was not enough for her? "Behave nicely," he answered. That is, keep a low profile. For the time being, at least.

The night passed, an eternity. Gili tossed and turned on his foul-smelling bed, envying his snoring neighbors. Bagel was truly sleeping round the clock, and Jumbo had finally landed.

When everything has ended well, I'll also buy myself some "sleeping bagels." With a lot, a lot of sesame, he smiled bitterly. He could not remember the last time he had slept more than four or five hours a night.

There were a few cries from different rooms throughout the night; the more disturbed patients occasionally gave bloodcurdling screams, the kind of shouts that he had heard during his nocturnal visit to Kiryat Bialik the night before. At three in the morning he gave up: He left the room and went to the nurses' station to ask for a sleeping pill. "You poor thing, you can't sleep?" The nurse took pity on him and gave him two Valiums. Gili took one of them, and moments later was deep in sleep.

He passed a difficult, anxious day. Jumbo spent much of his time synchronizing his watches and Bagel would not stop chattering. Gili did not dare call Rav Yoske to find out what had gone wrong. He went to the bathroom every hour to freshen his makeup. He was certain that Shuki Zucker's identity would be discovered any minute now. The war of nerves was almost at its end, and a day more precious than gold had been completely wasted. Everything was lost...

42

Dr. Seiden was a suspicious man.

He waited two days. The next night, a little after midnight, he decided to verify the story of the dead neighbor, Davy Cohen. He called the number Pinny Klein had given him.

Mendy Sofer was an older student, and as such was allowed several privileges, including a cellular phone. When the instrument chirped in his pocket he ran out of the yeshivah's *beis midrash* into the hallway, and pressed the SND button. A metallic voice was on the other end.

"This is Dr. Seiden, head of the Goldman Psychiatric Center. I wanted some clarification of an incident to which you were eyewitness."

Mendy was a cheerful lad, and everything was a joke to him. He could not really remember exactly what this was all about. "What incident?"

Dr. Seiden was one of those careful men who did not volunteer information. "Were you an eyewitness to a criminal incident, a murder perhaps?"

Now Mendy understood. Rav Yoske had not been kidding him. "Oh, when the psycho killed his neighbor."

"You're a neighbor too, aren't you?"

"Of course. I live in the second house, on the left."

"By the way, what was the madman's name?" Dr. Seiden asked.

Mendy banged his forehead, rummaging frantically through his pockets for the slip of paper with all the details. The paper had disappeared, of course, and he hardly remembered a word of it. "I think his name was Shuki. That's right, Shuki Zucker. He fell on the poor guy and finished him off then and there."

"The victim, your neighbor, his name was — " Dr. Seiden waited for a moment, giving him time to finish off the sentence. But as much as he tried, the name eluded Mendy. All he remembered was that it was a common one.

"Oh that's right, his name was Levy. Davy Levy."

"Davy Levy?"

"Yes, yes. For sure."

"Not Cohen?"

And now Mendy remembered. Cohen it had been, surely. "That's right, that's right, I got confused. Davy Cohen, of course. They had some kind of fight about a water sprinkler if I'm not mistaken."

That was enough for Dr. Seiden.

The phone rang in the home of Rav Avram Roosenthal, three series of three rings each. Choni picked up the receiver. He did not recognize the tinny voice.

"May I speak with the rav?" the frosty, metallic voice asked.

Choni, curious, transferred the call to Rav Avram, snuck into the kitchen and picked up the extension.

"This is Dr. Seiden. I wanted to let the rabbi know that we received a patient yesterday by the name of Shuki Zucker. He seems okay and his papers are entirely in order. That's what I thought, but now his story is beginning to fray at the edges. I think the matter bears investigation."

"What room is this Zucker in?" Rav Avram asked.

"Room 12, third floor. You've got the keys, right?"

"Of course. Thanks, you've done well."

"Will you use the information?" the doctor asked in an offhand tone. What he really meant was, "How much will you pay me for this?"

Rav Avram was quite used to Dr. Seiden's manner of conversation. It had already cost him plenty of money. He spoke feelingly, in a shrill tone that grew louder until it reached a crescendo: "What will I do? I'll tell you exactly: I'm leaving hundreds of my followers this minute and am coming to Kiryat Bialik, right now!"

❧⊰❦⊱☙

Rav Avram came looking for Choni. The boy just managed to hang up the receiver; his cheeks turned as red as a ripe tomato.

"Choni, where's Gili Dinar?" Rav Avram asked.

"Dunno," he muttered. "It's at least a week since we've seen the guy around here."

"Good. I have to leave the house now. Help Zabik and Muli take care of things."

Choni promised that everything would be fine. Rav Avram returned to his room and spoke with a bearded man, who told him of the terrible crisis that his *shidduch* was undergoing. Rav Avram made a further appointment with him, urged him out, and began to speed towards Haifa.

As soon as the rabbi's automobile had left, Choni called Meshulam. He updated him on the latest development, though he could not give details. "It's true that it's unusual for Rav Avram to leave all the people waiting?" Choni asked, fishing for a compliment.

"Absolutely true," Meshulam said generously and then, in a 180-degree turnaround, he began to rail at him. "Tell me, Mr. Smarthead, why did I pay you thousands of shekalim?" he thundered. "For these crumbs? First you lost Gili, now Rav Avram. Why didn't you go with him?"

Choni was dumbfounded. Meshulam's passing rages were nothing new; he had already seen how he'd acted in the ambulance with Paysi. Now it was his, Choni's, turn to be the sacrifice.

"Dunno, thought we didn't need to," he muttered.

"Of course we didn't need to," Meshulam said in a deceivingly soft tone. "Have you heard about the guy who lost first place in the idiot's olympics?"

"No," Choni trembled like a leaf in the breeze, yet he could not help laughing at Meshulam's way of putting things.

"They called him to take the prize, but he was so stupid he thought they meant somebody else."

Choni tried to giggle, but it ended up sounding more like a sob, a sob that mixed with the sound of the dial tone and told him that Meshulam had already hung up.

Four hours earlier...

At 7 o'clock in the evening the head nurse, Bella, went into Room 12 to give the patients their medicine. Gili received a dummy pill, as Rav Yoske Friedman had arranged with her. "Good night everybody," she said cheerfully. "Behave nicely now. Have a pleasant flight, Jumbo; a good night's sleep, Bagel. Shuki, attention!"

"Yes, sir!" Gili called out, jumping up and saluting.

As she left she put a full bag into his small drawer. He waited until 9 o'clock, hardly moving, then added still another half-hour as an extra security measure.

At 9:30 Gili turned the lights on in the room. Bagel and Jumbo were sleeping deeply after their nightly dose of Valium. They did not react at all as Gili rummaged through the bag.

He smiled. The nurse's uniform was there, as agreed upon, and within the rolled-up clothing lay a large, impressive-looking ring of keys. He counted at least 30 of them, of all sizes. These would open all the doors of Goldman Psychiatric Center before him this night.

A paper rolled up and held together by a rubber band was also concealed within the clothing. This was a sketch of the building, with all of its wards. A memo was scrawled in the margin: "Beyond the showers is service elevator G, that leads two floors beneath ground level."

And here was the key to the service elevator. Long live the mighty dollar! When all this was over he would have to liquidate every last asset he had, in order to fund this project. The bribes alone would reach over $10,000 dollars, if not more. But it was worth it, to achieve what he planned.

Assuming he had not made any errors in his calculations. Assuming that he would not come up with absolutely nothing...

It was exactly midnight when he put on the white nurse's uniform and opened the locked door. The building was absolutely silent. Even the tough cases had been calmed down with their sleeping pills.

The nurses' station in the center of the hallway was empty. Bella had done good work: She had offered to take the midnight shift, and had sent away the previous shift's nurse a bit early.

He walked with a catlike tread, his skin crawling and mouth dry. He could feel his heart thumping wildly. Rav Yoske had bribed Bella — but not the GSS. His every step now was calculated, but he did not see the metal chair in the corner...

The chair flew down with a bang that could have woken the dead. The echoes flew everywhere, a ringing that seemed to grow louder and louder endlessly.

Gili hugged the wall and froze. *That's it, you can say goodbye to the whole plan.*

At the end of the hallway a door opened and an orderly put his head through and glanced around, scrutinizing the entire length of the hallway. Gili prayed that the dim lighting would hide him from the orderly's curious eyes.

"Kiki, you see something there?" a sleepy voice asked from within a room.

"I'm checking, Gili," the orderly answered, approaching Gili's shrinking form with heavy steps.

Gili bent even lower. The orderly had mentioned his name! He knew all, he knew that Shuki Zucker was Gili Dinar, knew that he was hiding here!

Here he came; the blow was about to fall. What should he do, when Kiki approached? Hit him with the stupid key ring?

Kiki was two steps from the corner. Gili held his breath.

The orderly approached with silent steps. Gili could see gleaming eyes and the wicked face of a beast of prey about to pounce. Centimeter after centimeter he came closer. Gili felt that the end was near.

This orderly, Kiki, looked like a gorilla. He was close to six feet tall, a massive collection of muscle and sinew. He looked like a professional boxer who had not had a target for his fist in quite some time. One blow from him, thought Gili, was enough to send someone to heaven.

The distance between the two shortened. Two or three more steps...

A sudden call broken the tense silence. "Kiki, come back already! You're just wasting time; I think you're learning from our patients. One of the patients or some idiotic cat bumped into a chair and you're turning detective?"

Kiki, it seemed, was deeply insulted. He returned to the room with heavy steps and opened the door with a flourish. His rough voice did remind one of a gorilla. "Gili, are you hinting that I'm crazy? I'll show you! You talk to me that way?"

"Kiki, n...n...no," the other orderly stuttered, obviously frightened. "I didn't mean to offend you. I just meant to say that it's not likely that anyone would break into this pathetic hospital in the middle of the night; at worst, it's one of the crazies wandering around for no reason." His voice held a flattering note. "Kiki, it's not worth your wasting your few hours of sleep."

Kiki softened. "You may be right, Gili. One of the patients must have been wandering around." He gave a loud yawn. "The truth is, the two years I've been here have been one big bore. It's a shame to waste my energy."

Another few murmurs and a heavy silence again descended, broken only by the sound of the orderlies' snores.

Gili was in a cold sweat; his entire body trembled. He felt he had aged years in those few nightmare minutes, in the frightening shadow of the gorillalike staffer.

And you're not the only one with the name Gili, he chided himself. *A worker in a hospital can share the name!*

It took another quarter-hour before the cold sweat began to fade from his brow. Only then did he dare leave his hiding place.

He stared at the note that the head nurse had left for him. "Beyond the showers is service elevator G, that leads two floors beneath ground level."

Gili reached the showers with muffled steps. He listened: Had some-one decided to take a shower at this time? No, everything was completely silent.

Gili's face contorted; he felt the sour taste of failure in his mouth. Bella had written nothing of a locked metal gate in the middle of the hallway, blocking access to the service elevator.

Bella had taken the money and led him into a trap!

His nervous fingers rummaged through his pockets. The sound of the keys clanking together reminded him. He pulled out the key ring. Yes, each key was carefully marked in tiny letters. One of them bore the word "hallway."

He breathed easier as the key turned in the lock.

In absolute silence he passed through the hallway. His legs pulled him forward: His head felt heavy and a cardiologist examining his EKG would probably have fainted. This rushing between his thudding heart-beats was brutal. It was as if he were standing before a lion crouching, ready to spring.

No, worse than that, thought Gili. He was standing before the unknown. And he was afraid, deathly afraid.

Service elevator G brought him down to floor "2E," a floor that did not, to all appearances, exist. He stuck out his trembling head and looked right and left. A dusty light bulb hung from a black cord, casting an or-ange beam in the short hallway.

There was no one there.

His heart thumping, he left the elevator. A swift glance showed him six doors. Where should he begin? These were cages in a zoo: Every room could contain a wild, bestial patient, waiting to spring unless he was con-fined to his bed or in a strait jacket.

He had no information on which was Mickey Gadish's room. Rav Yoske had kept this last card close to his vest, afraid that if he told Bella for whom they were searching her professional instincts would overcome her deep greed and she would tell the administration.

Gili decided to begin numerically. Room 1.

The keys were in order, sparing him a prolonged search. The door opened with a blood-chilling screech. Gili's heart skipped a beat. Two fiery red eyes stared out at him from the dimness. That was enough for him: It was the most horrifying sight he had ever seen.

He hastily locked the door and walked towards the second room.

For one minute he stood before the locked door, hesitating. The gurgling sounds he heard within left no room for doubt: This was not what he was looking for.

Perhaps he should do the opposite, try the last door?

Gili decided to follow his instincts. He slowly tiptoed to the end of the hallway and listened next to the door of Room 6.

Absolute silence.

The key trembled in his fingers. This was the minute. Either he was right, or...

This time the door opened silently. Gili turned on the light. On the left, in a wretched-looking bed, an inert figure lay beneath a shabby woolen blanket.

Gili approached the bed on tiptoe. He had tried to prepare himself for this moment, but everything dissipated. His heart pounded like a drum and his body trembled. He stared stony faced at the figure on the bed. Staring and refusing to believe. "Is that him?" he whispered. "G-d protect us; what have they done?" The first tears began their path down his cheeks.

The man lying on the bed had aged terribly. Deep wrinkles of anguish were carved near his lips, once-robust cheeks had sunken, his black hair had gone gray and his eyes seemed to be sunken deeper. But Gili had no doubt, no doubt at all.

This was his father.

Udi Dinar.

Rav Avram Roosenthal's hands gripped the steering wheel firmly. He had suspected that this might happen from the very beginning. He understood Gili far better than Meshulam Yaakovi did, and he knew that this stubborn young man would achieve his goal, never letting go until he had achieved what he wanted.

With studied movements he pulled out a thin brown cigar from a gold case, lit it and inhaled the thick smoke.

The car surged ahead. He would try to stop Gili before everything blew up, but he had made some plans in case he was too late. He had perfected it down to the last detail some time ago.

And not even Meshulam Yaakovi knew what he was going to do.

"Abba, Abbaleh," Gili whispered gently.

The man turned over and buried himself in his pillow. Gili trembled like one suffering from malaria. "Abba. It's me, Gili. Get up. I've found you!"

The man suddenly sat up in bed. He could be seen in all his pathetic misery, looking like a stray dog on a rainy day. His eyes looked down, beaten and degraded, lacking any spark of life. He yawned. "Oh, my dream, my dream comes back to me always." He pushed Gili with his hands. "Go away, my dream, it's time for you to fade away."

"Abba, it's true, it's no dream. I've come to you, I've found you! Isn't it amazing?"

The man rubbed his forehead and stared indifferently at Gili.

"Abba, don't you recognize me?" Gili hesitantly approached. Maybe he was mistaken; maybe this was not his father. He looked deeply into the blue eyes, searching for a sign of recognition, for a tiny spark of his soul. He looked for the eyes that he remembered so well, the eyes that loved to laugh, that knew the magical secret of a half-smile, that could light up with mischief or share a moment between father and son.

No doubt about it: These eyes were the eyes of Udi Dinar. But now they were empty, all expression gone.

"Abbaleh, what's happened to you?" Gili sobbed brokenly, hugging his father. "What have they done to you? You've been drugged for six years now."

"What do you want?" the man asked apathetically, his tone melancholy. He felt cold beneath Gili's hot hands.

Disappointment seared Gili like white-hot metal; he felt absolutely defeated. Six years you mourn, an orphan; suddenly, you find that it is all a mistake, that your father is alive, and you plan your emotional reunion. *I was naïve,* Gili mocked himself, *I thought Abba would jump on me with hugs and kisses. A man who was hidden for six years in a cellar beneath the earth, never seeing the sun — would he jump for joy at the first minute?*

"Abba, say that you recognize me, it's me, Gili." He started to weep, but held back his tears with an intense effort of will. *Maybe happiness will help: Smile, laugh, let Abba see you rejoicing...*

Gili gave a weak smile, a smile that seemed to melt away like that of a clown painted on a helium balloon.

"Who are you?" the man demanded. His wall of apathy was beginning to crack a little.

Gili trembled convulsively. "Abba, don't you recognize your son? I'm Gili! Say something, Abbaleh, recognize me!"

He pulled the *kippah* off his head. "Maybe you don't recognize me because of this? I've become observant, I'm a religious man today, like you once were."

The man settled back into his bed, pulling the blanket up to his shoulders. "I have no son. I have no son."

Maybe I've made a mistake. He felt the doubt fill his heart. "What's your name?" he asked the man.

A vacant stare was his reply.

Gili looked around him. A medical file was hanging from the wall, bearing the name Mickey Gadish.

Mickey Gadish!

This was the final seal. Now he knew for certain that he had not made a mistake. He had heard that name in London, from Chedvi, quoting her brother Paysi.

His confidence increased. "Abbaleh, you're not Mickey Gadish, you're Udi Dinar, you're Udi Dinar!"

The empty look gazed back at him, cold and strange.

Gili felt a keen stab of frustration. Who knew what medications his father was getting? It seemed that they had hypnotized him into a new identity, an identity that did not even recognize his only son.

He banged at the buttons of his cellular phone. "Yes?" he heard the voice of Rav Yoske on the other end.

"I'm calling from the yeshivah," Gili said. "Bentzy is crying in the dormitory, and it's hard to comfort him."

That was the code they had arranged between themselves just two days ago, though it seemed to Gili that years had passed since then. Rav Yoske had been realistic, and had envisioned the possibility of difficulties in communicating.

"Try to work it out on your own," Rav Yoske answered, "and if he won't stop crying call his mother."

The phone was hung up. Gili knew that Rav Yoske Friedman would be there within 10 minutes. Time was short.

The first flash of curiosity appeared in the man's eyes. He stared beyond the bed. "What's that in your hand?"

"A cellular phone," Gili answered calmly.

"What's that?" the man asked.

"The message goes through special relays and antennas of certain frequencies and is received by free cells, without need for telephone wires or cables."

"Let me see," the man asked. Gili hesitated; what if he damaged the instrument?

He backed away slowly towards the door. Rav Yoske should be here any minute now; he had to meet one more challenge: opening the institution's main entrance.

"Forgive me, Abbaleh, for leaving you for one minute. I'll be back soon. In the meantime, listen to this."

He pulled a chair next to the bed and turned on the small tape recorder. From within came the sound of the rebbe of Kiltz: "And what is the source of the Dinar family? Was that your grandfather's name as well?"

"No." Now Gili's voice could be heard. "No, my grandfather was Rabbi Shmuel Dinburg. My father changed his name to Dinar, and also switched from Moshe to Udi."

At the time Gili had not understood the sudden urge to reveal everything to this venerable rebbe. Now he knew. Everything had its purpose; nothing was coincidence.

"Ahhh, your grandfather was Reb Shmiel Dinburg?" Here was the rebbe speaking again. "I learned with your grandfather in the Chayei

Olam *cheder*. We were in the same class. He was a special boy. *A kleine velt* — it's a small world. Your father was his only son, Moshe Dinburg. I was his *sandek* and said the blessings at his *bris*." An echo rolled through the cellar as the rebbe gently rubbed his cheek. "How your grandfather loved him. 'Moishike,' he called him. How much anguish he felt when his only son turned from the proper path. His heart couldn't take the suffering and simply gave out. Just two days before his stroke he was with me. He wept bitterly. 'I have nothing left in this world. My Moishike, my only son, the joy of my life, has thrown his *kippah* off his head, and has become completely lawless.' I spoke to him, assured him that his son would repent one day and bring him *nachas*, true joy. But alas, my words fell on deaf ears; he would not be comforted. Now I see that I was right: Your father has repented. Look, here is his son, wearing a large *kippah*."

Suddenly they could hear Gili's voice, bursting out in bitter tears. "I'm sorry, I'm sorry to disappoint the rebbe, but my father is no longer alive. The gates of repentance are closed to him forever and who knows what judgment he was given above? I just hope that his terrible death was his atonement."

"What? What a tragedy. I can't believe what I'm hearing. When did it happen?"

"It's already five years." Gili answered. "Five full years for me to feel incredible waves of longing, night and day. Dear Rebbe, my world was destroyed when I was 18 years old. I became an orphan, and I can't bear the pain. My heart goes out towards my father. I loved him so, and I still love him. I see his smiling face before me as if he were still alive. You're the first to hear a word about this. I'm living in a cruel world, a hard world that has no room for emotions. Someone who cries is considered a weakling but you, Rebbe, you are such a good person, and I'm not ashamed."

Now they could hear the scuffling sound of the rebbe as he walked on swollen feet through the room, all the while murmuring to himself, his emotion plain to hear. "But I was his *sandek*. How could he have died unrepentant? Didn't I bless him? Didn't I say, 'Living G-d, our Portion and our Rock, may You issue the command to rescue the beloved soul within our flesh from destruction, for the sake of His covenant that He has placed in our flesh...' How did Moishke Dinburg fall into the depths of the River Dinar? And I was his *sandek*..."

Mickey Gadish moved weakly in his bed. This was clearly some illusion, a mirage trying to remind him of a forgotten past that someone had erased from his life, to bring to life a dead past that perhaps never existed. Yes, he remembered: He had to press the button that said REW and bore two arrows. He rewound the tape and listened again, his face a mask of concentration.

He felt a slight awakening, the beginnings of a transformation. Suddenly he wanted to speak with this nice young man.

"Hey, boy," he called aloud, but there was no one in his room. Gili had gone up to the entrance to open the gates.

* * *

Rav Yoske had proved that the power of money was boundless. Gili was surprised to find the nurses' station near the entrance abandoned. Rav Yoske must have gone way over the $4000 mark: Bella wouldn't have done this kind of work without getting an extra thousand or two.

He approached, his stomach turning, and saw that not only was the station empty, but a note had been left for him, neatly setting out the instructions for opening the gate.

Gili stopped. This was a trap, that was clear.

But the writing was identical to that in the note that Bella had left him in his room. What was going on here? Was Bella some kind of all-powerful wizard here in Goldman?

"Don't be a 'fraidy cat," he whispered to himself. "It seems that Rav Yoske knew what he was doing. The way is clear: Go."

The buzz of the intercom suddenly broke the silence, like the sound of a broken electric cable. Gili flew to the button and pressed it.

Rav Yoske was not alone. Rabbi Schmidt had come with him. He had decided to stay in Haifa until the affair had been concluded.

The two rabbis were clearly moved and looked exhausted and drained. Their presence in this silent place reminded Gili of a Biblical image: two angels come to pull Lot out from Sodom's destruction at the very last second.

Gili raced towards them. "Be quiet," he said, panicking. "You made a terrific noise with that bell."

Rav Yoske looked around him. His glance fell on several reproductions of lovely scenic views. Rabbi Schmidt stared interestedly at collages that the inmates had put together as part of their occupational therapy, hung in large frames on walls painted in soothing pastel shades. "There's something strange about this place."

"Absolutely," a thin smile appeared on Rav Yoske's face. "Don't forget who is incarcerated here."

"Let's not waste time," Gili hurried them. "Come to the elevator."

They rushed down the hallway. The sound of their footsteps seemed to Gili's fevered imagination like a thousand banging drums. If this was not a trap, the State of Israel was in trouble. Had the GSS gone bankrupt or something?

Udi Dinar was in a completely different position than 10 minutes before. He was listening to the tape of the rebbe of Kiltz for the third time. His eyes were fogged.

Rav Yoske Friedman and Rabbi Chaim Ozer Schmidt suddenly looked like the same man. Each stared at the inmate, approached, and stared longer. They then had the exact same reaction: Both wiped their eyes, looked once more at Mickey Gadish, and cried, together, "Moishike!"

The word flew through the air and returned to them, echoing and re-echoing from the room's walls.

"Moishike!"

43

"**R**av Yoske, Rav Schmidt. What's the matter with you? Another minute and the entire hospital will be here!"

The two rabbis belatedly realized the wisdom of Gili's reproof. Their emotional shout could bring the entire staff down. But the echoes reverberating through the room could not be recalled. For a few minutes they waited, trembling, staring at the doorway.

But nothing happened. Udi Dinar sat on his bed, silently looking with dead eyes at the friends of his youth.

The small tape continued to speak endlessly. The voice of the rebbe of Kiltz split the air with quiet strength. "But I was his *sandek*. How could he have died unrepentant? Didn't I bless him? Didn't I say, 'Living G-d, our Portion and our Rock, may You issue the command to rescue the beloved soul within our flesh from destruction, for the sake of His covenant that He has placed in our flesh...' How did Moishke Dinburg fall into the depths of the River Dinar? And I was his *sandek*..."

And suddenly there was a diamond sparkling in the light: A single tear flowed from the eyes of the weakened man on the bed. And after the first tear came a second, and a third...

"What's going on here? Who are you? Who am I?" The words contained a hint of chaos, the echo of a deep abyss.

Rav Yoske Friedman answered tranquilly, "You are not Mickey Gadish. Your name is Udi Dinar. The nice curly-haired young man standing to my right is Gili Dinar, your son. My name is Yoske Friedman. The man standing next to me is Chaim Ozer Schmidt. If you recall, we learned together in Yeshivas Ein Yisrael some 30-odd years ago."

The man stared out of expressionless eyes. Two minutes, as long as eternity, passed.

"Why have you come here?"

"We've come to take you out of here. You don't belong here," Gili said.

"Why? It's good here. They take care of me, they give me medicine." The man's head nodded from side to side.

Gili walked closer and gazed deeply into Udi's eyes, as if trying to connect with his soul. For a long while they stared at each other. A deep silence fell on the room. Udi breathed heavily, like a man fighting some kind of battle. Suddenly a light dawned in his eyes.

"You're my son?" his voice quavered.

"Yes, Abba. I'm alive and well, and Ima, too, is healthy, thank G-d." Gili's voice was choked. He had hoped to grab some tiny thread and here it had happened: They had made the connection. Abba was coming alive!

And then the eyes were again veiled, the spark extinguished. Gili thought in frustration of that thread, evaporating between his fingers.

"They give me medicine every day." Udi spoke in a blank monotone. "I think I know this young man, he reminds me of my dream, the dream I have seen many times, a dream of someone whom I loved once, who is no more." His voice became melancholy, as one who has made peace with a loss of long ago, in the distant past.

His dull gaze fell on the two rabbis. "And you say you were my friends in yeshivah. I think I know you. Why have you come here?"

"I told you, we've come to take you out of here," Rav Yoske said. "I think we should hurry. I've brought you clean clothing. Change into them and come with us."

Udi refused. "No! I like it here. They take care of me, worry about me. I'm insane. I'm not allowed to be outside!"

Rav Yoske was filled with a burning rage. In the name of G-d, what had they done to this good man, who had never hurt a fly? How had they turned him into a worm without an identity, a worm that had burrowed itself deep within the reeking innards of a rotten vegetable, certain that there was no better place on this earth?

Rabbi Schmidt wanted to shake Udi Dinar, grab him and forcibly return him to the world of reality. He looked so normal: Why was he so stubbornly clinging to the swamp in which someone had thrust him?

"Abba, you're completely healthy," Gili pleaded. "They've hypnotized you, planted a new identity in your brain. You're not Mickey Gadish, you're Udi Dinar. Come with us!"

Udi lay down in his bed and covered himself with the woolen blanket. "No! I'm Mickey Gadish. You've come here to confuse me."

Gili felt as if a mighty fist had hit him in the stomach. This was it, the efforts were wasted, the man was staying here. And time was short: The GSS was bound to get here soon.

Rav Yoske whispered feverishly to Rabbi Schmidt, "One step forward — two steps back! This is typical of men in his condition. Say something! We're losing precious time."

Rabbi Schmidt walked towards Udi, sat on the stained sheet and warmly patted Udi's frail hand. "Udi, I'm going to call you Moishike, like I used to do in yeshivah. Do you remember how we learned together? Do you remember the *sugya*, 'money taken in doubt'? How many *chiddushim* you made in *Perek Shnayim Ochzim*: You had full notebooks of them. Moishike, have you forgotten Moshe Shiffer and his cast-iron stomach? How he would finish off plates full of chickpeas on Friday nights? Who ate a bucket of sabras and got his intestines stuffed up?"

Yoske Friedman took over. "Moishike, do you remember Eli Leiker, the clown from Brooklyn? How he stuck his head out the back window in the yeshivah's old shed and screamed, 'Long live Nasser!'? How we laughed. And now he's the captain of a TWA airplane, can you imagine? Eli Leiker — a pilot! I still keep up with him; he visits my house sometimes. Do you remember how we donated things for Tzion Batat, the porter? And how the *mashgiach*, Rav Shmuel Bergman, *shlita*, got so angry?"

The name of his beloved *mashgiach* lit a small spark of interest in Udi's dull eyes. He sat up in bed and leaned his head weakly on the wall.

"Rabbi Bergman, Rav Shmuel the *tzaddik*," he murmured, his voice breaking.

Rav Yoske and Rabbi Schmidt wanted to jump for joy. Two sparks of life in five minutes. He was beginning to wake up!

And then Udi's head lolled. "No, I can't, they told me I'm insane," he repeated.

"Who told you?" Rav Yoske's patience was giving out.

"He did," Udi pointed towards the door. "That man."

Too late, the three of them turned around.

"What a lovely picture," Rav Avram Roosenthal said. He was wearing a multicolored shirt, his rabbinic garb discarded. In his hand he held a revolver.

Yoske Friedman and Chaim Ozer Schmidt stared, paralyzed. Rav Avram's cold, mocking voice pierced them like an icicle. "Important rabbis sneak into closed wards of psychiatric hospitals?"

Gili spoke calmly. "This is the first time I'm seeing you as you are. Without a uniform, not masquerading."

"Don't be impertinent, Gili," Rav Avram gave him one of his piercing stares. "I went to the third floor, Room 12, and found your real identity card, Shuki."

"I'll never be a really good GSS agent," Gili said serenely. Only the sharpest ear could catch the sarcastic note.

Rav Avram's eyes turned into a pair of flashing lanterns. "Gili, don't be smart. What are you looking for here?"

"Me?" Gili was invulnerable to his rabbi's hypnotic gaze. "I'm organizing a reunion."

"A reunion?" Rav Avram paled.

"Absolutely. And not just any reunion: This is a historic occasion. A foursome, all the former roommates of Yeshivas Ein Yisrael; everyone's here. Yoske Friedman, Chaim Ozer Schmidt, Moishike Dinburg and ... would you please meet and make welcome — Manny Schwartz!"

Time stood still. A person could have cut the tension with a knife.

Rav Avram was the first to recover. "What are you babbling about, Gili?"

Gili chuckled derisively. "What's that in your hand, a 'vessel of blessing'? Who ever heard of a rabbi, an honored and respected holy man, threatening innocent people with a drawn revolver?"

Rav Avram wasn't stymied; he'd expected the question and had prepared an explanation. But suddenly he felt that whatever he said would sound strange, with a drawn revolver hovering in the background. He tried to buy time.

"Why did you call me that name? What did you say? Manny, Manny...Weiss?"

"Incredible. You've even forgotten your name." Gili was completely in control of the situation: He would not let the reins fall from his hands. With a magician's speed he whisked a folded piece of paper out of his pocket. "This is a page from your diary, Abba, the diary of Moishike Dinburg, Ein Yisrael, *Shevat* 5723. You do permit me to use it, right?"

Udi looked at him indifferently, but deep in his pupils a small fire began to burn. Gili opened the yellowed piece of paper carefully and began to read:

"Sunday afternoon, 9 Shevat 5723 (February 3, 1963)

There was a flu outbreak in yeshivah, and half the students were in bed this week. In our room, too, everyone was sick. Yoske Friedman was burning with fever, Manny Schwartz said his throat was on fire, and I trembled with the chills all night under my thick blanket.

Now I feel better and am helping out Yoske and Manny. I brought hot tea to their beds and fixed up Manny's blanket. The two of them have gone to sleep and I've got time to write. My diary is my biggest secret: the last island of privacy that Manny hasn't taken from me. (Abba always says that I have a way with words.)

We exploded with laughter before, when Manny asked me for the peninsula.

'What?' I asked. 'What in the world do you mean?'

He was burning up and hardly heard me. 'Bring me the peninsula already,' he fumed.

'What? What do you want?' I asked again.

Suddenly he realized and began to laugh. 'I got mixed up: I meant the penicillin.'

'So say so,' I muttered, bringing him a small bottle of penicillin and two pain relievers.

Yoske Friedman started to kid around and said, 'When the doctor comes, tell him the medicine is on an island surrounded by water on three sides.'

I got into the spirit and said, 'How much geography do you have to learn in medical school?'

Yoske started to go wild; his fever really made him let loose. He stood up on his bed and said, in the voice of a radio announcer: 'For a cold, you need an island. For flu, a peninsula. And if you feel really bad — try two tablets of Australia!'

I almost fell down, I was laughing so hard, and I dropped the pain reliever. 'Enough,' Manny begged, 'I'm not allowed to laugh, it hurts my throat.'

And after our laughing fit the two of them fell asleep like babies... Sometimes I'm surprised that such a bright boy as Manny will make these little mistakes. Maybe he's got some disease that makes him mix up words. This was not the first time."

Udi's eyes began to clear a little. "I think I remember that."

"Oh, I can remember it as if it happened yesterday," Rav Yoske held his head in his hands.

"Bingo," Gili said. He spoke only to Rav Avram. "On the day after Benny Gabison's funeral you warned me not to forget Paysi's 'peninsula.' I didn't pay any attention; mild dyslexia is a common phenomenon and everyone gets mixed up sometimes. But when I begin to be suspicious of you and just then the Creator enlightens me and lets me find just this particular relevant passage in my father's diary, I start doing some reckoning. One plus one makes two, not three as you wanted me to believe. And that's why I'm here. Isn't that right, Manny Schwartz?"

Rav Avram stayed calm. He put his hand on Gili's forehead. "I think you've got fever; you're burning up."

Gili would not be swayed. "Manny, your time is up, the game is over. You took everything into consideration, planned every step carefully. But you missed two points: my father's diary, and the old rebbe of Kiltz. It's true, I'm no superman, and as a GSS agent I'm pretty much a washout: You led me by the nose most of the time. The rebbe of Kiltz is no superman either, but he's a *tzaddik* and a man of complete integrity and so he has the secret weapon, the one we call *siyata diShmaya*. The GSS does not have that *siyata diShmaya*, and that's why it looks the way it does. The rebbe of Kiltz passed you right by. You never dreamed we would exhume the bodies of Udi Dinar and Manny Schwartz."

Manny is made of steel, as he always was, Rabbi Chaim Ozer Schmidt thought. *His mighty hands aren't trembling, not moving even a millimeter.*

Rav Avram continued to point his revolver at Gili. "This is all foolishness, penicillin, peninsula... You're not much of a detective, Gili. I never heard of Manny Schwartz. You're coming with me now."

"No problem," Gili said. "I made a mistake: You're not Manny Schwartz. But can I tell you a quick story?"

He didn't wait for Rav Avram to agree. He began to speak.

"In Antwerp a boy grew up, a boy with deep, dark eyes. A bright boy, unusually gifted, a genius. The boy's name was Menachem Schwartz, and his friends all called him Manny. The nickname stuck.

"Manny Schwartz's parents lived near the court of a famed rebbe, Rebbe Itzikel Gewirtzman of Antwerp. Manny would often visit his *beis midrash* and was enraptured by Reb Itzikel's personality. More than anything, he was enchanted by the reverence the *chassidim* felt for their rebbe. He misunderstood this reverence, seeing it as the rebbe's absolute domination of his followers, who gave him blind obedience.

"Manny himself was blessed with an unusual gift for control, both of himself and others. The desire to rule was the dominant trait of his character. He decided to become a rebbe, the leader of *chassidim*. He wanted to rule over thousands of people, perhaps tens of thousands. He had one problem, though: His father was a simple man, not a rebbe.

"When Manny grew up he understood the truth: Rabbi Itzikel didn't rule men, he served his Creator with all his might, for the sake of Heaven. He prayed long and ardently, fasted, mortified his body, learned Torah day and night. That was why men looked up to him and were prepared to do all he asked.

"That part Manny didn't like. From childhood on he'd fantasized about becoming a rebbe, but he wished to dominate people without working too hard on serving G-d. After his *bar mitzvah* he hid his dream away. He understood that it was unrealistic to become a rebbe without either family connections or incredible effort. The ambition was hidden, but never abandoned. In the back recesses of his mind remnants of his fantasy remained, a glowing ember, a passion never fulfilled.

"When Manny came to study in Israel, in Yeshivas Ein Yisrael, he found greener pastures. He met several obedient students who were easy to dominate, among them Moishike Dinburg, a sensitive boy who found it hard to adjust to yeshivah, who had trouble coping with his homesickness and the long hours of study. With his senses as sharp as a predatory bird's, Manny cast his eyes on this easy target, attacking from the beginning. When they first met on *Rosh Chodesh Elul* 5718, Manny stole Moishike's trunk key from him, thus allowing the student from Antwerp to come to the little Yerushalmi's 'rescue.'

"Domination and rule were easy; Manny had captured Moishike completely. Manny became his guardian; Moishike, completely dependent on his protector. Moishike admired Manny, was ruled by him — but at the same time was deathly afraid of him. He kept just one private corner in his life, his diaries. Manny would have given his right hand to know just what he was writing in them.

"One day the boys in Ein Yisrael got mixed up in mischief, at Manny's instigation, and the *mashgiach* sent them home for a week. Manny spent the time in Moishike's house in Batei Ungarin."

Four pairs of eyes stared eagerly at Gili; even Rav Avram was silent. Gili felt like an entertainer on stage. He continued.

"In Moishike's house, a new, or rather old, channel opened to Manny. My grandfather, Rav Shmuel Dinburg, in the innocent naivete of that day, showed Manny the book *The Vessel of Blessing*, that he planned on bequeathing to his only son Moishe after his death. With his rare sense

Manny smelled the scent of power. He realized immediately that this was no mere book, this was a bomb, and if it should fall into his hands he could realize his longheld dream of becoming a great leader of Jews without much spiritual effort.

"With characteristic slyness Manny hid his desire for the book, but slowly, carefully, and with extraordinary cunning he devoted all of his many talents to the ultimate goal of obtaining the book, in a roundabout way, of course. From that day on his spiritual energies were focused with laserlike intensity on the book, only the book.

"I don't know all the details, but it's clear that Manny played a significant part in the spiritual downfall of Moishike Dinburg. He encouraged him to join the army as part of a well-thought-out plan. He knew that a secular Moishe Dinburg wouldn't have a ghost of an interest in some old book of mysticism and kabbalah, wisdom and charms.

"He was wrong. Moishike Dinburg did become a secular Jew in the army, turned into Udi Dinar, but he didn't become a fool. He knew that the book was worth a fortune.

"Manny kept a low profile, to all appearances lost any interest in the antique book, and carried on his business. He kept his relationship with Udi on a back burner and waited for his opportunity.

"At about the same time the heads of the GSS decided to find a way to weaken the *chareidi* community in the nation. Secular Israelis are terribly afraid of the burgeoning *chareidi* population. They feel threatened: From a tiny minority, the *chareidim* turned into a huge group that must be taken into account in every step and question. This group has opinions on every issue. It's almost impossible to put together a government without the *chareidim*. And this trend is growing stronger: The religious population grows from year to year, while the same demographic realities mean that the secular group grows smaller. The secular Israeli fears the day that the *chareidim* will become a majority in this land. The time will come when the prime minister will be some old, fanatic, bearded rabbi. It's the nightmare of the secular world: The Council of Torah Sages will give orders to the Knesset!

"The heads of the GSS faced a dilemma. How do they keep the *chareidim* in check? They couldn't shoot them or send them off to exile!

"And then came Meshulam Yaakovi, head of the Psychological Warfare Division, with the incredible suggestion: Place a spy, a 'mole,' deep within the *chareidi* world: a rebbe with *chassidim* from all walks of life, one who will magically entrance thousands of the more credulous. He will use his position to find out secret after secret: family secrets, communal secrets, and he will hold the information until one important day, a day when the Pandora's box will be opened and a civil war will be sown within the *chareidi* community in Israel.

"And here's where the interests of the GSS and Manny Schwartz coincided. Meshulam had heard about Manny from his father, antiques dealer Pinny Yaakovi. He knew that Manny Schwartz, an authentic megalomaniac, wouldn't hesitate to take any step, and would agree to cooperate fully. The rest was simple. Manny was burned up on the Carmel and, donning a new identity, traveled abroad. He underwent plastic surgery there to change his look: his hawklike nose now turned up. He got a new name, too: Rabbi Avram Roosenthal. With the help of *The Vessel of Blessing* he turned into a beloved rebbe; later, he drafted naive Gili Dinar into becoming an agent for the GSS, without this top spy even knowing about it. Brilliant, no?"

Gili grinned at Rabbi Avram. "Shall I continue? Or is this enough? You are the 'Puppeteer Rabbi'! You've got the entire *chareidi* community on a string, dancing to your enchanted pipes, dancing right into the grave! You'll move them right into incredible hostilities, controversies that will destroy all the good there. You will sow an unparalleled hatred between brothers!

"Or do you have another explanation for the presence of the book *The Vessel of Blessing*, stolen from my father, in your safe? What is the purpose of the news clippings and the high-tech tape equipment with its three microphones?"

Gili still kept himself under cold control. "At the time I was shocked that you didn't let me go to America to join *The New York Times*. Hadn't you encouraged me to return to journalism? But then I understood that I had myself destroyed that chance, the moment I mentioned the yeshivah at which you had studied. You trembled with fear then, terrified that I would unmask you, and that's why you objected. Rabbi Avram Roosenthal from America is a myth; there never was any such person. You never set foot in the United States. You're a Belgian, and you were afraid that if I went there you would be found out."

Suddenly his face turned a bright red. He hissed in controlled fury, never raising his voice. "You betrayed me. Your apartment was my second home, and you led me astray, you scoundrel! You buried my father alive for six years in an insane asylum, stole his identity from him, hypnotized him and erased his true self. What did you say to me once? 'I can change any sane man to a raving madman.' You turned my father into a lunatic named Mickey Gadish; you poisoned him for six years with your terrible medicines."

His face contorted with unshed tears; only with difficulty did he control his urge to lunge at Rav Avram with his balled fists. "For six years my mother is crying; go and tell her she's not a widow. That her husband is alive but it's not him, it's Mickey Gadish, a robot. And me, you led me around like a sheep. Why? Is nothing too terrible for you? Where have your desires led you?"

Rav Avram's voice remained faithful to him. "Quiet! You can't prove one word of all this infantile prattle. Enough, I'm sick of you. Come with me now!"

Gili paled. This man was made out of reinforced steel. How had he not buckled under yet?

The barrel of the revolver was turned onto the two rabbis, particularly on Rabbi Schmidt, who stood just a step away from him. "You're not moving. One move, and I shoot."

"A rebbe shooting?" Gili murmured. "Rabbi Avram, you're going to get yourself into the Guinness Book of World Records."

Rabbi Schmidt gripped his chest, a look of extreme pain on his face. "Water, water! I don't feel well."

He swayed as one about to faint. As he went down heavily, he grabbed onto Rav Avram's shirt to steady himself.

There was the sound of cloth tearing; Rabbi Avram's forearm appeared beneath the ripped shirt. Even in the dim lighting of the cellar one could see a strange mark on it, a red-brown mark in the shape of an asymmetrical star.

Rabbi Avram jumped away as if bitten by a snake, his face white. He tried to cover his arm, but the brown mark stubbornly refused to disappear.

Rabbi Yoske Friedman had been frozen until this moment. Fear had paralyzed him: Never before had he faced a drawn gun. Now he woke up and rubbed his eyes. "Chaim Ozer, you were right. It's Manny, without a doubt. No one else could have the exact same birthmark."

"Only Manny. I recognized him right away, from his eyes," Rabbi Schmidt said, from his perch on the floor. "But I wanted to be sure. You remember what Manny said one day to the *rosh yeshivah*, Rabbi Aharon Rapaport, during class. 'My wife will never be an *agunah*. I've got an identifying mark.' Everyone laughed; we all knew that Manny had this star-shaped birthmark on his arm. And that's why you wouldn't meet with me that night, when Gili brought me to you; you were afraid I might recognize you. Right, Manny?"

Rav Yoske joined in. "My dear Rabbi Avram Roosenthal," he said mockingly, "if you wanted to change identities, you should have cut off your arm, not just your Jewish nose."

Rabbi Avram was beginning to lose his incredible confidence. The gun trembled in his hand. The flashing lightning in his eyes lost its glow.

Rabbi Yoske continued. "Menachem, the moment of truth is here! You must decide where you belong, in Ein Yisrael with Rabbi Aharon Rapaport and Rabbi Shmuel Bergman, or in the grave with Meshulam Yaakovi and his evil friends."

His voice softened. "Manny, you're not a child, you're a man 53 years old, if I'm not mistaken. In another few years you'll grow old; you'll die. What will you tell the Creator on that Day of Judgment, what will you say when He will ask you, 'Why did you join in destroying Torah and *mitzvos*, why did you help smash religious Jewry in *Eretz Yisrael*, why did you sow discord and controversy, poison and destruction, hatred and bloodshed?' What will you tell Him? 'I sold my soul for the desire for honor'? What will you tell the King of kings? 'I was playing a game, I wanted to be a rebbe of *chassidim*.'"

Rabbi Avram's face changed color. He stood for a few seconds, frozen and motionless.

Rabbi Chaim Ozer Schmidt saw the scarlet change to snow-white and then gray. Now is the time, he thought. We've got to touch his emotions.

"Manny, how could you, how? You wanted to be a rebbe. Okay, you succeeded. Do you know what? 'From doing without intention one comes to intention.' You've done thousands of good deeds, you've helped people: the brokenhearted, the unfortunate. You've collected millions of *zechuyos*, merits. And what next? You'll stab the people who believed in you completely in the back?"

Rav Yoske unconsciously stroked his beard. He spoke again, forcefully, with great strength. "Menachem, the gates of repentance are not locked. If you decide to do *teshuvah*, perhaps you can still right the wrongs. But if you don't... You can threaten me with that gun if you want. I was afraid of it before, but not any more. I'm not afraid."

He pointed to his chest. "Shoot me now, if you want," he said with open emotion. "I'm not afraid. I'm coming before my Creator with clean hands. But you, Manny? You'll go to *gehinnom* alive!"

Rabbi Schmidt stood up from the floor, dusted off his clothing. "I've never agreed with something quite so much," he said quietly. "I second every word of Rav Yoske's."

Gili made his contribution. "You killed my father spiritually long ago. Our Sages have said it is worse to make someone sin than to kill him. Then you destroyed his personality. Now go and kill his body, him and me together."

Rabbi Avram looked much less confident and proud. His eyes were lowered. "Good. Let's sit and talk. I have something to say to all of you, particularly Gili."

44

Meshulam Yaakovi's Mazda was parked about 20 yards from the Goldman Psychiatric Center. He waited impatiently, glancing at his watch every two minutes.

It was already 3 a.m. How much time would it take Rabbi Avram to take care of things inside?

A few times he hesitated and almost walked into the hospital, but he immediately squelched the temptation to see what was happening with his own eyes. "No, you won't go in," he whispered to himself. "You've remained in the shadows until now, pulling all the strings behind the curtain. You can't reveal yourself now!"

He sat alone in the car, staring at the little stuffed wolf swinging back and forth on a string. Meshulam loved wolves; when he was a youngster in kindergarten his teacher was horrified to learn that little Meshulam identified not with Little Red Riding Hood, but with the wolf who wanted to eat her. His eyes would light up when the wolf ate Grandma... *Something in this boy's head is completely warped,* she thought worriedly. She had planned on reporting it to the boy's parents, but when she saw the father, the gigantic, scarlet-faced Pinny Yaakovi, she backed down, and instead praised the boy's unusual talents, which gave him the nickname "the little genius."

Meshulam himself shared many of the traits of the lone wolf. He wanted only to work alone, to take the responsibility by himself. If he succeeded, all the praise belonged to him and him alone. If he failed, only a few would know of it or, conversely, the entire GSS would be accused.

S, head of the GSS, had been anxious these past few days. "Meshulam, zero hour is approaching," he told him time and again. "If we wait longer we'll miss the boat. When are you putting 'The Puppeteer Rabbi' into motion? The agents are waiting instructions."

Meshulam wasn't pleased by S's impatience. He dreamed of the moment his boss would read in the morning headlines, "Civil war among *chareidim*! Bloodshed in Bnei Brak! Riots in Jerusalem yeshivos!"

He wanted to surprise him. He hoped that his incredible plan wasn't being endangered in these few moments, in the Goldman building.

❧❦

"You're not much good as an analyst," Rabbi Avram told Gili. "I thought you'd manage to find out more."

They sat around the small table in Udi's musty room, two stories beneath the ground. A small vase set on a pink embroidered tablecloth was the sole decoration in the dreary room. Rabbi Avram felt at home here, pulling over a few chairs he obtained from other rooms with the help of Gili's key ring, and seated them all around the table. Only Udi chose to stay in bed, his gaze still vacant.

"What did you want to say?" Gili asked in hostile tones.

Rav Avram put the gun back in its holster, closed it with a quiet click, and leaned back in his old wooden chair.

"Your story is good, but it's full of holes," he said in a neutral, unemotional voice. "You're missing some vital details."

"That's what's bothering you?" Gili interrupted, his hostility apparent. "I know a lot more, but I'll give you the honor of revealing yourself and your motives."

Rav Yoske took a cup off Udi's tray, filled it with water and gave it to Gili. "Have a drink," he said gently. "Let your anger cool off a little."

Rav Avram was silent. He lowered his eyes, deep in thought. After a minute he shook his head. "Okay, you're right. I am Manny Schwartz. I created a perfect image of Rabbi Avram Roosenthal; there wasn't a hole in the net. My plastic surgery changed my looks completely; still, I worried about every detail. Even these." He pulled three small black and white pictures out of his wallet. They were faded, and their edges were serrated, like stamps. Pictures of life long ago... "Do you see? Me and Moishike on the long balcony of Batei Ungarin, near the doorway of his home, summer 5722. Moishike and me in the orchards of Ein Yisrael. Moishike and me in the dining room, singing, during the dedication ceremonies for the new building, donated by the philanthropist Sir Isaac Wolfson. The Wolfson family gave a lot to Ein Yisrael. It was the second son, Shmuel Wolfson, who gave them their dormitory."

"To replace the hut that burned down on Yom Kippur in 5719, right after Kol Nidrei," Rav Yoske said thoughtfully. "Do you remember?"

The paradox was astonishing: enemies bound together for a moment by their mutual memories, staring at old pictures of two young yeshivah boys sitting, friends leaning on each other, shoulder to shoulder. Both cheerful, full of the joy of life. Pictures that made one nostalgic; photos you could look at for hour upon hour.

Gili stared alternately at the pictures and at Rabbi Avram. The face had changed completely, unrecognizably. With difficulty, he saw the resemblance in the eyes, those piercing and wise eyes.

"I was even afraid of these pictures; I made sure they didn't stay in Udi's album," Rabbi Avram gave a small smile.

"Yes, those were the days. My story really starts in Antwerp, in the court of Rabbi Itzikel of Pshevorsk. We were neighbors, once he came to Antwerp from Paris.

"You never merited meeting Rav Itzikel. I merited it. He was a giant, a *tzaddik*, humble. I'll never forget the young Israeli boy who came to the rebbe's court with his widowed mother. His name was Shlomo, Shlomo Manheim. Because of his mother's difficult situation he had to go to work polishing diamonds for a Jewish diamond dealer.

"After a month the boy brought home his first paycheck, a large sum that he'd earned with his own hands. He proudly showed the money to the rebbe.

" 'How much does your mother need for the month?' the rebbe asked.

"It turned out that his paycheck was about double her expenses.

" 'Listen,' said the rebbe, 'an orphaned bride was just here. Can you contribute something for *hachnasas kallah?*'

" 'Gladly,' said Shlomo. At great personal sacrifice, he gave half of his salary without raising an eyebrow.

"A day passed, two days. The boy was a regular frequenter at Reb Itzikel's, just as I was. He waited for a compliment, an acknowledgment. He had, after all, done a truly noble deed. But the rebbe saw him and didn't say one word.

"On the third day, Shlomo's patience ran out. He approached the rebbe and tried to find a roundabout way to mention the money. At first Reb Itzikel didn't remember a thing about it; then it came to him. He looked at the Israeli boy in disappointment and said, 'What? You're still thinking about it? I thought you'd forgotten. If you still remember that you gave money to charity, you have nothing to gain from me here. Go find yourself a different rebbe!'

"Do you understand?" Manny said. "That was our vision, a giant of a man who reached heaven."

"And you're certainly a wonderful student," Gili could not resist the dig.

Manny said quietly, "I understand, Gili, that you're angry with me."

"Me, angry?" Gili said with overdone innocence. "I'm absolutely thrilled. Just look at your handiwork lying on the bed. You turned my father into the living dead."

Manny shook his head. "Soon you'll understand everything. And what happened to your father is not irreversible."

"Six years in an insane asylum is irreversible?" his anger poured out.

"Calm down, Gili," Rabbi Schmidt begged him. "We've got to talk with Manny, to hear exactly what's happened. Go on, Manny."

"Gili was right in his analysis of my personality," Manny continued. "I'm ambitious. I have the power to rule and a deep desire to dominate. It's in my blood, just as anger is in yours, Gili. I confess it freely: I did some terrible things in order to realize my great ambition to become a rebbe. In Yeshivas Ein Yisrael I took several boys of weak character and practiced domination on them. I rode Moishike Dinburg the hardest; he hadn't a clue as to how to shake me off."

He spoke in a mild tone that again set Gili's blood boiling. Rav Yoske felt his fury and gently motioned him to keep quiet. Manny continued:

"I set my eyes on *The Vessel of Blessing* and from the minute I saw it I plotted how to get it out of Moishike's hands. I pretended that the author was an ancestor of mine.

"Moishike was a good boy, but weak in character. Schmidt and Friedman undoubtedly remember how the *mashgiach*, Rav Shmuel Bergman, would tell him he was 'missing a spiritual backbone.' That was what he told a boy whose fear of Heaven was not an integral part of his being.

"I knew that it wouldn't be hard to take Moishike off the right path, to make him secular so that he wouldn't have any interest in the book. At a certain point I began to persuade him. I would tell him, 'Look, neither of us will ever be the great men of the generation. All the positions in the yeshivah world are already taken, so why shouldn't we go and learn a trade so that we can earn some money?'

At first, Moishike was shocked. "A trade? Leave yeshivah? They'll draft us into the army immediately!"

" 'That's right,' I told him. 'First we'll go to the army, have some fun, enjoy ourselves.' I put the thought in his head, slowly, slowly. I also began doing failed experiments with *The Vessel of Blessing*."

Gili's wandering glance fell upon his father, Udi, who quickly pulled his eyes away. Udi was listening to Manny's story!

"I convinced Moishike to bring the book to yeshivah, and proved to him that it was all nonsense, that none of the charms worked. Innocent Moishike didn't understand a thing; I changed the order as it appeared in the book, and that's why they were useless."

Rabbi Yoske asked curiously, "And when you experimented with the book by yourself, without Moishike, were you able to perform miracles? Did angels come?"

Manny gave him a meaningful glance but did not answer.

"Moishike used me as a personal example. And that's how the two of us wound up one sunny day in the military camp at Tzrifin, enlisting in the army. In the middle of my tour of duty I threw the *kippah* off my head. When Moishike saw that I, Manny the *tzaddik*, had left religious observance, he didn't hesitate a moment, and he followed in my footsteps. Not because he wasn't religious, but because his role model, Manny Schwartz, had done so.

"There was a small difference between us, though. For me it was a game. I actually continued to be religious, putting on my *tefillin* and doing other *mitzvos* secretly. Truthfully, I found myself in a deadlock: I wouldn't marry a nonobservant woman, and what religious woman would agree to marry a Marrano like me? In any case, as the folk saying goes, only two know a person as he really is — G-d and his wife. I didn't want anyone to know of my double life; that was the second reason I decided to forgo a normal home and family."

"So the end justifies the means," Rabbi Schmidt said in amazement. "To give up a family to become a shady rebbe?"

"You should have asked me that 30 years ago," Manny said sadly. "That's all in the past now."

He continued, eagerly removing a stone that had weighed down his heart for three decades. "Moishike didn't have my problem. He changed drastically, became a completely secular Jew in almost an instant. He changed his old name to a new and modern one, Udi Dinar.

"After his marriage I visited his home often. When you were a year old, Gili, I would sing you lullabies until you fell asleep in my arms. But then your mother forbade my visits."

"A wise woman," Gili interrupted.

"That's true," Manny agreed unexpectedly. "You'll be glad to know that she called me a charlatan and a scoundrel, and complained that I was overpowering her husband. Our relations were all but severed. But I'm still smarter than she is. After a few years I began to visit again, this time in the Tzalmon Studios, behind her back. In the meantime I had become an open *baal teshuvah*, wearing a big black yarmulke. I also became an antiques dealer, and that's how I met a much greater merchant than I, who helped me a lot in the business, though I wasn't anywhere near his caliber: Pinny Yaakovi.

"At that time Udi Dinar was facing a severe cash-flow problem. He wanted to develop his studio into a network. Forgive me, Gili, but Monica, too, had big eyes: She wanted to be among the aristocrats, part of Israeli 'high society.' Udi had made a fortune, but it wasn't enough for her. She wanted more and more and more. He used to complain to me. 'Monica is a paper shredder,' he used to say. 'She shreds dollars.'

" 'So what will you do?' I asked him.

" 'I'll sell *The Vessel of Blessing*,' he answered.

" 'Are you crazy? To sell a treasure like that? That's a desecration!' I told him, with feigned shock. Actually, I wanted to jump with joy.

" 'I have no choice, I need a lot of money,' Udi said.

"On the way home I almost got into an accident, I was so preoccupied. My dream was going to come true. That very day I went to Yaakovi and suggested he buy the book. Yaakovi agreed. In his crooked mind he was already planning how to sell forgeries of the work. He was prepared to resell it to me by lending me $100,000 at a high rate of interest, to be paid in four payments.

"It was tough, but I figured that after I had become a rebbe money would flow like water and I would be able to repay the debt.

"The plan began to take form. We intimated that Sotheby's was interested. We phoned your father, pretending to be Dr. Ralph Stern, then manager of Sotheby's in Israel. 'I heard from a friend that you're interested in selling the rare book *The Vessel of Blessing*. How much do you want for it?'

"I was shocked by the astronomical price Udi was asking: $650,000!

" 'I'm sorry, but Sotheby's doesn't estimate its value at more than $100,000,' I told Udi.

" 'But it's the only one of its kind in the whole world, and I'm very attached to it,' Udi said excitedly.

" 'Why are you selling it?' I asked with pretended, polite wonder, as would befit a man such as Dr. Stern.

" 'I need a lot of money. One hundred thousand is not a price for me.'

"I had to keep up the pretense. 'Wait a day or two and I'll check it with our branch in Holland. I may have a wealthy purchaser in England who would be interested in giving you a quarter of a million pounds sterling.'

"I then went to Yaakovi, my face downcast. 'I need more money,' I said.

" 'Impossible,' Pinny declared. 'As an antique it's not worth more than a $100,000. Forget your dream: You'll never be a rebbe.'

"I was crushed; my lifelong dream was fading away. But that very night I saw Providence intervene for me.

"At 2 a.m. the phone rang. Pinny Yaakovi screamed into the receiver, 'Manny, you're going to be a rebbe after all!'

"I was confused. 'What are you talking about?'

" 'With all honor to the great rebbe, Reb Manny,' Pinny yelled, 'you're going to be what you wanted to be: a rebbe, a miracle worker, a magician!'

" 'How?'

" 'My son Meshulam will tell you all about it.'

"At 3 a.m. I drove over to meet with Meshulam. It turned out that that very week there had been a meeting in the GSS, an emergency consultation and request for plans regarding the future of the *chareidi* world in Israel. No one had any serious ideas. The *chareidim* are a homogeneous, tightly knit group, and if you weren't born one of them you were immediately cast out. Only *baalei teshuvah* could make a mistake now and then and not be noticed; the tiniest slip-up on the part of any of the GSS spies gave them away. All the undercover agents had been discovered almost immediately."

"And that's when you became a rav?" Rabbi Yoske asked.

"Patience. Not so fast," Manny smiled.

☙✺❧

"On the day that Pinny had told Meshulam about *The Vessel of Blessing*, they had come up with the plan.

"Meshulam first shrugged the idea off. 'How can some book written 500 years ago help me?' he asked his father.

"Suddenly, at 1 a.m., the whole thing became clear to him.

"Manny Schwartz would disappear, take on a new name, undergo plastic surgery, and build himself a new identity as a great rebbe, a wise man who gave advice, blessings, good-luck charms. He would solve people's problems and connect with the masses.

" 'Ingenious!' Meshulam jumped out of his bed like a cricket. He could see it now: Manny Schwartz, the popular rebbe, collecting secret information from the *chareidim*. At the same time, the GSS would be able to sow more agents in that world, in the guise of *baalei teshuvah* recommended by that famous rav, each also collecting his data.

"And on the specified day, the GSS would let go the safety catch. The agents would get the order. All the classified information, all the secrets would be out. There would be shocking revelations, and some disinformation — slander, libel, that would hit all the people, all the levels, from the greatest rebbes and *roshei yeshivah,* to the politicians, businessmen, and, finally, to the prime target: the *chareidi* family structure itself."

"Are you sure of what you're saying?" Rav Chaim Ozer Schmidt's face was white as snow. "How could they penetrate the family circle?"

"Oh, it's easy!" Manny gave a derisive chuckle. "Do you have any idea how many families I could destroy right now, if I would just reveal 5 percent of what I know?"

"I've known about the plan for quite some time now," Rav Yoske said quietly.

"I know that you knew," Manny said. "Was it for nothing that they put listening devices all over your apartment? The GSS has marked 'K' — that is, Kalman Weiss, your brother-in-law, your wife's brother — as having given you classified information."

Rav Yoske's face didn't move a muscle, but his trembling fingers showed his fear. "Why didn't they assassinate him, as they did Eric Meisels?"

"Because they can't replace him; he's the best head of the Arab Section that they've had in years!" Manny answered. "But they're careful of him; he's always under surveillance. And you too."

" I know that," Rav Yoske said.

Manny smiled. "The GSS knows that you know; you've been using way too much water.

"In any case, Meshulam's plan was perfect. How did he put it? 'I've been after those *chareidim* for quite some time now. Though they're united against us, among themselves there is also conflict, controversy, discord. We've just got to help them out a little, take existing disagreements and enlarge them, sow disunity among the divisive. The rest of the work they'll do for us — one will kill the other.'

"That very night we perfected the plan.

"Udi had told me that day about a wedding in Kiryat Motzkin, a high-society affair that would include the Who's Who of Israeli life. I hardly knew the groom's family, but decided that I would attend. Half an hour before leaving I phoned Udi, pretending once again to be Dr. Stern of Sotheby's. I told him that the London connection was making progress and it was possible that in the next day or two he would have a buyer at Udi's price. We chatted about this and that for a few minutes. Udi began to seem politely impatient, but I didn't take the hint. Finally, I heard Monica yelling in the background, 'Tell him that we're in a rush.'

" 'I'm sorry,' Udi said apologetically, 'but I've got to cut this short. We're getting ready to leave to a wedding.'

" 'Where is it?' I asked nonchalantly.

" 'In Kiryat Motzkin, near Haifa.'

" 'That's funny,' I said, with restrained excitement. Dr. Stern was always a cool one. 'I'll be in Kiryat Motzkin tonight too. Maybe you could bring the book with you; I'll hop over to the wedding to see it.'

" 'Okay,' Udi answered coldly. That's why I wasn't certain until the last minute if he'd brought the book with him or not. I updated Meshulam, and we decided to go on with the plan.

⊙✤⊙

"The plan had six stages: 1. Bribery of Efraim, Udi's usual driver, so that I would take the wheel. By noontime he had been neutralized. 2. Emptying of the Mercedes gas tank. 3. Drugging the family at the wedding, with haze-inducing drugs. 4. Extinguishing the lights on the Carmel. 5. Landing a helicopter in the Carmel forests. 6. Getting possession of the book.

"It was to be a simple, easy operation.

"At the wedding I waited for the proper moment. When I saw Udi holding a large olive between his teeth, I shared a good joke. Udi laughed and the pit got stuck in his throat. I waited for him to choke, then I came like some guardian angel, performed the Heimlich maneuver, and he spit out the pit.

"While he was still flustered I gave him some liquor that was spiked with the drug Ecstasy."

"There was no limit to your degradation?" Rav Yoske fumed. "No limit?"

"Just a small amount," Manny said apologetically. "We had to drug the whole family properly."

"What is this drug Ecstasy?" asked Rabbi Schmidt.

"It's good that you don't know," Manny said. "Ecstasy is a hallucinogen and amphetamine in one. It takes about 20 minutes to take effect. Its chemical name is MDMA. It's synthesized in illegal labs, which makes it even more dangerous: not only does it cause hallucinations, but there is no supervision of its production or on the materials put into it. It's produced by chemically combining a number of materials. By a small mistake in the procedure, one can manufacture something entirely different, which can have much worse side effects, and it can occasionally even cause loss of consciousness or death. It's no wonder that Ecstasy was declared illegal back in 1985, and was named a high-risk drug."

"You're some organization, the GSS," Gili interrupted.

"I was talking about pirate Ecstasy," Manny hurriedly tried to correct the impression he'd made. "The GSS use only pure materials synthesized in a certified laboratory. In your case the worst that would happen was some weakness and hallucination."

"I'm thrilled to hear it," Gili said dryly. "When you die of this stuff you die with a smile on your face, with proper drugs and not some pirate mixture, Heaven forbid..."

Manny accepted the insult.

"We continued as planned. After Udi, I offered the drugged drinks to Monica and Gili. And then we went on our way.

"I was the driver. You were all drugged, and I acted as though I were drugged too. I got lost and somehow wound up climbing the Carmel. Then I began to speed down like a madman, knowing that they would make me stop.

"Monica acted as I expected; she demanded that Gili take over. I left the car, let Gili move from the back to the driver's seat, helped Udi change places with Monica. Then you left, by yourselves — I was no longer with you."

"What?" Gili yelled. "I don't believe this! You weren't with us in the car?"

"That's right," Manny laughed. "That's the power of the drug: complete confusion of fantasy and reality. You were sure I was in the Mercedes, while all the time I was outside."

"You planned on killing us," Gili approached Manny threateningly. "You let me drive under the influence of a drug that causes severe coordination problems, public enemy number 1 when it comes to driving. What was that, if not a prescription for murder?"

Manny grabbed his chest. "No! My plan was exact. The gas tank was almost completely emptied, so you couldn't drive far, just until the Carmel forests. When I left the car there was hardly a drop of gas inside it. I figured you'd manage to get 500 feet further down, and come to a stop near the forests, close to a clearing where a helicopter was to land."

"Abba said he heard a helicopter over us," Gili shuddered. "But how could he have heard it, when he, too, was drugged?"

"I told you, the drug is both hallucinogenic and an 'upper' as well. It made your father even more alert than usual; he was the only one who realized how dangerous my driving was, and the only one to hear the chopper."

All turned to stare at Udi, lying on the bed, gazing vacantly at them. "He was the most alert," Rav Yoske said sadly, "but if I'm any judge, he's lost now."

Manny seemed indifferent to Rav Yoske's sorrow. "Time is passing. Another few minutes and I'm through. The helicopter contained a few masked men who were supposed to take over the car by the threat of gunfire, tie up all the passengers, and steal the book. They were to take all the money in the car too, as camouflage.

"The plan called for me to arrive during the operation, take my place with you again, and be left tied up together with you. It should have been a sterling procedure.

"What I didn't know then was how low Meshulam could sink. He tricked me. When his men were emptying the gas tank they partially damaged the brakes as well, figuring that during the trip they would fail completely. I think that that's what happened after I left the car."

"Of course that's what happened. The car was racing and on the sharp curve it swerved to the left," Gili remembered. "I couldn't understand what was going on. I kept hitting the brakes, but nothing happened."

"It seems that Meshulam did want you dead," Manny explained calmly, "to send the car into the ravine. I didn't understand why he changed the plan at the last minute. He had called me right before I left to the wedding and warned me not to travel with you in the car, as we'd planned. I agreed with him, but I liked the original plan, and after the wedding I decided to drive in your Mercedes. I might have been killed with you, and his entire plan would have been for nothing.

"Meshulam was a true genius. He had three alternative plans: 1. If the car would run out of gas and stop, they would get out of the helicopter. It would be a classic theft, without a hitch. 2. If the car went down the ravine, his men would have to get the book from the car and call the police to get out the bodies. 3. If the car went down and not everyone was killed, there would be a stage-managed fire.

"And this is what happened..."

45

A deep blackness hung over Mt. Carmel that night. At 1 a.m. two of Meshulam's men reached the electric company's main generator on the mountain's summit. They were wearing proper work clothes and showed the security guard in charge urgent instructions from the regional manager of the company in Haifa to immediately cut off the electricity because of a main cable that had fallen onto the highway. One minute later the mountain was bathed in darkness.

The Mercedes sped through the night. It reached a sharp curve, swerved off the road and rolled noisily onto the mountainside. The horrible sound of rending metal could be heard, but actually not much happened to it. It turned over and rolled into some small tree roots and six yards later bumped to a halt in a mound of dirt.

Gili and Monica, both strapped in seat belts, flew out of the car, together with their seats. They hit the earth and lost consciousness from the strength of the blow. Udi remained trapped in the car, also unconscious.

Manny Schwartz reached the spot in another automobile in two minutes. To his horror he saw two other drivers who had stopped to see what had happened.

He asked them for their identification and quickly sent them off. Police cars then blocked the road in both directions, two kilometers away. Anyone who managed to pass the roadblocks could not see anything, because of the thick darkness.

Minutes later an unmarked helicopter arrived, illuminating the hillside with its powerful beams of light. Meshulam and his men sat inside the chopper. When it had landed in a nearby clearing the men jumped out and raced towards the overturned car. Meshulam himself stayed in the helicopter, giving his orders via walkie-talkie. With trembling hands Manny pulled the book out of the glove compartment, stroking the soft binding lovingly.

The agents examined Udi. "He's lightly wounded; soon he'll regain consciousness," one hard-faced man said.

"Leave him in the car. We'll be making a bonfire here soon," said another grim man, the commander of the operation to all appearances.

"What are you talking about?" Manny asked, horrified, putting the book into a briefcase.

"Him," one of the agents pointed mockingly at the unconscious man. "Meshulam told us to make roast marshmallows out of him."

"Absolutely not," Manny hissed. "Get me Meshulam."

He grabbed the walkie-talkie in his hand. "Meshulam, you ordered them to burn Udi up?"

"Why?" Meshulam asked innocently.

"Because I'm giving the whole story to the papers tomorrow. I won't have anything to do with the murder of a friend, an innocent man."

"Quiet!" Meshulam shouted into the instrument. "I give the orders, not you. What do you need your friend for anyway, you religious hypocrite? He's only going to give you away. Whatever you call yourself, he'll destroy everything. Burn him up. You're still sentimental about yeshivah?"

For a minute Manny was baffled; the scenario had occurred to him too. Meshulam urged him on. "Manny, Udi will identify you under eight *shtriemels* and 20 kilo of silk coats!"

"That's true, but to kill a friend? I have an alternative."

Meshulam thought for a minute. "What is it?"

"I have the ability to make men mad," Manny said. "I can make him lose his sanity, and have him institutionalized in an asylum."

"And the family?" Meshulam asked.

"Forget them. They were drugged and are now unconscious. The boy looks badly hurt; it's not clear if he'll live or not. They'll never search for the truth."

"You know what?" Meshulam said enthusiastically, "You've got it! And I've got an idea." He was silent for a moment's thought, then he spoke in short, staccato bursts. "In 15 minutes I'll arrange to have two ancient skeletons brought there by chopper."

"Are you crazy?" Manny asked.

"Me? No. You just don't understand a thing." Meshulam explained himself with characteristic brutality. "You and Udi are about to be burned to death."

"What?"

"Quiet! Stop bothering me with your 'what, what?'"

Manny listened to Meshulam's plan in silence. "I can get two fresh bodies from a hospital, but that'll take a few hours. But getting ancient skeletons is no problem. A friend of mine in Haifa works in the Archaeological Authority and he has cases full of old bones. We'll burn up the car, tell the papers tomorrow that Manny Schwartz and Udi Dinar were burned alive, and we'll kill two birds with one stone. You can wear a new identity without anyone bothering you, and Udi will disappear into the asylum forever. And if anyone ever comes digging around the graves they won't find anything: Old bones disintegrate quickly."

☙❧

"The car was doused liberally with gasoline and then burned," Manny replayed the night's scene. "Gili and his mother were taken to the hospital. Udi was the least seriously hurt. I kept him in my house for two days, worked hard on him. I succeeded in convincing him that Monica and Gili had been burned alive. He went wild, wanting to go to the funerals. I told him he'd been unconscious for three days and the funerals had already taken place.

"I took away his reason slowly, placing him in a deep depression. Finally I brought him here to Goldman, and told them he was a schizophrenic by the name of Mickey Gadish.

"When the nurse called him Mickey, he screamed, 'My name is Udi Dinar.'

" 'You see?' I whispered to the nurse, 'That's how it starts. Ask him who Moishike Dinburg is.'

"The nurse asked. Udi fell into the trap like a baby rabbit. 'That's right, I had another name: They used to call me Moishike Dinburg.'

"'Do you see?' I again whispered to the nurse. 'This is an interesting case of multiple personalities involving three identities, not two. You can do some research on him. He also has a mania; he can get very happy, and do a wild tango on the roof when the moon is full. He might fall off the roof and die. Since he did that he's been receiving Elidal pills regularly, to control the mania.'"

"If I don't stand up right now and break every bone in your body it's not because I'm a *tzaddik*, but because of the honor of Rabbis Friedman and Schmidt," Gili growled like a wounded animal, his balled fists in Manny's face. "You're a degenerate without a conscience. You caused him to be so depressed, you killed him. Why? What did he do to you? How could you shut him into a cellar with the most severe cases?"

"That's Dr. Seiden," Manny answered. "He'd sell his twin brother for $5,000."

"You bribed him. And what next?" Gili asked furiously. "What did you do once you laid your hands on the book?"

Manny flinched somewhat; Gili was growing more and more heated with each passing minute. "Gili, I'm not your enemy. Your real enemy is outside."

"What does that mean?" Rav Yoske jumped up like one bitten by a snake.

Manny nodded his head. "I can see through walls, remember? At this very moment Meshulam Yaakovi is sitting in his car, a short distance from this building. He's waiting for the minute that we leave."

❦

"It's a ruse!" Gili declared. "Don't believe him. I already know his style. Rabbi Avram Roosenthal sees through walls, Rabbi Avram Roosenthal can read minds..."

Manny wouldn't give up. "That's just a figure of speech. I know how people work. I know Choni, my little tattletale, and I know the thought processes of Meshulam Yaakovi. Put the two facts together and what do you get? Meshulam sitting outside of Goldman, waiting for us to go out."

"Does he have the GSS men with him?" Rabbi Schmidt asked fearfully.

"Not now," he said with clear confidence. "But later, when we go out — he'll call his men to go after us."

"I don't care about Meshulam," Gili said indifferently. "Let him wait a little longer. I'm at the point where you stopped. Abba is in the asylum, Monica and Gili are slowly recovering. What next?"

Manny took a deep breath. "You are obviously taping my every word on your small tape recorder, and that's why you're referring to yourself in the third person. Gili, as always, you're completely transparent. You're looking for evidence to be given in court? We'll never get to that."

Gili pulled the tape recorder out from under the table and put it on top. "Cards on the table?"

"Absolutely open," Manny promised. "I'll tell everything; I won't conceal a thing."

The tape continued to go round, transcribing every word of the confession.

"I traveled to America for a while. I successfully underwent plastic surgery, and I returned with a new name, a reasonable American accent, and a reputation for being a wonder-worker.

"In Israel several friends that Meshulam had found for me were waiting. They bought me an apartment on the outskirts of Petach Tikvah, spread the word of my powers, a miracle worker who could see the hidden, give incredible advice, solve all sorts of problems — what wasn't I? I began to see people; success brought more success. I turned into a great rebbe. Thousands came to my door. If I wasn't accepted by the elite, by the rabbinical leaders suspicious of my methods, it didn't matter: The masses were hypnotized by my talents, my reputation, and my obvious knowledge of things hidden.

"The book *The Vessel of Blessing* was as good as its name: It sent me billions of miles forward. If one just knows how to read it, he can bring down heaven and earth. I know a person from within, better than he knows himself.

"But all the time I lived with a doubt. I knew that Gili had suffered a tiny amount of brain damage as a result of the accident. I kept up with his medical file —"

"Nu, it seems the GSS has its hands everywhere!" Rabbi Schmidt interrupted.

Manny ignored him. "Gili's neurologists ascertained that most of his memory was untouched. His injury was a rare one, which took expression primarily in tiny short circuits in the brain — his blackouts — that damaged the electrical connections between the neurons in the area of memory. A similar disturbance has been noted in medical research among marijuana users. The active ingredient in the drug, THC, causes short breaks among the brain cells in the same area as the memory, causing drug users to undergo short-term memory loss. Gili, too, had just minimal damage and loss, right?"

"Medical file number 664947528, Rambam Hospital, Haifa. Name of patient: Gili Dinar. Page 7, left column," Gili declared. "You've done your homework very well."

"Meshulam is a perfectionist," Manny answered. "In any case, I knew that your memories might come back at any time.

"I did the reckoning. Gili Dinar is an intellectual, possesses a high IQ and phenomenal talents. Do I need the danger that he may discover the operation and reveal everything someday?

"And so I came up with a brilliant scheme: to put Gili on my side. To tie him to my apron strings and use him as part of the GSS plan of sowing destruction among the *chareidi* community. I'd be killing three birds with one stone. First, Gili, with his unusual talents, managed, in the course of writing his articles, to quickly learn many of the community's weak points. As a *baal teshuvah*, he was accepted in that world, an area in which the GSS has shown particular interest. Gili became a pawn in a chess game without realizing it. The GSS, through me and through his paper, used him, squeezed his brain dry. In the meantime, all his suspicions of me were allayed."

"That's where you're wrong," Gili said. "My suspicions grew from day to day."

"We'll talk about that," Manny said mockingly. "You worked as well as a radio. You push one button and it makes music, another and you get a different tune. You reacted to every stimulus just as I expected. I pulled you towards me on a definite timetable, and I didn't have to change a thing. Insulting, no?"

"Everything was well planned, right?" Gili sounded interested, not offended.

"Everything," Manny said proudly. "From the moment you were employed by *HaYom HaZeh* you were taking the route we'd put you on. I arranged an *Arachim* seminar for you in Teveriah. Because of you Benny Gabison also became a *baal teshuvah*. But his play-acting became a reality. You 'discovered' 'Big Yaakovi,' he caused your blackout, excited you with the help of a snuffbox with Halpern/Halperin written on it. He's an expert in such staging... Everything was done to pull you to me.

"You worried me when you went to learn at Rabbi Schmidt's yeshivah in Jerusalem, but I figured that you'd be crushed by the extended learning hours and you'd return to the paper. And I was right. Even your blackout on the way to Jerusalem was planned with Choni. You remember? It was the first time you were visiting Kiltz, and he started to remember the 405 bus that fell into the ravine near Telz-Stone. You had a blackout there on the road; Choni told me all about it."

"I saw," Gili enjoyed his tiny victory. "When I was sitting with Rabbi Schneidman in the office I saw the little spy giving over his information on the public phone."

Manny wasn't impressed. "Could be. I taught him what to tell you; I was taking your pulse. And when you weren't paying attention, the little puppy wagged his tail to his real master, Meshulam Yaakovi, and told him about the chandelier. Meshulam, the obedient son, passed the information on to his father. The result? One stolen chandelier."

Gili seemed tranquil. "And what would have happened if we would have turned over on the highway because of my blackout?"

Manny stammered, confused. "Uh...that is...uh...you're right...I didn't think of that."

"That's one mistake," Rav Yoske said quietly.

Manny recovered his composure. He continued. "The second advantage: You were close to me. I'm not bragging, but I do possess powers of suggestion that others do not have, partly because of *The Vessel of Blessing*.

"I managed easily to turn you into a disciplined soldier. Wherever you went I followed, via your friend, the late Benny Gabison, who unknowingly turned into a detective shadowing you. But at the time the one who did the most was that scoundrel Choni, Meshulam's faithful slave."

"Benny Gabison was your strike force," Gili concluded. He felt as though he was disconnected from his body, from all feeling. This lengthy consultation was discussing someone entirely different. "You planted him in the newsroom so that he would lead me to *teshuvah*. You worked on my emotions and made me overwhelmed with feelings of guilt, guilt that wasn't mine!"

"Absolutely right," Manny agreed. "I instructed Benny during the seminar in Teveriah, in the middle of the night. I prophesied when you would reach the breaking point as a secular Jew, and I was right. I wanted you to become a *baal teshuvah*, as an atonement for having destroyed your father and taken him away from Torah observance. But Benny really was a good friend of yours. Perhaps he knew about the bomb in the car and sacrificed himself for you!"

Gili was silent, astounded. Manny continued.

"Another nightmare of mine was when you would wake up and discover *The Vessel of Blessing*. I planted two forgeries in 'Big Yaakovi's' library."

"So you're a con man as well," Gili said in a patient voice.

Manny wiped his brow and smoothed some blond hairs in his beard. "Oh, this is something new, Gili managing to control his temper."

"Careful, Manny, I'm close to the bursting point," Gili warned him.

"I've got nothing to lose," Manny said serenely. "It's worth your while to hear the rest. It's absolutely fascinating. Yaakovi provoked you at the public auction at the Holiday Inn, by mentioning *The Vessel of Blessing*, and caused an immediate blackout. Then you went after him. Poor man, it was so hard for him, having you pull out the details of Rabbi Avram Roosenthal — just as I wanted it to be. At the same time, you found out that Yaakovi had two copies of *The Vessel of Blessing*. I gained a double advantage here: First, we impressed upon you the fact that there were more copies of the book extant, so if you would ever hear of Rav Avram's connection with the book, your suspicions would not be aroused. After all, if there are several copies of *The Vessel of Blessing*, what's wrong with one of them having come my way? Second, I was beginning to learn how your brain, with its blackouts, worked, and how your memory might return. Which brings me to the third goal of bringing you close to me: I'd be able to keep an eye on you."

"Manny, you're really something."

They turned their heads around in surprise. Udi Dinar had opened his mouth, for the first time since Manny had begun his confession.

"Abba, what did you say?" Gili cried out excitedly. But Udi had again buried himself between his sheet and his blanket, covered his face, and turned his back to them.

"You see?" Manny said. "He's beginning to wake up. Don't worry."

"Of course," Gili answered. "In seven or eight years he might even remember how to smile."

Rav Yoske again patted Gili's shoulder. "Manny, continue."

Manny complied. "When Gili came in the guise of Francois Germaine, to buy the book from 'Big Yaakovi,' together with his friend Moshe Vayden, he didn't know that he'd fallen into a trap that Pinny and Meshulam had set for him.

"In order to do so, Pinny took a risk and raised the price of the book to $800,000, in order to make the forgery seem more authentic. It was all a game, really: Gili had no intention of buying the book, and Yaakovi didn't dream that Francois Germaine would be so foolish. It was a war of nerves, and when Gili insisted on his right to authenticate the work, bringing with him an antiques merchant, Yaakovi had to swallow hard and take it, so to speak. But everything was part of the game.

"Yaakovi immediately reported to his son, Meshulam, that Gili knew it was a forgery. The conclusion: We had to be careful of Gili Dinar. Meshulam updated me, but he decided on his own, without involving the GSS in his decision, to assassinate Gili.

"That he didn't tell me, but knowing Meshulam's thought processes as I did, I realized that it was inevitable that he would do so. From then on

I fortified my surveillance of Gili, in order to protect him from the GSS murderers."

"'A righteous man will sprout like a date tree,'" Rabbi Schmidt murmured. "Gili's protector, Manny Schwartz..."

Manny's eyes were now tired and melancholy. "I had a reason. Soon you'll understand why.

"The GSS almost succeeded in their Operation Puppeteer Rabbi. Their agents have been waiting these past few days for zero hour. The minute the command will be given they will begin to pass on their information and their rumors, stories true and untrue, causing chaos in the chareidi sector, destroying it from the roots. They'll damage all the various groups, their economic base, everything!

"The plan was almost complete, but Meshulam Yaakovi didn't know that his father's greed would cause him to make a fatal error like the theft of the chandelier from the *chassidus* of Kiltz. That turned on an alarm light in Gili's head. He began to wonder about my connection with Yaakovi. He suspected that it wasn't a holy connection between *chassid* and rabbi. And that's when Gili began to distance himself from me.

"I also made a mistake. I forgot about a sick, unfortunate soul. I never thought that Paysi Brent would turn into a confederate of Gili's, and would become a fifth columnist in this war of nerves."

"The small details," Gili sighed. "The mistakes are always in the little things. Meshulam never dreamed that an empty gas tank would cause another blackout; he never expected that Gili would inspect the gas gauge, when his head was full of alcohol and drugs."

"No, it's the big things," Manny returned, "those were the failures. In his blackest nightmares Meshulam never envisioned what would happen next.

"You're not asking me why I'm giving you such a full confession? What caused me to do it? Isn't it strange?"

"We don't know what to think about this all," Rav Yoske answered. "I can't figure out if you're a chameleon, a scorpion, or a salamander."

Manny had the hide of an elephant; Rav Yoske couldn't manage to insult him. "You don't understand me; I'm more powerful than all of you together. If I wanted, I could hypnotize the three of you in a minute, cause you temporary memory loss, and sneak out of here the way I came. Why am I sitting here and chatting with you? Why didn't I do anything when Choni and Muli reported that Paysi was speaking with Gili in sign language? Why did I let Paysi stay home by himself on the night of Yaakovi's daughter's wedding? Didn't I know that Gili might come and break into my safe? Why did I let Gili fly to London? Why did I save him from certain death, when a GSS agent tried to plant a bomb beneath his car when it was parked in the lot near my apartment? Why did I stop giving the GSS tapes? Why did the GSS try to liquidate me after Benny Gabison's funeral?"

They followed his words with every fiber of their being. Manny stared at them, stone faced.

Gili hadn't forgotten Eric Meisels. "How did you make peace with the assassination of the paper's assistant editor?"

"Did I know about that?" Manny shuddered. "Meshulam Yaakovi is a lone wolf. He's got a long list of assassination victims, and my name is on it too. One of my devoted *chassidim* heard Bumi Porat ask his employer, Pinny Yaakovi, Meshulam's father, right after I left the wedding, 'Is Rav Avram loyal to us?' 'Big Yaakovi' immediately answered, "Of course not. He'll be liquidated soon."

Rav Yoske stroked his silvered beard with his hand. He shook back and forth and said in the singsong of the yeshivah, "Our rabbis have taught us, when there are 20 questions on one concept, don't look for 20 different answers, look for one answer that will answer all the questions at once."

"Absolute truth," Manny said in the same melody. "All the questions can be solved with one answer: I had ceased to cooperate with the GSS.

"I've been conducting a deadly war of nerves with Meshulam for the past few months now. When we put together Operation Puppeteer Rabbi, I identified with its goal. My passion for domination blinded me and captured all my senses. I so wanted to see my childhood dream come true and become a rebbe that I was ready to stab my own people, the *chareidi* community, in the back.

"Meshulam Yaakovi thought that he'd be able to keep my cooperation forever, with the threat of revealing my true identity.

"You won't believe it, but when I began to help others, without my wishing for it to happen, the saying 'one *mitzvah* brings another' came true. I came to people's aid, solved crises, brought domestic peace, made matches between girls and boys, served as *sandek* at the *brissim* of many infants in whose birth I had a hand."

Manny's voice broke. "I began to love the people I was treating. It's an iron-clad rule: When you do something for someone, you love him! The more you do for him — the more you love him! I feel part of the *chareidi* community today, in a way I never did before. I know it better than all of you, how wonderful it is, and I'm screaming: Save us!

They looked at him stone faced, unbelieving. Rabbi Schmidt asked, "Manny Schwartz wants to save someone? Perhaps himself?"

Manny's steely eyes were moist. "Chaim Ozer, believe me. I'm a true penitent, believe me. First and foremost, I want to save the *chareidim* from the hands of the GSS."

"And what about you?" Rav Yoske said. This was too good to be true; he didn't trust the man. Maybe this was still another show by Manny, the inveterate actor.

"I won't lie and tell you that I don't care what happens to me. The opposite: I'm asking that you save me too. I can't be a part of such a desecration. What will people say if they find out that a famed rebbe is a fraud, a traitor the likes of which we haven't seen since Shabtai Zvi?

"Help me," he begged, in broken tones.

"We've got to discuss this," Rabbi Schmidt said.

And then Gili's voice was heard. "I've already solved the puzzle of The Puppeteer Rabbi! And we can't believe Manny! Once a liar, always a liar!"

"Why do you say that?" Rav Yoske said sternly. These young people, they had no patience.

Gili had his answer ready. "Have you forgotten how he came here? His revolver drawn, threatening us. Suddenly he's a *chassid*, a *baal teshuvah*. Be careful of hypocrites: It's a trap!"

Rabbi Schmidt and Rabbi Friedman exchanged glances. Gili was making sense! "What do you have to say to that?" Rabbi Schmidt asked him.

Manny Schwartz lifted his eyes to the dim light bulb that gave off its weak ray. "I knew it. That's the punishment of the liar: Even when he says the truth, no one believes him. With my hand on my heart, I will tell you what I was thinking the entire way from Petach Tikvah to here: Master of the Universe, for six years I've been imprisoned by the hand of the GSS; for a year and a half I've been tortured by secret feelings of penitence and remorse; for half a year I've been leading Gili to uncover the truth. Now I feel Your presence; send me a rope before I sink into the mire; help them to believe me."

The room was silent, a thick and heavy silence. Three men (maybe four?) considered Manny's heartfelt words. Rabbi Schmidt spoke first.

"A man can feel the truth. I believe that you're not lying. And I have some simple proof," he said, waving his thumb as he would during a lecture. "If you wanted to, what would have stopped you from shooting all of us when you snuck in here?"

Manny took a deep breath. "And now you can laugh," he said. "Take a look at my cap gun."

He pulled the revolver out of the holster; they jumped back, terrified. "Cowards," Manny chuckled, as he put the revolver on the table. Three heads automatically bent forward.

The gun wasn't loaded.

⚜️

"I had to play out the game," Manny explained. "Rabbi Avram is a man with a style; he can't give in without a fight. And I didn't know just how far Gili would go. When I saw you all around Udi I pulled the revolver out almost as a reflex. I never hurt even a fly. Gili can attest to that."

Rav Yoske suddenly hit his temple with his hand. "Now I understand!" he cried excitedly.

"What do you understand?" Gili asked, his face still cold.

"Manny Schwartz was stuck in the 49th level of impurity. He wasn't far from the gates of hell. He may be the greatest informer of all time. His sin is too heavy to bear. The angels of below should have fanned the flames in expectation of his arrival. But what pulled him out of there? What merit remained?"

Manny said two words. "The sabras."

"That's right." Rav Yoske jumped up to his full height; his head touched the ceiling, bringing down a hail of black dust. "You really do know how to read minds. I'm beginning to be afraid of you... You had a great merit. When Moshe Shiffer almost died from 60 sabras in his stomach, who gave the *mashgiach* the idea that saved him? Manny Schwartz!"

Gili didn't join in the general clamor. "I'd forgotten that you were old friends, " he said furiously. "Only my father isn't taking part in this beautiful reunion of yours. Manny, I insist you restore his sanity."

"Not in an instant," Manny defended himself. "It's a protracted process. Give me some time and you'll see him return to what he once was. But we have to get out of here first, and that's not an easy operation. Meshulam is waiting for us outside."

"You have any ideas?" Rabbi Schmidt asked.

"Yes, but on one condition."

"Which is?"

"That you help me get out of this swamp, without *chillul Hashem* and without humiliation."

The two rabbis answered almost simultaneously, " 'If one comes to purify himself, others must help him.'"

In the next minutes Manny proved his worth. Udi refused to leave the bed. He hung onto the blanket in terror and repeated over and over again how much he liked it there. They were out of ideas, until Manny approached him.

"Like magic," Rav Yoske whispered, amazed. Manny effortlessly hypnotized Udi, putting him into a deep trance. After a minute he found the way to reach Udi's poor, warped brain. It seemed that Udi had been promised a computer in his room. Manny told him that he would get an even better computer in his house. Then Udi insisted on taking his blanket and pillow...

After a few minutes of coaxing, using all of Rabbi Avram's power of persuasion, Udi agreed to accompany them.

The car's windows had misted over. Meshulam Yaakovi stared at the dashboard for the 20th time. It was absolutely ridiculous, how much time he was taking in there.

At 3 a.m. he was certain that Rav Avram had failed. Gili must have overpowered him. He was about to call his assistant when his eyes widened.

"What's this?" he whispered in shock. "Five people leaving? Manny Schwartz, you traitor!"

Five shadows had passed beneath the street lights and hastily entered a Subaru Legacy parked a short distance away from the institution's gates. One of them tripped, and was supported by a tall shadow's hands. The car started and sped off.

Meshulam's Mazda took off after Rav Yoske's Subaru, following it — with its lights darkened — at an ever decreasing distance.

"Have you noticed?" Rav Yoske said to Manny sitting beside him, "A car is following us."

Manny chuckled mockingly. "Meshulam, the lone wolf. Now he's trying desperately to decide if he should call for help. Every second he takes his cell phone, then hangs it back up. He hits the SND and the END buttons ceaselessly. In the end he'll ask for assistance. If you know how to get rid of him, good; if not, give me the wheel."

"Absolutely not!" Udi suddenly shouted from his place in the rear.

"Abba," Gili said feelingly, "you're right; it's a bad idea."

But Udi had disconnected and was again in his twilight world.

The Subaru had left the environs of Kiryat Bialik and was speeding on the highway. The Mazda maintained its distance. Manny, as always, was right: Meshulam had, after long consideration, decided to break his strict rule. He hit his assistant's number and asked for help.

The GSS went out on attack.

46

Two Volvo automobiles and one Mazda determinedly gained on the Subaru Legacy. Rav Yoske tried desperately to reach his city, Haifa, in the hope of shaking his pursuers off in the city's back streets. He ran around the GSS men in spirals and dangerous curves, jumped from lane to lane, crossed streets, and soon left the main highway between Kiryat Bialik and Haifa behind. The chase was so swift that none of the passengers, in any of the cars, had the slightest idea of where they were. Only the twinkling lights of the port city hinted that they were still in the environs of Haifa. All the cars had extinguished their lights, and the night's darkness still surrounded them, but the few streetlights placed with a miserly hand here and there showed the Subaru's passengers just how desperate their plight was.

The chances of the Subaru outrunning its three pursuers were like those of a fleet deer being chased by three swift cheetahs on an open plain.

Rav Yoske hit the gas and the Subaru lurched forward, but still the three cars behind it were closing their distance.

"We're lost," Rabbi Schmidt whispered through white lips.

"Rav Chaim Ozer, a little faith. What's this despair?" Manny asked. His words grated on Gili's ears.

"How far is it to Haifa?" Gili asked.

"Three kilometers," Rav Yoske answered.

"What's that?" Manny said suspiciously, looking through the side mirror. Suddenly he shrieked wildly, "Get down!"

Only Manny's sharp eyes could have seen the young man putting his head and shoulders out the front window of the Volvo. The man was brandishing a revolver. With a steady hand he aimed at the Subaru's tires. A circular flash of light spewed out of the gun as he shot it.

Rav Yoske swerved hastily to the right; all the passengers fell on top of each other. The bullet missed the rear tire by inches.

"Let's stop and give ourselves up," Rabbi Schmidt screamed in fright. "We've got no chance against them."

His suggestion was rejected by a general consensus. "Absolutely not," Rav Yoske said with a strange serenity. "Tomorrow you'll see the head-lines: Car Plunges in Wadi, All Occupants Killed. No one will ever know that we were shot."

In the back Udi made little growling noises. His eyes protruded and stared with terror at the road before them.

The cars behind them continued to advance closer. They planned on catching their fleeing prey in a pincer movement. The young man behind them was now holding a Galil rifle, and was continuously shooting at the tires. Rav Yoske flew from right to left and left to right and somehow managed to evade the deadly bullets. Gili wrung his hands. "Rav Yoske, you don't need to be very smart to know you haven't 10 seconds left on these tires."

Manny balled his fists. He closed his eyes tightly and seemed to be pulling on some inner energy reserves from deep within him. "Yoske, lis-ten to me," he said resolutely. "Give me the wheel."

"We'll get to Haifa; I know the roads," Rav Yoske said stubbornly, his foot firmly on the gas pedal. The speedometer diligently reported their speed of 110 mph. The wind howled in an ever-increasing wail.

Manny wouldn't give up. "The Volvo has a stronger engine. Another minute and they've got us."

A bullet whistled by with a nerve-shattering shriek. The young man kept shooting.

Manny unbuckled his seat belt. Before Rav Yoske could say anything he'd maneuvered into the driver's seat, his two hands firmly gripping the wheel. Yoske, shocked, wordlessly moved over to the other side.

"Hang on tight," commanded Manny. "We're going to fly now."

The car was driving down the side of the mountain, on a winding road on the outskirts of Haifa. Four yards below them, on a terraced portion of the mountain, was the lower road.

The Subaru drove onto the road's shoulder. "Hold on," Manny shouted again, in a terrifying voice.

They left the road. For two horrifying seconds the car hovered in the air; then it thumped down onto the lower road. It landed firmly on its tires, and the terrible bump took the wind out of their lungs.

Manny recovered, hit the gas again; the car lurched forward.

"We made it alive," Rav Yoske patted himself on the chest in disbelief. "How'd you do that?"

"Concentration, my friend, concentration," Manny answered. "Absolute self-mastery and concentration. You'll see the damage later, Yoske: It seems I've shattered your exhaust," he said without a smile.

"But the main thing is, thank G-d we've lost them," Rabbi Schmidt murmured, his teeth chattering. "It will take them at least five minutes to catch up now."

"Not quite," Manny said. "One of the geniuses on top is copying me."

Gili looked up in disbelief. The Mazda and one Volvo were still racing down the winding road, but the second Volvo had tried the same shortcut that they had taken. For a second it stood on the shoulder as if hesitating, then it jumped forward.

It was doomed to failure from the start. The Volvo hadn't had enough velocity to get it to the road; it rolled heavily on the side of the mountain, and fell upside down onto the road, its tires spinning with a sickening screech.

No one said a word.

Manny was obviously an incredible driver. He brought the car to Haifa with a confident and steady hand, leaving the two other cars far behind.

The car stopped in the Ramat Dania neighborhood, near a luxurious villa. They left the car behind them and jumped into two waiting taxis which Gili had summoned on his cell phone.

"Where are we going to?" Rav Yoske asked, one foot on the sidewalk and the other in the cab. He looked all out of ideas. "The GSS knows all of our addresses; we've no place to hide."

"I've got a great shelter," Gili volunteered. "Effie Green's house. It's not far, on Herzl Street, further down the city."

He told them of the eyewitness that he'd met when he was investigating the accident on the Carmel. "It was as if he'd come down from Heaven that night, helping me to unravel the mystery."

"He truly did come down from Heaven," Manny agreed. "Look at this! I sent him away after the accident, and just the night that you decide to try and figure out what happened, he turns up again!"

"I took his address," Gili concluded, "and he's one of the five to whom I sent my sealed envelopes. I wrote to each of them, explaining what they had to do in the event of my disappearance. Besides the letter, I phoned him and asked him to prepare a safe haven for us. He's waiting for us."

Rav Yoske and Rabbi Schmidt were thrilled by the idea. Manny was less enthusiastic. "He'll recognize me."

Gili waved away his objection. "If only that were your worst problem, Manny. You have a lot more serious things to take care of."

Gili gently took his father by the hand and put him into the taxi. Rav Yoske, Rabbi Schmidt, and Manny took the other cab.

After a few minutes they met at Effie Green's apartment. The lights were on inside, and the shutters were down. Effie was waiting for them, and had followed all of Gili's instructions.

"How did you know this would happen?" Effie asked, as he poured them all cups of tea. He was fully dressed despite the hour; understandably rather confused. Since the terrible night of the accident six years earlier, he'd never felt such emotions.

"I figured it out," Gili replied modestly.

Effie was thoughtful. He approached Manny and stared at his face. "You seem familiar," he said. "Where do I know you from? Ohhh..." he gave a yelp and pulled Gili into a small room on the side filled with electronic equipment. "Gili, listen," he whispered, "I've recognized him. That's the man who sent us away the night of the accident. I think he may have had some plastic surgery on his nose, but I've got a good memory for faces, and I'd recognize those eyes anywhere!"

"I know all about it," Gili calmed him.

Effie rolled his eyes. "I don't understand. Is he a friend or an enemy?"

Gili sighed. "That's what happens when somebody wants to dance at two weddings at once." He yawned. "I know I'm talking in riddles. Another few days, Effie, everything will be behind us and you'll get a complete explanation."

Meshulam Yaakovi burned with rage. This had been the worst night of his life. Not enough that he'd had to ignore his pride and call for help, he'd been humiliated in front of his men when he'd lost Manny and Gili during the failed chase. And if that wasn't enough, two of his best men had been hurt when they'd taken the Volvo off the road in a failed attempt to emulate Manny's incredible feat.

"Your friends are complete idiots!" Mesulam squawked into his phone to his men in the other Volvo. "A Volvo can't take it! Why did they jump?"

The agents kept quiet; they'd learned something after all these years. Meshulam gritted his teeth in fury. Ten years he'd been diligently paving the way to the lofty heights of the GSS. His superior, S, had been feeling him nipping at his heels for two years now. Operation Puppeteer Rabbi was to begin in just a few days, and with it Meshulam was hoping to move into the boss's chair.

And now everything was up in the air. If Operation Puppeteer Rabbi were to fail, S would blame only him, and his GSS career would come to an end.

He could not let it finish with such disaster.

Meshulam was blessed with an extraordinarily sharp mind. He knew that in this war the winner would be the one who would get in the first shot.

He was not going to let Gili be the one to shoot first.

When he reached the GSS offices early in the morning he issued a series of orders to all of his agents spread within the *chareidi* world in the guise of *baalei teshuvah*. "Tomorrow at 12 noon, Operation Puppeteer Rabbi goes into effect."

He gave still another order to just a few of his top men. They were told to discreetly uncover the whereabouts of Gili Dinar and that most terrible of traitors, Rabbi Avram Roosenthal. His order specified very clearly what was to be done to them.

Meshulam then phoned the head of the GSS and asked for an emergency meeting of all division heads at midnight. "Everything's ready," he told his supervisor. "The agents are prepared for tomorrow. The long knives will be unsheathed in all of Bnei Brak, Jerusalem, Beitar, Beit Shemesh, Emanuel and Tzefat. Blood will be shed tomorrow in all the *chareidi* concentrations."

"I'm not so certain," S said doubtfully. "Don't count your chickens..."

"What do you mean by that?" Meshulam asked suspiciously. Surely S had no idea of the night's failed mission.

"I have a lot of experience with *chareidim*. They're not wimps; it'll take a while before the information we let loose will have effect. They'll have to stew in their own juice a little."

S suddenly grew angry. "We've got a long day ahead, and I didn't even get half an hour's sleep tonight. You're not human, Meshulam, what possessed you to call me at 5:30 in the morning?"

He hung up the phone, leaving Meshulam with a sour taste in his mouth. This call should have been his moment of triumph; why had it ended on a discordant note?

Meshulam's strength, and his weakness, were rooted in his fundamental refusal to look back. He would always go after the target, pursue his prey without a thought for what was behind him. The strength of it was that he wouldn't let past defeats weaken him. The weakness? He never, ever learned a lesson.

The five chosen people received their envelopes that day. Gili had planned for problems, but the postal service worked beautifully this time.

Monica read: "Ima, the material in your hands is a time bomb. If you don't hear from me in 48 hours, give the pages to Ami Kedmi. He'll know what to do with them."

She rolled her eyes and immediately turned to attorney Gadi Bental, one of the most illustrious lawyers in the country. He read the material with interest for more than an hour, asked his secretary to make several copies, and promised to take care of everything in the event of any problems.

Rabbi Yehoshua Schneidman stared indifferently at the brown envelope. The name Yehoshua Zucker meant nothing to him. He tore open the envelope and swiftly ran his eyes over the pages. The indifference had vanished as if by magic. Thoroughly shaken, he put on his overcoat and ran as fast as he could to the rebbe's house, leaving his hat behind in his agitation. He handed the sheaf of papers to the venerable rabbi.

The rebbe pulled out his reading glasses from their gold case. After a few minutes he told the impatient administrator, "He's a bright boy."

"And the material? The danger?" the administrator asked, trembling.

The rebbe raised his hands heavenward; Rabbi Schneidman didn't know if it was a prayer or a gesture of despair.

Moshe Vayden phoned the newsroom of *HaYom HaZeh* immediately after receiving the letter, and asked to speak with Ami Kedmi, chief editor. Kedmi promised to call back within two hours.

Effie Green had received a full explanation even before the mail arrived.

Ami Kedmi himself had received the stiff envelope from the hands of his secretary.

"Yehoshua Zucker?" he rubbed his head thoughtfully. "That handwriting looks familiar."

As he read the 10 pages the veins on his temple throbbed and his eyes protruded. With the sharp senses of a veteran journalist he knew that he had never held a time bomb like this one in his hands. It was the dream of every scoop-seeking reporter.

For an hour he sat in solitude in his office, thinking. Finally, he summarized what he'd come up with. On the one hand, he had done all he could until today to help the GSS in its Operation Puppeteer Rabbi. He had accepted Gili as a reporter for religious affairs, though Gili could have better served the paper as a national affairs journalist. If he made this report public tomorrow, he would severely harm the GSS plans, perhaps lay them to rest completely.

He read the last page once again, scanned the lines written on the bottom. "If you don't want to publicize this material, for whatever reason, it will be published in your competitors' papers. The editors of *Yediot Acharonot* and *Maariv* would grab a scoop like this one. They'll thank you from the bottom of their hearts for your loyalty to the GSS and will be happy to increase their readership by a significant amount in the next few days."

Gili hadn't relied solely on the letter; even as Ami was reading the material he received a phone call from a man who introduced himself as a friend of Gili's. He insisted on staying anonymous and asked if Ami had received the material. When Ami tried to avoid answering, the mysterious man said, "If I don't get your confirmation within the next two hours, the material will be sent to your competitors."

So should I be a better Catholic than the pope? Ami asked himself. *Whose interests are more important to me, the GSS or the paper? I have this time bomb in my hands, and I should keep quiet?*

With one more thought, Ami came to his conclusion. *Circulation of HaYom HaZeh is going to go through the roof tomorrow,* he crowed. He jumped from his office recliner and with the enthusiasm of a child called his secretary in.

"Two cups of cappucino, and quickly please," he gave the command with characteristic impatience. Then he called his assistant, the managing editor, and members of the security matters' newsdesk. They sat to discuss the report and its consequences. After two hours of stormy debate they decided to publish their exclusive report the next day, maintaining absolute secrecy until the last moment.

Ami sat by the phone waiting for its ring. When Moshe Vayden called a second time, Ami shouted into the receiver, "Yes, yes! We're running the story in tomorrow's edition. Not a word to another paper, understand?"

Moshe Vayden was not to be convinced so easily. "I want a draft copy of tomorrow's front page tonight at 9 p.m. And don't try to make a dummy copy that you don't intend to print, because I've got journalistic connections, and several spies in your organization. If by 4 a.m. I get any word that the story is not appearing, I'll fax it immediately to the other papers!"

"You've got nothing to worry about," Ami said, running a hand over a sweaty brow. "Do you think I'm made of stone? I'm a journalist, first and foremost!"

"How did you work it out with Goldman?"

They were closeted in the guest room of the Green family of Haifa. Rav Yoske and Rabbi Schmidt had decided to stay in this stranger's house until things quieted down. According to Gili, the whole thing would blow over tomorrow or the next day, one way or the other. Either Gili would win, or the GSS would hastily put Operation Puppeteer Rabbi into action earlier than they had planned.

Rav Yoske Friedman sat next to Manny Schwartz, who looked deeply depressed. Rav Yoske was looking for information that would help them extricate Udi Dinar from his sorry situation.

"Only money," Manny explained. "For six years I've been giving Dr. Seiden huge bribes. When he took in Mickey Gadish I enriched him with a few thousand dollars. Then the amount of the bribes went down significantly; there was even a time when it seemed I'd forgotten about the patient. But with all that, occasionally I would give the dedicated administrator a cheerful little bonus, just to remind him to take good care of Mickey Gadish, give him proper treatment, keep him carefully controlled with his medications, and to ensure that he never found out what was happening in the outside world.

"Mickey Gadish had been kept alone in a dark underground room in the hospital for six years. For six years he hadn't seen the sunshine.

"Sometimes my conscience would reproach me. What was I doing? But Dr. Seiden never felt a qualm. Keeping a sane man in an asylum is not on the list of medical ethics; it goes against all justice and righteousness. But what are justice and righteousness compared to occasional bonuses — in dollars?

"Now it seems that money is a two-edged sword. The head nurse, Bella Bar-Dror, learned the lessons well, and the student became wiser than the teacher: Her price was much higher!"

"What will you do with me?" Manny asked.

He was used to going without sleep, and despite his despondency he looked fresh and awake. Rav Yoske and Rabbi Schmidt were less so. Black circles shadowed their eyes. For the thousandth time they all thought of the future of Rabbi Avram Roosenthal.

Effie Green did not go to work that day. He took good care of his visitors: It was not every day that such a distinguished group arrived at his home.

"What should we do?" Rav Yoske asked, between sips of hot tea.

"The question is how to get me out of this mire without a *chillul Hashem*. And by the way, my life is in danger: The GSS wants to kill me."

"We're all in the same boat," Rav Yoske took another sip.

"There's no comparison," Manny declared. His cup of tea stayed full; only the lemon slice found its way to his mouth. "I've got the status of an agent turned traitor; you're honest citizens who somehow got involved in this mess. You're in the eye of the storm: If you're all assassinated, the public will once and for all rise up against this killer-happy group. The GSS is being very careful to let sleeping dogs lie. But me? I've gone underground, so I'd be easy to kill."

Rav Yoske thought for a while, then he said, "I think we've got to send you abroad. You'll disappear, find some excuse to give your adherents here, your *chassidim*. Maybe we'll tell the media that you've gone to Latin America for an unlimited amount of time. You'll go to Brooklyn. You can live in Boro Park or Flatbush, take on a new identity there."

"You can be a big rebbe there," Gili interrupted brutally, "wear a chassidic coat, buy a magic wand and silver turban, make miracles and coin money."

Rav Yoske turned blazing eyes on Gili. "Gili, enough! You're not being fair now. The man feels sorry for what he did and is trying to rectify what he's destroyed. Give him a chance." He turned to Manny and continued. "I suggest that you get married and try to build a beautiful Jewish family, raise a new generation to Torah and fear of God, busy yourself with true good deeds, and in this way honestly try to atone for your terrible actions."

"Atonement in New York? Let him wake my father up here and now," Gili repeated his demand and pointed at Udi, lying in a bed staring vacantly before him.

Manny stood up. His eyes were moist. "Gili, if you give me a quiet room, within a month I'll get your father back to normal. Before I flee abroad, he'll be perfectly okay."

"I don't believe you!" Gili interrupted, wounded. "You're just making it up. The harm you've done to him is irreversible. For six years I thought I was an orphan, then I found out I was wrong. Now I know once again that I was orphaned, an orphan like Choni, like Paysi. My father is alive, and I'm an orphan. A living orphan!"

෮෴෮

The lights were on in the offices of the General Security Service, but the heavy curtains concealed all signs of life. The conference had been called for midnight, but at Meshulam's request it had been put off another two hours. He was still missing some technical data and props for the big show he was planning for his colleagues that night.

The conference room was still quiet, but everyone felt a storm in the offing. The division heads sat around the oval table. Each had been previously briefed. But exactly what the subject of this meeting was, no one had a clue. A dark cloud of secrecy had been placed on this meeting; the topic was classified, more sensitive than any in the past.

It was, once again, the Night of the Pipes. Meshulam thought of another nickname: Night of the Propaganda. On this night they would insure that a *chareidi* civil war would break out, one that would tear the community apart and leave it splintered, group after group fighting. He was certain that blood would be shed.

The head of the GSS, Shlomo Templer, rested a cold gaze on Meshulam Yaakovi, head of the Psychological Warfare Division. The pipe in Templer's mouth gave off the sweet scent of rum-vanilla, but the tone of his voice did not contain even a drop of sweetness. Meshulam thought his superior was overdoing it: Was his sleep the holy of holies? Since that morning's incident Templer had been sour faced.

"Gentlemen, Meshulam has something to say to us."

Meshulam stretched in his chair, leaned back weakly and then straightened up. His fingers were forcefully pressed together.

"The time has come to put Operation Puppeteer Rabbi into action," he said with a tranquility that belied the pressure he had been under since the previous night.

The room filled with the sound of whispers. Shlomo Templer hit the table with his fist. "He hasn't even started, and you're already talking?"

Meshulam looked at him with concealed gratitude. Meshulam knew how to keep discipline, but right now he simply did not have the strength. He began to speak.

"Honored friends, Operation Puppeteer Rabbi is about to burst, it's so ripe. Everything's ready, the agents are waiting for action. It's a shame to waste a minute. We've got a six-part plan ready to begin."

"What happens during the first part?" Gavriel Reit, assistant to the director, asked.

Meshulam touched his briefcase, pressed a secret code. The lock opened with silent metal obedience. Meshulam pulled out an envelope marked "Top Secret" in bright red. His face wore a halo of importance. He began to read:

"Operation Puppeteer Rabbi. Plan of execution, in six parts:

"Part 1: One hundred sixty-eight agents, planted throughout the *chareidi* and religious sectors, are distributing sensitive material throughout the length and breadth of the land. First step: distribution of audio and video cassettes in populated areas in the three large cities. Jerusalem: Kikar Shabbat and Rechov Malchei Yisrael in Geulah, the area of the 'shtieblach,' Zichron Moshe, Meah Shearim, and Beit Yisrael. Bnei Brak: Rechov Rabbi Akiva and Chazon Ish, the Izkovitz and Lederman shuls, and the Beit Knesset HaGadol. Haifa: Rechov Geulah, the Hadar neighborhood, including the Tiferet Yisrael shul, and the chassidic neighborhood on top of the mountain. Smaller *chareidi* concentrations: Beit Shemesh, Beitar, Ashdod, Tzefat, Teveriah, Rechovot, Netanya,

Petach Tikvah, Kiryat Sefer, Telz-Stone, and Emanuel in the Shomron.

"Time of distribution: between 2 and 3 a.m."

"Very nice," Gavriel puffed on his pipe, "but you haven't given us an example of this explosive material."

Meshulam had waited for this moment. He winked at Mutty, the communications officer.

Mutty pulled a large projection screen from a corner of the room and unrolled it. It took two seconds to get the video recorder working and then the face of a well-known *chareidi* activist appeared on the screen.

47

The activist sat in a darkened room. He was speaking to someone sitting across from him. The ones with sharp hearing could quickly identify the voice of Rabbi Avram Roosenthal speaking with his visitor.

The activist was in deep distress, and spoke vehemently. The GSS men were amazed by the insults he was hurling at one of the most admired personalities in the *chareidi* world.

Cut.

A second picture: a man with an American accent complaining that his daughter cannot get accepted to a school in his neighborhood because he doesn't learn in a *kollel*.

Cut.

Another man, this one dark skinned, accusing a yeshivah of refusing his brilliant son because they were Sefardim.

And more. This well-known man spoke against that famous personality. Men from one group told hair-raising tales of men from other groups. *Chassid* against Litvak; Ashkenazi against Sefardi; brother against brother.

Then there were the family secrets, facts kept carefully concealed, now brutally revealed. These people, who came looking for advice and counsel, never imagined in their worst nightmares that every word of theirs would be recorded and used against them.

"And that's just a small sample, rather *pareve* compared to some of the stuff we have on the tapes," Meshulam explained with pleasure. "The continuation is even more detailed and damning."

He continued reading.

"Part 2: Anonymous phone calls in which a person will hear a clear tape of what another thinks of him. We have hundreds of such tapes; actually, close to 1000. Everyone who's anyone has been mentioned at some time. Afterwards, each person will get the tape in the mail, to erase any doubt.

"Part 3: Posters hung up all over the streets, with the worst of the libels and slanders. I promise you a lot of salt and pepper here.

"Part 4: Intervention in various controversies. There are existing conflicts between the heads of various institutions. In the name of 'the public's right to know' we'll reveal — and 'enhance' — all.

"Part 5: Family secrets. With all the diligence of an ant, Rav Avram collected incredible data, an ocean of information. We know who is sick in body and who in mind, which marriages are troubled, what families are fighting, who is taking whom to *din Torah*, and all sorts of hair-raising events that should be kept under wraps. Everything will come out, in careful prearranged ways, with the help of our various agents.

"Part 6: Disinformation. Sowing of false rumors that cannot be disproved, against personalities, families, and institutions, and particularly against the *teshuvah* movement, one of our main enemies. We'll link the names of well-known people in the underworld with the *teshuvah* movement. In the poisoned atmosphere that we will create in the *chareidi* world, everything will be believed."

A murmur of admiration swept through the conference room. At the beginning of the meeting some of the men had been yawning, but now eyes were opened and fists clenched. They looked like a pack of foxes that had come upon a defenseless flock of sheep.

Meshulam's face radiated happiness and a clear arrogance that followed the release of tension. He had waited for this moment for six years, for the recognition by all the division heads of his shining wit and powerful personality. He glanced at Shlomo Templer. His boss was beginning to feel the pressure. Meshulam was on his heels, now more than ever. It would not be long now; someone would come and give voice to all their thoughts: *Shlomo, our dear Shlomo, it's time to replace you. You have an heir, Meshulam Yaakovi, and he's got you beaten by a wide margin...*

The room grew silent. Meshulam continued to speak. "Can you imagine what the *chareidi* streets will look like after all of that? I'm not even talking about the conflicts among the leadership; I mean the destruction of the community's most secure fortress: the family!"

Meshulam rubbed his hands happily. "Imagine it. *Shidduchim* will come apart, couples will divorce. The *chareidi* family will come apart. And that's what we want. The family is the foundation of a healthy society. Among us it's already unstable. But among the *chareidim* it's still iron clad. The last two parts of the plan will spread a cancer among them, poison them!"

Boaz Shamir, head of Jewish Affairs, sipped his coffee and asked, "It sounds good. What are we waiting for?"

Templer had expected this reaction from Boaz, a powerful man who relished taking difficult steps, particularly against his fellow Jews. He was what he always was: overenthusiastic.

Teddy Philo, head of the Manpower Division, asked, "Do you need my people? I can give you 400 field workers to help."

"Thanks, Teddy," Meshulam answered graciously, "but I'm managing fine without you. My 168 agents will do the job skillfully, quietly, and, most important, neatly. Efficiency is the name of the game. There won't be any accusations: The GSS will stay completely out of the picture during the world war that's going to break out tomorrow or the next day in the *chareidi* community of Israel. No one has any idea that we're behind the business! Brilliant, no?"

"Snob," Teddy whispered.

"Did you say something?" Meshulam asked gently.

"No, no. Nothing," Teddy recoiled, embarrassed, and his beer can fell from his hand and rolled on the table, leaving a trail of sodden fizz in its wake.

Meshulam would not relinquish his prey. His heavy jaws ground out the words. "I'll tell you the truth, I know your crowd. They're a little bit clumsy, and they can spoil the whole show. My people are well trained, they're above suspicion. Most of them started in the *baalei teshuvah* yeshivos, have been absorbed into the *chareidi* world, and are now a part of it. No one suspects my agents. They won't make stupid mistakes like wearing *tefillin* on Shabbat or a *shtriemel* on Wednesday. You won't even find them making a mistake in the slang. They know it all!"

Kalman Weiss, head of the division of Arab affairs, drank neither juice nor cola, despite the dry, bitter feeling in his mouth. He was as coiled as a spring, and almost broke his fingers knocking beneath the table. The conference was about to close with a specific resolution, and if nothing happened they would all leave in a few minutes. What could he do?

He sent a tiny note to his neighbor, Danny Lavie, who was in charge of security for public officials. "Don't you think the movie was too short?"

Danny Lavie was one of the most talented men in the organization, part of it since its inception. His road to the top lay open before him, or so said well-placed sources. He had but one weakness: He loved a good movie. Kalman had heard him sigh in disappointment when Meshulam's little presentation had come to an end, too soon for Danny's taste.

Danny rose to the bait, unknowingly doing Kalman's work for him.

"Meshulam, why'd you show us such a small portion?" he demanded. "We want to see what else you've prepared for these people. Are you afraid of us? This is a serious matter, perhaps the most serious we've ever put into operation against any sector of the population. The material we've seen is important, but not enough to convince us."

He waited for a consensus, which was not long in coming. All the others also wanted to see Meshulam's masterpiece. The wave of requests grew stronger, forcing Meshulam to leave off the rest of his prepared speech and instead screen a two-hour film for his colleagues.

In the meantime, the printing presses worked at full speed...

୧ᕽᕽ৩

At 5:30 a.m., at the height of a scene with tremendous potential for arousing hostilities, Yossie Golan, general secretary of the GSS, walked in, a newspaper in his hand. His chest rose and fell in sharp, quick breaths, as if he'd just run a long distance.

"Yossie, has something happened?" Shlomo asked worriedly. The room was half dark but his sharp eyes had caught the terrible pallor of his talented assistant's face.

Yossie whispered into his ear. "About half an hour ago I got a call from a friend of mine who works in the distribution department of *HaYom HaZeh*. I ran to the printer and this is what I found."

Shlomo Templer took the freshly printed paper into his hands. Only seconds later he leaped up from his chair, his eyes almost bursting out of their sockets.

The headlines, in huge red letters, read: "*Chareidim* on Verge of Civil War. GSS Plan Revealed!"

A smaller headline underneath announced, in black: "Operation Puppeteer Rabbi of the GSS, to destroy the *chareidi* community from within, begins today. By a special team of *HaYom HaZeh* reporters."

The story continued: "Plans have been revealed for a grandiose scheme on an unprecedented scale by the GSS to cause a civil war among the *chareidim* and destroy the community from within, with the help of 168 agents who have integrated themselves into the yeshivot and chassidic courts, as well as dozens of other sensitive positions and openings into the *chareidi* world. The plan, in its entirety, was revealed yesterday to this newspaper by a top source. This source, whose name may not be mentioned, handed the newspaper a complete list of all 168 GSS agents spread through the *chareidi* community, who are ready to begin working today according to a detailed plan of operation.

"If Operation Puppeteer Rabbi goes on as planned, the next few days should bring some unexpected headlines, such as 'Civil War in Meah

Shearim and Bnei Brak.' And that would just be the beginning: The continuation could get worse."

The rest of the story brought clear details, as if the reporter had sat that night in the GSS conference room, taping the meeting and putting it into print. There were also photographs, retouched by a computer, of the various heads of the divisions. There was Meshulam Yaakovi's face, touched up ever so slightly...

Templer cleared his throat; he was almost suffocating from his fury, and could not believe what he was seeing. His eternal mask of steel began to dissolve just a little. Never had the GSS been revealed in all its shame. To publicize a top-secret plan on the day of its operation, with a detailed list of all its agents? Who was responsible for this debacle?

"Stop the movie," he roared in a thunderous voice.

The screen darkened and the room's lights went on. The shocked division heads had never seen their always-calm boss act like this. When they saw the red letters emblazoned across the width of the paper, they understood.

Shlomo waved two balled fists, as if seeking to fell some unseen opponent. He stared at his nervous staffers and pulled his cellular phone out of his pocket.

"Get me the phone number of the *HaYom HaZeh* printing press," he barked in controlled fury. "Maybe we can stop the distribution. What time is it? Twenty to six? Maybe we can do something. Get me that number!"

His yell was undoubtedly heard outside the conference room. His assistants rushed to the telephone directories as the phone in the room gave a ring.

Shlomo lifted the receiver. "Hello, who is this?" he yelled hastily.

"Hello, it's me, Manny Schwartz," the voice said calmly on the other side. "Put on the intercom; I want everyone to hear this."

"Who? Who is it?" Shlomo asked, trying to buy time.

"Shlomo, it's me, Manny." The voice was firm and steady, strong and disciplined. "You know that it's me. Only Manny Schwartz could infiltrate your closed meeting. You recognize my voice well, so stop this nonsense. Put on the intercom; press the 'speakerphone' button immediately."

Shlomo complied. Manny Schwartz knew how to make men obey, even at the other end of a phone line.

The conference room was covered with a cloud of smoke, as if in a magic show. The division heads ceased their whispers as Manny's voice came through.

"Hello, everyone, and good morning. This is Manny Schwartz speaking. You know me better under another name: Rabbi Avram Roosenthal."

A cry of consternation filled the room. Manny Schwartz continued. "You're surprised? I know that you're in a state of shock. I've left you all, forever! I've had enough of your wicked games and the hunt that you've arranged against the best people in Israel.

"I confess: I have sinned, I have erred, I have been a traitor. For many years I've misled people. Men trusted me blindly and I betrayed them. I speak 10 languages, and in 10 languages they confided in me. They came to me from all corners of the earth, and I taped their most intimate stories, in Hebrew and Yiddish, English and French, German and Swiss-German. I worked like a machine, giving over all the tapes to you.

"About a year and a half ago I awoke and stopped taping my patients. But Choni Vardi, an unfortunate young man whose difficult background you took advantage of, continued the practice.

"By putting a gun to my head, Meshulam managed to squeeze some more information from me, always with the threat of revealing my identity. I couldn't stand the pressure, but I managed to trick him. Meshulam is no fool, but I used his ignorance of the *chareidi* world and fooled him completely. The scenes that Meshulam has on his video are fakes. They are actors in costume who said exactly what I told them to say; not one word is true. Other times I used videos of real people, but I had actors read a completely different script and put that on the audio track. All of those vile slanders are lies. I have the names of all the people who were filmed, and if necessary they will appear in court to tell the truth."

Meshulam recovered first and screamed furiously towards the phone, "You liar! Those scenes are real!"

"Meshulam, you know that I'm not lying. You can't accept defeat," the infuriating answer came over the speaker. "If you compare the lips of the activist whom you saw on screen to the words he's saying, you'll see that they don't match at all. The video is a fake. A *chareidi* activist would never use such language against a beloved personality! Computer analysis will also prove that the voice on the tape doesn't belong to the activist!

"Don't bother prolonging this conversation in order to give you a chance to trace me through your telephone equipment. I know your methods. I have another four minutes before the technician can trace me, and that's enough time to give over my message."

The voice continued relentlessly. "Shlomo, I know that at the end of this conversation you'll send your men out to confiscate the newspapers before they get to the stores. They'll have to work very hard, and they won't succeed in confiscating all of them! I made certain that 200 copies were printed earlier and sent to certain people. The heads of the *chareidim*, the ones you're so afraid of, have already read the paper. They were the first to know of this plan that you've hatched, and they'll know how to protect themselves from 'Operation Puppeteer Rabbi.'"

"You are the Puppeteer, don't forget," Shlomo said quietly.

"I was," Manny answered with stoic calm. "But now it's merely the name of a failed operation. By the way, there are certain *chareidi* personalities who can rock this entire nation. They, too, have received the paper. Just think what they'll be able to do, with the names of all your 168 agents. Another thing: The electronic media and other newspapers will be receiving this, the hottest story of the year, today. And even if you put a blackout on the news, as is your habit, you can't black out *The New York Times*, *The Washington Post*, and the *Times* of London. And after that it will be legitimate to publicize it the length and breadth of this land — after all, the rest of the world knows about it, no?"

Manny was openly mocking them and they did not know how to respond. Only Meshulam broke the silence, screaming like a wounded animal, "Tell us what you want."

"Meshulam, take a drink and calm down. I'm almost finished. If you call off the operation, only a handful of people will know about it. I can't tell you for certain — maybe some clerk or diligent housewife in Tel Aviv will get up early and happen upon one of the 200 copies. We don't know how these things work out. But if you do go on with 'Puppeteer Rabbi,' I promise you a storm like you've never seen here in the State of Israel. Think about it. Goodbye."

The speakerphone emitted an irritating buzz.

Two technicians walked in. "The man knows his technology. He cut off four seconds before we could trace him. But he was speaking from Haifa, that's for sure."

"Find him," Meshulam shrieked.

The room was quiet, a silence that was heavy, that filled the space. Then the commotion began.

"I knew it!" Shlomo Templer yelled. His terrible rage surged through him, until it came out almost of its own accord. "From the first minute I knew that this was a crazy plan that was doomed to failure."

Meshulam's round face was devoid of color. The first obligation of a commander was to give total support; Shlomo was doing the exact opposite. He was blaming him!

"Shlomo? I don't believe it. You know what you are? You're a snake in the grass," he attacked him vehemently. "Who's been supporting me for six years, telling me to continue Operation Puppeteer Rabbi? Who's been pressuring me these past few days to put it into operation before it's too late? You tell me!"

Templer flinched slightly beneath his staffer's assault. "Your words are all on tape," he finally said.

He pulled out a top-notch miniaturized recording device from a matchbox and started it.

"It's brilliant," an exultant voice came out of the tiny speaker. "An incredible procedure that should in theory destroy them from within. But on second thought, it seems to me crazy, too grandiose. Who could possible do such a thing?"

Meshulam answers: "A good friend of my father's, by the name of Manny Schwartz. He will turn into a rebbe with a new identity, and he'll make a goulash of all the *chareidim*."

Shlomo Templer's voice, hesitant. "Think about it again; it's too difficult, too long and complicated. There are simpler ways."

The tape came to a stop. Everyone looked at Meshulam, sitting and trembling. The big bully who had frightened all the others now was revealed as a dwarf. He could hardly breathe and he searched for something to say.

Shlomo did not allow him time to recover. His words were strident, harsh, and biting; he spoke without mercy. "Meshulam, I noted some time ago in your evaluation that you were a genius, but weak in staff work. It's impossible to go on like this. The GSS isn't the business belonging to your father, that thieving merchant, and you can't organize operations behind all of our backs and wait, if it succeeds, for all the kudos to redound to you, while, if it fails, the GSS takes the rap. It doesn't work that way. You've humiliated the GSS in an unprecedented manner. We've become a caricature: The entire country — what am I saying, the entire world! — will be laughing at us today. A bunch of idiots whose biggest secret exploded on the day of the operation!"

He crossed the room, circled the large oval table and stood next to Meshulam. "What have you done to us?" he screamed in rage. "You've turned our top organization into a zoo! It's not the GSS, it's...it's..." he stammered slightly, looking for the perfect phrase, "it's a barn full of stinking cows, a security service worthy of Zimbabwe or Uganda!"

Shlomo finally concluded with a biting shout, "Meshulam, the game's over. Your time is up. Gather your things together and leave me your letter of resignation on my desk. You have until noon. Explain in the letter that you are resigning because of the failure of Operation Puppeteer Rabbi, and that you take full responsibility."

48

Meshulam left the conference, his head bowed. He did not look behind him, and did not wait for the storm that followed his departure.

The conference room was in a ferment, with each man blaming the other for the fiasco. While the recriminations flew, precious time was wasted. The agents that came to the *HaYom HaZeh* printing press managed to confiscate the papers a short time before they hit the streets. But the analog counter of the press showed that 51,000 papers had been printed, while a painstaking count of the number under GSS control came to 50,300. Add another 500 or so damaged copies, and that meant that about 1200 newspapers had managed to slip out of their hands.

Operation Puppeteer Rabbi was mortally wounded: The project was canceled at the last moment possible.

At noon there were soft knocks on Meshulam Yaakovi's door. The Filipino housekeeper led Choni into a brightly lit anteroom. "Oh, Choni, you've grown again," she gushed in her accented Hebrew. "Want to drink something cold, something hot? I bring you what you want."

Choni ignored the pleasantries. "Where's Meshulam?" he asked, worried.

"Speaking on telephone. Soon be finished. Wait in his room."

Meshulam ended the conversation. Pinny Yaakovi had tried to calm his son down, to explain that one newspaper was not the end of the world. "Tomorrow there'll be new headlines," he promised. "Everyone will forget what it said today."

Meshulam did not bother arguing. He hastily ended the call and received Choni in the luxurious study that had always been Choni's dream. It was a room that contained everything: a Pentium computer with oversized screen and a vast library of multimedia games, a realistic air-force flight simulator, four huge television screens that broadcast programs from all over the world, brought in by the satellite dish on the roof — all the electronic toys a high-tech baby could want. Posters of scenic views lined the walls, and in a small cage three elegant cockatoos joined in melodic chorus. In the light-filled courtyard, a gentle breeze made little ripples in the blue waters of the swimming pool.

"You see, Choni," Meshulam said despondently, waving his hand around the room, "I've got everything, and I've got nothing."

Choni trembled. "What are you talkin' about?"

"It's all over."

"What are you saying?"

Meshulam gave a deep sigh. "It was a good plan; they were top agents. Everything went like clockwork. There was just one thing I didn't know. You know what?"

"What?" Choni asked, his heart thumping wildly.

"There is a G-d."

Meshulam stood up, put on his gray jacket, checked that his revolver was loaded, and prepared to leave the room. Choni raced after him. "Meshulam," he cried beseechingly, "I'm coming with you."

Meshulam shook his head in dissent. "No, Choni," he said in decided tones. "I'm going on a trip from which there is no return. In my world there's no place for failures. The Japanese are right! You've failed? Hari-kari!"

Choni ran after him through the hallway, tears in his eyes. "Meshulam, no!" he begged brokenly. "You taught me always to fight. Why should you surrender?"

Meshulam was already on the street. He buzzed his remote-control unlocking system, and the car responded with a blink of its lights and a shrill beep. They had reached the automobile now, and Meshulam leaned heavily on the roof.

"This is the finger of G-d!" he told Choni, avoiding the boy's eyes. "How do I know? You have to be blind not to see it. The plan went on like a Swiss chronometer; everything moved perfectly. A grand scheme such as this never went wrong."

"So what happened?" Choni demanded.

The lowered eyes rose up and gave the broken lad a piercing gaze. "What happened? The finger of G-d! When G-d wants it, a broom can shoot bullets. A boy suffering from cystic fibrosis and a brain-damaged journalist defeated the best of the GSS. How else can you explain it?"

Choni was silent.

Meshulam leaned weakly on the metal gate of his blooming garden. He spoke slowly; Choni followed his every word. "I once was part of another world, a world with different values, a better world.

"That's right. If my father isn't one of the *tzaddikim* of our generation — his greed brought him to forgery — still, he instilled a belief in G-d, Torah and eternal values within me. I gave it all up, went much farther than my father ever did. He named me for his father, Rabbi Meshulam Yaakobovitz, the *maggid* of Meah Shearim. I mocked my grandfather's heritage, hoped to cover the streets of Meah Shearim with the blood of the *chareidim*. Now I know how wrong I was. There is a G-d in heaven and on earth and He pays back measure for measure. What I wanted to do to others, He has brought down on my head."

His hand smoothed Choni's wild hair fondly and patted his pimply face. "Go back home, boy, go back home," he said slowly, in choked tones. "Go back and make peace with your father while you still can. There's nothing better than a life of Torah and *mitzvot*. I have tried all the fun that the twentieth-century can offer to a youth; there's not a sin in the Torah that I haven't committed, may G-d forgive me. Choni, Yochanan. Don't exchange 20 centuries for the 20th century. Go back to your father! It's true, he didn't know to give you attention, and traveled far distances to do *mitzvot* and good deeds at the time that his son was shriveling up for a little of his time. Forgive him; no doubt he didn't act that way out of wickedness. There's nothing like home, like the love of a parent."

He got into the car. The Mazda started with a cough. The electronic window opened for a moment. "Choni, those two gangsters, Zabik and Muli, will no doubt take over Rabbi Avram's house. Don't go back there, your life is in danger. Go back to your father and mother — they miss you. Shalom, Yochanan Vardi."

The car left with a roar and disappeared around the corner. Choni leaned on the wall, put his head on his arm, and sobbed. He cried for his wasted childhood, for Meshulam the fallen idol, for his two friends, Paysi and Gili, who had truly wanted to help him and whom he had paid back with evil and pain. He only hoped that they had forgiven him.

Effie Green's drainpipes were blocked. The stench in the house grew unbearable. He called his regular plumber, Partush Plumbing, leaving a request for emergency service on the answering machine.

Within an hour two pleasant plumbers turned up. "Partush sent us; he can't come himself."

They were equipped with the most modern of tools. They scanned walls and broke a few tiles in the bathroom. After an hour and a half one of the plumbers walked into the living room, sat quietly down at the table, and asked for payment. His sharp eyes stole a glance at the others in the room.

The plumbers left with the money.

A simple Ford automobile was parked near Effie Green's house. Behind the wheel sat a bored driver reading the daily paper. He had headphones on, and his head was nodding back and forth with the rhythm. He looked just like someone who was sincerely enjoying his music.

Two hours earlier, the GSS computers had achieved what their electronic equipment had failed to do. The computer had narrowed down the call to a small area in Haifa, in the middle of Herzl Street. But even their top equipment had not been able to pinpoint which house, and certainly which apartment.

The information was transferred to Shlomo Templer. He stared at the report and wrinkled his forehead. "The middle of Herzl Street; that's a long street. Go find a needle in a haystack."

But then he jumped up with a yell. There was someone who could help him!

Jackie Wallace, an American programming genius and former Pentagon employee, was hustled into his office. When Jackie had moved to Israel he'd been drafted into the GSS and had built the security service a cutting-edge computer department that was the envy of the world.

Shlomo showed Jackie the computer's listings. "Can you help?" he asked.

Jackie chewed on the edge of his Cuban cigar. "Sure. It's a small problem. Give me the tape, and together with the phone company we'll be able to do something."

That "something" of his turned out to be the exact apartment number, found within a half-hour.

Manny had walked on a thin rope. Too thin.

During step one, a young man holding rags walked into the lobby and secretly took care of some pipes. A half-hour later Effie Green's drains were blocked. Step two, Effie called Partush the plumber. He had no idea that someone had tampered with his phone lines. The call never reached Partush; it came to a man sitting in a small truck nearby. The staff had done their homework: On the other side, Effie heard the recording from Partush Plumbing's answering machine.

The plumbers came as part of step three. No one noticed the little button that the plumber left on the bottom of the dining room table while Effie wrote the check.

The driver of the dusty Ford listened to the conversations going on in the house. The problem was that much of what came over his headphones was of no value. He was upset: Sitting here for so many hours, he might arouse suspicion. And one of the neighbors might want his parking space.

Patience pays off. After a few wasted hours the important conversation began.

"What do we do with you, Manny?" Rabbi Schmidt asked. "How do we get you to New York?"

A short silence. Rav Yoske Friedman shouted, "I've got it! Do you remember..."

A heavy truck got stuck in the street and blocked the road. Twenty angry drivers began to honk impatiently. The shrill honks deafened the man in the Ford for a few fatal seconds.

"...We've got to check with TWA. He'll probably be coming soon."

"*Chevra,* you're not being careful. You don't know the GSS. I'm walking a tightrope. This is zero hour, and I've got to get out of here as fast as I can."

Then came a moment of unclear murmurs. Suddenly, everything grew quiet. Shlomo's men came in a few minutes later, but they found an abandoned apartment. Effie Green, too, had disappeared.

Shlomo received the news in fury. "I knew it! My idiots managed to lose them! Truly, a Zimbabwe security service. This Manny is like quicksilver: put your hand on him and he's gone."

Gavriel Reit, his assistant, tried to quell his anger. "Look, the cup is also half full. We know that he's going to New York on a TWA flight. From today on we'll step up surveillance in Lod. Manny doesn't stand a chance against us."

Shlomo Templer took heart. "There's something in that," he said after a few second's thought. The flush returned to his cheeks. "Manny will get to New York in a coffin."

These were terrible days, in which Israel was struck by a round of terror beginning with the bombing of Egged Bus 18 in Jerusalem, and reaching its nadir when a group of young people were hurt by a suicide bomber in Diezengoff Square in the heart of Tel Aviv. The hands of Israel's security services were busy fighting outside enemies. And yet, astonishingly, they still managed to give their attention to one of their own.

Every TWA flight was closely scrutinized, with almost fanatical supervision of the passenger roster. The section whose responsibility included protecting political personalities took two agents from the Manpower Division, who were attached to every flight of the American airline to New York. They were searching for Manny, the agent who had betrayed them.

In their personal briefcases they had sketches of him in every possible guise: a long-bearded *chassid*, a Lithuanian rabbi, a typical American businessman, clean shaven and sporting a tie. There was even a drawing of Manny as bohemian, wearing a loud scarf around his head, a ponytail, and an earring. The computer had taken care of all possibilities.

But on all the flights there was not even one man who answered to the varying descriptions, and occasional suspicions of a fair-bearded rabbi all petered out to nothing.

Flight #884 to New York on Purim eve was different.

The plane landed in Kennedy Airport in New York around noontime on Purim. When the last of the passengers had left the plane and been swallowed up by the vast complex of buildings in JFK, the time came for the crew to leave.

"Thanks a lot," the bearded guest said to the American captain. "I'll always remember this. And don't forget to visit me in Flatbush."

"You're welcome, Manny," Captain Eli Leiker replied. "Once friends, always friends. Since Rav Yoske turned to me, I've been ready. I had to put a little pressure on, but a veteran pilot like me can occasionally host a friend in the cockpit. I assume no one will complain."

"A terrific idea," Manny gloated. "To search in the pilot's seat? Even the GSS wouldn't have dreamed of such a thing. The sky's the limit."

Eli gave his friend a piercing look. "And where are your limits? You've gone a long way since the days of Ein Yisrael. A long, long way!"

Manny hung his head.

Good-hearted Eli couldn't bear to see his friend's distress. "The main thing is that you've done *teshuvah*, and in the place where *baalei teshuvah* stand..."

"They stand more than 33,000 feet up in the air," Manny answered with a sad smile. "I'm still quite far from the level of a *baal teshuvah*. I've done an enormous amount of wrong. I just hope I can correct a small part of it."

"Be an optimist, Manny," Leiker said encouragingly. "Operation Puppeteer Rabbi went down the tubes, and a person is judged for the majority of his actions."

"Udi Dinar — Moishike Dinburg — lies like a millstone on my conscience," Manny said, his face darkening. "I thought that I would succeed in restoring his sanity and I didn't have the chance. I ran away from the GSS agents like a scared rabbit, and because of me Udi will doubtless remain handicapped all his life. Goodbye, Eli. I'll be hiding my blonde beard for a little while, but between you and me I'm afraid that the long arm of the GSS will capture me here one of these days. They won't forgive the humiliation."

They left the jet, and walked through the long corridor into the terminal. Manny disappeared into the TWA staff bathroom.

Half an hour later an elderly woman wrapped in a black coat walked out. She walked heavily, pulling a laden suitcase behind her. A cab picked her up at the building's entrance. The old lady sat down in the back seat.

One minute later a black Chrysler pulled out behind the cab. "Manny thinks he's the smartest of everyone," the driver chortled. "We've got you, Manny. Three weeks you eluded us, but he who laughs last laughs best. We figured you might go out as a woman."

The man sitting next to him was skeptical. "Who knows what a chase he'll lead us? He's an expert."

At that minute Manny turned his head and spotted the Chrysler. During his war of nerves Manny had developed razor-sharp senses. He knew that his time was running out, and felt the noose tightening slowly around his neck. No covert agency ever forgave an agent who betrayed it, certainly not the GSS.

"Speed it up," he told the driver. "I'll give you 10 times the fare if you manage to lose that black Chrysler."

The driver, surprised, looked into his rear-view mirror. Was that a male voice coming from the elderly lady he'd picked up? Shocked, he saw that the old woman had gotten out of her clothing, and was busily donning the garb of a *chassid*.

"Don't look behind you," Manny cried hastily. "Make it fast; use your horn until we've gotten to Boro Park."

The driver laughed in comprehension. "You're filming a movie! What luck to have picked you up," he shouted merrily. "Put me in also; my wife, Margaret, won't believe this."

The cab picked up speed, honking the entire way, as it made it way towards Boro Park.

❦

The Brooklyn neighborhood of Boro Park is divided into squares. Even a 5-year-old can easily find his way through the area. Once you know the street and avenue numbers, you can get where you want to go.

Only one road deviates significantly from the rest: New Utrecht Avenue. The elevated tracks of the B train run above this street that cuts diagonally through a large part of the borough.

The cab reached New Utrecht Avenue, at the corner of 43rd Street, and stopped. A large group of youngsters wearing costumes and holding huge balloons enjoyed a Purim carnival, blocking the entire street. From the cab alighted a thickly bearded *chassid* wearing a *shtriemel* and *kappatah*. His black pants reached his knees, and his white knickers ended in classic chassidic shoes. The youngsters greeted the man with a merry "a *gutten* Purim." A laughing little boy with curly blond *payos* smiled with cherry-red lips, handed him a small bottle of wine and a disposable cup, and called out in a shrill voice, "Drink a *l'chayim!*"

Inside the car a young man put his eye to his binoculars. "Manny, man of 1000 faces, I've found you! You were an old lady, now you're a *chassid*. Fine, let's get to work: You'll die as a *chassid*."

Manny pushed the merry children to the side. From the corner of his eye he could see the rifle butt being aimed at him from the window of the black car. He bent over for a moment: the whizzing bullet exploded a red balloon of a tiny King Achashverosh, continued its shrieking flight, and landed in a nearby wall.

Manny fled with every ounce of energy he possessed. He crossed Twelfth Avenue, passed a series of red-fronted apartment buildings, and reached Thirteenth Avenue.

Boro Park's bustling commercial center was busier than usual. Though many of the stores were closed, a celebrating crowd lined the street. Someone noticed the chase going on. "Hey, look at that," he said in shock. "That's the real thing!"

"Yaakov Moshe, what's with you? It's Purim!"

Manny raced like a beast in the jungle. He was surrounded by people, yet no one was as alone as he. His fleet-footed pursuers had left their car and followed him through the streets, revolvers with silencers faithfully hidden beneath their wide jacket sleeves. To Manny's good fortune, they didn't dare shoot him while he was surrounded by passersby, but when he turned onto a quieter street the bullets whistled by.

Please, Hashem, help me, he turned his eyes heavenward. *I so want to re-build that which I've destroyed.*

Now he was in the heart of Boro Park, in its center. His lungs burned; his legs would no longer carry him. For a millisecond he stopped to inhale. He turned around, panting. The two energetic young men were right behind him; his fine-tuned ears could hear their footsteps on the concrete beneath them. Threatening footsteps, footsteps that meant death and murder, coming closer, closer... In despair, he turned around once more. The building near him took on another cast entirely.

His face lit up. *Why didn't I think of it before?* There, on the side, was a metal fire escape, so prevalent in older Brooklyn apartment buildings. These emergency exits had saved many lives during fatal blazes: Now they could save him as well!

With lightning speed he jumped onto the suspended ladder, and climbed up higher and higher, towards the roof. His legs were exhausted, but the instinct of a hunted animal carried him on, whispering to him that the assassins were gaining on him. He reached the top.

The two down below came to the fire escape. "What to do now?"

"Climb up after him."

A group of Purim merrymakers stared at them with interest. "What's happening here?" an elderly Jew asked excitedly.

"They've prepared a drama for us, a *Purim shpiel* on the street," a younger man answered with equal fervor. His arms were laden with a heavy basket of *mishloach manos* for his son's *rebbi*.

The agents had already climbed up two stories. A large crowd gathered on the bottom and were watching them, fascinated. Someone screamed, "We've got to call the police. This is something criminal. Look at their eyes! They're killers, murderers!"

"Mutty, what do we do now?" one of the agents whispered.

"Yoram, things are getting complicated," Mutty replied. "That's all we need, that they should get the police or the FBI involved. Let's wait for him downstairs."

Manny could hear their words. The mention of the FBI sent shivers down his spine. Even if the American agency got involved, he was still in trouble: They'd immediately deport him to Israel!

In his moment of despair he made his decision. He flew across the roof to the other side and immediately made his way down another fire escape near the front of the building.

Downstairs, Manny took a deep breath. He was standing in front of the beautiful *beis midrash* of one of the largest chassidic groups in the neighborhood. In an instant he had vanished into the building and was encircled by a large group of *chassidim* heading to their rebbe's *tish*.

The agents ignored the hostile looks all around them. They had but one mission: assassination. And they would hang onto their target to the end.

They whizzed through the group of *chassidim* and tore into the marble-fronted building. As if possessed by demons they raced up the steps into the *beis midrash*.

More than one thousand *chassidim* swarmed throughout the large room, standing on bleacherlike platforms on two sides of an enormous table. The teenaged students on the highest level reached almost to the ceiling. The *chassidim* sang lively Purim melodies in a mighty roar. Many of them were dressed in a dazzling variety of Purim costumes. The thick-bearded *chassid* was lost among them.

The singing halted. On the table which now served as a stage, a *Purim shpiel* began. The star of the show played the rebbe's *gabbai*, who was pressed into service as rebbe because the rebbe was ill. The other *gabbaim*, in need of cash, tried to train him to serve as rebbe because of his resemblance to the great man, but the head *gabbai* wasn't too bright and couldn't manage to remember the *berachos* he was to give. Another actor tried to explain to the imaginary rebbe how he should bless someone: "If a woman comes in with her little boy, tell him he should grow and grow like a rose." The "*gabbai*" sat down on the rebbe's chair and his first client immediately entered: a hunchback seeking a blessing for the hump. The rebbe told him, "May it grow like a rose."

The huge *beis midrash* shook with laughter. The show continued. The hunchback exited, mortally offended, and the substitute-rebbe's handlers were left to tell him what he'd done wrong. "Hunchbacks get told, 'May it grow smaller and smaller until it disappears entirely!'"

Another minute and a woman and her sick daughter entered. The *gabbai* stared at his notes with huge gold-rimmed glasses, but he got his papers mixed up, and blessed the little one, "May you grow smaller and smaller until you disappear entirely!"

Some of the *chassidim* on the bleachers actually fell to the ground, rolling with laughter.

The GSS agents didn't understand a word of the actors' anglicized Yiddish. "Primitives," Yoram spit out. Mutty shuddered. "Careful, Yoram," he warned. "They're no fools."

They walked through the bleachers, stared at the faces, pulled at beards, checked out costumes.

The *chassidim*'s patience wore away. "Who are these bums? Coming to destroy the rebbe's *tish*, his special *Purim shpiel tish!*"

In one of the corners of the room a *chassid* with a light beard whispered in the ears of his neighbor. The *chassid* turned to the man with shocked eyes, then quickly passed the tale to the next man.

The famed Brooklyn battle cry, the cry of the religious Jew against the anti-Semite, came out of hundreds of mouths and echoed through the *beis midrash*:

Chaptz'em! Get them!

In an instant the two agents were surrounded by infuriated *chassidim*. Strong arms held them by the chest. They were dragged to the entrance way and thrown down the stairs.

And Manny disappeared like a stone in the depths of the sea.

49

They waited in line outside the rebbe's study. The rebbe of Kiltz had recovered somewhat from his illness and had been persuaded to annul the life-threatening vow that he'd made so long ago. Now he had asked that all of them visit that evening. Gili put his father, Udi, into an upholstered chair; the older man sat silently. At his side stood Monica, pale and tense. There had been many moments of shock after the meeting several days ago, the meeting that seemed like a fantastic dream. How many widows, after all, are beneficiaries of such a gift: to welcome back a husband dead these six years...

But then had come the great disappointment. He had not returned after all! The body was there, but it was empty, a mere shell of flesh and blood. The joyous spirit of her Udi — dead. She now put all her hopes on this meeting with the rebbe. Gili had aroused great expectations.

Rav Yoske's look was full of mercy. "Gili, there's been no improvement?"

"None," Gili answered sadly. "Ask my mother. She speaks to him night and day, shows him pictures of the past, and he doesn't react at all."

Rabbi Schmidt lifted his eyes from the small Gemara on the table, and tapped Gili lightly on the shoulders. "Don't give up, Gili. He'll come out of it."

Udi looked at him when he said those words, as if he wanted to join in the good wishes. But Rabbi Schmidt didn't notice the stolen glance.

"One thing I still don't understand," Rabbi Schmidt continued. "How did Paysi know about Mickey Gadish and Kiryat Bialik?"

Gili rummaged through his jacket pocket and pulled out an envelope bearing the stamps of the United Kingdom. "I got a letter from Paysi, from Harfield Hospital. *Dear Gili, I am feeling better and can finally answer your letters. The doctors give me a good chance to recover and I hope to come back to Israel soon. You ask who told me the secrets of Mickey Gadish, Kiryat Bialik, and the rest. The truth is, everyone thought that I heard about them wandering through Rav Avram's house, or that Choni told me. But that's not true. I didn't know anything. Everyone in Rav Avram's house kept the secret.*"

This was a bombshell. "What? Paysi didn't know anything?" Rav Yoske expressed everyone's thoughts.

"That's not all," Gili almost purred with satisfaction. "Listen to the rest. *It seems that the big man who was so wild in the ambulance thought the same thing. He was sure that I knew everything, and never realized that it was he himself who revealed the secret. He asked me, in a furious rage, 'What does Gili know about the Puppeteer Rabbi, about Mickey Gadish, and Kiryat Bialik?' He spoke slowly, so that I could read his lips, and that's what I did. I realized that if he didn't want Gili to know those names, they must be really important. Maybe he realized afterwards that in his stupidity he'd revealed the hidden names. I assume that's why he sent those two lovely guards to me in the hospital. Be well, my dear Gili. With eternal fondness, Paysi.*"

Gili quickly stuffed the letter back into his pocket, before anyone had a chance to read the final line, the one he hadn't read aloud: *P.S. Chedvi says that she's planning a surprise for you and my sister Simi when we get back to Israel. Mazel tov, my dear brother-in-law.*

"I think I'm becoming a *chassid* of Kiltz," Rabbi Chaim Ozer Schmidt said impulsively. "Wasn't it the elderly rebbe who sent Gili to London, without knowing anything? And by the way," he continued, "where did you get the idea of sending those five copies through the mail, and where did you get the list of the agents?"

Gili smiled. "I once read about a businessman who saw the tax authorities approaching his store. He knew that they wouldn't like what they found... So he quickly left the office, his hands full of brown manila envelopes. 'I'll be right back,' he explained to the representatives of the law who were already skimming through his files. 'I've got to send out these estimates to my clients.' He raced to the nearest post office and sent most of his papers right back to himself, via registered mail. So it was the post office that saved him from the tax people! Their automated systems are like robots: The mail service could protect secret documents, even from the all-powerful GSS."

"And the agents' names?" Rabbi Schmidt wouldn't give up.

"I didn't know a single name," Gili objected.

"Yes, yes. I'm the one who had the list," Rabbi Schmidt laughed, straightening his tie.

"Let me finish my sentence. It was Manny who gave us the names, on the day the report was publicized. He said that he wanted to try to atone for his deeds and destroy the GSS plan. He pulled out a small pad from his pocket, and faxed the 168 names and addresses to Ami Kedmi."

Rabbi Yehoshua Schneidman arrived from the cold street, wrapped in a heavy winter coat. His eyeglasses were fogged, and he wiped them with a tissue. "Gili, *shalom*," he called out happily. "Have you seen the chandelier?"

"I haven't been in the *beis midrash* yet," Gili answered. "Has it been returned?"

Rabbi Schneidman glowed with happiness. "The police confiscated it from Sotheby's. The nuclear testing proved without a doubt that it had been taken from our *beis midrash*. Sotheby's apologized profusely; the firm had been a victim of fraud."

Rav Yoske Friedman measured his words carefully. "The stolen chandelier illuminated the darkness of Operation Puppeteer Rabbi."

The words reminded Gili of why they were here. He grabbed Rabbi Schneidman's sleeve. "Yehoshua, what are we waiting for? Why isn't the rebbe receiving us?"

Rabbi Schneidman had finished cleaning his glasses. "The rebbe has just gone into his study. You'll be the first to enter. But have some pity and make it short: Even with his reduced schedule, there's a long line."

Ten minutes later they were led into the modest room. Here, in this place, Gili had recorded the rebbe's bitter tears for the terrible fate of Moishike Dinburg, for the way he'd fallen into the destructive depths of the River Dinar.

The rebbe warmly shook all their hands; astonishingly enough, his handshake was firm and powerful. He pulled out a bottle from a small antique buffet. The liquor was poured into small plastic cups; the gay sounds of *l'chayim* filled the room.

The rebbe looked at Udi Dinar with eyes blue as the sea. He poured him a cup. "Moishike, make a *shehakol*."

Udi gazed vacantly at him.

"Abba, answer the rebbe," Gili beseeched his father. "He was your *sandek*, the rebbe of Kiltz."

The rebbe gently touched Gili's hand. "Leave him," He took the small cup and put it near his lips. "I will make the blessing and drink a little. Then you will do that same. Okay?"

Udi nodded slightly.

The rebbe put his cup near his white lips, said the blessing out loud, and took a few sips. Udi stared at him, entranced. "Nu, Moishike," the rebbe said. "Now it's your turn."

Udi put out a hand like a robot, grabbed the cup in trembling fingers, and quietly said, word after word, "*Baruch Atah Hashem ... shehakol nihiyeh bidvaro.*"

"*Amen*," everyone answered with dawning hope.

The rebbe bent over and whispered in Gili's ears. "Does your father have a song that he loves?"

A song? Were there songs, then, in hell? Six years in hell — a song?

The rebbe repeated his question.

Gili searched his memory. Yes, though Abba was not religious, he never enjoyed secular music. He liked religious music and would often listen to well-known religious musicians. He particularly liked to hum one song, "*Lev tahor.*" Gili would look at him strangely when he sang the poignant tune: What did his father have to do with these religious songs?

He whispered in the rebbe's ear.

The rebbe began to sing quietly. "Hashem, a pure heart create for me." The melody was a well-known one, full of emotion, a quiet tune that grew more powerful with the words.

Hashem, create a pure heart for me,

and renew a proper spirit within me.

Cast me not away from You

and do not take Your holy spirit from me.

The *gabbai* disappeared for a minute, returning with a large tape recorder. He turned on the instrument and the speakers emitted the heart-rending melody. Those in the rebbe's study sang together, a chorus, against the background of the recording. They sang the words as the sound of violins filled the room.

Gili was the first to break down. The sobs came out of him like a storm. He fell on Udi's shoulders, hugging him with all the burden of longing and love, all the hurt of the years.

"Don't cast me away, Abba," he sobbed. "You've been cast away enough, enough. Wake up, don't take your spirit from me, don't let them have taken your holiness away. Come, leave your prison."

Udi looked at him with tears in his eyes. Something was growing within him, ever so slowly. The fire grew stronger from minute to minute.

His mouth opened. He began to sing with the tape: "Cast me not away from You." He repeated the words again and again. The inner fire became a blaze; the violins wailed on.

Udi fell onto Gili, hanging onto him, hugging him with all his might, and burst into tears.

Six years of silent weeping came out of its prison, into the walls of the room. It was the cry of a soul trapped, still looking for a way out.

They watched him, and they did not understand. Whoever had not undergone torture of the spirit, whoever never felt the soul's torment, could not understand. The worst physical pain could not compare to this spiritual agony.

They could not understand, but they felt. They saw Udi Dinar, battered by mortal agony. They heard his cries, coming from deep within his soul, and they covered their faces with their hands.

And then there was silence. The tape ended. Only Udi's broken voice could be heard. "Monica, my dear. My Gili. All these hard years, only one dream remained, the dream that my Monica and my Gili were alive. But I would wake up and the dream would vanish. And then I knew that I was Mickey Gadish, without a wife or a child.

"And now here you are, Monica, here you are, Gili. And you're no dream, you're no dream!"

⊙⋟⋞⊙

The rebbe of Kiltz spoke with controlled emotion. "I prayed at his *bris*, 'Rescue the beloved soul from destruction.' I knew from the moment you were with me that it could not be: The only son of Shmuel Dinburg would not die like a gentile!

"He'll be all right, but it will be a long, arduous process," the rebbe explained to Gili and his mother. "There will be progress and setbacks. We'll have to sweat together and pray together, until your father returns to us. But these first emotions have broken through the walls. He has left his prison."

"There are no words..." Gili whispered. "We're finally seeing the light that will end the darkness."

The rebbe bent his head modestly. "Only Heaven's mercy will help. Pray a lot, Gili, pray. And learn."

Rabbi Schmidt joined in. "When I sent Gili to the newspaper, I said he'd be back one day."

"I'm coming back, Rabbi Schmidt, I'm coming back," Gili exulted. "I missed the yeshivah every day."

The room was filled with the sound of joyful voices. Everyone spoke at once.

The rebbe of Kiltz lifted a thin hand, and all grew quiet.

"Gili had a mission. He accomplished it and is returning to yeshivah. But the mission is not ended."

"What mission?" Rabbi Schmidt asked, voicing everyone's question.

The rebbe laughed quietly, a bitter laugh. He began with a *midrash*. " 'When the axe was created all the trees began to tremble. Said the axe to the trees: Why do you tremble? If none among you trees join me, none will be harmed!' That is, if none of the trees volunteer to serve as the handle for the axe, the axe will not be able to chop down the trees!

"Do you understand? Our destruction comes from ourselves! They wanted to harm the *chareidi* world. Could they have done so without help from within? Don't we cooperate with our enemies when we speak against each other? Is there peace and tranquility among us, no controversy? Are there no cliques and no partisanship? Why should a 3-year-old boy not be able to be best friends with the child from across the hall, just because one father belongs to this group and the other to that?"

The rebbe's voice grew stronger; his pale face reddened with effort. "Let us unite together, all the different factions. Let's leave the reckonings behind. Forgive each other. We're all brothers, sons of one Father, and we all serve the same Creator. Why should we waste our energy on disunity?

"There are those who take advantage of our conflicts, seeking to put a wedge in between us and deepen the rift.

"And by the way," the rebbe asked, "what's happened to Rav Avram Roosenthal?"

Rav Yoske spoke quietly, as if still afraid of eavesdroppers. "I spoke with Eli Leiker. He's staying underground until the heat dies down."

The rebbe nodded. "Very good. His passion for domination caused him to stray. His vast spiritual powers would have raised him to greatness in any event. But he was in a hurry and he grabbed. He ran — and he sinned! As terrible as his downfall, so great was his atonement, and in this merit he will be forgiven. If he hadn't regretted what he'd done, we would be in the midst of a raging civil war now. May we learn to make peace, each with his brother, and live together, united."

His words of reproach rang in a gentle voice. Rabbi Schmidt could almost hear the wind playing on the strings of a harp, giving off a wonderful melody.

The rebbe looked at Gili. "And to you, Gili, just a few more words. When you came to me you were completely lost. You thought the world had ended. But the moment you told me that the background of the story was a book by the name of *The Vessel of Blessing* I knew that the GSS would fail, completely, and that no controversy would erupt!"

"Why?" Gili asked.

Rabbi Schmidt understood immediately, and jumped up from his seat. The rebbe laughed. "Scholars understand everything immediately. They wanted to make controversy among G-d-fearing people with a book called *The Vessel of Blessing*?

"We already have a promise on this: 'The Holy One, blessed is He, did not find a vessel of blessing for Israel, except that of peace'!"